EMPIRE
of
MAN

BAEN BOOKS
by JOHN RINGO

EMPIRE OF MAN,
with David Weber:
March to the Sea • *March to the Stars* • *March Upcountry* • *We Few* • *Empire of Man* (omnibus)

BLACK TIDE RISING:
Under a Graveyard Sky • *To Sail a Darkling Sea* • Islands of Rage & Hope (forthcoming) • Strands of Sorrow (forthcoming)

TROY RISING:
Live Free or Die • *Citadel* • *The Hot Gate*

LEGACY OF THE ALDENATA:
A Hymn Before Battle • *Gust Front* • *When the Devil Dances* • *Hell's Faire* • *The Hero* (with Michael Z. Williamson) • *Cally's War* (with Julie Cochrane) • *Watch on the Rhine* (with Tom Kratman) • *Sister Time* (with Julie Cochrane) • *Yellow Eyes* (with Tom Kratman) • *Honor of the Clan* (with Julie Cochrane) • *Eye of the Storm*

COUNCIL WARS:
There Will Be Dragons • *Emerald Sea* • *Against the Tide* • *East of the Sun, West of the Moon*

INTO THE LOOKING GLASS:
Into the Looking Glass • *Vorpal Blade* (with Travis S. Taylor) • *Manxome Foe* (with Travis S. Taylor) • *Claws that Catch* (with Travis S. Taylor)

SPECIAL CIRCUMSTANCES:
Princess of Wands • *Queen of Wands*

PALADIN OF SHADOWS:
Ghost • *Kildar* • *Choosers of the Slain* • *Unto the Breach* • *A Deeper Blue* • *Tiger by the Tail* (with Ryan Sear)

STANDALONE TITLES:
The Last Centurion

Citizens (ed. with Brian M. Thomsen)

BAEN BOOKS by DAVID WEBER
HONOR HARRINGTON:
On Basilisk Station • *On Basilisk Station 20th Anniversary Edition* • *The Honor of the Queen* • *The Short Victorious War* • *Field of Dishonor* • *Flag in Exile* • *Honor Among Enemies* • *In Enemy Hands* • *Echoes of Honor* • *Ashes of Victory* • *War of Honor* • *At All Costs* • *Mission of Honor* • *A Rising Thunder* • *Shadow of Freedom*

HONORVERSE:
Crown of Slaves (with Eric Flint) • *Torch of Freedom* (with Eric Flint) • *Cauldron of Ghosts* (with Eric Flint, forthcoming) • *The Shadow of Saganami* • *Storm from the Shadows*

THE STAR KINGDOM:
A Beautiful Friendship • *Fire Season* (with Jane Lindskold) • *Treecat Wars* (with Jane Lindskold)

Edited by David Weber:
More than Honor • *Worlds of Honor* • *Changer of Worlds* • *In the Service of the Swords* •
In Fire Forged • *Beginnings*

House of Steel: The Honorverse Companion (with BuNine)

Also by David Weber
with Eric Flint:
1633 • *1634: The Baltic War*

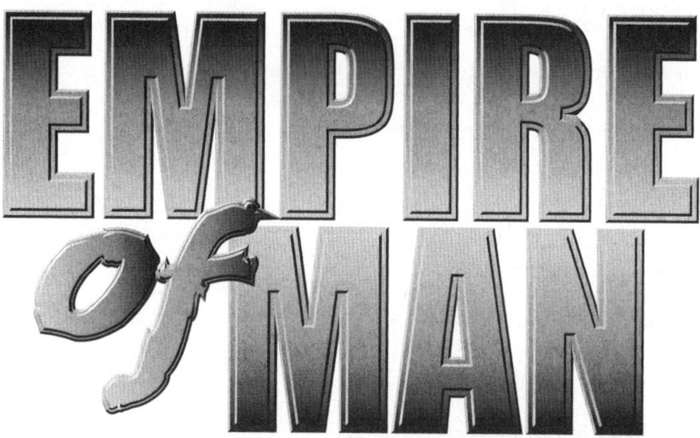

DAVID WEBER
JOHN RINGO

EMPIRE OF MAN

This is a work of fiction. All the characters and events portrayed in this book are fictional, and any resemblance to real people or incidents is purely coincidental.

A Baen Books Original

Baen Publishing Enterprises
P.O. Box 1403
Riverdale, NY 10471
www.baen.com

ISBN: 978-1-4767-3624-2

Cover art by David Seeley

First Baen paperback printing, February 2014

Distributed by Simon & Schuster
1230 Avenue of the Americas
New York, NY 10020

Library of Congress Cataloging-in-Publication Data

Weber, David.
[Novels. Selections]
Empire of man / David Weber, John Ringo.
pages cm
ISBN 978-1-4767-3624-2 (pbk.)
1. Life on other planets--Fiction. I. Ringo, John, 1963- II. Weber, David. March upcountry. III. Weber, David. March to the sea. IV. Title.
PS3573.E217E77 2014
813'.54--dc23

2013049292

Printed in the United States of America

10 9 8 7 6 5 4 3 2

CONTENTS

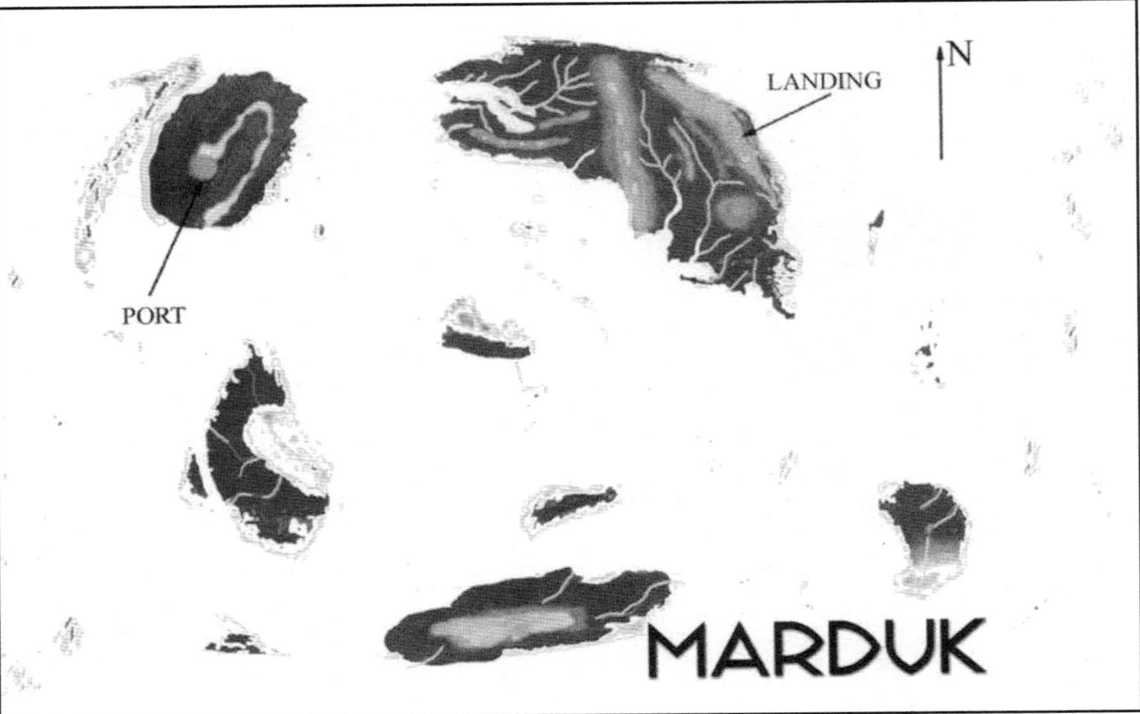
PORT
LANDING
N
MARDUK

MARCH UPCOUNTRY

This book is dedicated to our mothers.

To Alice Louise Godard Weber,
who put up with me, taught me,
edited me, believed in me,
and encouraged me to believe I could
be a writer . . .
despite all evidence to the contrary.
I love you. There. I said it.

To Jane M. Ringo,
for dragging me to places I didn't want to go
and trying to make me eat stuff that would
turn a monkey's stomach.
Thanks Mom.
You were right.

CHAPTER ONE

"His Royal Highness, Prince Roger Ramius Sergei Alexander Chiang MacClintock!"

Prince Roger maintained his habitual, slightly bored smile as he padded through the door, then stopped and glanced around the room as he shot the cuffs of his shirt and adjusted his cravat. Both were made from Diablo spider-silk, the softest and sleekest material in the galaxy. Since it was protected by giant, acid-spitting spiders, it was also the most expensive.

For his part, Amos Stephens paid as little attention as possible to the young fop he had so grandly announced. The child was a disgrace to the honorable name of his mother's family. The cravat was bad enough, and the brightly patterned brocade jacket, more appropriate for a bordello than a meeting with the Empress of Man, was worse. But the hair! Stephens had served twenty years in Her Majesty's Navy before entering the Palace Service Corps. The only difference between his years in the Navy and his years in the Palace was the way his close-cropped curls had shifted from midnight black to silver. The mere sight of the butt-length golden hair of the farcical dandy Empress Alexandra's younger son had become always drove the old butler absolutely mad.

The Empress' office was remarkably small and spare, with a broad desk no larger than that of a middle-level manager in any of the star-spanning corporations of Earth. The appointments were simple but elegant; the chairs sensible, but elaborately hand-crafted and covered in exquisite hand-stitching. Most of the pictures were old master originals. The one exception was the most famous. "The Empress in Waiting" was a painting from life of Miranda MacClintock during the "Dagger Years," and the artist, Trachsler, had captured his subject perfectly. Her eyes were open and smiling, showing the world the image of an ingenuous Terran subject. A loyal upholder of the Dagger Lords. In other words, a filthy collaborator. But if you stared at the painting long enough, a chill crept over your skin and the eyes slowly changed. To the eyes of a predator.

Roger spared the painting one bare glance, then looked away. All of the MacClintocks lived under the shadow of the old biddy, long dead though she was. As the merest—and least satisfactory—slip of that lineage, he had all the shadows he could stand.

Alexandra VII, Empress of Man, regarded her youngest child through half-slitted eyes. The carefully metered bite of Stephens' ironic announcement had apparently gone over the prince's head completely. Roger certainly didn't seem affected by the old spacer's disdain in the slightest.

Unlike her flamboyant son, Empress Alexandra wore a blue suit of such understated elegance that it must have cost as much as a small starship. Now she leaned back in her float chair and propped her cheek on her hand, wondering for the hundredth time if this was the right decision. But there were a thousand other decisions awaiting her, all of them vital, and she'd spent all the time she intended to on this one.

"Mother," Roger said insouciantly, with a micrometric bow, and glanced at his brother in the flanking chair. "To what do I owe the honor of being summoned into two such august presences?" he continued with a slight, knowing smirk.

John MacClintock gave his younger brother a thin smile and a nod. The galaxy-renowned diplomat was dressed in a conservative suit of blue worsted, with a practical damask handkerchief poking out of one sleeve. For all that he looked like a doltish banker, his poker face and sleepy eyes hid a mind as insightful as any in the known worlds. And despite the developing paunch of middle-age, he could have become a professional golfer . . . if the job of Heir Apparent had allowed the time for it.

The Empress leaned forward abruptly and fixed her youngest with a laser stare. “Roger, We are sending you off-planet on a ‘show the flag’ mission.”

Roger blinked several times, and smoothed his hair.

“Yes?” he replied carefully.

“The planet Leviathan is celebrating Net-Hauling in two months—”

“Oh, my God, Mother!” Roger’s exclamation cut the Empress of Man off in mid-sentence. “You must be joking!”

“We are not joking, Roger,” Alexandra said severely. “Leviathan’s primary export may be grumbly oil, but that doesn’t change the fact that it’s a focal planet in the Sagittarius sector. And there hasn’t been a family representative for Net-Hauling in two decades.” *Since I repudiated your father*, she didn’t bother to add.

“But, Mother! The smell!” the prince protested, shaking his head to toss an errant strand of hair out of his eyes. He knew he was whining and hated it, but the alternative was smelling grumbly oil for at least several weeks on the planet. And even after he escaped Leviathan, it would take several more weeks for Kostas to get the smell out of his clothes. The oil made a remarkable musk base; in fact, it was in the cologne he was wearing at the moment. But in its raw form, it was the most noxious stuff in the galaxy.

“We don’t care about the smell, Roger,” snapped the Empress, “and neither should you! You will show the flag for the dynasty, and you will show Our subjects that We care enough about their reaffirmation of alliance to the Empire to send one of Our children. Is that understood?”

The young prince drew himself up to his full hundred ninety-five centimeters and gathered the shreds of his dignity.

“Very well, Your Imperial Majesty. I will, of course, do my duty as you see fit. It is my duty, after all, is it not, Your Imperial Majesty? *Noblesse oblige* and all that?” His aristocratic nostrils flared in suppressed anger. "Now I suppose I have some packing to oversee. By your leave?"

Alexandra's steely gaze held him for a few moments more, and then she waggled her fingers in the direction of the door.

"Go. Go. And do a good job." The "for a change" was unstated.

Prince Roger gave another micrometric bow, turned his back quite deliberately, and stalked out of the room.

"You could have handled that better, Mother," John said quietly, after the door had closed on the angry young man.

"Yes, I could have." She sighed, steepling her fingers under her chin. "And I should have, damn it. But he looks too much like his father!"

"But he *isn't* his father, Mother," John said quietly. "Unless you create his father in him. Or drive him into New Madrid's camp."

"Try to teach me to suck eggs, why don't you?" she snapped, then inhaled deeply and shook her head. "I'm sorry, John. You're right. You're always right." She smiled ruefully at her older son. "I'm just not good at personal, am I?"

"You were fine with Alex and me," John replied. "But Roger's carrying a lot of loads. It might be time to cut him some slack."

"There isn't any slack to cut! Not now!"

"There's some. More than he's gotten in the last several years, anyway. Alex and I always knew you loved us," he pointed out quietly. "Roger's never been absolutely sure."

Alexandra shook her head.

"Not now," she repeated more calmly. "When he gets back, if this crisis blows over, I'll try to . . ."

"Undo some of the damage?" John's voice was level, his mild eyes unchallenging, open and calm. But then, he looked that way in the face of war.

"Explain," she said sharply. "Tell him the whole story. From the horse's mouth. Maybe if I explain it to him it will make more sense." She paused, and her face hardened. "And if he still is in New Madrid's camp, well, we'll just have to deal with that as it comes."

"But until then?" John met her half-angry, half-saddened gaze levelly.

"Until then we stay the course. And get him as far out of the line of fire as possible."

And as far from power as possible, as well, she thought.

CHAPTER TWO

Well, at least he's an athlete. Watching the prince drift out of the free-fall and flip to a lithe touchdown on the padded landing area, Company Sergeant Major Eva Kosutic had to admit that she'd seen experienced spacers handle the maneuver worse. *Now if he'd only grow a spine.*

First Platoon of Bravo Company, Bronze Battalion, The Empress' Own Regiment, was drawn up at attention in serried ranks on the forward side of the shuttle boat bay. The platoon's turnout was better than the Fleet's, which was only to be expected. The Bronze Battalion might be the "lowest" in the hierarchy of The Empress' Own, but they were still among the most elite bodyguards in the known universe. And that meant both the deadliest *and* the best looking.

It was Eva Kosutic's job to make sure of that. The thirty-minute Guard Mount had been, as always, precise and painstaking. Every centimeter of the uniform, equipment, and toilette of the individual Marines had been minutely inspected. In the five months she'd been Sergeant Major of Bravo Company, Captain Pahner had never found a single fault after she'd checked over the troops. And he never would, if Eva Kosutic had anything to say about it.

Admittedly, there were very few "gigs" for her to find. Before winning assignment to "The Regiment" all candidates went through an exhausting washout course. The five-week Regimental In-Processing, or RIP, was designed to remove the wannabes, and combined all the worst aspects of commando training with intense inspections of uniform and equipment. Any Marine found wanting—and most were—was sent back to his unit with no hard feelings. It was understood that "The Regiment" accepted only the best of the best of the best.

Once a recruit survived RIP, of course, he found another hierarchy to deal with. Almost all of the recent "Rippers" were assigned to Bronze Battalion, where they had the inexpressible joy of guarding an overbred pansy who'd rather spit on them than give them the time of day. Most of them suspected that it was just another test. If they stayed hardcore and professional for eighteen months, they could either take a promotion to stay in Bronze or else vie for a position in Steel Battalion and protect Princess Alexandra.

Personally, Eva Kosutic was counting down. One hundred and fifty-three days and a wake-up, she thought, as the prince stepped off the landing mat.

The last notes of the Imperial Anthem died, and the ship's captain stepped forward and saluted.

"Your Royal Highness, Captain Vil Krasnitsky, at your service! Might I say what an honor it is to have you with us on the *Charles DeGlopper*!"

The prince gave the ship's captain a languid one-handed wave, and turned to look around the boat bay. The petite brunette who'd trailed him out of the tube stepped forward and around him with an almost unnoticeable flare of her nostrils and took the captain's hand.

"Eleanora O'Casey, Captain. It's a pleasure to be aboard your fine vessel." Roger's former tutor and current chief of staff gave the captain a firm handshake and looked him directly in the eye, trying to project some semblance of leadership since Roger was in one of his sulks. "We've been told there's not a crew in this class that can touch yours."

The captain glanced sideways at the distant nobleman for only a moment, and then turned back to the chief of staff.

"Thank you, Ma'am. It's good to be appreciated."

"You've won the Tarawa Competition two years in a row. That's proof enough for this poor civilian." She gave the captain a blinding smile and nudged Roger lightly with her elbow.

The prince turned to the captain and gave him a thin, remote, and fairly meaningless smile. The captain, blinded by the sight of royalty, gave a sigh of relief. Presumably, the prince was pleased and his career would avoid the shoals of royal disfavor.

"May I introduce my officers?" Krasnitsky asked, turning to the line of waiting personnel. "And if His Highness wishes, the ship's company is prepared for inspection!"

"Perhaps at a later time," Eleanora suggested hastily. "I believe His Highness would prefer to be shown to his cabin."

She smiled at the captain once more, already rehearsing her future explanation that the prince had suffered a slight case of motion sickness in the free-fall tube and that was why he was distracted. The excuse was weak, but having "spacephobia" would go over better with the ship's crew than explaining that Roger was being a pain in the ass on purpose.

"I understand completely," the captain said sympathetically. "Changing environments can be stressful. If I might lead the way?"

"Lead on, Captain. Lead on," Eleanora said with yet another blinding smile. And another elbow jab to Roger.

Just let us make it to Leviathan *without Roger embarrassing me too hideously,* she thought earnestly. *Surely that isn't asking too much!*

"Oh, Christ on a Crutch. It's Mouse."

Kostas Matsugae looked up from the day-jackets he was unpacking from their traveling containers. The equipment bay was rapidly filling with Bronze Barbarians . . . and from the way they were putting their own equipment into lockers, it looked to be a permanent arrangement.

"What is the meaning of this?" the diminutive valet asked, in a precise, spare voice.

"Oh, don't get your titties in a wad, Mouse," the first speaker, one of the longer service privates, said. "There's only so much space on one of these assault transports. I guess you're gonna have to shoehorn into the space heavy-weapons would take up. Hey, all," the private went on, raising his voice slightly to be heard over the conversations and clatter of equipment. "Mousey's in the compartment. So nobody start doin' the nasty on the benches."

One of the female corporals sashayed past the middle-aged valet, stripping out of her dress uniform as she went.

"Mousies, how I love them. Mousies is what I love to eat."

"Nibble on their toesies, nibble on their tiny feet!" the rest of the platoon chorused.

Matsugae sniffed and went back to unloading the prince's accoutrements. His Highness would want to look his best for dinner.

"I'm not going to take dinner in the damned mess," Roger said petulantly, pulling at a strand of hair. He knew he was being a spoiled brat, and, as always, it drove him crazy. Of course, the whole situation seemed expressly designed to drive him mad, he reflected bitterly, and gripped his hands together until the knuckles went white and his forearms quivered.

"I'm not going," he repeated adamantly.

Eleanora knew from long experience that arguing with him was probably a lost cause, but sometimes, if you ground away at one of Roger's sulks, he came out of it. Sometimes. Rarely.

"Roger," she started calmly, "if you don't take dinner the first night, it will be a slap in the face to Captain Krasnitsky and his officers. . . ."

"I'm *not* going!" he shouted, and then, almost visibly, gathered control of his anger. His whole body was shivering now, and the tiny cabin seemed too small to contain his rage and frustration. It was the captain's cabin, the best one on the ship, but compared to the Palace, or even the regal ships of the Empress' Fleet that Roger had traveled on previously, it was the size of a closet.

He took a deep, cleansing breath, and shrugged.

"Okay, I'm being an ass. But I'm still not going to dinner. Make an excuse," he said with a sudden boyish grin. "You're good at that."

Eleanora shook her head in exasperation, but had to smile back. Sometimes Roger could also be disarmingly charming.

"Very well, Your Highness. I'll see you tomorrow morning."

She took the single step backward to open the hatch and stepped out of the cabin. And almost ran over Kostas Matsugae.

"Good evening, Ma'am," the valet said, skipping aside despite an armful of clothing and accoutrements. He had to dodge again to avoid running into the Marine standing guard outside the door, but the Marine remained utterly expressionless and motionless. Any humor she might have felt at the frantic hopping about of the valet was quashed by iron discipline. The members of The Empress' Own were renowned for their ability to remain stone-faced and still through virtually anything. They occasionally had contests to determine who had the most endurance and stoicism. The former sergeant major of Gold Battalion held the record for endurance: ninety-three hours at attention without eating, drinking, sleeping, or going to the bathroom. It was the last, he'd admitted, which had been the hardest. He'd finally passed out from a combination of dehydration and toxin buildup.

"Good evening, Matsugae," Eleanora replied, and fought her own urge to smile. It was hard, for the fussy little valet was so bedecked with outfits that it was almost impossible to find him under the pile. "I'm sorry to say that our Prince won't be taking dinner in the mess, so I doubt he really needs those," she continued, gesturing with her chin at the mass of clothes.

"What? Why?" Matsugae squeaked from somewhere under the pile. "Oh, never mind. I have the casuals for after dinner, so I suppose that will do." He gave his neck a little twist, and his balding head and round face rose like a toadstool from the pile of clothing. "It's a terrible shame, though. I'd picked out a lovely sienna suit."

"Maybe you can calm him down with some clothes." O'Casey's smile took on a tinge of resignation. "I seem to have set him off, instead."

"Well, I can understand his being upset," the valet said with another sharp squeak. "Being sent off to the back of beyond on a pointless mission is bad enough, but to send a prince of the Blood Royal on a barge is simply the worst insult I can imagine!"

Eleanora pursed her lips and frowned at the valet.

"Don't go making it any worse than it already is, Matsugae. Sooner or later, Roger has to begin taking up his responsibilities as a member of the Royal Family. And sometimes that means sacrifices." *Like maybe the sacrifice of enough time to get a staff to go with the "Chief,"* she added silently. "He doesn't need his sulks encouraged."

"You care for him in your way, Ms. O'Casey, and I will care for him in mine," the valet snapped. "Push a child around, despise him, revile him and cast out his father, and what do you expect to get?"

"Roger is no longer a child," she retorted angrily. "We can't coddle, bathe, and dress him like he is one."

"No," the valet replied. "But we can give him enough space to breathe! We can make an image for him and hope he grows into it."

"What, an image of a clotheshorse?" the chief of staff shot back. It was an old and worn argument that the valet seemed to be winning. "He's grown into *that* one beautifully!"

The valet stared back at her like a fearless mouse confronting a cat.

"Unlike some people," he sniffed with a glance at her painfully plain suit, "His Highness has an appreciation for the finer things in life. But there's more to His Highness than a 'clotheshorse.' Until some of you begin to acknowledge that fact, however, you'll get exactly what you expect."

He glowered at her for an instant longer, then gave yet another sniff, hit the latch for the hatch with an elbow, and stepped into the cabin.

Roger leaned back on the bed in the tiny cabin, eyes shut, and tried his best to radiate a dangerous calm. *I'm twenty-two years old,* he thought. *I'm a Prince of the Empire. I will* not *cry just because Mommy is making me angry.*

He heard the blast-door of the cabin open and shut, and knew immediately who it was; the cologne that Matsugae wore was almost overpowering in the small compartment.

"Good evening, Kostas," he said calmly. Just having the valet present was soothing. Whatever anyone else thought, Kostas always took him at his face value. When that value was below par, Kostas would tell him, but when it had merit on its own level, Kostas would acknowledge it where no one else would.

"Good evening, Your Highness," Kostas said, already laying out one of the light *gi*-like chambray outfits the prince preferred to lounge in. "Will you want your hair washed this evening?"

"No, thank you," the prince responded with unconscious politeness. "I suppose you heard I'm not taking dinner in the mess?"

"Of course, Your Highness," the valet responded as the prince rolled upright on the bed and looked sourly around the cabin. "Pity, really. I had a beautiful suit picked out: that light sienna one that complements your hair so well."

The prince smiled thinly. "Nice try, Kosie, but no. I'm just too frazzled to be polite at dinner." He slapped the sides of his head with both hands in frustration. "Leviathan I could take. Net-Hauling I could take, grumbly oil and all. But why, oh *why*, did Mother Her Regalness choose to send me on this goddamned tramp freighter?"

"It isn't a tramp freighter, Your Highness, and you know it. We needed room for the bodyguards, and the alternative would have been to detach a Fleet carrier. Which would have been a bit much, don't you think? I will admit, though, that it's a bit . . . shabby."

"Shabby!" The prince gave a bitter laugh. "It's so worn I'm surprised it can hold atmosphere! It's so old I bet the hull is welded! I'm surprised it's not driven by internal combustion engines or steam power! John would've gotten a carrier. *Alexandra* would've gotten a carrier! But not Roger! Oh, no, not 'Baby Roj!' "

The valet finished laying out the various outfits to be chosen from in the limited space of the cabin and stood back with a resigned expression.

"Will I be drawing a bath for Your Highness?" he asked pointedly, and Roger gritted his teeth at the tone.

"So I should stop whining and get a grip?"

The valet only smiled very slightly in return, and Roger shook his head.

"I'm too worked up, Kosie." He looked around the three-meter-square space and shook his head again. "I wish there was someplace I could work out in peace on this tub."

"There's an exercise area adjacent to the Assault Complement Quarters, Your Highness," the valet pointed out.

"I said in peace," Roger commented dryly. He generally preferred to avoid the troops that filled the compartment. He'd never actually worked out around the Battalion, despite being its nominal commanding officer, because he'd had his fill of weird looks and sniggers behind his back in four years at the Academy. Getting the same treatment from his own bodyguards would be hard to take.

"The majority of the ship's company is eating at the moment, Your Highness," Matsugae pointed out. "You would probably have the gym to yourself."

The thought of a good workout was awfully attractive. Finally Roger nodded his head.

"Okay, Matsugae. Make it so."

As the dessert was cleared, Captain Krasnitsky looked significantly at Ensign Guha. The mahogany-skinned young woman blushed a darker hue, and stood up, wine glass in hand.

"Ladies and gentlemen," she said carefully, "Her Majesty the Empress. Long may she rule!"

After the chorused "The Empress," the captain cleared his throat.

"I'm sorry His Highness is unwell, Captain." He smiled at Captain Pahner. "Is there anything we can do? The gravity, temperature, and air pressure in his cabin are as close to Earth normal as my chief engineer can make them."

Captain Pahner set down his almost untouched wine glass and nodded to the captain. "I'm sure His Highness will be fine." Various other phrases crossed his mind, but he carefully suppressed them.

After the completion of this voyage, Pahner would move on to a command slot on a very similar ship. But larger. As with all COs in The Empress' Own, he was already on the promotion lists for the next grade, and at the completion of his rotation, he would take over as the commander of the 2nd Battalion, 502nd Heavy Strike Regiment. Since the 502nd was the primary ground combat unit of Seventh Fleet—the Fleet usually found in any face-off with the Saints—he could expect to see regular action, and that was good. He had no love of war, but the heat of battle was the only possible place to truly test whether a person was a Marine or not, and it would be good to be back in harness.

With over fifty years in the service, enlisted and officer, the two commands—Empress' Own and Heavy Strike—would be as good as it got. From there on out, it would all be downhill. Either retirement, or else colonel and then brigadier. Which was as good as saying a desk job: the Empire hadn't fielded a regiment in a couple of centuries. It was a somber thought that he could see a light at the end of the tunnel and it was a grav-train.

Captain Krasnitsky waited for further elaboration, but decided after a moment that that was all he was getting from the taciturn Marine. With another frozen smile he turned to Eleanora.

"Has the rest of the staff gone ahead to Leviathan to prepare for the Prince's arrival, Ms. O'Casey?"

Eleanora took a slightly deeper gulp of wine than was strictly polite, and looked over at Captain Pahner.

"I *am* the rest of the staff," she said coldly. Which meant that there had *not* been anyone to send ahead as an advance party. Which meant that once they got there, she would be running her ass off trying to set up all the minor details the staff should be handling. The staff that she was apparently chief of. That mysterious, magically invisible staff.

The captain was now well aware that he was wandering through a field of landmines. He smiled again, took a sip of wine, and turned to the engineering officer at his left to engage in casual chitchat that wasn't going to tick off a member of the Imperial Household.

Pahner moistened his lips with his wine again and looked over at Sergeant Major Kosutic. She was chatting quietly with the ship's bosun, and caught the look and simply raised her eyebrows as if to say, "Well, what you want me to do about it?" Pahner shrugged millimetrically in reply, and turned to the ensign at his left. What could any of them do about it?

CHAPTER THREE

Pahner tossed the electronic memo pad onto the desk in the tiny office of the Assault Complement Commander.

"I think that's about all the planning we can do without actually seeing the dirtside conditions," he told Kosutic, and the sergeant major shrugged philosophically.

"Well, frontier planets full of rugged individualists rarely spawn assassins, anyway, Boss."

"True enough," Pahner admitted. "But it's close enough to both Raiden-Winterhowe and the Saints to have me twitchy."

Kosutic nodded, but she knew better than to ask most of the questions that came to mind. Instead, she fingered her earlobe, where the sun-painted skull and crossbones glittered faintly, and then glanced at the antiquated watch on her wrist.

"I'm going to take a turn around the ship. Find out how many of the posts are asleep," she announced.

Pahner smiled. In two tours with the Regiment, he'd never found a post other than fully alert. You just didn't make it this far if you were the type to even *slouch* on guard duty. But it never hurt to check.

"Have fun," he said.

Ensign Guha finished sealing her ship boots and looked around the cabin. Everything was shipshape, so she picked up the black bag at her feet and touched the stud to open her cabin hatch. Somewhere in the depths of her mind a little voice was screaming. But it was a quiet voice.

She stepped out of the cabin, turned to the right, and shouldered the ditty bag. The bag was unusually heavy. The materials within would have been detected in the security sweep of the ship which was standard operating procedure before a member of the Imperial Family took transit . . . and they had been. And then accepted. The assault ship was designed to take a full Marine complement, after all, which included all of their explosive "loadout." The six ultradense bricks, formed out of the most powerful chemical explosive known, should do the job perfectly. The thought was a pleasing one, and, of course, her own position as logistics officer gave her full access to the material. Even more pleasing. Taken all in all, she practically scintillated with pleasure.

Her cabin was on the outer rim of the ship, along with most of the personal quarters, and she had a long trip to Engineering. But it would be a happy trip . . . despite the quiet little screams within.

She strode down the passage, smiling pleasantly at the few souls about in the depths of ship-night. They were few and far between, but no one questioned the logistics officer. She'd been taking deep-night strolls for her whole tour, and it was put down to simple insomnia. And that was fair enough, for she did suffer from insomnia, however far from "simple" it might be on this particular night.

She traveled the curved passages of the giant sphere, taking elevators to lower levels on a circuitous route that brought her closer and closer to Engineering. The route was designed to avoid the Marine guards scattered at strategic locations around the ship. Although their detectors wouldn't spot the demolitions unless she got very close, they would easily detect the fully charged power cell of the bead pistol in the same bag.

The horizon of the gray painted passages shrank as she neared the center of the vast ball. Finally, she exited one last elevator.

The passage beyond was straight for a change, the far end sealed by a blast-door. To one side of the blast-door, covering the controls, was a single Marine in the silver-and-black dress uniform of the House of MacClintock.

Private Hegazi came to attention, one hand sliding automatically towards his sidearm as the elevator opened, but he relaxed again almost immediately when he recognized the officer. He'd seen her any number of times on her perambulations of the ship, but never by Engineering.

Guess she got bored, he thought. Or maybe I'm about to get lucky? Nonetheless, his duty was clear.

"Ma'am," he said, remaining at attention as she neared. "This is a secure space. Please exit this secure area."

Ensign Guha smiled faintly as an aiming grid dropped across her vision. Her right hand, hidden inside the bag, flipped the bead gun off of safe, and triggered a five-round burst.

The five-millimeter steel-coated, glass-cored beads were accelerated to phenomenal speeds by the electromagnets lining the barrel. The weapon's recoil was tremendous, but all five of the beads had cleared the barrel before recoil began to take effect. Ensign Guha's hand was thrown violently out of the now smoking bag, but the beads continued their flight towards the Marine guard.

Hegazi was fast. You had to be in the Regiment. But he also had less than an eighth of a second between the instant his instincts shrilled a warning and the impact of the first bead on his upper chest.

The outer layer of his heavy uniform was a synthetic that simulated buff wool but was fire resistant. It wasn't ballistic resistant. The next layer, however, was kinetic reactive. As the beads struck, the polymers of the uniform reacted instantaneously, their chemical bonds shifting under the imparted energy to change the textile from soft and flexible to solid as steel. The armor had weaknesses and was vulnerable to cuts, but it was light, and well-nigh impregnable to small-arms fire.

Yet any material has a breaking point. In the case of the Marines' uniform armor, that point was high but not infinite. The first bead shattered on the surface, the metal and glass bits flicking out in a fan to pepper the underside of the Marine's chin even as his hand reached once more for his own sidearm. The weight was coming off his feet as he started to drop to a kneeling position when the second bead hit a few centimeters above the first. This bead also shattered, but the extra energy began to splinter the molecular bonds of the resistant material.

The third bead did the trick. Coming in on the heels of the second and slightly lower, it shattered the kinetic armor like glass, finally throwing some of its mass into the now unprotected Marine's sternum.

Ensign Guha wiped the blood off of the keypad and attached a device to the surface temperature scanner. She shouldn't have had the codes to enter Engineering, or the facial features, for that matter. But any system is subject to compromise, and this one was no exception. The security systems saw the IR features of the *DeGlopper*'s chief engineer and received the correct codes timed in just the way the chief would have tapped them. She stepped through the open blast-doors and looked around, pleased but not surprised that there was no one in sight.

The engineering spaces of the ship were huge, taking up well over one-third of the interior volume. The tunnel drive coils and the capacitors to feed them took up the majority of the space, and their keening song filled the vast compartment as they sucked in energy voraciously and distorted any concept of Einsteinian reality. The light-speed limit could be violated, but it required immense power, and the tunnel drive gobbled up internal volume almost as greedily as it did energy.

But the field of the tunnel drive system was more or less fixed and independent of mass. Like the phase drive, there was a specific limit to the maximum volume of the field which could be generated, but the mass within that field was unimportant. Thus the huge ship carriers of the various Imperial and republican navies that battled among the stars. And thus the vast size of the interstellar fleet transports.

But all of it depended on power. Enormous, barely controlled power.

Ensign Guha turned to the left and followed the curving passage as the tunnel drive thumped out its keening star song.

Kosutic nodded at the guard on the magazine deck as she stepped back out the hatch. The guard, a newbie from First Platoon, had stopped her at the hatch and insisted that she pass the facial temperature scan and key in her code. Which was exactly what she was supposed to do, which was the reason for the sergeant major's nod of approval. However, Kosutic also made a mental note to talk to Margaretta Lai, the trooper's platoon sergeant. The trooper had clearly loosened up when she recognized the sergeant major, and she needed to learn to doubt everything and everyone. Eternal paranoia was the entire purpose of the Regiment. There was no other way to guard effectively in this day and age.

Despite early gains in processing, it had taken humanity nearly a millennium after the invention of the first crude computers to develop a system of implanted processors that interfaced completely with human neural systems without adverse side effects. The "toots" were still cutting edge and being constantly refined . . . and they were a security planner's nightmare, because they could be programmed to take over a person's body. When that happened, the unfortunate victim had no control over his own actions. The Marines called people like that "toombies."

Some societies used specially modified toots to control the actions of convicted criminals, but in most societies, including the Empire of Man, such a use of the hardware was illegal for all but military purposes. The Marines themselves used the system to the fullest as a combat aid and multiplier, but even they were wary of it.

The big problem was hacking. A person whose toot had been "hacked" could be forced to do literally anything. Just two years ago, someone had mounted an assassination attempt on the prime minister of the Alphane Empire by using a human official with a hacked toot. The hacker had never been found, but once the security protocols were solved, it had been a ludicrously simple thing to do.

The toots were designed for radio-packet external data input, and a small device disguised as an antique pocket watch had been found in the official's possession. It was speculated that it had been given to him as a gift, but wherever it had come from, it had taken his toot over. It was as if the official had been possessed by a demon hidden in the ancient Pandora's box.

Since then, all members of the Regiment and all close servitors of the Imperial Family had been required to go through random scans, and the security protocols of their toots had been updated yet again. Kosutic knew that, but she also knew there was no such thing as a perfect defense.

She made a note to hunt down Gunny Lai on her toot and smiled at the ambiguity of her own actions. She'd started off in the Marines before the day of the devices; but she'd become as dependent on them as everyone else. It was a humorous irony, in a bitter sort of way, that she now saw them as the single biggest threat to her charges.

She stepped onto the elevator and checked the duty roster again. Hegazi was on Engineering. Good troop, but new. Too new. Hell, they were all too new; eighteen months was just enough time to get very good at their jobs, then most went on to Steel. The few who stayed were rarely the best. She thought of Julian and laughed. Of course, there was best and best. But she intended to remind Hegazi, who was a good troop overall, that he needed to be totally one hundred percent paranoid at all times.

She stood in the pool of the Marine's blood. She hadn't bothered to check his pulse; nobody who'd lost that much blood was alive, and she was too busy considering what to do to waste time on pointless gestures. She didn't consider for long—the Marines didn't exactly pick ditherers as the senior noncoms of The Empress' Own—but there was always enough time to screw up, so there had to be enough to make the right move, as well.

She tapped her communicator.

"Sergeant of the Guard. Full load out to Engineering. We have a breach. Do not sound General Quarters."

She cut the communication. The guards would contact Pahner,

and the assassin wouldn't be alerted, for the Marine communicators were encrypted. Of course, the saboteur—and sabotage had to be what the killer contemplated—could have left any of half a dozen telltales along his backtrail to warn him that he'd been discovered.

Kosutic plucked the sensor wand off the dead guard's belt and swept the hatch. No obvious traces there. She keyed in the entry code and went through the hatch fast and low as it opened. The blood was already coagulating, and the body was cooling, so the assassin probably wasn't on the far side of the hatch. But Eva Kosutic hadn't survived to be a sergeant major by depending on "probably."

"Engineering, this is Sergeant Major Kosutic," she said into her communicator. "Do not, I say again, do *not* sound an alert. We have a probable saboteur in Engineering; your guard is dead." She swept the sensor wand around. There were heat traces everywhere, but most went straight ahead. All except one. A single trace split off from the pack, heading to the sergeant major's left, and it looked fresher.

"What?" the communicator demanded incredulously. "Where?"

"It looks like somewhere in quadrant four," she snapped. "Get on your scanners and vids. Find them."

There was a moment of silence from whoever was on the other end of the line. Then—

"Roger," the communicator responded.

She hoped like hell it wasn't the saboteur.

Ensign Guha paused and looked left and right. She brought up a measuring grid and used it to locate the precise point she needed on the right-hand bulkhead, then reached into her satchel and extracted a one-kilo shaped charge. She stripped the covering plastic off the bottom, affixed it to the bulkhead with the provided adhesive, and examined her handiwork for a moment, to ensure it wasn't going anywhere. Then she pulled a pin and depressed a thumbswitch. A small red light blinked on, then went out; the bomb was armed.

She turned to her left once more and continued her circuit. Only three more to go.

Captain Pahner closed the front of his chameleon suit and

configured his helmet to seal the whole system as the elevator descended. Gunnery Sergeant Jin, already suited, stood beside him with Kosutic's helmet slung at his side and her chameleon suit over his shoulder. The standard issue Marine suits offered better ballistic protection than dress uniforms, faded the wearer into the background, and were designed for vacuum work. They weren't as good as combat armor, but there wasn't time for full armor. He had one platoon warming theirs up anyway, of course, but if this didn't go down in the next few minutes his name wasn't Armand Pahner.

"Eva," he snapped into the helmet mike. "Talk to me."

"Three so far. One-kilo shaped charges right over plasma conduits. They've got anti-tamper devices in them. I can smell it."

"Captain Krasnitsky, this is Captain Pahner," Pahner said sharply. *Surprise is a mental condition, not reality,* he reminded himself. "We have to shut down those conduits."

"We can't," Krasnitsky answered. "You can't just shut off a tunnel drive. If you tried it, you'd come out at a random point somewhere in a nine-light-year-radius sphere. And the plasma has to be slowed down, anyway. If you just try to shut off it . . . backfires. We could lose everything."

"If we were about to be hit in Engineering by enemy fire," Pahner asked, "what would you do then?"

"We'd be under *phase* drive!" Krasnitsky snapped back. "You can't *be* hit in tunnel space. There's no procedure for this!"

"Shit," Pahner said quietly. It was the first time anyone had ever heard him swear. "Sergeant Major, get the hell out of there."

"I don't see any timers."

"They're there."

"Probably. But if I can get the shooter . . ."

"They could be on a dead-man's switch," Pahner said, gritting his teeth as he stepped off the elevator. "This is an order, Sergeant Major Kosutic. Get out of there. Now."

"I'm closer to getting out going through the shooter than going back," Kosutic said mildly.

Pahner looked at the first bomb. As Kosutic had said, there were no telltales but it smelled like it had anti-tamper devices. He turned to the sergeant of the guard, Sergeant Bilali from First Platoon, who looked as cool as a cucumber for someone standing within a few feet of a bomb that could go off at any moment. The private next to him wasn't quite as cool; she was watching the sergeant's back and breathing deeply and regularly. It was a common method of dealing with combat stress, which she obviously was. Pahner arched an eyebrow at Bilali.

"Demo?"

"On the way, Sir," the sergeant replied crisply.

"Okay," Pahner said with a nod and a glance around. If the bomber gave them time, they could try blowing the bombs in place. The explosion of a charge placed next to one of them would tend to break up the plasma jet from a shaped charge, and the bulkheads were armored to protect the plasma conduits. Without a shaped-charge jet, there was no way the explosions would penetrate. Of course, that assumed that they didn't go off before the demolition teams could get to them.

"'If you can keep your head when all about you . . .'" Pahner whispered, thinking furiously.

"Excuse me, Sir?"

"Is there someone following up the Sergeant Major?"

"Yes, Sir," Bilali said. "There are teams coming from either end, and we have one cutting across the middle of Engineering, as well."

"Okay, we all know we're brave, but there's a fine line between hardcore and stupid. Let's get the heck out of here and seal this passage in case these things go off."

"Roger that, Sir." The expression on Bilali's midnight-black face didn't even flicker as he touched his communicator. "Guard. Everyone but the point teams, out of the passage. Seal it at both ends." The passage made a circuit of the ship. Although there were side connections, those stayed sealed as a matter of course. It was only the central passageway hatches that remained open. And the intervening blast-doors. If worse came to worst . . .

"Captain Krasnitsky," Pahner said, "what happens if we shut all the doors and the bombs detonate anyway?"

"Bad things," a female voice snapped. "This is Lieutenant

Commander Furtwangler, Chief Engineer. First of all, the blast-doors aren't designed for multiple plasma failures. They might not stop it from flooding Engineering. And even if they do keep the plasma from killing us all, we still drop out of TD. We probably don't get the drive back with that much damage, and even if we do, we lose most of our range. Satan only knows what secondary damage would occur. Bad things," she repeated.

Pahner nodded as the blast-doors shut on his Marines. Bad things seemed to be happening all over.

Kosutic had noted the pattern of placement, and as the sixth blast-door came up, she leapt forward, skidding on her stomach into view of where the next bomb would be.

Ensign Guha triggered a burst of beads that shrieked through where the sergeant major would have been had she come around the corner running upright. The kick from the powerful pistol threw it up over the ensign's head despite her two-handed grip, and she never had time to get back on target.

Eva Kosutic was a veteran of a hundred firefights and fired thousands of bead rounds every week just to keep in practice. No hacked assassination program, however well-designed, could beat that experience. Her own bead pistol tracked onto the young ensign's throat, and she triggered a single round.

The five-millimeter bead was accelerated to four kilometers per second in its twenty-centimeter flight up the barrel. When it struck the ensign's neck, one centimeter to the left of her trachea, it shattered, converting all of its kinetic energy to explosive hydrostatic shock in a fraction of a second.

The ensign's head exploded off her body and was thrown backwards as the severed carotids jetted blood all over the unarmed bomb at her feet.

Before the decapitated body had hit the floor, Kosutic was up and running. The armed bombs were probably remotely triggered, but they would also have a backup. Any plan this meticulous was bound to have a backup. The simplest would be a timer, but a good addition would be a dead-man's switch controlled by the assassin's toot. When the ensign died, which she more or less had just done, the toot would send out a signal—probably when all brain activity ceased—to detonate the bombs. But although the ensign-zombie was for all practical purposes dead, brain activity in a case of severance continued for a few seconds. Which was why the sergeant major had shot her in the throat, not the head.

All of the bombs were behind Eva Kosutic, and she intended to ensure that they stayed as far away as possible. She keyed her communicator. "*Fire in the hole! Shut all blast-doors!*" she shouted as she leapt over the sprayed blood and past the ensign's head, still accelerating.

Captain Pahner had just opened his mouth to repeat the sergeant major's order when there were a whole series of thumps, and the world went sideways.

CHAPTER FOUR

Roger was never sure afterwards if it was the General Quarters alarm or the rough hands of the Marines that startled him awake.

The Marines' faces were unfamiliar to his mostly sleeping brain in the dim red emergency lights, under the banshee howl of the alarm, and he reacted violently as he was slammed roughly into a bulkhead. As a member of the Imperial Family, his toot was equipped with several bits of software not available to the general public, including a complete "hardwired" hand-to-hand combat package and an "assassin" program which did several interesting things. Moreover, the prince had always been athletic. He held black belts in three separate "hard" martial arts, and his *sensei* (not surprisingly) was one of the best in the entire Empire of Man.

With all of that going for him, he was *not* a safe person to jump upon, without warning, in the dark, whatever Bravo Company might have thought of him. Even taken by surprise in a sound sleep, he managed to kick backward, trying for a knee strike as one arm was wrenched to the left and inserted in a sleeve. Considering his surprised, sleep-groggy state, it was a remarkably well-executed attempt . . . and accomplished absolutely nothing.

If the members of The Empress' Own were surprised by his response, they had a surprise or two for him, as well. Like the fact that *their* toots offered hardwired booster packages of their own . . . and that all of them had spent even longer training in the martial arts than he had. He was spun around and struck in the solar plexus for his troubles.

The two Bravo Company privates seemed unconcerned by his chokes and gasps as they expertly stuffed him into an emergency vac suit, and once they had him in the suit, with his helmet on, they sat on him. Literally. He was pushed roughly to the deck, where the two bodyguards pinned him down and sat on him, weapons trained outward.

Due to the oversized cretin sitting on his chest, he couldn't reach his suit controls, and since the com was in its default "off" mode, he couldn't even call Captain Pahner and order him to get these slope-browed bruisers to let him up. Although he was technically their commander, the privates paid no attention to his first few queries, shouted through the plastron of the helmet. As soon as he realized his efforts were ineffective, he gave up. The hell if he was going to be ignored by these goons.

After what seemed an eternity, but couldn't have been more than ten or fifteen minutes, the compartment hatch opened to reveal two Marines in battle armor. The guards sitting on him stood up, one of them giving him a hand to help him to his feet, and left the compartment. The two new guards, faceless nonentities behind the flickering visors of their powered armor, sat him on the bed and sandwiched him between them, weapons trained outward once again. But in this case, the weapons were a quad-barreled heavy bead gun and a plasma cannon trained, respectively, toward the door and toward the next compartment. If boarders came slicing through the wall, they were in for an uncomfortable surprise.

He now had time to examine the vac suit and found that—surprise, surprise—the com was limited to the emergency "Guard" frequency only. It was an unforgivable sin, roughly comparable to eating one's own young, to use that frequency in anything but a true emergency. That was a lesson (one of the few) he'd learned quite painfully during his mandatory ordeal at the Academy, and since the troopers didn't seem to be hostile—just very, very determined to keep him safe—this probably didn't count as a "true" emergency. So no communicator.

Which left him to ponder what was going on with virtually no data. There was air, but the emergency lights were on. He reached for the latches on his suit to take the helmet off, but one of the armored Marines tapped his hand away from them. The tap was obviously intended to be polite but firm, but the pseudo-muscles of the armor turned it into a stinging slap.

Rubbing his knuckles, Roger leaned over until his helmet was in contact with the Marine's.

"Would you mind telling me what the hell is going on?"

"Captain Pahner said to wait until he got here, Your Highness," a female soprano, badly distorted by the helmets, responded.

Roger nodded and leaned back against the bulkhead, flipping his head inside the helmet to try to make his ponytail lie flat and smooth. So, either there'd been a coup, and Pahner was in on it, or there'd been some sort of emergency, and Pahner wanted to be able to give him a complete report rather than a garbled version second- or third-hand.

If the second scenario were correct, well and good. He would just cool his heels here for a while, then find out what the problem was. If it was a case of the first scenario . . . He looked at the armored Marine with the bead cannon pointed at the door. There was probably a snowball's chance in hell that he could actually wrest it away from the Marine and kill Pahner with it, but if this was a coup, his life was worth less than spit anyway. Might as well go out like a MacClintock.

He walked mentally back over every step of the event, and noticed that the floor had stopped vibrating. The background hum of the various life-support and drive systems had become so familiar that it was unnoticed, but now, with it gone, its absence was obvious. If those systems were off-line, they were in deep trouble indeed . . . which at least militated against the coup theory.

Then he thought about the two troopers who'd dragged him out of bed. They'd suited him up and literally sat on him for a good ten minutes before anyone showed up to relieve them. And they hadn't had suits. If the cabin had lost pressure, they would have died rapid and unpleasant deaths. So the privates, at least, thought he was worth keeping alive. Which also argued against the coup theory.

They'd also risked their lives to protect him, and while that willingness to risk or lose their lives to keep their charges alive was assumed on the part of the Imperial Family, Roger had never been in an emergency. There'd never been a situation in which his bodyguard's life was threatened. Well, there'd been that one disastrous encounter on a vacation, but the bodyguard was never actually in danger, whatever the young lady had threatened. . . .

But in this case, two people whose names he didn't even know had risked an awful death to protect his life.

It was a confusing thought.

Nearly two hours passed before "Captain" Pahner appeared, accompanied by Captain Krasnitsky. Pahner was in a chameleon suit, while the ship's captain was in a Fleet skin suit, with his helmet flopped back out of the way.

Pahner nodded to the two guards, who left the cabin, closing the hatch behind them. Roger took a good look at Krasnitsky, and promptly waved him into the station chair at the small desk. While the Fleet captain collapsed into the seat, Pahner touched the stud to lock the hatch, then turned and faced the prince.

"We have a problem, Your Highness."

"Oh, really, Captain? I hadn't noticed." The prince's voice was muffled through the plastron of the helmet. After a moment's fumbling, he released the standard catches and dumped the helmet on his bunk. "By the way," he continued sourly, "there wouldn't happen to be a skin-suit in *my* size on board, would there?"

"No, Your Highness, there wouldn't," Pahner answered stoically. "I've already checked. That detail was overlooked. As were others, apparently." He turned to the miserable-looking captain. "If you'd care to continue, Captain Krasnitsky?"

The captain rubbed his face and sighed.

"We were sabotaged, Your Highness. Badly."

"Sabotaged?" the prince repeated incredulously. "By whom?"

"Now *that* is the million-credit question, Your Highness," Pahner admitted. "We know the who as in 'who actually did the sabotage.' That was Ensign Amanda Guha, the ship's logistics officer."

"What?" Roger blinked in confusion. "Why would she do that?"

Captain Krasnitsky opened his mouth to answer, then looked at Pahner, and the Marine shrugged his shoulders and continued. "We're not positive, of course, but I believe she was a toombie."

"A toot zombie?" Roger's eyes widened. "Here? Are there any more?" Then he shook his head at the stupidity of his own question. "We wouldn't know, would we?"

"No, Your Highness, we wouldn't," Pahner replied with considerable restraint. "However, there are some indications that she was the sole toombie. It's vanishingly unlikely that anyone else in the Company is at risk. Everyone who is expected to have contact with you is regularly swept and has up-to-date security protocols. And everyone in the ship's company was swept before the voyage. Including Ensign Guha. But we found a device in her cabin. . . ."

"Oh, shit," Roger said.

"I can think of at least twenty ways the device could have made it on board," Pahner continued. "However, that's not the most pressing issue at the moment."

"Your Highness," Captain Krasnitsky said finally, with a nodded thanks at Pahner, "Captain Pahner is correct. How they got to Guha is less important than what she did to us, I'm afraid. She managed to attach explosive devices to several of the tunnel drive plasma conduits. When they went off, we nearly lost Engineering entirely from an unvented plasma core leak. When the plasma breach was detected, the automated systems were *supposed* to shut off deuterium flow, but the next bead in the magazine was a worm program that she apparently dumped into the control systems. It cut out the safety interlocks, so the plasma kept venting. . . ."

The captain stopped and wiped his face, trying to find the right words to report the disaster, but Pahner did it for him.

"We've lost all but one fusion plant, Your Highness," the stone-faced Marine said. "Tunnel drive is off-line. Phase drive is off-line. The chief engineer got the flow shut down manually, but a plasma blast took her out right after she did it. And she was our only fully qualified engineering repair officer."

"A physical and cyber attack." The prince sounded stunned. "Against a member of the Imperial Family?"

"Yes, Your Highness," Pahner said with the bleak smile of the truly pissed professional. "Lovely, don't you think? And it wasn't as if they were going to stop there. We've got worm programs and viruses in every major subsystem: Navigation, Fire Control—"

"And Environmental," Krasnitsky interrupted with a shake of his head. "Well, had. I'm pretty sure we got them all wiped out, but we've taken some heavy casualties in Engineering, and—"

"I was 'pretty sure' there wasn't anything like them on board to begin with!" Pahner snapped angrily. "We need to be more than 'pretty sure,' Captain."

"Agreed, Captain," the captain said shortly. He stood and straightened his back. "Your Highness, with your permission, I need to get back to my ship. I have high hopes that we can make sufficient repairs to get us to a habitable planet. Although," he turned and looked at the granite-faced Pahner again, "the system we have to make for . . ."

He let his voice trail off and shrugged, and Roger nodded, with a dazed expression.

"Of course, Captain. You need to get back to work. Good luck. Call me if you need anything."

He realized how fatuous the last sentence sounded even as it dropped from his lips. What the heck could he do that trained and experienced crew members couldn't? Cook? But the already exhausted captain paid no attention to the silliness of the remark. He simply bowed, and stepped past Pahner and out of the cabin.

The hatch closed behind him, and Pahner gave the prince another bleak smile.

"What the Captain didn't mention, Your Highness, is where we're headed."

"Which is where?" the prince asked warily.

"Marduk, Your Highness."

The prince searched his memory, but found nothing. A quick check of his implanted database found the planet, but it was simply listed as a Class Three imperial planet. A toot had a fairly large memory, but much of it was taken up by the interaction protocols. The remainder was filled with data which, in Roger's case, anyway, was selected at the user's discretion. Now the entry flashed across the surface of his consciousness as figures and pictures scrolled across his vision. Most of the data was textual and symbolic, the better to crowd into the memory allocation, and he frowned thoughtfully as he scanned it. The world maintained an imperial post with what sounded like very limited landing facilities, but it wasn't even an associate member—just a place where the Empire had planted its flag.

"It's one of ours," he stated carefully.

"Nominally, Your Highness. Nominally," Pahner snorted. "There's a port, but no repair facilities—certainly none capable of repairing one of these assault ships. There's an automated refueling post over one of the gas giants which is owned by TexAmP, but the port is locally managed. Out on the back of beyond like it is, who knows what's actually going on?"

Pahner consulted his own toot and frowned much more unhappily than Roger had.

"The only intel note I have on the region is that the Saints might be active out here. On the other hand, Your Highness, out here on the frontier about half the time you turn around there's a Saint SpecOps team nosing under the tent." He smiled faintly. "Of course, they probably feel the same way about us."

Pahner consulted his notepad, with its much greater memory, and frowned again.

"The locals are hostile and primitive, the fauna is vicious, the mean temperature is thirty-three degrees centigrade, and it rains five times a day. The region is notorious for Dream Spice smuggling, and piracy is rampant. Of course." He shook his head. "Frankly, Your Highness, I feel like I'm taking you down Fourteenth Street at oh-three hundred on a Saturday night in August dressed in thousand-credit chips."

Fourteenth Street had been in existence since the days when Imperial City had been the District of Columbia, the capital of the former United States, and it had never been a good place to wander.

But that was the last thing on Roger's mind at this particular moment, and he rubbed his face and sighed.

"Is there any good news?" The question had a note of a whine in it, and he kicked himself for being such a shit. Everyone else was busting their butts to save his sorry ass. The least he could do was not whine about the situation!

Pahner's face tightened.

"Well, you're still breathing, Your Highness. So I haven't failed my charge yet. And I think the Captain can get the ship *to* Marduk, which is a blessing. At least in a military ship they can reroute the fixed control runs, although that's going to take a week or more, with most of the Company pitching in alongside the crew to do, pardon the pun, grunt work.

"It's good news that the senior engineer was in the compartment in the middle of the night and reacted fast enough to shut down an out of control reaction. It's good news that we're on a military ship. It's good news that we only got knocked six or seven light-years off course, and not clear into Saint territory. It's good news that we're still breathing. But other than that, no. I can't think of any."

Roger nodded. "You have an interesting definition of good news, Captain. But I see your point. What can I do to help?" he asked, carefully controlling his voice.

"To tell you the truth, Your Highness, the best thing you can do is to stay in your cabin and out of the way. All your presence would do would be to distract the crew and make my guys have to run around using up extra oxygen. So, if you'd stay put, I'd appreciate it. I'll have your meals delivered."

"What about the gym?" Roger asked, his eyes flicking around the tiny cabin.

"Until Environmental comes back online, none of us are going to be doing much working out, Your Highness. Now, if you'll excuse me, I have to get back to work."

Without waiting for permission, Pahner hit the hatch key and let himself out. The hatch cycled shut behind him, leaving Roger to stare at the walls that seemed smaller than ever.

And to listen for the returning circulation of air.

CHAPTER FIVE

Prince Roger's patience had worn thin.

The better part of a day had passed since the crudely repaired, shuddering tunnel drive had kicked off and the in-system phase drive had cut in, and he was tired of being good. He'd been stuck in his cabin, half the time in this ill-fitting vac suit, for three weeks while the repairs proceeded and the ship limped through tunnel space toward Marduk, and the noise and vibration of the patched-up drive systems hadn't been designed to make him any happier about it.

The TD normally emitted a smooth, almost lulling background hum, but the jury-rigged repairs had produced something that whined, shuddered, and sometimes seemed to threaten to tear the ship apart. Pahner and Captain Krasnitsky had been careful to underplay the problems on their infrequent visits to update him, but the repairs weren't much more than "5k cord and bubble gum," according to Matsugae, who'd become friendly with some of the guards. They'd held together, though, and the awful journey was almost over. All they had to do was land on Marduk and commandeer the first imperial ship back to Earth. He might even end up being able to avoid Leviathan completely. Problem solved, crisis resolved, danger past. So Roger, Prince of the House MacClintock, was not by God going to stay cooped up, incommunicado, in his stinking cabin.

He smoothed down his hair, patted a few stray strands into place, touched the hatch control, and stepped out into the passage. The stink in the dim corridor was even worse than in the cabin, and for a moment he considered donning his helmet. But he was obviously clumsy putting it on and taking it off, and damned if he was going to give these Myrmidons a reason to laugh at his expense. He turned to one of the armored guards.

"Take me to the bridge," he ordered in his most imperious tone. He wanted to be absolutely clear that he was done cowering in his cabin.

Sergeant Nimashet Despreaux cocked her head inside her helmet and regarded the prince from behind the shield of her flickering visor. The helmet system was intended to cause the eye to shift away, enhancing the effect of the chameleon camouflage they all wore. But it also made it impossible for anyone on the outside to see a Marine's expression, and, after a brief pause, she stuck her tongue out at him and turned toward the bridge. She also sent a biofeedback command to the radio control and opened a channel to Captain Pahner.

"Captain Pahner, this is Sergeant Despreaux. His Highness is headed for the bridge," she reported flatly.

"Roger," was the terse reply.

It was going to be interesting to be a fly on the wall for this one.

They finally cycled through the double airlock system to the bridge, and Roger looked around. He'd familiarized with the *Puller*-class at the Academy, but he'd never actually been on the bridge of one before. The company-sized assault transports were the backbone of the Corps support groups, which meant they were under-emphasized by the Academy. An Academy graduate wanted to be posted to Line or Screen forces, where the promotions and the action were, not to an assault barge. Might as well captain a garbage scow.

But this garbage scow had survived the crisis, and that said a lot for the captain and crew, Academy graduates or not.

There was evidence of the damage even on the bridge. Scorch marks on the communications board indicated an overload in the maser com, and most of the front panels were missing from the control stations. Control runs were normally formed directly into the hull structure when a ship was grown, but since military ships had to assume that they would suffer combat damage, there were provisions for bypassing them with temporary systems. In this case, hastily installed relays, some of them even made out of *wire,* for God's sake, snaked across the floor, and the compartment was filled with the faint pulse of optic transmissions leaking from the joints.

Roger stepped over the cables littering the deck and joined the captain where he and Pahner were examining the tactical readout. The hologram of the system buckled and rippled as the crippled tactical computers struggled to keep it updated.

"How are we doing?" he asked.

"Well," Captain Krasnitsky answered with a grim, utterly humorless smile, "we *were* doing fine, Your Highness."

As he finished speaking, the General Quarters alarm sounded. Again.

"What's happening?" Roger asked over the wail, and Captain Pahner frowned and shook his head.

"Unidentified warship in the system, Your Highness. They're over a day away from intercept, but we don't know what else might be lying doggo nearby."

"What?" Roger yipped, his voice cracking in surprise. "How? But—" He stopped and tried to put on a better face. "Are they part of the sabotage? Could they be waiting for us? And who are they? Not imperial?"

"Captain?" Pahner turned to the ship's commander.

"Currently, who they are is unknown, Sir. Your Highness, I mean." For once, the captain wasn't flustered by the presence of royalty. The overriding necessity to fight his ship was all he had mind for, and the last three weeks of hell had burned out most of his other worries. "Our sensors are damaged, along with everything else, but it's definitely a warship, from the phase drive signature. The filament structure is too deep for it to be anything else." He frowned again and thought about the rest of the questions.

"I doubt that they're part of some deeply laid plan, Your

Highness. When the tunnel drive was damaged, it threw us badly off our planned flight path. I doubt that the conspirators, whoever they were, could believe we're still alive, and if they'd made preparations to 'make sure of the job,' they would have done so in systems closer to our base course. Marduk is off our baseline by almost a full tunnel jump, almost seventeen light-years. I don't see how anyone could have anticipated our ending up here.

"So, no, I don't think they're 'waiting for us,' but that doesn't necessarily make their presence good news. The drive and emissions signatures look kind of like a Saint parasite cruiser, but if that's so, that means the Saints have had a Line carrier in-system."

"And that means the Saints have probably taken the system," Pahner snarled.

The ship captain smiled thinly and sniffed, tapping the edge of the crippled tactical display. "Yes, it does."

"So the planet is under hostile control?" Roger asked.

"Possibly, Sir. Your Highness," Krasnitsky agreed. "Okay, probably. The orbitals, at least. They haven't necessarily taken over the port."

"Almost certainly," Pahner concluded. "Captain, I think we need a council. Myself and my officers, His Highness, your officers who are available. We have time?"

"Oh, yes. Whoever this is, he waited to bring up his phase drive until we were deep enough inside the tunnel wall to be sure no merchant could make it back out without being overhauled. Which probably means our signature is changed enough from our damage that he thinks we're a merchie instead of an assault ship. But even with our accel towards the planet and his accel towards us, we have several hours to decide what we're going to do."

"What are our choices?" Roger asked. The blinking red icon of the possible hostile cruiser held his eyes like a lodestone, and Krasnitsky smiled faintly.

"Well, there isn't much choice, is there, Your Highness? We can't space out . . ."

". . . so, we'll have to fight," Captain Krasnitsky said.

The wardroom was crowded. Besides Krasnitsky, there were his executive officer, the acting engineer, and the acting tactical officer. On Bravo Company's side of the table there was Prince Roger, who was flanked by Eleanora O'Casey and Captain Pahner. In addition, Pahner had brought two of his three lieutenants. According to the ideal universe of The Book, there were supposed to be seven lieutenants a line company, but that happy state of affairs was rarely found in dreary reality. It was especially hard to find in The Empress' Own, which had even higher standards for its officers than its enlisted men.

In general, the need for an executive officer and "chief of staff" for a company commander was seen as overriding the need for a platoon leader, so Third Platoon was officerless. Its platoon sergeant, who normally would have been in the meeting, was busy getting it prepared for whatever the CO decided to do, and the navigator was on the bridge, bluffing the oncoming cruiser which was looking more and more like a Saint parasite.

"I don't want anyone to have any doubts," Krasnitsky went on. "We might win, and we might not. Usually, I'd say we could take a single cruiser—we've got more missiles, and heavier, and we've got him licked on beam armament." He paused and stared at the deckhead for a moment. "We've got all the normal advantages of a tunnel drive ship. We aren't mass-limited; the drive only cares about our volume, so we can afford to mount ChromSten armor, which he can't. That right there is a major factor, since it will shrug off some of the missiles that get through, whereas ours will all hammer him. And we've got more internal volume, so we can absorb more of the damage that does get through.

"The downside is, we're in sad shape. We can hardly accelerate at all, and our sensors and targeting systems are screwed. We're a damned big target, too, so it's not like they're going to miss. All the normal disadvantages of a TD ship, with a few extra thrown in. So we'll take damage, no question. Even if we win, we'll be in worse shape than we are now."

He paused again and looked around the compartment. The Marines, combat veterans all, looked grim but determined. His own people, none of whom had actually been through a ship-to-ship action, looked a bit white, but focused. The prince's chief of staff was trying very hard to look as if she had any idea at all of what was going on. The prince, though . . . The prince was a sight. It was obvious that, whatever else he'd taken at the Academy, no-win simulations hadn't been on the program. As the briefing had gone on, his eyes had just gotten rounder and rounder. . . .

"What about punching the assault shuttles?" Pahner asked, leaning a chin on one fist and looking so calm he appeared almost disinterested. Krasnitsky had dealt with some cool Marines in the course of his career, but the commander of the prince's bodyguard was obviously one of those rare people who simply got calmer when disaster loomed. The Fleet officer was willing to bet that the Marine's blood pressure and heartbeat were so low they were dropping off the scale.

"I'd suggest loading them," Lieutenant Commander Talcott, *DeGlopper*'s XO, said, "but don't punch them. Putting their additional armor between the Prince and incoming fire would be good, but you'd have a helluva time making the planet without us from here."

"Have we received any transmission from the other ship?" Eleanora asked.

"Not yet," Krasnitsky said. "Lag. The soonest we can expect to receive a com is sometime in the next half hour, and they'll be receiving our own message about the same time. And before you ask: we're the Nebula Lines freighter *Beowulf's Gift*, out of Olmstead. We've had a tunnel drive failure, and we're looking for a port to await a repair ship."

"Whether they believe it or not," snorted Lieutenant Gulyas, the Second Platoon leader. Since Marine companies were designed to operate independently, which meant their COs needed their own *de facto* staffs, he also wore the "hat" of intel officer.

"Indeed," Lieutenant Commander Talcott said. "Just as much as we believe them."

"There's no reason for them to suspect us," Captain Krasnitsky pointed out. "With our phase drive damage, we can't make any sort of acceleration, and the damage also masks our tendril signature.

Frankly, we do look like a damaged freighter. They'll practically have to do a hull map to tell the difference."

"By which time," Sublieutenant Segedin declared, "we'll have them locked up and ready to blast." The acting tactical officer seemed to be looking forward to the action. Nervous but ready, like a racehorse at the starting gate. "The good news is how long they waited to fire up. They have to be assuming we're a merchie, so they'll come calling for us to heave to or follow them to the planet. We'll play along, but not decel. The closer we get to the planet, the better."

"We're down one missile tube," Talcott commented. "The local server was flattened by the power surges, and we're out of spares, but that leaves us seven. And all the laser mounts are online. Fire control is . . . spotty. But it should hold for a short engagement."

"So the ship blasts the cruiser," Prince Roger said, twining a golden strand of hair around one finger. "Then what? How do we get back to Earth?"

"Then the port submits, or we drop kinetic weapons on it, Your Highness," Pahner said flatly. "And after that, we wait for a ride home."

"And if the carrier comes back?" Roger was surprised at how calm he sounded. He looked at the piece of hair in his hand as if in surprise, and then patted it back into place. "I mean, the cruiser had to be dropped off by a carrier, right? And a carrier has collapsed armor and even more missiles than we do. Right?"

Pahner and Krasnitsky shared a look, and Pahner answered.

"Well, Your Highness, I think we'll have to cross that bridge when we come to it. It could just be lying low somewhere. But," he glanced at Segedin, "what about other ships in the system? Other cruisers or destroyers?"

"Right now, we don't detect any," the acting TACO replied. "But if the cruiser hadn't lit off its drive, we never would have detected him, either. There could be a carrier or another cruiser—or a hundred little fighter bastards—out there, and we'd have no idea."

"Okay," Pahner said, "we'll cross that bridge when we come to it, too." He turned to the Marine lieutenants who were making notes on their pads. The electronic devices would convert the entire meeting to text for reading, but the notes brought out the highlights. "Get the assault boats prepped. Full loadout. When we hit orbit, we should be prepared for a hot drop on the port."

"Are we talking an extended fight here, Sir?" Lieutenant Sawato asked. The First Platoon leader was the senior lieutenant and *de facto* operations officer for the company. If there was going to be an extended fight, it would be her job to ensure that the plans were in place to support it.

"No." Pahner shook his head. "We'll call on them to surrender. If they do, we'll drop on them like a ton of lead. If they don't, we'll hit them with kinetic strikes, *then* drop on them like a ton of lead. We'll work up a full mission order around that in the next few hours. Take this as a warning order. "

"Will that be strictly necessary, Major?" Eleanora asked. "I mean, you're the Bronze Battalion, not an enforcement company. It's your job to protect Prince Roger, not to retake planets from people like the Saints. If we hold the orbitals, can't we just wait for reinforcements to arrive and handle the situation on the ground?"

Pahner looked at her woodenly for a moment.

"Yes, Ma'am. I suppose we could," he said finally. "But, frankly, I think it's important that whoever has taken over the system understand that when you dick around with an imperial base, all it gets you is bloody and bruised. More to the immediate point, we might end up hiding on the ground. I'd prefer that base be neutralized if we do."

"You mean if the cruiser's support ship comes back?" Roger asked.

"Yes, Your Highness. Or if it's still around somewhere," Pahner replied shortly.

"Will His Highness be on the assault?" Krasnitsky asked in a diffident tone.

"Yes!" Roger said quickly, his face lighting at the thought of getting off the ship.

"No!" Pahner and O'Casey spoke simultaneously, and it was difficult to say which sounded more emphatic. They looked at each other, then at the prince. The two of them flanked him like lions at the gate, and O'Casey leaned out over the table to fix his eye, since he was steadfastly looking across the table at Captain Krasnitsky.

"*No*," she said even more firmly.

"Why not?" Roger asked, wincing inwardly as he heard his own whining tone. "I can carry my own weight!"

"It's too dangerous," O'Casey snapped. "The very idea is ludicrous!"

"If we're performing an assault, Your Highness, I can't have my troops guarding you at the same time," Pahner pointed out in her support.

"*My* troops," Roger said petulantly. He hated the tone, but he didn't know how else to say it. "*Mine*, Captain. I'm the battalion commander; you work for me." He smoothed his hair and pulled a couple of imaginary wayward strands into place, and Pahner's face turned to clenched-jawed iron.

"Yes, Your Highness, you are." He leaned back, crossed his arms, and gazed impassively up at the deckhead. "What are your orders, Sir?"

Roger had already opened his mouth to protest the next infringement on his prerogatives, and the sudden lack of resistance left him with his mouth hanging wide. He had absolutely no idea what orders he should give, nor did he want to give any. He just wished that people would start treating him like an adult and the commander of the battalion instead of an appendage only important as something to guard. But suddenly the image of a Marine, out of his chameleon suit, exposed to vacuum, sitting on his own vac-suited chest, waiting to see if the ship was going to depressurize, flashed across his vision, and he knew he had to find a way out of the corner he'd painted himself into. He thought about the conversation which had been going on around him, to the point of doing a quick check of his toot. The device had been set to a one-minute memory storage, a technique that had stood him in good stead in school and on numerous social occasions, and he felt a surge of relief as he spotted an out.

"Well, Captain, I think we should get started on drafting an operations order while the platoons prep the shuttles. We'll settle who's going to be included on the mission in the operations order." He glanced sideways at Eleanora, but she refused to meet his eye, as did the embarrassed-looking officers across the table. "Do you have anything further, Captain Krasnitsky?"

"No, Your Highness," Krasnitsky said. "I think that's it."

"Very well," the prince said. "Let's get to it!"

Krasnitsky looked at Pahner, who nodded, and with that, the meeting adjourned.

CHAPTER SIX

"Prince Roger to the bridge, please. Prince Roger to the bridge."

The intercom announcement, backed by a ping on his implant, caught Roger at an inopportune time. He was finally being fitted for a suit of armor, and the process was not going well.

The decision had been made, not without some heated discussion, that although Roger would not be permitted to join any assault on the port facilities, he would go down with the second wave of technical support from the ship. It was only half a victory, from his perspective, but at least Pahner had admitted that since there might still be some hostile fire, breaking out a suit of armor and fitting it to the prince was probably a good idea.

Roger suspected that the captain's rationale was intended as much to get the Marines' charge out of his hair as anything, but it only made sense to put as much security around the Imperial Person as possible. Unfortunately, the fitting was going to be interrupted, and he felt some trepidation as he looked over at the armorer who was glaring at the intercom with his lips drawn back in a snarl.

Since good armorers were much harder to find than good guards, and since their function was an "out of sight, out of mind" one, armorers assigned to The Empress' Own went through a far less stringent winnowing process than the guards and faced only one true criterion: extreme competence. And when there weren't enough volunteers, extremely competent armorers were sometimes "volunteered." This occasionally led to the assignment of persons who, while more or less suitable to take out in public, were not the sort with whom Roger normally dealt.

"So what do we do now?" the prince asked, staring at a hand frozen in an alloy gauntlet. The gauntlet's interface was proving cranky, and the armorer had been deeply engrossed in the debugging process when the announcement came in.

"Will, Yer Highness," said the slight Marine, whose name tag read *Poertena*, "I guess we git a pocking can opener and cot you out."

It took Roger a moment to translate the sergeant's thick Pinopan accent. Pinopa was a world of widespread archipelagoes and tropical seas which had been settled in the first wave of slow-boat colonization by refugees from the Dragon Wars in Southeast Asia, and although the planet's official language was Standard English, the Pinopan had obviously grown up in a non-English household. Despite the accent, Roger was pretty sure he had "pocking" translated correctly. He hoped, however, that the corporal was exaggerating the rest.

"Should I call them and tell them I'm busy?" Roger asked, unsure how they were going to get him out of the ill-fitted armor in any short period of time. Normally, it was a matter of hitting controls which opened the armor along numerous seams, but given the problems this particular suit had been evincing, the experienced armorer had locked down and tagged out most of the controls. The alternative, in which he wasn't particularly interested, was the possibility of intercepting several hundred amps of current or getting cold-cocked by a flailing fist. Now it would be necessary to reconnect all the contacts before the prince could be extracted.

"New, Yer Highness. I'll have you out in a pocking minute. Tell them yer gonna be ten mikes, and that'll cover it. Besides, I got all this udder pocking suits they need pix." His arms swept around the Armory, where half a dozen suits were up on racks awaiting repair. "Pocking gun-bunnies alles breaking t'eir suits. Pocking passers."

The armorer crossed the room to a disused tool chest and extracted a one-meter wrench. He dragged the mass of metal back over to the prince, who was immobilized by the armor, and looked the noble right in the eye.

"Now, Yer Highness," the slight, dark Marine said, grinning nervously, "t'is ain't gonna hurt a bit."

He swung the giant wrench back like a batter, and, with a grunt of effort, slammed its head into the left upper biceps of the suit with all his might.

Roger grimaced when he realized what was about to happen, but other than an unpleasant vibration, the only effect on the suit was that the connection from the arm piece to the shoulder popped free. The collapsed molecules of the ChromSten armor barely noticed the impact, but Poertena dropped the ersatz hammer and shook his hands.

"Pocking vibration."

He looked at the disconnected arm in satisfaction, then picked the wrench up and maneuvered to the other side.

"I used to use a hammer fer t'is." The right biceps was disconnected with another grunt of effort and another noisy clang. "But my cousin-in-law, he said, 'Ramon. Gets you a wrench, pudder-mocker.' So I gets a wrench. An' tee pudder-mocker was right." He dropped the wrench and reached up into the gap created by the detached arm piece. "Wonce you get tee arms detached, it all over but tee counting." He slid his small hand and forearm up along the prince's back. Roger could feel him fumbling for something, then there was a release of tension as the seam along the rear of the suit's carapace opened. Unfortunately, the suit bent at the shoulders, and that trapped the armorer's forearm in the gap. "Pock," was his only comment. Then—

"Prince, can you sock it op an' push you shoulders pack?"

With a few more contortions, the prince found himself standing in the middle of scattered bits of powered armor. He looked down at his singlet, and chuckled. "So much for modesty."

The armory hatch whooshed open and a female sergeant in chameleon dress stepped in. She had a cool face with high Slavic cheekbones, and her long brown hair was done up in a bun at the back of her head. The rippling distortion of the chameleon fabric denied any impression of shape, but her quick tread and lithe movements indicated a high level of athleticism. She didn't bat an eye at the half-naked prince or the scattered armor.

"Your Highness, Captain Pahner requests your presence on the bridge."

"Com the Captain and tell him that it took a bit to get out of the armor," Roger said testily. "I'll be there in a minute."

"Yes, Your Highness," the sergeant said blandly and tapped the transmitter button on her side as Roger began getting dressed in the clothes he'd chosen for these few, tense hours. He'd considered combat dress, but decided that it was just too uncomfortable and finally chosen a safari outfit made of a brushed cottonlike material. It wouldn't be appropriate for combat, but it gave a fine aura of adventure and was much more pleasant than the chameleon cloth everyone else had changed into.

Roger watched the sergeant surreptitiously as he dressed. At first, he thought that she was wiggling her jaw to work a bit of food out of her teeth, but he eventually realized that she was having a long subvocal discussion or argument with someone. The throat microphone was almost invisible against her long, tanned neck, and the receiver, of course, was embedded in her mastoid bone.

Finally he was dressed, and he gave the multipocketed shirt a tug and flipped off a bit of lint.

"Ready."

The sergeant touched the hatch control, but stayed behind as the prince left, escorted by the two guards in the passage outside. As the hatch closed, she turned to the armorer who was reassembling the suit on a mannequin rack.

"Poertena," she said in severe tones, "did you do the hammer thing to the Prince?"

"Of course I didn' do tee hammer ting," the armorer said nervously. "I don' do tee hammer ting no more."

"Then what the hell is that wrench doing on the floor?"

"Oh, t'at. I don' do tee hammer ting, I do tee wrench ting."

"Poertena, you start fucking around with the Prince, and Pahner will have your ass for breakfast."

"Pock Pahner," the armorer snapped, gesturing around the compartment. "You see t'at? I got six pocking sets of pocking armor to get ready. You see Pahner helping? You see you helping? I gonna go get reamed by Pahner, or I gonna pix suits?"

"If you need help, ask!" The sergeant's blue eyes flashed, and she crossed her arms and glared at the half-pint armorer. "We're finished loading the boats. I've got two squads sitting around with their thumbs up their butts. They can be down here in a second."

"I don' need a buncha ham-fist clowns pocking up my suits," the armorer said petulantly. "Every time I gets help, they pock up my suits."

"Okay," the sergeant said with a nasty smile. "Tell you what. I'll get Sergeant Julian to help you."

"Oh, nooo," Poertena said as he realized that he'd put himself in a trap with his bitching. "Not Julian!"

"Hey, Troop!" Julian entered the weapons bay, walked up to the nearest trooper, who was a recent join from Sixth Fleet, put a hand on her shoulder, and grasped her hand for a firm handshake. "Glad you could make it." He gestured with his chin at the plasma rifle the trooper was preparing to disassemble. "You need some help with that there plasma thingamajig?"

The plasma rifle was the IMC's version of a squad automatic weapon. It weighed six kilos, and was supplied by external powerpacks which weighed two kilos each and were good for three to twelve shots, depending on the weapon's discharge settings. The "basic load" for a plasma gunner was twelve packs, the gunners normally carried up to thirty packs in their rucksacks, and their squad mates usually distributed another thirty among them. If there was one thing in the universe a Marine squad hated, it was running out of plasma ammo.

This particular squad from First Platoon had gathered in the bay for one last cleaning of weapons, and since the plasma rifle had a mass of subcomponents, it was natural that the gregarious Julian, from Third Platoon, would offer to help. The new private had just started to smile when her fire team leader spoke up.

"Don't do it, gal," Corporal Andras said.

"What?" Julian affected a hurt expression. "You don't think I can help this rookie trooper?"

The trooper, Nassina Bosum, had just spent six months in the Husan Action before reporting as a Bronze Barbarian. She opened her mouth to retort angrily that she was anything but a rookie, but was cut off by her team leader.

"Oh, you'll help all right. . . ." Andras muttered.

"Seven seconds," Julian said with a smile, and the corporal eyed him beadily.

"No way." There were over forty subcomponents in the M-96 plasma rifle. There was no way to disassemble it completely in seven seconds. Not even for the legendary Julian.

Julian reached into a breast pocket and extracted a chip. "Ten creds says I can do it in seven seconds."

"Impossible!" Bosum snapped, forgetting the implied insult. The standard was over a minute; nobody could disassemble a plasma rifle that fast.

"Put your money where your mouth is," Julian said with a smile, and tossed the chip onto the table.

"I'll take some of that," a grenadier said from down the table, and the squad leader, Sergeant Koberda, pushed forward to manage the piles. Finally there were two chips on Julian's side, and a pile of five- and ten-credit chips opposite.

"Who bet on Julian?"

"I did," Andras said sourly. "He's taken my money every other time."

"We ready?" Julian asked, his hands hovering over the plasma rifle.

"Uh, hang on," said one of the bead riflemen, pulling a helmet out from under his station chair and putting it on his head. "Okay," he said, tapping a control so that the ballistic-protection visor extruded. "Fine by me."

Sergeant Koberda touched the plasma gunner on the shoulder.

"You might wanna step back," he said with a little warning wrinkle of the nose. He suited action to words himself, then put his arms over his head, and the gunner saw others do the same.

"Wha . . . ?" Bosum began, but the squad leader had already activated the timer in his toot and said: "*Go!*"

Removing the compression pin to begin the disassembly process took the longest, just over a third of a second. The new troop watched in awe until the first magneto ring bounced off her skull. Then she realized that pieces of the weapon were flying all over the compartment and started to yell for the sergeant to stop . . . just as the last bit of component flew across the open space and bounced off a bulkhead.

"*Done!*" Julian yelled, raising his hands.

"Six point four-three-eight seconds," Koberda announced morosely, consulting his toot as he kicked aside a capacitor.

"Thank you, thank you, ladies and gentlemen," Julian said, bowing and splitting the heap of chips into two equal piles. He slid one across to Andras, picked up his own, extracted a bundle of other chips large enough to choke a unicorn, and added the squad's offerings to the bundle. "Always a pleasure," he added, and headed for the next compartment.

Corporal Bosum looked around the compartment, trying to figure out where all the pieces of her weapon had gotten to.

"Does he do this often?" she asked sourly.

"Every chance we give him," Andras said. He picked up a capacitor ring and tossed it to her. "But sooner or later, he's gotta lose."

"Sergeant Julian to the Armor Bay," chimed the intercom. "Sergeant Julian to the Armor Bay."

"Oh, man," Koberda said. "That was Despreaux. Despreaux, Poertena, and Julian all in the same compartment! I'd rather be on the bridge!"

Roger tugged down the skirts of his safari jacket and flipped off an imaginary bit of fluff before nodding at the guard to trigger the hatch command. The guard waited patiently, then tapped the green square and stepped through the hatch to do an automatic sweep for hostiles. What the sweep turned up was a massive amount of tension.

Roger stepped over the now tape- and padding-covered control runs and crossed to the tac center. He took a stance with his feet shoulder-width apart and his hands behind his back, nodded coolly at Krasnitsky and Pahner, and then glanced at the rippling tactical display. His cool demeanor vanished abruptly, and his hand flew forward to point at the red icon in the hologram.

"Look! There's a—"

"We know, Your Highness," Pahner said stonily. "Another cruiser."

"It hasn't moved out yet," Krasnitsky said with a sigh. "It's probably warming up its pulse nodes because we haven't slowed down." He rubbed his stubbly jaw and sighed again. "The XO has been hailing the first one. It wants us to begin decelerating to prepare for boarding. It's claiming to be an imperial cruiser, HMS *Freedom*, but it's not. For one thing, the *Freedom* is a cruiser carrier, not a cruiser. For another, its captain has a Caravazan accent."

"Saints." Roger's mouth felt dry.

"Yes, Your Highness," Pahner said. He didn't comment on the obviousness of the conclusion. "Probably," he corrected. "Whoever they are, the worst-case scenario is Saints. So we assume it's them."

"But, Captain," the prince said, looking at Krasnitsky, "can your ship win against *another* cruiser?"

Krasnitsky looked around the bridge. Not a hair had twitched, but he knew better than to have *that* discussion in public.

"Perhaps we should step into the briefing room," he suggested.

Once the hatch had closed, he turned to the prince. "No, Your Highness. There is zero chance that we can survive taking on two cruisers. We're not a full-scale Line ship, just a heavily armed and armored transport. Were we at full strength, without damage, maybe. As it is, there's no chance."

"So what do we do?" Roger looked from Pahner to Krasnitsky. "We have to surrender, right?"

It was Pahner's turn to sigh. "That's . . . not really an option, Your Highness."

"Why ever not?" Roger asked. "I mean," he turned to the grim looking Fleet officer, "you're going to *die* if you don't!"

Pahner bit his tongue on a sharp rejoinder, but Krasnitsky simply nodded. "Yes, Your Highness, we will."

"But why?" Roger asked, his eyes wide in amazement. "I mean, I know it isn't the proper thing to surrender, but you can't run, and you can't win. So why not?"

"He can't risk their getting their hands on you, Your Highness," Pahner snapped finally.

"But . . ." Roger began, then stopped to think about it. He pulled his ponytail in frustration. "Why not? I mean, what could they do with . . . with *me*, for God's sake? I mean, I could understand if it was Mother, or John, or even Alexandra. But who the heck cares about Roger?" he ended a trifle bitterly. "I don't know any secrets, and I'm not in immediate line for the throne. Why *not* turn me over to them?"

The prince's face hardened with resolution.

"Captain, I insist that you surrender. As a matter of fact, I order you to. Honor is all well and good, but there is a line between honor and stupidity." He lifted his chin and sniffed. "I will surrender to them myself, with honor. I'll show them who's a MacClintock." The stance would have been improved if there hadn't been a slight quiver in the pronouncement.

"Fortunately, Your Highness, you're not in my chain of command," Krasnitsky said with a wry smile for the bravado. "Major Pahner, I'm going to go get ready for the change in plans. Do you want to try to explain it to him?" With that, he nodded at the prince and left the compartment.

"What?" the prince gasped as the hatch closed behind him. "Hey! I gave you an order!"

"As he said, Your Highness, you're not in his chain of command," Pahner said with a shake of his head. "But you might at least thank him for committing suicide, not berate him."

"There's no reason for them not to surrender," Roger said stubbornly. "This is just stupid!"

Pahner cocked his head and looked at the prince darkly.

"What happens if the Saints get their hands on you, Your Highness?"

"Well," Roger said, thinking about it. "If they tell the Empire, it's war, or they hand me back over. I suppose they could force a few concessions, but they don't want a war."

"And what if they don't tell the Empire right away, Your Highness?"

"Uhmmmm . . ."

"They can't tamper with your toot, Your Highness; not with *its* security protocols. But what about psychotropic drugs?" Pahner tilted his head to the other side and raised an eyebrow. "What then?"

"So I make funny noises and bark like a dog," Roger scoffed. Until they were finally fully banned, psychotropic drugs had been common at comedy clubs for the terminally humorless.

"No, Your Highness. My guess—and I'm not privy to these sorts of scenarios—but my guess is that they would have you babble all the state secrets that you know to their 'free and independent' news services."

"But that's the point, Captain Pahner," Roger said with another laugh. "I don't *know* any state secrets."

"Sure you do, Your Highness. You know all about the Empire's plans to invade Raiden-Winterhowe."

"Captain," the prince said warily, "what are you talking about? Not only are we at peace with Raiden-Winterhowe, but taking them on would be stupid. They've got nearly as good a navy as we do."

"In that case, Your Highness," Pahner said with another smile, "what about the Empire's conspiracy to enslave all the alien species we can find and to terraform planets that have been reserved because of their unique flora and fauna?"

"Captain Pahner, what are you *talking* about?" the prince demanded. "I've never heard of any of this! And that sounds like Saint rhetoric. . . ." He stopped. "Oh."

"Or about how your imperial mother eats fetuses for breakfast, or about—"

"I get the point!" the prince snapped. "You're saying that if they get their hands on me I'll be their mouthpiece for all that bullshit they're always spouting."

"Whether you want to or not, Your Highness." Pahner nodded. "And I don't even want to *think* about what they'll do with your big game hunting record. For that matter, it would make the lives of the rest of the Family worth less than a plugged millicred. If they could kill the rest of the Family, that would make you heir."

"Parliament would impeach me," Roger said with a bitter laugh. "Hell, Parliament would probably impeach me even if the Saints *weren't* putting words into my mouth. Who the hell is going to trust *Roger* at the controls?"

"It takes two-thirds to impeach, Your Highness," the captain said darkly.

"Are you suggesting that the Saints could influence a third of Parliament?" Roger was beginning to think he'd stepped through a looking glass and into some sort of weird fantasy universe. There'd always been bodyguards around him, certainly, but no one had ever seriously suggested that he might be a target of another empire's designs. He'd always assumed that the guards were there mainly for show or to keep off the occasional overly smitten female fan. Now he suddenly realized that what they were there for was . . . sitting on his chest, waiting for the air to evacuate.

"Why?" he asked, quietly, wondering what would make people serve and protect someone that even he didn't like looking back at in the mirror.

"Well," Pahner replied, not understanding the true question, "the Saints want to ensure that humanity doesn't expand further into uncontaminated worlds. It's a religion to them." He paused, unsure how to go on. "I'd assumed that you'd been briefed, Your Highness."

Actually, it was common knowledge. The Church of Ryback had a few outlets in the capital, all heavily financed by the Saints, and they ran regular commercials. For that matter, it was a common subject for discussion in civics and history classes, which made Pahner wonder about the prince's education. Asking what the Saints wanted made no sense at all, given that O'Casey had been Roger's tutor for years and she had a quadruple doctorate in, among other things, history.

"No. No, that's not what I meant. I meant . . ."

Roger looked into the bleak face of the Marine and realized that this was not a good time to get the question off his chest. And even if he asked it, Pahner—as most people seemed to do when Roger asked questions—would probably just provide some opaque answer that ensured deeper confusion.

"I meant, 'What.' What do we do now?"

"We're going to go for the long shot, Your Highness," Pahner said, nodding now that the question made sense again. He suspected that something else had gone on in that airhead, but what it had been he neither knew nor particularly cared. There was a mission to perform, and it looked to be a long one.

"We're going to reload the boats. With the cruiser topside, taking the port by assault is out. So we're going to have to land on the planet and make our way to the port on foot. We can't let anyone know we're there, or they'll slaughter us, so we're going to have to come in on a ballistic approach and land quite a way around the planet from the port. Marduk was an afterthought to the Empire, so it's never been fully surveyed, and there's no satellite net, so the port won't be able to detect us as long as we stay out of line of sight. Once we reach the port, we capture a ship and head for home."

It sounded easy put like that. Right.

"So we're going to land on the backside then take the shuttles across . . . um, I can't remember the term. Low to the ground so they don't get spotted?"

"Nape of the Earth," Pahner answered somberly. "No, Your Highness. Unfortunately, we're going to have to launch nearly five light-minutes out. We're going to put three platoons and a few support personnel from the ship in four assault shuttles: enough room for a reinforced company. The rest of the load is going to be fuel for deceleration. When we're down, if we have enough fuel to do a couple of klicks we'll be lucky."

"So how are we going to get to the port?" Roger asked, dreading the answer.

"We're going to walk, Your Highness," the captain said with a grim smile.

CHAPTER SEVEN

"It says here, 'Marduk has a mean gravity of slightly greater than Earth normal, and is a planet of little weather change,'" Sergeant Julian said, reading off his pad. He'd managed, along with Poertena, to get two more suits up and running before the call came to drop everything and change the loadout on the shuttles. Currently, they were unloading.

He was perched on one silver wing of an assault shuttle as his squad moved out nonessential materials. The space-to-ground assault craft's variable geometry wings could sustain in-air flight at speeds as low as a hundred KPH or as high as Mach three, but it also had hydrogen thrusters for space maneuvering. Similar to a ground support pinnace, it had lighter weapons and a single top-mounted quad-barreled bead cannon, and thus correspondingly more room for personnel and equipment.

"'. . . with a median temperature of thirty-three degrees and a median humidity of ninety-seven percent,'" he continued. There'd been nothing in the Marine databases on the planet, but it turned out that one of the corporals in Second Platoon had a *Fodor's Guide to the Baldur Sector*. Unfortunately, it offered only a limited amount of data on the planet . . . and what data there was only made a gloomy situation worse. "Jesus Christ, that's hot!"

"Oh, just fucking great," Lance Corporal Moseyev said as he

trotted out of the shuttle with a case of penetrator ammunition in his hands. "I only had three weeks and I was transferring to Steel!"

"'The native culture is at a stagnant level of low-grade firearms technology. Politically, the Mardukans—' Hey, there's a picture!"

The Mardukan native, a four-armed biped from a hexapedal evolutionary line, was pictured next to a human wiredrawing for size. From the scale, the Mardukan was the height of a grizzly bear, with broad, long feet on the ends of long, backcurved legs. The hands of the upper and lower arms were about the same size, with the upper shoulders wider than the lower, which were in turn wider than the hips. The upper arms ended in long, fine, three-fingered hands with one fully opposable thumb each. The hands of the shorter, lower arms were heavier and less refined, with a broad opposable pad and two dissimilar fingers. The face was wider and flatter than a human's, with a broad nose and small deep-set eyes. Two large horns curled up and back over the head. They were obviously functional weapons; the inner curve looked razor-sharp. The rubbery-looking skin was a mottled green and had an odd sheen to it.

"What's that?" Moseyev asked, pointing to the sheen.

"Dunno." Julian tweaked the cursor over the skin and rolled up the magnification. "'The skin of the Mardukan is covered in a polycy . . . polyss . . . in a something something coating that protects the species from casual cuts and the various harsh funguses of its native jungle home," he read, then thought about it for a second. "Ewww."

"It's covered in *slime*," Moseyev laughed. "Yick! Slimies!"

"Scummies!" Sergeant Major Kosutic snapped from the hatchway, and strode into the launching day. "I thought you were told to get the extraneous equipment out of the shuttle, Julian?"

"We were getting updated on the mission, Sergeant Major!" Julian was suddenly at attention, the pad held alongside his trousers. "I was briefing my squad on the enemy and conditions!"

"The enemy are the fucking Saints or pirates or whatever-they-are that hold the port." Kosutic stalked up to stand so close to the braced sergeant that he could smell her breath mint. "The scummies are what we're going to have to cut our way through to get there.

Your mission, right now, is to get the shuttle unloaded—not to sit around on your ass cracking wise. Clear?"

"Clear, Sergeant Major!"

"Now get your asses to work. We're on a tight time schedule."

"Moseyev!" Julian said, turning hastily back to his squad. "Get your team unloading that ammo. We don't have all day-cycle! Gjalski, your team on the powerpacks. . . ."

"Not the powerpacks," Kosutic said. "Leave all of them. We're going to add extra, as a matter of fact. Thank Vlad we don't have a heavy weapons platoon with us."

"Sergeant Major," Julian asked as the squad began to scurry around, "you called the Mardukans 'scummies.' Where'd you hear that?"

"Knew somebody that went through here once." The sergeant major pulled at an earlobe. "Didn't sound like much fun."

"Are we really gonna have to walk all the way across the damn world?" Julian asked, aghast.

"There ain't many choices, Sergeant," the sergeant major snarled. "You just stick with the mission."

"Roger, Sergeant Major." The sergeant glanced at the "scummy" on the pad. It looked big and nasty . . . but, then, that also described the IMC. "Will comply."

There weren't a lot of options.

"Okay, I want options, people," Pahner said, and looked around the briefing room. "First of all, let's be clear about something: what's the mission?"

The group was limited to the prince's party: himself, Pahner, O'Casey, and the three lieutenants. O'Casey was panning through the limited data on Marduk on a pad. The old-fashioned academic always seemed to prefer holding data in her hand. Roger, for his part, had looked at it nine ways from Sunday already on his toot, and there wasn't much good in it.

"Take the port while avoiding detection," Lieutenant Sawato answered. The slight officer gestured at the limited-scale map depicted in the hologram over the table. It had been extracted from the *Fodor's*, and, with the exception of the area around the port, offered virtually no detail. "Land on the northeast coast of this large continent, cross a relatively small ocean, and move inland to take the port."

"Sounds easy," Lieutenant Gulyas snorted. He was about to go on, but Pahner raised a hand.

"You forgot one thing, Lieutenant," Pahner told Sawato mildly. "While ensuring the security of His Highness Prince Roger."

Roger opened his mouth to protest, but was elbowed by O'Casey. He knew those elbows of old, and knew better than to try to go on.

"Yes, Sir," Sawato said to Pahner, but with a nod to Roger. "That was, of course, assumed."

"You know what they say about assumptions," Pahner said. "Let's not assume Prince Roger's safety, okay? The Navy has a plan for getting us onto the planet, and there's not a thing we can do to affect that. But we need to do everything we can to ensure that item above all else. His Highness' security is job one."

He looked around to make sure the other officers understood that and then nodded.

"In that case, I think we need to look at the conditions and threats next." He turned to Lieutenant Gulyas. "Conall, normally that would be your brief. However, I've been talking to Doctor O'Casey, and she has some insights." He turned to the civilian. "Doctor?"

"Thank you, Captain," she replied formally, and tapped the display to bring up a picture of Marduk. "You are all, by now, familiar with the limited data we have on Marduk and its inhabitants.

"Marduk is classified as a Type Three world," she continued, and tapped another control. This time the picture was a large beast of some sort, with six stumpy legs, an armored forehead, and a triangular, fang-filled maw. The human scale model next to it indicated that the creature was a bit larger than a rhinoceros.

"That, by the way, is probably the same classification Earth would have had at the same technological and development level. Marduk, however, has not only an unfriendly climate—it's extremely hot and steamy, which will have a negative effect on electronics—but also unfriendly inhabitants and wildlife. This particular specimen, called a damnbeast, is a good example. The first survey crew ended up shooting several specimens. The planet is warm enough that the dominant species are all cold-blooded, which makes a higher ratio of predators to prey possible. Whereas a mammal this size would require half a million hectares to support, one of these has a territory of less than forty thousand hectares." She smiled faintly. "And this is the only recorded carnivore species listed in our onboard databases. Further inquiries referenced the official Survey Service report."

She smiled again at the general groan.

"The resident autochthons, the Mardukans, are at a pre-steam level of technology. Obviously, their tech level varies from area to area of the planet, but some of their most advanced cultures have discovered gunpowder, although that's scarcely uniform and even the ones which have it don't have anything resembling mass production or cartridge weapons."

She tapped another control, bringing up a view of some odd weapons.

"These are the primary projectile weapons of the Mardukan societies which have mastered gunpowder: the matchlock arquebus and the hooped bombard. These weapons were used on Earth in the distant past, primarily in Europe, although the arquebus was rapidly superseded by flintlock muskets, and then rifles. The hooped bombard is a distant cousin of one of your Marine howitzers."

She brought up another screen, this time a map of the Mediterranean.

"The Mardukan sociological climate has few direct counterparts in human history, but there are similarities to the Earth during the early Roman Republic. The Mardukans are broken up into city-states and small empires that are distributed along fertile river valleys, so these areas between the rivers are primarily barbaric. Although the barbarians do have a few gunpowder weapons, they rely primarily upon spear-hurlers and lances. The precise nature of the barbarian tribal structure is unknown."

"Why is it unknown?" Lieutenant Gulyas asked, wondering where she'd gotten all this information.

"Well, probably because they ate the researchers," O'Casey said deadpan, then grinned. "Or because it's never been researched. From what I've been able to find, anything more than a thousand klicks or so from the spaceport is very much terra incognita. Either way, the data in my database stopped there."

"Where did you have that?" Gulyas asked curiously.

"I always travel with my history and sociology databases," O'Casey said with another smile. "I need them to work on papers." She turned back to her pad.

"To continue, not only are the barbarians at war with each other—when they're not raiding the borders of the city-states—but the city-states are continually at war with each other, as well. Any state of peace can be assumed to be a temporary truce, awaiting the slightest spark to ignite a war." The smile she gave the officers of this time was grim. "I think that we can assume a Marine company is going to constitute a spark."

She paused for a moment, then shrugged.

"That pretty much exhausts the primary data. I'll make the full outtake available to you right after the meeting."

"Thank you, Doctor," Pahner said somberly. "That was a nice overview. I'm sure you also noticed that we can eat the food. The biochemistry's a long way from Earth standard, but our nanites ought to be able to break down anything we can't digest naturally, and they should keep anything in the local biosystem from actively poisoning us. On the other hand, not even the nanites can put in what isn't there, so we'll require supplements, especially of vitamins C and E and several amino acids. Which means we'll be humping those." He looked up when there were no groans from the lieutenants. "No complaints? My, we must be feeling sobered."

"We've been discussing it, Sir," Lieutenant Sawato admitted. The XO shook her head. "I listed out all the parameters, but, as Lieutenant Gulyas indicated, there are tremendous problems."

"True." Pahner leaned back and rested his chin on his hand. "Tell me what they are."

"First of all, Sir, there's the matter of time. How long will it take us to cross a world?"

"A long time," Pahner replied calmly. "Months."

The entire compartment seemed to draw a deep breath as someone finally said the words. They were no longer talking about a short drop on the planet, but about an extended stay. They had all realized it, but no one had wanted to say it.

"Yes, Sir," Lieutenant Jasco said into the silence after a moment. The tall, broad CO of First Platoon was in charge of logistics, and he shook his leonine head. "I don't see it, Sir. We don't have the food or the power. We carry combat rations for two weeks, and power for one week's use of the armor, but we're looking at three to six months to cross the planet. We may be able to forage, and our nanites will help with digestion problems, but if we're going to be dealing with hostiles, foraging will be limited. And given the intensity of the threat, we need the powered armor to survive, but it won't begin to last that long. With all due respect, and not wanting to be a quitter, I don't see a way to do this mission, Sir."

"All right." Pahner nodded. "That's your input. Does anyone see a way to accomplish the mission?"

"Well, we can strip the ship of spare power systems," Lieutenant Gulyas suggested. "There are powerpacks all over the place."

"How do we get them where we're going?" Jasco shook his head. "It's a situation of diminishing returns when you overload suits carrying stuff—"

"We can preposition caches!" Gulyas gestured enthusiastically with his hands. "We send out a team that puts down a cache. Some of the team stays behind to guard it, while the rest come back to get supplies. They take them to the cache and use some of the cache to take them a little further. They leave a team with that cache and go back for supplies. . . ."

"We'd be defeated in detail if we strung ourselves out that way," Sawato said severely.

"And that would take *six times* as many supplies!" Jasco snapped.

"We could carry the armor," Roger suggested diffidently, and looked around at the lieutenants. Jasco rolled his eyes and leaned back and crossed his arms, while Gulyas and Sawato simply refused to meet his gaze. "It would save power . . ."

"Ahem," Jasco said. "Your Royal Highness, with all due respect . . ."

"I think," Roger said, "that it would be better in these sorts of meetings to use my proper military rank."

Jasco cast a quick glance at Pahner, but the captain returned it blandly, and the lieutenant was suddenly reminded of one of those Academy tests where there was no right answer.

"Yes, um, Colonel. As I was saying, the suits weigh nearly four hundred kilos apiece," he continued with a not particularly friendly chuckle.

"Oh," Roger said with a chagrined expression. "I . . . oh."

"Actually," Pahner said quietly, "that was exactly what I had in mind." He looked around at the stunned lieutenants and smiled kindly. "Ladies and gentlemen, you are a credit to your training. 'Hit 'em hard and hit 'em low, grab their balls and don't let go,' right?"

The lieutenants smiled at the Academy drinking song. Even though most officers in the IMC, like Pahner himself (although usually with less . . . spectacular career summaries) were former enlisted, it was well known in the officers corps.

"Well, we will indeed hit these 'scummies' hard and low when we have to. But we don't have the power to smash our way across the planet, so we're going to have to make treaties when possible, trade when necessary, and only kick ass as a last resort. When we kick ass, we'd better kick ass with a vengeance, but we parley first.

"One platoon each day, on a rotating basis," he continued, "will be detailed as bearers. We will carry one squad's armor. We'll take Second Squad of Third Platoon's; they have the most veterans and the highest combat scores, currently." He looked at Roger, obviously weighing pros and cons, then nodded. "And we'll take the Prince's. He doesn't have much background in it, but it goes along with ensuring his survival.

"But we have to remember that crossing the planet only gets us halfway to our objective. The real mission is to take the port and get our hands on a ship home, and we'll need the armor to take the port even more than we should need it on the way there. Initially, until we get the lay of the land, we'll keep one team in armor at all times.

Once we become comfortable with our ability to survive, we'll make our way in normal uniforms to conserve power until we reach the port.

"Initially, we'll maintain our security with bead rifles and plasma weapons. But we can assume that they, too, will become exhausted. So from our first encounter with the Mardukans, we will ensure that all Mardukan weaponry is gathered, and we'll begin training with it."

He looked at the lieutenants again. Jasco, at least, appeared to think he'd lost his mind. The other two were trying, unsuccessfully, to keep their thoughts off their faces, but the prince, to give him credit, just seemed confused. It amused Pahner to turn the lieutenants' worldview on its ear; making them think was good for them, whatever the junior officers might believe. In the case of the prince . . . Pahner found himself moving from annoyed towards amused, which was another surprise.

Pahner had always considered the prince his charge, but never one of "his" officers. Or, for that matter, whatever the Table of Organization might say, his superior. But now the captain realized that what he actually had on his hands was a terribly confused, brand-new lieutenant. And since "Captain" Pahner had spent a good part of his life as "Gunny" Pahner, teaching confused lieutenants the rules of the game, the prince suddenly switched from a hindrance to a challenge. A tough challenge—Pahner had never seen a lieutenant with a lower likelihood of making a decent officer—but an approachable one, nonetheless. And the only kind of challenge worth facing was a tough one. With that realization, the mission, in Pahner's mind, suddenly went from impossible to simply very difficult.

"Train with scummy weapons, Sir?" Lieutenant Jasco asked, looking at the other officers. "What are we going to do with them? Sir?"

"We'll use them to hold off attacking Mardukans or hostile fauna until heavier weapons come online. And when we get to the point that our power supplies are at the minimum necessary, in my opinion, to take the port, we'll use them exclusively."

"Sir?" Lieutenant Sawato said diffidently. "Are you sure about this? Those—" She gestured at where the hologram had been. "Those . . . weapons aren't very good."

"No, Lieutenant, they aren't. But we'll just have to learn to get by. Our chameleon suits have limited ballistic protection, so we'll be highly resistant to fire from their arquebuses. As for lower-velocity weapons like spears and lances and swords and everything else . . . we'll deal with that as it comes.

"Now," the captain continued. "What, other than charges for the weapons and armor support, are our largest issues?"

"Communication," Lieutenant Gulyas said. "If we're going to trade and negotiate, we have to be able to communicate. We have a 'kernel' of the Mardukan language, but that's for one dialect on the subcontinent surrounding the base. We don't have any kernels for other areas. Without kernels, our toots can't translate for us."

"I can work on that," O'Casey said. "I've got a good heuristic language program I use for anthropological digging. I may have some trouble communicating with the first few groups we run across, but once I pick up a regional language base, even vast dialect changes won't affect things. And I can create kernels for other toots."

"Well, that's that one solved," Pahner said with a smile. "But you'll need to get that program to other toots. We can't have you as a point failure source."

"That might be a problem," she admitted. "It's big. It will take a very capable toot to handle it. I've got one custom designed for me, but without a huge amount of processor capability and storage, this program runs like a slug."

"I'll load it," Roger said quietly. "Mine's . . . pretty good." There was a slight, general chuckle at the understatement, for the Imperial Family's implants' abilities were almost legendary. "We might have some trouble loading it, but I'll guarantee I can run it."

"Okay," Pahner said. "What's next?"

"Food," Lieutenant Jasco said. "We don't have the rations for the trip, and we can't forage and carry the armor and keep the Prince safe all at once." His tone was respectfully challenging.

"Correct," Pahner acknowledged calmly. "And what is the answer to *this* dilemma?"

"Trade," O'Casey said definitively. "We trade high-tech items for whatever the Mardukans use for portable wealth. That might not be metals, by the way. The ancient North Africans traded salt. But whatever they use here, we trade the largest mass of advanced technology at the first city-state for our basic needs and a 'nest egg,' and then portion the rest out slowly as we go."

"Exactly." Pahner's nod was firm. "So, what do we have that would make good trade goods?"

"Firestarters," Jasco said promptly. "I saw a case of them in the supply room last week." He consulted his pad. "I've got an inventory here—let me cross load."

He set his pad down on the table to transmit the inventory data, and the other lieutenants and O'Casey captured the data and began perusing it while Roger was still pulling out his own pad. By the time he had it opened and configured to receive, Jasco had cut the transmission and was back to looking at the data.

"Lieutenant," the prince said in a lofty tone, "if you *don't* mind?"

Jasco looked up from the lists in surprise. "Oh, sorry, Your Highness," he said, and set the list to transmit again.

Roger nodded as his pad picked up the data.

"Thank you, Lieutenant. And, again, it's 'Colonel' under these circumstances."

"Yes, of course . . . Colonel," Jasco said, going back to his data.

"What do we see?" Pahner asked, apparently ignoring the byplay. He didn't have a pad out, nor had he received a download.

Roger transferred the data to his toot and put his own pad away. He would've taken the data straight into the toot from Jasco's pad, but the implant had so many security protocols that filtering through the pad had been easier and faster. As Roger was going through these circumlocutions, the officers and O'Casey were studying the inventory.

"Virtually anything in here would be tradable," and O'Casey said, her eyes bugging out at the thought. "Space blankets, chameleon liners, water carriers . . . not boots. . . ."

"We'll be space and mass-limited," Pahner noted. "The ship's going to have to drop us fairly far out, and we'll have to come down in a long, slow spiral to avoid detection. That means internal add-on tanks of hydrogen, and those will take up volume and mass. So the higher the potential profit, the better."

"Well," O'Casey continued, "not uniforms. Rucksacks. There are five spares; that might be good. Spare issue intel-pads? No. What are 'multitools'?"

"They're memory plastic tools," Lieutenant Sawato said with a nod. "They come with four 'standard' configurations: shovel, ax, pick-mattock, and boma-knife. And you can add two configurations."

"We've got fifteen spares," Jasco said, flipping through the data. "And each Marine in the Company has one."

"Of course," Gulyas observed with a chuckle, "some of those have some . . . odd secondary settings."

"What?" Sawato smiled. "Like Sergeant Julian's 'out of tune lute' setting?"

"I was actually thinking of Poertena's 'pig pocking pag' setting," Gulyas snorted.

"I beg your pardon?" O'Casey blinked, and looked back and forth between the two lieutenants.

"The armorer controls the machine that resets the adjustable configurations," Pahner told her in a resigned tone. "Julian used to be Bravo's armorer before Poertena. Both of them are jokers."

"Oh." The prince's ex-tutor considered for several seconds, then snorted as she finally completed the translation of "pig pocking pag" in her head. "Well, in this case the setting makes sense. We're going to need lots of . . . large bags to carry equipment."

CHAPTER EIGHT

"Hey, Julian, old puddy!" Poertena yelled across the shuttle bay. "Gimme a hand what t'is pag!"

"Jesus Christ, Poertena!" Julian hefted the carry handles on the outside of the quivering memory plastic sack. "What the pock . . . I mean, what the heck do you have in here?"

"Every pocking ting I could pocking pack," the armorer answered. "Tee pocking suits don' run on t'eir pocking own. You know t'at!"

"What the hell is in here?" Julian asked, reaching for the mouth of the sack. It was heavy as hell.

"Get chore pocking hands out o' my pocking pag!" Poertena snarled, slapping at the offending member.

"Look, if I'm gonna help you hump it, I'm gonna know what the hell I'm carrying." Julian popped the sack opened and looked in. "Jesus Christ, Poertena!" he repeated. "The fucking *wrench*?"

"Hey!" the little Pinopan shouted, practically hopping up and down in fury. "You got your pocking way of doin' it, an' I got *my* pocking way! You never can get people out, they power goes off? Huh? Have to blow tee pocking seals! Only ting holding t'em seals is tee pocking secondary latches! You get tee secondary latches loose, you got tee armor open, and tee seals not damaged! Bot *no*! Big time billy badass soldier always gotta blow tee pocking bolts!"

"That's what it says to do in the manual," Julian said, throwing his hands up in the air. "Not *bang* on 'em until they come apart!"

"*Hey!*" Sergeant Major Kosutic shouted from the entrance to the bay as she strode across to break up the incipient fight. "Am I gonna have to jack both of you up?" she asked, glaring up at Julian.

"No, Sergeant Major," he said. "Everything's under control." He should have known she'd show up. She popped up like a damned Djinn every time anything got out of whack.

"Well, keep it strack! We've got a hard, cold mission to perform, and we don't need any sand in the gears. Do you understand that?"

"Yes, Sergeant Major!"

"And, Poertena," the sergeant major said, rounding on the braced Pinopan. "One, you'd better learn not to tell any more sergeants 'pock you' in public, or I will have your ass. Do you understand me?"

"Yes, Sergeant Major," Poertena said, looking for a convenient rock to melt away under.

"Two, you'd better learn a new word to replace 'pock,' because if you say it *one* more time in my hearing, I will *personally* tear off your stripes and feed them to you—raw. You are in The Empress' Own now, not whatever rag-bag line outfit you came from. We do not say 'pock' or 'rap' or any of those other words. We *especially* do not say them while rigging the pocking *Prince*. Do I make myself pocking clear?" she finished, pounding a rock-hard index finger into the lance corporal's chest.

Poertena's eyes flickered for a moment in panic. "Clear, Sergeant Major," he answered, finally, obviously unsure if he could get along without his verbal comma.

"Now what's in the Santa bag?" she snarled.

"My pock . . . my tools, Sergeant Major," Poertena answered. "I gotta have my po . . . my tools, Sergeant Major. Tee armor don' run by itself!"

"Sergeant Julian?" the sergeant major said, turning to the sergeant who'd started to drop out of his braced position as Poertena seemed to be getting the worst of the chewing out.

"Yes, Sergeant Major?" Julian snapped back to attention.

"What was your objection? You seemed to have one."

"We have mass limitations, Sergeant Major!" the NCO barked. "I objected to certain of Lance Corporal Poertena's tools that I didn't believe were strictly necessary, Sergeant Major!"

"Poertena?"

"He doesn't like my po . . . my wrench, Sergeant Major," the lance corporal answered somewhat sullenly. He was fairly sure he was going to lose the tool.

The SMaj nodded and opened the bulging sack. She glanced at the packrat's nest inside, and nodded again. Then she turned to the armorer and fixed him with a glare.

"Poertena."

"Yes, Sergeant Major?"

"You know we're humping across tee whole . . . this whole planet, right?" the top sergeant asked mildly.

"Yes, Sergeant Major." Poertena didn't brighten up; he'd been on the receiving end of mild and bitter before.

The NCO nodded again, and pulled on her earlobe.

"Because of your unique position, you will probably be exempt from helping to hump the ammo, power, and armor."

Kosutic looked around the bay, then back into the sack.

"But I'm not going to have any of these people carrying unnecessary stuff," she growled.

"But, Sergeant Major—"

"Did I ask you to speak?" the NCO snapped.

"No, Sergeant Major!"

"As I say, I'm not going to have anyone carrying unnecessary stuff," she continued, fixing the Pinopan with a frigid eye. "However, I'm not going to tell you, the armorer, what you really need to do your job, either. I'm going to leave that entirely up to you. But I *will* tell you that nobody else in the Company is going to hump one item *for* you. Is that perfectly clear?" she ended, with another rock-hard index finger, and the armorer gulped and nodded his head.

"Yes, Sergeant Major." He winced internally at what that meant.

"You are being given slack on what you've got to carry," Kosutic said, "*because* you have your own stuff to hump. Not, by Satan, so that other people can hump it for you. Clear?"

Index finger.

"Clear, Sergeant Major."

"So, if you want your hammer, or wrench, or whatever, fine. But *you*—" index finger "—are gonna hump it. Clear?"

"Clear, Sergeant Major." Poertena's voice sounded more strangled than ever, not least because Julian stood grinning at him behind Kosutic's back. The sergeant major gave the armorer one last glare . . . then turned to the squad leader with cobralike speed.

"Sergeant Julian," she said mildly, "I'd like a moment of your time out in the passage."

Julian's smile froze, and he cast a burning glare at the Pinopan before he followed the top sergeant out of the shuttle bay. Poertena, for his part, could have cared less about the glare. He was trying to figure out how to fit two hundred liters of tools into a ten-liter space.

"We can't fit that in," Lieutenant Jasco said, slowly and carefully so that Lieutenant Gulyas could understand. He pointed to his pad, where the loading program was already in the yellow. "We're . . . gonna . . . be . . . overloaded," he continued in the simplest possible terms, and Gulyas gave him a friendly smile that stopped at the eyes. Then he reached up to clap the much larger platoon leader on the shoulder.

"You know, Aziz, you're an okay guy, most of the time. But from time to time, you're a real prick." He went on as the other lieutenant's face colored up. "We need trade goods. We need ammo. We need power. But if we don't have enough supplements to last the whole trip, we're all gonna die anyway!"

"You've stripped the ship of every last vitamin and herbal remedy!" Jasco snapped, slapping the hand off his shoulder. "We don't need three hundred kilos of supplements!"

"No," Gulyas agreed. "By exact calculation, we need two hundred and thirty precisely balanced kilos for six months with no casualties. If we take no casualties. And if we stay six months. Neither of those is likely, so we probably need less. But what about waste? And we don't *have* the *precise* supplements we need. And what about a trooper's opening up his kit and finding that mold has eaten his stash overnight? If we don't have enough supplements, we're all *dead.* So we've gotta have all the supplements we can hump; it's that simple."

"We're overloaded!" Jasco snapped, waving the pad. "It's *that* simple!"

"Can I be of assistance, gentlemen?" Sergeant Major Kosutic appeared as if by magic between the two lieutenants. "I only ask because some of the troops seemed to be interested in this discussion, as well."

Gulyas looked around the shuttle bay and noticed that work had almost stopped as the troopers slowed down to watch the two lieutenants argue. He turned back to the sergeant major.

"No, I think we have it under control." He looked at Jasco. "Don't we, Aziz?"

"No, we don't," the junior lieutenant said stubbornly. "We're running out of room for the loading. We can't afford three hundred kilos of supplements."

"Is that all we're taking?" Kosutic sounded surprised. "That doesn't sound like enough. Hang on." She keyed her throat mike, and used her toot to bring the two lieutenants into the circuit. "Captain Pahner?"

"Yes?" came the growled response.

"Priority. Supplements, or trade goods?" she asked.

"Supplements," Pahner said instantly. "We can raid instead of trade if we have to, but all the trade goods in the ship won't keep us alive without supplements. The order of priority is fuel, supplements, food, the suits for Third Platoon, power, ammo, trade goods. Each person may bring ten kilos of personal gear. How many kilos of supplements do we have?"

"Only three hundred," Kosutic answered.

"Damn. I'd hoped for more. We'll have to eke it out with rations. We go on short rations from the moment we board the shuttles. And confiscate all the pogie bait. Most of it won't have much in the way of nutritional value, but it's something. No more than one ration per day, and we hope we have one a day all the way through."

"Understood," Kosutic said. "Out here." She raised her eyebrows at the lieutenants. "Does that clear the air, Sirs?"

"Yes, Sergeant Major, it does," Jasco said. "I still don't think we're going to run out, though."

"Sir, may I make an observation?" the sergeant major asked, and Lieutenant Jasco nodded.

"Of course, Sergeant Major." He was an Academy graduate, with a previous stint as a platoon leader and four years in the IMC under his belt, but the sergeant major had been beating around the Fleet long before he was born. He might be stubborn, but he wasn't stupid.

"In a situation this screwed up, Sir, planning for the worst is just good sense. For example, I would strongly suggest that you not put all the supplements on one bird. Or any other point failure source, such as spare ammo or power. Spread it across the shuttles. When the shit hits the fan, there's no such thing as being overparanoid."

She nodded and stepped lightly out of the shuttle bay, and Jasco stood shaking his head as he looked at the pad in his hand.

"Do you think she was looking at the load plan?" he asked Gulyas.

"I dunno. Why?"

"Because I had *all* the spare food, ammo, and power on Shuttle Four!" the logistics lieutenant said angrily, and shut the pad with a snap. "It would have carried the heavy weapons platoon in a standard drop, and since it was empty . . . What a cherry mistake! Damn, damn, damn it to hell! Time to start cross-loading."

"And that, Your Highness," Pahner said, gesturing towards the memo pad, "is why I don't consider it advisable for you to bring the three cartons of personal gear."

The wardroom was empty, except for the two of them, although Doctor O'Casey was expected soon.

"But what am I going to wear?" the aghast prince asked. He pulled at the chameleon fabric of the uniform he'd changed into. "You can't expect me to go through each day every day in *this*? . . . Can you?"

"Your Highness," Pahner said calmly, "each of the military personnel will be carrying on his own back six spare pairs of socks, a spare uniform, personal hygiene equipment, five kilos of proteins and vitamin supplements, rations, additional ammunition and power packs for their weapons, additional ammunition for squad and company level weaponry, a bivy tent, his multitool, a rucksack fluid pouch with six kilos of water, and up to ten kilos of personal gear. The load will total out at between fifty and sixty kilos. In addition, the entire Company will be switching off carrying powered armor and additional trade goods, ammunition, and powerpacks."

He cocked his head and regarded his nominal commander steadily.

"If you order the Company, in addition to all these necessities, to carry your spare pajamas, morning clothes, evening clothes, and a dress uniform in case there's a parade, they will." The company commander smiled thinly. "But I find the idea extremely . . . ill advised."

The prince looked at the officer in shock and shook his head.

"But who's going to be carrying all that stuff for *me*?"

Pahner's face became closed and set as he leaned back in the station chair.

"Your Highness, I've already made arrangements for the support material for Doctor O'Casey to be distributed and field gear to be issued for Doctor O'Casey and Valet Matsugae." The captain regarded the prince steadily. "Am I to assume from that question that I should make the same arrangements for *your* personal gear?"

Before Roger could even think of a proper reply, he found his mouth, as usual, running away with itself.

"Of course you should!" he half-snapped, then nearly quailed as Pahner's face darkened. But he'd already climbed out on the limb; might as well saw with abandon. "I'm a *prince*, Captain. Surely you don't expect me to carry my own bags?"

Pahner stood and placed his hands flat on the tabletop. Then he drew a deep, calming breath, and let it out.

"Very well, Your Highness. I need to go make those arrangements. By your leave?"

For just a moment, the prince appeared to be about to say something, but finally he made a small moue of distaste and waved a hand in dismissal. Pahner gazed at him silently, then gave a jerky nod and strode around the table and out the hatch, leaving the prince to contemplate his "victory."

CHAPTER NINE

Captain Krasnitsky leaned back in his command chair and rotated his shoulders in his skin suit.

"All right. Let's bring the ship back to General Quarters, if you please, Commander Talcott."

The captain hadn't slept in thirty-six hours. He'd had a sonic shower before climbing back into the stinking skin suit, but the only thing keeping him going at this point was Narcon and stimulants. The Narcon was to keep him from going to sleep. The stimulants were to keep him thinking straight, since the *only* thing the Narcon did was prevent sleep.

Even with the combination, his brain felt wrapped in steel wool.

"Wait until they open fire, Commander," he repeated, for what seemed the thousandth time. "I want to get as close as possible."

"Aye, Sir," Talcott said, with rather less exasperation than Krasnitsky thought he would probably have shown in the commander's position.

The captain's mouth tried to quirk a smile, but his amusement was fleeting, and his mind flickered back over his options with a sort of feverish monotony.

DeGlopper was an assault ship, not a true warship, but she was a starship, out-massing the in-system cruiser by nearly a hundred to one, and had enormously heavy ChromSten armor. The combination of mass and armor meant she could take damage that would shatter her opponent. But she was also slower, and not only were her sensors damaged, but her entire tactical net had taken a hit from the sabotage. So like any blind, drunk bruiser faced with a clear-eyed and nimble, but much smaller, foe, she wanted to grapple. She only had a good right remaining, but one uppercut was all it would take.

The plan called for her to maintain the appearance of a damaged freighter, desperate to make landfall, for as long as possible. She was finally starting to decelerate, and the cruiser was piling on all the gravities of deceleration it could stand, as well, but the transport would still flash by the smaller ship at nearly three percent of light-speed. At those velocities, there would be a very, very limited envelope of engagement.

Which meant every shot had better hit.

"We're coming into radar and lidar detection range, Captain," Commander Talcott said a few minutes later. "Should we paint their hull?"

"No. I know we'd get better lockup, but let's play unarmed merchie as long as we can. Be ready to paint them the minute they do it to us, though. And we're going to be close enough that our antiradiation HARMs should be in range. When they paint us, launch a flight."

"Aye, Sir," Talcott said, and moved over beside the ship's defensive systems officer.

Now if the shuttles only came through it alive.

Prince Roger hunched closer to the tiny display, trying to discern anything from it, but the same flickering and distortion that had been evident on the bridge's tactical plot was even more pronounced on the smaller flat screen of the shuttle.

"Give it up, Your Highness," Pahner suggested, and there was actually an edge of humor in his voice. "I've tried to follow ship-to-ship battles on these things when the systems were all *working*. All you're going to do is strain your eyes."

Roger rotated in the station chair to face him, careful where he put his feet, arms, and hands. Nearly his first action on boarding the shuttle had been to smash a readout as the unfamiliar powered armor lived up to its reputation for strength. And for clumsiness in the hands of the untrained.

The station chairs were designed for use by armored or unarmored Marines, so they were hardened. The same could not be said for all the items surrounding them, and there wasn't much space in which to move. The simple fact was that a shuttle loaded with troops and supplies was always overcrowded.

The troops in the cargo bay sat packed like sardines in four rows, two back-to-back down the center of the bay, and one down either side, facing inward. The rows were composed of memory plastic cocoons, but the cocoons were thin walled to either side, so that their occupants were practically shoulder to shoulder, and each row faced another, so close that the Marines' knees intertwined. Their individual weapons and rucksacks were on their knees, piled on top of each other, and each cocoon top sprouted a combat helmet, currently configured to do service as a vac helmet for the chameleon suit of the trooper inside it.

Between a near-total inability to move their legs, the fact that the slightest movement resulted in punching a neighbor, and the fact that getting up or out required going through four layers of gear, it was no place for a claustrophobe. But at least troops in chameleon suits didn't have to worry about how to go to the bathroom. Since the suits were designed for space combat, they had all the comforts of home.

There were armored suits scattered through the cocoons as well, and halfway down the compartment the rows of troops were abruptly broken by a mass of hydrogen cylinders. The red painted battle steel ovals, each the size of an old-fashioned natural gas tank, were piled halfway to the shuttle roof and strapped down nine ways from Sunday. The shuttle might crash, a nuclear-tipped missile might detonate at point-blank range, but nothing was going to move those cylinders. Which was the point. If they kicked loose during the maneuvers of the shuttles or their mothership, the passengers might as well give up and open their suits to vacuum, because without the hydrogen in those tanks, the shuttles would never be able to make reentry.

Beyond the cylinders, which were placed just forward of the shuttle's center of gravity, was the rest of the armored squad and general cargo. In the case of this shuttle, putting the armored squad behind the cylinders, along with the cargo, which had a higher density than the troopers forward of the cylinders, balanced out the load. Since the ships were going to have to make a nearly "dead stick" atmospheric reentry, balance of the cargo was critical. But the whole setup made for terrific crowding.

At least Roger didn't have to put up with the conditions in the cargo bay, but the small compartment he shared with Pahner wasn't all that much better. It offered just enough room to swing a cat . . . assuming it was a very small cat. It contained two tactical stations, wedged into the starboard side of the shuttle, forward of the cargo compartment that separated it from the cockpit. It was the most hardened part of the ship, which was one of the reasons Roger was there, and it also had umbilicals, like those in the cargo bay, to provide local power and recycling support to armor or vac suits. But the low overhead (the position was wedged in above the starboard forward thruster plenum) and the limited space to move around meant that it, also, was no place for a claustrophobe. And just to make the crowding complete, Pahner and Roger's rucksacks hung from the cramped compartment's forward bulkhead.

Roger managed to get his knees out from under the tac station without breaking anything else and looked at the back of Pahner's helmet.

"So," he said testily, "what do we do now?"

"We wait, Your Highness," the company commander replied calmly. He seemed to have gotten over his anger at the prince's refusal to carry his own gear. "The waiting is supposed to be the hardest part."

"Is it?" Roger asked. He found himself out of his depth. This was something he'd never planned for—not that he'd been given many options in planning his life—and it was something he wasn't prepared for. He was accustomed to the challenge of sports, but one reason he had embraced that sort of challenge was because no one had ever taken him seriously enough to make any others applicable to him. Now he was face to face with the greatest challenge of his life . . . and making a mistake on this ballfield would mean death.

"It is for some," Pahner replied. "For others, the worst part is the aftermath. Counting the cost."

He turned his own chair to face the prince, trying to decipher what was going on behind the flickering ball of the boy's faceplate.

"There's going to be a pretty high cost to this operation," he continued, carefully not allowing his tone to change. "But that happens sometimes. There are two sides to any wargame, Your Highness, and the other side is trying to win, too."

"I try very hard not to lose," Roger said quietly. "I discovered early on that I didn't care for it a bit." The external speaker was the highest quality, but the sound still echoed oddly in the little compartment.

"Neither do I, Your Highness," Pahner agreed, turning back to his command station. "Neither do I. There aren't any losers in The Empress' Own. And damned few in the Fleet."

"We just got painted, Sir." Commander Talcott's quiet tone was totally focused. "Sensors confirm that it's a Saint lidar. A Mark 46." He looked up from the tactical system. "That's standard for a *Muir*-class cruiser."

"Roger," Krasnitsky said. "They'll realize their mistake in a moment. Go active and open fire as soon as you have a good lock."

Sublieutenant Segedin had been poised for the order like a runner in the blocks, and his hand stabbed the active emissions button just as the launch alarm sounded.

The Saint parasite cruiser was underarmed for the engagement. Although she was large for an in-system ship, she and her sisters were nothing compared to a starship.

Since the tunnel drive was dependent on volume, not mass, starships could be made extremely large and incredibly massive. Max-hull warships were over twelve hundred meters in diameter, and all interstellar warships were plated with ChromSten collapsed matter armor. That armor normally represented a third of the total mass of a ship, but since their systems were volume dependent, it hardly mattered. They also had immense room for missiles, and the capacitors that drove their tunnel drives gave them enormous storage for their energy batteries.

But once they were inside the TD limit, they found themselves limping along on phase drive, and phase drive *was* mass dependent. Which meant that starships were relatively slow and awkward to maneuver.

That was where the parasites came in.

Parasite cruisers and fighters could be packed into max-hull warships in terrific numbers. Once the starships entered a system, they could send out their cruisers and fighters to engage the enemy, but the cruisers were designed to be fast and nimble, rather than heavily armored, and lacked the ChromSten of starships. But *this* cruiser had come well within *DeGlopper*'s engagement range and was at the mercy of the heavier ship.

The CO of the Saint parasite quickly realized that he'd screwed up by the numbers. His initial launch started with a single missile, which had clearly been intended as a "shot across the bows," but the rest of his broadside followed swiftly. Within moments, a half-dozen missiles came scorching towards the assault ship, and the next broadside followed seconds later.

"He's firing at his launchers' maximum cycle rate, Sir!" Segedin announced, and Krasnitsky nodded. The Saint captain was firing as rapidly as he could, using a "shoot-shoot-look" tracking system. It would take nearly four and a half minutes for the missiles to cross the distance between the two ships, which meant that at his current rate of fire, he would have shot his magazines dry before the first salvo impacted. It was exactly what Krasnitsky would have done in his place, because given the difference in the sizes and power of the two opponents, the cruiser's only chance at this point was to overwhelm and destroy the heavier ship before they closed to energy range.

But that wasn't going to happen.

"All right, let's delta vee," he told Segedin. "I want a max delta towards this Saint P-O-S. Take him, Tactical!"

"Aye, Sir!"

Radar and lidar had an iron lock on the cruiser, and despite the crippling effects of Ensign Guha's sabotage, the tactical computers quickly finalized firing solutions.

DeGlopper was a four-hundred-meter-radius sphere. She was an assault ship, which meant she had to build in room for six shuttles, but that left more than enough room for missile tubes and ample magazines, and the missiles in those magazines were larger and heavier than any parasite cruiser could carry. Now all eight of her launchers began hammering fire at the Saint, and mixed in with her more dangerous missiles were jammers and antiradiation seekers.

It looked like a totally unfair fight, but *DeGlopper*'s tactical net was far below par. Most of her missiles were under autonomous control, which meant the transport's computer AI couldn't adjust their flight profiles to maximum effect. And it also meant her point defense was far less effective than normal.

"Vampires! I have multiple vampires inbound!" There was a series of thuds as the ship's automated defenses reacted to the inbound missiles. "We have auto-flares and chaff. Some of the vampires are following the decoys!"

"And some of them aren't!" Krasnitsky snapped, watching his own plot. "Sound the collision alarm!"

Some of the Saint missiles were picked off by countermissiles and laser clusters. Others were sucked off course by active and passive decoys, and the entire first salvo was destroyed or spoofed. But one missile from the second salvo, and three missiles from the third, got through, and alarms screamed as pencils of X-ray radiation smashed into the ChromSten hull.

"Direct hit on Missile Five," Commander Talcott reported harshly. "We've lost Number Two Graser, two countermissile launchers, and twelve laser clusters." He looked up from his displays and met Krasnitsky's eyes across the bridge. "None of the damage hit any of the shuttles or came near the magazines, Sir!"

"Thank God," the captain whispered. "But still not good. Navigation, how long to beam range?"

"Two minutes," the Navigator reported, and smiled evilly. She'd successfully fooled the Saint captain for hours, playing the role of a panicked merchant skipper while he reviled her parentage, knowledge, and training. Now let him suck laser!

"Hit!" Segedin called. "At least one direct missile hit, Sir! She's streaming air!"

"Understood," Krasnitsky replied. "How are we doing on the computers?"

"Rotten, Sir!" Segedin snapped, euphoria vanished. "I had to shift resources to the defensive systems. Most of the birds are flying on their own at this point."

"Well, this will be over soon," the captain said, just as another salvo of Saint missiles came streaking in. "One way or another."

CHAPTER TEN

Roger grabbed the arms of the command chair as another concussion rocked the shuttle like a high wind.

"This," he remarked quietly, "is not fun."

"Hmmm," Pahner said noncommittally. "Check your monitors in the troop bay, Sir."

The prince found the appropriate control and tapped it, turning on the closed-circuit monitors in the troop bay. What they revealed surprised him: most of the troops were asleep, and the few who were awake were performing some sort of leisure activity.

Two had electronic game pads out and appeared to be competing in something with one another. Others were playing cards with hard decks or, apparently, reading. One even had a hard copy book out, an old and much thumbed one from the look. Roger panned around, looking for anyone he recognized, and realized that he only knew three or four names in the entire company.

Poertena was asleep, with his head thrown back and his mouth wide open. Gunnery Sergeant Jin, the dark, broad Korean platoon sergeant of Third Platoon, had a pad out and was paging slowly through something on it. Roger scrolled up the magnification on the monitors, and was surprised to see that the NCO was reading a novel. He'd somehow expected it to be a military manual, and he spun the magnification still higher, curiously, so that he could read over the sergeant's shoulder. What he got was a bit more than he'd bargained for; the sergeant was reading a fairly graphic homosexual love story. The prince snorted, then spun the monitor away and dialed back on the magnification. The sergeant's taste was the sergeant's business.

The monitor stopped as if by its own volition on the face of the female sergeant who'd summoned him from the armor fitting. It was a face of angles, all high cheekbones and sharp chin with the exception of the lips, which were remarkably voluptuous. Not a pretty face, but arguably a beautiful one. She was looking through a pad as well, and for a reason he wasn't sure he would have cared to explain, he hunted until he found a monitor that would permit him to look over her shoulder. He panned the camera down, and felt a sudden rush of relief—although exactly why he was glad that what she was reading was the briefing on Marduk was something he didn't care to consider too deeply.

Flipping back over to the original monitor, he zoomed in on the sergeant's chameleon suit. There it was. On the right . . . breast. *Despreaux*. Nice name.

"Sergeant Despreaux," Pahner said dryly, and the prince hit the trackball and panned the monitor off the name.

"Yes, I recognized her from when she crashed my fitting," he said hurriedly. "I was just realizing how few of these guards I know by name." He cleared his throat uncomfortably, happy, for some reason, that the captain couldn't see his face.

"Nothing wrong with getting to know their names," Pahner said calmly. "But what you might want to catch is their attitudes," he continued, as another salvo slammed into the ship.

"We just lost Graser Four and Nine, and Missile Three. We're down twenty-five percent on our countermissile launchers. More on the laser clusters," Commander Talcott said. He didn't bother to add that *DeGlopper* had also suffered severe hull breaching, since everyone on the bridge could feel the draw of the vacuum around them. The executive officer had just turned toward the captain, when there was a crow of delight from Tactical.

"There she blows!" the sublieutenant shouted. The Saint cruiser had come apart under the hammer of the missiles, without even having come to grips at energy weapon range.

"Put us back on course for the planet—and shift to Evasion Able Three!" Krasnitsky snapped to the helmsman. "We're not out of the woods yet. There are still incoming missiles."

"Yes, Sir," Segedin agreed with a triumphant grin. "But we still got her!"

"Yes, we did," Talcott whispered so quietly that only Krasnitsky could hear. "But what about her mate?"

The tac officer shut down the guidance channels to the remainder of the offensive missiles and shunted all the processor power they'd been using to the defenses. Then he picked up half the defensive net and waded in. Between the added processor power, the loss of the cruiser's support, and the addition of Segedin's experience, the remainder of the missiles were quickly shredded. All that was left, for the time being, was to pick up the pieces.

"So that's it, Your Highness," Captain Krasnitsky finished, looking up from the pad in his hand. His skin suit was sealed, and the orange vacuum warning light behind him was clearly visible. "We used less than half our missiles in this engagement, but the other cruiser has already broken orbit and is accelerating towards us. We'll drop your shuttles in two hours, and it will take us longer than that to get patched up and restore pressure again. So I would suggest that you stay where you are, Your Highness."

"Very well, Captain," the prince said. He was aware that all the captain was seeing was the distorted ball of his powered armor's helmet-visor, and he was just as glad. He was beginning to understand why *DeGlopper* had to, effectively, commit suicide, but he was still uncomfortable with it.

Pahner's company, at least, were official bodyguards for the Imperial Family, with the tradition of taking rifle beads to protect their charges; "catching the ball" as it was called. But the company's personnel had to survive—some of them, at least—if they were to accomplish their mission of keeping him alive; *DeGlopper*'s entire crew had to *die* to do that. Spoiled he might be, but not even Roger

MacClintock was immune to the sense of guilt that produced. Yet nothing in Krasnitsky's tone or attitude suggested that he had ever even considered any other course of action. In the captain's place, Roger suspected that he might be thinking about how . . . convenient it would be if something happened to remove the prince from the equation. After all, if Roger were dead, there would be no reason for Krasnitsky's remaining crew to die to save him, now would there? Somehow, the fact that Krasnitsky and all of his people seemed totally oblivious to that glaringly logical point only made him feel guiltier.

"I suppose we'll talk again before separation," he said after a moment, awkwardly. "Until then, good luck."

"Thank you, Your Highness," the captain said with a tiny nod. "And good luck to you and the Company, as well. We'll try to do the *DeGlopper* name proud."

The communications screen blinked out, and Roger leaned back and turned to Captain Pahner. The Marine had doffed his helmet and was scratching his head vigorously.

"Who was DeGlopper, anyway?" the prince asked, fumbling with the controls and latches of his own helmet.

"He was a soldier in the American States, a long time ago, Your Highness," Pahner said, cocking his head at the angle Roger had begun to recognize as a subtle sign that he'd stuck his foot in it. "There was a plaque right outside the cabin you were in, listing his medal and the citation for it. He won their equivalent of the Imperial Star. When we get back to Earth you can look up the citation."

"Oh." Roger pulled the pin and let his hair down so that it cascaded across the back of the armor, then scratched his scalp with both hands at least as vigorously as Pahner. "We weren't in these things all that long. What makes your head itch so badly?"

"A lot of it's psychosomatic, Your Highness," Pahner said with a snort. "Like that itch between your shoulder blades."

"Agggh!" Roger rolled his shoulders as well as he could in the constricting armor and squirmed, trying to rub his back against the internal padding. "You would have to mention that!"

Pahner just smiled. Then he frowned ever so slightly.

"Can I make a suggestion, Your Highness?"

"Yesss?" Roger replied doubtfully.

"We're not going anywhere for two hours. I'm going to go roust out the troops and tell them they can undog their helmets and do a little stretching. Give them about a half-hour, and then come down and talk to a few of them."

"I'll think about it," Roger said dubiously.

He did, and his thoughts didn't make him all that happy.

CHAPTER ELEVEN

Chaplain Pannella placed his hands behind his back and sniffed.

"Lord Arturo isn't going to be happy," he observed.

Captain Imai Delaney, skipper of the Caravazan Empire parasite cruiser *Greenbelt*, refrained from snarling at the ship's chaplain. It wasn't the easiest restraint he'd ever exercised, and it got even harder as he looked around and recognized his bridge officers' stunned disbelief. He drew a deep breath and wiped his face. They'd obviously gotten sloppy, and "not happy" was a very pale description of what Lord Arturo would be when he heard about this one.

At the same time, he understood exactly how it had happened. There had been no problems at all since the two parasites had been put on station, and they were mainly there to make sure that no one noticed the Saint presence in the system. They'd let a few transports—the ones with registered schedules—through and taken a few of the tramps as prizes. But their primary job wasn't commerce raiding; it was supporting the tactical operations that were being staged through the system, and it had become routine. Too routine.

"It's a *Puller*-class transport," the tactical officer reported as he studied his readouts. "There was one flash of nearly full power. They're masking their drive, somehow, but that flash was clear."

"Why would the Earthies send in a single armed transport?" the chaplain demanded. "And why is its acceleration so low?"

The captain decided that screaming would probably be unwise, however tempting. The answer to both questions was obvious, but if he simply stated them bluntly he might be accused of "insufficient consideration" for the chaplain's feelings and opinions. As if a chaplain should have a voice in military matters!

He looked around the bridge. His officers' uniforms were the somber and slightly off-color tones that bespoke preparation in low-acid processes. The textiles were all natural, too . . . which meant that unlike in most navies, if there was a sudden shipboard fire the crew was subject to immolation.

Captain Delaney had been aboard an Empie parasite cruiser once. The bridge had been all cool tones and smoothly rounded edges; on his own ship, the edges were jagged and unfinished. Finishing and "trim" were considered unnecessary frills. Unnecessary frills used excess energy. Excess energy, eventually, was bad for planetary environments. So, no trimming for *Greenbelt*'s bridge.

The same philosophy extended throughout the ship. Everything looked rough hewn and badly fitted. Oh, it worked. But it wasn't as smooth as it would have been aboard a damned Empie warship. Nothing was . . . not even the command relationships. On an Empie ship, the captain was king. He might be under the command of an admiral, but on his own ship he was lord and master.

On the Saints' ships, though, the chaplain always had to be considered. Adherence to the tenets of the Church of Ryback was as important, to the higher-ups, as capability. So besides fighting the damned aristos for command slots, Captain Delaney had been fighting the Church for his entire career.

Not that there was going to be any difference of opinion about what to do in this instance.

"I believe she might be damaged," he said, allowing no trace of his thoughts to color his tone. "That one burst of power is probably all their phase drive could stand."

"Well . . . I suppose that makes some sense," the chaplain said doubtfully. "What are we going to do about it?"

We are going to kill it, Delaney thought. Which would be easier to do if you would just get your eco-freak butt back to the chapel and off my bridge!

"The data from *Green Goddess* indicates that the enemy's tactical net is probably damaged," he said aloud. He scratched his beard and thought about it. "We'll stay at the edge of the powered missile envelope and pound her to scrap. She can't maneuver, and we should have the better tac net." He nodded his head in self-agreement. "Yes. That should work."

"How much damage will we take?" the chaplain asked nervously. "Damage repair will do great harm to the environment. We must limit our use of resources in every way we can. And it will surely damage the *ki* of the crew."

"Do you want the ravening imperialists to fully colonize this world?" Delaney asked rhetorically. "That ship is filled with Marines, carrying their humanocentric infestation with them to new worlds. What would you have me do? Let them go?"

"No," the chaplain snapped, shaking his head. "They must be destroyed. The infestation must be ripped out root and branch. This fine world shall not be polluted by man!"

Fine world, indeed, the captain thought behind a smile of agreement. It's a green hell. Killing these Marines is probably doing them a favor.

Sergeant Major Kosutic reached across the narrow compartment and tapped the prince's chief of staff on the shoulder.

"You can undog your helmet now," she said, suiting action to words and removing her own.

O'Casey undid the latches clumsily, and looked around the cramped compartment.

"Now what?" she asked.

"Now we wait a couple of hours, and hope His Evilness Who Resides in the Fire decides we get to live," Kosutic answered, scratching the back of her neck. She set down the helmet and reached under the command station. "Aha!" she said, and pulled out a long plastic tube with a faint ripping sound.

"What is that?" O'Casey asked, looking up as she opened her pad to begin an entry.

"It's a wiring harness cover." Kosutic leaned forward and inserted the flexible tube into the neck of her suit. "Most of these shuttles have had them stripped out already." She began rubbing the corrugated tube up and down her back. "Ahhh," she gasped. "I forgot mine, by Satan."

"Oh," Eleanora said, suddenly noticing the itchiness of her own back. "Can I, um, borrow it?"

"Check by your left knee. I don't mind your borrowing it, but you might as well find your own. Best back scratcher ever created."

Eleanora found the wiring harness where the sergeant major had indicated and pulled its cover out.

"Ooooh," she sighed after a brief try. "Boy, this is good!"

"And for telling you that deep, dark secret, known only to Old Marines," Kosutic said, "you have to tell me something."

"Like what?"

"Like what's eating the Prince," Kosutic replied, propping her heels on the command station in front of her.

"Hmmm," Eleanora said thoughtfully. "That's a long story, and I'm not sure how much of it you're cleared for. What you know about his father?"

"Just that he's the Earl of New Madrid; that he's on the watchlist, which means he doesn't get within a planet of the Empress; and that he's quite a bit older than the Empress."

"Well, I'm not going to get into why he was banished from Court, but Roger not only looks like his father, he acts very much like him. New Madrid is a gorgeous man, who's a terrible dandy. And he's also very much involved in The Great Game."

"Ah." Kosutic nodded. The intrigues of the Empire had gotten deeper and deeper during the reign of Emperor Andrew, Alexandra's father. While things had never, quite, come to the point of outright civil war, they seemed to be edging closer to it. "So is the Prince involving himself in the Game?" she asked carefully, and Eleanora sighed.

"I'm . . . not sure. He's been in contact with some of the known conduits in his sports clubs. I mean, one of the other fellows on his polo team is a known member of New Madrid's clique. So, maybe. But Roger hates politics with a purple passion. So . . . I'm not sure."

"You should know."

"Yes, I should," the chief of staff admitted. "But it's not the sort of thing he would confide in me. I'm an appointment of his mother's."

"Is he . . . conspiring against the *Empress*?" Kosutic asked even more carefully.

"I doubt that very much," Eleanora said. "He seems to truly love his mother, but he might be being used as a dupe. The way he acts, the . . . frivolity. It just doesn't make any sense. With his background, with what his father did, Roger has to realize that presenting such a front lays him open to charges of following in New Madrid's footsteps. So half the time I'm certain he's doing it on purpose, and the other half . . . I just don't know."

"Maybe it's a double-blind," Kosutic suggested. "He might be putting on these airs as a cover for being really, really capable?"

She was aware that she was engaging in wishful thinking, but there had to be at least a shred of light in the darkness. Otherwise, the Marines had stuck their heads into a guillotine for an enemy of all they held dear.

"I doubt it," Eleanora said with a grim chuckle. "Roger's just not that subtle." She gazed down at her pad for several moments, then sighed. "And, frankly, however subtle he is or isn't, he's always been the odd one out in the Imperial Family."

She tapped at the pad's controls for several seconds, then closed it and turned her chair to face the sergeant major.

"At the expense of possible *lesse majeste*," she said, "Roger can act like a real pain in the ass sometimes. No, let's be honest—he can *be* a real pain in the ass. But I think it's fair to point out that it's not entirely his fault."

"Ah?" Kosutic kept her face carefully expressionless, but mental ears pricked at the chief of staff's tone. Despite the fact that Bronze Battalion was specifically charged with the task of guarding the Heir Tertiary, and despite the amount of time the Bronze Barbarians had spent in their charge's presence (not with any particular sense of pleasure for either party), no one in the company really *knew* Roger at all. O'Casey obviously did, and if she was prepared to give Kosutic any insight at all into the prince, the sergeant major was more than ready to listen.

"No, it's not," O'Casey told her, and shook her own head with a crooked smile. "He's a MacClintock, and everyone knows that all MacClintocks are brave, trustworthy, fearless and brilliant. They're not, of course, but everyone *knows* they are, anyway, and the fact that Crown Prince John and Princess Alexandra actually live up to the stereotype—like their mother—only makes it even harder on Roger. The Crown Prince has a record as a diplomat anyone could envy, and even without her family connections, Princess Alexandra would be respected as one of the finest admirals in the Fleet. And then there's Roger. Decades younger than the others, always on the outside, somehow . . . the classic 'bad boy' of the Imperial Family. The never-do-well, spoiled, pampered aristocrat." She paused and cocked her head at the sergeant major.

"Sound familiar?" she asked with a quirky half-grin.

"Well, yes, actually," Kosutic admitted. It wasn't something any Marine, and especially any member of Bronze Battalion, had any business admitting to anyone, anytime, anywhere, but she admitted it anyway, and O'Casey chuckled without humor.

"I thought it might. But when you consider the cloud his father is under, the fact that no one really knows where Roger himself stands, and the fact that the Empress' own attitude towards him often seems . . . ambiguous," she chose the word with obvious care, "it's probably inevitable that he should turn out at least a bit that way." She snorted sadly. "Kostas Matsugae and I have argued about it often enough, but I've never disagreed with Kostas' insistence that Roger wasn't exactly dealt the fairest possible hand. But where Kostas and I differ is on where we go from where we are *now*. I wasn't Roger's first tutor, you know. In fact, I've only been with him for a little over six years, so I wasn't there when he was a hurt little boy dealing with the unfairness of life. I can feel for that little boy's pain, I suppose, but I have to be more concerned with getting Roger the theoretical adult to face up to the fact that life isn't fair and learning to deal with it as a MacClintock and as a prince of the Empire. And," she admitted heavily, "I don't seem to be doing a very good job of it."

"Well," Kosutic told her, picking her words with equal care, "I can't say I envy you. I've done my share of kicking wet-behind-the-ears lieutenants into Marine officers, but the Corps gives me a lot better support structure for that kind of thing than you seem to have."

"It *would* be nice if I could use the sort of judo I've seen you using on Captain Pahner's officers," O'Casey agreed wistfully. "But I can't. And, frankly, Roger has a positive genius for digging in his heels. He may not be the overachiever his brother and sister are, but he's certainly got every bit of the MacClintock stubbornness!"

She paused with a sudden laugh, and Kosutic raised an eyebrow at her.

"What's funny?" the sergeant major asked.

"I was just thinking about Roger and stubbornness," O'Casey replied. "Well, that and God's peculiar sense of humor."

"I beg your pardon?"

"Have you ever been to the Imperial War Museum?" the academic asked, and the Marine nodded.

"Sure. A couple of times. Why?"

"I take it you've seen the Roger III Collection, then?"

Kosutic nodded again, though she wasn't at all sure where O'Casey was headed with this. Roger III had been one of the many unreasonably capable emperors the MacClintock Dynasty had produced, and, as seemed to be the norm among his relatives, he had been a man of passionate (and, some would say, peculiar) interests. One of them had been military history and, particularly, that of Old Earth between the twelfth and sixteenth centuries, CE, and he had assembled what was probably the finest collection of arms and armor from the period in the entire history of the human race. When he died, he had bequeathed the entire collection to the Imperial War Museum, where it had become and remained one of its star attractions.

"Ever since Roger III's time," O'Casey went on a bit obliquely, "the continuance of his hobby interest in ancient weaponry has been something of a tradition in the Imperial Family. Oh, there's an edge of affectation to it, of course—something that makes good PR as a 'family tradition' that imperial subjects can ooh and ah over—but there's also more than a little truth to it. The Empress and the Crown

Prince, for example, can spend hours explaining more than you ever wanted to know about things like Gothic armor and Swiss pikemen." She grimaced with so much feeling that Kosutic chuckled.

"But not Roger," the academic continued. "I said he can be stubborn? Well, he dug his heels in and flatly refused to have anything to do with the 'tradition.' I suppose it was a fairly harmless way to express his rebellion, but he was certainly . . . firm about it. Maybe it's partly because it was all started by another Roger who also happens to have been another of those MacClintock figures everyone *respects*—unlike our Roger—but despite his family's very best efforts, he never showed the least interest in the entire subject, which is a pity really. Especially now."

"Now?" Kosutic gazed at her for a moment, then barked a laugh as understanding struck. "You're right," she said, "it *would* be handy if he knew anything about it, given the local tech level on Marduk."

"Absolutely," O'Casey agreed with another sigh, "but that's our Roger all over. If there's a way to do it wrong, he'll find it every time."

Roger watched Pahner make his way down the center transom of the shuttle bay and shook his head. With the troops squashed into the shuttle like old-fashioned sardines in a can, the only way to move up and down the troop bay was by walking on the transom on which the center seats were mounted. That meant, of course, that he was walking at head level to the seated Marines.

The problem was that while Pahner was in a relatively light and fairly nimble skin suit, which he'd donned in preference to armor for just this reason, Roger was wrapped in ChromSten. He could no more make his way down that narrow strip in armor than he could walk a tightrope, and he rather doubted that any of his bodyguards would feel happy about being stepped upon, however daintily, by armor that weighed as much as a tyranothere.

"Well, Your Highness?" Pahner asked as he reached the end and swung easily to the floor.

"I'm going to have a hard time making my way down the bay in this," Roger said, gesturing at his armor. Pahner glanced at the gray battle steel and nodded.

"Take it off. We're going to be rattling around for a couple of hours."

"Take it off where? There's not enough room in the compartment."

"Right here," Pahner said, gesturing at the small open area. The patch of deck was the only open area in the bay, a tiny sliver of room for the shuttle crew to move around in. A ladder led up from it to a small landing with two hatches, one to the command compartment, and the other to the bridge. There was another hatch on the troop level portside. It was a pressure door leading to the exterior.

"Right here?" Roger juggled the helmet under his arm to give himself a moment to think while he looked around. Most of the guards were still doing their own things. A few had gotten up to move around, but most of those had headed to the rear of the bay where the palletized cargo afforded room to stretch out. It seemed awfully . . . public, though.

"I could get your valet," Pahner said with a faint smile. "He's back there," he continued, gesturing towards the rear of the troop bay.

"Matsugae?" Roger's face brightened. "That would be grea—I mean, yes, of course, Captain. Do you think you could fetch my valet?" he ended in a refined drawl.

"Well," Pahner said, his face closing down again, "I don't know about 'fetch.'" He banged the nearest sleeping guard on the shoulder. "Pass the word for Matsugae."

The Marine yawned, shoved the next Marine in line, passed on the word, and promptly went back to sleep. A few moments later, Roger saw the small form of the valet emerge from under a pile of rucksacks. He bent down and spoke to someone, then climbed onto the transom and made his way toward the prince.

Vertical pillars ran up from the transom to the roof every two meters, and if Matsugae was far less nimble on the uncertain footing than Captain Pahner had been, he had the overall idea down. He would hold onto a vertical, then move forward of it, using it to balance as he shuffled out on the transom as far as he could before making a hopping lunge for the next. Using this technique, he slowly made his way forward to the prince's position.

"Good—" the valet paused, obviously checking the clock in his toot "—evening, Your Highness." He smiled. "You're looking well."

"Thank you, Valet Matsugae," Roger said, much more careful to maintain his formality in front of so many listening ears. "How are you?"

"Very well, Your Highness. Thank you." Matsugae gestured to the rear of the compartment. "Sergeant Despreaux has been a mine of helpful information."

"Despreaux?" Roger lifted an eyebrow and leaned sideways to look down the line of troops, and caught the brief flash of a refined profile.

"She's a squad leader in Third Platoon, Your Highness. A very nice young lady."

"Given their resumes," Roger said with a smile, "I doubt that you could categorize any of the young ladies in The Empress' Own as 'nice.' "

"As you say, Your Highness," Matsugae said with an answering smile. "How can I be of service?"

"I have to get out of this armor and into something decent."

Matsugae's face crumpled.

"I'm sorry, Your Highness. I should've known. Let me go get my pack." He started to scramble up onto the transom again, preparing to retrace his route.

"Wait!" Roger said. "I have a uniform packed up in the command compartment. I just need help getting out of the armor."

"Oh, well then," Matsugae said, climbing back down. "If Captain Pahner could give me a hand? I don't actually know all that much about armor, but I'm willing to learn."

As they disconnected the armor's various latches and controls, Roger became curious.

"Matsugae? Am I to understand that you have spare uniforms for me in your pack?"

"Well, Your Highness," the valet said almost shyly, "Sergeant Despreaux told me that you weren't able to bring all your clothes. And why. I didn't feel it appropriate that you have only one suit of armor and a single uniform, so I packed a few extra outfits along. Just in case."

"Can you carry it?" Captain Pahner sounded skeptical. "Of course, if that's *all* that you're carrying . . ."

"I will admit, Captain," the small valet said in a pert voice, "that I'm not carrying the weight of ammunition most of your Marines are. However, I *am* carrying my full equipment load and a share of the squad load for the headquarters group. His Highness' gear is, so to speak, my ammunition allotment."

"But can you carry it?" Pahner repeated darkly. "Day after day."

"We shall simply have to see, Captain," Matsugae replied calmly. "I think so. But we shall have to see."

He returned to his task of peeling the prince, and Roger soon found himself once again standing in the midst of scattered pieces of armor.

"I'm forever putting this stuff on and taking it off." He brushed an imaginary fleck of dust from the singlet he'd worn under the armor as Matsugae scrambled up the steps to the command compartment.

"Not for much longer, Your Highness," Pahner pointed out. "Once we land on the planet, it will hardly ever be used. But if we need it, we're *really* going to need it."

CHAPTER TWELVE

"What else do we need?" O'Casey asked, thumbing through the list of supplies the Marines had loaded.

"Whatever it is, it better not weigh much," Kosutic replied. The sergeant major was doing a recalculation of fuel use, and she looked up with a grimace. "I don't think we have much margin."

"I thought you could glide one of these things in," Eleanora said uncomfortably. It was hardly her area of expertise, but she knew that the shuttles' swing-wing configuration gave them a tremendous glide ratio.

"We can." Kosutic's tone was mild. "If we have a runway, that is." She gestured at one of the monitors, where the small map from the *Fodor's* was displayed. "Do you see many airports? In glide mode, one of these things needs a nice, old-fashioned runway. You try to land without one, and you might as well give your soul to His Wickedness."

"So what happens if it were running out of fuel, then?"

"Well, if we were headed in for a standard atmosphere insertion, we could correct at the last minute and do some atmospheric skipping to slow down. The problem is, if we do an orbit, we'll be detected. Then the whole plan goes out the airlock, and we have a cruiser and the garrison hunting us dirtside.

"If, on the other hand, we do a steep reentry—which, by the way, is what we're planning—and run out of fuel, we'll just pancake."

"Oh."

"Make a hell of a hole," Kosutic snorted.

"I can imagine," O'Casey said faintly.

"I imagine that this is about where we should be detecting the Saint, Sir," Sublieutenant Segedin said.

"Understood." Captain Krasnitsky looked at the helmsman. "Prepare for course change. Quartermaster, pass the word to the Marines to prepare for separation."

"They should have detected us by now," Captain Delaney said. "Why are they still decelerating for the planet?"

"Could they still intend to land their Marines?" the chaplain asked, leaning over the tactical display beside him.

Delaney's nose wrinkled at the sour smell of the chaplain's unwashed cassock. Washing among the faithful was an occasional thing, since it used unnecessary resources. And such harmful chemicals as deodorants were, of course, right out.

"They must," Delaney mused. "But they're still too far out." He smiled as the display changed. "Ah! Now we have a feel for their sensor damage. There's the course change."

"Prepare for separation. Five minutes," the ennunciator boomed.

Roger looked up in surprise from his conversation with Sergeant Jin. The Korean was surprisingly well versed on current men's fashions, and after Roger had circulated briefly around the compartment (doing his best imitation of Mother at a garden party), he'd settled down for a long talk with the sergeant. Better that than a long talk with the fascinating Sergeant Despreaux. Something told him that getting "interested" in one of his bodyguards in a situation like this one probably was a bad idea. Not that it would have been a *good* idea under any circumstances, he reflected with a familiar moodiness.

"You'd better get your armor back on, Sir," Jin said, glancing at the chameleon suit Roger had changed into. "It'll take you at least that long."

"Right. Talk to you later, Sergeant." Roger had become accustomed to walking the transom, and now he sprang lightly onto it and skipped forward, swinging gracefully from pillar to pillar.

"Show off," Julian muttered as he shifted the rucksack across his knees. It wasn't particularly uncomfortable, since it was supported by his armor, but the confinement got to him after a while.

He'd been awakened by the prince's circuit, and hadn't yet gotten back to sleep. He realized that his responses to the fop's rote questions had been a bit surly, but the prince hadn't seemed to notice.

"I don't think he was showing off," Despreaux said tartly. "I think he was hurrying up front."

Julian raised an eyebrow. Since Despreaux was seated across from him, it gave him the perfect opportunity to needle her, and it would have violated his most deeply held principles to pass it up.

"Ah, you're just jealous because he has better hair than you do."

She glanced sideways to get a glimpse of the rapidly undressing prince.

"It is nice," she murmured, and Julian's mouth dropped open as the realization dawned on him.

"You *like* him, don't you? You've got the hots for the *Prince*!"

Her head snapped back around, and she glared at the other squad leader.

"That is the stupidest thing—Of course I don't!"

Julian started to tease her further, but then the full implications hit him. There was no way the Regiment would allow one of the guards to carry on with a member of the Imperial Family. He looked around, but all the other troopers seemed to be asleep or had earbuds in. Fortunately, no one had caught his earlier outburst, and he leaned forward as far as the packed equipment permitted.

"Nimashet, are you nuts?" he hissed softly. "They'll have your ass for this!"

"There's nothing going on," she replied just as quietly, fingering the gray chameleon cover of the rucksack on her knees. "Nothing."

"There'd better be nothing!" he whispered fiercely. "But I don't believe it."

"I can handle it," the sergeant said, leaning back. "Don't worry about me. I'm a big girl."

"Sure you are. Sure." He shook his head and leaned back as well. *What a cock-up,* he thought.

On the opposite side of the transom, Poertena managed to turn a laugh into a cough. He rolled his head around as if half-asleep, and coughed again. *Despreaux and the Prince,* he thought. *Oh, t'at's pocking funny!*

"What's so funny, Sir?" Commander Talcott asked. The XO had just returned from a survey of the ship, and the news wasn't good. Four of *DeGlopper*'s eight missile launchers had taken enough damage to put them out of play for the next bout, and the dead cruiser's fire had gouged deep wounds into the ChromSten-armored hull. Some of them threatened loaded magazines, and although the laser-pumped fusion warheads wouldn't detonate from impact, the power systems of the missile drives would . . . and take the entire ship with them.

But at least the phase drive had suffered no further damage. In fact, it was actually in better shape than for the last encounter, so they'd have a few more gravities to play with and more time on the power. And while they'd lost launchers, they'd also used less than half the total missile inventory against their first opponent, so the next fight would be nearly even.

Except for the cruiser's ability to dance rings around them.

"Oh, I was just thinking about our ship's namesake," Krasnitsky answered the question with a grim smile. "I wonder if *he* ever thought 'What the heck am I doing this for?'"

Roger watched the external monitors as the giant docking hatches opened. The perfect blackness of space beckoned as the tractor moorings cut loose, and the shuttles drifted forward. As they cleared the ship's field, *DeGlopper*'s artificial gravity fell away, and they were in freefall.

"I forgot to ask, Your Highness," Pahner said tactfully. "How are you in microgravity?" He carefully avoided any mention of the excuses O'Casey had made to explain the prince's "indisposition" the first evening aboard.

"I play null-gee handball quite a bit," the prince said in an offhand manner as he swiveled the monitor around to watch the ship disappearing in the distance behind them. "I don't have any problems with freefall at all." He smiled evilly for just a moment. "Eleanora, on the other hand . . ."

"I'm gonna *diiie*," the chief of staff moaned, clutching the motion sickness bag to her mouth as another wave of wracking nausea washed over her.

"I've got a Mo-Fix injector around here somewhere," Kosutic said with the half-malicious chuckle of one who possessed a cast-iron stomach. Even the smell of the ejecta was survivable; it wasn't like she hadn't smelled it before.

"I'm allergic." Eleanora's voice was muffled by the plastic bag. Then she leaned back and zipped the bag shut. "Oh, Goddd. . . ."

"Oh," Kosutic said in more sympathetic tones. She shook her head. "We're going to be out here for a couple of days, you realize?"

"Yes," Eleanora said miserably. "I do realize that. But I'd forgotten these shuttles don't have artificial gravity."

"I don't think we can rotate, either," the sergeant major told her. "We're going to do a long, slow burn. I don't think we can do that and rotate at the same time."

"I'll live . . . I think." The chief of staff suddenly ripped the bag open and buried her face in the contents. "*Arrggg.*"

Kosutic leaned back and shook her head.

"I can see this is gonna be a great trip," she said.

CHAPTER THIRTEEN

"On a scale from one to ten," Captain Krasnitsky muttered, "I give this trip a negative four hundred."

He coughed and shook his head to clear the mist of blood the cough brought up. The instructions on the box were fairly clear. Now if he could just hold together long enough to enter the codes.

Finding the keys for this particular device had been tough. Talcott, who'd had one, had been cut in half on his way back from Engineering. And, of course, the third had been in the suit of the acting engineer. He'd felt awful about having to cut it off of her to get to the device, but he'd had no choice. Tactical had had the fourth, and Navigation the fifth; those two had been easy to snag after the hit on the bridge.

Somewhat to his surprise, the ship had held together. And now, the Saints, after receiving the surrender transmission and the recording of the prince ordering Krasnitsky to surrender, were practically salivating. Capturing the prince would set every member of the ship's crew up for life, even in the austere Saint theocracy.

There was no plot here in the armory, but he didn't need one to know what was happening. He could hear the parasite cruiser docking onto the larger ship, and the concussion as the Saint Marines forced the airlocks for boarding.

Lessee. If I have all five keys, but only one activator, I have to set a delay. Okay. Makes sense.

* * *

"Captain Delaney, this is Lieutenant Scalucci." The Caravazan Marine paused and looked around the bridge. "We've taken the bridge but no prisoners. We are encountering resistance from the crew. So far, no prisoners. They're fighting hard—some of them in powered armor—and not surrendering as I would've expected. We have yet to encounter the Prince's bodyguards." He paused and looked around again. "There's something about this I don't like."

"Tell him to keep his opinions to himself!" Chaplain Panella snapped. "And find the Prince!"

Captain Delaney glanced at the chaplain, then keyed his throat mike.

"Continue the mission, Lieutenant," he said. "Be careful of ambushes. They apparently haven't surrendered after all, whatever their captain said."

"It doesn't appear that way, Sir. Scalucci, out."

The captain turned to face the chaplain squarely.

"We'll find the Prince, Chaplain. But losing people doing it is stupid. I wish we'd had a pinnace to send the Marines over." An unlucky hit to the boat bay, unfortunately, had settled that. "If the Prince weren't on board, I'd put this down as a trap!"

"But he is," the chaplain hissed, "and there's no way they'd risk *his* life playing some sort of ambush game!" He grinned like a rabid ferret. "Although, if they had any sense, they'd cut his throat themselves to keep him out of our hands. Imagine what we can do with a member of the Imperial Family of that damned 'Empire of Man'!"

"Captain!" It was Lieutenant Scalucci. "The shuttle bays are empty! The shuttles must have already punched!"

The Saint captain's eyes flew wide.

"Oh, pollution!" he swore.

"The Saint is matching the last known accel of the *DeGlopper*," Pahner said.

"How can you tell?" Roger asked, eyes aching from the strain of staring at the tiny screen. "I can't tell a thing from this."

"Bring up the data records, instead," Pahner advised. "I've always said there's no reason we couldn't have larger screens in these things. But the command station was an afterthought in the design, and nobody's ever changed it."

"Well, we will!" the prince smiled as he banged the side of the recalcitrant instrument. "Oops."

He'd forgotten the power of the armor, and he withdrew his hand carefully from the fist-sized hole driven into the side of the workstation.

Pahner spun his own chair around and typed commands on the secondary keyboard at the prince's station. The now flickering monitor switched from a wider view of power sources in near space to a list of data.

"There's the last known velocity and position of the *DeGlopper*," the captain said. "And there's her current probable position and velocity." He sent a command through his toot, and a different screen came up. "And this is the Saint data."

"So they're alongside?" Roger asked, noting the obvious similarities in the data.

"Yep. They've matched course and speed with the *DeGlopper*. Which means they fell for Krasnitsky's little deception hook, line, and sinker."

Roger nodded and tried to reflect some of the Marine's satisfaction, but it was hard. It was odd, he thought. Pahner was military, like Krasnitsky, and he knew as well as Roger that the Fleet captain and his entire crew were committing suicide to cover their escape. Somehow, the prince would have expected that to produce more emotion in the Marine. He'd always suspected that people who chose military careers had to be a little less . . . sensitive than others, but Pahner had been quick to let *him* know, however respectfully, whenever he stepped on one or another of the Marines' precious traditions or attitudes. So why was Pahner so detached and clinical over what was about to happen when he himself felt a hollow void of guilt sucking at his stomach?

This wasn't the way things were supposed to happen. People weren't supposed to throw away their lives to protect *him*—not when even his own family had never seemed quite certain he was worth keeping. And when gallant bodyguards and military personnel offered to lay down their lives for their duty, weren't they supposed to get something out of it besides simply *dying*?

The questions made him acutely uncomfortable, and so he decided not to think about them just at the moment and reached for some other topic.

"I didn't sound all that good on the recording," Roger said sourly.

"I think you sounded perfect, Your Highness," Pahner said with a grin. "It certainly suckered the Saints."

"Uh-huh," Roger acknowledged even more sourly. Until he'd heard the edited playback of him ordering the officers to surrender which Krasnitsky had sent to the Saint cruiser, he hadn't realized how truly childish he'd sounded. "Surrender with honor." What poppycock.

"It worked, Your Highness," Pahner's voice was much colder, "and that's all that matters. Captain Krasnitsky has them right where he wants them."

"If there's anyone left to detonate the charge."

"There is," Pahner said firmly.

"How do you know? Everybody could be dead. And unless there's at least one officer left who knows the codes . . ."

"I know, Your Highness." There was no doubt at all in Pahner's reply. "How? Well, the Saint cruiser is still alongside. If it had captured one of the crew and made him talk, it would be accelerating away at top speed. It isn't; so the plan has to be working."

And God bless, Captain, the Marine thought quietly, allowing no trace of his inner anguish to show as he watched the data codes and thought of the men and women about to die. *You've done your part; now we'll do ours to make it worth something. He's a pain in the ass, but we'll keep him alive somehow.*

"It's not working," O'Casey said to herself.

The sergeant major had drifted into the troop bay to buck up the troops, leaving the civilian to fend for herself. Which was ironic, because Eleanora was feeling seriously in need of bucking up herself.

Of course, even the sergeant major might have gotten tired of the smell, which could help explain whose morale she'd decided to improve.

To take her mind off the situation, O'Casey had started reviewing the plan—if it was really fair to call it that. From the moment the second cruiser had been spotted, there'd been no time for anything as deliberate and orderly as formulating anything Eleanora O'Casey would have called "a plan." Everything had been one frantic leap of improvisation after another, and she'd been sure something vital had to have been overlooked. For that matter, she still was, but she'd never had time to stop and reflect, and now she was feeling so out of sorts and woozy that her brain was scarcely in shape for critical analysis.

Unfortunately, it was the only brain she had, and despite its grumpy complaints, she insisted that it apply itself to the problem.

They'd loaded the trade goods. She'd suggested adding refined metals, as well, but Pahner had rejected the suggestion. The captain hadn't felt that the weight-to-cost ratio would make metals worth carrying, and besides, most of the material available consisted of advanced composites, impossible for local smiths to work at the Mardukans' technology level. And, as Pahner had pointed out, material that couldn't be adapted to the locals' needs would be effectively useless to them.

There'd been no great stock of "precious" metals or gems on the ship, either. A smidgen of gold was still used in some electronics contacts, but there'd been no way to get it out. Captain Pahner had ruthlessly appropriated the small store of personal jewelry, but there hadn't been a great deal of that, either. At least what there was ought to be very attractive to a barbarian culture, even though it was little more than costume jewelry by the standards of the Empire of Man. She doubted that anyone on Marduk had ever heard of a synthetic gem!

But even if one assumed that Mardukans valued such items as highly as human cultures of comparable tech levels had valued them, there simply weren't enough of them to even begin to meet their needs. The trade goods would be worth far more in the long run, yet Eleanora still felt she was missing something. Something important.

It bothered her that she had all this incredible store of knowledge about ancient cultures and—

Knowledge.

Chief Warrant Officer Tom Bann ran the calculations for the fifteenth time. It was going to be close, closer than he liked. If everything went perfectly, they were going to have less than a thousand kilos of hydrogen when they landed. To a groundhog, that might have sounded like a lot; a pilot, on the other hand, knew that it was nothing over the distance they were traveling. The margin of error was more than that.

He glanced at the monitor and shook his head. He was a "Regiment" pilot, not one of the shuttle pilots assigned to *DeGlopper*, but it still hurt to watch a sacrifice like that. They were all Fleet, whether they were Marines or Navy, and Krasnitsky had sure taken the highroad. He shook his head again and looked at the number. It would really suck if it all turned out to be for nothing.

"Hello? Pilot?" He didn't recognize the voice in his earbud at first, but then he realized it was the prince's chief of staff.

"Yes, Ma'am? This is Warrant Bann." He wondered what the airhead wanted at a time like this. It had better be important to interfere in a deathwatch.

"Can we still get a connection to the ship's computers?"

Bann thought about all the things wrong with the request and wondered where to start.

"Ma'am, I don't think—"

"This is important, Warrant Officer," the voice in his earbud said firmly. "Vital, even."

"What do you need?" he asked warily.

"There's a copy of the *Encyclopedia Galactica* in my personal database. Why we didn't bring it with us, I don't know."

"But . . ." Bann said, thinking about the problems of connecting to the ship. Even if there were surviving antennae, he'd have to use a whisker laser, and with the Saints attached to the hull, there was a good chance that they would detect it, which would give away the shuttle's location.

"I know there's hardly anything on Marduk in it," O'Casey said quickly, anticipating part of his objection, "but there *is* data on early cultures and technologies. How to make flintlocks, how to make better iron and steel. . . ."

"Oh." The warrant officer nodded in his helmet. "Good point. But if I try to connect with the ship, we might be detected. And then what?"

"Oh." It was O'Casey's turn to pause in thought. "We'll have to take the chance," she said after a moment, her voice firm. "This data could make or break the expedition."

Bann thought about it as he warmed up the laser system. He saw her argument—it could be vital data—and there certainly wasn't much time to kick the idea around. If he tried to find Captain Pahner's blacked-out shuttle first to ask for permission, *DeGlopper* would almost certainly be gone before they could get anything. Which meant that *he* had to decide if it was worth endangering the entire mission to get some possibly useless data.

On the whole, he decided, it was.

"Whisker laser!" The lieutenant at Ship Defense Control turned towards her superior. "It appears to be sending a data request to the Empie assault ship. From . . . two-two-three by zero-zero-nine!"

"The shuttles," Delaney said. "It's the shuttles, trying to sneak away to the planet."

"We're too far out," the chaplain objected. "You said so yourself. They can't brake and make a reentry. And even if they could, we'd still be here to control the planet."

"True." Delany nodded. "But they *could* hide on the surface for a time."

"Only until the carrier detected them," Panella said dismissively. "They'd be mad to try to sneak down to the surface. Besides, we can still run them down, and we would've detected them soon after they started their deceleration."

"Maybe," the captain said dubiously. "But those shuttles use a hydrogen reaction jet that's fairly hard to detect much beyond a light-minute." He scratched his beard in thought about it for a moment. "Still, you're right. They must have expected to be detected."

He thought for a moment more, and in his eyes flew open wide.

"Unless they know we won't be here *to* detect them!" He wheeled to his bridge crew.

"Detach the ship! *Detach now!*"

"What to download?" O'Casey asked the empty compartment. "What? What, what? Come on, load!" she snapped.

Warrant Officer Bann had experienced great difficulty finding a connection, but Eleanora was in now, and waited as the final connects were made. When the screen finally came up, she sent the command through her toot.

"Search 'survival,'" she whispered, watching the results of the query come up. "Scroll down, scroll down, 'hostile flora and fauna' download, 'medicine' download. Search 'fuels, shuttle.' Scroll down. 'Expedient' download. Search, 'military, primitive.' Refine, 'arquebus.' Scroll down, scroll." She kept one eye on the loading diagram. The whisker laser was a relatively small bandwidth system, and the first download on hostile flora and fauna survival wasn't complete yet. She hissed, and then shook her head as a default message came up. "Four thousand three hundred eighty-three articles. *Damn.*" She didn't have time for this.

"Refine . . . 'generals.' Refine, 'greatest.'" She viewed the results. There was only one name she recognized offhand, despite her doctorate in history. She'd been more interested in societal developments than in military destructiveness, and arquebuses were as distant as ancient Rome and its fabled legions. But one name stood out in both the military and societal continuum.

"Download, 'Adolphus, Gustavus.'"

"Damn," Pahner snarled.

Roger nodded, more comfortable with the information now. "Disconnection."

"Yes," the captain replied in a quiet voice, watching the simple text "TOS" which had replaced the data feed from DeGlopper.

Termination of Signal. Such a . . . sanitary acronym. The letters held his eye, and then the sensor readouts on the Saint cruiser disappeared, as well.

"Ah," he said sadly, and Roger nodded again.

"Well," the prince said after a moment, trying to lighten the atmosphere, "at least they got them."

Without even turning around, he felt the temperature in the compartment drop, and swore at himself for putting his foot into his mouth yet again. He'd been wrong about the Marine's lack of feeling, he realized.

"Yes, I suppose they did. Your Highness," Pahner said flatly.

"*Damn!*" Eleanora shouted, slamming her hand down on the panel. The transmission had shut off in mid-line, and she'd only gotten part of the way through the entry on Gustavus Adolphus, King of Sweden.

She'd hunted for other data after entering that article, and as she had, she'd realized the incredible reach of the information available. The Marines could use data on improved metallurgy, agriculture, irrigation, and engineering. On chemistry, biology, and physics. It had all been sitting there the whole time, available for translation to pads or even toots. They could've loaded the whole thing into individual toots and had a walking encyclopedia!

But only if she'd thought of it in time.

"What's wrong?" Sergeant Major Kosutic asked, coming back into the compartment. She glanced at the monitors and nodded. "Oh. The *DeGlopper*'s gone. But they got the Saint."

"No, no, no. That's not it!" O'Casey snapped, banging the workstation again. "I realized after you'd gone that I had the whole universe in my hand. I had a copy of the *Encyclopedia Galactica* in my personal system on the ship. I hardly used it, because it was only outline information. But there were all *sorts* of things that we could've downloaded if we'd only thought of it in time. I started grabbing articles, but the signal terminated on me."

"Oh? Did you get anything?"

"Yeah," O'Casey replied as she brought up the data. "I think I got the most critical stuff. Survival and hostile environments, survival first-aid, something on expedient shuttle fuels and the beginning of a download on a general from Earth when they used arquebuses." She frowned and looked at the files. "The one on shuttle fuels looks a little slender."

Kosutic's mouth worked as she tried not to smile while the academic brought up the data on shuttle fuels.

"Oh. According to this, the field expedient shuttle fuel can be made by using electricity to break down water and—"

"And there's a system on the shuttle that can do it," Kosutic interrupted. "They get the power from solar cells . . . and it takes about four years to fill a shuttle's tanks."

"Right." O'Casey turned from the monitor. "You already knew that?"

"Yep," Kosutic admitted, still fighting back a grim chuckle. "And before anyone joins the Regiment, she goes through a Satan-Be-Damned course that includes combat survival skills. In fact, Captain Pahner is a survival instructor."

"Oh," O'Casey said. "Damn."

"Don't worry about it," Kosutic advised her, and this time the sergeant major allowed her chuckle to escape. "The Empire's worlds have an enormous variety of tech levels, and the Marines recruit from almost all of them. You'd be amazed by the stuff some of the troops know. When we need something done, most of the time there'll be a troop who has the skill. You just watch."

"I hope you're right."

"Trust me. I've been riding herd on Marines for almost forty standard years now, and they *still* surprise me sometimes."

"In that case, I guess we just sit here and wait for the landing," O'Casey said sourly.

"Pretty much," Kosutic agreed. "You play pinochle?"

CHAPTER FOURTEEN

"Oh, joy."

Pahner tapped the monitor control, but the picture didn't get any better. Not that there was anything wrong with the sensors or their readouts.

For the last three days the shuttles had been on a pursuit arc headed to overtake the planet from behind. The port was on a small continent or a large island, depending on how one chose to look at it, and their flight plan had been carefully calculated to bring them down just on the far side of the local ocean. That would have put them within a thousand klicks of their objective, and the Mardukans were supposed to have seafaring capability, so most of the trip could be accomplished on shipboard. All they'd have to do would be to hire a ship or ships to carry them across.

It had been, Pahner admitted modestly, a neat and tidy plan. The only real drawback had been that it pushed the parameters of the shuttles' range envelope. The deep-space burns required to put them on the proper intercept course for the planet had consumed so much of their total fuel that they had just enough left to complete their approach and land.

Unfortunately, there was a ship in orbit above the port.

She was powered down, or *DeGlopper* would have detected her, but she was probably the carrier for the parasite cruisers. And whoever she was, parked in that position, she would be able to detect and track the shuttles' reentry unless they landed, literally, on the far side of the planet.

The good news was that the second Saint cruiser obviously hadn't realized the shuttles had escaped—or, at least, hadn't realized in time to alert her carrier. If she had, the carrier would have moved to watch the side of the planet which the port's sensors couldn't cover in order to prevent the shuttles from sneaking in. The *bad* news was that the carrier's mere presence, and the diversion that would force upon them, would add some ten thousand kilometers to their dirtside journey.

And, of course, that they wouldn't have enough fuel for the landing, anyway.

"Oh, this is bad," Roger said, looking over the captain's shoulder. "Very, very bad."

"Yes, Your Highness," Pahner said with immense restraint. "It is."

He and the prince had been at close quarters for three days, and neither was in the best mood.

"What are we going to do?" Roger asked, and that faint edge of whine was back in his voice.

Pahner was spared the necessity of an immediate response by the attention chime of the communicator. He managed not to let his relief at the interruption show as he hit the button that acknowledged the com request. Rather than answer immediately, however, he switched the system to holo-mode and waited patiently. It wasn't a long wait, and he smiled thinly at the series of holograms which soon hovered in the compartment.

"I take it that you've all noticed our friend," he said dryly once his audience—all three lieutenants, all four pilots, Sergeant Major Kosutic, and Eleanora O'Casey—was complete.

"Oh, yeah," Warrant Bann said. "The planned IP is out, and so are aborts one and two."

"We should have had a plan in place for this!" Chief Warrant Officer Dobrescu snapped. The pilot of Shuttle Four looked at Pahner as if this were all his fault. Which, in a way, it was.

"That's true enough," Bann said, "but the fact is that we never did have the fuel for a conventional powered landing, no matter where we set down. We needed that atmospheric braking even to hit the prime site."

"Which site is completely out of the question with that damned carrier sitting there," Pahner pointed out. It was, he decided, almost certainly the most unnecessary observation he'd ever made, but he made himself continue with the thoroughly unpalatable corollary. "We'll have to land in the backlands, instead."

"We can't," Dobrescu said. "You can't land one of these things in a jungle unpowered!"

"What about these white patches?" Roger asked, and Pahner and all of the holograms turned to look at him as he tapped the limited chart he'd been feverishly reviewing. The map on the handheld pad had been prepared from a cursory spatial survey and had virtually no detail, but certain features stood out, and he tapped the image again.

"I don't know what they are," Pahner said. He took the pad and gazed thoughtfully at the irregularly shaped patches in a mountainous region on the far side of the planet from the port. "Whatever they are, they aren't created structures; they're too big for that."

He started to say that they wouldn't help, then stopped. They weren't jungle or water or mountain, and that was about all the planet had to offer. So what were they?

By now others were studying their pads.

"I think . . ." Lieutenant Gulyas began, then stopped.

"You think what?" Warrant Bann asked. He too was drawn to the white patches.

"They're one of two things," Gulyas said. "I can't tell if they're above or below sea level, but if they're low enough, I *think* they might be dry lakebeds."

"Dry lakebeds on a jungle world," Dobrescu snorted. "That's rich. And very convenient if they are. But if we aim for them and they're not, we're dead."

"Well," Bann replied, "a planet is a damned big place, Chief.

There almost have to be dry lakebeds on it *somewhere*, and we're dead anyway if the carrier sees us or we auger into a mountainside. Might as well try the possible lakebeds and hope."

"I agree with Lieutenant Gulyas," Roger said. "That's why I pointed them out. This looks like the sort of folded mountain formation where you'd get them. If the mountains folded around them and cut off their water sources, that would leave dry lakebeds." He scanned across the rest of the map. "And there are others, closer to the port. See? It's not just here."

"But the rest of the world is swamps, Your Highness," Dobrescu pointed out. "You need desert terrain for dry lakes, and why would there be desert only there?"

"I'd say that whole mountain range is probably arid," Pahner said. "The surface color is brown, not green. And there are other arid regions—they're just few and far between. So there's a good chance these really are dry lakes."

He gazed at the pad a moment longer, then set it aside and looked back at the pilots.

"Whether we're in agreement or not, the possibility that they're lakebeds is our only way out. So begin recalculating for an extended burn to slow us and a sharp descent behind the planet for a dead stick landing."

Dobrescu opened his mouth to protest, but Pahner held up his hand.

"Unless there's an alternative plan, that's what we're going to do. *Do* you have an alternative?"

"No, Sir," Dobrescu replied after a long moment. "But, with all due respect, I don't like the idea of risking His Highness' safety on a guess."

"Neither do I. But that's exactly what we're going to do. And the good news is, that we're going to be risking the rest of our lives right along with his. So if it doesn't work, none of us will have to explain it to Her Majesty."

After they'd hit zero G and the likelihood of being shot out of space by the cruiser had passed, the troops had floated around the troop bay, lacing into their low-grav hammocks and chilling out. Three days on the shuttle without a damned thing they had to do but sleep were on the order of heaven to most of the experienced Marines. But as they neared the planet and landing, the hammocks and loose gear were secured, and the troops buckled down and put on their mission faces. It had been a nice little interlude, and everyone felt fairly refreshed.

Of course, there were still a few small problems to deal with.

"Hold on a second," Julian said as the shuttle began to skip through the outermost reaches of atmosphere. "Are you trying to tell me that they *think* there's a landing zone?"

"More or less." Despreaux smiled. "It looks like there is, but, you know, we don't exactly have the best maps in the galaxy."

"Oh, this is *truly* good," Julian said, slamming his helmet into place while the assault shuttle began to shake and shudder. "Wrrflmgdf," he continued, as the helmet muffled his voice.

"What was that?" Despreaux held a hand up to her ear as she reached for her own headcover. "I think I missed it."

"What I *said* was," Julian cut in his suit speaker to tell her, "this is truly fucking good!"

"What's the problem?" Despreaux settled her helmet and brought her own speakers online. "Just another day in the Marines."

"This is the sort of shit I wrangled my way into the Regiment to avoid," Julian snarled, wiggling deeper into the enveloping memory plastic of his cocoon as the shuttle hit another bump. "If I wanted to make lousy drops on hostile planets under insane commanders I could've stayed with Sixth Fleet."

Despreaux laughed.

"Oh, Zeus, that's rich! You were in the Sixth?"

"Yep, under Admiral Helmut, Dark Lord of the Sixth." He shook his head in memory. "Now there was a character. Kill you as soon as look at you."

Despreaux smiled, and her eyes crinkled as the shuttle gave another lurch. "You know you love it."

"Like hell!" Julian shouted as the roar of reentry filled the compartment and began to grow. He worked his tongue at a bit of ration caught between his teeth for a moment, and looked around quizzically.

"Is it just me, or do we seem to be coming in a little faster than usual?"

"*We're too steep!*" Bann shouted, and his hand cocked, ready to override the automated reentry system if the computer got confused.

"Stay on profile," Dobrescu said calmly. "We're in the pipe. It's just a shaky pipe, is all."

"We're exceeding parameters!" Bann snapped. Shuttle Four felt as if it were shuddering apart, and there was zero maneuver fuel left. All the pilot could do was hang on and hope she stayed together. "I've got overheating on all surfaces, and stress warnings on the wings!"

"We are exceeding the manual numbers," Dobrescu admitted as his toot flashed a series of numbers across his vision. Every system was in the yellow, but he'd performed over two thousand drops in training and combat, and had a far better feel for the real, as opposed to the specified, capabilities of the rugged drop shuttles than whatever dweeb had written the manual. "The computer doesn't like that, but the numbers are conservative. We'll be fine."

"This is insane!"

"Hey, you're the one who said 'go for the lakebeds'!" Dobrescu chuckled nastily. Then shrugged. "Would you rather be target practice for that carrier?" he asked in a milder tone. There was no answer. "Then shut up and hang on."

The shuttles flashed across the eastern ocean at five times the speed of sound, and the thunder of their crossing hammered the uncaring waves. Their speed dropped steadily, and the outer barrier range of mountains—the upthrust giants that turned the region beyond into a desiccated wasteland—reared before them. They swung out their wings, clawing now for enough speed and lift to make the tiny dots of their possible landing areas, and the faces of their pilots were grim and taut.

The craft were heavily laden, and even with their wings swept forward for maximum lift, their greatest danger now was that they would simply fall out of the sky. They had to retain altitude to cross the soaring ranges, yet maintain a tightly calculated flight path to their hoped-for landing areas, and the final descent would be steep and tricky.

Shuttle Four cleared the final ridge by barely nine meters, and Warrant Officer Bann let out a whoop.

"*Yeeha!* That's a dry lake if I've ever seen one!"

The glittering white salt bed reflected the intense G-9 sun like a mirror. The pilots' helmet visors darkened automatically, and their eyes swept back and forth over the glowing instrument readouts projected onto their visor heads-up displays.

The dangers of landing on salt lakes were as old as flight. The flat, white expanses made perfect airports but for one thing: perspective. With nothing to give a feeling of depth, a pilot trying to land visually was unable to determine whether he was going to land or just dig a big, nasty hole. The answer, of course, was technology, and the shuttle pilots pulled in their heads like turtles and shut out everything but their instruments. Radar and lidar range finders measured airspeed, velocity over ground, flight-angle, and all the other myriad variables that made the difference between a landing and a fireball and pronounced them correct. Nonetheless, each pilot continued to monitor his systems, hoping that no further demons would rear their ugly heads at the last moment and snatch defeat from victory.

Chief Warrant Dobrescu checked his instruments, studied the computer-calculated glide path on his HUD, and shook his head. They were actually doing it. He'd given up on performing any sort of decent landing when they picked up the Saint carrier; now it seemed that the entire company might actually make it to the ground intact.

Then the hard part would start.

CHAPTER FIFTEEN

Julian popped the seals on his helmet, took a sniff of the air, and grimaced as the temperature overcame the residual cool from his suit chiller.

"Christ, it's hot!"

The sweat that instantly popped out on his skin disappeared just as quickly. The blinding light from the salt flats was mixed with a light, parching wind, and the temperature was at least forty-nine degrees Standard—over a hundred and twenty degrees in the antiquated Fahrenheit scale still used on a few backward planets.

"Whew, this is gonna be funnn."

He gave a brief, unamused chuckle, and beside him Lance Corporal Russell juggled her grenade launcher into the crook of her arm and popped her own helmet.

"*Yah!* It's like being in a furnace!"

There was nothing to be seen but the four shuttles, scattered over a kilometer or so of blazing, empty salt, and the distant mountains. Julian's squad, as the only one with armor, had been unloaded first. The ten troopers had spread out with scanners on maximum, but they were barely detecting microorganisms. The salt was as dead as the surface of an airless moon—deader than some, for that matter.

Julian sent a command to his toot and switched to the company command frequency.

"Captain Pahner, my squad doesn't detect any sign of hostile zoologicals, botanicals, or sentients. The area appears clear."

"I see." The captain's tone was as a dry as the wind in Julian's face. "And I suppose that's why you took off your helmet?"

The sergeant rolled his tongue in his cheek and thought for a moment.

"Just trying to use all possible sensory systems, Sir. Sometimes smell works where others don't."

"True," the captain said mildly. "Now put it back on and set up a perimeter. I'll have the rest of Third move out to support. When they're in place come into the center as a reserve."

"Roger, Sir."

"Pahner, out."

"Modder pocker."

Poertena dropped the case of grenades onto the stack, wiped sweat off his face, and looked around. He'd spoken quietly, but Despreaux heard him, and she snorted as she ticked the item off her list. Despite the intense heat, she looked as cool as if she were standing in snow.

"Don't worry," she said. "We're nearly finished unloading. Then the fun begins."

Poertena took on the cross-eyed, inward look characteristic of someone communicating with his toot.

"Modder . . . we've been at t'is for hours!" He looked toward the horizon, where the sun was still well up. "When do tee sun go down?"

"Long day, Poertena," Despreaux said with another cool smile. "Thirty-six hours. We've got nearly six more until dusk."

"Pock," Poertena whispered. "T'is suck."

"And you know what's really gonna suck?" Lance Corporal Lipinski demanded of the universe in general as he affixed a large square of solar film to the top of his rucksack. All members of the company had been issued squares. The combined area was designed to partially recharge the powerful superconductor capacitors that drove the human technology. While the power gathered would never support the company's bead guns, plasma rifles, and powered armor, it would serve to maintain a charge in their communicators and sensors.

"What?" Corporal Eijken asked.

The Bravo Team grenadier jerked at the belt feed over her shoulder. If the feed wasn't aligned perfectly, the grenades had a tendency to jam, and that was something she really didn't want to happen. They were going to be walking a long way through really bad stuff. That much had already become evident.

The company had unloaded and prepared through the remainder of the day and into the night. As the sun went down, the temperature went with it, and by local midnight it was well below freezing. Even with their chameleon blankets, it had been a long, miserable night, and many of the troopers remembered why they'd signed up for the Regiment in the first place. Pride of position was certainly one reason, but another was so that they wouldn't have to do stuff like huddle under a thin covering in below-freezing temperatures on a surface hard enough for an interplanetary transport landing apron.

They'd been up and at it again before dawn, loading rucksacks and overbags, piling the spare gear on stretchers, and generally preparing to move out. As the sun came up, the cold came off, but now it was building into another scorcher. Which made for a certain amount of bitching, no matter how good the troops.

"What's really gonna suck," Lipinski replied, "is humping all of *his* gear."

He gestured cautiously with his chin in the direction of the prince, and Eijken shrugged.

"It's not that much spread across the Company. Hell, I've been in companies where the CO makes his clerk carry his gear."

"Yeah," Lipinski agreed quietly, "but they're not good companies, are they?"

Eijken opened her mouth to respond, but stopped as Despreaux left a gaggle of NCOs and headed their way.

"Company," the grenadier said instead, and she and Lipinski trotted towards the sergeant as she made an "assemble here" gesture at her scattered squad. Despreaux waited until everyone had gathered around, then pulled out her water nipple.

"Okay, drink."

The water bladders were integral to the combat harness of the chameleon suit: a flexible plastic bladder that molded into a trooper's back under his rucksack. The bladder held six liters of water, and had a small, efficient chiller driven by a mechanical feedback system. As long as the trooper was moving, the chiller was running. It didn't make icewater, but what it produced was generally at least a few degrees below ambient temperature, and that could be awfully refreshing.

"Uh, I gotta get mine," Lipinski said.

Sergeant Despreaux waited as the lance corporal and a private from Bravo Team retrieved their combat harnesses and the others took swigs from their bladders. Once everyone had gathered again, she glanced around mildly.

"The next time I see anyone without her harness," she noted, and then glanced pointedly at one of the plasma gunner's flat bladders, "or with an empty water bladder, I'm putting her on report. Your nanites may help you keep going even when you dehydrate, but only to a point."

She glanced around the team again, and then shrugged one shoulder. It was the one her rifle was slung over.

"And I'm also gonna put you on report if I see anyone without a weapon again. We don't know a thing about this planet, and until we do, we will consider it hostile at all times. Understood?"

She listened to the chorus of agreement, then nodded.

"The Captain is going to give a little talk before we get started. Get your teams together and get loaded up. We've got fifteen minutes before move-out. I want you to mostly finish your bladders, then refill from the tanks on the shuttles. I want you sloshing when we start out." She glanced around one more time. "Let's go over this again. Drink?"

"Water," the squad responded, more or less in unison and with a few smiles.

"When?"

"Always."

"How much?"

"Lots."

"And carry . . . ?"

"Your weapon."

"When?"

"At all times."

"Very good," she said with a blinding smile. "You're a credit to your squad leader." She gave them a wink and headed back over to where Sergeant Major Kosutic was standing.

Kosutic waited until the company's NCOs had gathered around, then raised an eyebrow.

"Well?"

"Just like you said," Julian said, taking a sip of water from the bladder in his armor. "Nobody had finished his water. Only a couple had refilled."

"Same here," Koberda said. "You'd think they'd learn. We're all vets, and we all went through RIP. Hell, most of us have spent time in Raider units! This is just same shit, different day."

"Uh-huh." Kosutic nodded in agreement. "How's your water level, George?"

"What?" Koberda's hand tapped the bladder on his back. "Oh." The bladder was mostly full, and Kosutic chuckled as he popped the drinking tube into his mouth.

"This is gonna be a long mission, By His Wickedness," she said, scratching her ear. "And we need to get the right habits right at the beginning. Most of your troops think they're tough. Hell, they *are* tough. But there's tough and there's tough, and, frankly, they're the wrong kind of bad news for this. Give me a bunch of fringe world mercenaries for an op like this one. We're used to having everything on a silver platter, and all we gotta do is drop, kick ass, and go home. This is about staying in the fight for months. That's not something we train for or plan on.

"The troops are gonna get worn out. They're not gonna want to eat. They're not gonna want to drink. They're not gonna want to keep alert. They are not, By His Evilness, going to care.

"So you've gotta be their momma and their poppa. You've gotta make them eat. You've gotta make them drink. You've gotta make sure they keep up their hygiene. You've gotta make sure they keep up their heads.

"Let the troops keep on the lookout for the bad guys. You squad leaders and platoon sergeants have to keep an eye on the troops.

"And I'll keep an eye on *you*," she finished with a laugh. "Now, drink!"

"Have you had anything to drink this morning, Your Highness?" Captain Pahner asked as he watched the prince unpack his weapon.

The rifle would have been a point of contention if Armand Pahner had had an ounce of strength left for silly arguments. He had nothing against the weapon as a hunting rifle: the Parkins and Spencer eleven-millimeter magnum was a gem among heavy caliber rifles. True, it was a "smoke-pole" rather than a bead gun, but the selectable action weapon (it could be fired in either bolt-action or semi-automatic mode) was the end product of over a millennia of development. The big, chemical-propelled round had excellent penetration and muzzle energy, and in the hands of an expert, it was deadly out to nearly two kilometers with the Intervalle 50x variable hologram scope mounted on it.

Yet whatever its virtues, it was also incredibly heavy, nearly fifteen kilos, and used nonstandard brass-cartridge rounds, which meant the prince would be unable to trade ammunition with the other weapons. Eventually, the prince's own ammo would run out, and he would be left with an extremely expensive, very heavy stick.

But Armand Pahner was done arguing with the arrogant young prick. About most stuff.

"Not recently," Roger replied with a headshake as he snapped the receiver into the walnut stock.

"Then might I suggest that His Highness drink water?" Pahner said through gritted teeth. He knew that the prince had all the military's nanite and toot enhancements, and a few that even his bodyguards didn't have. But he still had to have some water in his veins for the nanites to swim in.

"You can suggest it," Roger said with a slight smile. "And I even will, in a minute. But I'm going to get my rifle assembled first."

"Very well, Your Highness," Pahner said after a calming breath. It was hot as the hinges of hell already, and he didn't need this. "We're going to be moving out in a few minutes." The captain smiled faintly. "O'er Marduk's sunny plain."

"I'll be there," Roger said with a glance at the captain. The Marine's last phrase had not made sense to the prince, but he had other things to worry about, and he started loading ammunition into his combat vest. The handspan-long cartridges would eventually cover the chameleon cloth harness, actually providing an ersatz armor. He had a pack at his feet which was intended to accept additional rounds, and there were loops sewn into the legs of his combat suit. He would eventually be covered in bullets.

God help us if he gets hit by a stray bead, Armand Pahner thought.

Pahner glanced at Poertena. The armorer was racked out in the shade under one net-draped wing of the shuttle. The captain knew most of the troops had bitched about hauling the camo nets into place and staking them down, but he'd been adamant. The shuttles' hulls and wings were essentially one huge crystal display; as long as their internal power held out, their programmable skins could produce better reactive camouflage than a chameleon suit or even powered armor. But even though the power requirement wasn't huge, it was more than enough to eventually drain the shuttle capacitors, at which point the craft would stand out like elephants on a golf course if anyone happened to overfly them and look down. Even if that hadn't been the case, the best reactive skins in the universe couldn't do much about the shadows they cast, so he'd ordered the nets out. Not only would they take over when the power did run out, but they broke up the artificial angularity of the shuttle hulls and wings, which also broke up the artificiality of the shadows they cast.

Roger, predictably, had considered it a waste of time, although at least he'd managed to restrict *his* bitching about it to Pahner himself instead of whining in front of the troops. The captain had wanted—badly—to ask why he'd been so upset when no one was asking *him* to do the grunt work, but he'd decided against it after only a brief struggle. They'd already gone around and around about his decision to maintain a round-the-clock listening watch on all frequencies. It would only require a single trooper to monitor them through the sophisticated com equipment engineered into his helmet, which would hardly pose a crippling drain on their manpower. Despite that, the prince had done a deplorably poor job of concealing his opinion that worrying about possible communications traffic when the entire mass of the planet lay between them and the only high-tech enclave on it made no sense at all, and Pahner had no doubt that Roger had written him off as a terminally paranoid security dweeb.

Fortunately, the captain had discovered that he was remarkably immune to worries about the prince's good opinion of him, and Roger's arguments hadn't changed his mind about the listening watch *or* the camo nets. No doubt the prince was right when he pointed out that the chance of anyone coming in low enough to see the shuttles, assuming there was any reason to be looking in the first place, on the completely opposite side of the globe from the only spaceport or landing facility on the entire planet was virtually nonexistent. Armand Pahner, however, was not in the habit of exposing his people or his mission to avoidable risk, however remote, even if the "extra work" did piss them off.

And it was remarkable how the troops' attitude had shifted when the sun came back up and they realized what nice shade the nets provided for anyone who could come up with an excuse to get under them. Like Poertena, who looked indecently comfortable as he snored with his head propped on a gigantic rucksack. The captain wondered, briefly, what was in it, then walked over and kicked the Pinopan on the sole of his boot. The armorer's eyes popped open, and he scrambled to his feet.

"Yes, Sir, Cap'n?"

"Circulate around. Leader's conference. Here. Now."

"Yes, Sir, Cap'n," Poertena acknowledged, and trotted off towards the knot around Kosutic, bead rifle at high port.

Pahner turned and looked towards the distant mountains. Trees were faintly visible on the lower slopes.

CHAPTER SIXTEEN

The trees were spindly and very tall. There were branch scars on their lower surfaces, but the first actual limbs were nearly twenty meters up the trunk. From there, the trunk continued upwards another ten or twenty meters in a spreading crown. They looked misshapen, like some sort of odd, oversized toadstools. The bark was generally gray and smooth, but some of the trees showed gouges that reached nearly to the spreading crowns.

Roger glanced up at the trees through the extruded plastron of his helmet and shook his head.

"Bad sign. Strop marks," he commented. There'd been chatter about the gouges on the tactical net, but he was still having a hard time making out what everyone was talking about. Now, looking up the trees, some of the comments made more sense.

"Pardon me, Your Highness?" Eleanora said, pausing to take a couple of deep breaths. The pace Captain Pahner had set wasn't fast—he knew better than to rush forward in terrain about which he had no knowledge—but combined with the heat, it was terribly debilitating to a woman who'd practically never set foot outside a city. She'd kept up with the Marine company so far, but only by dint of iron determination, and it was obvious that she was exhausted.

The company had been walking for nearly six hours, marching

for fifty minutes and then taking a ten-minute water break as per doctrine for the environmental conditions. It had taken them that long to get off the salt flats, and now they were entering an alluvial outflow from the mountains. The outflow, unlike the salt flats, had some vegetation. But not much, and the trees that made up the majority of it were widely spaced. And scarred.

"Strop marks," Roger repeated, absently offering the academic the left arm of his armor to support some of her weight. The prince was sweating profusely, but didn't look particularly worn. That might have something to do with carrying less gear than the rest of the company or being in powered armor, but mostly it had to do with the fact that he preferred being on safari to anything else.

He'd traveled, hunted, and studied in more unpleasant, out-of-the-way places than almost any of the Marines realized. And he rarely hunted game that didn't hunt back.

"Marks on a tree like that come from two things," he explained. "Animals eating the bark, and territory marking. And if it were bark-eaters, *all* the trees would be marked."

"So," O'Casey asked with another gasp, "what does that mean?" She knew it should be obvious, but she was wilting in the heat. She checked her toot and suppressed a whimper. Twenty minutes until the next rest.

"It means that there's something around here that's territorial," Roger said with a glance at the marks high overhead. "Something really, *really* big."

Sergeant Major Kosutic watched the point guard, PFC Berent, from Julian's squad. The company was moving with two platoons forward of the headquarters unit, and one behind, and they'd started with Third Platoon forward, since Third had the only squad with armor. The private on point not only had her suit sensors on maximum, she had a hand-held scanner in her left hand. The hand-helds were more sensitive than the suits' systems, and this one was dialed to maximum. So far, though, there'd been no signs of the predators the brief entry on the partial planetary survey report had alluded to. Kosutic had just opened her mouth to make a comment on that to Gunny Jin when the point held up a closed fist. Almost as one man, the company jerked to a stop.

"Well, if we run into whatever it is," Eleanora said, taking a deep gulp of water, "just let it kill me, okay?" She suddenly realized that she was talking to herself and that the whole company had stopped. "Roger?" she said, and turned to look back.

Pahner had a repeater of the scout's data on one-quarter of his visor, and general data on the company and its formation on two other quarters. The fourth was left for figuring out where to put his feet. Currently, the only one he was paying attention to was the repeater from the scout.

The beast that had come into sight around a pile of boulders was dark brown and nearly as high in the shoulder as an elephant, but longer and wider. The head was armed with two long, slightly curved horns that looked useful for fighting or digging, and the neck was protected by a ruff of armor. Massive shoulders were covered in armored scales that faded back to pebbly hide, and it had six squat, forward-thrust limbs and a fleshy tail that flailed back and forth as it pounded from left to right across the company's path. As it ran, it bugled in rage at whatever it was chasing.

The captain examined it for just a moment. The beast was fearsome looking, but a closer examination confirmed his initial judgment. There was no sign of canines or any analog; only grinder teeth were revealed when it opened its maw to scream. Nor did the beast have the sort of long, lean look one found in virtually all predators. It was undoubtedly something to keep an eye on and could be a problem, but it wasn't a carnivore, and was therefore unlikely to attack the company.

"All units," he said, knowing that the tac-comp in his communicator would set the radio to all-frequency broadcast. "Don't fire. It's an herbivore. I say again, do not fire."

There was chatter on the net, and although Roger's inexperience with the com link kept him from following it at all clearly, he could certainly understand its excited overtones. He looked at the creature and its paws. They were odd for a desert creature, webbed and clawed like those of a carnivorous toad. And it was just about the right length and design to be able to rear up on those trees. It was obviously an herbivore, but it was just as obviously a part of whatever herd had marked these trees as its territory. That put it in the "dangerous" slot, and Roger wasn't about to let it circle around and hit the company from behind like a Cape buffalo, or a Shastan rock toad. Or go and get the rest of the herd to squash them all to paste.

He put the rifle to the shoulder and drew a breath. *Lead it, easy squeeze.*

Pahner's jaw dropped as the giant beast snapped at its side. It turned on its tail once, then slammed over sideways in a self-made hurricane of dust and gravel. The ground shuddered underfoot with the impact, and it lashed and snapped at the air for several seconds until it was still. He watched it for one sulphurous moment more, and took a deep breath.

"*Okay! Who the hell fired?!*" There was complete silence on all the nets. "I *said*, 'who fired?'!"

"That would be His Highness," Julian said ironically.

Pahner cut out the snickering on the squad leaders' net and turned to where Roger stood with a smoking rifle propped on his thigh. The prince had the Parkins and Spencer set for bolt action, and Pahner watched as he jacked the spent round out of the chamber and caught it in midair. He pulled a fresh round out of his vest, chambered it, and put the empty case where the new one had been. Each of the movements was precise, but jerky and over-muscled. Then he reached up and cleared the chameleon field from his helmet so that he could meet Pahner's eye.

Pahner stepped over to where the prince stood and switched to the command frequency they alone shared.

"Your Highness, could we talk for a moment?"

"Certainly, Captain Pahner," the prince said sardonically.

Pahner looked around, but there was nowhere to have a private conversation. So he touched the control that opaqued the prince's visor again.

"Your Highness," he began, then drew a deep, calming breath. "Your Highness, can I ask you a question?"

"Captain Pahner, I assure you—"

"Your Highness, if you please," Pahner interrupted in a strangled tone. "May. I. Ask. You. A. Question?"

Roger decided at that moment that discretion was better than valor.

"Yes."

"Do you want to live to get back to Earth?" Pahner asked, and Roger paused before responding carefully.

"Is that a *threat*, Captain?"

"No, Your Highness, it's a *question*."

"Then, yes, of course I do," the prince said shortly.

"Then you'd better get through your overbred, airheaded brain that the only way we are going to survive is if you don't *fuck me over every time we turn around*!"

"Captain, I assure you—" the prince started to respond hotly.

"*Shut up!* Just shut up, *shut up*! You can have me relieved once we get back to Earth! And I am *not* going to wrap you up in ropes and carry you the whole way, although right now that sounds like a good idea! But if you don't get a grip and start figuring out that we are *not* on some backwoods adventure where you can go and blast anything in sight and walk away without consequences, we are all going to get *killed*. And that would *really piss me off*, because it would mean that I *failed* to get you back to Earth so that I can *give you back to your mother in one goddamned piece*. That is *all* I care about, and if you don't get with the program, I will *sedate* you and *carry* you to the spaceport *unconscious on a stretcher*! Am I making myself absolutely, positively, crystalline clear?"

"Clear," Roger said quietly. He realized there was no way he could possibly explain the situation as he saw it to the enraged captain. He also realized that with the helmets opaqued and on a restricted frequency, no one else had heard the dressing down.

Pahner paused for a moment longer, looking around the desolate wasteland. It might look flat, but he knew it hid dozens of little dips where enemies and predators could be hiding. The whole march, for months on end, was going to be like that. And all the Marines, as opposed to the civilians they were guarding, knew that. He shook his head and switched to the all-hands frequency.

"Okay, show's over. Let's move out."

Great. Just great. Just what a unit in a situation like this needed: an obvious argument in the chain of command right at the start.

"Woo, hoo, hoo," Julian whispered on his suit mike. "I think the Prince just caught himself a nuke."

"I bet Pahner didn't even ask why he took the shot," Despreaux said.

"He *knows* why Princy took the shot," Julian shot back. "Big, bad big-game hunter saw the biggest game in town. Time to try out the rifle."

"Maybe," Despreaux admitted. "But he *is* a big-game hunter. He's dealt with big nasty animals a lot. Heck, he does it as a hobby. Maybe he knew something Pahner didn't."

"The day you find out something the Old Man doesn't know," Julian commented, "you come look me up. But bring some CarStim; I'll need it for the heart attack."

"I t'ink he just like to kill stuff," Poertena said soberly. They'd reached the carcass of the giant herbivore, and he examined more closely. It would have made a fair trophy for any hunter.

Despreaux glanced over at the armorer. Despite the huge rucksack that made him look like an ant under a rock, he'd come up behind them so quietly she hadn't noticed his presence.

"You really think so?"

"Sure. I hear about his trophy room," Poertena said, sipping water out of his tube. "There are all sorts of t'ings in there. He likes to kill stuff," he repeated.

"Maybe," Despreaux repeated, then sighed. "If so, I hope he can learn some control."

"Well, I guess we'll see the next time we have a contact," Julian said.

"*Contact!*" the point guard called.

CHAPTER SEVENTEEN

Kosutic tapped a bead rifle outward.

"There are three people covering one scummy," she commented to the trooper as she stepped past him. "Watch your own Satan-Be-Damned sector."

". . . just appeared out of nowhere," the point guard was saying as the sergeant major walked up. The PFC waved the sensor wand at the scummy. "Look, there's hardly any readout!"

"That's what your eyes are for!" Gunnery Sergeant Jin snapped. He looked at the scummy standing quietly just outside the perimeter, and shuddered. He hadn't seen the being until the point yelled, either.

The Mardukan stood two and a half meters tall. He—it was clearly and almost embarrassingly a "he"—carried a figure-eight shield nearly as tall as he was. A lance that was even taller was cast over one shoulder, and he had a large leather covering thrown over his head. It was obviously an attempt at a parasol, and his need for something like it was clear. Given the fact that Mardukans were covered in a water-based mucus, the fact that he could have survived all the way to the edge of the salt flats was amazing. He should have been dead of dehydration long before he got this far.

Kosutic tossed her bead rifle over one shoulder in a manner similar to the way the Mardukan carried his spear, stepped past the three troopers covering the stranger, and held out one hand, palm forward. It wasn't a universal sign of peace, but humans had found it to be close.

The Mardukan gabbled at her, and she nodded. The gesture meant no more to him than his handwaving at the horned beast did to her. He could be angry that they'd killed his pet, or happy that they'd saved his life. Her toot took a stab at the language, but returned a null code. The local dialect had very little similarity to the five-hundred-word "kernel" they'd loaded into the toots.

"I need O'Casey up here quick," she subvocalized into her throat mike.

"We're on our way," Pahner responded. "With His Highness."

Kosutic held up one hand again, and turned to look over her shoulder. As she did, she noticed the two bead rifles and the plasma gun still leveled at the apparently benign visitor.

"Go ahead and lower them, Marines. But keep them to hand."

She half-turned at the crunch of gravel, and smiled at the group approaching from the center of the company's perimeter. The diminutive chief of staff was virtually invisible behind the bulk of Pahner and Roger's armor. And surrounding Roger was a squad from Second Platoon that looked ready to level the world. All in all, it looked like a good time to fade, and she bowed to the visitor and drifted backwards, wondering how it would go.

Eleanora O'Casey wasn't a professional linguist. Such people not only had specially designed implants, they usually also had a flair for language that interacted with their toots so that the final translation was synergistically enhanced. She, on the other hand, was dependent on an off-the-shelf software package and a general knowledge of sentient species to carry her through. There were quite a few "ifs" in that equation.

The regions around the spaceport used a four-armed bow as a sign of parley. Unfortunately, there were a variety of nuances to it—none of which had been very clear in the explanation—and she had only two arms.

Here went nothing.

★ ★ ★

D'Nal Cord examined the small being before him. All of the beings in this tribe—they looked like *basik,* with their two arms and waggling way of walking—were small and apparently weak. However, most of them blended into the background as if they were part of it. It was probably an effect of their strange coverings, but it was also disconcerting. And some weapon or magic among them had killed the *flar* beast. Both features bespoke great power. And since the *flar* beast had nearly had him, it also spoke of an *asi* debt. At his age.

The being bowed in a nearly proper fashion and gabbled at him in a strange guttural tongue. It was different from the words which had been spoken between the beings.

"I seek the one who killed the *flar* beast," he answered, gesturing at the aggressive herbivore. The beasts burrowed during the day in the dry hills, and he'd been blinded by the light of Artac shining off the sands, beaten down by the heat and dryness and, truth to tell, feeling his age. He hadn't noticed the depression around the snorkel at the surface, and he'd survived only because it had been a rogue bull with no herd mates to help it kill him. And because of the altruistic act of a stranger.

Damn him.

The slight one at the fore spoke again.

" . . . kill . . . flor . . ."

Cord spoke very slowly this time.

"I . . . seek . . . the . . . one . . . who . . . killed . . . the . . . *flar* . . . beast. That rogue bull over there, you ignorant little *basik.*"

"I need the second person, damn it," Eleanora gritted through her teeth. She touched her chest. "I . . . Eleanora." She pointed at the Mardukan, hoping it would understand.

The scummy gobbled and clacked at her again. It seemed to be becoming agitated. As well it should, for it was terribly hot and dry out here for it. Which brought up an idea.

"Captain Pahner," she turned to the CO. "This is going to take a while. Could we set up some sort of shelter from the sun?"

Pahner looked up at the height of the sun and consulted his toot.

"We've got three more hours of daylight. We shouldn't stop for the night."

Eleanora started to protest, but Roger held up a hand at her, and turned to Pahner.

"We need to communicate with these people," he said, gesturing at the scummy with his chin. "We can't do that if this guy dies of heatstroke."

Pahner took a breath and looked around as he suddenly realized that the comment was coming in on the command frequency. Apparently the prince had listened to the previous lecture about debating in front of the troops. But he was still wrong.

"If we take too long, we'll run out of water. We only have so much supply. We need to get into the lowlands where there's resupply."

"We need to communicate," Roger said definitely. "We take as much time for that as Eleanora needs."

"Is that an order, Your Highness?" Pahner asked.

"No, it's a strong suggestion."

"Excuse me." Eleanora couldn't hear them, but she could tell that they were debating and thought she ought to make a point. "I'm not talking about all night. If I can get this guy into some shade and get him a little water and humidity, this will probably go fairly fast."

Roger and Pahner turned to glance at her, then turned featureless faceshield to featureless faceshield and debated some more. Finally, Pahner turned back to her.

"Okay."

A couple of privates, impossible to tell apart in identical uniforms and camouflage helmets, came forward and rapidly erected a large tent. The temperature inside wasn't going to be all that wonderful, but they sprayed a few milliliters of water around on the inside of the walls, and the evaporation both cooled it a bit and raised the humidity. The relief would be brief, but it would help the Mardukan.

Cord stepped inside the structure and sighed. It was not only cooler, it was not so dry. His *dinshon* exercises had prevented complete desiccation, but the experience had been anything but pleasant. This was still far too arid for permanent survival, but it was a welcome respite. He nodded to the small interpreter (such as he was) and the two slightly larger beings in their strange hard coats like stang beetles.

"My thanks. This is much better."

He also noted the two additional beings in the background. Their strange weapons weren't pointed at him, but he'd seen bodyguards enough among the city magnates to recognize them for what they were. He wondered which of them was the leader.

"I'm Eleanora," O'Casey said, gesturing at herself. Then she pointed, carefully, at the Mardukan. Pointing in some cultures was an insult.

"D'Nal Cord . . ." The rest was a senseless gabble.

"*Flar* beast?" she asked, hoping to get more context.

"I . . . knowledge . . . *flar* beast . . . kill."

"You want to know how the beast was killed?" she said in the best approximation of the local dialect her toot could create. The known words were increasing, and she felt that the toot would soon have a full kernel. But understanding was still elusive.

"No," the Mardukan said. " . . . killed the *flar* beast? You?"

"Oh," Eleanora said. "No," she answered, gesturing at Roger. "It was Roger." She stopped as she realized that she'd just pointed out the prince for retribution if the act was considered hostile.

Roger tapped a control and cleared his visor of its concealing distortion.

"It was I," he said. His toot had been loaded with the same program, and he'd been following Eleanora's progress. For that matter, his toot had considerably more processor capability than hers, and he suspected that his own program might have made more progress than hers. He was pretty sure, for example, that he was further along on the Mardukan's body language. The individual seemed at least partially unhappy, but not really angry. More like resigned.

The Mardukan, Cord, stepped toward Roger, but paused as the two Marines in the background hefted their weapons. He reached out, carefully, and placed his hand on Roger's shoulder. There was a gabble of syllables.

"... brother ... life ... owe ... debt ..."

"Oh, shit," Eleanora said.

"What?" Roger asked.

"I think," she said with a snort, "that he just said the something like you saved his life and that makes you his blood-brother."

"Oh, hell," Pahner said.

"What?" Roger repeated. "What's wrong with that?"

"Maybe nothing, Your Highness," Pahner said sourly. "But in most cultures like this, those things are taken seriously. And sometimes it means the brother has to join the tribe. On pain of pain."

"Well, we're probably heading in the direction of his tribe," Roger pointed out. "I'll drink the deer's blood, or whatever, and then we'll pass on through. Nice story to tell at the club, and all that."

Eleanora shook her head.

"And what happens if you have to stay with the tribe or it's going to be a big problem?"

"Oh," Roger said. Then, "Oh."

"This is why you don't shoot until you have to," Pahner told him on the side circuit.

"Let me see if I can talk our way out of this," O'Casey said.

"Fat chance," Pahner muttered.

" ... Chief Roger ... regrets ... honor. Travel ... way ... pass ..."

Cord laughed.

"Well, I'm not all that happy about it, either. I was on a very important spirit quest when he had the temerity to save my life. Don't you people have any couth? Never mind. That doesn't matter a *rid* fly's fart. I still have to follow him around like a demon-spawned *nex* for the rest of my life. Oh well. Maybe it will be short."

He watched the little spokesman working through the translation, and finally gestured impatiently.

"This tent is nice, but if we hurry we can reach my village before the *yaden* arise. Unless you have skin like a *flar* beast, we'd best be under cover. I suppose you can cut up the *flar* and use it for cover, but it would take time. Time we might not have."

* * *

"I think he said—"

"Tough noogies," Roger finished with a laugh. "He said we're just going to have to live with it. And something about hurrying."

"I didn't get that full a translation," Eleanora said with a shake of her head. "And there was more than the basic cultural background. There's something definitely sticky about this translation. I got a real gender malfunction, at first. It's settled down to male though."

She glanced at the naked Mardukan and then away.

"Of course, I don't see how it could possibly mistake the gender," she added with a smile.

"I got most of it," Roger said. "I think I'm more attuned with him or something. He also says we'd better get moving or something nasty is going to happen."

"Did he indicate what?" Pahner asked.

"He called it the *yaden*. No context. I think it's related to night." He turned to the Mardukan and tried the toot's voice control function. "What are the *yaden*?"

Roger discovered that the software was giving him images in response to some form of subcommunication involving his background, the gestures of the Mardukan, and known words. In cases where it had clear translations, it shut down the direct auditory feed and substituted the "translated" words. But in this case, it obviously had no clear translation, so it was giving ephemeral images of possible translations, and the general outline, although startling, was clear. He almost laughed.

"He says the *yaden* are vampires."

"Oh," Pahner said blandly.

"He's very emphatic about it, though," Elenora said, nodding in agreement. "Yes, I get that, too, now. Vampires. You're good with this, Roger."

Roger smiled in pleasure at the rare compliment.

"You know I like languages."

"So the scummy thinks we should move out?" Pahner asked, just to keep things straight.

"Yes," Roger said, somewhat coldly. He was beginning to develop a distaste for the epithet. "He has a problem with something that apparently comes out only at night. He wants to hurry to make it to his village before whatever it is comes out."

"That's going to be tough," Pahner said consideringly. "We've got a pass to cross, then quite a bit of jungle. We'll barely make it up to the top of the ridge before dark."

"He seems to think we ought to be able to make it before dark without *too* much trouble," Eleanora put in.

"He may be right," Pahner responded. "But if he is, then his village has to be a lot closer than I think he's suggesting."

"Then *I* suggest that we'd better get moving," Roger said.

"No question there," Pahner agreed. "First we've got to get this tent taken down, though."

"Hang on." Roger pulled his drinking tube down. "Here," he said, gesturing with it to the Mardukan. "Water."

They didn't have that word yet, so he used Standard. To demonstrate, he took a drink out of it and dribbled a few drops onto his hand to show the Mardukan what it was. Cord leaned forward and took a swig off of the tube. He nodded at Roger in thanks, then gestured to leave the tent.

"Yeah," Roger said with a laugh. "I guess we're all on the same sheet of music."

But playing in different keys.

It quickly became apparent to Roger where the disconnect between Cord's and Pahner's estimated travel times lay. Cord's giant legs drove him forward at a far quicker pace than humans were able to maintain. The Marines, had they been less heavily encumbered, could have jogged and kept up with the Mardukan, but Matsugae, O'Casey, and the Navy pilots were unable to make anything like the same rate of movement. As the sun set behind the mountains and the alluvial outflow narrowed into a mountain gorge, the Mardukan became more and more voluble in his worries, and translations became clearer and clearer.

"Prince Roger," Cord said, "we must hurry. The *yaden* will suck us dry if they find us. I'm the only one with a cover cloth." He gestured to his leather cape. "Unless you have those 'tents' for everyone?"

"No," Roger said. He grasped a boulder and pulled himself up onto it. The vantage point gave him a clear view of the company scattered up and down the narrow defile. The tail of the unit was just starting up the narrow, steep canyon while the head was nearing the top. As mountain canyons went, it wasn't much, but it was slowing them as the heavily laden troopers struggled up the ravine, pulling themselves from boulder to boulder. They blended into the background well, but for the flash of solar panels on the rucksacks and the occasional reflection off a weapon's barrel. The parties with the stretchers were in particularly bad straits, wrestling their heavy and cumbersome loads over rocks and around corners. All in all, the company was moving very slowly.

"No, we don't have enough large tents for everyone. But we have other covers, and everyone has a personal bivy tent. How large and fierce are these *yaden*?"

Cord mulled over a few of the words that obviously weren't quite right.

"They are neither large nor fierce. They are stealthy. They will slip into a camp full of warriors and select one or two. Then they overcome them and suck them dry."

Roger shuddered slightly. He supposed that it could be superstition, but the description was too precise.

"In that case, we're just going to have to post a good guard."

"This valley is thick with them," Cord said, gesturing around. "It is a well-known fact," he finished simply.

"Oh, great." Roger jumped nimbly down off the boulder. "We're in the Valley of the Vampires."

CHAPTER EIGHTEEN

The wind was constant and enervating. It blew through the pass incessantly, funneling from the high-pressure upland desert to the lower pressure jungles. It dried the surroundings here at the head of the pass, creating one last patch of arid ground before the all-enveloping triple-canopy rain forest barely a hundred meters below.

Captain Pahner looked down at that canopy and, for the sixth time, reconsidered his decision to stop in the pass itself. Cord hadn't cared one way or the other; he insisted that anything short of returning to his village was a veritable death sentence, and now he sat by a fire as the cold settled in. Pahner didn't blame him a bit; the cold-blooded scummy would be virtually somnolent once the full cold hit.

The Marine scratched his chin for a moment, pondering what they'd so far learned from the native. He was forced to admit, albeit grudgingly, that Roger had had a point about the need to acquire the ability to communicate with the locals as quickly as they could. And the delay for the initial conversation probably hadn't mattered all that much in the end. Not that Pahner intended to say anything of the sort to Roger . . . or even to O'Casey. There could be only one commander, especially in a situation as extreme as this, and whatever the official table of organization might have said, "Colonel" His Royal

Highness Prince Roger wasn't fit to be trusted with the organization of a bottle party in a brewery.

Now that the moment of pure, incandescent rage which had possessed him when the young jackass went right ahead and killed the *flar* beast had passed, the captain rather regretted his language. Not because he hadn't meant it, and not because it hadn't needed saying—not even, or perhaps especially, because of the potential impact their little *tête-à-tête* might have upon the future career of one Captain Armand Pahner (assuming the captain in question survived to worry about career moves). No, he regretted it because it had been unprofessional.

On the other hand, it seemed to have finally started making an impression on the sheer arrogance and carelessness which seemed to be two of the prince's more pronounced characteristics. Which was the reason Pahner had no intention of admitting that *this* time the kid might have had a point. The last thing they needed was for the prince to feel justified in continuing to butt heads with the professional who was his only chance of getting home alive.

Setting that consideration aside, however, it was beginning to look as if Cord might prove very valuable indeed, at least in the short run, and the debt he felt he owed to Roger might actually work out in the company's favor. It appeared that the Mardukan was a chief or shaman of the tribe whose territory they were about to enter, and that suggested that Roger might just have secured the best introduction and intermediary they could hope for.

Exactly why he'd been headed towards the lakebed remained less clear. He insisted that he'd been on some sort of vision quest, and it seemed evident that whatever problem he'd been seeking answers to must be pressing to drive him into such a hostile environment, but just what that problem was remained elusive despite his efforts to explain it. On the other hand, his conversations with Roger and Eleanora during the hike to this first camp had nearly completed the task of gathering a workable kernel for the language program. By tomorrow, translations should be as clear as the software could make them.

Pahner allowed himself a few more seconds to hope that would be the case—it would be really nice to have *something* break their way—and then put that particular problem away in favor of more immediate concerns. He turned and walked back through the camp perimeter, running one last personal visual check. Everything was in place: directional mines set, laser detectors on sweep, thermal detectors up and watching. If anything tried to get through those defenses, it had better be invisible or smaller than a goat. He completed his check and crossed to where Sergeant Major Kosutic waited with the portable master panel slung over her shoulder.

"Turn it on," he said, and she nodded and hit the trip switch. Icons flashed on the panel as the sensors came online and the weapons went live, and he watched her eyes move as she ran the visual checklist. Then she looked up at him and nodded again.

"Okay, everybody," Pahner announced, using both his external suit speakers and the all-hands frequency. "We're live. If you have to take a dump or a piss, do it in the latrine."

The latrines, like everything else about the camp, met the guidelines for a temporary camp in hostile territory. The latrines had been set up on the jungle side of the camp, and were dug to regulation depth and width. Inside the sensor parameter, each two-man team had dug in its own foxhole, and most of the party would sleep in them. The two-meter trenches were uncomfortable, but they were also safe. Those who weren't assigned to a fire team, like the Navy personnel (or Roger), had erected temporary shelters with their one-man "bivy" tents within the perimeter enclosed by the foxholes, and the company would maintain fifty percent watch all night long, with one trooper covering the other as he or she slept. It was a technique which had kept armies relatively safe on multiple worlds and through thousands of wars.

Relatively safe.

"How are the troops, Sergeant Major?" he asked quietly. He didn't like having to ask, but the constant wrestling with Roger was dragging him away from the troop time he preferred.

"Worried," Kosutic admitted. "The marrieds, especially. Their spouses and kids will have gotten the word by now that they're dead. Even if they make it back after all, it's going to be hard. Who's going to provide for their families in the meantime? A death bonus isn't much to live on."

Pahner had considered that.

"Point out to them that they're going to be up for plenty of back pay when they get home. Speaking of which, we're going to have to get some sort of a pay cycle in place when we get to whatever passes for civilization on this ball."

"Long way off to think about," Kosutic pointed out. "Let's make it through this night, and I'll be happy. I don't like this *yaden* thing. That big scummy bastard doesn't look like the type to scare easy."

Pahner nodded but didn't comment. He had to admit that the Mardukan shaman had him spooked, too.

"Wake up, Wilbur." Lance Corporal D'Estrees nudged the grenadier's boot with her plasma rifle. "Come on, you stupid slug. Time to take over."

It was just past local midnight, and she was more than ready to rack out for a couple of hours. They'd been trading off, turn and turn about, since sunset, while it got colder and colder. There'd been a few little things moving in the jungle below, and the sort of strange, unfamiliar noises any new world offered. But nothing dangerous, nothing to write home about. Even with both of the planet's double moons below the horizon, there was enough light for their helmets to enhance it to a barely dusky twilight, and there'd been nothing doing. Just hours to wait and watch and think about the straits the company was in. Now it was Wilbur's turn and the bivy tent was calling to her. If she could just get the stupid bastard to wake up, that was.

The grenadier was sleeping in his bivy, a combination of one-man tube-tent and sleeping bag less than a meter behind the foxhole. If it dropped in the pot he could be in the hole in a second; *would* be in the foxhole before he was fully awake. It also kept him in reach to be awakened for guard duty, but it had been a long day and it looked like he was sleeping pretty hard.

Finally, she got annoyed and flipped on her red-lens flashlight. It had the option of infrared, but prying open an eyelid and shining infrared in was an exercise in frustration.

She pulled back the head of the tent to flash the light in the sleeping grenadier's eyes.

Roger rolled to his feet at the first yell, but he could have spared himself some bruises if he'd just stayed put. The instant he came upright, two Marines tackled him and slammed him straight back down on the ground. Before he could sort out what was happening, there were three more troopers on his chest, and more around him with weapons trained outward.

"Get off me, goddamn it!" he yelled, but to no avail. The limits of his command authority were clear; the Marines would let him make minor choices, like whether they lived or died, but not large ones, like whether *he* lived or died. They ignored his furious demands so completely that in the end he had no choice but to settle for chuckling in bemusement.

Several minutes passed, and then the pile began to erupt as arms and legs disentangled. There were a few good-natured wisecracks that he pointedly did not hear, and then a hand pulled him to his feet. He noticed in passing that it was as dark as the inside of a mine, and he was wondering what had changed their minds and convinced them to let him up when his helmet was placed on his head and the light amplifiers on the visor engaged. Pahner was standing in the doorway of the tent.

"Well," the captain said wearily, "we've had a visit from your friend's vampires."

The grenadier was twenty-two, stood a shade over a hundred seventy centimeters, and, according to his file, weighed ninety kilos. He'd been born on New Orkney, and he had light reddish hair that ran thick on the backs of his freckled hands.

He no longer weighed ninety kilos, and the freckled hands were skeletal and yellow in the beam from the flashlight.

"Whatever it was," Kosutic said, "it sucked out just about every drop of blood in his body." She pulled up the chameleon cloth and pointed to the marks on his stomach. "These are at all the arteries," she said, turning the head to show the marks at the neck. "Two punctures, side-by-side, just about the width of human canines. Maybe a little closer."

Pahner turned to the lance corporal who'd been the grenadier's buddy. The Marine was stonefaced in the light from the lamp as she faced the company and platoon leadership with a dead buddy at her feet.

"Tell me again," Pahner said with iron patience.

"I didn't hear a thing, Sir. I didn't see a thing. I was not asleep. Private Wilbur did not make a sound, nor were there any significant sounds from the direction of his hooch."

She hesitated.

"I . . . I might have heard *something*, but it was so faint I didn't pay it any attention. It was like one of those sounds in a hearing test, where you can't really tell if it was a sound or not."

"What was it?" Kosutic asked, checking the inside of the bivy tent for any indication of what had slipped in and out of the camp with such deadly silence. The small, one-man tents were shaped like oversized sleeping bags with just enough room inside for a person and his gear. Whatever had killed the private had entered and left the tent without any apparent trace.

"It . . . sounded like . . . a bat," the plasma gunner admitted unhappily, fully aware of how it was going to sound. "I didn't think anything of it at the time."

"A bat," Pahner repeated carefully.

"Yes, Sir," the Marine said. "I heard a real quiet flapping sound once. I looked around, but nothing was moving." She paused and looked at the semicircle of her superiors. "I know how it sounds, Sir. . . ."

Pahner nodded and looked around.

"Fine. It was a bat." He drew a deep breath and looked back down at the body. "To tell you the truth, Corporal, it sounds like just another creature on another world we don't know much about.

"Bag him now," he told Kosutic. "We'll have a short service and burn him in the morning."

The Marine body bags could be set to incinerate their contents, which allowed bodies to be recovered rather than left behind. After the cremation, the bag was rolled up like a sleeping bag around the ashes and became just another package which could be carried with a minimum of weight and space.

"A bat," he muttered, shaking his head again as he walked back into the darkness.

"Don't worry about it, Troop," Gulyas told D'Estrees definitively with a tap on the arm. "We're on a new planet. It might have real vampire bats, and those are sneaky suckers, let me tell you." The lieutenant had grown up in the mountains of Colombia, where vampire bats were an old and known enemy. But *Terran* vampire bats didn't suck a corpse dry.

"It might have been real vampires," the corporal said dubiously.

The morning dawned with a sleepy, nervous company of Marines praying the fierce G-9 star back into the sky. After recovering the mines and sensors and conducting a brief service for Wilbur, they moved out down the valley on the jungle side of the mountains with a much more cautious attitude toward their new home.

Roger continued to walk with Cord as they moved down the gentler valley on the western side of the range. The pass was high and dry, which gave it some of the temperature characteristics of the desert beyond, and the morning was very cool when they first broke camp. The low temperature caused the Mardukan to move slowly, almost feebly; the isothermic species was obviously not designed for cold weather. But as the day progressed and the sun cleared the peaks at their backs, the oppressive heat of the planet came on full force and the shaman awoke fully, shook himself all over, and gave the grunt Roger had come to recognize as Mardukan laughter.

"Woe for my quest, but I will be happy to leave these awful mountains!"

Roger had been looking around at the banded formations in the walls of the valley and thinking the exact opposite. They were beginning to reach the low hanging clouds, the second cloud layer that obscured the lowland jungles, and the humidity was already increasing. Along with the gathering heat it made for conditions well suited to a steam bath, and he wasn't particularly elated by the thought of wading deeper into them.

But for now, the steep valley had temporarily plateaued, and Roger stepped aside from his slot in the column again as he paused to examine the small cirque. The valley was obviously a product of both runoff and glaciation, so temperatures must have been much lower at some point in the planet's geologic history. The remnants of that geologic event had produced a valley of surpassing beauty to a human's eyes.

The kidney-shaped valley was centered by a modest lake, about a half-hectare in area, fed from small streams that plumed down the rocky walls, and a primary stream that was apparently intermittent stretched up into the heights. The company had already refilled its bladders from the pool, and the water had been proclaimed not only gin-clear but fairly cool.

The upper and lower ends of the valley were marked by moraines, small mounds of stones, which had been dropped by the glacier in its retreat. The upper moraine would have been a perfect spot for a house with a breathtaking view of the lake and the jungles laid out below it. By the same token, the lower moraine could have provided a prime source of building materials.

The striated walls of the valley were clearly a product of the uplift that had formed the entire chain, but their strata indicated that at one point, long, long, long ago, they'd been part of a plain or shallow seabed. Roger noted evidence in different places of both coal and iron formations, specifically of banded iron, which was the richest possible form. The fairly pleasant, for a human, valley was perfect for mining development. Of course, as Cord's comment reminded him, for any scummies exiled to it, it would be a lesser ring of Hell.

"Oh, I don't know," he disagreed. "I like it here. I love mountains—they offer up the soul of a planet to you if you know what you're looking at."

"Pah." Cord snorted and spat. "What does a place like this hold for The People? No food, cold as death, dry as a fire. Pah!"

"Actually," Roger said, "there's a lot of good geology up here."

"What is this 'geology'?" the shaman asked, shaking his spear at the valley walls. "This 'spirit of stone'? What is it?"

It was Roger's turn to snort as he took off his helmet and ran a hand over his hair. He'd put it up in a bun, and the lake looked awfully inviting. He badly needed a shampoo, but the Mardukan's question intrigued him away from that thought.

"It's the study of rock. It's one of the things I found interesting when I was in college." Roger sighed and looked at the line of Marines hell-bent on protecting him from harm. "If I hadn't been a prince, I might have been a geologist. God knows I like it more than 'princing'!"

Cord considered him quietly for a moment.

"Those who are born to the chiefs cannot choose to be shamans. And those who are shamans cannot choose to be hunters."

"Why not?" Roger snapped, suddenly losing his temper at the whole situation and waving his arms at the company as it trudged past. "I didn't ask for this! All I ever wanted to do was . . . well . . . I don't know what I would've done! But I sure as hell wouldn't have been His Royal Highness Prince Roger Ramius Sergei Alexander Chiang MacClintock!"

Cord looked down at the top of the young chieftain's head for several moments before he finally decided on the best approach and drew a knife from his harness. A half dozen rifles snapped around to train on him, but he ignored them as he tossed it up for a grip on the long iron blade . . . and thunked the prince smartly on top of the head with the leather-wrapped hilt.

"*Ow!*" Roger grabbed the top of his head and looked at the Mardukan in consternation. "What did you do that for?"

"Quit acting like a child," the shaman said severely, still ignoring the readied rifles. "Some are born to greatness, others to nothing. But no one chooses which they are born to. Wailing about it is the action of a puling babe, not a Man of The People!" He flipped a knife in the air and resheathed it.

"So," Roger growled, rubbing the spot which had been hit, "basically what you're saying is that I should start acting like a MacClintock!" He fingered his scalp and pulled away slightly red-stained fingers. "*Hey!* You drew blood!"

"So does a child whine at a skinned false-hand," the shaman said, snapping the "fingers" on one of his lower limbs. The hand on the end had a broad opposable pad and two dissimilar-sized fingers. It was obviously intended for heavy lifting rather than fine manipulation. "Grow up."

"Knowledge of geology is useful," Roger said sullenly.

"How? How is it useful to a chief? Should you not study the nature of your enemies? Of your allies?"

"Do you know what that is?" Roger demanded, gesturing at the coal seam, and Cord snapped his fingers again in a Mardukan sign of agreement.

"The rock that burns. Another reason to avoid these demon-spawn hills. Light a fire on that, and you'll have a hot time!"

"But it's a good material economically," Roger pointed out. "It can be mined and sold."

"Good for Farstok Shit-Sitters, I suppose," Cord said with another snort of laughter. "But not for The People."

"And you trade nothing with these 'Farstok Shit-Sitters'?" Roger asked, and Cord was silent for a moment.

"Some, yes. But The People don't need their trade. They don't require their goods or gold."

"Are you sure?" Roger looked up at the towering alien and cocked his head. There was something about the Mardukan's body language that spoke of doubt.

"Yes," Cord said definitely. "The People are free of all bonds. No tribe binds them, nor do they bind any tribe. We are whole." But he still seemed ambivalent to the human.

"Uh-huh." Roger put his helmet back on, carefully. That tap had hurt. "Physician, heal thyself."

CHAPTER NINETEEN

The jungle wore mist like a shroud. This was a cloud forest more than a rain forest—a condition of eternal damp and fog rather than a place of rain.

But it was also a transition zone. Soon the company would pass out of it into the enveloping green hell of the jungle below. Soon their vision would be blocked by lianas and underbrush, not mist. Soon they would be in the cloaking darkness of the rain forest understory, but for now there were only tall trees, very similar in many respects to the trees on the desert side of the mountains, and the omnipresent mist.

"This sucks," said Lance Corporal St. John, (M.). Sergeant Major Kosutic required him to respond that way—"St. John, M."—because he had an identical twin in Third Platoon, St. John, (J.) She also required each of them to have a distinguishing mark at all times. In St. John (M.)'s case, it was that one side of his head was shaved bald, and he reached up to scratch under his helmet as he looked around at the steamy twilight.

The temperature was over 46 degrees, 115 Fahrenheit, and the fog was dense and hot, like being in a steam bath, and nearly impenetrable. Visibility was no more than ten meters, and the helmets' sensors were overwhelmed by the conditions. Even the sonics were defeated by the swirling, choking steam. St. John (M.)

turned to bitch some more to the plasma gunner behind him . . . just in time to be hit by a high-pitched squeal in his right ear.

"Eyow!"

"What?" PFC Talbert asked as the lance yanked off his helmet. The two of them were covering the right flank of the company, slightly out of line with the point man and fifty meters back.

"Ow!" the grenadier said, banging the helmet into a convenient tree trunk. "Goddamn feedback! I think this damned steam blew out a circuit."

Talbert laughed and let her plasma rifle dangle on its sling as she slapped a stingfly on her neck and fished in her jacket with the other hand. She extracted a brown tube.

"Smoke?"

"Nah," St. John (M.) snarled. He put the helmet on his head and yanked it off again. "Shit." He reached into the depths and pulled a harness plug, then held it up to his ear again. "Ah, that got it. But I just lost half my sensors."

Talbert popped the brown tube into her mouth and tapped the end to light it, then paused and looked around at the mists.

"Did you hear something?" she asked, hitching up her plasma rifle cautiously.

"I can't hear shit," St. John (M.) said. The big lance corporal rubbed his ear. "Nothing but chirping crickets!"

"Doesn't matter," Talbert said around the nicstick. The mild derivative of tobacco had a low-level of pseudonicotine and was otherwise harmless. It was, however, just about as addictive as regular tobacco. "Sensors can't do shit in this cra—"

St. John (M.) spun in place like a snake as the scream began behind him.

Talbert, shrieking like a soul in hell, was connected to one of the trees by a short, wiggling worm. The worm stretched down from perhaps a meter over head height and was connected to the curve where shoulder met neck. Even as the corporal watched, frozen, the juncture spurted bright red arterial blood, and the worm snatched Talbert up into the air.

St. John (M.) was shocked out of coherent thought, but he was also a veteran, and his hands jacked the belt of high explosive rounds out of his grenade launcher without any conscious order from his brain. They were reaching for a shotgun shell when Gunnery Sergeant Lai appeared out of the mist. The senior NCO paused for no more than a heartbeat to take in the situation, then blew the worm off the tree with her bead rifle.

The plasma gunner hit the ground like a sack of wet cement, then broke into convulsions. The ululating shrieks never stopped as her arms and legs spasmed on the ground, tearing up handfuls of dark, wet soil.

Lai dropped the bead rifle and ripped the first-aid kit off her combat harness. She threw herself onto the writhing plasma gunner and covered the spurting wound on her neck with a self-sealing bandage. But even as she did so, the wound erupted with red, streaming jelly. The smart bandage expanded to cover the bleeding areas, looking for clear undamaged tissue to bond to, but the damage spread faster than the bandage as flesh-eating poisons began dissolving the proteins under the skin that bound the private's flesh together.

Lai cut the gunner's camouflage jacket open with a combat knife as the subcutaneous hemorrhaging spread. She whipped out another bandage, but it was obviously useless as black-and-red pools of destruction crossed the private's tanned torso. The skin around the initial puncture broke, and a slit ripped open down Talbert's ribs as blood, fats, and dissolved muscle poured out onto the forest floor.

The plasma gunner went into fresh paroxysms as the blackness spread and both of her exercise-flattened breasts melted into pools and washed out through the slash in her chest.

Lai backed away in horror as the black blood spread up the Marine's neck and the skin and muscles of her face fell flaccid against the bones of her skull.

Final dissolution didn't take all that long. It only seemed like hours until the private stopped thrashing and screaming.

"What the fuck is this, a picnic?" Sergeant Major Kosutic snarled.

She shoved one private towards the perimeter and looked the platoon sergeant in the eye. "We need a perimeter, not a cluster fuck!"

The group around the incident broke up, scattering towards guard positions, as she strode through them.

"Okay, what happened?" She looked down at the skeleton at her feet and blanched. "Satan! What did that? And who is it?"

"It was jus' . . . it was . . ." St. John (M.) said incoherently. He was swinging from side to side, training his grenade launcher up into the treetops of the surrounding forest. He was obviously still in shock, so Kosutic looked at Lai.

"Gunny?"

Lai hefted her bead rifle and looked around at the trees, wide-eyed.

"It was some sort of worm." She kicked what was left of the invertebrate where it had fallen at the base of the tree. "It bit her, or stung her, or something. When I got here, it was pulling her up into the tree. I shot it off of her, but she just . . . she just . . ." The sergeant stopped and retched, still searching the enveloping mists for more of the worms.

"She just . . . *that*," she finished, gesturing to but not looking at the partial skeleton at her feet.

Kosutic pulled out her combat knife and prodded the alien carcass. It was darkly patterned, with noticeable blue patches along its back. All that was left after Lai's bead rifle had blown it apart was ten centimeters or so of the base. What appeared to be the back end had several pod-feet with hooks. One of them still had a bit of bark attached, indicating where it hung out. Literally. And the business end apparently . . . dissolved people. She stood up, stuck the knife back into her combat harness, and wiped her hands.

"Nasty."

Captain Pahner appeared out of the mist, trailed by Prince Roger and his pet scummy. The captain padded up and looked down at the casualty.

"Problems, Sergeant Major?"

"Well," she said grimly, pulling at an earlobe, "point's not going to be a favorite spot."

Cord walked over to the group gathered around the skeleton and snapped his lower fingers.

"*Yaden cuol*," he said, and Kosutic raised an eyebrow at Roger.

"'Vampire' what, Your Highness?" Her toot had picked up the "*yaden*," but the second word wasn't yet in its vocabulary.

"Vampire . . . baby?" Roger suggested doubtfully. He wore an odd, introspective expression, and the sergeant major realized he was communing with the software. "I'm beginning to think this language program is making too many assumptions. I think it means larva of whatever the vampires are."

"How do we fight it, Sir?" Gunny Lai was beginning to get over her shock, and she turned almost pleadingly to the prince. "Talbert was a good troop. St. John (M.), too. I doubt they were fucking off. And it's camouflaged to the max. How the fuck do you fight something like that? No motion, no heat, hardly any electrical field?"

Roger let loose with a stream of liquid syllables and clicks. The scummy knocked his lower hands together and let loose a string back. Then he looked around, knocked his hands together again, and shrugged his cape up to cover his head, shoulders, and neck.

"Well," the prince said doubtfully, "he says that you need to start paying attention. He says he's watched us walking, and we never look 'hard enough' or we look at the wrong things. He also says that these worm-things hang out in the trees and are hard to see, so if you put something up to cover your head and shoulders you're better off."

Cord produced another spurt of syllables and gestured around the woods. He pulled the cape back down and clapped his hands again, and Roger nodded and gave a grim snort.

"He also says that they're just about the most horrible things in the woods, but not the most dangerous. They can't move very fast, except to strike, so you can easily kill them with a spear. He said, 'Wait until you face an *atul-grack*,' whatever that is. And these . . . killer caterpillars . . . sometimes come in groups.

"He's pretty philosophical about it," Roger added. "That handclapping gesture is a shrug. Basically, 'Life's a bitch—'"

"'—and then you die,'" Kosutic finished with a nod. "Got it."

★ ★ ★

Eleanora's feet slid out from under her on the muddy hillside, and she landed flat on her rump. The jarring impact sent shooting pains all the way up her spine and into her skull, and she started to slip down the hill. She scrambled wildly for some sort of braking grip, but without success until a hand snapped out and caught the light rucksack on her back. She looked over her shoulder and smiled wearily at her savior.

"Thank you, Kostas," she said with a sigh.

She rolled over on her stomach and tried to struggle to her feet, but it was no use. She'd been barely staggering along as it was, and between the mud, and the heat, and the biting flies, and the screaming muscles in her back and legs from the last two days of exertion, it was just too much.

"Oh, God," she whispered. "I just want to die and get it over with."

A Mardukan insect, more from curiosity than malice, landed on her ear and started to investigate her ear canal. She summoned a burst of energy to shake her head violently and swat at it, but then she slumped back into the mud.

"Now, now, Ma'am," Matsugae said with a smile. "We're nearly to Cord's village. You can't give up now." The valet hooked a hand in her rucksack's straps and helped her claw her way to her feet.

She swayed in exhaustion and leaned on a tree . . . carefully. Her arm was covered in a welter of swollen bites from the defenders of a previous support, and since that incident she'd become much more careful where she put her hands. But this tree, at least, didn't seem to want to kill her, and she leaned into it gratefully.

They were below the clouds now, and into the fringe of the planet's all-encompassing jungle. They'd followed the river out of the valley as it grew larger and larger, until finally the ground around it became too marshy to continue along its banks. The company had turned off to the south, but continued to parallel the watercourse, although the gurgle of its passage could be barely distinguished through the background racket of the jungle.

The incessant hum of flying insects was everywhere. The Mardukan version was eight-legged and had a six-winged pattern, as opposed to the terrestrial six-limb/four-wing arrangement. The local bugs also used an aramid polymer, similar in some respects to Kevlar, as the hard core of their exoskeletons. Since it was both lighter and stronger than chitin, it allowed the existence of species which would be considered extremely large on Earth—or on most other planets, for that matter.

There were thousands of different kinds of beetle analogues, some of them huge. Most of them seemed to be turners of the detritus on the forest floor, while a few joined forces with the midge analogues to take turns biting the humans. Dozens of species swarmed on the human intruders, ranging from tiny creatures that looked so much like mosquitoes that the Marines simply named them skeeters, to a slow-flying beetle the size of a blue jay that had the troopers pulling out their multitools and swinging axes during its infrequent attacks. The chameleon suits were impervious to even the local insects' best efforts and could be sealed up completely, but while the chameleon cloth actively transpired carbon dioxide and oxygen, the rate was too low to support heavy activities. The Marines would occasionally close up their suits to escape the insects, but soon enough they were forced to open their helmets back up and take deep gasping breaths. Then spit out the midges they'd swallowed.

But the hum of the insects, as up-close and personal as it was, was overwhelmed by the rest of the bedlam.

The air rang with strange cries—here a shrill whistle, there a grunting roar, in the distance a banshee howl as some beast celebrated a victory or defended its territory, or perhaps simply called longingly for a mate.

Besides the sounds, the atmosphere was suffused with weird smells. The odor of rot was a near universal on oxygen-nitrogen planets, and overpowering in any jungle, but here there were thousands, millions, of other scents.

Nor was vision left unassaulted. The entire jungle was a riot of bright colors in the oppressing gloom. The combination of the double layer of cloud cover and triple-canopy jungle made the understory tenebrous to a degree rarely found on Earth, but the depths of that overarching gloom offered beauty of its own.

A dangling liana near O'Casey's head was decorated with tiny carmine blossoms. The blossoms released a heavy perfume that had attracted dozens of similarly colored butterflies. That was the tag which came to the sociologist's mind, at least. The insectoids' covering was smooth, instead of the furry look of terrestrial butterflies, but they were just as brightly patterned. As she watched the swarm of fluttering beauties, a purple spider/beetle dropped from a branch into their midst and snagged one of their number. The flock of nectar eaters took off in a crimson cloud that briefly surrounded the chief of staff in a fall of gorgeous red, then dispersed.

O'Casey took a deep whiff of the glorious blossoms' perfume as the tiny predator finished off its tiny prey, then pried herself back off the tree. A good part of the company had stumbled past as she rested, and now she would have to hurry to catch up to her assigned position.

Pahner had put the "hangers-on," as he phrased it, just behind the command group. Beside Eleanora and Kostas, that included the pilots of the four shuttles. If they could retake the port, those pilots would be their only hope of capturing an interstellar ship and escaping the system, so it was nearly as important to keep them alive as it was to keep Roger that way.

Eleanora had realized, however, that neither she nor Matsugae were as high on Pahner's list. The Marine captain was determined to reach the port with as few casualties as possible, but if he had to lose the odd academic or valet along the way, then so be it.

She couldn't fault his logic, for there was no margin to spare on this operation, but she didn't have to like it. And she doubted that Roger had made the connection, for the prince would probably object if it ever came down to losing either member of his "staff."

The conclusion that the man responsible for keeping all of them alive had earmarked her as, regrettably, expendable was disturbing. Throughout her entire life, she'd always functioned under conditions where she could move at her own pace. Academically, that pace had been quite fast, and she remembered looking down on those who fell by the educational wayside, but even those unfortunates had simply found less satisfying and successful positions.

That wouldn't be the case here. Now she faced a physical challenge that was, literally, life or death, and she knew instinctively that if she asked for some respite, it would be denied. She was unimportant to the mission, and the safety of the entire company couldn't be jeopardized for her sake. So for her and Matsugae, it was "march or die."

She was fairly certain it was going to be both for her, but Matsugae seemed to be taking to the change in conditions fairly well. The fussy little valet carried a pack nearly as large as the armorer's, but he was keeping up with the company without complaint, and had helped her along the way several times. She was, frankly, astounded.

She straightened up and started along the muddy track which had been smashed through the undergrowth by the passage of most of the company. The Marines around her were paying as much attention to the back trail as to the sides, so she knew she was dangerously close to the tail of the company. As she picked up the pace to catch back up to the center of the force, she glanced up at the valet, still doggedly tailing her.

"You don't seem to be having any troubles with this march at all, Matsugae," she said quietly.

"Oh, I wouldn't say that, Ma'am," the valet answered, adjusting the straps of the internal frame rucksack which, along with the chameleon suits they both wore, had come out of the company's spare stores. He idly slapped a "skeeter" and winked at the academic. "I'm afraid I've spent rather a lot of time following Roger through places almost this bad on safari, although, to be fair, never under conditions quite so . . . resource-limited and extreme. But I think this is hard on everyone, even the Marines, whether they show it or not."

"At least you don't have any trouble keeping up," she said bitterly. The backs of her legs felt as if someone were sticking hot knives into them, and they'd just gotten to the bottom of the hillside. That meant crossing a shallow stream and climbing another hill that looked even taller. Slipping and sliding in the sweltering muck, not being able to hold onto the trees for fear of something eating you, constantly tired and constantly afraid.

"You just have to put one foot in front of the other, Ma'am," the valet said reasonably. He planted a foot on the worn path up the hill and offered the chief of staff his hand. "Alley-oop, Ma'am!"

O'Casey shook her head and took the offered hand.

"Thank you, Kostas."

"Not much further, Ma'am," the valet said with a smile. "Not much further at all."

CHAPTER TWENTY

The village nestled on a hilltop, surrounded by a log and thorn wall.

The hill itself sat in an angle where a large stream intersected the river the company had been paralleling. Just upstream from the junction, the river thundered over a cataract, and downstream from the hill, the combined flows created a deep, wide river that was probably navigable by barges. As they'd gotten lower and lower in elevation, however, the signs of frequent floods had become obvious. Clearly, the village was situated atop its hill to avoid this recurring phenomenon, and it was likely that frequent flooding would also interfere with navigation.

It began to rain as they approached the hill. Not a slight, steady rain as a cloud parked itself and motheringly watered the parched soil. Not even the hard, firm rain of a powerful weather front. This was the pounding, drowning rain of a tropical thunderstorm—rain like a waterfall, hitting so hard that weaker members of the party were actually knocked off their feet by its first rush.

"Is this normal?" Roger yelled to Cord as the company struggled up the hill.

"What?" Cord asked, hitching his general-purpose cape up a little higher.

"This rain!" Roger yelled, gesturing at the sky.

"Oh," Cord said. "Of course. Several times a day. Why?"

"Joy," Pahner muttered, having monitored the conversation. Roger had fed the language kernel he'd collected during the day's walk to all of the party's toots, and the company's members were now capable of translating the local language on their own. It was expected that they would be able to pick up each dialect quickly as they progressed from area to area, now that they had a local kernel.

"I should go to the head of your group," Cord pointed out. "I'm sure I have been watched as we approached, but I should go to the head so that they're sure I'm not a prisoner or a *kractan*."

"Yeah," Roger said, and turned to look at Pahner. "Are you coming, Captain?"

"No," the Marine said, and triggered his communicator. "Company, hold up. Our local is going up to pass us through."

"I'll stay here," he continued to Roger, and raised one hand in a beckoning gesture. "Despreaux!"

"Yes, Sir!" the NCO snapped. She'd been scanning the bushes with a hand-held scanner, and she didn't like the fact that she'd kept getting twitches but hadn't been able to lock them down.

"Take your squad up front with the Prince and Cord."

"Roger, Sir." She gestured at the squad and pointed to the front. "Up and at 'em, Marines."

She put the scanner away and glanced off to the north one more time. There was something out there, she was sure, but what it was eluded her.

Cord and Roger moved up to the front of the company, surrounded by Despreaux's squad. The company had spread out in a standard cigar-shaped perimeter, and now most of the Marines were down in the prone, covering against any attack. There was no such thing as "safety" in a combat zone, but a unit temporarily at rest like this was in the worst possible situation. Unless an enemy has had time to prepare an ambush, a moving unit is a hard target to hit. Similarly, a unit which has had time to prepare defenses is a tough nut to crack, but a company which has just stopped can be hit at any moment and isn't prepared for the attack.

It makes soldiers who are well trained—like those of The Empress' Own—very nervous.

* * *

Cord followed a beaten track up to the single opening in the palisade. As he approached, another Mardukan of the same height and general demeanor appeared in the opening. At the sight of Cord, followed by the humans but clearly not threatened by them, the second Mardukan waved his upper arms in welcome.

"Cord," he called, "you bring unexpected guests!"

"Delkra!" the shaman shouted back, waving his spear. "As if you hadn't been shadowing us these last few hours!"

"Of course," the greeter agreed imperturbably as Cord and Roger's party reached the top of the hill.

The last portion of the path was so steep that steps had been cut and reinforced with logs and rocks. The top of the hill had been roughly leveled, and now Roger could glimpse the village through the palisade opening. It looked much like other villages on other planets. A large communal fire pit was at its center, surrounded by an open area which was currently deserted. Immediately inside the walls were rude, thatch and wattle huts, open to the inside of the palisaded area. The similarity to villages once found in the Amazon basin and other tropical areas on Earth would have amazed Roger if he hadn't spent enough time hunting on primitive planets to realize that there was only so much that could be done with mud and sticks.

"D'Net Delkra, my brother," Cord said, clapping the greeter on his upper shoulder, "I must introduce you to my new *asi-agun.*" He turned to Roger. "Roger, Prince of the Empire, this is my brother, D'Net Delkra, Chief of The People."

The greeter, Delkra, hissed and clapped all four hands together in agitation.

"Ayee! *Asi-agun?* And at your age? Foul news, brother—foul news, indeed! And your quest?"

Cord clapped right true-hand to left false-hand in a gesture of negation.

"We met on the way. He saved my life from a *flar* beast without clear need, without threat to his life, and being not of my tribe."

"Ayee!" Delkra repeated. "*Asi* debt, indeed!"

The Mardukan, who was a bit taller than the shaman, turned to the prince, who'd doffed his helmet. The armor was more comfortable than the steamy heat of the jungle, but Roger felt it was more diplomatic to face this Delkra, who was presumably senior in the local hierarchy, without the obscuring head gear.

"I thank you for my brother's life," Delkra said. "But I cannot be happy for either his enslavement or the failure of his quest."

"Whoa!" Roger said sharply. "What's this 'enslavement' thing? All I did was shoot a . . . a *flar* beast!"

"*Asi* bond is the tightest of all bonds," the chief explained. "To save another's life, without fear or favor, binds him to you through this life and beyond."

"What?" Roger was trying to get over the "slave" concept. "You guys never help each other out?"

"Of course we do," Cord said, "but we are members of the same clan. To help another is to aid the clan, and the clan, in turn, aids us. But you had no such reason to kill the *flar* beast. For the life of me, I'm not sure that you should have."

"It could have attacked the Company," Roger pointed out. "That was the real reason I shot. I didn't even see you."

"Fate, then," Delkra said with a hand clap. "It wasn't threatening you or your . . ." he glanced over the Marines scattered down the hillside " . . . clan?"

"No," Roger admitted. "Not at the time. But I could tell it was dangerous."

"Karma," Cord said with a double hand clap. "We will complete the binding tonight," he continued with another gesture. "Delkra, I request shelter for the night. And shelter for my *asi*'s clan."

"Oh, granted," the chief said, stepping out of the palisade opening and waving into the jungle. "Granted. Come in out of the rain!"

"We're getting sensor ghosts all along the perimeter," Lieutenant Sawato had just taken a tour of the company while Captain Pahner kept an eye on the negotiations of the top of the hill. Now she looked around at the curtaining rain and shook her head. "I've got that funny feeling. . . ."

"We're surrounded by the warriors of this tribe," Pahner said in a distant tone. "They're good. They move slow, so the motion sensors aren't sure if they're really there, and they're isothermal, so the heat sensors can't pick anything up. No power sources, no metal except a knife or spearhead, and we don't have the sensors dialed in for scummy nervous systems." He pulled out a pack of gum and absentmindedly extracted a stick and popped it into his mouth. He shook the pack a couple of times to get the water out, and put it away, all without looking. "Take a glance over to the left. There's a big tree with spreading roots. Halfway up, there's a limb covered in . . . stuff. Go out the limb five meters, just before a red patch. About a half a meter to the right of the red patch. Spear."

"Damn," Sawato said softly. The scummy was as hard to spot as any professional sniper she'd ever seen. He appeared to be covered with a blanket that broke up his outline. "So, what do we do about it, long-term?"

"Dial in the nervous system sensors. We'll have enough data after tonight to do that. After that, any scummy comes within fifty meters of us, we'll be able to detect them. And warn everybody that they're out there. We don't want any accidents."

"I'll pass that on then, shall I?" Sawato asked. Pahner seemed awfully detached about the whole thing, she thought.

"Yeah. Might as well. Looks like the negotiations are going all right after all. I was waiting to see if it dropped in the pot."

"You know," Julian said, "I've been shot, blown up, deep frozen, and vacuum dried. But this is the first time I ever worried about being washed away."

The rain had yet to let up, and the position the squad leader occupied—a slight depression behind a fallen and rotting tree—was rapidly filling. The combination of rising water and the weight of his combat armor meant he was slowly sinking in quickmud.

"Or drowned," he added.

"Ah, come on," Moseyev said as he gently moved aside a bit of fern with the barrel of his bead rifle, "it's just a little rain." He was sure there was something watching them, but he wasn't sure what it was.

"'A little rain,' he says." Julian shook his head. "That's like saying Sirius is 'a little hot,' or that New Bangkok is 'a little decadent.'"

"It's not like it's gonna kill you," Moseyev said. "The armor has air for nearly two days." The fire team leader jerked his head to the side as his helmet highlighted another possible contact. But then it faded again. "Damn. I wonder what's causing that?"

"I'd say it was the wet," Julian said, lowering his own rifle. "But since we're all getting the same ghosts, I'd say it's something in the jungle."

"All hands." The radio crackled with Lieutenant Sawato's calm soprano. "Those sensor ghosts are the local tribesmen. Be calm, though; the natives are friendly. We're going to be going into the village soon, so they'll probably make themselves evident. No firing. I say again, no firing."

"Everybody get that?" Julian called, standing up to make sure he could see all the members of the squad. "Check fire for partisans."

"Got it, Sarge," Macek replied from the far end. "'The natives are friendly.' Riiight."

The private's position was the edge of the squad's area of responsibility, and Macek was the member with the least time in the unit. If he'd gotten the word, everyone else probably had, but Julian wasn't in The Empress' Own because he settled for "probably."

"Yeah, and 'The transfer's in the system,'" the sergeant responded with a laugh. "Give me a thumbs up on that check fire," he added more seriously, and made sure he saw a thumb from everyone before he resumed his position in the puddle. He might bitch about it, but the depression was still the best location for him. Even if it *was* turning into a lake.

"'I'm from the Imperium,'" Moseyev continued with a litany as old as government, "'I'm here to help you.'" He gave a thumbs up.

"'Don't worry, it's a cold landing zone,'" Cathcart added from behind his plasma gun. Thumbs up.

"'We're getting air-trucked to the barracks,'" Mutabi said in an evil tone. Middle finger up.

"Oh, man, you *would* have to say that one!" Julian chuckled. "My aching feet."

★ ★ ★

"Modderpocker," Poertena said. "Chus what we need. Surrounded by tee cannibals."

"Chill, Poertena," Sergeant Despreaux advised. "They're friendly."

"Sure they are," Poertena replied. "Why fight tee roc if you can get it to fly into tee pot."

Even as he spoke, his helmet registered another contact. Then another. It began popping up icons everywhere, and an entire line of Mardukans materialized magically out of the rain.

"Modderpocker," Poertena said again, quietly. "Neat trick."

CHAPTER TWENTY-ONE

The company barely fitted inside the walls of the village. The Marines and their equipment were packed into every nook and cranny as the women of the village, significantly smaller than the male warriors, came out with hoarded foodstuffs for what was shaping up as an evening of celebration. The company reciprocated in building the menu as best it could. Despite the critical importance of the food supplies they'd brought with them, some of the Marines' rations were never going to survive conditions on Marduk, and they brought those out to add to the various edibles being produced by the Mardukans.

Platters of grain, similar in texture to rice but tasting more like barley, were scattered about among the residents and visitors, along with carved wooden bowls of fruits. The predominant fruit species appeared to be a large, brown oval with a thick, inedible skin but a ripe red interior that tasted something like a kiwi fruit. Since it grew on palmlike trees, the humans promptly christened it a "kiwi-date" or "kate" fruit. In addition to the grain and fruit, there were steaming platters of unrecognizable charred things. Most of the humans passed those up.

There was also a sort of wine made from fruit juices, but it was obviously distilled and not just fermented. Like humans, the Mardukans metabolized alcohol for pleasure, and after one tentative sip of the potent beverage, the sergeant major growled at the platoon sergeants. Her growls then wandered down the chain of command until even the lowliest private was aware of the penalty for getting plastered in the middle of a potentially hostile jungle. There was also a heavy and bitter beer that some of the Marines relished and others found disgusting.

The Marines followed the custom of their hosts, reaching into the piles to extract handfuls of grain and fruit and brushing away gathering insects, livestock, and pets.

Pride of place was given to a large lizardlike creature roasting on a spit at the center of the camp. The head had been removed, but the bulky body was a meter and a quarter in length, with a longer tail dragging off into the fire. The spit was turned, with serious and dedicated attention to the responsibility, by a Mardukan child—one of several running about the stockaded village.

The Mardukans were viviparous and bore live young, but they had "litters" of four or more. Baby Mardukans were extremely small, barely the size of a Terran squirrel, and mostly stayed glued to their mothers' backs, mired into the mucous from which they also derived nutrition. Half-grown Mardukans were everywhere underfoot, inextricably mixed with livestock, pets, and, now, Marines.

O'Casey stopped tapping at her pad and shook her head.

"They must have an enormous infant mortality rate," she said with a yawn.

"Why?" Roger asked.

As one of the stars of the evening, he was seated in a place of honor under the awninglike front section of Delkra's hut. He took one of the charred things off the broad leaf that served as a platter and tossed it to a lizardlike creature which had been looking at him with begging eyes. It started to pounce on the morsel, but was pushed aside by a larger version. The larger beast, patterned red and brown with pebbly skin like the *flar* beast's, and with the ubiquitous six legs and a short, wide tail, came over to the prince, sniffing at his platter, but Roger shooed it away.

"I mean," he continued, still looking at the smaller beast, "what makes you say that?"

The little beast was interesting, he thought. The legs, instead of being splayed out like a lizard's, were directly under the body, like a terrestrial mammal's. And the eyes looked much more intelligent than any Terran lizard's.

But it still looked like a six-legged lizard.

"All these children," O'Casey said, snapping her pad closed. "There are six children below what I would guess to be reproductive age for every adult. Now compare that to humans, and you can see that they must have either a tremendous rate of population growth, or a high infant mortality rate. And there's no evidence of population growth. So—"

"What would cause it?" Roger asked absently, holding out another charred bit to the lizard. It shuffled forward hesitantly, sniffing at the tidbit and looking around cringingly. Reasonably sure that it was in the clear, it bared two-centimeter long fangs and hissed, then darted forward with the speed of a striking snake to take the offered treat out of Roger's fingers. It was a precise strike; Roger was left holding a tiny bit of the meat, which had been sheared off cleanly within a millimeter of his fingertips.

"Youch," he said, wiping off the carbon on his fingers.

"Oh, various things. I suppose barbarism is probably the biggest single factor." O'Casey leaned back on Matsugae's rucksack. The valet had left the overstuffed container in her "care" while he went around the camp, examining the cooking methods of the Mardukans. He was currently discussing something with a Mardukan female who'd emerged from one of the huts to lather a substance on the lizard being cooked in the center.

"People evolve to barbarism and usually stop there. Little civilizations rise and fall under the tide of barbarism." She yawned and thought about the history of Earth and some of the less well-prepared slow-boat colonies. "Sometimes, it seems that barbarism, for all its horrors—and they are many—is the natural state of a sentient species. So many, many times humanity has slid into barbarism in one area or another on one planet or another. In fact, we came within a centimeter of it on an interstellar scale during the Dagger Years; I think only your great-to-the-umpteenth grandmother prevented it. Not that that was what she was thinking about—"

She broke off as a yawn interrupted her, then winced as she

stretched.

"God, I hurt," she observed, and lay back and closed her eyes. "Which, I might add, is a consequence of another mortality factor: living in a jungle ain't easy. It's a very competitive environment. Something is always trying to eat you, and finding things *you* can eat is hard."

She reopened her eyes looked up at Roger as the rain began to fall once more. The thunder of it on the thatch was lulling, and she yawned again.

"Roger, we're in a jungle," she said, and her tone was oddly ambiguous. "Jungles try so hard to kill you. They're always trying to." She stopped and smiled at him. "I've tried to get you to listen to me so often, but I'm going to try again. You have to check your tongue. You have to keep your temper. *Learn* from Pahner, don't piss him off, okay?"

He opened his mouth to protest, but she waved him quiet.

"Just . . . try to bite your tongue from time to time, all right? That's all I ask."

The last two days of strain had drained her, and she could feel herself drifting off despite every intention of staying awake. Not only was the social organization of the natives fascinating, but opportunities to catch Roger in a mood to learn anything but sports and hunting tricks were rare. Yet, despite that, she simply couldn't keep her eyes open.

"Jungles are beautiful," she continued in a mumble, "until you have to live in them."

Her eyes closed, and despite the heat, flies, and noise of festive preparation, she slept.

"You're making me proud, brother," Cord said, watching the gathering feast. Its lavishness would extract a price from the tribe, but it showed they were of good status. Something that would be important for this "Roger" to remember.

"It's the least I can do for my brother," Delkra replied. "Ayah! And for these odd strangers." He paused for a moment, then gave a grunting laugh. "They look like *basik*, you know."

Cord clacked his teeth sourly. "Thank you so much for pointing that out, brother. Yes, I'd made the same connection."

The small *basik* were often found around open areas in the jungle. Their mid-legs were foreshortened, and when they were frightened—which was virtually all the time—they ran on their hind legs with their upper limbs flopping loosely about. They were a beast of choice when it came to training young children to hunt, since they were small, harmless, cowardly, and stupid.

Very stupid.

"Get used to it, brother," Delkra said with another grunt. "Others will make the same connection."

"I suppose," Cord conceded. "And, demons know they're just about as stupid in the jungle. But although I've only seen those weapons of theirs used twice, I know to fear them. And rarely is the guard of a lord taken from among the most foolish. I don't underestimate them."

Delkra clapped his lower limbs together and changed the subject abruptly.

"*Asi*, at your age!"

"You keep saying that, brother," Cord observed. "You're not that much younger."

"Tell me a truth unknown," the chief replied somewhat sourly.

Cord understood, of course. Both of them would soon have to leave the Warrior Path, and although those who'd survived it enjoyed great status, few lived long thereafter. It was a thought neither enjoyed contemplating, and the shaman looked around, searching for a neutral change of subject. His gaze flitted about the familiar village which he soon would leave behind forever, and his eyes narrowed as he noticed a puzzling absence.

"Where is Deltan? Hunting?"

"One with the mists," Delkra said, rubbing his hands together to drive away bad luck. "An *atul*."

"What?" the shaman gasped. "How? He was surprised?"

"No," the chief snapped. "The spearhead broke."

"Ayah!" the shaman said, but he refused to show the emotion that threatened to overwhelm him. He'd never had children, not even daughters. A single pairing as a youth had resulted in the death of the brood wife from an infection that was, unfortunately, all too common. Since then, he'd never taken another mate, and his brother's children had become as his own. Delkra certainly had enough to go around; half the females in the tribe had brooded a litter for him at some point. And he ran heavily to males in his broods.

But Deltan had been one of the special ones. He'd shown a flair for the learning of the shaman, and Cord had hoped that someday the fine young warrior might follow in his own footsteps. Now that was done, and it boded poorly for the tribe that he must leave with his *asi* and there would be no shaman to pass on the traditions. He'd hoped to pass on a few critical pieces of knowledge to Deltan before leaving, or perhaps to have him accompany them on the first leg of the humans' travels.

"Ayah," he repeated. "Evil times. The iron?"

"Bad," the chief spat. "Soft and rotten beneath a brittle exterior. It looked fine, but . . ."

"Aye," the shaman said, "but—"

"There's no other choice," the chieftain interrupted. "It must be war."

Cord clapped opposite hands in negation.

"If we war with Q'Nkok, the other tribes will pick our bones."

"And if we don't," the chief pointed out, "Q'Nkok will continue taking our lands and giving *feck* back! We must have the lands or the tribute. As it is, we have neither."

Cord clasped all four arms around his knees and rocked back and forth. His brother was correct; the tribe was in a lose/lose situation. They could neither survive a war with the local city-state nor permit the present intolerable trends to continue, yet war was the only way to stop it. There seemed no way out.

"Q'Nkok is to be our first stop," he observed after a moment. "The humans want to trade for such things as only the shit-sitters can provide. We will discuss this with the humans."

"But—" his brother started to object.

"The humans aren't good in the jungle," Cord overrode the objection, "but they are very wise, nonetheless. I know they're shit-sitters, but they're smart and, I think, honorable shit-sitters. If I had my old master here, I would ask him for advice. But I don't. Far Voitan is fallen, and all its heroes with it. I can't ask my master; therefore, we will ask the humans."

"You're a stubborn *flar* beast," Delkra told him.

"But I'm also right," Cord retorted with a grunting laugh.

CHAPTER TWENTY-TWO

Eleanora awoke to a high-pitched, atonal chanting and a low-tempo, muffled drum beat. Her eyes flickered open, and she froze in adrenaline shock at the sight of a swaying vampire larva. The perspective was weird as the flickering firelight of full dark combined with the swaying dance of the creature to make it seem a strange hallucination. It seemed to shrink to the size of a caterpillar, and then swelled suddenly up to the size of a . . . Mardukan in a mask.

The dancer swayed in the firelight, and as Eleanora blinked at him the long, dripping fangs of the beast were revealed as a crown about his head, the camouflaged body as a painted wrap. Behind the shuffling figure were more dancers: a giant, pincer-armed beetle, a two-armed snake like the legendary Naga, and a low, writhing, six-armed beast whose maw was filled with sharklike teeth.

The fog of sleep and firelight, the swaying of the dancers, the singing and drumbeats were hypnotic. Eleanora lay in a spell, trapped by the symbolism of the animistic rite as the drumbeats increased and the singing shifted through patterns of atonality. The tempo increased, and the dancers' rhythm became more frenzied, until with a final burst of song, now perfectly blended with the drums in tone and pitch, there was a final crash, and the dancers froze.

The audience was left with a feeling of pleasant incompleteness as the dancers departed and conversation broke out among the Marines and Mardukans. Eleanora tried to shake off her fog and looked around for something to help with the attempt, only to find herself rather dreamily contemplating a boot.

She blinked, and her eyes moved upward. The female Marine to whom the boot was attached stood at parade rest by her head, one arm behind her back, plasma gun cocked forward. Eleanora looked around, and discovered another one—this one a grenadier—at her feet. How interesting.

She sat up and rubbed her eyes. It didn't help. She still felt like death warmed over, but at least her brain was a little clearer than before the nap. She looked up at the Marine at her head.

"How long was I out?" She hadn't checked the time at any point in the afternoon, so the current time, halfway through the local evening, told her nothing. Nor did her question communicate very much to the Marine. It came out mostly as a croak, so she cleared her throat and tried again.

"Corporal . . . Bosum, isn't it? How long was I sleep? And, thank you, but guarding me was probably unnecessary."

"Yes, Ma'am." The Marine looked down and smiled. "But His Highness told us to make sure no one bothered you." She thought about the other question. "I don't know how long you were asleep before we got here, but we've been on guard for three hours."

"Five or six, then," was Eleanora's mumbled guess. "I should feel better than this after five hours' sleep," she muttered plaintively.

She stood up, and every joint in her body seemed to creak or pop. Her legs hurt so much that she felt lightheaded and queasy, and she swayed for a moment until the Marine corporal steadied her.

"Take it easy, Ma'am," the plasma gunner said. "You'll get used to it after a few more days."

"Oh, sure," Eleanora said bitterly. "That's easy for you Marines to say. You've got so many nanites running around in you, you're practically cyborgs! And you're trained for this, too."

"But we don't start out that way," the male Marine put in. "They start us off systems-free in Basic."

"He's right," Bosum agreed with nasty cheerfulness. "We all go through this the first few days in Basic. It's just your turn," she added with an evil grin.

O'Casey twisted her torso and gasped as she felt her back crack in half a dozen places. Rotating her shoulders, arms, and legs extracted more crackling, and she decided that with a shower, a bath, another shower, a couple of tubes of heating gel, and two days' sleep, she'd be just fine. Barring that . . .

"Where is His Highness?" she asked, as she glanced around the clearing without seeing either Roger or Pahner, who was bound to be close by the prince.

"I'll lead you to him," the plasma gunner replied, and the male Marine fell in behind as they wove their way across the stockade.

Roger, Pahner, Kosutic, and the senior Mardukans were in a nearby hut, watching the festivities. Roger looked up from feeding the lizard he'd apparently adopted and smiled as Eleanora hobbled in.

"Ms. O'Casey," he said formally. "You're looking better for your nap."

The creature swarmed onto his lap at the chief of staff's approach and hissed at her faintly. His Highness tapped it lightly on the head, and it ducked down and stretched out its neck to sniff at her. Apparently, it decided she was part of the pack, because it gave one last sniff, then twisted around and curled up on the prince's lap, exactly as if it belonged there.

"I feel like death warmed over," she answered. "If I'd known you were going to be taking me on adventure tours, I would have had the appropriate upgrades before we left."

She nodded at Matsugae as he handed her a plastic cup of water and two analgesic tablets.

"Thank you, Kostas." She took the tablets and a sip of the water, which was surprisingly cool. It had obviously been chilled by one of the bladders. "Thank you again."

She looked around the gathering. The Marines were scattered throughout the village, interacting much more fully with the Mardukans than they had been. Some of the humans were cleaning weapons, and some were quite obviously on alert, but most were socializing. Poertena had produced a pack of cards from somewhere and appeared to be teaching some of the younger Mardukan warriors poker while other Marines were demonstrating their entertainment pads or simply talking. Warrant Dobrescu had apparently set up an aid station and was doing a little "hearts and minds" work.

Dobrescu, it turned out, was a pearl beyond price in more ways than one. The chief warrant officer had gone to flight school as a second career track after spending sixteen years as a Marine Raider medic.

Normally, the Navy provided Marine units in combat environments with corpsmen, but the Raiders were the Empire's version of Saint special ops teams. They were designed to be out of contact with support for long periods of time, and thus needed specially trained medics who could do more than slap on a bandage and decide who went into the cryochambers and who didn't. The training was intense, and included everything from primitive methods of reducing gangrenous infection to serving as the hands of a remote surgeon for thoracic trauma surgery.

Since Prince Roger's company had never been intended for detached duty, none of the Powers That Were had ever considered the need to assign it an integral, dedicated medic. Unfortunately, *DeGlopper*'s sickbay attendants had been needed to support the transport's final battle, and somehow not even Eva Kosutic had thought to point out that the company would require medical services on the planet. All of which made it extremely fortunate that Dobrescu was along.

At the moment, he was examining the Mardukans who were willing to let him and doing his best to repair the various wounds and infections that any jungle inflicts on its inhabitants. As in other jungles, both on Earth and other planets, surface lesions were the main complaint. The Mardukans' mucus covering helped in that regard, however, and only in spots where the coating had been damaged did the sores break out.

Dobrescu had analyzed the lesions and determined that they were primarily fungal in nature. A universal antifungal cream seemed to work on them and didn't cause negative side effects. Better yet, the cream was produced by yeast in an auger jelly which could be replaced with sterilized meat broth. That made it one of the few regenerating systems that they had, which meant he could be relatively spendthrift in its use. Since some of the Marines already sported similar infections, that was going to be a good thing.

With the cream and self-sealing bandages, he'd just about fixed all the simple problems in the village. There were a few advanced cases of infection that he was less sanguine about, and a couple of other cases where something was attacking eyesight had him scratching his head. But in general, he'd done good service to the village that day.

"What did I miss?" O'Casey asked as she watched the slight warrant officer packing up his tools. He'd obviously worked through the celebrations that *she* had slept through, and the realization made her even less thrilled with her physical weakness.

"Oh, you would've loved it," Roger admitted in Standard English, scratching the lizard's head. It hissed with pleasure and rubbed its chin on his chest.

"We had a nice little ceremony. Very symbolic of all sorts of things, I'm sure. Cord forswore all previous allegiances in my favor, while I promised not to throw his life away pointlessly. Then we had all sorts of bonding oaths: the usual suspects. Last, but certainly not least, it involved eating a small bit of slime from Cord's back," he finished with a grimace.

Eleanora chuckled and seated herself carefully on the ground with the rest of them. The hut was walled on three sides by bundled branches with mud packed in the cracks between them. There was a rolled up covering for the open front, woven out of some sort of fibrous grass or leaves, and the sleeping areas arranged along the back and sides were also covered with the woven mats, which appeared to be designed to be staked down. It would be an awfully warm way to sleep in the muggy heat.

"I'm sorry I missed it," she said, and meant it. She'd initially taken her third doctorate in anthropology because it was a traditional complement to sociology and political science. But she'd quickly found that one developed a richer and fuller appreciation for the politics of a culture if one looked at its underlying premises, which was what anthropology was all about.

"I don't understand all the fuss." Roger pulled his hair up off his neck. "I can't believe they treat all visitors like this."

"Oh, I'm sure they don't," O'Casey said as her mind gradually cleared of fog. "You do understand the meaning of all this ritual, don't you?"

"I suppose I don't," Roger said. "I don't really understand most rituals, even the ones on Earth."

O'Casey decided that it would be more discreet to avoid agreeing overenthusiastically with him, and took another sip of her warming water while she considered how best to respond.

"Well," she said after a moment, "this was a sort of cross between a wedding and a funeral."

"Huh?" Roger sounded surprised.

"Did Cord maybe take something off or put it on? Or maybe give something to someone?"

"Yeah," Roger said. "They gave him a different cape to replace the one he was carrying. And he gave a spear and a staff to one of the other Mardukans."

"I talked a little to Cord on the way down from the plateau," Eleanora said. "This *asi* thing is a form of slavery or bondage—you realized that?"

"Today I did," Roger said angrily. "That's crazy! The Empire doesn't permit slavery or bondage of any form!"

"But this isn't an imperial world," she pointed out. "We've barely planted the flag, much less started on socialization. On the other hand, I think you misunderstand the situation. First of all, let's take a look at the definition of slavery."

She considered how to go about explaining slavery, marriage, and the similarities between them that had existed for thousands of Earth's years to a man of the thirty-fourth century.

"For most of history—" she began, and saw him glaze over immediately. Roger was always interested in the battles, but get onto the societal structures and faction struggles, and he completely lost interest.

"Listen to me, Roger," she said, meeting his eye. "You just married Cord."

"What?"

"That got your attention, didn't it?" she asked with a laugh. "But you did. And you also took him as your slave. For most of history, the rituals of marriage and slavery were practically identical. In this case, you performed an action that required that you 'marry' the person whom you'd saved."

"Oh, joy," Roger said.

"And you are now required to 'keep' that person, for the rest of his life and into the afterlife, most likely."

"Another mouth to feed," Roger joked.

"This is serious, Roger," his chief of staff admonished, but she couldn't help smiling. "By the same token, Cord must obey your wishes religiously. And to his family, it's as if he's dead. Which is probably the origin of the big festivities at weddings, by the way. In most primitive cultures, there are practically no rituals involved in marriage bindings, but elaborate rituals for funerals. There's a strong theory that the wedding rituals eventually evolve out of the funeral rites because the bride and groom are leaving their families . . . just as would have been the case if they'd died.

"Now, I used the term 'marriage' because I knew it would get your attention," she admitted. "But I could have said 'permanently binding oath of fealty,' 'slavery,' or 'indenture.' The rites and customs for all of them were practically identical in most early human societies, and we've found parallels for that in almost all of the primitive nonhuman societies we've studied. But any way you look at it, it's a very important sacrament for the Mardukans, and I'm really sorry I missed it," she concluded.

"Well, the dance of the forest animals was apparently the climax," Roger told her. He picked up one of the blackened bits of meat and popped it into his mouth, following it up with one for the tame lizard. Her explanation made quite a few little bits which had been confusing him fall into place. He would worry about the ones that hadn't at another time.

"But I'm glad you woke up," he went on. "If you hadn't, I would have had to send someone for you. Cord has just broached an interesting subject."

"Oh?" She picked a leftover bit of fruit off a plate . . . and set it back down hastily when she saw that several of the "seeds" were moving.

"Yes. It seems that his tribe is in need of some advice."

The hut was hot, dark, and close.

The party had gradually broken up, and as people left the square, the front covers of the huts had come down. They were, indeed, designed to be pegged down, and the Mardukans had also laced up the sides. Most of the Marines were packed into the huts, while a few were in tents, but at least the entire company was under cover, and most of its members were asleep.

But in Delkra's hut, the futures of both the company and Cord's tribe were under discussion as Cord explained why the interruption of his vision quest and his departure with Roger constituted such a bitter blow.

"In the days of my father's father's father, traders came up the Greater River to the joining of Our River and the Greater River. Traders had long come upriver, but this group made peace with my father's father's father and took up residence on a hill at the joining. We brought the skins of the *grack* and the *atul-grack*, the juice of the *yaden cuol* and the meat of the *flin*. In my father's day, I was sent to Far Voitan to study the ways of the sword and the spear.

"The traders brought with them new weapons, better metals. Cloths, grains, and wine. The tribe flourished with the wealth that was brought in.

"But since that time, the town has grown greater and greater, and the tribe has become weaker and weaker. During my father's time, we were at our greatest. We were more numerous and more fierce than the Dutak to the north or the Arnat to the south. But as the city has grown, its people have taken more and more of our hunting lands. Starvation has loomed more than once, and our reserves are always scanty."

The shaman paused and looked around, as if trying to avoid an awkward truth.

"My brother has been overgenerous in this celebration. The barleyrice is purchased from the city, Q'Nkok, at great price. And the other foods. . . . There will be hungry mothers in weeks to come.

"The problem is the city. It has extended its fields too far, yet that's hardly the worst of it. Their woodcutters are not to go beyond a certain stream, and even in that stretch where they are permitted, they are only to take certain trees. That is the treaty. For that, we are to be given certain goods—iron spears and knives, cooking pots, cloth. Yet these goods have become of worse and worse quality, while the woodcutters drive deeper and deeper into the forest. They do not restrict themselves to the proper trees, and their intrusion drives out the game or kills what remains."

He looked around again and clapped his hands.

"If we kill the woodcutters, even if they are beyond the line, it breaks the treaty. The Houses of Q'Nkok will gather their forces and attack." He ducked his head in shame. "And we will lose. Our warriors are able, but we would have to defend the town, and we would lose.

"But if we attack Q'Nkok, without warning, we can take it by surprise as the Kranolta took Far Voitan." He looked around the humans, and Roger was forced to recognize that a fierce look was nearly universal. "Then we feed on their hoarded grains, kill the men, enslave the women, and take the goods that are rightfully ours."

"There is, however, a problem with this," Delkra said, and leaned forward as he took over the thread. "We will lose many warriors even if the attack is successful, and then Dutak and Arnat will fall upon us like *flin* on a dead *flar* beast. We didn't know which way to go, so Cord went on a spirit quest in search of a vision of guidance. If he'd seen peace in the future, it would have been peace. If he'd seen war, it would have been war."

"What if he hadn't come back?" Pahner asked. "He nearly didn't."

"War," Delkra replied simply. "I'm in favor of it anyway. Without Cord to hold me back, we would have attacked last year. And, in all honesty, probably have been eaten by Dutak and Arnat."

"Make peace with Dutak and Arnat," Roger said, "and attack in concert."

He felt O'Casey's elbow connect with his ribs and realized what he'd just said. He supposed that advising the local barbarians to cooperate with one another in the destruction of this Q'Nkok would hardly advance the cause of civilization, and he remembered what his chief of staff had said about barbarism and infant mortality rates. On the other hand, *these* "barbarians" were his friends, and he didn't particularly care for either of the possible outcomes Cord had described.

He started to glower at her, then stopped and looked down at his hands, instead. His history teachers—including Eleanora, when she'd been his tutor—had harped incessantly and unpleasantly on a ruler's responsibility to weigh the possible impact of his decisions with exquisite care. He'd never cared for their apparent assumption that he wouldn't have weighed such matters carefully without their pointed prodding. But now he suddenly realized just how easy it was for purely personal considerations to shape a decision without the decider's even realizing it had happened.

He drew a deep breath, decided to keep his mouth shut, and went back to scratching his pet dog-lizard. He'd seen larger specimens around the camp, and if this one grew as large as some of the larger ones, it was going to be interesting. The biggest had been the size of a big German Shepherd, and the species seemed to fulfill the role of dogs in the camp.

Delkra, unaware of the prince's thoughts, clapped his hands in resigned negation.

"The chiefs of both tribes are crafty. They have seen us weaken. They feel that if they just let us wither a bit more, they can take our lands and squabble over the leftovers."

"So how can we help?" Captain Pahner asked. From his tone, Roger decided, it was pretty obvious that he knew at least one way they could help . . . and just as obvious that he was unwilling to do so.

"We don't know," Cord admitted. "But it's obvious from your tools and abilities that you have great knowledge. It was our hope that if we described our quandary to you you might see some solution which has eluded us."

Pahner and Roger turned as one to look at Eleanora.

"Oh great," she said. "Now you want my help."

She thought about what the two Mardukans said. And about city-state politics. And about Machiavelli.

"You have two apparently separate problems," she said after a moment. "One on the receiving side, and one on the giving side. They might be connected, but that's an assumption at this point."

She spoke slowly, almost distantly, as her mind ranged back and forth over the Mardukans' description of events, and she scratched the back of her neck while she thought.

"Have you been actively offered offense in your dealings with the rulers of the city-state?"

"No," Cord answered definitively. "I have been to Q'Nkok twice recently to discuss the problems with the quality of the tribute and the unlawful intrusions of the woodcutters. The King has been very gracious on both occasions. The common people of the city don't like us, nor we them, but the King has been very friendly."

"Is wood-cutting a monopoly?" Eleanora asked. "Does one house cut all the wood? And what are these houses? How many are there, and how are they organized?"

"There are sixteen Great Houses," Cord told her. "Plus the House of the King. There are also many smaller houses. The Great Houses sit on the Royal Council and . . . there are other rights attached to them. No single house has the right to cut wood, and the woodcutters who offend are not from a single house."

"And the tribute? Is it supplied by the Houses or by the King?"

"It is supplied by the King through taxes on the Houses, Greater and Lesser. But it is usually conveyed by one of the Great Houses."

"Expansion of the city-state is inevitable," she said after a moment's thought. "And as long as they need the wood as a resource, they'll encroach farther and farther on your lands. Wars are usually about resources—about economics—at the base. But your concerns are certainly justified.

"I can't know what's going on from here. As I understand it, we're traveling to this Q'Nkok next?" She made it a question and looked at Pahner, who gave a confirming nod and then looked at their hosts.

"I ask that you hold off on any attack until we visit the city," the Marine said. "I ask for two reasons. One is that we need to trade for goods and animals to make our journey; Q'Nkok is the closest and most accessible source of what we need. The second is that we might be able to come up with a third option that would avoid the needless bloodshed of a war. Let us do a reconnaissance of the town, then we'll send back word of what we find. As outsiders, we might be able to discern something that you can't."

Delkra and Cord looked at one another, and then the chief clapped his upper hands in agreement.

"Very well, we won't rush to attack. When you go to the town, I will send some of my sons with you. They'll aid you on the trip and act as messengers." He paused, and looked around at the gathered humans, and his body language was sober. "I hope for all our sakes that you are able to find a third way. My brother is *asi* now, and dead to his family, but it would grieve him if his family were dead in truth."

CHAPTER TWENTY-THREE

The city-state was a larger version of the village of The People and was obviously expanding. The company had followed the river from Cord's village downstream to its junction with a still larger river, and the city sat on a small ridge on the eastern side of the new one. The ridge was near the apex of the confluence of the two streams and more or less covered with structures. A wooden palisade surrounded the intersection, but the palisade was obviously a temporary expedience, and several sections of it had already been replaced with a high stone curtain wall. It was nearing evening as the travelers came to the cleared boundary of the city-state's lands, and the sky over the town was gray with the smoke of the evening's fires.

The jungle ended with knife-sharp abruptness at the border of the city-state's territory. The stream that marked the boundary was the fourth one they'd crossed, but this crossing had significant differences from any of the earlier ones.

On the west side of the stream—the "civilized" side—there were large mounds every few hundred yards. They were surmounted by oddly constructed houses, and more mounds and houses were scattered throughout the valley of fields and orchards. The houses had no lower-floor doorways, and the upper floors extended out to overhang the walls of the lower sections, which were very stoutly constructed. For the life of him, Roger couldn't figure out why they were designed that way, but from their placement, they were clearly intended to defend the fields.

Also scattered along the banks of the irrigation ditches and poor roads were very simple huts. Compared to them, the huts of Cord's village were masterpieces. These were more stacks of barleyrice straw than true dwellings, and Roger was fairly sure they were temporary shelter for the peasants who worked the land. No doubt they were expected to wash away with the regular seasonal floods, for they could certainly be "rebuilt"—if that wasn't too grand a term—easily enough.

The cultivation of barleyrice took up the majority of the several square kilometers of cleared land. Unlike Terran rice, it was dry farming, and Roger thought it might be a tradable grain in the Empire. It was as easy to prepare as rice but had more and better taste, and if it lacked some amino acids, so did rice. Combined with the proper terrestrial foods, it would provide a balanced diet.

It was clear that the single biggest difficulty in cultivating the grain around Q'Nkok wasn't the jungle, but rains and floods. Most of the fields, especially in the lower areas near the river, were surrounded by dikes intended to keep water out, not in. Lifting pumps, like a sort of reverse waterwheel, were everywhere, pulling water out of depressions cut into the corners of the fields. Some were driven by peasants pushing circle wheels, but most were attached to crude windmills.

What was not evident were reasonably sized domestic animals. As they emerged from the jungle, they'd seen a line of what Cord identified as pack beasts entering the distant city, and Roger, along with several of the Marines, had used his helmet to zoom in on the large creatures. They'd been surprised, for the beasts were apparently identical to the *flar* beast which had threatened Cord. When Roger commented on it, Cord had responded with a grunting laugh and indicated that although the pack beasts, which he called *flar-ta*, might look the same as the creature he called *flar-ke,* which Roger had killed, there were huge differences between the two obviously related species.

The peasants who worked the grain were scattered throughout the area, weeding and planting. Some were done for the day and were drifting back to their dwellings, whether those were the temporary huts, the blockhouses near the jungle, or the distant town, when they spotted the travelers' approach and slowed abruptly.

As the humans followed the twisting roads towards the town, the crowd of workers became thicker. Some who'd gone ahead turned and retraced their steps, and others looked up from the fields and began to flow towards the roadside. Pahner had started to get a feel for Mardukan body language, and he didn't care for the hostile looks and gestures thrown their way. Nor did he like the occasional, half-understood insults . . . or the way one or two of them waved agricultural implements.

The hostility seemed to be directed more towards Cord and Delkra's sons than at the humans, although the strangers came in for some heaped abuse, as well, and as the crowd grew larger, its mood got uglier. By the time they neared the city walls, a large mob had gathered, and more people flowed out from inside the walls to join it. Shouts and the local equivalent of catcalls grew louder and bolder, and Pahner recognized a building riot with the Marines as its object.

"Company, pull in. I want a coil perimeter around Roger. Standard riot procedure. Armor to the front, link arms. Second layer, fix bayonets and prepare to repel rioters."

The Marines responded with automatic precision, folding the spread-out formation in which they'd been moving into a circle around the command group. Julian's armored squad moved to the section of road facing the city and passed their weapons back. The ChromSten-clad powered armor was capable of lifting five times its own weight, and no known Mardukan weapon could damage it, so mere weapons would only have been in the way for riot work.

The poorly graded road was about ten meters wide and bordered by high dikes, which allowed the coil formation to block it like a cork. The group at the Marines' back was relatively small—no more than fifty or sixty individuals. For it to join with the larger group spilling from the city, it would have to trample the growing crops to either side of the road. That balked them, since farmers tended to care about such things. A few of them rushed the rear ranks instead, trying to break through, and they went over the line from crowding to attacking. The bayonets protruding over the wall of Marines in the rearmost rank drove them back despite their large size. One Marine was badly injured by a threshing flail that cracked his clavicle, but his companions beat the Mardukans back without being forced to open fire.

At the front, the armored squad stymied the movement of the mob from the city. The newcomers obviously weren't farmers, for they were far more ready to spread out over the fields, but they were also less aggressive than the group at the rear. They threw a few stones, but their main weapon was lumps of fecal matter. The armored Marines quickly learned to dodge the stinking projectiles after one of the first hit Poertena. His sulphurous comments were a clear violation of his orders from the sergeant major, but she forbore to point that out, and some of them were so accidentally accurate it was hilarious.

Unfortunately, the situation was a stalemate. The town-dwellers couldn't get past Julian's squad, but neither could the Marines get past *them* without employing a level of force guaranteed to cause serious Mardukan casualties. Pahner was tempted to do just that as the rain of stones and other matter became denser, but killing or crippling several dozen members of the local citizenry, whatever the provocation, would scarcely endear them to the Q'Nkokans with whom they'd come to trade.

On the other hand, the rioters or protesters or whatever the hell they were were creating sufficient bedlam that whoever was responsible for maintaining what passed for civil order in the city could hardly fail to figure out something was going on outside his front door. Which *ought* to mean that any minute now—

A group of Mardukan guards suddenly emerged from the city. They were the first Mardukans the Marines had seen wearing any clothing, and even Roger recognized it as armor.

The leather armor was worn like a long apron, open at the back, and doubled in critical spots over the chest and at the shoulders. It stretched from shoulder to knee, painted with a complex heraldic device, and each guard also carried a large, round shield with an iron boss.

Their weapons were long clubs, apparently designed for riot work, not swords or spears, and they waded in with abandon. They didn't maintain any sort of formation. Each simply found a rioter to attack and charged, and the mob scattered away from them like pigeons from hawks, running out into the fields and back around the knot of soldiers into the town.

The guards paid no attention to those who ran away, concentrating instead on any who stood and fought or didn't run away fast enough. Those laggards were brutally beaten down with the long, heavy-headed clubs, and the guards seemed to have no compunction about the use of deadly force. Their weapons might not be edged, but when they were done, at least one of the rioters was obviously dead. His head had been split like a melon, but the guards showed no particular concern as they dragged the corpse—and several other inert bodies, most of which were probably simply unconscious—off the road before they gathered back together between the Marines and the city gate.

Cord passed through the cordon of Marines to approach the regrouped guards, trailed by Roger and a couple of nephews. Pahner rolled his eyes as the prince followed the shaman, then signaled Despreaux to take a group with him. She snapped her fingers at Alpha Team, and the six Marines chased after the prince as Cord approached the apparent leader of the group of guards—or the one who had been shouting the most, at least—and nodded.

"I am D'Nal Cord of the Tribe. I come to speak to your king on matters of treaty."

"Yeah, yeah," the guard answered surlily. "We greet you and all that." He looked at the Marines following Cord and snorted. "Where'd you find the *basik*? You could feed a family on one of these!"

At those words, Roger stopped abruptly. It hadn't occurred to him that although the Mardukans were no more cannibalistic than humans, they might not put humans in the same category as "people." He'd intended to make his own announcement along with Cord, but the guard's suggestion made that seem . . . less attractive, somehow.

"I am *asi* to their leader," Cord said definitively. "Thus they are bonded to my tribe and should be accorded the same privileges as The People."

"Oh, I don't know," the guard leader argued. "They seem like regular visitors, so they should fall under trader's rules. Besides, no more than ten of you barbs are permitted in the city at the same time."

"Hey," another guard put in, "let's not be hasty, Banalk! If you consider them traders, does that mean we don't get to eat them after all?"

He meant it as a joke—probably—Roger thought, but Pahner had been monitoring the conversation through a feed off of Sergeant Despreaux and decided that it was time to nip this particular discussion in the bud. He looked around for something relatively useless and found it quickly. The hills that supported the town were igneous basoliths, ancient granite extrusions from a deep magma rift. Their surroundings had slowly worn away until the erosion reached the stony outcrops, but although the refractory granite was much more weather resistant than the soil around, it still tended to crack and fissure over time. That had produced large boulders that congregated at the base of the hill, which the locals had dragged away from the town's wooden palisade when it was erected. One such boulder was no more than a hundred meters from the road, in easy sight of the guards and the few bystanders who'd remained outside the walls.

"Despreaux." Pahner placed a targeting dot on the boulder. "Plasma rifle."

"Roger," the squad leader responded, spotting the dot in her own visor HUD, then waved her arms to get the attention of the arguing group.

"Excuse me," she said in a pleasant soprano. "We think this conversation has gone far enough."

She'd already relayed the targeting dot to Lance Corporal Kane, and now the slight blonde hefted her plasma rifle and triggered a single round.

The plasma bloom left a scorched track through the green corn of the field, but that was nothing compared to what it did to the boulder. It struck with an explosive whipcrack of sound, and the transmitted heat caused diffusive expansion through the meter-and-a-half boulder that shattered it like an egg. Pieces flew in every direction, from head-sized lumps down to relatively fine gravel, some of which reached clear back to the roadway before it pattered to the ground.

As the last echo faded, the last bit of gravel plunked into silence, and Sergeant Nimashet Despreaux, Third Platoon, Bravo Company, turned back to a suddenly frozen and speechless group of guards and smiled.

"We don't care if you treat us as The People or as traders, but they won't find enough to bury of the next one who suggests eating us."

CHAPTER TWENTY-FOUR

The front hall of the king's castle was a vaulted arch in a gate bastion of the outer curtain wall. Unlike most of the city, the king's citadel was built of a combination of the local granite and limestone. The lower portions of the walls were the dark gray of the granite, but they were surmounted by the limestone in a pleasing duotone pattern. Although it was obviously intended for greeting and ceremony as much as for defense, the hall was unornamented aside from the pattern, and it was floored with simple paving stones. The far wall sported large, open windows, which revealed gardens in the bailey and an inner line of defenses.

The local ruler, along with a sizeable bodyguard of his own, greeted Roger's party in this public arena. Their passage uphill through the town had been much more muted than their reception, and Pahner had become increasingly suspicious that the mob scene had been staged.

"Welcome to Q'Nkok." The king, accompanied by a much younger son, greeted them with grave courtesy and glanced at the humans curiously and a bit warily. Pahner smiled behind his flickering visor; clearly, the king had already been apprised of their demonstration at his gates.

"I am Xyia Kan, ruler of this place," the king continued, and gestured to the youth at his side. "This is Xyia Tam, my son and heir."

Roger nodded calmly in response. He had taken off his armor's helmet, both so that his face would be clear and as a gesture of respect. The ruler appeared old. He had the slightly flabby skin and patchy mucus that Roger had noted on Cord, although it was worse in Xyia Kan's case.

"I am Prince Roger Ramius Sergei Alexander Chiang MacClintock, of the House MacClintock, and Heir Tertiary to the Throne of Man," he said formally. "I greet you in the name of the Empire of Man and as the representative of my mother, Empress Alexandra."

He really hoped that the toot was getting these terms right. He was becoming increasingly convinced that the translation software was screwing up something major. Little glitches were appearing in translation left and right and this was too important a meeting to get things wrong.

The "repeat" of his translation which the software played back to him had his mother momentarily as a male, which was a hoot. It had actually formed an image of her as a guy, and she really wasn't all that bad looking. His lips twitched, fighting to smile as he visualized her response to the image, but then, in response to another repeat query, he got an image of himself dressed as a fairy-tale princess, which quashed all humor. This software was definitely buggy as hell.

"We are travelers from a far land who have been stranded in this one," he continued with the story which had been decided upon as easier than trying to explain the truth. "We are passing through your kingdom on our way to a place where we can obtain passage to our home.

"We bring you these gifts," he continued, and turned to O'Casey, who deftly handed him one of the Marine multitools.

"This device can change its form into any of several useful objects," Roger said. It wasn't the sort of thing one commonly gave to a ruler, but they didn't have anything else that was better, and Roger quickly demonstrated the settings to Xyia Kan. The king watched closely, then nodded gravely, accepted the gift, and handed it to his son. The younger Mardukan was no more than a child, judging from what Roger had seen in Cord's village, and looked much more interested in the multitool, but restrained his curiosity admirably.

"Estimable gifts," the king said diplomatically. "I offer you the hospitality of the visitors' quarters of my home." He looked at the line of Marines and clasped his hands together. "You should be able to fit your force in there."

Roger nodded his head again in thanks.

"We appreciate that kindness," he said, and the king nodded in return and gestured to a hovering guard.

"D'Nok Tay will lead you to the quarters, and we shall meet more formally in the morning. For now, take your rest. I will have food and servants sent to your quarters."

"Thank you again," Roger said.

"Until then," the king responded, and walked out of the bastion, trailed by his son. The younger Mardukan, unlike his father, kept looking over his shoulder at the Marines until they were out of sight.

Roger waited until the king was decently gone, and then turned to the guard.

"Lead on."

D'Nok Tay turned without a word and walked out of the far door, but whereas the king had turned to the left on exiting, the guard turned to the right.

They proceeded across an open bailey and up a steep ramp. The ramp ran between the outer curtain wall and the base of the citadel proper, and the fairly narrow way was dark and dank. As they started to ascend it, the skies opened up in another monsoon-quality rainstorm and filled the narrow track with vertical water. The sound of pouring water and flying spray in the slotlike space was like the underside of a waterfall, but D'Nok Tay paid it no more attention than Cord or his nephews, and the humans did their best to emulate the natives. Fortunately, the ramp turned out to be well designed for the storms, and a slight outward slope carried the water to regular openings in the outer wall and thus out of the castle.

The whole town had obviously been designed to take advantage of the regular rains. The main road up which they'd traveled from the city gate had switched back and forth with very little rhyme or reason, but it, too, had been well designed to handle the water. Both sides had been lined with gutters which linked with others to carry the water around to the river side of the hill, where, presumably, it was dumped into the river.

The efficient storm water system also reduced, but did not eliminate, the problem of hygiene in the city. Clearly, the Mardukans had never heard of the concept, for the road had been strewn with feces from the Mardukans and their pack beasts. According to O'Casey, this was normal in lower technology cultures, but at least with the rains the majority would get washed away.

And it certainly explained The People's epithet for the townspeople.

The narrow ramp finally opened out to the level of the curtain wall's battlements, and the company was afforded a spectacular view of the surrounding countryside. The clouds had broken momentarily, the rain had stopped as abruptly as it had begun, and the larger moon, Hanish, was rising over the mountains to the east. They were about a hundred meters above the floodplain, and the valley of Q'Nkok spread out below them in the moonlight. The city was surprisingly dark to humans who were used to the streetlighting found in even small towns on the meanest worlds of the Empire, but the valley was a fairy-tale place under the primary moon.

The river glittered a silver tracery across the plain and the shimmer of water through the fields and irrigation ditches echoed it. The evening fires of farmers dotted the plain here and there, and the coughing roar of some beast from the jungle across the river could be heard even at their height.

Roger paused to take in the vista and found Despreaux beside him. Her squad had never been taken off "close protection," and she was still following him doggedly.

"You can probably drop back into the Company now," he said quietly, and raised one arm of his armor with a smile. "I don't think anything local is coming through this."

"Yes, Sir," she said. "You're probably right, but we haven't been relieved by our CO."

Roger started to open his mouth to object, but decided not to for two reasons. One was that scathing ass-chewing from Captain Pahner about interfering with the chain of command. The other was, frankly, that it was a pretty night and Despreaux was a pretty young woman, and he would be a fool to trade her for a random choice replacement. He looked back over the valley as the company passed, and smiled in the gathering darkness.

"When it's not awful, this can be a pretty place."

Despreaux sensed that the prince wanted more than a simple "yes, Sir; no, Sir," and nodded her head.

"I've seen worse, Your Highness." She thought about one assignment, in particular. The planet Diablo had the highest tectonic instability rating of any inhabited planet in the Empire, with air quality so low children were routinely kept inside until they were old enough to wear a breath pack properly. "Much worse," she said.

Roger nodded, and sensed that the tail of the company was catching up with them in the darkness of the ramp. He didn't want to break the spell, but it was time to move on again.

"We need to get moving, Your Highness," Despreaux said, as if she'd read his mind.

"Right," he said with a sigh. "Time to find out what new joy awaits us."

The "guest quarters" of the castle were odd. To reach them, the company passed through a doglegged tunnel sealed with two gates. At the far end, the tunnel led into a small open area, a bailey, and a single door into the building which was, effectively, a separate keep. The entryway was very low for a Mardukan—low enough that D'Nok Tay had to bend nearly double to lead the way—but about right for the humans.

The building beyond had three levels. There were no interior partitions on the first two levels, and no windows on the lowest one. The second level had small windows and a simple wooden floor that was accessible through a single trapdoor. The third level was also accessed through a single trapdoor, but was separated into six wooden-walled rooms grouped along a common corridor. All six of the rooms had large windows, with wooden shutters to seal them. On the ground floor was a simple latrine kept "flushed" by rainwater from the roof.

Roger stood in the largest of the rooms, looking out over the vista of the valley once again, with his hands on his hips.

"This is the strangest building I've ever seen," he commented to Pahner.

Matsugae had been laying out Roger's bedroll when the company commander entered the room. He looked up at the captain and winked, but Pahner just shook his head.

"Not really, Your Highness. It's a fort designed for visiting dignitaries. We can defend it even if the King turns on us, and he doesn't have to worry about us trying to take over from within. The gates in the tunnel may seal us in, but getting in here without our permission would be hard. For example, that door is offset so that you can't get a good run up with a ram. I'm happy with it."

Roger turned away from the view and looked at the Marine. The captain stood in the pool of shadow cast by the camp light in the corner, and his face was obscured. Not that Roger could have gotten anything from seeing it; except when he was really enraged, Pahner was very hard to read.

"Do you think Xyia Kan would turn on us?" the prince asked. The idea surprised him. The Q'Nkok monarch had seemed friendly enough to him.

"I didn't think there was a toombie onboard the *DeGlopper*, Your Highness," Pahner said bitterly, and Roger nodded.

"What are we going to do about it?" he asked reasonably.

"Get our stuff traded, get the supplies we need, and get out of town as fast as possible, Your Highness," Pahner said, and Roger nodded again and clasped his hands behind him.

He started to reply, then stopped himself. O'Casey's little lecture had been perking at the back of his mind, and he decided that now was a good time to start biting his tongue. And he had no *specific* problems with what Pahner had just said, only vague reservations. Until and unless they became more specific, it would be much smarter to just let it ride.

"I suppose we'll see tomorrow," was all he said.

"I'll go see about the arrangements downstairs then, Your Highness," Matsugae said. He'd set up the prince's sleeping area and laid out a fresh uniform.

The sight of the uniform sent a fresh prickle through Roger from the itch down his back, and he felt a sudden overwhelming desire to get out of the armor. The equipment had a cooling unit, so he hadn't suffered from the heat and humidity as much as the rest of the company, but it was still uncomfortable to wear hour after hour.

"I'm going to get out of this damn armor and have a good rubdown with a cleaning cloth," he announced.

"Yes, Your Highness," the captain said, with a faint frown.

"What?" Roger asked, stripping off the uniform.

"Well, Your Highness," the captain said carefully. "You might see about your rifle first."

The officer chuckled and shook his head at the prince's frown. "Just thinking of an old service poem, Your Highness. It ends 'mind you keep your rifle and yourself just so.' "

Roger nodded. "I take your meaning, Captain." He glanced at the weapon and nodded again. "I know better than to go to bed with a fouled weapon; you never know if you'll wake up with a banshee in your tent. I'll take care of that first. But I'm not sure I'll be down for supper. I might just have a ration and go to bed."

"Yes, Sir," Pahner said. "If not tonight, I'll see you in the morning. We should discuss the audience beforehand."

"Agreed. In the morning then."

"Goodnight, Your Highness," Pahner said, and vanished into the shadows.

CHAPTER TWENTY-FIVE

Roger bowed to the king and presented his documentation as a member of the Imperial Family. The piece of paper was in Standard English, utterly unintelligible to the locals, and he had no idea if it was a protocol that they observed. But the king looked it over, and it was certainly impressive enough with its gold lettering and vermillion seals. He handed it back after several moments, and Roger launched into his prepared speech.

"Your Majesty," he said, throwing back his head and interlacing his hands behind him. "We visit you from a distant land. In our land we have come far in the areas of technology, the knowledge of making things, yet we continue to seek more knowledge of all aspects of the world, and that search often takes us upon long journeys. We set out on such a voyage of discovery, but our ship was blown far off course, and we crashed on the eastern shores of this land."

Eleanora O'Casey stood back and watched the prince's performance. The toot seemed to be adequately translating the speech into the clicks and growls of the local dialect. It was impossible to be certain without any reliable native to return the translation, but Roger had tried most of it out on Cord, who had pronounced it fit, so it should be okay. At least so far there'd been none of the laughs or grimaces which were normal signs of a flop.

"The eastern shores are beyond the high mountains," Roger

continued, gesturing out the windows which ringed the throne room. The room was near the pinnacle of the citadel, and had high windows on every side to catch the breezes. It was, for Marduk, remarkably cool and comfortable, with a temperature that couldn't have been much over thirty degrees Standard.

The throne itself was elevated and elaborately carved out of some lustrous wood. The room was paneled in carefully contrasting multihued and grained woods, and each panel was itself a work of art. The panels depicted scenes of everyday Mardukan life, alternating with images of the various gods and demons of the local pantheon. Given the monsters the local wildlife gave the natives as models, the demons were particularly good.

It was a beautiful and obviously expensive display, and, just as clearly, no expense was spared for the security of the king. The walls were lined with guards in the same leather apron armor as the ones who'd escorted the humans to the palace, but this armor was reinforced in strategic spots by plates of bronze. And instead of clubs, these guards carried spears that were nearly three meters long. Those spears were apparently designed not only for stabbing, but also for slashing, given the keen edges of their broad, meter-long heads.

"We traveled over those mountains," Roger was continuing, "for we do not share your form or your desire for damp and heat, and met upon the edge of them with my good friend and companion, D'Nal Cord. He has since guided us to your beautiful kingdom, where it is our desire to trade and prepare for a great journey."

The prince had a deep, rich baritone which had been trained (often over his strenuous objections) as an oratorical instrument, and it seemed the Mardukans responded to oratory in many of the same ways humans did. O'Casey had begun to develop a feel for Mardukan body language, and the speech had so far evoked a positive response. Which was good, because Roger was about to shock them.

"We know little of your lands, but we do know a place where a trading mission from our own land exists. It is a long journey from here, which will take many, many months. And it will take us through the lands of the Kranolta."

The group of Mardukan nobles gathered at the audience began to buzz with conversation, and there were occasional grunting laughs, but the king simply looked grim.

"This is sad news," he said, leaning forward in the throne. His son, sitting on a stool at his feet, on the other hand, looked very excited at the pronouncement. But he was young. "You know that the Kranolta are a vast and fierce tribe?"

"Yes, Your Majesty." Roger nodded gravely. "Nonetheless, we must pass through that region. Far to the northwest lies an ocean we must reach. I have spoken with Cord, and he tells me that most of your trade goes to the south. As you know, the ocean in that direction lies several months' journey further away. We . . . don't have that much time."

"But the Kranolta are fierce and numerous," Xyia Kan's son put in. He glanced at the team of armored Marines, and tapped his half-hand fingers nervously.

Roger had been surprised by the amount of backstage negotiations which had gone on to set up this meeting. Pahner and O'Casey had been up half the night negotiating with the local equivalent of the palace chamberlain about who was going to be allowed into the king's presence.

The problem was the guards.

Pahner wasn't about to let Roger wander into the king's presence without at least a squad of guards. First of all, it wasn't done. A member of the Imperial Family didn't meet with a barbarian king without *some* retainers. But even more to the point, there was no reason at all to trust the monarch, so both protocol and sense dictated having guards in attendance. But the locals were no dummies. It was clear that the town was highly factionalized, and the king had long since mandated specific limits on the number of guards permitted in his presence.

Commoners and merchants weren't allowed to bring guards or weapons of any form into the royal presence. Nor were members of the lesser houses of the city-state. The heads of the Great Houses who made up the town council could each bring up to three guards, but no more than fifteen total as a group. Since the council numbered fifteen, it had become the custom for each counselor to bring a single guard as a token of his status. Which meant that Pahner's insistence that it was impossible for the prince to travel with less than eight guards was a major sticking point.

The number finally settled on was five, and despite the stubbornness with which he'd held out for eight, Pahner had to admit that Roger in armor and Julian with his Bravo Team, also fully armored up, probably had the king's guard outnumbered.

Hell, they probably had all of *Q'Nkok* outnumbered!

"Even with your fierce guardians and your powerful weapons, you will surely be overwhelmed," the king commented now, in apparent agreement with his son.

"Nonetheless," Roger said grimly, "it is to the north we must go. We will try to make peace with the Kranolta." He shook his head and clapped his hands by his waist in an attempt to replicate the Mardukan version of a shrug. "But if they will not have peace, then we will give them war to the knife."

The king clapped his upper arms and grunted in agreement.

"I wish you luck. Well it would be to be rid of the Kranolta. They have never attacked this side of the mountains. Indeed, they have been much weaker in my generation than in my father's. But the mere fear of them keeps many traders from coming up the river. Any aid we can give you will be proffered."

He looked around the throne room and grunted again.

"And speaking of war to the knife, I fear that I know why D'Nal Cord is back so soon." The words were strong, but the intent appeared to be friendly. "Come forward, counselor and brother of my friend Delkra, and tell me what transgression has brought you from your beloved forest hell this time."

Cord strode forward gravely, and raised his hands towards the monarch.

"Xyia Kan, I greet you in the name of The People and the name of my sibling D'Net Delkra. I bring sad tidings of continued cutting beyond the Treeline. Further, much of the last shipments of spears and javelin heads have been of unacceptable quality. I am deeply grieved to inform you that my nephew and apprentice D'Net Deltan was killed when the spear he was using snapped. It was of inferior quality, or he would still be alive."

The shaman stepped forward and carefully withdrew a reversed spearhead from his cloak. He handed it to the king, who examined it with care. On the surface, it appeared to be good iron, but one tap on the arm of the throne revealed the rotten tone of poorly smelted material, and Xyia Kan's expression was grim as he set it down and gestured for Cord to continue.

"This has gone beyond the pale." The shaman clapped his hands emphatically. "There is now a blood debt." He clasped his hands gravely and looked at the floor.

"I am now . . . *asi* to this young prince. I go with him on his quest to reach Far Voitan and the fabled lands beyond. I shall not be here to see the results if this is not resolved quickly and clearly." He looked up again and clacked his teeth in anger. "But, yes, I would think that if the words sent back are once again simple platitudes and promises that it will indeed be war to the knife.

"And the burning of Q'Nkok will rise to the sky to mingle with fallen Voitan's."

CHAPTER TWENTY-SIX

Xyia Kan entered the audience chamber and ascended his throne. The Council had been summoned immediately at his insistence. And, also at his insistence, the single traditional armed retainer of each councilor had been stopped at the chamber door. The only visibly armed Mardukans present were his guards, lining either side of the room, where, at a single gesture from him, they could stop the intrigues that were plaguing him in their tracks forever.

And ensure the end of his dynasty.

Once he was settled, he simply sat and looked at them. Just . . . sat. He let seconds tick by, then a full minute. Two minutes. Even the hardiest of his councilors looked away, confused and perplexed or confused and angry, depending upon their personalities and exactly how much they understood about the stakes for which they played, under the insulting weight of his baleful gaze. He felt the tension singing about him, but he made no move to break it until, finally and somewhat predictably, W'hild Doma burst with fury.

"Xyia Kan, I have a House to manage!" he snapped. "I don't have time for games. What is the meaning of this?"

Since Kan was particularly furious with the W'hild, he almost cracked. He wasn't furious because the house-leader had switched out good weapons in the tribute for bad. Among other things, if that had been done in the House W'hild, the monarch was virtually certain Doma was unaware of it. No, he was furious because Doma, whom he trusted to be both capable and loyal, had let someone sucker his House so thoroughly.

But he managed to not even flinch, simply looked at the fulminating W'hild and stared him down. Doma was hardly the sort to cower, but even his angry eyes finally fell under the unrelenting weight of Xyia Kan's, and the heavy silence returned until, finally, the king relented.

He leaned sideways and spat on the audience chamber floor.

"*Women!*" he snarled. His councilors, already simultaneously uncertain and angry, looked at one another in confusion, and he spat on the floor again.

"Women," he repeated. "All I see before me are stupid women!"

This time, there was no confusion. Fury at the carefully chosen insult overwhelmed any other emotion, and three or four of the councilors actually came to their feet. Fortunately, Xyia Kan had warned his guard captain, and his warriors' spears remained at their sides, but his own hands slammed down on the arms of his chair.

"*Silence!*" The pure venom of his wrath sliced through the shouted posturing of their outrage like a whetted spearhead. "Be seated!"

They sank back into their chairs, and he glowered at them.

"I've had another visit from D'Nal Cord. He will be leaving for good when the humans leave, for he is now *asi* to the human leader."

"Good!" W'hild shot back. "Maybe with Cord gone, Delkra will understand that we cannot control every peasant who sneaks into the forest!"

"*Delkra will have our heads!*" Kan snapped. "It has been Cord restraining his brother all along, you fools! Without him, the X'Intai will roll over us in a day! Either I must have more guards, or I must have command of the household guards in the event of an attack!"

"Never!" P'grid shouted. "If the barbarians attack, however unlikely that is, the Houses will provide for their own defense, as always. It is the duty of the King to protect the town as it is the duty of the House to protect itself. This is as it has always been!"

"In the past, we weren't looking at being overrun by the X'Intai!

And if you think that after having a spearhead break and kill the son of Delkra, the protégé of Cord, that they are *not* going to attack, you are a greater fool than even I believe you can be!"

"Spearheads break," P'grid said with a grunt of laughter. "One less barbarian for you to lose sleep over."

"Especially spearheads like *this*!" the monarch snarled. He whipped out the offending weapon and hurled it at the floor, and it shattered, scattering splinters of iron among the councilors.

"Where did that come from?" Doma demanded sharply. "Not out of the last shipment!"

"Yes, Doma," the king retorted. "Out of the demon-cursed shipment. *Your* demon-cursed shipment. That you were responsible for! I ought to send the X'Intai your head!"

"I am *not* responsible for this!" the councilor shouted. "I shipped only the finest wrought iron spearheads. *I took a loss!*"

"Nevertheless," the king said flatly, "this is what the X'Intai received. And what killed Deltan. So if anyone has anything to say about this, now would be a good time!"

Again there was much glancing around, but none of the eye contact seemed to mean much. And not many of the eyes were willing to meet Kan's. Finally, Kesselotte J'ral clapped his false hands.

"What would you have us say, O King?" he asked. "Would any of us jeopardize this fair city? The city that is our home, as well as yours? What purpose would it serve?"

"Most of you would sell your mothers for a hunk of scrap bronze," the monarch hissed. "Get out of my sight. I doubt that we'll have another council meeting before the X'Intai come over the wall. And woe betide you then, for the gates of this citadel shall be shut against you!"

"—shall be shut against you!"

"Interesting," Pahner said. The video from the nanitter bug was extremely grainy. There was only so much any system can do with a nanometer of visual receiver, but the audio enhancement at the receiving end did a much better job with the sound. "Hmmm. 'It was an August evening and, in snowy garments clad . . .'"

The nanite transmitter resembled, in many respects, a very small insect. It could move itself, not just stay in one place, and this one had jumped from the spearhead Cord had given Xyia Kan to the king's ear. From there, it was party to every conversation the king had, and it had made it evident that the king was either on the level or a very good actor.

"I think he's serious." O'Casey wiped her face with a cloth that came away sopping with sweat. "I can think of a double-blind situation where he might be trying to crack the Great Houses through the threat of Cord's tribe, but I don't believe that's what he's trying for two reasons. First, he sounds *awfully* angry, and I don't think he's that good an actor. And second, even if he was, any attempt like that would be terribly risky. He'd have to have a second force available to act as the cavalry. Where is it?"

It was a particularly hot and muggy day and the room had both windows open to catch the breeze. One of Marduk's gully washers had just finished, and even the skeeters seemed to be sluggish as they struggled through the incredibly humid air.

"He could be collaborating with Cord's enemies," Kosutic suggested, tugging at an earlobe. "The other two tribes. The . . ." She paused to consult her toot and slapped at a bug. Her hand came away red. "Hah!"

"Dutak and Arnat," Roger said offhandedly. He was holding a bit of meat up, trying to teach the dog-lizard simple obedience. "Sit!"

It wasn't working. The dog-lizard measured the distance to the meat, the gravitational forces, and Roger's own reactions, and flashed out like a snake.

"Damn," Kosutic said with a laugh, wiping her hand on the tabletop. "Down another morsel, Your Highness?"

"Yeah," Roger said sourly. The animal was friendly enough, and seemed to be intelligent, but it was completely uninterested in learning tricks. It came when called, but not if too much time elapsed between treats. Although, even when it wasn't called, it followed Roger around most of the time now. When he went to the audience, it had been closed up in one of the smaller rooms and, from reports, none too happy about it. It had two vocalizations: a sort of hissing purr that it made when it was happy, and a battle-roar. The dog-lizard was still young, but its roar was already rather loud.

"You should name it," Kosutic told him. "Call it 'Bullseye.'"

"'Cause it's so accurate at taking bits from my hand?" Roger sounded testy.

"No, because one of these days you're gonna shoot it!"

"If we can get back to business?" Pahner suggested. "Sergeant Major, do you actually find it likely that Xyia Kan is collaborating with the other tribes?"

"Nope. That was more in the nature of brainstorming, Sir. I'm fairly sure that Cord or his brother has some intelligence on those tribes, and we should check that out with Cord. If they do, they'd be bound to know about something that large."

"Agreed." O'Casey said. "Cultures at that level usually know, in a broad sense, what's going on with surrounding tribes. If one of the tribes were preparing for a full-scale assault, it would be known."

"And these people don't seem to have roving mercenaries," Pahner observed. He pulled out his pack of gum and counted the slices, then carefully put it back away in its sealed container. "What's the upside for one of the other Houses?"

"Unknown." O'Casey consulted a pad and snorted. "What I wouldn't give for a copy of *The Prince* right about now! Fortunately, I've got most of it memorized, but we need more information."

"Right." Pahner scratched his chin. "I think we need to bug the Great Houses."

"What pretense could we use?" Kosutic asked. "Why do they let us in?"

"Well," O'Casey mopped her brow again, "we're going to have to buy equipment and supplies anyway. Why don't we send a squad and one of the officers around with a list of bids?"

"That could work." Pahner started to fish out his gum again, and stopped. "We'll just send Julian along."

"Why do we care?" Roger asked. He had, with difficulty, placed a morsel of meat on the dog-lizard's nose. Now he slowly withdrew his hand, planning on stepping back before giving the dog-lizard the word that she could have the choice bit.

The dog-lizard had other ideas. The instant the pressure of his hand on her snout was relieved, she flashed her muzzle in two directions with an intervening "Clop."

"Damn." Roger gave up for the time being and looked up with a shrug. "I mean, why should we care if these barbs beat each other bloody? We just need to get our supplies and get out of the way. Let The People overrun them. Or not."

He looked around at the staring faces, and gave another shrug.

"What? We're not here to save the world; we're here to get off it. Isn't that what you've been telling me, Captain Pahner?"

"We're going to be here for a few days at least, Your Highness," O'Casey pointed out carefully. "We need a fairly stable area to prepare in before we head out."

"And we need the local boss backing us," Kosutic said, without meeting the prince's eye. "Having strong backing is a whole different thing from just having him say 'ain't that nice.' If the King is really backing us, we'll have a much easier time. The troops will have an easier time."

"Correct, Sergeant Major," Pahner said formally. "I strongly recommend, Colonel, that we obtain more intelligence before we fail from either action or inaction."

"Oh, very well," Roger said. "But I hate the thought of staying in one place any longer than necessary." He looked out the window towards the distant jungle. "Maybe Cord and I can see what sort of game there is in the jungle."

"If you do, Your Highness," Pahner said in a painfully expressionless tone, "might I ask that you take a significant force with you. Also, we won't be able to spare the armor. We seriously drained the power systems on the march here; we'll need to pack the gear from here on out."

"And that means we need some of those big pack beasts, Sir," Kosutic said. "And handlers for them."

"And we need local weapons," Pahner agreed. "We have to have the advanced equipment to take the port and for emergencies, but we need to obtain local weaponry and start training with it as soon as possible."

"And all of that will take money and time," O'Casey said. "And *that* will require a stable base."

"I got it." Roger sounded even testier than he'd intended, but the heat and humidity were starting to get to him. "I'll talk to Cord about the training. He's been wanting to teach me the spear already. I'd prefer a sword, though."

"Be hard to make a good sword with this rotten metal they've got." Kosutic looked around as the others regarded her with surprise and shrugged. "It's not a big deal; I know that much about swords. Good ones are made out of fine steel, and I don't see much steel around here."

"We'll have to see what we can find," Pahner said. "Sergeant Major, I want you to get with the platoon sergeants. We don't let the troops out until we get the lay of the land. I'll assign that to you, initially. Move out with a group and get a feel for what we're dealing with and what sorts of trade we can get for our items. And when the troops *do* go out, I want them moving in groups. Understood?"

"Understood, Sir. What are we going to do for pay?"

"Is that a problem?" Roger was surprised. "We're feeding and clothing them, and they are getting paid. We just don't have access to it."

"It will be, eventually, Your Highness," Pahner told him. "The troops will want to buy souvenirs, local food . . ."

"Alcohol," Kosutic grunted.

"That, too," Pahner admitted with a grin. "And that takes pay. We'll need to factor that into our budget."

"Arrgh!" Roger clasped his head in his hands. "I don't care *what* we get for those shovels and lighters. It won't be enough!"

"All the more reason to have a friend at court, Your Highness," Pahner pointed out, then glanced at the others. "I think that wraps it up. I'll pass on the relevant sections to the lieutenants, including the intel pass. Sergeant Major, tomorrow I want you find the local market and check it out. Take a squad and a couple of the headquarters people with you."

"Yes, Sir," Kosutic said. She already had the relevant group in mind.

"Your Highness," Pahner said, "I know you feel cooped up here. But I'd really prefer that you not go hunting in that jungle."

"I understand," Roger sighed. Maybe the heat was sapping him, but he just didn't feel like getting into an argument. "But I can circulate in the city?"

"With sufficient security," Pahner conceded with a thankful nod. "At least a squad and fully armed."

"But not armor," Roger argued.

"Fine," Pahner said with a slight smile, then nodded briskly. "I think we've got us a plan, people."

CHAPTER TWENTY-SEVEN

Lieutenant Gulyas looked elsewhere as Julian dealt with the guards.

"My officer has come upon matters of trade," the sergeant said grandly. "He wishes to speak to the Kl'ke." The Mardukan guard might overtop him by a meter and a half, but a Marine could out hauteur any old barb. "We are expected," he concluded with a slight sniff of derision.

The guard looked down his nose at the diminutive human, but turned and banged on the door.

The House of Kl'ke was of a piece with the other Great Houses the squad had visited. The walls were granite, unlike the wood of the rest of the town, and coated in highly decorated plaster. The walls of the Great Houses were covered in bas-reliefs and decorative arches, and the dominant theme of each House's art was its primary trade. In the case of Kl'ke, the bas-reliefs depicted a variety of forest prey, for the House had been founded on the skin and leather trade. There were no windows on the first floor, and, as in the citadel visitors' quarters, the narrow openings in the second-story walls were more like arrow slits than windows.

As with all the other Houses, the front door was massive—over two stories high and constructed like a castle gate. The heavy wood was a Mardukan equivalent of ironwood that was virtually impervious to fire, and the door was banded and studded with bronze. Knocking it down would require time and a good battering ram.

Set into it, again, was another of those odd doors like the entrance to their visitors' quarters. Low enough to require a Mardukan to duck to enter it, it not only put a visitor's head in position to be opened up like an egg, but also symbolically caused him to bow to the holder of the House.

The lower portal opened to reveal another impassive guard. This worthy waved them in, and they entered one by one. Unlike Mardukans, the humans could walk through standing up.

The interior was similar to a series of concentric Roman villas. The outer wall held inward-facing rooms on all levels, but there was also an "inner" building of wood which was where the majority of the House's business was conducted. The area immediately behind the gate was a vaulted entranceway, with several doors to either side. It was open on the inner side, revealing the gardens that surrounded the inner sanctum.

The guard led them through the gardens and from there into the inner house. This was also open at the center, and surrounded yet another garden. Passing around the edge of this garden, they entered the back of the house, where Gulyas and Julian were separated from their squad of guards and led to a small, high-ceilinged room. The room was open on both sides to let in the air, and the walls were of multiple woods, cunningly crafted to give an impression of rolling waves. It held a high table, behind which the Kl'ke stood making notes in a ledger.

Gulyas had the spiel down pat now and nodded to Julian, who began laying out samples.

"As you know, Sir," the lieutenant began, "we are visitors from a far land. The items that we carry are very few, but of such surpassing workmanship that each is, in itself, a jewel of craftsmanship."

Julian had laid out the chameleon cloth, and now began demonstrating the utility of the multitool. The part that got to the Kl'ke was the same as the one which had so intrigued all the house-leaders: the final "blade" function which cut cleanly and easily through one of the soft iron spearheads.

"There are only a limited number of each of these items, and when they're gone, they're gone. We'll be holding an auction for each of them," the lieutenant continued as Julian demonstrated Eterna-lights and fuelless lighters.

"The auction is to be held in the public square on the fifth of T'Nuh." That was six days from now; time enough for the Houses to conspire to cheat them if they so chose. Of course, the humans would be listening to every word if they did.

"In conclusion," Gulyas said, stepping forward, "let me offer you this lighter. It is useful for starting any type of fire, and is impervious to wind."

The lieutenant demonstrated this time, ensuring that the bug was well and truly planted on the alien. He'd let Julian plant the others, but he wanted to do at least one himself.

"Does the Kl'ke have any questions?"

The Mardukan thumbed the lighter and held it to a piece of the local paper until it flamed. He put the small fire out quickly, and cocked his head at the humans.

"You say 'not many' of these devices," he said, gesturing with the technological artifact. "How many is 'not many'?"

"That hasn't yet been determined," Gulyas admitted. "For the multitools, somewhere between seven and twelve."

"Ah." The house-leader made a Mardukan gesture of agreement. "Not many, indeed. Very well, I shall ensure that a factor is present to bid and has full instructions."

"Thank you, Sir," Gulyas said. "And, of course, most of the money will be coming back to Q'Nkok. We'll be purchasing food, equipment, and pack beasts for our long journey."

"Ah, yes." The Mardukan lord grunted a laugh. "Your quest for fabled Voitan."

"It isn't actually Voitan we seek, Sir," Gulyas corrected tactfully. "But from Voitan there are routes to the northeast. Thus we must pass near Voitan."

"Well, it's still a waste of good transport," the Mardukan said with another grunt. He seemed undisturbed by their probable death. "But I have a full stable of the beasts. The best in the city."

"We'll keep that in mind," the lieutenant said, bowing his way out of the room.

"See that you do," the house-leader snapped as he went back to his ledger.

Roger looked into the distorted mirror and turned his head to the side. The ponytail left hair dangling everywhere, especially in this damp heat. What he really needed was a braid but there was a problem with that. Finally, he took two more leather ties and wrapped the ponytail in the middle and at the bottom. Now if they'd just stay in place, his damned hair would stay out of his face.

The knock on the door was followed by its opening so quickly that the two blended. He spun in place to scorch whoever it was, but paused when he saw that it was Despreaux. Just because he was having a bad hair day didn't mean the sergeant should be blasted.

"What?" Unfortunately, the question came out before he could control his irritated tone. So even *without* meaning to, he managed to sound like a jerk.

"Captain Pahner has called a meeting for 14:30," the sergeant replied blandly.

"Thank you, Sergeant!" the prince snapped, then sighed. "Let me try that again, if you don't mind. Thank you, Sergeant."

"You're welcome, Your Highness," the Marine said as she closed the door.

"Sergeant?" the prince called hesitantly. They were going to be on this planet for a long time, and he might as well bite the bullet on this one.

"Yes, Your Highness?" Despreaux replied, opening the door again.

"Could I have a moment of your time?" Roger asked, quite sweetly.

"Yes, Your Highness?" the sergeant repeated rather more warily as she stepped into the room.

"If you don't mind," Roger said, clearing his throat, "this is somewhat private. Could you close the door?"

Despreaux did, then crossed her arms.

"Yes, Your Highness?" she said for a third time.

"I know you're not a servant," the prince said, fiddling with his hair, "but I have a little problem." He took a deep breath and went on despite the hammerlike look on the sergeant's face. "It's something I can't do for myself: Could you possibly braid my hair for me?"

"There's no reason for them to notice the plant, Sir," Julian said as they walked away from the building.

"So why am I drenched in sweat?" Gulyas asked.

"Because . . . it's hot?" Julian suggested with a smile. "Sir?"

Gulyas smiled at the NCO's quip and stopped to look back at the building.

"What do you think?" he asked quietly. As long as they used Standard, no one was going to be able to know what they were talking about. But it never hurt to be careful.

"Like shooting fish in a barrel, Sir," Julian responded. "Two exits. Complex interior, but not bad. All the guard rooms at the front, servants at the back, family in the middle. If we need to take one, or even two or three, it won't be much of an op." He paused and then continued ruminatively. "Of course, it would use up ammo."

"Not much," Gulyas responded. "Okay, only three more to go. You can plant those; that was too much fun for me."

"Ah, that's nothing, Sir. Did I ever tell you about the time I stole a space limo?"

"You never learned how to braid your own hair?" Despreaux asked. The prince had the best hair she'd ever run across, solid without being too coarse, and long as a Mardukan day. "This is gorgeous stuff."

"Thanks," Roger said calmly. He wasn't about to tell the sergeant how sensuous it felt to have her brushing it. "Just another legacy of illegal gene engineering."

"Really? Are you sure?"

"Oh, yeah," Roger said ruefully. "No question. I've got the twitch muscles of a shark, the reactions of a snake, and *way* more endurance than I ought to have. Somebody on either Mommy or Daddy's side, or both, did a lot of engineering back in the Dagger Years, but I guess anyone who had the cash would have done the same thing then, rules or no rules. I even got enhanced night vision out of it."

"And Lady Godiva's hair. But you'd better learn how to do this yourself."

"I will," Roger promised. "If you'll show me. I've always had *someone* to do it for me, but I think servants are going to be in short supply on Marduk, and Matsugae didn't know how, either."

"I'll show you how. And it can be our little secret."

"Thanks, Despreaux. I really appreciate it. Maybe you can get a medal for it," he added with a laugh.

"The Order of the Golden Braid?"

"Whatever you want. As soon as we get back to Earth, I'm rich again."

"Rich city," Kosutic said.

This was the third bazaar the team had found, and it was of a piece with the others. The majority of the market was permanent, wooden stalls set side-by-side on narrow alleyways. There were also occasional open areas where temporary carts were set up, selling everything imaginable, but most of the trade was in the back alleys.

Kosutic had initially entered those with care. She'd been on enough planets and around enough alleys to know that they contained both the best and the worst available on worlds like this. The Marines had dispensed with armor, and if she gave them the chance, these Mardukans could be a nasty proposition at close quarters. So she was slow. And careful.

As it turned out, the alleys were generally the best part of the market. The small shops were very old and established, and had not only the best items, but better prices. Unfortunately, the products weren't what they wanted.

The region was a supplier of raw material and gems. There was more than sufficient food and leather goods available for their purposes, but what they really needed—pack beasts and weapons—were expensive and hard to find.

She stopped at one of the small booths selling weapons as a sword on its back wall caught her eye. The Mardukan running the booth squatted on a stool, and still overtopped her. Even by Mardukan standards he was a giant, and it appeared that he might not always have been a merchant. His left true-arm ended in a stump at the elbow, and his chest was an Escher painting of scars. Both horns had been capped with bronze points that were wickedly sharp, and a hook depended from the arm stump.

He looked up at what she was staring at, and slapped his hook with his remaining true-hand.

"You know that?" he asked.

"I've seen it before," she said carefully. "Or something similar."

The weapon was unlike the others she'd seen in the bazaar, for the steel was damascene. The black and silver water pattern was clear as day. The blade was long for a human, short for a Mardukan, and curved to a slightly widened end. It was neither precisely a katana nor a scimitar, but something in between.

And it was flat out beautiful.

She'd seen swords of that type on several worlds, but all of them were much more advanced than this one's tech level. Or than the local tech level, at least.

"Where is it from?" she asked.

"Ah," the merchant said, clapping his cross hands. "That's the sad part. This is a relic of Voitan. I have heard of you visitors, you 'humans.' You are from a far land, so do you know the story of Voitan?"

"Some of it," Kosutic admitted. "But why don't you tell it to me from the beginning?"

"Have a seat," the local invited, and reached into a bag to extract a clay jug. "Drink?"

"Don't mind if I do." Kosutic looked over her shoulder at the small group which had been following her around. Besides Koberda's squad, it consisted of Poertena and three of Cord's nephews. "You guys go circulate." They'd each been given an Eterna-light and a lighter. "Do a little trading. See what they bring. I'll be here."

"Do you want someone to stay with you, Sergeant Major?" Sergeant Koberda asked. His tone was mild, but the orders had been fairly strict.

Kosutic raised an eyebrow at the merchant, who grunted in reply.

"No," she said with a headshake. "I'm just gonna sit here and shoot the shit for a while. I'll give a holler when I'm ready to head back, and we can link up."

"Aye." Koberda gestured at his squad; he'd seen a place that looked a lot like a bar a few alleys back. "We'll be circulating."

Poertena followed Denat down the alleyway. He figured that three of Cord's nephews counted as "a group," and the Mardukan swore he knew the best pawn shop in the city.

The shopkeepers and artisans to either side of the narrow way looked up with interest as he passed. Word of the humans' arrival had spread through the grapevine, but he was surprised that there wasn't more overt curiosity. On most human planets, there would at least have been a group of children following him around, but not here. For that matter, he didn't see any children or women, and hadn't since they arrived in the area.

"Where are tee women?" he asked Denat as the Mardukan took another turn. Poertena decided that if they got separated he would be in trouble finding his way back.

"The shit-sitters lock them away," the tribesman said with a grunt of laughter. "And the children. A stupid custom."

"Well, I'm glad you got pocking respect for tee locals," Poertena said with a bark of laughter of his own.

"Pah!" Denat spat and made a derisive hand gesture. "Shit-sitters are for killing. But if we kill one, it's the knife for us, as well."

"Yah." Poertena nodded. "I guess they probably give a fair trial and slit your throat."

"No." Denat stopped for a moment to get his bearings. "The town law doesn't apply to us. If we violate a town law, we're turned over to the tribe. But for a killing, the tribe will give us the knife as quickly as the town. And any townsman found violating our laws is turned over to the town. Just as our tribe judges us more harshly than the town would, the town judges its people very harshly.

"Ah." He'd obviously located the landmark he sought. "This way. It's close now."

"Put why do tee town kill t'eir folk for breaking your laws?" Poertena was confused.

"Because if they don't," Tratan said from behind him, "we'll burn their abortion of a shit-city to the ground."

Denat grunted in laughter but clapped his hands in agreement.

"They dare not offend us too greatly, or we'll attack them. Or camp outside Q'Nkok and pick them off in the open until they don't dare step outside their gates to relieve themselves. But they can also attack us, attack our towns. We had a war soon after this city started to grow, and it was terrible on both sides. So we keep the peace."

"For now," Tratan said with a hiss.

"For now," Denat agreed. "And here we are."

The shop was similar to all the others, if a bit smaller. Made of some hardwood, it was abutted on both sides by other shops and looked to be about five meters deep, but the opening was half covered with a leather curtain that shadowed its interior. Inside, dim shapes of piled skins and containers could be barely discerned, but there were more goods piled outside on a leather ground cover spread out into the narrow alley.

The products were a magpie's nest of gewgaws. There were a few spearheads, some jewelry (ranging from decent to quite bad), tools for wood and metalworking, cups and platters, candle holders of ruddy brass, leather and wood boxes (some elaborately decorated), spice containers, and a myriad of other items piled haphazardly.

Squatting in the midst of this disorder was an old scummy. His right horn was broken at the tip, and the mucous covering his body was patched and dry, but for all that, his eyes were bright and interested.

"Denat!" The merchant got creakily to his feet. "You always bring such interesting things!" he continued, eyeing Poertena.

"Time to do a little trading, Pratol," Denat laughed. "I brought a few things, and my friend here wants to show you some others."

"Of course." The merchant pulled a bottle and some cups out of one of the boxes. "Let's see what you brought. I know you'll cheat me, as you always do, but if you promise not to take too much of my money, perhaps we can bargain!"

"T'at sounds like we goin' to tee cleaners," Poertena observed with a chuckle of his own. It felt like home.

CHAPTER TWENTY-EIGHT

The "tavern" was a large tent, open on all sides and located on one side of the square that defined the beginning of the bazaar. A series of upended barrels at one end served as the bar, and behind the barrels the carcass of some unknown beast turned slowly over a large brazier.

There were several long tables scattered throughout the tent, and the Mardukans gathered at them shoveled in the barleyrice, meat, and vegetables being served with gusto.

The square was a bazaar in its own right, with temporary booths scattered around its periphery. It wasn't a planned opening—simply a space between one of the Great Houses, a warehouse, the bazaar, and a drop off. Two roads led out of it: one down past the warehouse, and the other up past the Great House. The square was also, clearly, a hangout for the guards from the House. They strode around in their leather armor and carrying their broad headed spears as if they owned the area, which in a way, they did. The merchant eyed them warily, and Koberda doubted that they paid for most of their trifles.

The NCO looked up from his heavily spiced stew and waved to Poertena. The armorer had picked up another scummy, this one an old guy, and he looked pleased with himself.

"Hey, Corp," the Pinopan said. The tables everyone else was standing at came nearly to his head, so he found an empty barrel, rolled it over, and upended it to provide himself with a highchair. "Watcha eating?"

"Some *hot* shit," Andras said, taking a pull on his beer and waving at his mouth. "I don't know what they're putting on that damn stew, but it is hot, hot, *hot*."

"Sounds good!" Poertena headed for the bar.

"I made a deal with the guy," Koberda said. "We all eat free for one of those Eterna-lights."

"Ayah!" The new scummy clutched his head. "That I didn't need to hear! I'll go see if I can negotiate being included in it!"

Denat laughed and picked up the jug in the middle of the table. He shook it, took a sip, and grimaced.

"Pah! Shit-sitter piss!"

"Better than that rotgut you served," PFC Ellers said with a laugh. The grenadier took another bite of meat and sipped more beer. "At least you can taste something of the beer."

"Hey," Cranla, the third of Cord's nephews, protested. "We just expect some taste in our drinks."

"Taste, sure," Ellers agreed. "But did you have to add the turpentine?"

Poertena turned back up with a large platter and put it on the table. The table was long, constructed of a thick slab of almost black wood taken from a single trunk. The humans had occupied one end, and the tribesmen gathered around them, snatching at the hot slices of meat on the platter. There were also slices of fruit, and a sliced root the humans didn't recognize. It was good, though—somewhere between a sweet potato and a white potato.

"Smells good," Denat said, popping a piece of the highly spiced meat into his mouth, then choked. "Ayeeeeii! Peruz!" He grabbed for the beer jug as the spice kicked in.

"Pock!" He took a huge gulp of beer and gasped. "Whai-ee! I guess that beer's not so bad after all!" he wheezed.

"Where are you, Koberda?" Kosutic asked over the communicator.

"Ah, my squad is just finishing up lunch, Sergeant Major," the NCO replied, putting down his cards and looking around.

The squad was sprawled around the tables, taking it easy. The heat of the day had been building, and most of the Mardukans had beat it for cooler climates. But it wasn't really all that bad under the tent: no more than 43 Standard, or 110 on the old Fahrenheit scale.

Poertena had started up a poker game. He'd apparently taken the old Mardukan merchant for a ride dickering over a couple of Eterna-lights and lighters. Now the old guy was trying to get his own back . . . in a game he'd never played before.

Koberda picked his cards back up and looked at them in disgust. Poertena had let him exchange some of his imperial credits for a few pieces of the local silver and copper. He knew he should've kept them in his pocket.

"Fold."

Poertena looked over his cards at the old Mardukan. The merchant looked at his cards, then at the pot.

"I raise you," the Mardukan said. He thought about it, then tossed one of the Eterna-lights into the pot. "That should be worth more than that pile."

"Yeah," Poertena agreed with a smile. "Or lunch for twelve."

"Ayah! Don't remind me!" Pratol snapped.

"Pace it," the Pinopan said. "Koberda got taken!"

"Well," the squad leader said, wondering just how much the little Pinopan had squeezed out of the obviously experienced pawnbroker, "somebody did."

Poertena gave his cards another glance and shook his head.

"Fold."

"I like this game!" Pratol gave a couple of grunts and reached out with all four arms to scoop in the pot.

"Yeah, yeah," Poertena said as he dealt the next hand. "Just you wait."

"Hah!" Tratan said suddenly. He had gotten sense and dropped out while he still owned his weapons. "Look at those shit-sitter pussies!"

A group of five armed scummies was passing the eatery. The Mardukans were armed with swords, which they carried in the open, rather than scabbarded. The swords were long, straight, and broad;

they would have been two-handed weapons—at least—for any of the humans.

Unlike other guards the humans had seen, these wore full coverage leather armor, with plate patches on the shoulders and breast. They were obviously guarding the lone unarmored scummy in the middle of their formation, who carried a small leather purse slung on a strap around his neck. Apparently, he had less than total confidence in the stout-looking strap, since he also clutched the purse in both true-hands.

"What's t'at?" Poertena asked. He picked up his cards and stayed very, very calm.

"Gem guards," Pratol replied. He tossed in two for draw.

"Pussies," Tratan repeated. "They think all that fancy leather makes them immortal."

"I wouldn't mind some armor." Koberda picked up the beer jugs and shook them, looking for one that wasn't empty. "If Talbert'd had some armor, she'd still be here."

"Yeah," Poertena agreed as he drew two cards. It was down to three players, and that was too few for a good poker game. Denat was still hanging in, though. He'd traded a couple of nice gems to Pratol for some silver and credit on goods. Now he was trading on some of Tratan's silver and the edge of his credit. Poertena glanced up at him as he looked at his draw, then set his cards down in disgust.

"Fold."

Poertena looked at his own cards and didn't smile. Fortune favored the foolish.

"Raise you." He looked at his pile, and flicked over a tiny lapis lazuli. It was an exquisite royal blue, shot through with lines of raw copper.

"Hmmm." Pratol pushed over a pile of silver and added his own lapis, slightly larger and polished into a large oval. "See you and raise."

Poertena looked at the pile and rolled over a ruby.

"See you an' raise, ag'in."

Pratol tilted his head to the side suspiciously, then pulled out a tiny sapphire like a flick of blue fire, and placed it carefully atop the pile. The blue and red gems were of a piece, dark but translucent. The gems of the region were its greatest treasure, and watching them glow in the center of the table made it abundantly clear why that was true.

Poertena picked up the sapphire and the ruby and put them side-by-side. Then he looked at the rest of the items.

"I t'ink the pot's light," he said.

"Okay." Pratol tossed a few pieces of silver and a small citrine onto the table. "Now it's not."

"Call," Poertena said. "Four sevens."

"Crap!" The merchant slammed down his cards. "I still like this game."

"I'm out," Denat said. "I want to keep my weapons."

"Why, young tribesman?" a new voice asked. "I'd be happy to sell you more."

Kosutic and the merchant she'd stopped to talk with were both smiling as they watched everyone else jump. They'd approached the group so silently that no one had noticed them coming, and Koberda cleared his throat.

"Ah, Sergeant Major, we were just . . . uh . . ."

"Gathering energy for the coming march?" she asked. "Don't sweat it, Koberda. But you need to keep at least one person alert at all times. We're still not out of the woods here. Clear?"

"Clear, Sergeant Major," he said, and then an eyebrow crooked as he noticed the oddity sticking up over her shoulder. "Is that what I think it is?"

"Yep." Kosutic drew the sword over her shoulder. The ripples of silver and black were muted in the overcast gray sunlight, but it was clearly a work of art. "I like it, but I actually got it for the prince. It was designed for the child of a king, so it's human-sized."

"Yeah." Koberda nodded. "I can understand that. But what about other weapons?"

"Alas," the hook-handed merchant replied, "this isn't a good area in which to look for large supplies of weapons or armor. The weapons available here have mostly been made elsewhere. They're from T'Kunzi, or even relics from Voitan, as is this one."

"Folks, meet T'Leen. He used to be a trooper until he lost the arm. Now he sells swords."

"Spears and knives also. Anything with a blade. Mostly to the guards of the gem merchants and the occasional group of mercenaries," T'Leen said, fingering one bronze-capped horn. "Or the House guards, occasionally. There are both independent gem merchants and those of the Houses in the town. Although," he added, "the House merchants sometimes make it . . . hard on the independents."

"Pah!" Pratol said, looking up from his examination of the poker deck. He really liked this game. It was better than knucklebones because it included elements of bargaining and skill as well as luck. Very interesting.

"The Houses are all peopled by bastards!" he went on. "They squeeze us until we're dry, then have their bully boys come around to wreck us so that we leave town!"

"That has, admittedly, happened more often than one would like," T'Leen agreed soberly. "This is a piss-hole of a town."

As if to punctuate his remark, there was a crash of metal across the square.

Two groups, one a cluster of toughs from the local House, and five fighters from a rival, had clashed near the edge of the square. The home team far outnumbered their rivals, but they didn't use their superior numbers to overwhelm the invaders. Indeed, the invaders seemed to be far more proficient as individuals, particularly two who were each using a long dagger or short sword in a lower false-hand. The additional weapon was used almost purely for blocking, and Kosutic wondered why they didn't use something like a small buckler shield. Since the local fighters persisted in taking on their more skilled opponents one-on-one as scummy military tradition appeared to require, they were also taking heavy casualties despite their numerical advantage.

The spears were used somewhat like bayoneted rifles, Kosutic noticed. Their technique emphasized blocking and thrusting, but also parries and ripostes which humans weren't normally taught with bayonets. There was very little contact, but what there was was bloody, for the broad spearheads caused wide and deep wounds.

The injuries being suffered were serious, but clearly not life-threatening. If one of the local fighters felt he was getting ready to lose, he simply withdrew, and someone else took his place.

The rival house's fighters had so far not faced anyone who was their equal, but just as it seemed that the locals were going to lose totally, the doors of the House opened, and a group of guards in heavier armor emerged.

"Ah, now you'll see something," T'Leen said. "The guards from Crita were chosen from among their elite. They came here to see what the new N'Jaa guards are like, and now they will. The newcomers are N'Jaa's elite—they're considered the best in the city."

"Are they?" Kosutic asked.

"Possibly," the weapons merchant snorted. "But that's not saying much. The local bully boys aren't up to any but local standards. They should go collect debts for the House Tan."

The two groups squared off, and the battle began. The local elite was both more heavily armored and unwinded, so it was short and furious. When the two groups parted, two of the Crita fighters were laid out, apparently dead, and so was a N'Jaa. The surviving Crita had beaten a hasty retreat, chased by jeers from their N'Jaa opponents.

"There!" T'Leen said. "Did you see that riposte in *secundus* K'Katal made?"

"I don't even understand what you just said," Kosutic replied, tapping her mastoid bone to get the toot to translate into Standard. "What's *secundus*?"

"Down here." T'Leen gestured with a false-hand. "Great move! I've only seen it once before, in Pa'alot. Very difficult to execute—you have to have your feet positioned just so. But if you perfect it, it's very difficult to defeat." He pantomimed the move and grimaced when the necessary contortion drew a twinge from some scar tissue. "Ouch."

"Where'd you learn all this?" Koberda asked. "I mean, what? Were you a guard?"

"Yes," T'Leen said, abruptly losing the animation he'd drawn from his explanation. "But not for a long time. My fighting days are over."

"He was from Voitan," Kosutic said quietly.

"I was an apprentice weapons maker," the old merchant explained. "I'd traveled with a caravan to T'an K'tass when word came back that the Kranolta had swept down and taken all of the outlying cities. Gone was S'Lenna, shining city of lapis and copper. Gone was fair H'nar, perhaps the most beautiful city I've ever seen in all my travels. Gone were all the other sister cities of far Voitan.

"Voitan held, though. We had word through the few who could trade with the Kranolta without losing their horns. The barbarians attacked her repeatedly, but the walls of Voitan were high, and they not only had great stores of food, but could still trade across the ranges to the cities on the far side.

"T'an K'tass knew the worth of Voitan. No one in all the lands knew the making of weapons as did the Steel Guild of Voitan. No one else knew the secrets of the Water Blade. And Voitan and the region around it were the source of most of the metals that T'an K'tass and the other southern city-states depended upon.

"The Council of T'an K'tass called upon the other cities to send a force against the Kranolta, to drive through to the aid of Voitan. But no such thing had ever been done, and the other cities didn't see the need. They saw only the wealth of Voitan, as the Kranolta had, and laughed at the fall of all that fair land."

His face turned very bitter, and he became quiet, looking back over the years at that memory.

"The King of Pa'alot and the Houses of this stinking Q'Nkok both repudiated us. That was before the House of Xyia arose to the kingship. I will admit that Xyia spoke for us, or so I have heard.

"I was on the delegation from T'an K'tass that went to Pa'alot to plead our case, but they said that each state must survive or fall on its own. They asked what they had gotten from Voitan that they should risk their money and goods, and to that question I could make no answer." He clapped his false-hands in sadness. "I could not answer for my lords of Voitan.

"So T'an K'tass sent out a force by herself. And we met the Kranolta in the Dantar Hills." He clapped his false-hands again, softly. "We were defeated. The Kranolta were as numerous as the stars in the sky, as the trees in the forest! And fierce, fierce!

"We fought through the day and into the next, but we were defeated. Finally, we could fight no more and retreated in good order. But the Kranolta pursued us to T'an K'tass." He clapped his false-hands once more. "They followed us wherever we went."

"And they took that city," Kosutic concluded grimly. "And two others in the area. And that was the last news of Voitan that anyone has heard."

"Some few of us remain," T'Leen said sadly. "A few of the House Tan escaped with the force. They're doing well financially; they got out most of T'an K'tass' specie and went into the banking business. We talk from time to time.

"And there are a few left of Voitan. Such as myself. A few." The Mardukan shook his head. "So very few."

"How long ago was this?" Koberda asked.

"I was a youth," T'Leen admitted. "Long, long ago."

"No seasons," Kosutic pointed out with a shrug. "No sun. They don't count time like we do, and your guess is as good as mine how old any of these guys are."

"Hang on a second," Bosum said, setting down a glass of water. "This is the place we've got to go next?"

"You betcha," Kosutic said with a grim smile. "Or at least the *way* we have to go. Right through them Kra . . . Kra . . ."

"Kranolta," Poertena said helpfully.

"Yeah. Them bastards," Kosutic said with a laugh. "I'd suggest you make sure your plasma rifle's in good shape, Marine."

"Yeah," the newly arrived corporal agreed. "No shit."

CHAPTER TWENTY-NINE

Roger moved the blade across slowly, trying to remember the way the move felt.

"What is that?" Cord asked. The shaman had begun teaching the human his own half-remembered lessons in the sword, but this move had a look he didn't recognize.

"I took a semester of something called '*kendo*' when I was in school," Roger replied, frowning in concentration. His feet were wrong, and he knew it. "But I can't remember the moves!"

He made a small adjustment, but it was still wrong, and he growled inwardly in frustration as the ghost of Roger III and all those generations of MacClintock history fanatics enjoyed a hearty horselaugh at his expense. He'd fought tooth and nail to avoid his *kendo* classes. Officially, he had objected to them because they took time away from his other martial arts classes; in fact, as he'd made certain his mother knew, he had simply refused to embrace their stupid traditions. It had been a petty triumph, perhaps, yet one he had treasured at the time when she finally gave up and let him drop out.

Of course, that had been then, and this was now. . . .

Cord cocked his head and examined the stance. The four arms of the Mardukans meant that many of the methods of the humans, and not just weapons craft alone, were different in detail. But despite both the inevitable differences and the partial nature of what Roger recalled, Cord recognized a more advanced technique when he saw one.

The two had been working out with the sword Kosutic had procured for the past two days while the company rested and the commanders waited for better information. Pahner had joined them from time to time to watch Cord at work, and generally approved. The old scummy had been imparting far more than just weapons instruction; maybe what Roger had truly needed all along was a coach.

"It is always about balance, young prince," the Mardukan said, walking around Roger as the human moved through his *kata*. "You're off your center."

Roger stopped, and the Mardukan looked at his foot placement, then grunted. He tapped one foot with the butt of his spear.

"Try from there," he commanded, and Roger took the steps of the *kata* again, and smiled.

"You did it again, you old sorcerer."

"You need to learn to find your balance better," the Mardukan said, with a clop of teeth. "If you don't have your balance, *everything* is harder. If you have your balance it is not necessarily easy. But it is far easier than otherwise."

He looked up as PFC Kraft entered the salle. The training room was in a part of the castle distant from the visitors' quarters, so there was a squad of Marines outside the door, and the rifleman tapped his helmet to indicate that he'd received a transmission.

"Captain Pahner says he'd like to see you, Your Highness. At your earliest convenience."

Roger opened his mouth to retort angrily at the interruption of his session, then closed it again as Cord laid a hand on his arm.

"We'll be there in a moment," the Mardukan said. "Please send the Captain the Prince's regards."

Kraft nodded and withdrew, and, as the door closed, Cord grunted in laughter.

"Center, young prince. The wise monarch listens to his generals in matters of war, to his ministers in matters of state, and to his people in matters of morality."

"Ha!" Roger laughed. "Where did you hear that one?"

"It was in the writings of the Sage of K'land," the barbarian shaman admitted with a shrug.

"Why in the hell did you go back to the jungle?" Roger asked as he picked up a cleaner cloth to wipe down from the workout. He'd discovered that the shaman was as well read as any sage in the city, one of the reasons Xyia Kan listened to his pronouncements with such care. He was far more than just a "dumb barbarian," and now he clapped his false-hands in a Mardukan shrug.

"I had duties to discharge to my tribe. It needed a shaman; I was the shaman."

"I hope Teltan can fulfill the trust you placed in him."

Roger shook the cloth to clear the majority of the filth it had picked up. The cleaner cloths actively removed dirt and grime from any surface and were easily cleaned for reuse. Unfortunately, they eventually wore out, and soon the company would have to find a substitute, which wouldn't be easy. The Mardukans didn't bathe. They didn't need to, and their mucus coverings would have prevented the use of anything like soaps. They did have some cleaners designed for equipment, but they were unbelievably harsh. It would be an . . . experience to take a bath in them. Rather like lathering up with bathroom cleaner, Roger suspected.

There were many similar problems. Equipment had already started to break down in the oppressive heat and humidity. Several Marines were already without functioning helmets, and two plasma rifles had been deadlined by Poertena. As the journey went on, it would only get worse, and Roger wondered idly what they would look like at the end of the trip. Would they be covered in skins and swinging swords like the one he was putting away? It was an unpleasant thought when he considered that their ultimate objective was a fortified spaceport.

"We all have challenges to face," Cord said, and Roger had a sudden sense that the old Mardukan was responding to much more than the prince's comment about Teltan, as if he could read the other thoughts flowing through his *asi*'s mind.

"It is each man's life to rise or fall to *his* challenges," the shaman went on gently. "Thus are we judged."

* * *

The command group sat on pillows on the floor of the room which had been designated as the headquarters. It was the first time since they'd left the shuttles that they'd all been gathered in a single place, and Roger gave a silent snort as he thought about what one grenade in the room would do. However, the only grenades were in the hands of the Marines, and they, so far, were supporting the chain of command. Or Pahner, at least.

The captain stood at the end of the room at parade rest as Lieutenant Jasco, the last member of the command group, came in and grabbed a seat. Pahner waited to be certain all of them had their pads out, then cleared his throat.

"Lieutenant Gulyas and Sergeant Julian have finished analyzing the take from their listening devices, and they're prepared to report on just what we're facing here. Lieutenant Gulyas has suggested that Julian present the data. Julian?" he concluded, glancing at the noncom who'd been trying to stay inconspicuous in the corner.

The normally irrepressible sergeant was clearly ill at ease as he got to his feet and took Pahner's place, looked around the room at the assembled officers, and activated his own pad.

"Ladies and gentlemen," he began, glancing at Cord, squatting behind Roger, "this report has been developed from several sources besides our monitoring devices. However, *all* sources clearly point to one conclusion: we're in a snake-pit.

"There are several factions in this town, most of them working at one or another plot, and mostly to cross purposes. If any of the locals, including the King, have any idea of just how many of these plots and counterplots there truly are, I would be very surprised.

"The single plot that's of particular interest to us, however, is the one which focuses on the issue of woodcutting, and why the woodcutters continue to violate treaty provisions, despite repeated threats from Cord's tribe." He looked at Lieutenant Gulyas as if in question, but the officer only nodded and made a "go on" gesture with one hand.

"As it happens," Julian said, turning back to the rest of his audience, "the Lieutenant and I see a clear opportunity in this situation for us. What we need is to. . . ."

"Would you mind explaining that to me again?" the king said carefully.

Cutting through protocol to arrange the meeting, especially quickly, had been difficult. In the end, the "guest list" had come down to Xyia Kan, Roger, O'Casey, Pahner, H'Nall Grak, the commander of the king's guards (and the only one in the room with a visible weapon), and Sergeant Julian. The choice for the final human member had been between Julian or the intelligence lieutenant, but Gulyas had recommended that they take the NCO. It turned out that most of the plan had been Julian's from the first.

"You're in what we call *rok-toi*, Your Majesty," he responded now. "That's a complicated and nasty food in our . . . land . . . that smells to high heaven.

"There are three Houses involved in a complex plot against your House. They've been sending the woodcutters and hunters, managed through intermediaries, into the woods to stir up The People. They've also switched out the high-quality goods in the last two shipments for those of lesser quality, also to enrage Cord's people.

"At the same time, they've been resisting your calls for increased defense, because they plan on taking over the town, using a group of Kranolta."

"That's the part I'm afraid I don't understand," the king admitted. "Not even the C'Rtena could be stupid enough to believe they could control the Kranolta inside the city walls! Could they?"

"Frankly, Your Majesty," O'Casey replied, "that's exactly what they believe. The group of Kranolta they've hired is fairly small, only a few hundred, and most of them will be fighting The People outside the walls. But they've been promised that after the fighting they can sack portions of the city: specifically, the bazaars where the independent tradesmen are based. The conspirators are of the opinion that they can limit the depredations of the Kranolta to the bazaars and the lesser houses. Perhaps one or two of the great Houses who aren't part of their plot. But any damage to those groups would only leave them in a better position at the end."

"They're mad!" Grak snarled. The scarred old soldier grunted in grim humor at the thought. "If the Kranolta leave one stone standing on another, it will only be so that there's something left for the rest of their tribe to pick over!"

"Well, yes and no," Julian said. "Our . . . information includes data on the Kranolta which is apparently new. It appears Voitan did fall, finally, but the Kranolta were significantly reduced in number in the process. The tribe remains smaller than it was, and it's more or less stagnated since the fall of Voitan." The intel NCO shrugged. "Of course, even granting all of that, I still think the correlation of forces is adverse."

Grak translated the translation and laughed again. "Adverse. Yes. And what do they think we shall be doing, hmmm? When they let the Kranolta in through the gates?"

"What they think, General," Pahner answered, "is that most of you will be dead. The Royal Guard is responsible for the defense of the city, and you'll spend yourselves fighting The People. Then the Kranolta will come in, wipe out the remnants of both forces, destroy the competitor minor Houses, and sack the independents in the bazaars. The King, who enjoys support among both groups, will be left without either a support base or a guard. He may keep the castle, but it's more likely he'll be deposed by the remaining guards."

"I'm fascinated to hear this," the king said. "But I would be even more fascinated to know where *you* heard it."

The humans had discussed how to answer that question when it inevitably arose, and had come to the conclusion that there was no good response. Pahner had originally wanted to avoid telling the locals anything which might reveal their intelligence-gathering capabilities or, even more importantly, limitations. Then there'd been the ticklish point that admitting that they'd spied on the Great Houses—and how—would probably start the king wondering whether or not they'd spied on *him*.

It was O'Casey, backed by Kosutic, who'd put forth the counter-argument. By imperial standards, Q'Nkok and its monarch were primitive, but that certainly didn't mean Xyia Kan was unsophisticated. The likelihood that they'd spied upon him was going to occur to him whatever they said, so there was little point trying to hide the fact that they could. On the other hand, the king's confidence in them required that they at least make an attempt to convince him that they could gather otherwise unobtainable information reliably, and Julian faced the monarch squarely.

"Your Majesty," he said, "the information was gathered through what we would call 'technical means.'"

The king considered the sergeant's toot's translation effort for a moment, then grunted.

"'The way of pumps'? What in the Nine Halls of Kratchu does *that* mean?"

"I'm afraid our translations aren't quite up to explaining that, Your Majesty," Roger told him, and Pahner hid a smile at his unwontedly diplomatic tone. "Your irrigation systems and their pumps require the services of highly skilled mechanics, so the device which translates for us chose that term to substitute for one of our language's terms which refers to something which also requires great skill and long training. With all respect, you've seen our multitools and other devices. Could your artisans duplicate them? Or explain to another how they function?"

"No." The king didn't appear excessively pleased at making the concession, but he made it promptly.

"That's because *our* artisans have learned things yours have not yet discovered, Your Majesty," O'Casey stepped in, once again wearing her diplomat's hat. "And those same artisans have constructed devices which may be used to . . . observe and listen unobtrusively at a distance."

"You have mechanical *spies*?" The king glanced around the meeting room with a suddenly speculative expression, then returned to his attention to O'Casey.

"Ah, yes. That is to say, in a manner of speaking—"

"That must be a marvelous advantage . . . assuming that it's true. And that your description of what they've reported to you is accurate."

"You're wise to consider whether or not we might have motives of our own to deceive you, Your Majesty," Pahner said calmly. "But would it be possible, now that we've brought this information together for you, for you to confirm it by other means without allowing any of your enemies to realize you have?"

The king thought about that for a moment, and looked at Grak. The old soldier fluttered his hands, and then, finally, clapped them in agreement and turned to the humans himself.

"Yes," he answered.

"And if we do confirm it, the method by which you obtained it will be beside the point," the king told Pahner. "The question is, what shall we do about it if your reports prove accurate?"

"Actually," Pahner replied with a grim smile, "that's the easy part, Your Majesty."

"We kill them all," Julian said.

"And let the gods sort them out." Grak snorted. "Yes, I've heard that one. But how? Three Houses against the Royal Guard is still a . . . What was that term you used?"

"'An adverse correlation of forces,'" the sergeant answered. "Actually, you'd be at just about at parity, with the advantage of a single unified command against a bunch of conspirators who don't trust anybody—including each other—as far as they can throw them. Of course, they've been planning this for quite a while, so at best, you'd have about a fifty-fifty chance of kicking their butts. However, Your Majesty, General Grak, there's an intersection of needs here. We need equipment, supplies, and transportation across this continent. Frankly, we need funding."

"And *you* need a force to crack this conspiracy," O'Casey cut in, smoothly maintaining the double-team approach. "Our company can supply that force. We'll break the conspiracy, uncover all the evidence you need to prove the conspirators' intent to bring in the Kranolta, point out the other Houses that were aware of the woodcutting part of the plot, and force concessions from all of them in your favor. In return, we'll retain a portion of the seizure and fines, and you'll lend your weight to the filling of our needs so that we obtain the quality of goods and services we need."

"Mutual benefit, indeed," the king murmured. He rubbed his horns. "If, of course, there is such a conspiracy."

"There is," Pahner said. "But confirm it, by all means. Please. In the meantime, we'd like to begin cross-training our people in local weaponry with your guard. That will make a good cover for getting integrated with them.

"But we would greatly appreciate it if you could make your inquiries quickly, Your Majesty. We've discovered that we have a particular need to strike before the auction we've arranged for our goods. It turns out that the Great Houses have also conspired to fix the bidding," the captain finished sourly.

"Yes, they would." Xyia Kan gave a grunting chuckle. "Have no fear. I shall make inquiries quickly, and if they are, in fact, conspiring to release the Kranolta upon the city, then we shall act even more quickly."

"But beyond this," Roger said, "there's still the problem of wood. The crisis which the conspirators are busy exploiting isn't entirely artificial."

Pahner was a highly trained, superbly disciplined professional. Which explained why he didn't wheel around to glare at the prince. Roger had done quite well in helping to explain why they couldn't explain how their "mechanical spies" worked, but that contribution to the meeting had been discussed and agreed upon ahead of time. Given his rank among the human visitors, it had been all but imperative to put the weight of his princely status behind that explanation, and the fact that he had a flair for the local language had also been a factor.

No one, however, had suggested that His Highness had anything else to add. Certainly no one had *discussed* anything else he might contribute, which meant that whatever he was up to now was going to be ad-lib. So the captain gritted his teeth and reminded himself that he couldn't rip his royal charge's head off. At least, not in front of outsiders. All he could do was pray that whatever harebrained idea the young idiot was going to concoct this time wouldn't queer the deal just when things had been going so satisfactorily.

"No," Xyia Kan agreed with a hiss of dissatisfaction. "It isn't artificial. If it were, they wouldn't be able to use it so effectively. We must have a new source of wood if Q'Nkok is to survive, but we've exhausted our supply in the area the X'Intai permit us to cut, and the Kranolta hold the other side of the river. Woodcutters who cross to their side of the river do not return. Some solution to this must be found, for it would be pointless to stop the conspiracy and *still* have the X'Intai attack."

"As I understand it," Roger said, nodding in agreement, "besides building, the majority of the wood cut for Q'Nkok is used for cooking and metalworking. Mostly as charcoal. Is that right?"

"Yes," Grak answered. "The majority is used in cooking fires."

"For which coal would work just as well, wouldn't it?" Roger asked, tugging on his braid.

"Coal?" Xyia Kan produced a Mardukan frown. "Perhaps. It's used in some other cities, at any rate. But there's no coal source anywhere nearby."

"Actually," Roger said with a grin, "there's one on the other side of The People's territory. Just upriver from Cord's village, in the mountains. In fact, I saw indications of several unmined minerals up there, and just down the mountain from the coal, at Cord's village, the river becomes navigable."

"So the coal could be packed to the village on *flar-ta*," the king said with a pensive expression, "then transferred to boats for the trip to the city. But I've heard of this valley. It is filled with *yaden*. Who would be so foolish as to go there to dig mines?"

"Well," Roger said with a thin, cold smile, "I was thinking that you might *start* with the members of the deposed families and their guards."

This time Pahner did glance at the prince—not in irritation, but in surprise. He hadn't heard that particular tone of voice from Roger before, and he suspected that the ruthless side the prince had just revealed would have surprised any of his old acquaintances. His tone wasn't cruel, just very, very cold, and the captain suddenly realized that when the kid had delivered that suggestion he'd looked a good bit like his umpteenth-something grandmother, Miranda I. She'd been famous for a certain lack of pity where enemies were concerned.

Of course, such things could be taken too far, but it also might be the first symptom of a spine.

Now if only it could be moderated into decency.

The king, on the other hand, only grunted in laughter and glanced at his general before he looked back at Roger with a handclap of agreement.

"An elegant solution, young prince. You would make an excellent monarch someday. I've noticed that if you have only one problem, it is often insoluble, but that if you have many problems, they solve each other. We have a conspiracy to break, a need to fulfill, and hands to fulfill it. Excellent."

"In order to pull all of this together, we need some of my officers," Pahner said. "And we need to get down to planning quickly."

"Agreed," the king replied. "But we don't move until I've confirmed this."

"As you say, Your Majesty," Roger replied for the group. "We exist but to serve," he finished sardonically.

On the way back to their quarters, Roger found himself nearly alone with Captain Pahner. He glanced around to ensure that no one besides Marines were in the area, then sighed.

"At least Mom doesn't have to put up with conspiracies like this," he said. "I'd hate to deal with backstabbing bastards like N'Jaa and Kesselotte all day long."

Pahner stopped as abruptly as if he'd just taken a round from a bead rifle and stared at the prince, who continued for another step and a half before he realized the Marine was no longer beside him. He turned to the captain.

"What? What did I say this time?" He could tell he'd upset the officer, but for the life of him, he didn't have a clue how.

Pahner felt breathless. For a moment, he could only shake his head, speechless at the naïveté of the statement while he tried to figure out if the prince was trying to feel him out or if the young idiot really was that blind. He finally decided that it could be either, as impossible as that seemed. Which meant the truth was the best answer.

"You—" He stopped himself just before he called the prince an idiot and cleared his throat.

"Your Highness," he continued then, in a calm and deadly voice, "your Lady Mother deals with plots ten times as Byzantine as this every day of the week, and twice on Sunday. And she comes up with, I guaran-damn-tee you, better answers than this one. *She* would figure out a way to have all the Houses continue under current leadership on a completely different political track, and I wish to hell that we could do the same.

"However hard we try not to, we *are* going to kill innocents with this 'bigger-hammer' approach, and that doesn't make me a bit happy. Unfortunately, none of us are as smart as the Empress, so we'll just have to muddle through and hope she manages to survive all the crap headed her way while we're trying to get home!"

Roger stared at him, eyes wide, and the Marine snorted bitterly. Whatever the prince might think, Pahner knew only too well just how false the surface serenity of the Empire of Man was, for he'd had access to intelligence reports very few mere captains would ever see.

"You think I'm exaggerating, Your Majesty?" he demanded. "Well I'm not, so for God's sake wake up and smell the coffee! You think, perhaps, that all of us are here on sunny Marduk because we *want* to be? You think that *DeGlopper* just happened to have a few minor technical problems which had nothing at all to do with your presence? *Somebody* slipped a toombie onto your goddamned ship and marooned us on this God forsaken planet, and I guarantee you it wasn't N'Jaa!"

CHAPTER THIRTY

Julian looked around the rainy midnight square.

His armor's light-enhancement system made the details as clear as day . . . not that there was a great deal to see at the moment. The tavern had been taken down, and the food vendors had packed up for the evening. Which was normal. The city always more or less rolled up its streets at dusk, but this was still eerie. No people at all were moving on the streets, and the shutters on every house had been closed almost before the square emptied. Clearly, the common folk knew something was going down.

It had taken barely a day for the king to confirm the broad details of the humans' intelligence. The clincher had been a scouting foray by some of the city's few skilled woodsmen, who'd found the Kranolta force awaiting word to move on the city exactly where the humans had told them to look. That had been more than sufficient for the king to give his go-ahead.

The Council had been summoned once again, this time at night. Its members were currently at dinner, or so said the latest situation report. Now all three platoons were in position and ready to move.

Julian's own squad of armor had been spread throughout the company. Since the chameleon suits were going to be effectively useless against the low-speed impacts of swords and spears, Captain Pahner wanted the virtually impregnable armor on point for the entry. Which was why Julian found himself standing in front of the door to House N'Jaa, scanning the surroundings, checking his paltry power levels, and wondering if there was something that could penetrate ChromSten armor on this planet after all.

"Teams check in," the communicator said. Lieutenant Sawato had that remote, robotic tone down cold; she sounded like a bad AI answering machine.

"N'Jaa team in position," Sergeant Jin announced. Third Platoon had gotten N'Jaa, since it was the largest and toughest House. Lucky them. They might be the more experienced platoon, but they were also short a squad.

"Kesselotte team, in position," came the next check, and Julian wondered if the Old Man were listening. God knew that very shortly he was going to be busy enough his own self.

"C'Rtena team, in position." Lieutenant Jasco's response was late, and Julian called up the remote plot on his helmet HUD and grimaced. The remote reported that C'Rtena's backdoor still didn't have anyone covering it, but just as he thought that, the last few troopers got into position.

Each mansion, unbeknownst to its inhabitants, now had two-thirds of a platoon parked outside its front door under cover. Even worse, two troopers in powered armor were poised to lead the entry, with the rest of the force in support. In Julian's case, the backup was across the square, ready to jump off instantly when the word came. The unit had moved up in nearly complete silence, which, coupled with the chameleon systems of their uniforms and armor, made it extremely unlikely that anyone had even noticed their passage, despite the narrow, twisting streets.

The third squad of each platoon was on the backdoor of that platoon's objective, ready to plug the bolt-hole, and each detachment was also accompanied by a squad of Royal Guards. The remainder of the armored suits were at the castle, ready to move as reinforcements if they were needed.

Which they shouldn't be.

"All right," the XO said finally. "All the pieces are in position, and the dinner is underway. All teams: *Execute.*"

Julian drew a deep breath. He shouldn't be nervous; there ought to be zero danger in this for him. And worrying didn't help matters, anyway. It was time to do the deal, and he raised a hand and knocked on the door, hard.

K'Luss By paused just as he was about to throw the knucklebones. He'd heard that there was some new game going around, one that used pieces of paper, but he was a traditionalist. Knucklebones had been good enough for his father, and they were good enough for him.

"Who the hell is that?" he asked rhetorically, looking around at the other guards in the front room, and T'Sell Cob clapped his false hands and shrugged, then picked up his favored ax as the door boomed again.

"I don't know. But he's about to be in pieces."

"*Open in the name of King Xyia Kan!*" a voice boomed through the hallway.

"Ah," By said as he picked up his own spear, "maybe we ought to wait for the others to join us?"

It had always bothered Julian that there was no way to fidget effectively in armor. He wanted to pick at a finger, or bite fingernails. Nope. Pull hair? Nope. The best he could do was to fiddle with his bead cannon as the sensors indicated more and more guards gathering in the front area. A loud boom suddenly racketed through the night like a rogue thunderclap, and his sensors processed the sonics and electromagnetic flux and then announced that a full powered charge from a plasma cannon had just struck something at the facility the HUD designated "House C'Rtena."

Nice to know the sensors were working.

He nodded at PFC Stickles and stepped to the side of the vast door.

"Gunny, I'd say we've got about max participation here," he said, keying his helmet to darken. It was supposed to do that automatically, but it never hurt to make sure. Regrowing eyeballs would suck on this rock. "Stickles, darken your helmet."

"Yes, Sergeant," the PFC shot back just a tad testily. "Already done."

He was the junior guy in the squad, which was why Julian had picked him as his own backup. Better that Julian be stuck with the rookie, although, to be fair, a "rookie" in the Regiment was hardly the same thing as a rookie in a regular unit.

"We're ready here, Gunny," Julian said, and leaned into the wall and pointed his bead-cannon to the vertical as he took it off safe. Time to party.

"What was that?" N'Jaa Ide demanded. The booming echo was similar to thunder, but not identical. "It sounded like one of the weapons of these visitors, these humans," the house-leader went on with an ill-pleased glare.

Mardukan state dinners, in Q'Nkok, at least, were conducted on platters and covers on the floor. This one was no exception, and by careful manipulation of the seating arrangements, the human guests had been placed opposite the house-leaders considered particularly dangerous. And, just coincidentally, all of those humans were accompanied by Marines in armor.

"What was what?" Xyia Kan asked innocently. The monarch's power had been systematically hamstrung and undercut by the Houses for a generation, the very Houses which were about to be removed, and his dinner had been deliciously flavored with anticipation all evening.

"That noise," Kesselotte said in support of N'Jaa, sounding even more suspicious than his fellow house-leader. After the last acrimonious meeting, he'd insisted on bringing his full complement of guards to this one. Indeed, there were over twenty house guards present, far more than should have been allowed into the king's presence. Perhaps it was time to act. Sometimes even the deepest plots were improved by a willingness to take advantage of opportunities, and one such as this was unlikely to come again. He glanced at N'Jaa to see if the other leader was in agreement, but saw only worry.

Kesselotte was still considering the significance of the human weapon when two more booms echoed across the city. They were just as loud as the first one, and his eyes flew wide as other strange crackling noises followed them.

"Brothers!" He leapt to his feet. "It is an attack by the faithless Xyia Kan! We must—"

Before he could finish the sentence, two of the human leaders came to their own feet and drew weapons.

Pahner had been infuriated by Roger's insistence, but in the end, he could only accede to his demands. At least this time the prince had made them in private! So when the captain stood and drew his bead pistol, Roger stood up right alongside him. O'Casey, at least, had the intelligence to scuttle behind the armored trooper at her back, then out the door.

Each of the Houses involved in "The Woodcutters Plot" had brought its maximum of three guards. In addition, two other Houses which were fully aware of that plot and were involved in others of their own against the king, had brought their maximum, as well. It was up to the humans to ensure that none of those extra guards did anything unpleasant.

Two of Xyia Kan's bodyguards picked the king up and interposed their armored bulk between him and danger as the humans opened fire. Since each guest's guards were placed to watch his back, and since the prince and the captain been seated facing the plot leaders, all their targets were lined up in a neat, formal row down the opposite wall.

It was Hell's shooting gallery.

Armand Pahner had been shooting one weapon or another for the better part of his seventy-two years. The M-9 bead pistol was an old and dear friend, so as he began servicing targets, his hand moved as steadily as a metronome. The small bead pistols had tremendous recoil, which meant the maximum rate of accurate fire depended primarily on how fast the shooter could get the weapon back on target. Armand Pahner had plenty of bulk and plenty of forearm strength, so in the first four seconds, eight guards were slammed back against the far wall, staining the pale wood with huge splashes of blood before they slumped to the floor.

At which point, it was all over.

Sixteen of the guards had been designated as threats, and it had been decided that the bead-cannon of the armored Marines were a bit too overpowering for an enclosed space . . . particularly since the idea was for all the "lords" to survive. So it was up to the pistol-armed "officers."

Pahner had moved from right to left, concentrating on picking off the guards that were quickest to respond. The first to react were a couple of N'Jaa elite, but before either of them could draw a sword or hurl a javelin, they were both bloodstains. The rest went down nearly as quickly, but by the time he'd cleared "his" zone, the prince's zone was already empty.

He looked at the eight blood splotches, all high on the wall where Roger's assigned targets had stood, then at eight headless bodies, and turned to his charge.

"*Head shots?!*" he demanded incredulously.

Roger shrugged and then smoothed his hair as the house-leaders erupted in consternation, some wailing at the blood that covered everything—the people, the floor, the wall, the ceiling, the food.

"My toot has a *very* good assassin program, Captain," he said.

"Assassin program?" Pahner repeated. "There was no mention of any 'assassin program' in *my* brief, Your Highness!"

"I suppose that's because a secret weapon isn't very effective when it's not a secret," Roger said with a slight smile, then shook his head as the Marine's eyes narrowed. "I didn't mean to sound sarcastic, Captain. I didn't know you hadn't been told, and that's the only reason I can think of for your briefer, presumably Colonel Rutherford, *not* to tell you."

"Um." Pahner glanced at the bodies again. The pistol beads' damage was too extreme to be certain, but it looked as if every one of those shots had been dead center, and it happened that the Imperial Marines in general and The Empress' Own in particular knew quite a lot about combat enhancing toot software.

Pahner had several of the same sorts of packages tucked away in his own toot, for example. And because he was familiar with them, he knew that there were limits in all things. A package like the one the prince was suggesting was basically a shortcut for training, probably with some fairly impressive sight enhancing overlays to boost accuracy. But it was only a *training* device, one which had to have a human interlock if its possessor wasn't going to go around mowing down innocent bystanders in job lots, and no one knew better than a combat veteran how completely training could desert a man the first time it truly dropped into the pot.

That obviously hadn't happened here. Armand Pahner had a very clear notion of the sort of intestinal fortitude required for a combat newbie to stay focused—and confident—enough to take a single head shot, much less *eight* of them, rather than blazing away at center of mass.

"Head shots," he repeated, shaking his head, and the prince shrugged again. "Not even a samadh in your honor."

"Well, I didn't want anybody getting hit by accident," Roger said. "Safety first!"

"Now let's think safe here, okay people?" Gunnery Sergeant Jin admonished as First Squad entered the building. He was in the middle, watching everyone else's actions as the squad's troopers executed their dynamic entry. The most dangerous part of an entry like this was friendly fire. They had overwhelming firepower and good technique, but it was just as easy as ever to be shot by your own side.

He kept a careful eye on the squad's weapons. Each member had a zone to cover, including straight up, and the team leaders and Despreaux were ensuring that everyone covered his own area and not some random other.

"Julian," the gunny said over the com, scanning the upper stories as they came into the gardens around the inner house, "we're in the open. Be careful where you shoot."

The rounds from the powered armor's bead-cannons would go through the flimsy wooden walls as if they were tissue. There was plenty of evidence that the armored troopers had already been through; the swath of destruction looked like one of those pack beasts had gone on a rampage.

"No problem," Julian replied. "We're not firing much anymore. Most of them are being driven to the back. Make sure Third Squad is ready for them."

"Movement!" Liszez announced. "Balcony."

Jin saw two or three weapons twitch in that direction, then settle down on their own sectors, as he looked up. A single Mardukan, probably panicked by the fire, was running down the balcony to the right. It looked like one of the small females.

"Check fire. No threat."

"Check," Liszez responded. If the target had been clearly hostile, it would already have been an ink blot pattern. "Clear." She disappeared around a corner.

"Target!" It was Eijken, and the grenadier triggered a round as the Mardukan who'd charged into view drew back his arm to throw a javelin. The forty-millimeter grenade hit just to the left of the native and tossed him sideways like a mangled doll. "Clear."

"Center building clear," Julian reported. "Entering back rooms."

"Don't get too far ahead," Jin told him. He paused and looked around. "Time to split. Despreaux, take Alpha Team into the left wing. I'll take Bravo to the right. Clear front to back."

"Roger," Despreaux acknowledged, and jerked her head at Beckley to lead her team out. "Alpha, echelon left. Move."

The team leader nodded acknowledgment of the order. She'd already spotted a downstairs doorway, and now she spotlighted it with an infrared laser designator.

"Through there. Kane, take the door. Go."

The reconfigured team trotted towards the door with the plasma gunner in the lead. When she was fifteen meters away, the gunner triggered a single round into the heavy wooden door, which disintegrated in a roar of flame.

Kyrou and Beckley performed the primary entry. Kyrou went through and to the right and dropped to a knee. No more than five meters away a scummy was already starting to hurl the spear in his hand. Unfortunately for him, Kyrou reacted from thousands of hours of training, and the spearman was hurled backward by the hypervelocity beads punching into his chest. Another burst cleared a group further down before it could decide whether or not to attack.

"Right clear."

There was a burst from behind the private.

"Left clear," Beckley called. Another burst. "Really clear."

Despreaux set a cracker charge against the door opposite their entry point, and the thin, high expansion-rate charge shattered the simple bolts on the other side and scattered splinters of the door throughout the area.

She blasted the scummy on the other side of the doorway before she realized it was one of the females. Not only were they entirely untrained for combat, but this society sequestered them. This might have been the first time in this one's life that anything more exciting than sex had occurred. And it had been brief.

The sergeant gazed at the pathetic, shredded body, then inhaled sharply and looked around.

"Stairs," she called sharply. "Ground floor clear."

She stepped back out into the hallway, wiping at a line of blood from a flying splinter, and looked around. She pointed down the corridor.

"Kyrou, Kane," she said, then gestured at the stairs. "Beck, Lizzie." The team leader lead the way, and Despreaux followed. She carefully didn't look back at the pitiful shape sprawled in the shadows of the stairs.

Later for that. Later.

CHAPTER THIRTY-ONE

"Clear," Pahner said, nodding his head at the report over the helmet radio. It had nearly killed him to let Lieutenant Sawato take point on managing the company, but he'd had to be at the dinner. And better him on the line than anyone else in the company when that particular bucket of shit hit the rotary air impeller. Except, maybe, Roger. Which still had him floored.

Pahner was not the type to judge anyone by his ability to shoot. He'd known too many consummate bastards who happened to be good combat shooters to do that. But between Roger's surprising ability with weapons and the occasional depths he revealed, the captain was feeling distinctly whipsawed. Ninety percent of the time, he wanted to throttle the spoiled brat, but, lately, there'd been times when he was almost impressed. Almost.

He checked the maps and grunted at the report from Jin.

"Okay, I'll take it up with His Majesty. Make sure you hold the treasury, but don't get involved otherwise."

He looked over to where Xyia Kan was sitting. Most of the blood had been washed off, but the king was still a sight. Bits of dried blood clung to the decorations on his horns and on his face, but he looked up alertly at Pahner's motion.

"Yes? It goes well?"

It had, in fact, gone perfectly in the castle. The ringleaders had been seized, and their crimes had been detailed to the other house-leaders. Those leaders had then been instructed to send orders to their own Houses to stand down their guards on pain of the same sort of assault. Pending the delivery of proof of their crimes, the leaders of N'Jaa, Kesselotte, and C'Rtena had been separated and imprisoned. Those who apparently hadn't had any knowledge of the plot had been released to return to their homes; the others were still being held in the dining room, surrounded by the now rotting blood of the dead guards. The psychological effect was salutary.

"It goes okay," Pahner said. "We took casualties at C'Rtena, which I didn't expect. No one got hurt bad, though, and other than that, we got off clean. But we have fires at C'Rtena and Kesselotte, and the troops need somebody to come put out the flames. And your guards are looting. My people can't get them under control."

"They will," Grak said with a resigned handclap. "How do you stop soldiers from looting?"

Well, you can, for example, kill them until the survivors figure out it's not permitted, Pahner thought with a mental snarl.

"I don't suppose you can," he said aloud, calmly. That shrug-your-shoulders, what-the-hell attitude was the sort of thing he had to ensure didn't happen with Roger, he told himself. There was a fine line between ruthless and evil . . . and another between sloppy and barbaric. At the back of his mind, though, the song called. "I suppose that's what makes the boys get up and shoot."

"I'll send servants to put the fires out," the king said. "And soldiers whose job it will be to make sure they do so," he said pointedly to Grak. "And to *prevent* them from looting. Is that clear?"

"I'll go myself." Grak hoisted his broad-headed spear and grunted in laughter. "Maybe I can pick up a few pretties myself."

After the general left, Pahner found himself alone with the king. Roger had gone to wash, and the various guards had been dismissed. The situation was irregular, but the captain ignored that as he followed the movement and condition of the company on his pad.

The monarch, for his part, watched the human officer. So somber and serious. So precise.

"You see no difference between us and the barbarians of Cord's tribe, do you?" he asked, wondering what answer he would hear.

Pahner looked up at the king, then tapped a command, sending half the reserve to reinforce First Platoon while he considered the remark.

"Well, Sir, I wouldn't say that. Overall, I think it's better to support civilization. Barbarism's just barbarism. At its best, it's pretty awful. At its worst, it's truly awful. Eventually, civilizations have the ability to pull themselves up to a condition which is better for everyone."

"Would you have assisted me if you didn't need supplies for your journey?" the monarch asked, fingering the decorations on his horns and flicking off a bit of dried blood.

"No, Your Majesty," Pahner shook his head, "we wouldn't have. We have a mission: get Roger to the port. If this operation hadn't advanced that, we wouldn't have done it."

"So," the monarch observed with a grunt of laughter. "Your support for civilization isn't so deep as all that."

"Your Majesty," Pahner said, pulling at a stick of gum and carefully unwrapping it. "I have a mission to complete. I will continue trying to perform that mission, whatever it takes. And so will my Marines. That mission has damned little to do with our individual survival and *everything* to do with maintaining a degree of continuity in our political environment." Pahner popped in the gum and smiled grimly. "Your Majesty, that *is* civilization."

Roger watched the Mardukan mahout securing his armor on the giant pack beast. The creature looked very much like the one which had been chasing Cord, but the native insisted they were different. Roger thought Cord was probably right. The Cape buffalo looked very much like the docile water buffalo, and there was no more dangerous beast on Earth. Of course, these looked like giant horned toads, not buffalo. Capetoad. He wondered if he could get the translation system to start substituting the term.

He also wondered, not without some trepidation, if he could

master the local mahouts' skills himself. He'd always had a way with animals, and he'd been in the saddle of his first pony almost literally before he could talk and his first polo pony before he was ten, so it seemed possible. Despite that, he found the elephant-sized *flar-ta* daunting, and he didn't even want to consider how the rest of the company felt about them.

Still, they'd best get over it and learn. They'd been far luckier than they deserved when Portena and Julian turned up with D'Len Pah in tow, and Roger knew it even if the Marines as a whole seemed unaware of their good fortune. Of course, for all their survival training, they were much less accustomed to using animal transport in inhospitable regions than Roger was thanks to his taste for safaris, but the prince had been shocked by Pahner's apparent blithe assumption that they could simply buy their own animals and handle the beasts themselves.

Fortunately, D'Len Pah had made the company a better offer. *Flar-ta* were scarce in Q'Nkok, and even with the king's strong support, the prices being demanded had been astronomical. Just buying the necessary pack beasts would have come close to bankrupting the humans, despite the hefty slice of Xyia Kan's fines and confiscations which had come their way. They certainly wouldn't have had enough left for the other supplies they needed.

But D'Len Pah had turned up in the nick of time. He and his clan were something like a cross between Old Earth's gypsies and professional caravaneers—semi-nomadic freight carriers who owned and managed their own string of *flar-ta*. Roger had been astounded when he arrived at the citadel with Julian and Portena to offer his clan's services to the humans, since no one else in Q'Nkok had wanted to go anywhere near the lunatics who thought they could actually get through to Voitan. But D'Len Pah had gone by the Houses the Marines had taken down to make a personal examination of the wreckage, and he'd also talked to survivors who'd seen the humans' weapons in action. Clearly, he calculated that if anyone could get through and reopen the long-closed (and highly profitable) trading routes through Voitan, Bravo Company was that anyone.

Roger had come to suspect that there were other factors at work, as well. For one thing, he was pretty certain Xiya Kan had strongly "suggested" to D'Len Pah that it would be in his best interests to make the offer. For another, the chief mahout clearly hoped to pick up some of the offworlders' marvelous devices and knowledge for himself. And, finally, the scummy had insisted on receiving two-thirds of his payment up front, before leaving Q'Nkok . . . and extracted a promise that he would not be required to hand it back over if—or when—the humans actually encountered the Kranolta and realized they had no choice but to turn back or die.

For all that, though, D'Len Pah and his clansmen looked like tough customers in their own right. They were well armed, by Mardukan standards, and clearly accustomed to looking after themselves. No doubt they had to be, since their entire families, including women and children, traveled with them. They were likely to prove a worthwhile addition to the humans' forces in a great many ways . . . and whatever else, they would at least keep Pahner from losing a dozen or so of his Marines finding out that driving a *flar-ta* was just a *bit* more complicated than handling an air lorry!

Roger grinned at the thought and looked around as the company made its final preparations to leave. It was early, barely past dawn, and the heat wasn't really on the day yet. It would be soon—turning the humidity up into the customary steam bath—but for now, it seemed relatively cool.

Everyone was checking his personal gear, making sure that it was just right. A strap out of place would make for a sore day, so it made sense to check ahead of time. Weapons were being serviced, and ports sealed against the conditions. They were down another plasma rifle, and the Old Man had indicated that they might have to put them all away in sealable bags. Roger intended to have a few choice words with whoever had approved the weapons for deployment; they'd only been on the planet for a couple of weeks, and the complicated weapons were failing left and right.

He saw the captain coming up the line of pack beasts, checking the gear. Since the *flar-ta* were carrying so many items that were absolutely vital, not to mention valuable, the Marine officer had placed a small explosive charge on each of them . . . and demonstrated the devices to the mahouts. If one of the beasts tried, for whatever reason, to run away with the company's gear it wasn't going to get far.

Pahner hadn't even bothered to mention the tracker planted on each of them.

Nor was that the only "precaution" the human castaways had taken. Somewhat against his own better judgment, Pahner had given in to O'Casey's argument and agreed that the chief of staff could brief both Xyia Kan and D'Net Delkra on the true reason for their visit to Marduk. The captain was unhappy at the thought of telling anyone anything he didn't have to, but he'd had to admit that O'Casey had logic on her side when she pointed out that both The People and Q'Nkok already knew they were effectively shipwrecked. Telling their leaders and rulers how and why couldn't increase the risk that one or both of them might have designs upon them, but—like Pahner's radio listening watch—alerting people with reason to wish them well to the fact that their trail might need covering couldn't hurt.

"Your Highness," the captain said as he reached the pack beast Roger was examining. He looked up at the prince's armor, then back at the prince himself, and smiled. "Try not to get yourself killed, Your Highness."

Roger smiled back and hefted his rifle.

"I'll try, Captain. But it's going to be a long march."

"It will that, Your Highness." Pahner fingered his breast pocket, but decided to forego a stick. "A long march." He raised an eyebrow at the item at Roger's feet. "That looks . . ."

"Fairly full?" Roger hefted the rucksack and swung it into place. "Well, I couldn't let Matsugae carry it all, could I?"

"No, I suppose not," and Pahner said, then looked up as Kosutic caught his eye and made the circular hand motion that signaled everything was in order. In the years they'd been together, he'd never had reason to doubt her, and he didn't this time.

"Well, Your Highness, it looks like it's time," he said, looking up and down the line of pack beasts and the last-minute goings-on. O'Casey, still spouting Machiavellianisms from the top of her pack beast as the king said goodbye. Cord, having a last word with the delegation from The People which had arrived to negotiate the mining arrangements. Julian, making motions of kicking down doors to one of the female privates in First Platoon. Poertena, bickering with one last merchant. But, really, they were ready to go.

"Agreed, Captain," the prince said, looking at the hills across the river and shifting a strap of his bulging pack. The bridge had been lowered to let their caravan cross, now all they had to do was find a way through trackless jungles filled with vicious enemies to a fabled lost city. And from there, on into the true unknown. He looked to the northwest and tied the braid dangling from under his helmet into a knot.

"Time to head upcountry," he said.

CHAPTER THIRTY-TWO

Roger leaned over the big kettle and sniffed.

"Is that what I think it is?"

The company had waged an exhausting battle against nature across the brutal hills. Whatever paths had once existed had been erased over the years, and they were forced to create new ones. Driving a way through the choking undergrowth for the big pack beasts would have been bad enough under any circumstances, but the hills' vicious carnivores had made it nightmarish.

They had lost Sergeant Koberda to the carnivore Cord called an *atul* and the company just called a damnbeast. It was low, fast, and hungry. About two hundred kilos, it had a triangular head filled with sharklike teeth, and a rubbery, mucus-covered skin similar to that of the Mardukans.

A burst of bead fire had torn the beast apart, but not before it had savaged the sergeant. The tough old NCO had held on for a day, riding on one of the *flar-ta*, but he'd finally succumbed. Even the nanites and Doc Dobrescu's Magic Black Bag hadn't been able to heal all the damage, so they'd bagged the popular squad leader and fired him up. Captain Pahner had said a few words, and they'd moved on. Marching upcountry.

Along the way, they'd become accustomed to the constant danger. Roger saw it all around him, and even in himself. Everyone was getting better at reading the jungle, at anticipating the dangers. The Marines on the perimeter now made a game of spotting the killerpillars in the trees, and the ones that were on the path were harvested. The fangs of the horrible worms contained two poisons, both of which were considered valuable by the Mardukans.

The whole company was changing, getting a little wilder, a little wilier. They were learning about "waste not, want not," and that if something is attacking you, it's probably edible itself. Which brought Roger back to the stewpot.

Matsugae smiled, stirred, and shrugged.

"Damnbeast, Your Highness. The one you killed. Clean shot as well, which I appreciated. Not too torn up but well bled by the time I got it."

"I can't believe we're having *damnbeast* for supper," Roger said, and brushed a recalcitrant strand of hair out of his eyes.

"Well, the troops are having damnbeast stew," Matsugae said with another grin. "Just wait until you see what the *officers* are having."

"I still can't believe that was damnbeast," Roger said, leaning back and setting down his fork.

Matsugae had somehow secured not only a large quantity of a really good wine, but a variety of local spices. The troops had seen him at various times throughout Q'Nkok, talking to restaurant and tavern owners, and when the company started out on its journey, he had immediately established himself as a cross between chief cook and caravan-master.

The result was a smoothly functioning caravan. D'Len Pah's mahouts had experience of this sort of thing, and Matsugae hadn't hesitated to pick their brains. It was the mahouts who'd suggested unloading one beast and letting it break trail, for instance, thus lightening the load on the Marines. It was also the mahouts who'd pointed out that it was silly to waste good protein just because it was trying to eat you. And that there was nothing wrong with shooting for the pot.

That last point had nearly caused Pahner to go ballistic. Hunting on the move went against every bit of his training. Modern ground warfare required that troops move through the woods as if they weren't even there, since anything that could be seen could be killed. That a unit was "made out of mist" was a high compliment, and shooting at everything that moved and looked vaguely edible was noisy anathema to his dearest principles.

But in the end he'd been forced to concede that their situation was . . . unusual. After looking at their consumption rates and how far they'd traveled, he'd agreed—not without one last, severe tussle with his military professionalism—that they needed the supplement. Once he'd conceded the point, however, he'd implemented it with his customary thoroughness, and thereafter a member of the company who was a superior marksman was routinely put up front with the point specifically to look for game.

More often than not, and over Pahner's fuming protests, Roger could be found in the same area for the same reason. He usually rode the unencumbered *flar-ta*, like some latter-day raja on an extraterrestrial elephant. It should have been faintly ludicrous, but the elevation and the fact that the pack beast wasn't recognized as a threat by the local wildlife often gave him shots well before the "official" company hunter. And he rarely missed.

This day, the only thing he'd seen on the route hadn't been, to him, food game. The crouching damnbeast would have been invisible to the point until she reached attack distance. Given their increased awareness, and the guns pushed to the front of the formation, the point might have survived the encounter. And, then again, maybe not. The question was moot, however, for Roger had shot the beast while the lance corporal was still seventy meters distant.

Now he picked at a bit of the lightly spiced meat and shook his head.

"This was good! The last time you tried it, it was . . . well . . ."

"Rubbery," Matsugae said with a laugh. "Right?"

"Yes," O'Casey said. The academic was coming to her own terms with this world. She still resented the heat, the humidity, and the bugs, but they all did that, and at least she no longer had to slip and slide in the mud. Instead, she got to ride on one of the great pack beasts, and she thought she might live, after all. She'd felt bad about being "pampered" for a while, but one of the Marines had finally remarked that O'Casey had never volunteered for this, and she'd decided not to worry about it.

She wiped at her brow and drew a breath. The tent was hot and close, but it kept out the bugs and the *yaden*. The latter never seemed to attack when people were up and about, but better safe than sorry. And since the troops had taken to zipping their one-man tents closed at night, they hadn't lost anyone else, even if it did make for hot, fetid sleeping environments.

"But this is actually quite nice," she continued, taking another bite. "It reminds me of a light-tasting beef." Fortunately, it was also leaner than beef. A heavy meal in this climate would be devastating.

"Emu," Lieutenant Jasco said, taking another helping of barleyrice and meat. "It tastes a lot like emu."

"Emu?" Cord repeated. "I don't know what that is." The shaman rolled a ball of barleyrice and popped it into his mouth. He had pulled it from the communal bowl, as was his people's custom. Not for him these bizarre human notions of forks and such!

"Flightless bird," Roger said offhandedly. He pulled a bit of his portion of damnbeast off his plate and fed it to Dogzard, who'd been patiently waiting by his chair. "Originally from the South American pampas. It's distributed all over now. Fairly easy to raise."

"We raised 'em on Larsen," Jasco said nostalgically. "Almost tastes like home. Now, if you'd just chop up the leftovers and put them in a hotdish, I'd have to marry you," he told the valet with a grin, and Matsugae laughed with the others as he poured Roger another glass of wine.

"Sorry, Lieutenant. I already had one spouse. Once was enough."

"How'd you get it so tender?" Kosutic asked. She took a sip of wine and picked up one of the barbecued vegetables. The squashlike plant had been christened yuckini because, unlike zucchini, it had a bitter taste in its uncooked state. However, a combination of one of Matsugae's marinades and cooking over a slow fire resulted in a surprisingly delectable vegetable course. The cooking, or perhaps the marinade, left the slices with a sugary coating somewhat like a honey glaze.

"Ah," Matsugae said with another smile. "That's a chef's secret." He put his finger against his nose and smiled again, then, with a slight bow and a spatter of applause, he let himself out of the tent.

"All right," Pahner said. "I want to make sure everyone is clear on tomorrow's march. Gulyas wants to have a word."

"I've been talking with Cord and his nephews," the lieutenant said, swallowing a bite of barleyrice and clearing his throat with a sip of wine. The vintage was fairly heavy for the conditions, almost like a sherry. But wine was wine. "As everyone knows," he went on, "we're in Kranolta territory. So why haven't we been hit?"

"Yeah." Jasco nodded. "We must have passed right by that group that was waiting to attack Q'Nkok."

"They couldn't have stayed in one place for too long," Cord said. "The strip of flatland along the river is too narrow for good hunting. That's why The People have never taken it for their own."

"Apparently," Gulyas nodded at the shaman, "hunting parties go over there when game is sparse on their side of the river. The Kranolta hunt there also, but only occasionally. For the raiding party to stay there, they had to be broken up."

"Foraging." Kosutic nodded, tugging at an earlobe. "Of course."

"So we might have brushed some of them," Gulyas said. "And, conceivably, they could be on our back trail, catching up fast."

"Do you rate that as likely?" Pahner asked. He and Gulyas had already discussed this, but he wanted the entire group to hear the whole story.

"No, Sir," the lieutenant answered. "At least, not quickly. They'd still be waiting for word from the conspirators in the city. Even if a messenger preceded us, they'd have to assemble before taking us on. Even the Kranolta are going to recognize that we're a serious military threat."

"However," Cord said, scratching at the tent floor with his knife, "that was a raiding party outside its traditional territory. They wouldn't attack unless they had all the warriors necessary to destroy us. Once we enter the home territory of the tribes, they'll attack at every turn. The deeper we enter, the bolder they will become, and the more they will attack."

"So," Pahner said, "we need to begin being extra alert. The tribes don't hunt the hills we just passed through, but they do hunt the lowlands. Whether there's a big force on our back trail or not, we now face the probability of regular attacks. And we haven't the time to teach them the price of an Earthman slain."

"The troops are going to have a problem with that," Kosutic admitted. "I'm worried that they're getting sloppy. We told them to expect regular attacks through the last two weeks in the hills, and no Kranolta materialized: just big nasties. We'll need more than the Lieutenant's read on it for them to take it seriously."

Pahner nodded.

"Get with the chain of command," he told the lieutenants. "Make sure that they, at least, are aware of the likelihood. We need to make sure the troops are as alert as possible. These aren't half made recruits. Remind them of that."

Julian leaned on his rucksack and listened to the quiet of the sleeping camp. The clouds often seemed to break for just a bit after sunset, and tonight was no exception. The smaller moon, Sharma, cast a faint, ruddy light over the scene. Dim as it was, it would have been more than sufficient for his light enhancers, but he'd switched them off. The jungle seemed placid tonight, with hardly any animals stirring. Even the roars and gurgles of the normal night were muted.

That was just as well. He had two more hours as sergeant of the guard, and then he could get some sleep. Tomorrow would be another long march through the jungle, and being stuck as sergeant of the guard meant damned little rest, but for the time being, he could chill out. All the posts were placed, and he'd done a walk-around a half hour ago. Everybody was staying awake and alert, per normal.

He leaned on the rucksack a little harder and sniffed. You could still smell the stew Kostas had cooked up, and Julian shook his head. Who would have thought that the fussy little valet could have become such a tower of strength? Or turn out to be such a good cook? The actual work was done by a couple of the scummy beast drivers, but

Matsugae made sure it was done right and no one was about to complain about the result. The company definitely wasn't starving, although what might happen when they ran out of barleyrice and dried fruits and vegetables was another story. Hopefully, their supply would hold out to the next city-state—

He froze at the tiniest whisper of a scrape somewhere in front of him. The sound had been almost below the level of audibility, but the Marine had unusually sharp hearing. He considered turning on his helmet enhancers, but that scrape had sounded like it was right in front of him, and the helmet would take a second or to come fully online.

He reached up and flicked on the flash clipped to his combat harness.

The low-power red light blinked on instantly . . . and revealed five forms, crawling towards him. The creatures were shaped vaguely like moths, mostly black but with a spotted pattern that turned pale pink in the red light. A score of glittering red eyes gazed back at him, and ten poisoned fangs glistened. . . .

Roger was up, out of the tent, and halfway across the encampment before he realized he'd moved. He looked down, and discovered that he had his rifle in one hand, his bead pistol in the other, and nothing on but a singlet.

The discovery slowed him just long enough for Sergeant Angell to overtake and jerk him to a halt as his tent guards got in front of him.

"At least let us get there first, Sir," the NCO said with a laugh, and handed the prince his combat harness. "And always remember to grab ammo, too. It makes it easier on us."

Roger threw on the harness and resumed his progress more sedately, surrounded by his hovering bodyguards as he crossed to a cluster of troopers gathered in Third Platoon's area. Julian sat on the ground at the center of the small group, cradling a jug of the local wine and shaking his head.

" . . . low-crawling up on me," he said. The normally upbeat NCO was obviously shaken. "No wonder we lost Wilbur."

Roger looked at the shape on the ground while he pulled his hair up into a quick bun. It looked like a giant, six-winged moth, incongruously pinned down with a combat knife, and the area around it was torn up from its death throes.

Warrant Dobrescu ran a sensor over it and tapped the knife. The thing gave a few weak flaps of its wings, and the fangs quivered, but other than that it was quiescent. The warrant officer pulled the knife out and used it to expertly flip the thing over.

"Hmmm," he murmured and raised an eyebrow. "Fascinating."

"What happened, Julian?" Pahner asked. How long the big captain had been standing there nobody knew, but Julian shook his head again and capped the clay jug of wine.

"I was maintaining my post, Sir. I'd checked the posts a half-hour before, and I was just . . . sitting and listening. And I heard a scraping sound. So I turned on my flashlight, and—" He gulped and pointed at the "moth" on the ground. "And five of those things were low-crawling up on me. Just like a fire team."

"I'd say that this is the species that got Wilbur the first night," Dobrescu confirmed. The warrant officer had a Marine shining a white-light flash over his shoulder and was examining the fangs of the still twitching moth with a field-scope. "These are clearly evolved for drawing liquids," he said, and looked up with a black chuckle. "I don't think these are nectar-drinkers, either."

"Okay," Pahner said. "We know the enemy now. Break it up and get back to sleep, people. We've got a long day ahead."

He watched the gaggle break up, the Marines heading back to their shelters and zipping them tight, and then turned to Julian.

"You gonna be okay?"

"Sure, Captain. I'll be fine. I was just shook. They're so . . ."

"Horrible," Dobrescu offered, and looked at Pahner. "What do you want me to do with the specimen?"

"Move it closer to the center of camp. We'll burn it with our garbage in the morning."

"Aye," the warrant officer said. "I wonder if this is a foretaste of things to come?"

* * *

Roger rocked with the movement of the pack beast, his eyes half-closed in the dim morning light. It had taken a while for the camp to get back to sleep, and everyone seemed quiet and subdued.

He watched the point chopping away a large liana. A multitool's monomolecular edge could cut through even the thickest vines like a laser through paper, but the company's point Marines usually tried to move through the brush without cutting. The pack beast immediately behind them would clear the way through most obstructions, so additional clearance would only have been extra effort. Even pack beasts had problems with some of the jungle's lianas, however, so the Marines generally cut a few heavy obstacles.

In this case, Roger's mount lent its strength to the female private who had point today, lifting away the upper section of the liana as the Marine cut through it closer to the ground. While she worked, Roger and the point-guard maintained an overwatch. It was when they stopped like this that Roger always felt the most vulnerable, whether they actually were or not.

Dogzard sat up and stretched from where she'd been sleeping, leaning on Roger's back. She sniffed the air, turned around, and lay back down. Nothing happening, no threats, time to sleep.

Patricia McCoy slung her bead rifle and stepped over the severed base of the liana. She could have cut it a little closer to the ground, but there was no need, since the *flar-ta's* broad, hard pads would pound the stump to splinters as they passed. Besides, she had other things to think about.

McCoy always felt vulnerable with only a mono-machete in her hand, but Pohm was right behind her, guarding her back. And, to give the devil his due, the Prince was pretty good backup, too.

She stepped through a circle of smaller vines and looked around. The ground was getting wetter, and the vegetation even lusher, if that was possible. It looked like they were moving into a marsh, but it was all light brush. The beasts could clear all of this without her assistance.

She took another step . . . and dropped in her tracks, choking on blood, as the javelin appeared in her neck.

★ ★ ★

Roger's eyes widened as the flight of javelins erupted out of the jungle, but he reacted automatically. He kicked one leg over the back of the pack beast, rolled off and away from the javelins' source, twisted in midair with a contortion fit to shame a cat, and landed on his feet. He didn't stay there. Instead, he dropped to his stomach as two-tons of *flar-ta* tail whistled over his head.

The beast's driver was dead, with a javelin through him, and her own sides had been abruptly and impolitely feathered with light, iron-headed spears. She was not, to put it mildly, pleased, and she turned on her tail, snapping at whatever was biting her. But there was no enemy in biting range, so she turned her attention in the direction from which the bites had come. The little creature which had been intermittently riding on her was already pounding in that direction, and she saw movement that shouldn't have been there.

It looked like she'd found her enemy.

Roger scanned the brush for targets as the *flar-ta* gave a roaring bugle. He stayed prone as it charged off in Dogzard's wake and was rewarded with the sight of a scummy, scrambling to get out of the beast's way. There was heavy firing off to his right, from the main body of the company, but he had his own sector to cover.

Another scummy erupted into sight with Dogzard firmly attached to his arm. Roger removed him from view and dispatched the friend who'd been coming to his aid, then checked fire as Marines rushed into view.

It was time to follow his dog.

Pahner took one look at the flight of spears and snapped: "Ambush. Close."

There were two kinds of ambushes in the Marines' lexicon—close and far—and deciding which was which was the responsibility of the unit commander. The ability to tell the difference was one way to separate the schoolbook soldier from the true field tactician.

The difference was crucial because the reactions to each were diametrically opposed. In the case of a long-range ambush, the drilled reaction was for the company to take cover and use fire and maneuver to assault the ambushing force. It was massively more chaotic than that, of course, but that was the overall plan.

In the case of a close-range ambush, however, the doctrine was simply to turn into the ambush and charge. Even with the inevitable mines and booby traps, there was no percentage in taking cover if the enemy had you dead to rights where you were.

Kosutic was already in the brush and accelerating towards the concealed foes. Her bead rifle was on "automatic," and she was firing regular bursts from the hip, laying down a path of destruction to her front, "plowing the road." Again, with no enemy in sight and only ephemeral ghosts on the helmet sensors, there was no point in trying for aimed fire. Laying down massive firepower in the general area of the enemy was the best bet, and the hypervelocity beads chewed through lianas and tree trunks in a spectacular spray of sap, chlorophyll, and muck.

She burst through a curtain of undergrowth and saw a scummy rear up to hurl a spear. One burst spread him across the vegetation, and she spun in place, checking her surroundings. Nothing else was in sight, but that didn't mean anything. She knew she was ahead of the mass of the company; her helmet visor had blue "friendly" icons all over it when she looked behind her, but there weren't any in front of her. They were coming, though. The rest would be here any moment, and the only question was whether to go on or wait for support.

She paused indecisively, then hit the ground as the area to her left erupted in plasma fire. Somebody wasn't checking her helmet sensors.

Nassina Bosum swore as she realized she'd almost torched the sergeant major. She'd paused to lay down covering fire for her team, and the blast had nearly converted the company's top NCO to charcoal. A corner of Bosum's mind told her that Kosutic would have a little something to say to her about that later, but there was no time to worry about that now.

She walked her fire away from the sergeant major, across the line of cover that had produced the javelins, and smiled as a flaming native tumbled into view and was cut down by the bead rifle of her team leader.

The charge exhaustion warning tone sounded insistently, and she ejected the ammo clip and slapped in another. The magazine contained lithium-deuteride pellets and a power source to feed the laser compressors and initiate the fusion reaction that drove the weapon. The system was relatively simple for imperial technology, but to ensure that everything worked properly, the ammunition manufacturer's quality control had to be precise, or the condition of the weapon firing it had to be perfect.

In this instance, neither was the case. The pellet that dropped into the firing chamber was partially contaminated by carbon. The contamination level was low, barely a tenth of one percent of the mass of material, but the results were catastrophic.

When the packet of lithium-deuteride was lased, the carbon reacted chaotically, causing a "flare" in the fusion reaction. The flare, in turn, exceeded the design parameters of the magnetic containment field, but even that would have been survivable under other circumstances. There was a backup containment system, designed specifically to prevent uncontrolled discharge in situations just like this one.

Unfortunately, Marduk's climate had had its way with the capacitor ring managing the critical feature. When the containment spike hit the capacitor, it exploded.

The result was a small nuclear detonation in the lance corporal's hands.

Pahner cursed as the detonation's blast front punched outward through the jungle. Whether it was a string of grenades or a plasma gun hardly mattered. The general roar of combat had already begun to panic the pack beasts; now the explosion accelerated that process, and the hail of javelins continued unabated.

He called for reinforcements to fill in the sudden hole in the line in First Platoon's sector as he followed the Second Platoon squad which had been covering the headquarters section towards the concealing cover from which those javelins came. His helmet HUD was a welter of icons and images, but he'd had years of experience in deciphering them at an almost subconscious level, and the density of the spears and the width of the attack made it clear that they faced a large group of hostiles.

That was when he noticed a single gold icon on one end of the line.

"Roger! Your Highness! Damn it, get to cover! You're not supposed to be leading the damned assault elements!"

The grenade launcher appropriated from the late point-guard wasn't exactly familiar, but his helmet systems managed the conversion easily. Roger replaced the empty box of ammunition and hung the dead Marine's spares over his shoulder. The area had been cleared by the *flar-ta*, which was now headed into the distance, and cleared again by "His Royal Highness."

I really have to have a talk with Pahner about how I keep ending up on my own.

The com net was filled with chatter, and, as usual, it was impossible for him to sort out the conflicting calls. On the other hand, his visor HUD made it clear that he was behind the majority of the Mardukan ambushers and well in the lead of most of the company. He thought about that for just a moment, then smiled and looked down and shook his head as Dogzard trotted up to him.

"Am I crazy, Dogzard? Or just evil?

Kosutic pulled her knife out of the scummy's head and looked around. She was deep in the brush now, and the damned assault elements had bogged up in the middle of the ambush. No matter how many times you told them, no matter how many times they practiced it, the unit always seemed to stop on the objective instead of going *through* the damn thing. Now the surviving scummies and the Marines were inextricably intertwined. It was practically down to hand-to-hand, since to fire in any direction was just as likely to hit a friend as a foe.

She was just about to charge back into the fray when she was assaulted by friendly fire.

Again.

Pahner ducked as the scummy's spear whistled overhead and struck another Marine with a meaty "thunk!" He triggered a single round into the center of mass of the spearman, following the targeting caret of the helmet systems automatically, and looked around. Undergrowth restricted his line of sight, but everywhere he could see the Marines were locked in hand-to-hand combat with the larger Mardukans. He saw one private picked up and hurled away by a native who was nearly three meters tall, and shook his head angrily.

"*Move through the ambush!*" he bellowed over the com, and sprinted forward just as the trees around him started to come apart under the hammer of grenade rounds.

Roger laughed like a child. He'd figured out how to use the helmet systems to aim, and he was dropping grenades to the side of and above all the blue icons. Since the grenades threw out high-velocity shrapnel which, unlike javelins and swords, was stopped by the chameleon suits, theoretically the fire should be doing more damage to the enemy than to the Marines.

Theoretically.

Julian had just discovered that grappling with something with four arms and the size and disposition of a wounded Terran grizzly was a losing proposition. The Mardukan had him in a bear hug, and the knife was inching closer and closer to his throat when the world seemed to explode.

He and the native were thrown sideways into a tree, but the chameleon suit reacted to the strike, hardening to take the damage and puffing to pad the impact point.

The native wasn't so lucky. The explosion of the grenade tore off its head and one shoulder.

Julian stumbled to his feet, favoring his left hand, and looked around for his weapon. He finally found it under a pile of leaves thrown up by the explosion, then tried to get his bearings.

Throughout the ambush site, other Marines were doing much the same thing. Whoever had been firing the grenade launcher had apparently walked the things all the way down the ambush, and there were bruised Marines and dead scummies everywhere.

Pahner saw Julian and walked over to him.

"Sergeant, assemble your squad and sweep this area. Then move out another twenty meters and establish a perimeter." He started to move on, then stopped when Julian didn't start moving. "Sergeant?"

Julian shook his head and took a breath. "Roger, Sir. Will do."

Pahner nodded and moved on down the line, shaking the occasional Marine into coherence or calling for a medic. Most of the injuries were the result of the fighting with the Mardukans, not the grenades from whatever maniac had peppered the fight. Whoever *that* had been was not going to enjoy the ass-chewing he had coming.

As the captain reached the end of the line of impacts, he saw the prince striding towards him, appropriated grenade launcher propped on his hip like a big-game hunter surveying his kill.

"Did it work?" Roger asked with a grin.

Kosutic eeled out of the brush and looked around. The firing had died to nothing, and she'd found no sign of the scummies in the area beyond the ambush. It looked like the company had reacted so quickly that it had gotten every one of its attackers.

She walked over to Captain Pahner and was just opening her mouth when she realized he was rigid and shaking. She'd occasionally seen him perturbed, even angry, but she'd always wondered what he would look like if he was *furious*. Now she knew.

"What happened?" she asked.

"That arrogant, intolerable, insufferable little *snot* was the one with the grenade launcher!" Pahner said tightly.

"Oh," Kosutic said. Then: "Oh. So, was he an idiot or a genius?"

"Idiot," Pahner said, calming just enough to make a rational judgment. "We'd already taken most of the casualties we were going to take. The Mardukans were either going to run away or stay in place as we passed through. Either way, we could have taken them with aimed fire. Now we've got half a dozen broken wrists and cracked ribs, not to mention shrapnel wounds."

"So what now?" Kosutic asked. She had her own opinion of the prince's actions. And she suspected that the captain's might, eventually, moderate.

"Reassemble on the trail." The captain ground his teeth. "Move back to drier ground to make camp, send out parties to recover the pack beasts, and dig in. I think this was the group that was going to hit Q'Nkok, but that doesn't mean that we're out of the woods."

"Nope," Kosutic agreed, looking around at the vegetation flailed by the grenade launcher and the scattered bodies of the Kranolta attackers, "it sure don't."

CHAPTER THIRTY-THREE

Cord examined the blade in the firelight.

The weapon was a Mardukan two-handed sword. At nearly three meters in length, it would have been ridiculously oversized for a human, but its proportions were lean, lethal, and graceful, and its silver-and-black patterning and elaborate engravings reflected red in the flickering light.

"Beautiful craftsmanship," Cord whispered. "Definitely Voitan work."

Much of the pattern was covered in a patina of rust which had been inexpertly scrubbed in places, damaging the very artistry the scrubber had meant to reveal.

"Damned Kranolta," the shaman added.

"Yeah, but it's useless for us," Lieutenant Jasco said, shaking his head. His arm was cradled in a sling with a broken ulna as a result of the ambush. Fortunately, his quick-heal nanites were on the job and he'd be out of it in a day or two, none the worse for wear.

Others hadn't been as lucky.

Captain Pahner appeared out of the darkness. He tossed a short sword or long knife point-first into the ground beside the shaman and nodded to the lieutenant.

"True," he agreed. "But this will work just fine, and most of them were carrying at least one of them." He paused, looking speculatively at Cord, and then cleared his throat. "And a bunch of them were carrying something else, too. Horns that looked . . . sort of familiar."

The shaman clapped his true-hands in agreement with a shiver of disgust.

"The Kranolta take the horns of kills as souvenirs. They prefer the horns of champions, but in fact, any will do. The souvenirs of lesser enemies are made into musical instruments," he added, examining the knife before he tossed it down dismissively. "Well crafted, but it's only a dagger."

"Maybe for you Mardukans," Pahner replied, taking a seat by the fire. "But for us, that's a short sword. Combine it with large shields and a javelin, and I think we'll show you a thing or two."

"You're planning on using the Roman model?" Jasco asked. The need to use local equipment was a foregone conclusion. The ambush they'd just survived had depleted nearly ten percent of their plasma rifle rounds. At that rate, they would be "fired dry" before they made it to the next city-state, and that didn't even consider what had happened to Corporal Bosum. They had to start training on local equipment as soon as it could be obtained, but Q'Nkok, unfortunately, hadn't had sufficient supplies of human-sized weaponry to outfit the company.

Jasco had been arguing in favor of a technique using longer swords and smaller shields: the "Scottish model." He felt that the longer swords would be more effective against the reach of the Mardukans. Of course, against a weapon like the one the shaman was examining, any possible human reach with a sword wouldn't matter.

"I think the Roman model will be easier to learn," Lieutenant Gulyas put in. The Second Platoon leader joined the group gathered around the fire and took a seat as well. He slapped a bug on his neck and shook his head. "Not that it will help worth a damn, if today is any example."

The company had taken heavy casualties, particularly in First and Second Platoons. And while the majority of the deaths were from the spears and swords of the attacking Mardukans, there were numerous minor injuries from the grenades of the prince's bombardment.

Reactions to Roger's actions were mixed. It came down to those who'd been saved by his intervention being in favor of it, and those who'd been injured by it being against. The only undecided were those like Sergeant Julian, who'd been saved while being injured. He said he would make up his mind after the ribs healed.

"We survived it," Pahner said stoically. The company had been devastated by the ambush, and had lost Lieutenant Sawato, a platoon sergeant, and two squad leaders. But that didn't mean the mission was a failure. Or impossible. "We need to move smarter. From now on, we're going to put a squad out front on a three-pronged point. That should spring any ambushes before we get to them."

"It's not doctrine, Sir," Jasco pointed out, fingering his sling. "It won't spring a long-range ambush, and you're effectively offering a squad as a sacrifice instead of one Marine."

The captain shook his head angrily.

"We keep forgetting that the Mardukans are range-limited. Or these Mardukans are, at least—that may change when we finally hit some of them with gunpowder. But as long as we keep flankers out at thrown-weapon range to the front, the Kranolta can't ambush the main body. They don't have the range. So we change the doctrine."

"And pack up the goddamned plasma guns," Gulyas said with a grimace. Bosum's death had been spectacular, and most of the plasma gunners had already unloaded their weapons as a precaution. No one knew what had gone wrong, and no one wanted to be the next person to find out.

"Yeah," Jasco snapped. "No shit."

He was out half a squad and a team leader from the malfunction. Between Koberda's death and the loss of most of the squad's Alpha Team to the plasma rifle malfunction, Gunnery Sergeant Lai had been forced to roll what was left of Second and Third Squads together under the Third Squad leader.

"Well, like the King said in Q'Nkok," Pahner pointed out, "if you have one problem, it's sometimes insoluble. But if you have several, they sometimes solve each other. We took enough casualties that there are spare weapons for all the plasma gunners to switch over to something else. I'll have Poertena and Julian start going over the plasmas in the morning, but in the meantime, we'll limit ourselves to grenades and bead guns."

"As long as the ammo holds out, Sir," Jasco said.

"That too," the company commander admitted with a grim smile. "That too. Which brings this conversation full circle."

Roger knew that doing *kata* while angry was pointless. No matter how many times he tried to find his balance, he could never quite manage it, yet he couldn't stop, either. He spun in the darkness behind his tent, hair windmilling out in a golden halo, away from the eyes of most of the company while he tried to work out his frustration, anger, and fear.

He was shocked by the casualties the company had taken. Despite everything, it had never truly occurred to him that the Marines might be wiped out by this march. Oh, intellectually he'd acknowledged the possibility, but not emotionally. Not at the heart of him. Surely modern troops, armed with Imperial weapons, would be able to slash their way through an enemy armed only with spears and swords or the crudest of firearms.

But that presumed the enemy was unwilling to take casualties. And it also presumed that the Marines could *see* the enemy in time to kill him before he reached such close quarters that all of their advantages in range and firepower were negated. The failure of the automated sensors to detect the attackers before they struck boded ill for the rest of the journey.

Although the tactical sensors were, theoretically, designed to detect a broad range of possible "traces," it was now clear that the software depended heavily on infrared and power source input. If it had a possible contact, but the contact was "anomalous," it filtered by infrared tracing and power emissions, which made perfectly good sense against high-tech opponents who would be emitting in those bands.

But the Mardukans emitted in neither of them, so the sensors were throwing out most detections as ghosts. In some cases during the battle, the helmet HUDs had flatly refused to "caret" the enemy at all, which had thrown off the Marines, who were trained to depend primarily on their helmet sensors precisely because those sensors were so much better than the ones evolution had provided. Except that now they weren't.

Roger had dealt with that problem by ignoring the targeting carets—first by using the simple holographic sights on his rifle, and then by firing into a melee where he knew the Marines *weren't* on the theory that that was where the enemy had to be. Of course, the burst radius of the grenades had caused a few problems, but still . . .

He spun on the ball of one foot, carrying the heavy sword through a vicious butterfly maneuver. It wasn't fair. He'd personally broken the back of the ambush. So the method was a little drastic. It had worked, and whatever Pahner might think, his actions had stemmed from neither panic nor stupidity nor arrogant carelessness.

Now if someone besides the ever-worshiping Dogzard would just *realize* that, he might even—

He froze at the sound of a cleared throat and turned gracefully to face the interruption. His face settled into a practiced, invulnerable mask of hauteur as he placed the point of the sword on the toe of his boot. It was an incredibly arrogant pose, and he knew it, but he didn't really care just at the moment. Screw 'em if they didn't like it.

"Yes?" he asked Despreaux. He hadn't heard the soft-footed squad leader approach, and he wondered what she wanted.

The NCO regarded him carefully for a moment, taking in both the attitude and the picture. The prince had changed into a pair of shorts to work out, and the heat and activity had raised a heavy sweat. The greater moon, Hanish, was breaking through the clouds, and the reflected fire and moonlight dappled the sweat on his body like patina on a bronze statue. The image sent a stab of fire through the NCO's abdomen, which she firmly suppressed.

"I just wanted to say thank you, Your Highness. We probably would have cut our way through the ambush, but we were in the tight, no question. Sometimes you have to do things that seem crazy when it drops that far in the pot. Blowing the shit out of the Company isn't the dumbest thing I can think of, and it worked. So, from me, thanks."

She didn't add that the Mardukan who'd been blown all over her by one of the grenades had had her dead to rights when it hit. Another second, and the big bastard would've taken her head off before she could reload.

Since it was exactly what he'd wanted to hear, Roger couldn't understand why the statement caused him to flare with rage. But it did. He knew it shouldn't have, but it did. He tried hard—really tried—to swallow his contrarian reaction, but his inner anger leaked through his control.

"Thank you for your input, Sergeant," he replied tightly. "In the future, however, I'll try to think of a more . . . elegant solution."

Despreaux didn't have a clue what it was about her comment that had pissed the prince off so badly, but she was smart enough to back off.

"Well, thanks anyway, Your Highness," she said quietly. "Good night."

"Good night, Sergeant," Roger said more naturally. His intense flare of anger was already fading, and he wanted to apologize for his earlier tone, but he couldn't find the words. Which only made it worse, of course.

The rebuffed NCO nodded calmly to him in the moonlight and headed back into camp, leaving him to swing his sword and rage . . . now at both the world and his own stupidity.

CHAPTER THIRTY-FOUR

"I brought everyt'ing I could pocking pack," Poertena snapped. "How tee pock was I gonna pack a pocking plasma cradle?"

Captain Pahner had decided the company needed a day or two to repair and reconsolidate. His initial reaction had been to push on, trying to deprive the Kranolta of time to concentrate more warriors on their position. But although all the pack beasts had been recovered, many of them were injured, and the mahouts insisted that some of them needed a few days rest. Pahner had to admit that it would help the Marines as well, so the company had spent the next day improving the camp's defenses and recovering from the contact.

Well, most of them had. Julian and Poertena had a different mission.

The sides of the hide tent which had been turned into an *ad hoc* armory were rolled up, but they were still unpleasantly hot under it. Not as hot as the Marines digging stake-pits, perhaps, but at least the diggers didn't have to make bricks without straw.

"Tee pocking high-capacity tester for tee M-98 is a pocking tabletop pocking unit," Poertena went on sharply. "How tee pock was I gonna carry it? Huh?"

"Tell me something I don't know, Poertena!" Julian shot back. The two experienced armorers had already stripped down and inspected twelve plasma rifles, front to back. None of them had exhibited any sign that they would detonate like the late Nanni Bosum's, but they'd pretty clearly deduced what must have happened to Bosum, and they had no way to test the high flux capacitor systems. The machine that did that was, as Poertena had pointed out, a tabletop model which had become an expanding ball of plasma along with the rest of the *DeGlopper*.

Pahner walked into the tent and glanced at the disassembled rifles and parts strewn across its interior.

"Any luck?"

"No, Sir," Julian admitted tiredly. "Other than expected faults, we can't find anything. There's nothing to indicate a malfunction that would cause a blowout," he went on, and Pahner nodded.

"I heard you talking about capacitors. Nothing there?"

"No," Julian said. "Bad capacitors are the most common cause of breech detonations, but—"

"But we don't have tee pock . . . I mean, I couldn't hump tee test module, Cap'n," Poertena put in. "It was too po—It was too big."

"Oh." Pahner smiled. "Is that the only problem?"

"Yes, Sir." Julian gestured at the torn down weapons. "We've got a general meter, but we can't stress charge the capacitors. The charge exceeds the meter's capacity."

"Okay." Pahner turned to the Pinopan. "Poertena, go rip the system pack out of a suit of armor. Better make it Russell's." The grenadier had been one of Third Platoon's few casualties in the ambush, and would no longer require her powered armor.

"Roger, Captain."

The small armorer trotted off towards where the armor had been stored, and Pahner turned his attention back to Julian as he extracted a precious stick of gum and popped it absentmindedly into his mouth.

"Julian. Go get me a plasma rifle that's been positively deadlined, a section of twelve-gauge superconductor, and a cyber-pad."

"Yes, Sir." Julian stepped into the bowels of the tent to find the required items. He wasn't sure what the captain was up to, but he knew it was going to be interesting.

* * *

Pahner held the charge-couple ring steady in one hand and applied the edge of his combat knife to the base of the contact points.

"Essentially, the tabletop tester for these things is identical to the built-in system in the armor." He sheared the contact off cleanly and caught it in midair. "But the contact points are different. The old Mark Thirty-Eight used different contacts, too, but it had a field service kit. You should have heard the bitching and moaning about not having a portable tester when these Mark Ninety-Eights came out! But this trick had been around for a long time, so we just kept using it."

"Why didn't they specify the same design?" Julian asked. "Or a field tester?"

"You don't know much about procurement systems, do you, Julian?" Pahner smiled crookedly and wiped a trickle of forehead sweat off on the shoulder of his uniform while he concentrated on lining up the superconductor and the contact.

"The same company that supplies the plasma rifles supplies testing equipment. Naturally, they want to sell the equipment with the rifles. If they say 'Hey, you can use the same testers as you use on your armor,' there goes the sale. Not to mention the fact that the tabletop model is about three times as expensive as the field tester. I never have figured out why; it does exactly the same thing."

The captain shook his head, and this time there was very little humor in his smile.

"The Mark Ninety-Eight is about twice as powerful as the Thirty-Eight, but I think Kruplon Armaments just overcharged a Thirty-Eight and put on a new cover. The interior modules are practically identical. I'd heard the rumor that the Ninety-Eight had a tendency to blow, but this is the first time I've personally seen any evidence of it."

"But why doesn't somebody call them on it?" Julian demanded, then shook his head. "Never mind."

"Yeah," Poertena laughed. "You got any pocking idea how much pocking money 'e's talking about?"

"If they lose the sale, there goes the money for the senator's reelection campaign," Pahner agreed quietly. "Or the big dinners for the procurement officers. Or the high-paying jobs for the retired admirals."

He didn't bother to mention that the Imperial Bureau of Investigation had enough to do lately tracking down various conspirators against the throne without worrying about such minor matters as exploding weapons that killed the people using them. It was, frankly, a bad time to be a Marine.

He took the mated contact and superconducting wire and wrapped them with a piece of gum the size of a pea.

"The gum will harden when the current hits it," he said with a smile as he pressed the joint tight. "And you thought it was just a habit," he added, blowing a tiny bubble.

Out of two dozen plasma chamber capacitors, they found a distinct drop in current management on half a dozen. As the current flow increased, they faltered. In a spike situation, the capacitors would fail catastrophically, with predictable results.

And all of them carried similar lot numbers from the same manufacturer.

"Fuck." Captain Pahner popped another tiny bubble and smiled grimly.

"There's microscopic cracking in tee capacitor wall," Poertena said, examining one with a field-scope. A tiny pseudo beetle wandered across the field of view, but he didn't even notice. "They probably let tee moisture get in. Especially when they been used and tee capacitor is swell. T'at's death on these dry capacitors."

"So if you don't have a spike, everything is fine." Julian shook his head. "And if you do, but don't have a bum capacitor, everything is fine. But not both."

"Right," Pahner said. "Okay. Toss these crap capacitors into the fucking jungle, except for a couple of samples. When we get back, I think Her Majesty is probably going to hang a couple of subcontractors. Given how annoyed she's going to be over this entire little adventure of ours, I think that may be a literal statement. And I'll tie the rope for her.

"After you get rid of them, put together the best plasma guns you can, as many as you can. Check every component, every piece and connection. Go over all of them with a field-scope. Then put them in zipbags with something to keep them dry.

Julian grimaced.

"Losing the plasma guns is really gonna *suck*, Boss." The weapons were almost a security blanket for the ground-pounders.

"Can't be helped. I'm not losing another squad to a breech blow. We'll hold them in reserve until it really has dropped in the pot. If it turns out we can't survive without them, we'll bring them out."

"It'll take us a while to put them together," Julian said.

"I'll get you some help. You've got today and tomorrow."

"Okeedokee," Poertena acknowledged with a resigned headshake. "Nice pocking trick," he added. "Where'd you learn it?"

"Son, I'm seventy-two," the captain said. "I joined up when I was seventeen. After fifty-five years of being on the ass-end of the supply chain, you learn to make do."

Kostas Matsugae had always enjoyed cooking on a small scale, but preparing dinner for a wider audience was a challenge. That was especially true with completely unknown spices and foods, but he was learning to make do.

With the company stopped, he finally had some leisure to experiment. He knew the troops had started complaining about the sameness of the menu, and he didn't really blame them. With very little time each evening and a large number of meals to prepare, he'd been forced to fall back on stew almost every night. The running joke was that they'd have a different meal every day—today it was stew and barleyrice; tomorrow it was barleyrice and stew.

The valet might not be a Marine, but he recognized the importance of food to morale, and he meant to do something about it. Although he intended to stay with the basic "lots of stuff in a big pot" meal plan, those parameters permitted a variety of dishes, and he was working on a new one now.

The Mardukans grew a little-used fruit that was vaguely similar to a tomato. He'd purchased a large quantity of it, and now he was simmering it in a pot spiced with the blowtorch herb *peruz* and filled with a brown legume which filled much the same culinary niche as lentils in Q'Nkok. With any luck—and it was certainly smelling good—he had a Mardukan chili in the pot. Or, it might turn out to be inedible. In which case, the company would be having . . . barleyrice and stew. It was Wednesday, after all.

He smiled as Sergeant Despreaux leaned over the pot and sniffed.

"My," she said, "that smells heavenly."

"Thank you." Kostas stirred at the top of the large kettle with a wooden spoon and took a taste. Then he waved at his mouth and took a hasty drink of water. "A bit too much *peruz*," he said in a strangled voice.

Dogzard had been sleeping in a patch of sun that penetrated the enveloping canopy. But at the sound of a spoon hitting the side of the pot, the lizard flipped to all six feet and padded rapidly over to the cooking area, and Kostas picked a small bit of meat out of the ersatz chili and tossed it to the begging lizard. The dog-lizard had become a general company mascot, emptying bowls and cleaning up messes with indiscriminate zeal. Since leaving the village of The People she'd started to grow, and was already a fairly large example of the species. If she didn't stop growing soon, she was going to end up a veritable giant.

"It'll remind us to drink," Despreaux said. She looked around for a moment, then lowered her voice. "Can I ask you a personal question?" she asked seriously.

Kostas cocked his head to the side and nodded.

"I would never betray the confidence of a lady," he said, and Despreaux snorted a laugh.

"La, sir! Seriously, no lady I. Being a lady and a grunt are sort of contradictions in terms."

"No," Kostas said. "They're not. But ask your question."

Despreaux looked around again, then looked at the pot rather than meet the valet's eye.

"You've known the Prince for a long time, right?"

"I've been his valet since he was twelve," Kostas said. "And I was a general servant in the Imperial Household before that. So, yes, I've known him for quite some time."

"Is he gay?"

Kostas stifled a snort. Not because the question was unexpected—he'd almost answered it for her before she asked—but because it was such an incredibly normal question out of this enormously capable Amazon.

"No." He was unable to keep his amusement entirely out of his tone. "No, he's not gay."

"What's so funny?" Despreaux asked. Of all the reactions she'd anticipated, amusement hadn't been one.

"You have no idea, nor will I try to give you one, how many times I've heard that question," Kostas replied with a smile. "Or heard the suggestion. Or noted the rumor. On the other hand, I've heard the opposite question just as often. There are just as many—perhaps more—gay young men as straight young ladies who have hit Roger's armor and bounced."

"So it's not just me?" she said quietly.

"No, my dear." This time, there was a note of sympathy in the valet's voice. "It has nothing to do with you. Indeed, if it makes you feel any better, I would guess that Roger finds you attractive. But that's only a guess, you understand. The Imperial Family follows the core world aristocratic tradition of providing its children with first-class sexual education and instruction, and Roger was no exception. I also know that he's inclined to prefer women; he's had at least one sexual encounter I'm aware of, and it was with a young lady. But he's also rebuffed virtually every other advance that I'm aware of." He chuckled. "And I'm aware of quite a lot of them. Frankly, if Roger were interested, he could have more 'action' than a company of Marines, pardon the expression."

"No problem." The Marine sergeant smiled. "I've heard it before. So what's with him? He's . . . what's the term? Asexual?"

"Not . . . that, either." Kostis shook his head, and there was a thoughtful, almost sad, look in his eyes. "I haven't discussed it with him, and I don't know anyone who has. But if you want the opinion of someone who probably knows him better than most, I would say it's a matter of control, not disinterest. Precisely why he should choose to exercise that control, I don't know, but that in itself tells me quite a bit." The valet shook his head. "There are many things Roger won't discuss with most people; I think there are very few he won't discuss with me, but this is one of them."

"This is . . . weird," the Marine said. Her own lovers hadn't exactly been as numerous as the stars in the sky, but she wasn't counting them on the thumbs of one hand, either.

"That's my Roger," Kostas told her with a smile.

CHAPTER THIRTY-FIVE

"Looks like it's just you and me again, Pat," Roger said, patting the pack beast just below the bandages swathing its side.

Pahner had the three most heavily injured *flar-ta*, shorn of the company's supplies, breaking trail. The pack beasts' individual reactions to the ambush had been remarkably variable. Most of them had run away from the fire and confusion of the attack, but two of them—the one Roger had coincidentally been riding and one in Third Platoon's sector—had charged the attacking Kranolta. For obvious reasons, these particularly aggressive beasts were two of the three breaking trail.

Roger, who'd decided that near a *flar-ta* was the place to be in an ambush, was walking beside "his." She reminded him of a "Patricia" he'd known in boarding school, and the name the mahouts gave her was nearly unpronounceable, toot or no toot. So "Pat" it was.

The company had been hit three more times, but not only had the additional ambushes been on a smaller scale, the wider path being forged by the trio of pack beasts had prevented the Mardukans from surprising them at such close quarters. Coupled with Pahner's decision to beef up his point team and push it further forward, the humans had escaped the attacks unscathed.

It would be nice if anyone had expected that to remain the case.

According to Cord, they were nearing the region Voitan had

dominated in his father's day. Thus far they'd seen no sign of civilization, but neither had there been any sign of a Kranolta concentration against them, and the company was inclined to take the good with the bad.

Roger saw one of the point-guards raise a hand and drop to one knee. The mahouts drew the pack beasts to a stop instantly in response, and the prince trotted forward as the column accordioned behind them.

Dogzard looked up from where she'd been riding on Patty's rump. The dog-lizard raised her striped head as she sniffed the air and hissed. Matsugae wasn't cooking, and nothing was trying to eat anyone, so she jumped off her perch and followed Roger.

The point, Lance Corporal Kane from Third Platoon, was stopped at the lip of a marsh. The bank was short, barely a quarter of a meter of bare dirt, and then there was only water, covered with weeds.

The vista stretching into the distance wasn't encouraging. The swamp was choked with fallen trees and dead vines, and the live vegetation was gray and weirdly shaped, clearly different from the normal jungle foliage. Roger looked around, then walked over to a sapling and lopped it off with the sword he'd taken to carrying slung over his back.

He was probing the marsh with his stick while Dogzard sniffed at the water disdainfully when Pahner walked up behind him.

"You know, Your Highness," the captain said dryly, "sometimes there are things that *eat* people at the fringe of water like this." The Marine seemed to have at least partially forgiven Roger for blasting the company with a stick of grenades, but the prince was still inclined to watch his tongue with rather more care than usual.

"Yes, there are," he agreed. "And I've hunted most of them. This isn't exactly shallow," he continued, withdrawing the chopped off sapling and examining the sticky mud which coated the first meter of its length. A bubble of foul-smelling gas followed the probe to the surface.

"Or solid," he observed with a choking cough.

The company had spread out in a perimeter, and seeing that there was no immediate threat, Kosutic had wandered up behind Pahner.

She looked at the black, tarry goo clinging to the stick, then at the swamp, and laughed.

"It looks like . . . the Mohinga," she announced in hushed, hollow tones which would have done a professional teller of horror stories proud.

"Oh, no!" Pahner said, with an uncharacteristic belly laugh. "Not . . . the Mohiiinga!"

"What?" Roger tossed the sapling into the swamp. "I don't get the joke."

Dogzard watched the stick land and considered going after it. But only briefly. She sniffed at the water, hissed at the smell, and decided that discretion was the better part of getting in there. Balked of any possibility of "fetch the stick," she looked up at the humans speculatively. None of them seemed to be up to anything interesting, though, so she trundled back to the *flar-ta* with her thickening tail waggling behind her.

"It's a Marine joke," Kosutic told the prince with a smile. "There's a training area in the Centralia Provinces on Earth, a jungle training center. It has a swamp that I swear the Incas must have used to kill their sacrifices. It's been drained a couple of times in the last few thousand years, but it always ends up back in the military's hands. It's called—"

"The Mohiiinga. I got that much."

"It's a real ball-buster, Your Highness," Pahner said with a faint smile. "When we'd get Raider units that were, shall we say . . . a little more arrogant than they should have been, we'd set up a land navigation course through the Mohinga. Without electronic aids." His smile grew, and his chuckle sounded positively evil. "They quite often ended up calling for a shuttle lift out after a couple of days of wandering around in circles."

"You were a JTC instructor, Sir?" Kosutic sounded surprised.

"Sergeant Major, the only thing I haven't instructed in this man's Marine Corps is Basic Rifle Marksmanship, and *that* was only because I skated out of it." Pahner grinned at the NCO. Although the marksmanship course was critical to developing Marines, it was also one of the most boring and repetitive training posts in the Corps.

"All paths lead into the Mohiiinga," Kosutic quoted with horrified, quavering relish, "but . . . none lead ooout!"

"I won't say I *wrote* that speech," Pahner said with another chuckle, "because it was old when I got there. But I did add a few frills. And, speaking of the Mohinga . . ." The captain looked around and shook his head. "I certainly hope we can go around this one."

Cord walked up to look at the swamp as well, then walked over to where Roger and his group stood laughing in the human way. It was apparent that they didn't realize the full import of the marsh.

"Roger," he said with a human-style nod. "Captain Pahner. Sergeant Major Kosutic."

"D'Nal Cord," Roger replied with an answering nod. "Is there a way around this? I know it's been some time since you came this way, but do you remember?"

"I remember very clearly," the old shaman said, "and this wasn't here in my father's day. The fields of Voitan and H'Nar stretched outward through this region. But as I recall, they had been drained from a swamp that surrounded the Hurtan River." The shaman clapped his false hands in regret. "I fear that this may fill the valley of Voitan. It may stretch all the way to T'an K'tass."

"And how far is that?" Kosutic asked.

"Days to the south," Cord replied. "Even weeks."

"And north?" Pahner asked, looking at the swamp and no longer chuckling.

"It stretches as far north as I have knowledge of," the Mardukan said. "The region to the north, even in the days of Voitan, was held by the Kranolta, and they didn't permit caravans through their lands."

"So," Roger said dubiously, "we have to make a choice between going several weeks out of our way to the south, getting hit by the Kranolta the whole way. Or we can go north, directly into their backyard. Or we can try to navigate the swamp."

"Well, your Marines and my people may have some problems," Cord admitted. "But not the *flar-ta*. They can easily make it through a swamp no deeper than this."

"Really?" It was Kosutic's turn to sound doubtful. "That thing that was chasing you was in a desert. These things—" she jerked a thumb over her shoulder at Patricia "—don't look that different."

"The *flar-ta* and the *flar-ke* are found everywhere," Cord pointed out. "They prefer the high, dry regions because of the absence of *atul-grack*, but they can be found in swamps as well."

Pahner turned and looked at D'Len Pah. The chief mahout had taken over Pat when her original mahout was killed in the first ambush, and now waited patiently for the humans to make up their minds.

"Do you think the pack beasts can cross this, Pah?" the captain asked skeptically.

"Certainly," the mahout said with a grunt of laughter. "Is that what you've been jawing about?"

He tapped the beast in a crease in the armor just behind her massive head shield to get her in gear, and the *flar-ta* whuffled forward. She moaned dolefully when she saw the black muck, but she stepped into it anyway.

The pack beast's feet each consisted of four toes with leathery bases. They were equipped with heavy digging claws, and their pads were broad and fleshy. They were also webbed, and now Patricia spread her toes wide, more than tripling the square area of her foot. That foot sank into the sloppy mud but found "solid" footing well before the belly of the creature touched the water.

"Hmmm." Roger watched thoughtfully. "Can she move out into the swamp?"

Pah prodded again, and the beast grumbled but moved out into the black water. Obviously, she was as at home in the swamp as in the jungle, but a moment later she burbled and started to back up hastily as a "V" ripple started towards her from deeper in the swamp.

Roger picked up his rifle from where he'd leaned it against a tree and flipped it off safe. Beads from Marine rifles started bouncing off the surface as the panicking beast lumbered back up out of the water, but the prince only drew a breath and led the approaching ripple.

Pahner flicked the selector switch on his bead rifle to armor-piercing as he realized that the lighter ceramic beads were simply skipping off the water, but just as he was about to fire, Roger's big rifle boomed, and the ripple turned into a whitewater of convulsions. The creature jerking and flopping at the center of the maelstrom was longer and narrower than a damnbeast but otherwise similar, with the same mucus-covered skin as a scummy. The green-and-black-striped beast thrashed a few more times as the huge hole blown through its shoulder and neck bled out, then rolled over to float belly-up on the surface.

"Dinner," Roger said calmly, jacking another round into the chamber.

"Well," Pahner observed with a sniff, "that's half the problem solved. We'll pile the rucksacks on the beasts and follow them through the swamp."

"It will make Kranolta attacks less likely, as well," Cord said ruminatively as the mahouts waded into the water to retrieve the kill. "Such swamps are useless to the forest people. They won't be as at home there as in the forest, and they'll never expect us to cross it here. But," he continued, gesturing into the swamp with his spear, "somewhere in there is the Hurtan River. And *that* the *flar-ta* will be unable to cross."

"We'll build that bridge when we come to it," Kosutic said with a laugh. "First, we have to deal with—"

"The Mohiiinga," Roger and Pahner chorused.

Poertena slipped and went under for a moment before Denat could pull him, puffing and spluttering, to his feet. The armorer spat out foul-tasting water, but he'd still managed to keep his bead rifle from going under.

"T'anks, Denat," he began, then broke off as his helmet started to pop and hiss.

"Shit!" He tore off the helmet as the earphones began to howl. "Modderpockers are suppose a be waterproof," he grumped. He'd deal with it later.

The company had been slogging through the waist- to chest-high swamp all the long Mardukan afternoon. The going was slow and hard, with the black mud sucking at their boots and chameleon suits, and hidden roots and fallen branches grabbing at their ankles. Most of them were coated in muck from top to bottom after repeated falls.

The only exceptions were the marksmen sitting on the *flar-ta.*

"Look at t'at stuck up prig sittin' up there," Poertena grumbled, glaring at the prince who was on the lead pack beast.

"You'd be up there, too," Despreaux said, moving forward to check on her Bravo Team, "if, of course, you could shoot as well as he can."

"Rub it in," the armorer muttered. "An' watch where you step. One o' these modderpocker swamp-beast eat you!"

Roger's head twitched to the right, tracking a ripple in the water, but it was small and heading away. The ride wasn't much different from normal, although it was perhaps a tad smoother. The *flar-ta* crushed most of the fallen limbs or trees they encountered without even breaking stride.

The swamp's flora ran to smaller species than in the jungle, and many of those he'd seen seemed relatively young. Cord had indicated that these areas had been fields in his father's day, so perhaps that explained their lack of age. Which, in turn, might explain their smaller size, now that he thought about it.

He turned to look behind him at the Marines sliding through the swamp and patted the snoring Dogzard on her head. The poor bastards were covered in the thick black mud and looked as worn and dragged as he'd ever seen them. The necessity of holding their rifles up out of the muck and pushing their way through it was obviously telling on them. It was particularly hard on the grenadiers, who had their boxes and bandoliers of grenades piled on their heads and shoulders with the heavy grenade launchers held up out of the slop. All in all, it made him feel like a shit to be sitting on Patricia's back.

The only consolation was that he'd been contributing. The caravan had attracted a host of carnivores as it passed through the swamp, and the Marines' bead rifles, even when switched to the heavier tungsten-cored armor piercing rounds, weren't as effective in the water as his big 11-millimeter magnum "smoke-pole." The lower velocity, heavier slugs punched into the water, rather than tending to come apart on the surface.

But he wasn't happy about it, especially with night coming on.

Pahner moved forward, pushing against the drag of the swamp as he responded to a call from the lead mahouts. He sloshed up alongside, and D'Len Pah looked down from the slow-moving reptiloid and pointed his goad stick in the direction of the descending sun.

"We must rest the beasts soon," he said. "And it will be very difficult to move in the dark."

Pahner had recognized the inevitability an hour before. There was no end to the swamp in sight, and apparently no island-forming uplands. And even if there'd been islands, they would have been inhabited by *something*.

"Agreed," he said. "We're going to have to stop somewhere."

"And we need to unload the packs," the mahout said. "The *flar-ta* will sleep standing up, but we must unload them. Otherwise, they will be useless tomorrow."

Pahner looked around and shook his head in resignation. It was the same wet, weird vista as it had been for the last few hours, so he supposed here was as good as anywhere.

"Okay, hold up here. I'll go get started on unloading them."

"We can't just dump the stuff in the swamp," Roger said. It was meant as an observation, but his tone made it sound like a protest.

"I know that, Your Highness," Pahner said testily. Just when the prince started to get a grip, he said the wrong thing at the wrong time. "We're not going to dump it in the swamp."

"Going vertical?" Lieutenant Gulyas asked. Because he was a couple of months senior to Jasco, he'd taken over as XO when Sawato was killed, turning his platoon over to Staff Sergeant Hazheir, its senior surviving NCO. It didn't really require more. Second Platoon had been hit hard, both in the ambush and before, and was already down to half its original complement.

"Yep," Pahner responded, looking up. The trees in the area

weren't the giants of the rain forest they'd traveled under for weeks. They were lower, more like large cypresses, with branches that spread out to choke the light and red vinelike projections that reached up from their roots to search for oxygen.

"Start setting up slings. We'll sling the armor off one piece at a time, then sling the rest of the gear in bundles." The company had plenty of issue climbing-rope. The lines were rated to support an eighty-ton tank, but the forty-meter length that each team leader carried weighed less than a kilo. There was more than enough to lift all the gear.

"What about the troops?" Roger asked. "Where are they going to sleep?"

"Well, that's the tough part, Your Highness," Kosutic told him with a grin. "This is how you separate the Marines from the goats."

"Besides the usual method—with a crowbar," Gulyas said, completing a joke as old as armies.

"T'is really suck." Poertena didn't even bother to try to get comfortable.

"Oh, it's not all that bad," Julian said as he adjusted the strap across his chest. The ebullient NCO was coated from head to toe in black, stinking mud, and exhausted from the day's travel, so his manic grin had to be false. "It could be worse."

"How?" Poertena demanded, adjusting his own rope. The two Marines, along with the rest of the company, were tied with their backs to trees. Since they had no choice but to sleep on their feet, the ropes around them were designed to keep them from slipping down into the chest-deep muck. As tired as they were, there was a distinct possibility that they wouldn't wake up if they did.

"Well," Julian replied thoughtfully as the skies opened up in a typical Mardukan deluge, "something could be trying to eat us."

Pahner had the sentries walking the perimeter and shining red flashlights on each individual. It was hoped that a combination of the movement and the light would drive off the vampire moths. Of course, there were also the swamp beasts to worry about, and it was always possible that movement and light would *attract* them, but there wasn't a great deal he could do about that.

All in all, it looked like being a very bad night for the Marines.

"No, Kostas," Roger said, shaking his head at the item Matsugae had produced. "You use it."

"I'm fine, Your Highness," the valet said with a tired smile. The normally dapper servant was covered in black slime. "Really. You shouldn't sleep in this muck, Sir. It's not *right*."

"Kostas," Roger said, adjusting his chest rope so that he could keep his rifle out of the muck but still get to it quickly, "this is an order. You will take that hammock and sling it somewhere and then climb into it. You will sleep the entire night in it. And you *will* get some goddamned rest. I'm going to be on the back of that damned pack beast again tomorrow, and you won't, so I can damned well spend a night sitting up. God knows I've seen enough 'white nights' carousing. One more won't kill me."

Matsugae touched Roger on the shoulder and turned away so that the prince wouldn't see the tears in his eyes. Without even realizing it, Roger had started to grow up. Finally.

"Now *that* was something I never thought I'd see," Kosutic said quietly.

The sergeant major had managed to rig a line so that she was out of the water, dangling in her combat harness. She didn't know how long she could manage it, but for the time being at least she was off her legs. If she did sleep, she figured she was going to look like something from a bad horror holovid: a dead body dangling on a meat hook.

"Yep," Pahner said, just as quietly. He'd slung himself against a tree like the rest of the company. He had a hammock packed as well, but he'd bundled O'Casey into it. There was no way he was going to use it unless every member of the company had one. And Roger, apparently without prompting, had come to the same decision.

Amazing.

CHAPTER THIRTY-SIX

"Wake up."

Julian shook the private by the arm. The bead rifleman dangled limply from the tree, her face gray in the predawn light, and pried one eye open. She looked around at her wet, indescribably muddy surroundings and groaned.

"Please. Kill me," she croaked.

Julian just shook his head with a laugh and moved on. A few moments later, he found himself looking up at the sergeant major, spinning slowly on the end of her rope and snoring. He shook his head again, thought about various humorous possibilities, and decided that they wouldn't be good for his health.

"Wake up, Sergeant Major," he said, touching her boot as it swung into range.

The NCO had her bead pistol out and trained before she was fully awake.

"Julian?" she grunted, and cleared her throat.

"Morning, SMaj," the squad leader chuckled. "Wakee, wakee!"

"Time for another glorious day in the Corps," the sergeant major replied, and pulled an end of the rope to release the knot. She splashed into the water, still holding her bead pistol out of the muck, and came up coated in a fresh covering of mud. "Morning ablutions are complete. Time to rock and roll."

"Sergeant Major, you are too much," Julian laughed.

"Stick with me, kid," the senior NCO told him through her brand new mud. "We're gonna see the galaxy."

"Meet exotic people," Pahner said, untying himself and stretching in the early dawn light.

"And kill them," Julian finished.

After changing socks, the company moved out on cold rations and vague dreams of dryness. Pahner, recognizing the danger to the Marines' feet, started cycling the company up onto the *flar-ta* two at a time. Even with the company's reduced manpower, however, it would take most of the day to get everyone up for a brief respite. And it would be brief.

As the morning progressed, there was no sign of a break in the swamp, nor of the sort of increasing depth that might signal a river ahead. In fact, the humans could see no change at all in their surroundings, but the pack beasts seemed to be getting less and less happy about continuing.

Finally, when one balked, Pahner slogged up to D'Len Pah.

"What's wrong with the beasts?" he asked.

"I think we might be in the territory of *atul-grack*," the mahout answered nervously. "They're very frightened."

"*Atul-grack*?" Pahner repeated as Cord's nephew Tratan waded up, and the young tribesman started waving all four arms in agitation.

"We must go back!"

"What?" Pahner asked. "Why?"

"Yes," the mahout said. "We should turn around. If there are *atul-grack* around, we are in grave danger."

"Well," the human said, "are there, or aren't there?"

"I don't know," Pah admitted. "But the beasts act as if they're afraid, and the only thing that would frighten *flar-ta* is *atul-grack*."

"Would someone *please* tell me what the hell an *atul-grack* is?" Pahner demanded in frustration.

His answer was a deafening roar.

The beast that exploded out of the swamp was a nightmare. Solid and low, like a damnbeast, the gray-and-black-striped monster was at least five times as large—nearly as large as the elephantine *flar-ta*. Its mouth was wide enough to swallow a human whole and filled with sharklike teeth, and it sprinted across the swamp like a tornado, water fountaining skyward from every impact of its six broad feet, as the company's weapons opened up on all sides and the pack beasts erupted in pandemonium.

Roger rolled off of Patty's back as she hot-footed away from the charging carnivore. He came up sputtering, covered in mud, but he'd managed to keep the rifle out of the swamp.

Dogzard had followed him, spinning through the air out of a sound sleep and splashing into the water beside him. The sauroid planted her amphibian hind feet in the muck and shot her head above water just long enough to determine the problem. Then she promptly ducked back under and swam away at top speed. She was a scavenger, not a fighter. And certainly not a fighter of *atul-grack*.

The carnivore was intent on pulling down one of the *flar-ta* as its dinner. It was being bracketed by grenades and hit on either side by dozens of rounds from the bead rifles, but it charged on, ignoring the pinpricks, and Roger realized that it was charging dead at Captain Pahner, who was sliding out of its way as fast as he could while firing a bead pistol at it one-handed.

The prince put the dot of the holographic sight on the beast's temple, led it a little, and let fly.

Sergeant Major Kosutic stood up, coughing and spluttering. One of the pack beasts' tails had hit her hard enough to harden her chameleon armor and throw her ten meters through the air and into a tree. She spun around in place and immediately spotted the bellowing carnivore that had started the ruckus. The friction-sling of her bead rifle was still attached, and she raised the weapon, then froze and checked. A twig frantically inserted into the barrel came out dry, so she switched to armor piercing and took careful aim at the head of the beast.

The two shots sounded as one, somehow echoing clearly in a lull as the rest of the company was reloading. Armand Pahner abandoned dignity and comfort for survival and threw himself into a long, shallow dive out of the way as the beast slid to a halt where he'd been standing in an all-enveloping bow wave of water, muck, and shredded swamp vegetation.

He was back up almost instantly, pistol in a two-handed grip, but the emergency was over. The beast was down and quivering, its tail thumping a slow, splashing tattoo. The back of the tiger-striped beast overtopped the tall Marine by at least half a meter, and he looked over at Roger, who was shakily reloading.

"Thank you, Your Highness," he said, putting his pistol away with a steady hand.

"*De nada*," Roger said. "Let's just get the fuck out of this swamp."

"Yours or mine?" Kosutic asked. She stepped up to the beast and emptied half a magazine of armor piercing into its armored head.

"Uh." Roger examined what was left of the evidence. It sure looked like his 11-millimeter had done the main damage. "Mine, I think."

"Yeah, well," the NCO said as she carefully inserted another magazine, "you shoot it; you skin it."

The good news about the thing Mardukans called an *atul-grack* and the humans just called a bigbeast was that they were very solitary, very territorial hunters who required at least one high, dry spot in their territory. It took a while, but Cord's tribesmen found it.

And the river.

The large mound was clearly artificial, part of a dike system which had once contained the Hurtan River within its banks. The artificial island supported the remains of a burned gazebo, just a few charred sticks succumbing to the Mardukan saprophytes, and the barest outlines of a road paralleling the river it overlooked.

The Hurtan wasn't a huge river by any stretch, but it was big enough. And the current was noticeable, which was unusual in the swamp.

"No way," D'Len Pah said. "*Flar-ta* swim, but not that well."

Their raised elevation also permitted a view of the low mountains or high hills where their intermediate objective lay. They seemed to be within easy reach, no more than one day's march.

If, that was, they could get across the river.

"We could go upriver," Roger suggested. "Look for a crossing point. Was there a ford?" he asked Cord, who shook his head.

"A ferry."

"We could build a raft. . . ." Pah started.

"Huh-uh," Pahner said, cutting everyone else off. He'd been staring at the river and its far bank thoughtfully.

"Bridge it?" Kosutic asked.

"Yep," the company commander replied. "And we'll belay the pack beasts across. Pah," he turned to the mahout, "the beasts can cross on their own, but they have a problem with the current. Is that it?"

"Yes," the mahout said. "They're good swimmers, but we can't ride them while they swim, for if we fall off, we'll drown. Swept downstream, without us to guide them, they might panic and drown as well." He clapped his true-hands in agitation. "You don't want us to lose any, do you?"

"No, no, no," Pahner said soothingly. "But we will cross this river. Right here."

"Why tee pock do *I* have to do t'is?" Poertena demanded as he took off his boots.

"Because you're from Pinopa," Kosutic told him. "Everyone knows Pinopans swim like fish."

"T'at's stereotyping, t'at is," the armorer snapped. He struggled out of his filthy chameleon suit and stood in his issue underwear. The flexible synthetic material made for an adequate swimsuit. "Just because I'm from Pinopa doesn't mean I can swim!"

"Can't you?" Julian asked in an interested tone. "Because if you can't, it's going to be funny as hell when we throw you in."

Dogzard sniffed at the two of them, then walked down to the water's edge. She sniffed at it in turn, then hissed and walked away. Somebody else could swim that river.

"Well, yes," Poertena admitted.

"Fairly well, right?" Kosutic asked. She did have to admit that it was stereotyping. There could be a Pinopan who couldn't swim. It would be like someone from the planet Sherpa, which was basically one giant mountain chain, being afraid of heights. It *could* happen, but it would be like being afraid of oxygen.

"Well, yes," the armorer admitted again, sourly. "I was on a swimming team in high school an' you've gotta believe tee competition was pocking pierce. But t'at's not tee point!" he continued in protest.

"Right. Sure. Anything you say," Julian soothed as he tied a rope around the diminutive Pinopan's waist. "One sacrifice to the river gods, coming up!"

Roger shook his head at the good-natured wrangling going on below his tree and took his rifle off safe. The river appeared placid, but no one intended to settle for appearances.

The rifle normally mounted a three-round magazine to save weight, given how heavy the big magnum rounds were, but the manufacturer also offered a ten-round detachable box magazine as an option. Roger had never understood why anyone who could hit what he was aiming at would need ten rounds—unless, of course, he was trying to kill main battle tanks—but two of the ten-round boxes had come with the rifle, and he'd brought them along without really thinking about it.

Now that he was down on Marduk, he'd discovered that his original contemptuous opinion of the option had undergone considerable modification, and he snapped the first, fully loaded ten-round box into place, then slid an eleventh round "up the spout" before he closed the bolt. He also had additional standard magazines laid out on the broad branch in front of him, a box of ammunition opened on his belt, and Matsugae stood ready to reload empties for him on the fly, but even all of that wasn't enough to banish his fear that he might run out of ammo as the day wore on.

Marine sharpshooters were scattered in other trees along the river, but more and more, it was Roger the company depended on when an accurate shot was needed. The time he'd spent big game hunting was coming to the fore, as he invariably placed his big bone-smashing bullets in vulnerable spots.

Julian climbed into the tree next to his and Matsugae's and unlimbered his bead rifle.

"You really ought to have one of these," the NCO noted, gesturing with his chin at the ammunition scattered across the tree limb. "Fifty in a magazine beats three—or even ten—all hollow." The sergeant pulled one of the dual magazines out of the bead rifle and replaced it with one filled with armor piercing. "And now I've got a hundred."

"Tell you what," Roger said good-naturedly as he flipped his "smoke pole's" selector switch from bolt action to semi-auto. "What do you want to bet that I get more of whatever comes along than you do?"

Julian considered himself a fair shot, but he recognized it as a tough bet to win. The prince, for all his other faults, was no slouch with that big-game rifle. The entire company had seen ample proof of that, but the Marine couldn't resist.

"Okay. Fifty credits?"

"Three hundred push-ups," Roger retorted. "Fifty credits doesn't mean a thing here, and it's peanuts to me on Earth. But three hundred push-ups is three hundred push-ups."

"Done," Julian agreed with a smile. Watching as the little Pinopan gingerly lowered himself into the water. "But who's gonna judge?" he asked.

"One hundred and twenty-six," Julian grunted. "One hundred and twenty-seven . . ."

"Come on, Julian," Sergeant Major Kosutic said. "He beat you fair and square."

The sound of bugling *flar-ta* and the occasional crack of a bead rifle could still be heard in the distance as the elaborate bridge system was disassembled.

After Poertena had taken the lead line across, the company had swung into gear with a vengeance. The first rope bridge was being tautened within twenty minutes, and a security team went swarming across it. In another half hour, two more rope bridges were in place, and the *flar-ta* were being belayed across.

The first bridge was a simple affair: two taut ropes, one above the other and about a meter and a half apart, strung between trees on either side of the river. The ropes were tightened by tying a metal ring into the side over the river and then running the end of the rope through the ring. A fire team then pulled the rope as taut as possible, and a quick release knot was tied into it. Another rope was run above the first, and then the two lines were lashed together. The resulting bridge was crossed by holding onto the top rope while shuffling across the lower one.

The *flar-ta* crossing was, inevitably, a bit trickier.

That was what the two additional bridges were for. Unlike the personnel bridge, they were single lines, and the Marines attached metal clips to them, then ran a rope from one clip to a sling around each pack beast's middle. Another rope was run from the pack beast to the far shore, and a third ran from the beast to the near shore.

Even if the entire company had grabbed onto the far rope, there would have been no way they could have managed the beast's crossing with raw muscle power. But as it turned out, a simple trick permitted a single fire team of five to pull the beast across the river.

The rope to the far side was first bent around a tree, then back on itself. The team's members held the doubled up rope in their hands as the beast was coaxed into the water, and as slack came into the rope, they pulled it through. But whenever the big beast balked and tried to draw back, they clamped their hands around the rope. The steadiness of the tree and the friction of the clamped rope prevented even the powerful *flar-ta* from backing up.

Once they were in the river, the beasts started to swim. The line run to the taut "bridge" kept them from being swept downstream, and the alternate heaving and belaying of the team on the ropes drew them across whether they wanted to cross the river or not.

In the meantime, the expected wave of carnivores arrived. The Mardukan crocodilia were just pleased as pie to have all those big, toothsome *flar-ta* come into their area, and they decided to welcome them with open jaws. Roger and company, however, had a surprise for them.

Roger was glad he'd brought a couple of cases of ammunition down from *DeGlopper*. He'd thought it was ludicrous to bring more rounds on the expedition than he'd ever shot in his life, but he and his faithful loader Matsugae shot out all the rounds they had in the tree plus a hundred more Roger had asked Despreaux to get for him before the last *flar-ta* was out of the water.

Not all of them hit, of course. Even he missed the occasional shot, but at one point there had been fifty carcasses floating in view, more than two-thirds of them with an 11-millimeter entry wound. That had been the worst point—after the smell of the blood had gotten downriver and attracted the fast-swimming swamp beasts.

Roger, followed silently by Cord, walked up as Julian grunted, "One hundred and fifty-seven . . ."

"I think that's adequate, Sergeant Major," the prince said. He stood his rifle up against a tree and sat on the ground.

The far side of the river had turned out to be higher and drier, for which the company was giving elaborate thanks. Already, in the midst of constructing a fortified camp, uniforms and allegedly waterproof rucksacks were being dried out.

"We've all had a tough few days," Roger added. He picked up the rifle again and broke open the action to clean it, but that was as far as he could get. "God, I'm tired."

"Let me clean that for you, Sir," Corporal Hooker offered. The lance corporal held out her hand for the rifle. "I've got mine to clean, anyway."

"Oh, thank you, Corporal, but we're all tired," the prince demurred. "I'll get it."

Dogzard walked over to where he sat and sniffed to make sure he was okay after the river crossing, then spun around and curled up against his side. The lizard was growing like a weed. She'd gained at least fifteen kilos in the last two weeks, and it was all Roger could do to prop up her weight.

"Let her take it, Your Highness," Kosutic said. "You probably need to go coordinate with the Old Man while I finish ensuring that the Sergeant here learns to keep his mouth shut."

Roger had opened his mouth to protest, but shut it with a clop and a laugh.

"Very well, Sergeant Major. They say 'Never argue with the Gunny.' I presume that goes double for a sergeant major." He handed the rifle to the lance corporal. "Thank you, Corporal."

He looked at Julian, who gasped: "One hundred and seventy-eight . . . !"

"And to you, Sergeant Julian," the prince said with a twinkle, "good luck."

" . . . can expect an increase in attacks on this side of the river," Lieutenant Gulyas said.

The briefing was taking place in the command tent. The sides were rolled up to let in a bit of breeze, but the troops still kept their distance. Sometimes it was better to get the word through official channels rather than as a rumor.

"Do we stay here and let them concentrate to hit us while we're dug in?" Roger asked, flicking a bug off his pad. "Or do we move on, hoping to cut down on the contacts?" Even with the sun still high, the gray light through the perpetual overcast was dim under the trees. He squinted at the pad, then rolled up the light level. Better. Still not great, but better.

"They can probably figure out that we're headed for Voitan without any difficulty," Pahner said. "And there's something to be said for letting them come to us in a prepared position. But this isn't the sort of location I'd want to defend."

The area was a flat, heavily forested plain, higher than the swamp, but still prone to flooding. The flat plain, however, did not provide anything in the way of terrain features to use in defense. The company could, and had, cut down most of the secondary growth trees to improve their perimeter and fire lanes, but that was about it.

"If we reach Voitan," Cord said, deliberately, "we'll have many places to defend. Not only should there still be walls in places, but the quarries behind the city offer numerous fortifiable spots."

"What do you think, Captain?" Roger asked, yawning. Everyone was exhausted, including him. He just needed to drive on.

"I think that in the morning we pull out carefully, then make the fastest march possible to Voitan. We'll pile the packs on the beasts again and force the pace. I doubt they expected us to cross the swamp here. They probably have a crossing place they use, and if they've begun to assemble to hit us, they'll probably be assembling there. Unfortunately for them, we were too stupid to use the 'good' crossing."

"So we make a run for Voitan," Kosutic said.

"Right." Pahner considered the situation for a moment. "If it's as close as Cord thinks, then we should arrive by mid-afternoon." The long Mardukan day would work in their favor for once.

"And if it's not?" Kosutic asked.

"Then we will have exhausted ourselves for nothing," Pahner told her grimly.

Matsugae sampled the stew and gave the mahout who was stirring it a thumbs up. He walked on to where a Mardukan female was turning strips of meat battered with barleyrice meal on a large metal sheet over a fire. He pulled one of the strips off and blew on it to cool it enough to taste without burning his mouth. Again, he smiled and gave the cook a thumbs up.

The captain had backed the camp up against the river, and the company had spent the remainder of the afternoon digging in and cleaning up. Matsugae, for his part, had spent the same time working hard to put together a decent meal for the first time in three days. Many of the swamp beasts had been lassoed or hooked and dragged to shore. Although there was good flesh all over the carcasses, there were three or four particularly good cuts, and with all the bodies floating in the river, the mahouts had ended up taking only the skins and the very best of the meat.

Most of the mahouts were preparing the skins. The swamp beasts were fairly rare, and their skins brought a high price. The company, possibly Roger alone, had shot the cost of two or three pack beasts in one afternoon.

Matsugae grinned. The mahouts had been picking up the skins of all the beasts that the company shot along the way. The captain had nearly offered them to the drovers as a free benefit, but Matsugae had convinced him not to do that. The mahouts were being paid a straight rate, just as they would for any caravan. The skins, however, even after processing, were the property of whoever shot the beasts they came from. Give the mahouts a bonus for their work, certainly, but the skins of those predators were valuable. The beasts that had harassed them would help pay the company's way, and that gave the valet a simple sense of pleasure.

The dog-lizard wandered into the outdoor kitchen and sniffed at the strips on the fire. The Mardukan female tending them shooed her away, so she wandered over to Matsugae, looking pitiful. The beast had grown steadily since Roger adopted it. It was nearly the size of a dalmatian now, and its growth showed no sign of slowing. In addition, its tail was thickening. The *flar-ta*, which were similar to the dog-lizard in many ways, stored up reserves in their tails, or so the mahouts claimed. Certainly, they were skinnier now than when the company had left Q'Nkok. Apparently, unlike the pack beasts, the journey had been good for the dog-lizard.

Matsugae consulted his toot and smiled as he tossed the dog-lizard the last bit of damncroc tail. Nearly time for dinner.

"Kostas, that was wonderful, as always." A yawn interrupted Roger's compliment, and he grimaced. "Sorry."

"Don't worry about it, Your Highness," Pahner said. "We're all beat. I hope like hell we don't get hit tonight. I don't think Bravo of the Bronze could hold off a troop of Space Scouts tonight."

"I think you underestimate them, Captain," O'Casey said. The chief of staff had begun to adjust to the brutal regimen of the trip, shedding fat and putting on muscle. When she got back to Imperial City, she intended to recommend shipwreck on a hostile planet full of carnivorous monsters and bloodthirsty barbarians as a sovereign method for attaining physical fitness. Now the former tutor smiled warmly. "Your troops have been just magnificent. Her Majesty will be incredibly proud when we finally get back."

"Well," Pahner said, "we have a long way to go before we find out. But, thank you, Councilor. That means a lot to me, and it will actually mean something to the troopers as well. We don't just fight for pay, you know."

Roger shook his head sleepily.

"I never considered all the little stories around me all the time. Do you know Corporal Hooker's first name?" Roger asked as he fed Dogzard a scrap of gristle from the damncroc.

"Of course, Your Highness. Ima."

"She said her dad had a sick sense of humor," the prince confirmed in a tone of outrage. "I offered to have him thrown out an airlock."

"He's long dead," Kosutic said, taking another fingerstrip of damncroc tail. "Snorted himself to death on dreamwrack."

"Ah," Roger said with a nod. "And Poertena wanted to go to college on a swimming scholarship . . ."

" . . . but he got beat out in the finals," Pahner finished. "There's more to leadership than wearing the right tabs on your collar, Your Highness. Knowing the details of the troops is important, and for knowing the really intimate details . . ."

". . . you have sergeant majors and gunnery sergeants," Kosutic said with a frown. "Andras' wife was expecting when we left, and I doubt we'll be back before she's due. I don't suppose it will matter one way or the other, though; we're undoubtedly written off as dead."

"That . . . sucks," O'Casey said.

"Being a Marine sucks," Pahner told her with a quiet smile. It was rare for the academic to swear.

"Then why do you do it?" she asked.

"It's something I'm good at. Somebody has to do it, and better someone who's good at it. Not everyone is." The captain looked pensive for a moment. "It's . . . bad, sometimes. When you realize that what you're really good at is either killing other sentients in person or leading others in the killing of them. But everyone in the Regiment is an exceptional Marine. And reasonably presentable. And utterly loyal . . ."

"But there's more," Kosutic said with a grin. "That describes a surprising number of Marines. And even a surprising number that can make it through RIP. It's a big Corps, after all."

"Yes," Pahner said, taking a sip of water, "there is more. Every member of The Empress' Own has some odd skill that the selection board thought might conceivably be of use. You don't get in if the only thing you know is what you've learned since Basic."

"I knew Poertena could swim that river," Kosutic told the prince. "But I wasn't about to tell him that I knew he was an Olympic-class swimmer," she added with a laugh.

"You mentioned Corporal Hooker," Pahner said soberly. "Ima Hooker was an air car thief before a judge gave her a choice between the Marines and a long jail sentence."

"What the hell is *she* doing in The Empress' Own?" O'Casey asked with a gasp as she choked on a mouthful of wine.

"She can open and be driving an air car she's never seen as fast as you can open your own and drive away with a key," Kosutic said seriously. "If you think that's not a skill the Empress might need someday, you're sadly mistaken."

"She is also *utterly* loyal to the Empress," Pahner told the chief of staff. "She actually has one of the most stable loyalty indexes I've ever seen. Better than yours, I might add, Ms. O'Casey. The Marines took her out of a hellish existence and gave her back her honor and purpose. She's somehow transferred that . . . redemption to the *person* of the Empress. She's definitely one of the ones who's going to end up in Gold."

"How strange," the academic murmured. She felt as if she'd stepped through the ancient Alice's looking glass.

"So what's *your* skill, Captain?" Roger asked.

"Ah, well." The CO smiled as he leaned back in the camp chair. "They make exceptions for captains."

"He's taught himself to be a pretty fair machinist, and he can rebuild an air car from the ground up," Kosutic said with a grin at the captain. "You only thought they made an exception for you. He also does decent interior work."

"Hmph! Better than yours."

"What is yours, Sergeant Major?" O'Casey asked after a moment had passed and it was obvious that the sergeant major wasn't going to be forthcoming.

"Well, the main one is . . ." Kosutic paused and glared balefully at Pahner ". . . knitting."

"*Knitting?*" Roger looked at the grim-faced warrior, unable to keep the laugh completely out of his voice. "Knitting? Really?"

"Yes. I like it, okay?"

"It just seems so . . ."

"Feminine?" O'Casey suggested.

"Well, yeah," the prince admitted.

"Okay, okay." Pahner grin. "Let me point out that it's not just knitting. The Sergeant Major is from Armagh. She can take a hunk of wool, or anything similar, and make you an entire suit, given time."

"Oh," Roger said. The planet Armagh was a slow-boat colony of primarily Irish descent. Like many slow-boat colonies, it had backslid after reaching its destination and stabilized at a preindustrial technology level before the arrival of the tunnel drive. And unfortunately, also like many, it had broken down into factional warfare. The arrival of the first tunnel drive ships and the subsequent absorption of the planet into the Empire of Man had reduced the blood feuds, but it hadn't eliminated them. It had been suggested that nothing short of carpet bombing the surface with nukes and sowing it with salt would get the residents of Armagh to stop fighting amongst themselves. It was practically a genetic imperative.

"Hey, it's not that bad," Kosutic protested. "You're safer in downtown New Belfast than you are walking around in Imperial City. Just . . . stay out of certain pubs."

"Some *other* time, I'll ask you what it was like being a priestess of the Fallen One on Armagh. Everywhere I turn there are fascinating stories like this," Roger said. "It's like taking off blinders." He yawned and patted Dogzard on the head. "Get up, you ugly beast." The sauroid lifted her red-and-black-striped head off his lap with a disturbed hiss and headed for the tent door. "Folks, I'm exhausted. I'm for bed."

"Yes," Pahner said, standing up. "Long day tomorrow. We should all rest."

"Tomorrow," Roger said, getting up to follow Dogzard.

"Tomorrow," O'Casey said.

CHAPTER THIRTY-SEVEN

"We have found the nest of the *basik* outlanders!" Danal Far shouted. "Tomorrow we shall sweep down upon them and rid our lands of them forever! This land is ours!"

The shaman clan-chief of the Kranolta raised his spear in triumph, and the horns of defeated enemies clattered against the steel shaft. It had been long years since the Kranolta gathered in anything like the numbers in this valley. The crushing of the invasion by these "humans" would be the high point of his time as clan-chief.

"*This land is ours!*" the clan gathering echoed with a blare of horns. Many of them dated from the fall of Voitan, when the horns of champions had been common.

"I wish to speak!"

The statement took no one by surprise, and Danal Far grunted silently in laughter as the limping warrior stepped to the front. Let the young fool say his piece.

Puvin Eske was now the "chief" of the Vum Dee tribe of the Kranolta. As such, he was the representative of the tribe which had supplied the majority of the mercenaries to the N'Jaa of Q'Nkok. But now his tribe consisted only of many hungry females and a handful of survivors of their ambush of the human caravan. The tribe would be gone before the next full moon; the jungle and its competitors would see to that.

Puvin Eske was half the age of most of the leaders gathered for the council. Many of them had participated in the battles to take Voitan, long, long ago, and they remembered those days of high glory for the clan clearly. Few of them, however, saw the truth of the clan as it was, despite their complaints over the loss of spirit among their younger warriors.

"We face a grave decision," the young chieftain said. Only a few days before, he would have been far too hesitant, too aware of his youth, to speak in opposition to the clan elders. Now he'd looked into the face of Hell. After fighting Imperial Marines, no circle of weak, old men would bother him. "Our clan, despite its high standing, has faltered in my years. Every year, we have become fewer and fewer, despite the fertile lands we took from Voitan—"

"What is this 'we,' child?" one of the elders interrupted in a scoffing tone. "You weren't even a thought in your weakling father's head when Voitan fell!"

There were rough chuckles at the jest, but Danal Far raised his Spear of Honor to call for order.

"Let the 'chief' speak," the old shaman said. "Let the words be spoken in public, not in the darkness at the back of huts."

"I asked," the scarred and burned young chief continued, "are we not fewer? And the answer is, 'Yes, we are.' And I tell you this: the reason we are fewer is the fall of Voitan. We lost many, many of the host in the battle against Voitan. Now we recover slowly. Indeed, we seem to be faltering rather than recovering. I had many playmates in my years, but my son plays alone.

"Now the Vum Dee and Cus Mem are a memory. We brought the pride of our tribe against these 'humans,' and the warriors of Cus Mem joined us. We attacked them all unawares, with no warning."

He had, in fact, argued with his own father against the decision to attack. The runners who'd brought the tale of the fall of the House of N'Jaa had also brought word of the terror of the humans' weapons. Hearing that, and fearing for the tribe in its already crippled state, the young warrior had argued against taking losses among the flower of their warriors, but his arguments had been rejected.

"Yes, we surprised them," he continued, "yet still we lost a set of sets while the humans might have lost a hand pair."

The Kranolta's problems, although Puvin Eske didn't know it, were dispersion and death rate. The native sophonts had only two reproductive periods per Mardukan year. With the dispersion of the Kranolta to fill a huge hunting area very sparsely, the males of the tribe had been able to range at will in their hunting quests. Unfortunately, this meant that they weren't always around brooder females when their seed quickened.

Coupled with these missed opportunities to breed were the tremendous casualties taken in capturing Voitan. A single male could only implant a single female with eggs during mating season. With the multiple "pups" that this normally produced and a biannual reproduction, normal death rates were taken care of. But the death rate the Kranolta had suffered in capturing the city hadn't been anything like "normal," and despite the increase in hunting range, child death rates hadn't declined since.

All of which meant that the clan was recovering very slowly, if at all, from its "victory."

"If we lose the greater part of the clan's warriors to these terrible weapons," Eske continued, holding up an arm cooked by plasma fire, "we shall be ended as a clan. Some few tribes might survive, but even this I doubt."

"Who shall speak to this?" Danal Far asked. He himself would have spoken against it, but an image of impartiality was important. Besides, the answer was a massed roar, and he pointed to one of the other veterans of Voitan. Let him put the young puppy in his place

"The only thing that the loss of Vum Dee shows is that they were and are gutless cowards, as proven by these words!" Gretis Xus shouted. The old warrior limped forward on painful scars won not just in the destruction of Voitan but in constant skirmishing against the other city-states that bordered his tribe. "Vum Dee has sat on its behind since the fall of Voitan. But the Dum Kai have continued to battle against the shit-sitters. *We* are not so weak and gutless as to accept this intrusion. I say that Vum Dee is no longer true Kranolta!"

Xus' words drew a roar of approval, not just from the gathered tribe chiefs, but from the ring of warriors behind them. Puvin Eske heard it, and bent his head in sorrow.

"I have spoken my words. As I spoke them to my father, who is no more. Puvin Shee, who was the first over the walls of Voitan; who wore the horns of the King of Voitan on his belt. And who I saw cut in half before my eyes by fire from warriors it was nearly impossible to see."

He raised his head and regarded the other tribes.

"Vum Dee will be eaten soon enough by other tribes and the jungle. But if the Kranolta go forth to battle the humans, so also shall the rest of the Kranolta be eaten. You say the Vum Dee, whose fathers led the Kranolta over the walls of Voitan, whose warriors were the spear of the Kranolta all the way out of our ancient tribal lands, whose own flesh was the clan-chief of the Kranolta for the war against Voitan, are not true Kranolta? Very well. Perhaps it is true. But tell me this five days hence, for then it shall indeed be true. For five days hence, there shall *be* no Kranolta!"

The warrior turned and walked out of the circle of hostile faces. Many glared, but none tried to stop him. None would dare even now to touch a chief at the clan meeting. Let them wait the days.

Danal Far took center place again as the Vum Dee chief and his decimated retinue left the circle.

"Are there any other objections?" he asked. "Seeing none, I call for an attack against these humans as soon as we can reach them. They will move out on the morrow, probably for Voitan, but we shall intercept them before they reach there. They move slowly through the jungle, and it will be easy. They are only shit-sitters, after all."

"Move!"

Julian shouldered the private aside, hit the sixth setting on his multitool, held it at arm's length as it flicked into a 130-centimeter blade, and grunted with effort as he brought the mono-machete down on the thick liana. The girder-thick vine parted with a crack and swung towards him, and he grunted again as it hit him in the stomach—then yelled in fear as he had to roll out of the way of a descending pack beast paw.

The point gave him a glance of thanks and hurried to get in front of the pack beast again.

The company moved through the jungle at a trot. It was virtually impossible to maintain that pace, but they were doing it anyway. For the most part, the *flar-ta* were breaking trail, but occasional larger obstacles had to be cleared the hard way. That meant the point squads were kept busy hacking through the thicker lianas and finding ways around the occasional deep valleys which had begun to appear, none of which was designed to make people who'd survived the first ambush happy at the distraction from keeping an eye out for *future* ambushes.

The ground was rising towards the hills they had glimpsed by the river. Somewhere on the edge of that range of low mountains were the ruins of the city of Voitan, perched, according to reports, on the shoulder of a small peak. And somewhere—either at those ruins, or in the jungle—they were going to be hit again by the Kranolta. Better for it to be in the ruins, where there were places to defend, than in these open, defenseless woods.

Roger leapt a small fallen trunk that hadn't yet been smashed to splinters by the caravan of *flar-ta* and helped the squad leader to his feet.

"No lying down on the job, Julian," he said, and continued on without a pause. Cord, who'd just caught up with the prince, clapped his hands in frustration and trotted off in pursuit.

Julian wasn't sure if the prince was joking or not. The tone had been dead serious, but it could have been a very dry joke. Very dry.

The NCO shrugged and reformatted his multitool to fit into its pouch. If they survived, he might figure it out; if they didn't, it wouldn't matter anyway.

Pahner nodded to himself as his toot flashed a time alert.

"Second Platoon, onto the pack beasts. First Platoon, point!"

Humans, especially Marines, could almost certainly have outrun the *flar-ta* over time and in open terrain. In the jungle, it would have been a toss-up, at best. The company already had several badly sprained or broken ankles, and the strain of jumping logs and dodging limbs slowed them badly.

But the Marines got a breather by cycling the platoons onto and off of the big beasts. It was hard on the *flar-ta*, and Pahner hadn't needed the mahouts to tell him that they would have to rest for at least a couple of days when they reached Voitan, but it was the only way to ensure that the troops would be in any reasonable sort of shape if it dropped into the pot.

Pahner saw the prince pull himself up the ropes onto the *flar-ta* he'd christened Patty, and nodded. Roger had stated that for purposes of rotation he was in Second Platoon, and he'd apparently stuck to that. Which was good. The kid was coming along.

"Captain!" Gunny Lai called. "We've got movement front!"

Cutan Mett heard the tramping sounds of a herd of *flar-ta* and waved his warriors to a halt. They were the vanguard of the Miv Qist tribe, and he felt their hungry anticipation as they realized that the honor of first contact with the invaders was about to be theirs.

"Fire on the contact," Pahner said. Normally, he would have waited for more than a sensor reading. That was not only doctrine, it was also common sense . . . normally. But not here. Whether it was a bolting damnbeast or the vanguard of the attackers, it was time to "plow the road."

"Roger," Lai responded.

The Imperial Marine M-46 was a forty-millimeter, belt-fed, gas-operated grenade launcher. The advanced composition of the grenades' filler gave them the destructive force of a pre-space twenty-kilo bomb, but despite any advances in explosive fillers, the chemical-powered launcher had an old-fashioned kick like that of a particularly irritated Terran mule. Ripping off an entire belt in a mass of fire, as the prince had done a few days before, was the action of an idiot or someone who was very good with the weapon and big enough to handle the recoil.

Lance Corporal Pentzikis was neither a fool nor particularly massive. So when given the order to "flush" the detected Mardukans, the experienced Marine settled the big weapon into her shoulder, made sure the forty-round belt fed over her shoulder without a kink, and started a slow, aimed fire.

The rounds impacted with a deep jackhammer sound that raised the hackles on experienced troopers' necks, and the remainder of First Platoon spread out around her as she fired grenades into the area where the sensors had detected movement. Moments later, the ground and trees flashed white.

Mett shouted as the trees around him started to come apart in eruptions of thunder and lightning, and splinters flayed the warriors of Miv Qist.

"Forward!" he bellowed. "*This land is ours!*"

There were times when Ima Hooker felt like a distilled potion of fury. Whether that was nature or nurture—the father who'd given her her name had been cruel in many other ways—she neither knew nor cared. All that she cared about were the occasional moments when the Imperial Marines gave her an outlet for it.

Like now.

As the scummies burst out of the concealing foliage, she snugged the bead rifle into her shoulder, placed the laser targeting dot on the body of the leader, and flicked her rifle to its three-round burst setting. Time to get some back from the universe.

Pahner glanced at his tactical display and made a decision.

"They're trying to close the route," he snapped over the command circuit. "First, stay in place, screening our flank. As we pass, roll in behind us. Everybody but sharpshooters off the pack beasts. Third to the point, Second in the body. Pick up the pace, Marines. Let's *go*!"

Roger started to slide off Patty and got slapped on the leg by Sergeant Hazheir.

"Stay up there, Your Highness!" the acting platoon sergeant said. "You're probably who he *meant* by sharpshooters."

Roger laughed and nodded.

"Okay! " he yelled as the staff sergeant slid off the beast and trotted forward. "I'll try to remember who the good guys are!"

Corporal Hooker put another burst into the vegetation and cursed. The bastards were figuring out to stay behind cover.

"Behie! Flush those bastards for me!" she snapped, highlighting the cover with her target designator for the grenadier.

"Roger!" Pentzikis had just finished attaching a new belt and pivoted slightly, letting the launcher's sensors search for the target. "I need more grenades; I'm short."

"Roger," Edwin Bilali acknowledged. The NCO shot at a patch of gray and was rewarded by a scream. "Gelert! Get to the pack beasts and bring back three strings of grenades!"

"On my way, boss!" The newbie private put a burst into the vegetation in front of him and reared up to run for the passing beasts. He thought he knew where he could find the ammunition.

Ima Hooker popped out her first magazine and had just started to reload another of the half-kilo plastic packs when a scummy reared up from behind a log and hurled its javelin.

"Heads up!" she shouted, seating the magazine, and took aim.

The spinning HE grenade beat her to the shot, exploding a meter above the Mardukan's head and turning it into red jelly, but the burst also threw two more targets into her view. The fury within her howled like an enraged beast, for she'd seen the result of her momentary distraction, and she unleashed her rage and flicked the three-millimeter bead gun onto full automatic and cut the unfortunate natives in half.

"*Bastards!*" she screamed, and swept the muzzle onward, seeking still more targets and fresh vengeance.

Sergeant Bilali ran to the rifleman, but he knew he was too late. The private from St. Augustine scrabbled at the muck and loam of the jungle floor, choking on the blood that poured out of his mouth. Bilali pulled off the private's helmet and tried to roll him over, but the javelin pinned him to the forest floor, and the movement jerked a scream through the bright, scarlet flood.

"Ah, Christ, Jeno!" The NCO's hands fluttered helplessly over the wounds. Bullets didn't transfix their targets like specimens in some alien entomologist's collection, so all his training meant nothing. "Ah, God, man."

"Move!" Dobrescu was suddenly at his side. The warrant officer had already learned all he cared to know about wounds like this one. He figured the kid had about one chance in twenty, max, but it was worth going for.

"It's got to come all the way through," the medic went on as he pulled out a monomolecular bone cutter. The scissorlike device sliced open the chameleon suit and snipped the javelin shaft flush with the private's back effortlessly, with absolutely minimal movement, yet even that tiny twitch evoked another scream.

"Now comes the fun part," Dobrescu added through gritted teeth. "Gelert," he said firmly, applying a self-sealing bandage. "Listen to me. I got one way to save your life, and its gonna have to go quick. We are going to *flip* you onto your back. You're probably going to pass out from the pain, but don't scream. Don't."

Even as he spoke, he was running a drainage tube with frantic haste. The wound was going to have to drain somewhere, and if it drained into the lungs, nanites or no nanites, the kid was going to drown in his own blood.

Gelert was twitching and the blood was going everywhere as the company passed them by. Stopping for one casualty would get them all killed, but if Dobrescu couldn't get this kid evacuated soon, the company's advance was going to leave him behind the caravan.

"Bilali, I'm gonna need a stretcher party."

"Who the fuck is going to carry it?" the NCO demanded as fresh firing started to the front and another cry of "Medic!" cut through the bedlam. "We're getting hammered."

"Find someone!" the warrant officer barked. He wondered for a moment if he should just write the kid off and get him lashed to a pack beast until they could bag and burn him. But if he could get the holes patched and the bleeding slowed, the fast-heal nanites sometimes could perform miracles. Fuck it.

"And while you're finding somebody, we're going to need security!"

★ ★ ★

"Roger," Kosutic answered. "Shit!" She looked over her shoulder. "*Captain!*"

"What?" Pahner never looked away from his HUD. Second Platoon had just passed through in the leapfrog and reported that they were hitting signs of buildings and rock outcroppings. If they made it into the city, it was going to be by the skin of their teeth, and he could hear the howling of the Kranolta horns behind him. It was as if the Huntsmen of Hell had been loosed on their trail.

"Dobrescu is trying to get Gelert stabilized to move. He's already out of Third's coverage!"

That was enough to pull the captain away from his display, and he looked up in disbelief. The sergeant major looked as royally pissed as he felt, not that being in agreement made either of them feel any better.

"Dobrescu!" Pahner keyed his communicator. "Get your ass out of there—now!"

"Captain, I have Gelert stabilized. I think I can save him."

"Mr. Dobrescu, this is an order. Get your ass out of there!" He checked his HUD and realized that none of the private's fire team had moved out. "*Bilali!*"

"Sir, we're pulling out as fast as we can rig a stretcher," the NCO responded.

"Sergeant—!"

The company CO chopped off his furious command. Long, long ago at the Corps NCO combat leadership school, he'd been told something which had stood him in a good stead for fifty-plus Standard years: Never give an order you know won't be obeyed. He never had, and he didn't intend to start today.

"We'll be waiting for you in Voitan, Sergeant."

He knew he'd just written off their only medic, who was also an irreplaceable pilot, and a full fire team, but that was better than losing the entire company trying to cover them.

The line of *flar-ta* was pounding up a slope and through a ruined gateway partially choked by the rubble of the gatehouse. The area beyond was too large to hold for long—a fifty-meter-wide plaza surrounded by overgrown heaps of masonry—but it was a good place to rally.

"Hold it up on the other side," he called over the general company frequency. "Third Platoon on the gate, First and Second in support. I want a headcount."

He stepped up onto a liana-bound pile of masonry that had probably been the wall of a house, and looked around. A quick count showed him that all of the pack beasts had made it through, most of them with bead rifle or grenade-launcher-armed Marines on top. Then he took another look at the riders.

"Where," he asked with deadly calm, "is Prince Roger?"

CHAPTER THIRTY-EIGHT

Bilali triggered another burst and the group of scummies disappeared behind their log. He had them pinned for the time being, but he was also low on ammunition.

"Sarge," Hooker called, "you got any ammo? I'm dry."

He cursed silently. Hooker always put her rounds on target, but she always used too many of them.

"I'm about out here, too," he answered.

"I've got some," Dobrescu said. "Take 'em."

The medic had the patient fully prepped and was working on a field expedient stretcher: the trunks of two stout young saplings with the wounded private's chameleon suit stretched between them. It would be heavy and awkward and nearly impossible to get up to the city, but it was the only chance the wounded trooper had.

"Shit!" Hooker spun to the west. "I've got movement between us and the Company!"

"Calm down, Hooker," came the prince's voice. "We're coming in."

Roger was positive that he'd killed not only himself, but Matsugae and O'Casey as well. Eleanora was shaking like a leaf, but she still managed to hold up her end of the heavily-loaded standard-issue stretcher. Matsugae was smiling, as usual, as he carried the other end, but the expression was a rictus.

"Roger," the valet told him, "this is quite insane."

"You keep saying that." Roger ducked down behind a tree. "Doc, you're going to have to take the other end for Eleanora on the way back."

He gripped the butt of the grenade launcher between his arm and rib cage, stood up, and ripped out a string of fifteen grenades. The end of the string traveled upward and off target, but most of them hammered into the area where the scummies had taken cover. The shrapnel and splinters of shattered branches scourged the cowering natives like flying knives, and drove them to their feet, screaming.

While Bilali and Hooker blew their flushed targets apart, Roger ejected the mostly-used belt and picked another off the stretcher. The stretcher was covered in belts, as were his shoulders, and more of them bulged his rucksack.

"We'd better move, Doc."

"Got it!" The warrant officer dumped the munitions off the stretcher. "Bilali, Hooker, Penti, get loaded."

Roger kept an eye on the woodline beyond the smashed lane where the *flar-ta* had thundered through the jungle while the remnants of the fire team gathered up the ammunition the civilians had humped in to them and Dobrescu got Gelert strapped into the stretcher.

"Thank you, Sir," Bilali said. "But this is goddamn stupid."

"My blood for yours, Sergeant," the prince replied. "Why the hell should you try to save my life if I'm not willing to reciprocate?"

"*Break out the armor!*" Pahner shouted furiously over the general circuit. "Roger, where the *hell* are you?!"

"Ah," Roger said as Matsugae and Dobrescu lifted the stretcher. "Our master's voice."

Pentzikis was so nervous that she broke into giggles and put a few rounds into the woodline from the twitch.

"We're fucking dead," she giggled. "If the goddamn scummies don't kill us, Captain Pahner will!"

"I don't think so." Roger lifted another belt of grenades out of his rucksack and draped it across the top. "Personally, I refuse to die today."

"Come on, you stupid hunk of crap!"

Julian watched the power levels rise in his helmet HUD. The suit wasn't even on completely, but he could feel the crash of grenades through the heels of his armored boots.

Despreaux hooked on his gloves, working with furious haste as the crack of bead rifles got closer. A moment later came the furious blast of another string of grenades in the distance, and she knew that Roger, at least, was still alive.

"You'll make it," she said.

"I know I'll make it. But will I make it before Pahner decides to just kill us and start over with scummies as bodyguards?"

"It's not *our* fault Roger went haring off!" Despreaux protested, furious with the prince.

"No, but after we save ourselves, Pahner is going to kill us. We were supposed to be *watching* the little shit."

"Now that's not fair," the female sergeant snapped as she hooked up the gravity feed to the stutter gun. The quad-barreled bead gun hooked to an ammunition storage box on the back of the armor, but despite the mass of rounds in the box, it could still run through its ammunition in a surprising hurry. And they had only so many boxes. "Roger was trying to save a wounded Marine," she went on. "And watch your ammo."

"I will," Julian said. "And he was. But he's still a little shit. If he gets killed, I'm gonna frag his ass."

"You're up!" Despreaux made the last connection and flipped his visor up to give him some air. Until the things came online, the armored suits could be sweltering.

"Still waiting for the God *damned* computer to settle down," Julian snarled. Why the damn thing took so long to load was always a mystery to the Marines. It was worse than a pad.

"*Julian?*" Pahner roared from his perch on the rubble.

"Waiting for warm-up to complete, Sir!" Julian yelled back, looking around his troops. He couldn't even do his status check until the damned computer completed dumping its memory or pulling its cheek or whatever took so . . . so . . . so modder pocking long. Finally, the damned light turned green.

"*Up!*" He shouted, and raised one hand, thumbs up. A moment later, two more hands came up, then a third. But that was it.

"What the fuck?" He'd lost Russell earlier, but that still left nine in his squad. "Status check!"

"Red lights," Corporal Aburia reported tersely, stepping up to Cathcart and looking into his helmet. The plasma gunner was yelling behind his visor, and the team leader lifted it just in time to hear ". . . motherfuckingcocksuck . . ."

"We've only got four, Sir," Julian told Pahner over the captain's private channel.

"Poertena!"

"How you doin' for ammo, Behie?" Roger yelled as he laid down another string and a screen of lianas vanished in the explosions. A javelin had come from beyond that screen, and Roger had become a major proponent of peace through superior firepower. A ghastly shriek sounded even through the thunder of grenades, and something thrashed and bled in the bushes. "Fuck with a MacClintock, will you?" he yelled.

"I've got five belts left, Sir!" The grenadier popped a single round into a suspicious looking bush, exercising an economy of ammunition expenditure His Highness seemed constitutionally unable to match. "You might want to conserve your ammunition a little, Sir."

"We can conserve ammo when we're dead," he retorted. "Move, I'll cover you."

The grenadier just shook her head and darted from behind the fallen tree she'd been using for shelter. The stretcher team—the struggling doc and Matsugae, with the prince's chief of staff holding a bottle of drip fluid—was nearly twenty meters ahead of them, closely protected by the bead gunners as the grenadiers covered the retreat. She'd already tried to argue about who should move out first and who should stay behind in a movement. And lost. She was done arguing.

She ran to where Hooker sheltered behind another fallen tree. They'd cursed all day long at the obstacles the passage of the *flar-ta* had thrown down, but now they were lifesavers.

"Move, Sir!" Pentzikis shouted, and fired a round into another likely looking clump.

Roger pushed himself up with both hands and turned to run . . . just as a massive flight of javelins erupted out of the brush.

"Oh, fuck," the grenadier said mildly. She'd become expert at judging the flight of the spears, and she realized they were all aimed at their previous positions. Hers . . . and the prince's.

Roger didn't even think—not consciously, anyway. He simply bolted straight towards the source of that massive flight, grenade launcher blazing. There was no way he could outrun the flock of javelins, but he might be able to run *under* them.

Their angle of flight, partially because of the slope of the ground, was high, and the speed he'd found so useful on soccer fields finally came into its own somewhere else. As the steel-tipped rain fell all around and behind him, he charged forward, grenade launcher spitting a metronome of fire.

Julian and his three armored companions passed the stretcher team, bounding by in run mode at nearly sixty kilometers per hour. They could have gone faster on better ground, but not on a track torn by *flar-ta* and covered in fallen trees.

"Man, Bilali," Julian said as he passed. "You are fucked."

"What the hell was I supposed to do?" the squad leader demanded, falling back to cover the stretcher team. "Knock him over the head and throw *him* on the stretcher?"

"Probably," the squad leader snarled, then tripped over one of the fallen trunks and plowed into a tree that was still standing. "*Shit!*"

"You okay, boss?" Gronningen called. The big Asgardian had his M-105 plasma cannon trained outward. The company hadn't expected to be using them so quickly, so they hadn't been inspected with the same care as the M-98s. On the other hand, they were an older and more robust design which had never given any trouble. Yet.

"Yeah, yeah," Julian growled, scrambling to his feet. The impact had done far more damage to the tree than to his now sap-coated armor. It would take more than a sixty-kilometer-per-hour impact to damage ChromSten. "I'll be right there," he added as another flurry of grenades exploded ahead of them.

Roger dropped the empty grenade launcher and pulled his sword over his shoulder. The sensei in school was always talking about *The Book of Five Rings*, but the prince had never bothered to read it all. Another of those little acts of rebellion he was beginning to regret. Still, he remembered the technique for battling multiple opponents: reduce it to one at a time.

Nice to know, he thought, surveying the fifteen or twenty Mardukans filtering out of the brush with a variety of swords, spears, and other sharpened artifacts. *Now, how the hell do you* do *it?*

Some of them were wounded, a few quite seriously. Most of them, however, were just fine. And seemed really upset about something. Worse, the clear notes of hundreds of hunting horns sounded, coming up the hill behind them. All in all, it looked to be just a little dicey. Maybe they would leave him alone because his forehead didn't offer any trophies? Right.

The first Mardukan charged, holding a spear at waist height and screaming to wake the dead. Roger parried the spear down and to the side, let the momentum carry him through a spin and took off one of the scummy's arms as he passed. Then the rest of the group charged, and he picked out the weakest: a Mardukan with a bloody shrapnel wound on one leg.

Roger charged the wounded warrior, parrying another's spear and carrying the sword into a high parry of the wounded Mardukan's own blade. A butterfly twist, and the katana-like weapon came down and across, opening the Mardukan from shoulder to thigh as Roger passed through the closing circle.

He found himself several meters from his opponents, gazing at the group of warriors. He'd laid out two of them for nary a scratch, and the Kranolta seemed to be reevaluating the situation.

Roger was doing the same. He was fully aware that so far he'd survived on luck and a few tricks, but these Kranolta didn't seem to be very well trained. There were standard counters for both of the attacks he'd used. Cord knew them, and he'd taught them to the prince, but none of these tribesmen seemed aware of them. If all of them were this inept, he might last, oh, five more minutes.

But realistically, unless something broke soon, he was dead. Unfortunately, if he turned tail and ran, those spears could fly faster than he could run. So far, nobody seemed inclined to simply pincushion him and be done with it, and as long as it was hand-to-hand and more or less one-on-one he had a chance, however small.

Let's hear it for Homeric customs, he thought.

One of the scummies stepped forward and drew a line on the ground. Roger looked at it and shrugged; he had no idea what the gesture meant. He thought about it, then drew a line of his own.

The scummy clapped his false hands and stepped over his own line and fell into a guard position.

As he did, Roger thought of his pistol for the first time. There were only four spearmen; the others carried only swords. He could draw his pistol and kill all of his missile-armed opponents before the first spear could fly—he'd proven that conclusively in Q'Nkok—and he almost did it. It was the right thing to do, and he knew it. The idea of a prince of the Empire of Man fighting some four-armed barbarian with a sword on a neo-barb planet on the ass-end of nowhere was something from a really bad adventure novel. And if, by some fluke, he survived the experience, Captain Armand Pahner would personally break his neck for it.

He stepped over the line.

As he did, the scummy charged, sword held over his right shoulder. The weapon was one of the Mardukan two-handers and weighed nearly ten kilos. If Roger tried to block it, it would smash through his parry as if it weren't even there, so he waited patiently, sword at low guard, until the scummy began his swing. Then he darted in close to his towering foe, his sword held practically overhead.

The clash of steel was frighteningly loud as Hooker pounded into view. At every step, she'd expected to see the prince's dead body, for the ground was a pincushion of javelins. Instead, she found him in the midst of a half-circle of yelling scummies. She nearly tripped over a dead Mardukan as she skidded to a stop, but she managed to keep her feet . . . and not open fire as a dozen more scummies trotted up to join the shouting crowd. She knew instinctively that if she fired, the prince was dead.

Roger panted and looked at the next scummy in line. Already, three bodies had been pulled out of the de facto arena, and he was beginning to learn the rules. The line he'd drawn was a safe point. As long as he stayed on "his" side of it, they wouldn't attack, and if they were on the other side of their line, he couldn't attack in turn. However, the one time he'd waited too long to come out to meet an opponent, they'd gotten agitated. Obviously, he couldn't just sit and wait for rescue.

He didn't look around as he heard running feet behind him, but from the stiffening of some of the Mardukans, it had to be a Marine.

"There's a line behind me on the ground. Don't cross it!"

"Yes, Sir." He recognized Hooker's voice and hoped the angry little Marine would keep her cool. "Armor's on its way."

Roger nodded and flexed his shoulders. He'd long since dropped his rucksack, ammunition harness, and anything else that threatened to weigh him down. His sparring with Cord had taught him much that had, so far, kept him alive. As a mass, these scummies might be the most terrifying thing on this part of the planet, but as individuals, they were almost woefully ill-trained. On the other hand, it had been a long day already, and he was getting tired.

"Tell them to get here fast, but keep their cool," he said as another set of boots pounded up behind him. Then he looked at the scummy. "Come on, you four-armed bastard. I'm getting bored."

Julian passed the Mardukan shaman, hurrying towards Roger's position. The NCO wasn't sure exactly what the old scummy was saying, but it sounded a lot like cursing. The old geezer, who was fast enough on open ground, was having a bunch of trouble with the fallen trees, which was obviously the reason Roger hadn't included him on this little jaunt.

"Glad to see you're as happy with him as we are," the Marine yelled over his external speakers as he thundered by.

"I'll kill him," Cord snarled. "*Asi* or no *asi*, I swear I will!"

"Okay by me, but you'll have to get in line," Julian said as he passed out of sight. "A *long* line."

"I'm gonna kill him," Pahner said, almost calmly, as Bilali and the stretcher team pounded into view.

"Bilali?" Kosutic asked, rubbing her ear.

"Roger. Maybe Bilali, too."

The team leader marched up to the company commander and saluted.

"Sir, Sergeant Bilali reporting with party of one."

"And that one isn't the Prince, I see," Pahner said coldly. "I am far too enraged at the moment to deal with this. Get out of my sight."

"Yes, Sir." The sergeant walked over to where the medic was working on Gelert.

"Don't go ballistic, Armand," Kosutic whispered. "We have a *long* way to go."

"I keep telling myself that," Pahner replied. "And I'm trying not to. But if we lose the Prince, finishing the journey is next to pointless."

Kosutic could only nod at that.

Roger stepped back across his line and turned around.

"Who is the leader here?" he asked.

Over a hundred scummies had gathered to watch the contest by now. So far, Roger had won each match handily. A gouge on his helmet indicated the closest anyone had come to hitting him, and several of his own supporters—including Julian and his armored companions—had assembled with Hooker behind him. So far, the scummies had left his cheering section strictly alone while they concentrated on the main event.

A handful of seconds passed, and then a single Mardukan

stepped carefully onto the blood-soaked ground. He was older than most of the others, much scarred, and wore a necklace of horns around his neck.

"I am the senior tribe chief. I am Leem Molay, chief of the Kranolta Du Juqa."

"Well," Roger flipped the sword sideways to flick off the blood pooling on it, "I am Prince Roger Ramius Sergei Alexander Chiang MacClintock, of the House MacClintock, Heir Tertiary to the Throne of Man. And I finally have enough firepower to turn your pissant little tribe into meat for the *atul*." He took a rag from Hooker and began wiping down his blade as Cord came scrambling across the fallen tree trunks at last. "I don't intend to kill you one by one until I'm exhausted, and I don't intend to stand here jawing until darkness. So I propose a truce."

"Why should we let you live?" the chief scoffed.

"Julian?" Roger hadn't been able to see who was in the suits, and he'd long before turned his radio off. Listening to Pahner bitch had gotten on his nerves.

"Yep," one of the suits answered over its external speakers.

"Leem Molay, how many of your warriors do you want slaughtered to prove that you should let us walk away?" Roger sheathed his cleaned sword and took his reloaded grenade launcher from Pentzikis, but his icy eyes never left the Kranolta chieftain.

"Let me ask it this way," he went on calmly, tilting his head to the side. "Which half do you want us to kill to prove our point?"

"If you could truly kill us all, you would!" the chief retorted. "We are the Kranolta! Even Voitan could not stand before us! We will wipe *your* pissant little tribe from these lands!"

Roger inhaled sharply through his nostrils. The stench of dead Mardukans barely affected him at this point; he was far too deep into that dark world of battle.

"Watch carefully, old fool," he hissed.

The impromptu challenge matches had occurred on an open spot on the southern edge of the main battle zone. The Mardukans, for the most part, had been appearing from the northern woodline, so the southern one would make a better neutral target zone.

"Sergeant Julian." The prince gestured to the south. "Demonstration, please."

"Yes, Your Highness," the squad leader replied over his external speakers. He'd directed the response at the Kranolta, and his toot automatically translated it into the local dialect. "Gronningen, make these fine people a clearing to bury their dead in."

"Aye," Gronningen acknowledged, and turned to the south. "Shaman Cord, you might want to cover your ears."

The M-105 was a much heavier system than the M-98. That meant that, despite the all-pervasive, humid dampness of the jungle, the first shot from the plasma cannon left a trail of flickering fires on a ruler-straight line from the big Asgardian to the plasma bolt's impact on a tree in the middle of the area Roger had indicated. Where it shattered a divot into the woods.

The cannon's "*CRAAACK!*" was the loudest sound any of the Mardukans, even the survivors of the first brush with the company, had ever heard. It set their ears ringing, and the thermal pulse dried the surface of their mucus-covered skin, burning several of them painfully. And that was just from the secondary effects.

Twenty meters of the jungle giant which had been the gunner's target simply vanished as a lightning bolt carved from the heart of a star devoured it. The massive trunk shredded explosively for another five to ten meters above the impact point, and splinters longer than Roger was tall shrieked through the air far more lethally than any Kranolta javelin. The top of the tree flipped away into the burning jungle beyond, and the vegetation around it was turned into a finely divided, drifting ash surrounded by a dozen other burning, fallen trees.

And then Gronningen fired another round. And a third.

With those three rounds, he'd cleared a section of jungle fifty meters on a side and ringed with smoldering vegetation. Within that semicircle of hellfire, the ground steamed and smoked.

After a moment's stunned reflection, the chieftain turned from the destruction and asked the question.

"Why?"

"Because I don't intend to fight my way into Voitan. We walk into the city unmolested, or we kill every scummy in sight. Your choice."

"And on the morrow?" Molay was beginning to understand Puvin Eske's objections to this attack.

"On the morrow, you do your damnedest to kill all of us. Good luck. You had your chance to kill me as an individual . . . and couldn't. I suggest that you go home. If you do, we . . . I, Prince Roger Ramius Sergei Alexander Chiang MacClintock, will let you live."

The Kranolta chieftain laughed, although, even to himself, the sound was hollow. Or perhaps it was only the ringing in his ears.

"You think much of yourselves, humans. We are the Kranolta! I myself was one of the first over the walls of Voitan! Don't think to impress me with your threats!"

"We are The Empress' Own," Roger replied in a voice of iron, "and The Empress' Own does not know the meaning of failure." He smiled grimly, baring his teeth in that way which bothered most species except humans. "We rarely know the meaning of mercy, either, so count your blessings that I'm willing to show it to you this once."

The Mardukan glanced again at the flaming clearing and clapped his true-hands.

"Very well. We will let you go."

"Unmolested," Roger said. "To the city."

"Yes," the old Mardukan said. "And on the morrow, we will come, Prince Roger Ramius Sergei Alexander Chiang MacClintock. And the Kranolta will kill you all!"

"Then you'd better bring a bigger army!" Roger snarled, turning his back, and switched on his radio. "Julian, take the back door."

"Oh, yeah," the squad leader said. "Bet on it."

CHAPTER THIRTY-NINE

Most of the company was already gone when Roger walked through the gates. The hill ascended through the ruined city to a citadel on the upper slope, and it was obviously there that Captain Pahner had decided to make his stand.

Not everyone had been sent on to the citadel, however. A security detachment consisting of most of Second Platoon covered the gates, and Pahner sat waiting on his mound of rubble.

Roger walked up and saluted the captain.

"I'm back," he said, and Pahner shook his head slowly and spat out his gum at the prince's feet.

"First of all, Your Highness, as you've pointed out to me time and again, you don't salute me, I salute you."

"Captain—"

"I won't ask what you were thinking," the Marine continued. "I know what you were thinking. And I will admit here and now that it has a certain romantic attraction. It will certainly play well to the newsfeeds when we get home."

"Captain—"

"But it doesn't play well to *me*," Pahner snarled. "I've spent Marines like water to keep you alive, and having you throw that away on a stupid little gesture really pissed me off, Your Highness."

"Captain Pahner—" Roger tried again, beginning to get angry.

"You wanna play games, Your Highness?" the officer demanded, finally standing up. The two were of a height, both of them nearly two meters, but Pahner was by far the more imposing, a modern Hercules in bulk and build.

"You wanna play games?" he repeated in a deadly quiet voice. "Fine. I'm a master of playing games. I resign. *You're* the fucking company commander." He tapped the prince on the forehead with one finger. "*You* figure out how to make it across this goddamned planet without running completely out of ammunition and troops."

"Captain—" Roger was beginning to sound desperate.

"Yes, Sir, I'll just toddle along behind. What the hell, there's not a damn thing I can do *anyway*!" Pahner's face was turning a truly alarming shade of red. "I am really, really pissed at Bilali, Your Highness. You know why?"

"Huh?" Roger was confused by the sudden *non sequitur*. "No, why? But—"

"Because he can't forget he's a goddamned Marine!" Pahner barked. "I was a Marine before his *mother* was born, but when I came to the Regiment the first time, do you know what they told me?"

"No. But, Captain—"

"They told me to forget about being a Marine. Because Marines have all sorts of great traditions. Marines always bring back their dead. Marines never disobey an order. Marines always recover the flag. But in The Empress' Own, there's only *one* tradition. And do you know what the tradition of *your* regiment is, Colonel?"

"No, I guess not, but, Captain—"

"The tradition is that there is only one task. Only one mission. And we've never failed at it. Do you know what it is?"

"To protect the Imperial Family," Roger said, trying to get a word in edgewise. "But, Captain—"

"Do you think I *liked* leaving Gelert behind?!" the captain shouted.

"No, but—"

"Or Bilali, or Hooker, or, for God's sake, Dobrescu? Do you think I liked leaving our only *medic* behind?"

"No, Captain," Roger said, no longer even trying to rebut.

"Do you know why I was willing to lose those valuable people, troopers I've trained with my own hands, some of them for years? People I love? People that until recently you didn't even realize *existed*?"

"No," Roger said, finally really listening. "Why?"

"Because we have only one job: get you back to Imperial City alive. Until Crown Prince John's kids reach their legal majority and Parliament confirms their place in the succession, *you*—God help us all—are third in line for the Throne of Man! And whether you believe it or not, your family is the only damned glue holding the entire Empire of Man together, which is why it's our job—the *Regiment's* job—to protect that glue at any cost. Anything that stands in the way of that *has* to be ignored. Anything!" the captain snarled. "That's our mission. That's our *only* mission. I thought about it, and determined that I couldn't persuade them to retreat and abandon Gelert. But the company probably would have been lost if we'd settled into a meeting engagement on that ground. So I ran," he said softly.

"I abandoned them to certain death, cut my losses, and beat feet. For one reason only. And do you know what that was?"

"To keep me alive," Roger said quietly.

"So how do you think I felt when I turned around and you weren't there? After sacrificing all those people? And finding out it was for *nothing*?"

"I'm sorry, Sir," Roger said. "I didn't think."

"No," Pahner snapped. "You didn't. That's just fine, even expected, in a brand new, wet-behind-the-ears lieutenant. The ones who survive by luck and the skin of their teeth learn to think, eventually. But I can't take the chance on *your* not making it. Is that clear?"

"Yes," Roger replied, looking at the ground.

"If we lose you, we might as well all cut our throats. You realize that?"

"Yes, Sir."

"Roger, you'd better learn to think," the Marine said in a softer tone. "You'd better learn to think very quickly. I nearly took the entire company back out to get you. And we would all have died on that slope, because we couldn't have extracted you and then withdrawn successfully. We would have died right here. All of us. Bilali and Hooker and Despreaux and Eleanora and Kostas and all the rest of us. You understand?"

"Yes." Roger's voice was almost inaudible and he was looking at the ground again.

"And whose fault would that have been? Yours, or Bilali's?"

"Mine." Roger sighed, and Pahner looked at him unblinkingly for several moments, then nodded.

"Okay. As long as we have that straight," he said, and waited again until Roger nodded back.

"Colonel," he went on then, without a smile, "I think it's time we gave you another 'hat.'" He reached out again and tapped the prince on the forehead once more, more gently this time. "I think you need to take over as Third Platoon leader, Colonel. I know it will be a step down in rank, but I really need a platoon leader over there. Are you up for it, Colonel?"

Roger took his gaze off the ground at last, looked up at him, and nodded with slightly misty eyes.

"I'll try."

"Very well, Lieutenant MacClintock. Your platoon sergeant is Gunnery Sergeant Jin. He's an experienced NCO, and I think you could learn a lot from listening to his advice. I remind you that platoon leader is one of the most dangerous jobs in the Corps. Keep your head down and your powder dry."

"Yes, Sir," Roger said, and produced another salute.

"You'd better get up there, Lieutenant," the captain said soberly. "Your platoon is hard at work digging in. I think you should familiarize yourself with the situation as soon as possible."

"Yes, Sir!" Roger saluted yet again.

"Dismissed," Pahner said, and shook his head as the prince trotted up the ruined road towards the citadel. At least he finally had Roger unambiguously slotted into the chain of command, although he hated to think how the Regiment's CO was going to feel about the expedient to which he'd been driven. Now if he could only keep the young idiot alive! Platoon leader really *was* the most dangerous post in the Corps; which didn't mean that it wasn't *less* dangerous than watching Prince Roger ricochet around like an unaimed rifle bead on his own.

He watched the prince for a few more moments, then decided that he should hurry himself. He couldn't wait to see Jin's face.

"Gunnery Sergeant Jin?"

"Yes, Your Highness?" The gunnery sergeant turned from specifying positions and fields of fire with Corporal Casset and glanced at the prince. "Can I help you?"

The city of Voitan had been vast, but the citadel was the simplest of constructions. It was built into the slope of the mountain, backed up to a cliff which had been quarried sheer, undoubtedly for building material for the rest of the city. A seven-meter curtain wall ran in a more-or-less semicircle from cliff to cliff and surrounded a three-story inner keep. The curtain wall was thick, three meters across at the top, and tapered outward as it descended, with a heavy bastion built right into the cliff face at either end. The only entrances to the bastions were through small doors on the inner side at the level of the top of the wall. The original doors were long since gone, but temporary doors were already being constructed. The upper stories of the bastions had been of wood and had burned down long ago, as had the upper story of the keep, but the lower stories were built into the wall, and the interior partitions were stone. These had withstood not only the Kranolta assault but also the ravages of time and even the unceasing onslaught of the Mardukan jungle.

Slits for javelins and spears were arrayed on the "wall-level," pointing outward. No inner first-story slits faced the top of the wall, but upper-level slits did just that, designed so that if the top of the wall were taken, fire could be poured into the attackers. There were also slits at the level of the bailey, so that if the attackers made it over the wall they could be attacked as they assaulted the keep.

The keep itself was a large, burned-out, vine-covered shell. The upper story, like those of the bastions, had been constructed of wood and was now charcoal. The rear of the keep, however, was dug deeply into the hillside, its roof supported by cleverly constructed stone buttresses, which provided a large, cavelike area that could be used to shield the pack beasts, wounded, and noncombatants. The *flar-ta*, kept from stampeding by chains stapled into the naked rock, were on the ground level, while the wounded and noncombatants waited on a raised shelf on the north side, along with Julian and the other power-armored Marines.

There were spear slits at the keep's bailey level, but the only exterior door was on the second floor, up a staircase. Vines covered the walls, and trees had grown up through the flagstones of the bailey, but other than the vegetation and the damage to the gates, the gray stone of the fortress was intact.

Third Platoon, which was still more or less at full strength, had been assigned the left side of the wall, while First and Second shared the right. Teams from both groups were working feverishly to construct barricades to replace the broken and decayed gates, and Sergeant Jin had been noting the locations of the platoon's troopers and their fields of fire. It was important to ensure that all possible approaches were covered and that the heaviest fire could be directed at the point where the enemy would be most likely to attack in force.

With that in mind, Jin had placed his grenadiers in locations covering the primary avenues of approach. He'd also pointed out to them the locations that the enemy was most likely to use for cover. There were, unfortunately, a lot of those. The citadel overlooked what had once been a densely populated city, and the shells of buildings still loomed above narrow, twisting streets. That would have been enough to mask the approach of any attackers by itself, but the ruins were also massively overgrown with vines, creepers, small trees, and jungle ferns, producing what were effectively well-screened trenches up to the foot of the citadel wall. Those would be the particular target of the grenadiers, since they were the only troopers whose weapons would allow them to drop indirect fire behind obstacles.

The platoon also had two plasma cannon. Given the failure of the power suits and the fact that this would be a stationary defense, the heavy cannon had been set up on their tripods. Jin intended to use them only against the heaviest concentrations of enemies, both because the Marines had developed a healthy distaste for the possible repercussions of firing them and because of the need to conserve their precious ammunition.

He was going to be without Julian and his team of suit-users. The inoperable suits had been lashed back onto the pack beasts, with their cursing users still trapped inside them, and carried out into the citadel. The gear was now scattered on one side of the bailey with Poertena working on it, but the personnel whose suits did work were going to be used as a reserve for the company as a whole. So it was with too few troops to man the section of wall he'd been given, with his heavy troopers missing, and the possibility, however remote, of losing half his platoon to exploding plasma cannon, that the gunnery sergeant found out he had a new responsibility.

"I'm your new platoon leader," Roger said.

"Pardon me?" Jin looked around. Corporal Casset was standing with his jaw dropped, but other than the corporal (and the pissed-off and tired looking shaman standing behind the prince) no one else had heard Roger's announcement. "Is this some sort of joke, Your Highness?"

"No, Gunnery Sergeant, it isn't," Roger said carefully. "Captain Pahner has asked me to 'wear another hat.' He's appointed me to be your platoon leader."

"Oh," Jin said. He did not add "joy," for some unknown reason, but after a moment he went on with slightly glassy eyes. "Very well, Your Highness. If you'll give me a moment, I'll walk you through the defenses and explain the placements. I would ask for your comments and suggestions after that."

"Very well, Gunny. And, I think 'Sir' would be appropriate. Or 'Lieutenant.' I'm not really a prince in this assignment, as I understand things."

"Very well, Your . . . Sir," the sergeant said, shaking his head.

"Captain, we've gotten our people into position, and—"

"Shhh!" Pahner's hand waved Lieutenant Jasco to silence as the captain turned his head from side to side.

"Pardon me, Sir?" the lieutenant said after trying for a moment to figure out what he was looking at. All the lieutenant could see was the idiot prince talking to Gunny Jin.

"*Shhh!*" Pahner repeated, then grunted in satisfaction as he finally managed to get the directional microphone onto the conversation just as Jin realized what his company commander had done to him.

Lieutenant Jasco maintained a straight face as Captain Pahner did something the lieutenant would have flatly denied was possible. He giggled. It was an amazing sound to hear out of the tall, broad officer, and Pahner cut it off almost immediately. He listened for a few more seconds, then switched off the mike and turned to Jasco with a seraphic smile.

"Yes, Lieutenant?" he asked, still chuckling. "You were saying?"

"We've gotten all of our people into position, Sir. When do you think they're going to attack?"

"Lieutenant," Pahner looked at the sky, "your guess on that is as good as mine. But I think they'll wait until morning. It's getting late, and they've never hit us at night. I'll come by your positions in a bit. Go get with your platoon sergeant and figure out a chow rotation for right now."

He could smell Matsugae starting something on a fire.

Roger sniffed and looked towards the keep where Kostas had dinner well under way. The valet might just have put himself in harm's way to rescue a nobody trooper, but it didn't seem to have affected him at all. He'd simply gone back to organizing the camp. Maybe there was a lesson to learn there.

Roger turned and swept his gaze over the troopers still working all around him. Now that the basics had been done—setting up the heavy weapons, assigning fields of fire, putting up sandbags where stones had fallen from the battlements of the citadel wall—the Marines were improving their individual positions. Despite the intense heat, even more focused here inside the stone walls, the troopers worked without pause. They knew it would be too late to improve their chances of survival *after* the Kranolta hit.

Despreaux walked over to him, and he nodded to her.

"Sergeant," he said, and she nodded back and tossed him the small object in her hand.

"Nice folks."

Roger caught the item and blanched. It was a very small Mardukan skull, one side crushed. The horns were barely buds.

"There's a big pile of bones over in the bastion," she continued. "That was part of it. It looks like the defenders made some sort of stand."

Roger looked over the wall at the crumbled city below. He had enough experience now to imagine the horrors the castle's defenders would have observed as the rest of their city went up in roaring flame and massacre. And to imagine their despair as the gate crumbled and the Kranolta barbarians poured through. . . .

"I'm not really very happy with these fellows," he said, setting the skull gently on the parapet.

"I've seen worse," Despreaux said coldly. "I made the drop on Jurgen. Pardon me if I'm humanocentric, but . . . it was worse."

"Jurgen?" Roger couldn't place the name.

Despreaux's sculpted profile hardened, and a muscle in her jaw twitched.

"No place that mattered, Your Highness. Just a stinking little fringe world. Bunch of dirt-poor colonists, and a single town. A pirate ship dropped in for a visit. It was a particularly unpleasant bunch. By the time we got there, the pirates were long gone. The results weren't."

"Oh," Roger said. The attacks on border worlds were so common that they hardly ever made the news in the Home Regions. "I'm sorry."

"Nothing for you to be sorry about, Your Highness. Just something to remember; there's bad guys out there all the time. The only people who usually see them are the Fleet and the Marines. But when things get screwed up enough, this isn't so uncommon. The barbs are always at the door."

She touched the skull gently, then gave him another cool nod and walked back to where her squad was digging in. Roger continued looking out over the city, stroking the skull with a thumb, until Pahner walked up.

"How's it going, Lieutenant?"

"Just fine . . . Sir," Roger said distractedly, still gazing out over murdered Voitan. "Captain, can I say something as 'His Highness' instead of 'Lieutenant'?"

"Certainly," Pahner said with a smile. "Your Highness."

"I don't think it would be a good idea to leave an existing force in our rear, do you?"

"You're talking about the Kranolta?" Pahner glanced at the skull.

"Yes, Captain. How are we fixed for power for the suits?"

"Well," Pahner grimaced, "since we only have four of them up, not bad. Days and days with just four of them. But we need to get the rest up to have a hope in hell of taking the spaceport."

"But we have enough for a pursuit, don't we?"

"Certainly." Pahner nodded. "And you have a point about leaving remnants in our rear. I don't want to have to fight off ambushes from here to the next city-state."

"Good." Roger turned and looked the captain in the eye. "I don't think that the cause of civilization on this world would be advanced by leaving a single Kranolta alive, Captain. I would prefer that that not be the case after tomorrow."

Pahner regarded him steadily, then nodded.

"So would I, Your Highness. So would I. I think tomorrow we'll be building a samadh. To the honor of the Corps."

CHAPTER FORTY

Roger looked out from the citadel wall as the first overcast light of dawn stole across the dead, jungle-devoured cityscape.

The company had been up for nearly an hour, getting breakfast and preparing for these first moments of early morning light. This time, Before Morning Nautical Twilight, had been considered the most dangerous time of all for millennia. It was the time preferred for a "dawn attack," when sleepy-eyed sentries were at their lowest ebb and attackers could slip up under cover of darkness but attack with the gathering light.

The Marines' answer was the same one armies had used for centuries: get up well before time and be awake and alert when the moment of "stand to" came. Naturally, as had also been the case for centuries, there were some complainers.

Roger wasn't one of them. He'd been up for hours the previous night, reviewing his actions of the day before and worrying about what was to come. For all that he'd been fighting monsters and the occasional skirmish or ambush all the way across the continent, this would be his first true battle. Today the Kranolta would come to kill the company, and someone would lose, and someone would win. Some of them would die, and some would live. While it seemed likely that casualties would be light, there was still a risk. There was even a risk that the humans would lose, and then word of the treachery aboard the *DeGlopper* would never reach Earth. Roger had smiled at himself when he reached that point in his ruminations. It was amusing to realize that the main thing he thought about was that the word wouldn't get back to his mother, not that he himself would be dead.

Sergeant Major Kosutic padded up silently behind him and leaned on the lip of the adjoining embrasure.

"Still quiet," she said, and glanced over at Cord who stood silently at Roger's back. Since the events of the day before, the old shaman had attached himself firmly to his "master," and was rarely to be found more than five meters away.

The sergeant major had been up from time to time the night before. Not worried, just running through the practiced actions of an experienced warrior checking on changes. Still, she'd become slightly perturbed as every sentry throughout the night had reported more and more fires. The tactical computers were having a hard time pinning down numbers, but each fire sent the estimates up and up. The current balance of forces didn't look good.

"I wish we had some razor wire," she said.

"Do you think it will come to that?" Roger asked in surprise. "They've only got spears; we have plasma cannon."

"Your Highness—I mean, Lieutenant," Kosutic said with a smile, "there's an old story, probably a space story, about a general and a captain. They were fighting some indigs and an air car came in with a spear sticking out of the side. The captain laughed and asked how they could lose against people armed only with spears. But the general looked at the captain and asked how she thought they could win against people willing to *fight* an air car with only a spear."

"And the moral is?" Roger asked politely.

"The moral, Lieutenant, is that there is no such thing as a deadly weapon. There are only deadly people, and the Kranolta—" her hand waved over the battlements at the broken city "—are fairly deadly."

Roger nodded and looked around, then back into the sergeant major's eyes.

"Are we?" he asked quietly.

"Oh, yeah," Kosutic said. "Nobody who gets through RIP is a slacker in a firefight. But . . . there's gonna be a lot of those scummies, and there ain't many of us." She shivered slightly at the smell of woodsmoke from the thousands of fires in the jungle. "It's gonna get interesting. Satan damn me if it ain't."

"We'll get the job done, Sergeant Major," the prince said confidently.

"Yeah." Kosutic looked at the sword hilt jutting up over his shoulder. "I suppose we will."

Captain Pahner strolled up, checking the positions, and looked out at the mists curling around the ruined city.

"Beautiful morning, fellas," he remarked, and Roger chuckled.

"It'd be even more beautiful if half 'my' platoon were in armor, Captain. What's the status?"

"Well," Pahner said with a grimace, "it isn't pretty, 'Lieutenant.' Poertena found the fault, which is a mold eating the contacts coating of the joint power conduits. You can't remove the coating; it's a dissimilar metallic contact. The problem seems to be in a new 'improved' version."

"Oh shit," Kosutic chuckled grimly.

"Yeah." Pahner nodded with a grim smile. "Another improvement. The suits that hadn't been 'upgraded' are okay. But that's just the four."

"What are we going to do?" Roger's eyes were wide, for Pahner had stressed repeatedly that they had to have the suits to take the starport.

"Fortunately, the contacts tend to wear out, so each suit has a spare in its onboard spares compartment. The ones sealed up in the storage packets are okay, but . . ."

"But there's only a couple of spares per suit, normally." Kosutic shook her head. "So we're down to four sets of armor for everything except taking the spaceport."

"Right." The captain nodded. "We can cannibalize from suits that we lose the users for, or that go down with other problems we can't fix. So we can put His Highness in a suit if things look particularly bad. But until then, it's just 'The Four Horsemen.' "

"I guess that will have to do," Roger said with a shrug, then changed the subject. "So what's the plan for today, Captain?"

"Well," Pahner replied with his own shrug, "we wait until they have the majority of their forces in close, then engage with all the firepower we have. I won't say that I agree or disagree about whether they should be wiped out as a tribe, but we can't afford to have a large force following us to the next city-state. So they have to be eliminated as an operational threat at least."

"Can we do that?" Over the night, Roger's ardor had cooled, and he looked at the scattered weapons positions worriedly.

"Against what I'd estimate the maximum threat to be, yes," Pahner said. "There's a big difference between barbarian warriors and soldiers, and today these Kranolta are going to discover that."

"What's your estimate?" There were hundreds of fires in the jungle according to the taccomp in Roger's helmet—just under a thousand, in fact.

"I'm estimating a maximum of five thousand warriors with some camp followers. More than that is really hard to maintain logistically."

"Five *thousand*?" Roger choked. "There are only *seventy* of us!"

"Don't sweat it, Your Highness." Kosutic gave him a cold smile. "A defensive position like this gives us a ten-to-one advantage all by its lonesome. Add in the firepower, and five thousand isn't an impossible number." She paused and looked thoughtful. "Tough? Yeah. But not impossible. We're gonna get hurt, though."

"We'll make it through," Pahner said grimly. "That's the only thing that matters."

"What did Cord think of those numbers?" the prince asked, looking over his shoulder at the shaman. Despite the Marines' confidence, it still seemed like a lot of scummies to him.

"The Kranolta are said to be as numerous as the stars in the sky," the shaman said quietly. "They cover the ground like the trees."

"Maybe they do," Pahner said, "but that's not what you could call a hard and fast number. And it's really difficult to support more than five thousand in these sorts of conditions. I don't see any sign of a baggage train, for example."

"And if it *is* more?" Roger asked dubiously.

"More than the stars in the sky?" Pahner smiled wryly. "If it's more than five thousand, well . . . we'll just handle it. The important part is to survive and damage them badly enough that they decide that fucking with Imperial Marines is a short road to Hell."

"Oh hell," Corporal Kane whispered.

The humans had been working in shifts throughout the night to prepare their defenses, and she stood on one of the recently constructed platforms within the burned-out bastion, monitoring the sensor remotes planted along the approaches to the citadel. That gave her the dubious pleasure of an advanced look at the approaching horde, and a horde it was. She took one more look at the numbers estimate, blanched, and keyed her radio.

"Sergeant Despreaux, could you step over to the west bastion?"

The company command group had gathered atop the curtain wall gatehouse, watching the gathering horde on their visor HUDs. Captain Pahner's maximum estimate had unquestionably been exceeded.

"How the hell could they have gathered fifteen thousand warriors?" Pahner demanded irately. He couldn't seem to decide whether he was more incredulous or more offended that the Kranolta had not abided by his professional estimate.

"Between fifteen and eighteen, actually, Sir," Lieutenant Gulyas corrected, looking at the readout on his own helmet heads-up display.

"Should I have Poertena start warming up the other suits?" "Lieutenant" MacClintock asked.

"No," Pahner said, thinking furiously.

"We could engage them at longer ranges," Lieutenant Jasco suggested. "The plasma cannon would range from here, and they've got the punch to burn through the undergrowth. Hell, for that matter, they could blow through most of those *walls* without much sweat."

"No," Pahner said again, shaking his head. He pulled out a stick of gum and popped it into his mouth without any sort of ritual.

"This is gonna get real interesting, boss," Kosutic said, taking another look between the battlements.

"Pull the plasma cannon off the walls," Pahner said abruptly. "Put them in the bastions ready to move up. Put one on each of the bottom floors, and the rest at wall level. When we come to grips, it's bead rifles only. No grenades, no plasma."

"But—" Lieutenant Jasco said. "Sir, we'll lose the walls!"

"Yep," Pahner agreed with a grim smile. "Better make sure the door to the keep is heavily reinforced. And tell Julian his people stay put in there until I tell him different. And make sure those damned pack beasts are tied down!" If the elephant-sized *flar-ta* got loose in those close confines, it would doom anyone who wasn't in armor.

"I'll take care of that," Jasco said, heading out the door.

"Get those plasma cannon moved back," Pahner continued to Gulyas. "Remember, at least one downstairs in each of the bastions. We have five, so two upstairs in Third Platoon's bastion, and one downstairs. One up, one down in the east bastion."

"I'm on it," the lieutenant replied, already leaving, and Pahner turned back to the oncoming Kranolta.

"I still don't believe this." He shook his head. "Where do they get the food?"

"They've had word of our coming for some time now," Cord pointed out. "Undoubtedly they heard through rumors from Q'Nkok, and with that warning, the warriors would have gorged and gorged for days, then set off with packs of food for Voitan. We were lucky to arrive before the main host."

"They were probably waiting for us wherever the crossing of that Satan-damned swamp was," Kosutic agreed, nodding her head. "Good thing *we* didn't know where it was, or we'd be dead in the jungle."

"They can't stay together long," Cord admitted. "Only a few days, at most. But they don't intend to stay long; only long enough to kill us."

"And if we just hold them off," Roger continued, "they'll be waiting for us every few kilometers in the jungle."

"Which is why we have to do more than drive them off," Pahner confirmed. "And we will."

"Let's hope so," Roger said. "Let's hope so."

CHAPTER FORTY-ONE

All through the long morning, the enemy gathered in a swarm just inside the ruined outer wall of the city. The mass of natives blew their horrible trophy horns and pounded drums, taunting the humans hunkered down in the citadel. Finally, when their numbers were fully gathered, they started in good order for the citadel.

Pahner, watching the approach from the gate bastion on the HUD fed by the remotes, nodded as he surveyed their formation. The lead group carried scaling ladders, and about a third of the way back from the front of the formation a mass of warriors with ropes carried a large ram. They'd prepared well, he decided, but then, they'd taken this city before.

Of course, they've never tried to take a city away from The Empress' Own, he thought grimly.

"Third Platoon, when that ram gets to a hundred and fifty meters from the gate, take it out with plasma fire."

Roger watched from a position on the wall. The heavily reinforced firing point had been prepared for one of the plasma cannons, so it was a "safe" spot from which to watch the approach of the enemy. It seemed folly to wait for the Kranolta to overrun the company before using heavy weapons, but he was taking Pahner's lead. He keyed his microphone and passed on the order.

Corporal Cathcart was almost over the failure of his armor, but he was still pissed about being taken off the wall and told to hold his fire. So when the word came down to engage the ram, he was happy to oblige.

The designers of Voitan's original defenses had faced only muscle-powered weapon threats, and that had dictated the clear areas they had allowed as fire zones. The citadel's approaches had been paved and flat for approximately a hundred and fifty meters from the curtain wall gatehouse, and just a bit over a hundred meters from the rest of the wall. The city's buildings had begun beyond those ranges, and the wrecked, decaying, luxuriantly overgrown ruins of those buildings were what cut up the company's fire lanes and would have deprived it of the full use of its range advantage even if Captain Pahner hadn't opted to let the barbarians close. But those ruins were also liberally seeded with remote sensors, and Cathcart had been using them to watch the big log approach.

Now he rolled his plasma cannon over to a handy spear slot and mentally licked his chops as he positioned it carefully. The cannon was designed for use as either a crew-served weapon or from a powered armor mount. In its crew-served configuration, its mount included retractable wheels, which were really quite useful in situations like this. He got the gun lined up, and hit the switch to take it off the wheels and drop its firing platform firmly into place.

"Everybody stand back. There's liable to be some backblast."

The barrel of the weapon was aligned with the exterior of the mini-fort as he hunted until he spotted the ram again. It had advanced another fifty meters as the lead elements approached the wall. In fact, it was in direct line of sight from his position now, and he punched a button and grunted as the entire ram was outlined in red on his sighting screen. The computer recognized it as a target and began to track automatically.

There were quicker ways to do things like this, but he had plenty of time, and it never hurt to do the job right. He designated the entire ram as a target, then designated three specific target points along its length before he took his eyes from the display to look carefully around his position one last time. He was behind the blast shield, but anyone else nearby might be caught by backscatter as the plasma charge exited the spear slit. Fortunately, everyone was well under cover . . . helped, no doubt, he reflected, by memories of exploding plasma rifles.

"Fire in the hole!"

The three plasma charges hit like the micro-nuclear explosions they were. They didn't splinter the ram; they vaporized it, along with every one of its carriers and every Kranolta warrior within forty meters. Beyond that immediate kill zone, there were actually some survivors, although the mucus-covered Mardukans suffered horribly from the flash burns of thermal bloom. The entire horde bellowed in shock, but they hadn't been totally surprised, for the story of Julian's "demonstration" had spread among them.

Worse, from the humans' perspective, the narrow, twisting streets, choked with rubble and encroaching jungle wreckage, split the Kranolta advance into channelized tentacles, exactly as the Marines had feared. Had the horde been a more organized force, that might have wreaked havoc with its attack, but the barbarians' lack of organization actually worked in their favor in this instance. They were scarcely discommoded by the confusion of their approach to the citadel, even as the Marines were denied the full advantage of their weapons' range.

That was one main reason Pahner had selected his chosen deployment plan. If the scummies were prepared to accept sufficient casualties, they could close with the citadel whatever his people did, so he'd decided to make a virtue out of his weakness.

The trickiest element of his battle plan was the need to inflict sufficient casualties to enrage the barbarians into pressing the attack without hurting them badly enough to convince them to do the intelligent thing and back off until simple starvation forced the Marines to abandon their defensive position and run a gauntlet of endless ambushes in the jungle. Not that this particular bunch of barbarians seemed to require much in the way of enraging, he reflected as they surged forward around the huge, half-fused hole the plasma cannon had torn in their ranks.

Cathcart's shot had also acted as an effective start for the rest of the company's fire. The citadel's elevated position helped some, but the furthest out aiming stake was barely a hundred and fifty meters from the curtain wall. That was short range for a bead rifle . . . and meant the scummies had only a soccer field and a half to cross.

"*Fire!*" Gunnery Sergeant Jin snapped over the platoon net, and set the example himself. The first wave of burst fire from the company tumbled a windrow of the ladder-carriers in piles, but the mass of natives simply kept coming as the following ranks picked up the ladders and charged the walls.

Pahner nodded. The enemy was coming on more or less as expected, although the ladders were a surprise. There were even more Kranolta than the taccomp had estimated, though, and that was causing a few jinks in the plan. They were also much heavier on the west flank; Roger's side. It might be a good idea to thin them out a bit.

"I want two grenade volleys," he called. "Aim into the middle of the mass, about seventy-five meters out. I want to create a break in the assault."

"Roger," Lieutenant Jasco acknowledged. He'd taken over command of the right wall while Lieutenant Gulyas was in the keep.

The grenadiers filed out of the bastions and got into position as the bead riflemen on the parapets continued to pour aimed fire into the attacking Mardukans. The grenadiers readied their weapons and awaited the word as Pahner followed the timing. Right . . . about . . .

"Now!"

The twelve remaining grenadiers fired upon his command. For most of them, it was their first clear look at the enemy, but the numbers coming at them didn't throw off their aim. The twenty-four grenades arced out into the mass of the Mardukans, dropping behind sheltering walls and heaps of rubble which had blocked the bead fire, and detonated. The double string of explosions ripped holes in the Kranolta army, and hundreds of the four-armed natives writhed in shrieking agony as shrapnel from the mini-artillery scythed through their packed ranks.

"Again," Pahner called. "Down fifty meters."

Again the belt-fed launchers spat out their packages of death, tearing the ranks of the enemy apart. But still the natives closed up over the mangled bodies of their comrades and came on, blowing their horns and bellowing war cries.

"Okay," Pahner said, satisfied. "Back under cover." He pursed his lips and whistled. "'*When you're wounded and left on Marduk's plains—*'"

Most of the grenadiers filed back into the bastions, where the hastily constructed doors were wedged in place. The few who stayed on the wall picked up their bead rifles and opened fire again. The enemy was about to assault.

"Sir," Lieutenant Jasco said, with a grunt that carried clearly over the com, "I've got more ladders coming up than I've got hands to push down. I need some support here."

"Same here," Roger reported, and Pahner heard the distinctive sound of steel meeting flesh over the prince's radio. "We're about to lose the wall!"

"Too soon," Pahner whispered, peering through the slit that overlooked Roger's position. There were already Mardukans on the wall, in close combat with the Marines, and he saw Roger lop the head off one, while Cord speared another.

"Call out your grenadiers and plasma gunners! Push them off the walls!" he ordered. He'd held the grenadiers and plasma gunners under cover to protect them from the anticipated wave of javelins from the Mardukans, but very few javelins were flying. Instead, the Kranolta concentrated with fanatical determination on getting over the walls and coming to close grips with their smaller opponents. *When are they going to follow the plan?* he wondered with a grim mental chuckle. *Guess they've learned a little about the disadvantages of matching javelins against bead rifles at range. Too bad it's really true that no plan survives contact with the enemy!*

The fresh infusion of Marines and a barrage of grenades pushed the enemy off the walls, and Pahner was relieved to see no prone bodies and only a few Marines nursing wounds.

"Switch out weapons. Put the wounded in the bastions." He looked out the slit facing the enemy, who seemed to be getting back in shape rather quickly. "And get ready for another attack!"

* * *

"Inside, Despreaux." Roger thumbed towards the bastion.

"I'm not hurt that bad, Sir." She hefted her rifle with her left hand, and started to try to reload it one-handed.

"I said, get in the bastion!" Roger snatched the weapon out of her hand. "That's an order, Sergeant."

Her jaw clenched, but then she nodded.

"Yes, *Sir!*" She saluted with her left hand.

"And get Liszez to replace you."

"Aye," she answered, and he nodded and turned towards the gate.

"Kameswaran! I thought I told you to get your ass into the bastion!"

Jimmy Dalton stroked the butt of the bead rifle and shook his head. There sure were a shit-load of the damned scummies.

The plasma gunner had carried a bead rifle through about half his service, so he was familiar enough with the operation of the weapon. But he'd also inherited Corporal Kameswaran's ammo harness, and that was unfamiliar. Everyone had his own idiosyncrasies about what went where, and the corporal's were more idiosyncratic than most.

Dalton ran his hand across the positions of all the gear and shook his head. Just had to hope he didn't need any of the stuff in a hurry.

The prince came up and looked out of the mini-bunker the private occupied.

"Looks like they're getting ready to come back."

"Yes, Your Highness." The private wished he had his plasma rifle; that would slow them up. "When do we open fire?"

"When Gunny Jin gives the word." The prince grinned. "Even I don't fire until the gunny says it's okay!"

"Yes, Your Highness." The plasma gunner ran his hand across the ammo harness again and shook his head. They'd made it onto the walls the last time. Why not open fire further out?

The prince seemed to read his mind.

"This is hard, waiting for them to come to us. But it would be worse worrying about being ambushed from here to the sea. We need to suck them in and kill them all, Jimmy, not just drive them off."

Dalton hadn't thought the prince even knew his name.

"Yes, Your Highness."

"I'm not Prince Roger right now, Jimmy. I'm just your platoon leader. Call me Lieutenant MacClintock."

"Yes, Your—Lieutenant," the private said. As if he didn't have enough to worry about.

Most of the ladders were still at the base of the wall, so the Kranolta came on at an unburdened run in the second wave.

"*Fire!*" Jin barked as they passed the hundred-meter stake and picked out his own target—one covered with horn trophies. "Take that, you bastard," he whispered, as the chieftain and two followers fell away from the burst of fire.

Roger pulled out another magazine and inserted it even as he maintained fire. The double magazine system was made for situations like this. His accuracy was somewhat degraded during the switch, but as long as he fired into that incredible mass of targets he was bound to hit *something*.

The Kranolta packed the ground before the wall as they reached its base and the ladders started coming up again. They were more tangled than in the first assault, but a little thing like that was nothing in the chaos at the wall's foot. Thousands of them were packed dozens deep, each and every one of them determined to be the very first over the battlements.

"Grenades, Gunny?" Roger heard his own voice over the radio and was surprised by how calm he sounded. He triggered another burst into the back of the mass; leaning out over the wall to fire directly down at its base was hazardous to health.

"Yes, Sir," Jin approved and called the order. A dozen grenades sailed into the close-packed Kranolta, exploding with deadly effectiveness, but the close press of bodies actually lessened their effect by absorbing blast and fragments, and the holes they opened closed rapidly as the feet of fresh waves of tribesmen pounded their less fortunate fellows into paste.

Roger charged forward as the first ladder came up in his sector. He and PFC Stickles managed to heave it back over the side with a descending scream from the scummies on it, but three more came up in the time it took to push one off. The Kranolta were pushing forward again through sheer weight of numbers and there were nowhere near enough humans to cover the full length of the wall.

"*Grenades!*" Pahner barked. "All you've got!"

Roger ripped one of the hundred-gram cylinders off his belt with his left hand, thumbed the activator, and tossed it over the wall just as the first scummy appeared at the top of a ladder. The prince put two rifle beads into the attacker one-handed even as he threw two more grenades, but by then the Kranolta were over the wall.

His magazine clicked suddenly empty, and he tossed the rifle into "his" bunker and waded in with the katana as he had before. This battle was a complete madhouse, with dozens of screaming barbarians clambering over the parapets, their false-hands holding the ladders and both true-hands filled with weapons. Trading parries with a scummy who was better than usual, Roger found himself back-to-back with Cord and realized they were practically alone. Most of the Marines had retreated into the bastions, but there were a few human bodies scattered along the wall.

"Cord!" Roger ducked a swing and opened the attacking Kranolta from thigh to breastbone. "We have to get off the wall!"

"No doubt!" the shaman shouted back, and speared another attacker. The barbarian dropped, but Cord suddenly found himself facing three replacements, and they did not appear to be taking turns. "How?"

Roger was about to reply, when his eyes widened and he spun and lunged at Cord. He tackled the much larger shaman hard enough to drive both of them into his mini-bunker . . . just as the flight of grenades from Third Platoon's bastion landed.

The grenades temporarily cleared the wall, turning the Kranolta who'd scaled it into hamburger. Most of the Marines' chameleon-suited wounded were unaffected by the air-burst grenades, but the unarmored barbarians were slaughtered.

Fragments also tore into Cord's legs. Roger had thrown himself across the shaman's torso, preventing instant death, but the native was horribly injured, and Roger himself was considerably the worse for wear.

He was stumbling to his feet, ears ringing, vision doubled, and more than half stunned, when he felt himself lifted and thrown across a shoulder.

"Okay," Despreaux snapped. She seemed, he noticed, to be upside-down. "Are you done playing hero, Hero?"

"Get Cord," he croaked. It had to be either St. John or Mutabi carrying him, he decided; nobody else was big enough.

"Already done," she said, taking one corner of the shaman's stretcher. Wounded Marines were being dragged off all along the wall while others recovered their weapons.

The last thing Roger remembered was an upside-down scummy coming over the parapet, with his ax raised over Despreaux's head.

Pahner listened to the reports and nodded.

"One more time on the walls. But make sure everyone makes it back to the bastions this time."

He looked out at the sea of scummies and shook his head. The jam-packed mob looked as if it hadn't been reduced at all, but that was an illusion. They'd already lost almost a fifth of their force to the wall assaults and the grenades. Now it was time to start the real killing.

"Blow the gate."

The timber barrier replacing the ruined gates had been carefully constructed. The original purpose of the emplaced demolition charges had been to permit a sally by the armored suits, but the explosives designed to let Marines out worked just as well to let Mardukans in.

The loss of their ram had reduced the Kranolta at the gate to clawing and hacking at the timbers. Their howls of frustration had been clearly audible even through the din of battle . . . and so were their shrieks of agony as the demo charges' explosions mangled them and blew them backwards. The warriors behind them paid them no heed, however, except to stream forward over their writhing bodies, screaming exultant war cries as they fanned out across the bailey. The gate was down; the fortress was theirs!

"Oh, Captain, that was mean," Julian whispered as he peered through the firing slit at the open gateway. He watched the tide of scummies split, some charging for the keep, and others for the inner stairs to the bastions, and then he poked his bead cannon through the slit.

There were a number of available munitions for the weapon. Besides the standard ten-millimeter ceramic-cored, steel-coated beads, there were both armor piercing and "special actions" munitions. The armor piercing beads were designed to be effective against any known suit armor, and against most armored vehicles, as well. The "special actions" munitions were mixed. Some were crowd-control devices: sticky balls to coat rioters in glue, knockout gas, or puke gas. And some of them were for close quarter conditions where the object was pure, unmitigated slaughter. The company didn't have many of those with them, but this was just about the perfect time to use the one magazine he had.

He stroked the stock of the bead cannon with a feral grin.

"Come to Poppa," he crooned.

Pahner gazed down into the courtyard from the gatehouse's upper story, calmly masticating his gum and waiting. He blew a bubble when First Platoon reported that spears were being thrust into the ground floor slits of its bastion. He nodded when the keep reported that the Mardukans were chopping at its door, and he steepled his fingers when the sound of ax blows started beneath his own feet. Then he nodded again.

"Fire," he said, and stepped back from the spear slit.

Julian had already programmed his visor HUD to show the round's footprint, and he aimed his first shot carefully. The ten-millimeter cylinder was fired at very low velocity, relatively speaking, but the instant it exited the barrel, it blossomed like some hideous flower to deploy its twenty-five depleted uranium beads in a beautiful geometric pattern like a high-tech spider's web.

Strung with monomolecular wire.

The advanced adaptation of the ancient concept of chainshot was lethal almost beyond belief, yet it never made it across the courtyard. Its designers wouldn't have believed that was possible, for the wire sliced through weapons, limbs, and bodies almost effortlessly. But only *almost.* If enough flesh and bone was crowded together in its path, eventually even wire a single molecule thick would find sufficient resistance to stop it.

This wire did, but not before it had torn over a third of the way across the bailey and sliced every native in its path into neatly severed gobbets of flesh. The destruction sprayed blood and bits of Mardukan in every direction, and so did the second shot in Julian's magazine. And the third. And the fourth.

The paved courtyard was an abattoir, filled with Kranolta who'd finally seen sufficient concentrated slaughter to stem even their frenzied advance for just a moment. The survivors were frozen in momentary shock and disbelief, like lifesize sculptures coated in the blood of their hideously dismembered fellows.

Sculptures which were cooked an instant later by plasma cannon.

There were four of the weapons at ground level: one in each bastion, and two mounted in armored suits in the keep. Some of the natives had begun poking spears into the firing slits before Pahner gave the word, but a few blasts from bead rifles had cleared the Kranolta away. Now all four plasma gunners thrust the muzzles of their weapons outward, a moment after the "special actions" cartridges had scythed across the bailey, and filled the courtyard with actinic silver fury.

The charges from the cannon were five times as powerful as those from mere plasma rifles, and the volcanic impact of four of them within the confined space of the bailey flashed all of the remaining vegetation into flame and cooked every Kranolta inside the gates.

The remaining plasma cannon on the wall level opened up simultaneously. Their blasts of silver fire were less intense and concentrated than in the confined space of the bailey, but that made them no less effective. They turned the Kranolta attacking the bastions into charred stumps and flaming torches. The hydrophilic Mardukans were particularly susceptible to burns, and the silver death of the plasma cannon was pure horror to them as it swept the top of the wall.

The handful who survived threw themselves shrieking from the wall's height, accepting broken bones or death itself—*anything*—to escape that ravening, hideous furnace.

Pahner stepped back up to the spear slit and looked out over the area in front of the citadel. The true horror within the bailey and atop the walls had been invisible to most of the enemy outside the fortress, and its impact had been lost on them, for all their attention was concentrated on gaining entry themselves. As he'd expected, the horde continued to push forward into the citadel, although with slightly less haste.

"Check fire," he said calmly, face and voice leached of all expression as he gazed down upon the unspeakable carnage.

No need to rout them. Not yet.

"Pull back, you old *fool*!" Puvin Eske shouted. "*Now* will you believe us? This is the death of the clan!"

"Great rewards require great sacrifice," the clan leader said. "Do you think we took this town before without loss?"

"No," the chieftain snapped. "We obviously lost everyone with any sense! I'm taking the rest of my people to the camp. We will prepare to try to hold off the humans when they come forth to take our horns. And may the forest demons eat your *soul*!"

"You shall be cast out of the clan," the elder said calmly. "Coward. We shall deal with *you* after the victory."

"Go into that hell yourself, coward," the younger Mardukan hissed. "Then come tell me of '*victories*'!"

Eleanora O'Casey wore one of the "spare" helmets and the same uniform as the Marines, but unlike them, she'd never been trained to break down the net's clipped transmissions or the military technobabble which comprised them. For her, the majority of the bursts that came over her radio were cryptic "Tango at two-fifty" conversations which, unfortunately, her translator software was useless for deciphering, so she generally depended on some friendly Marine to interpret for her.

In this case, however, the only available translator was Poertena. Which created its own problems.

"What's happening?" she asked the armorer. She, Matsugae, and three of the pilots sat on a pile of ammunition boxes halfway back into the cave that made up the majority of the keep's interior. The noncombatants shared the space with the wounded, Doc Dobrescu, the mahouts, and nineteen nervous *flar-ta. Flar-ta* reacted in a predictable animal way to nervousness. It was a hot, smelly existence.

"Tee scummies, they off tee wall," the diminutive Pinopan said with a shrug, "but they getting ready to 'tack again. Tee Cap'n is gonna say somethin' soon."

"How is Roger?" Matsugae asked quietly. He had his own helmet and had heard the terse report of the prince's injury.

"He fine," Poertena said. "Jus' shock. He be fine."

"I'm pleased to hear that," Matsugae said. "Very pleased."

"Great," Pahner said, nodding as he listened to the transmission. "Great. Get him to Doc Dobrescu as soon as possible. I know you don't dare now, but as soon as we open that door, I want him in the keep."

He looked out the slit at the reforming enemy and shook his head. Bravo Company had really whittled them down that time, but the barbs were still coming back for more, and he sent his toot the command that opened the general frequency.

"Okay, people, they're coming back for another round. We took some wounded that time, so we're a little thin on the walls. I want platoon sergeants to select your best walking wounded for bead rifles and send out everyone else you can to stand by as grenadiers. They don't seem to be bothered by casualties, so I'll call for fire a little further out this time.

"Grenadiers, when they start coming through the gate, I want you to fill the bailey with their dead. I think they'll still come on in, so when they start coming up the stairs or over the walls, retreat to the bastions."

He thought of trying to say something stirring, but the only thing that came to mind was "once more into the breach, my friends," which was both technically inaccurate and too theatrical for him. Finally he just keyed the mike.

"Pahner, out."

There was silence over the com for several seconds, except for the occasional laconic transmission of firing points and targets. But then Julian's distinctive voice came over the Third Platoon net.

"Okay, Second Squad. I know I can't be up there with you, but I want you to remember that . . . that . . . you're members of The Empress' Own, damn it." There was a cracked sob, and he choked out the next words. "I want you to do me *proud*. Remember: long, *wildly* uncontrolled bursts!"

A tide of laughter welled up over the net. Gunnery Sergeant Jin was faintly audible, protesting the bad radio discipline, but it was almost impossible to understand him through his own barking belly laughs.

"Remember," the squad leader continued with another sob. "You're Marines, and The Empress' Own! We're the best, of the best, of the best. Well, maybe not the last best. That would be *Gold* Battalion, actually, but—"

"Juliannn," Jin wailed, "stoppp!"

"And, I just want to say . . . if these are our last moments together . . ." the NCO continued.

"Company, stand by to open fire!" Captain Pahner's voice crackled over the general frequency, oblivious of the transmissions on the platoon net.

"Gronningen," Julian said, with another choking sob, to the biggest, ugliest, most straightlaced private in the entire company, "I just want you to know: *I love you, man!*"

Eleanora looked up in surprise and fear as one of the armored plasma gunners fell over on her side, bent nearly double. The academic started to get up to try to render assistance, but Poertena held up his hand to stop her as he switched frequencies on his helmet radio. She watched in fear as his expression slid from worry through annoyance while the plasma gunner first tried to get to her knees, and then fell over again, twitching. O'Casey couldn't imagine what could have happened to the woman, but then the armorer began to laugh. He slid down from his perch on the ammunition boxes, holding his sides, and the civilian's eyes went wide as Doc Dobrescu opened his mouth and began to howl with laughter of his own.

"Third Platoon!" Pahner barked as a burst of bead fire went flying off into the distance and a grenade volley rolled through the enemy's ranks like a surf line of fire and death. "Sergeant Jin! What the hell is happening down there?"

"Ah . . ." Jin replied, then burst into laughter. "Sorry," he choked out. "Sorry, Sir, ah . . ."

A wild rip of bead fire lashed out from Third Platoon's position and sliced into the Kranolta like a hypervelocity bandsaw. Then another. The Mardukans went down like wheat before a reaper, and Pahner heard the distant sound of almost maniacal laughter from the parapet.

"Sergeant Jin! *What the hell is happening down there?*" He couldn't fault the effectiveness of the platoon's fire, but it wasn't like they had ammo to spare.

"Ah—" It was all the gunnery sergeant could say as he tore off his own wildly uncontrolled rip of automatic fire . . . and dissolved into helpless laughter of his own.

Pahner started to bellow furiously at Jin, but the firing quickly got itself back under control, and he clamped his jaw tightly. Then he tilted his head to the side and flipped to the platoon frequency just in time to hear " . . . no, man, really. I *love* you!" followed by hysterical laughter as Gronningen explained exactly what was going to happen to the NCO when he got his extremely heterosexual fingers around Julian's throat.

"*Juliannn!*" Pahner began, then paused as he realized that not only was the firing steadier, but he could actually see smiles on the faces of the troopers on the parapet. Some of those smiles might be a little crazed, but it was obvious that at least one platoon had stopped contemplating the likelihood of death in the near future.

"Buuut, Caaaptain!" the NCO whined.

"And," sobbed Jin, who was well known for his own interests, "I've gotta tell the Sergeant Major I love her, tooo!"

"Okay, people," Pahner said, shaking his head but unable not to do a little laughing of his own. "Let's settle down and kill us some scummies, okay?"

"Okay, okay," Julian said. "Sorry, boss."

"I'm still gonna kill your ass, Julian," Gronningen growled. A burst of fire echoed over the open link. "But I've got other things to do in the meantime."

And so Bravo Company, Bronze Battalion of The Empress' Own, went into battle against overwhelming odds . . . with an uncontrollable chuckle on its lips.

Morale is to the physical as ten is to one.

CHAPTER FORTY-TWO

"Are these stupid bastards ever going to realize that they're beaten?" Pahner wearily asked no one in particular.

Damage from repeated plasma blasts had finally forced him to abandon the gatehouse, which was now a pile of rubble, and move into the Third Platoon bastion. The Kranolta had taken unspeakable losses throughout the long Mardukan day, but still they insisted on charging the castle. And in so doing, they'd whittled their opponents down to practically nothing.

Of the seventy-two members of The Empress' Own who'd survived the initial Kranolta ambush, barely half were still on their feet. Pahner had come to the point of regretting his decision to immure Poertena and Cord's nephews in the keep. They were safe there, but he could have used them on the walls.

He shook his head. There were still several thousand Kranolta out there, and they'd stopped trying to take the keep. The last wave had avoided the smoldering killing ground of the bailey and hurled itself solely against Second Platoon's portion of the wall and its bastion. The attack had crashed in behind a massive javelin launch, and Second Platoon had taken terrific casualties before it could beat off the assault.

As always, the Mardukans' losses had been enormously higher than the humans'. Unfortunately, the Marines could kill hundreds of the barbarians for every one of their own casualties and still lose. It was insane. Whatever happened to the company, the slaughter of the Kranolta's warriors had already been so extreme that the clan itself was almost certainly doomed to extinction, but they didn't seem to care. Or perhaps they did. Perhaps they knew their people had already been effectively destroyed this bloodsoaked day, and all they wanted now was to drag down and kill the aliens who'd slain them.

Whatever they were thinking, they were also lining up for yet another attack on Second Platoon, and he lifted the visor of his helmet to scrub his eyes in exhaustion.

He could shift some of Third Platoon over to Second's area, but if he did that and the scummies hit Third's bastion simultaneously, they would sweep away the reduced defenders. No. The only option was to order Third to fire everything it had into the flank of the assault. That hadn't stopped the last one, but maybe it would work this time. Something *had* to break these bastards.

He shook his head again as the scummies surged forward. The ground was so thickly covered with their dead that they literally had to climb over drifts and hills of bodies just to reach the wall, but they didn't even seem to notice. They just came on through the hail of bead and grenade fire from front and flank until they hit the wall. Then the ladders went up again, and the Kranolta swarmed upward.

The plasma cannon in the keep and Third Platoon's bastion could bear on them as they topped the battlements, but the gunners had to be careful. Not only was there the danger that they might inflict human casualties in the wild melee atop the wall, but one twitch to the side, and the plasma bolts could blow the door right out of the other bastion.

Now that door rang to the sound of axes again, and bead gunners from Third Platoon's bastion picked off the axmen carefully. Again, a burst of beads in the wrong spot would do the scummies' work for them.

Only three of Third Platoon's spear slits overlooked the other platoon's doorway. Against any rational foe, that should have been enough, but these were Kranolta. A bead rifleman stepped back with a jammed rifle, and for the flicker of time required for someone to replace him, a single scummy was able to survive long enough to drive three more blows into the hastily assembled timber barricade.

The barrier had finally taken all it could stand. It crumbled, and a wild, hungry scream of triumph went up from the Kranolta as they saw their chance at last.

Pahner dropped down to the plasma cannon and slapped the gunner on the helmet. He pointed to the open doorway and the line of scummies clawing towards it against a solid wall of bead fire.

"Fire it up!"

"But, Captain—" the gunner began. The angle to the doorway was acute, and it the odds were better than even that none of the plasma bolt itself would carry through it. But they were just *barely* better than even, and even if the bolt itself didn't, blast, fragments, and thermal bloom through the doorway and its covering spear slits would be more than sufficient to turn the bastion's interior into a vision of Hell.

"Do it!" Pahner snapped, and keyed the general frequency. "*Second Platoon! Duck and cover!*"

The gunner shook her head and triggered three rounds into the mass around the doorway, clearing the narrow walkway. Someone shrieked over the radio as the rounds impacted, but there was no time to think of that, and Pahner leapt back to his previous perch as the Kranolta recoiled again.

But they didn't recoil far, and the Marine cursed. They'd barely retreated at all this time, dropping below the level of the now unmanned wall, which put them just out of the angle of fire from the defenders clinging to the bastions and the keep. His taccomp threw fresh strength estimates up on his HUD, and he swore again. There were still three thousand or so of them left. Which wasn't very many for a force which had begun with *eighteen* thousand, but his readouts showed only thirty-one of the company still mobile.

We can still win this thing, he thought. They're wearing us away, but we're wearing them away even faster. Two more assaults. Maybe three. That's all we've got to make it through, and—

The enemy's horrible trophy horns brayed as they worked themselves up for yet another assault, and Pahner's nerves tightened.

But then he heard another sound, an answer to the Kranolta horns. A harsher, deeper braying came from the west, and Pahner looked in that direction and his heart seemed to freeze.

Another entire army was deploying out of the forests beyond the ruined city. It was barely a fraction of the original Kranolta host, but it was also fresh and unbloodied as it marched to join the assault. The new warriors were heavily armed and armored, and they were accompanied by *flar-ta*—the missing baggage train the initial Kranolta army had left behind, no doubt. Some of the pack beasts seemed to be covered in glittering bronze, and as the taccomp projected the new numbers, Armand Pahner knew utter despair.

The Kranolta reinforcements outnumbered the mangled force at the foot of the wall, and their addition to the next assault would break the Marines' back at last.

He stared at the death of every one of his people for perhaps ten seconds, then sucked in a deep breath. If he and his people were going to go down, he would be damned if they died cowering in these holes like Voitan's last defenders.

"If you can make a heap of all your winnings. . . ." he whispered then opened the company frequency. "Bravo Company. All units, prepare to sally. A new force has just arrived. If we can hammer them badly enough in the open field, it will give us a little time to regroup. Immediately upon return to this position, I want everyone to fall back to the keep. We'll reform our line there." As if any of them were going to return, he thought bitterly. "All units, arm your wounded and prepare to sally."

"Oh, fuck," Julian muttered as he began to tear at the barrier across the keep door. Like the curtain wall gate, the keep doorway had been too large for them to hang a portal that could be easily opened and closed. Instead, it was barricaded by a pile of braced tree trunks, hammered together by the armored suits. Taking it down was a permanent operation; putting it back would not be an option.

"It's cool," Macek said unevenly. "We can do this."

"Sure, sure," Julian said as he ripped down another support with the mechanically enhanced power of the armor. "We'll live until the juice gives out. While we watch the damned Kranolta kill everybody else. Then we'll have a choice between opening up or suffocating."

"We'll kill them at the same time," the private said. "We'll kill most of them that are left."

"Sure, but they'll wipe out the company while we do it. Which is why the Old Man didn't send us out in the first place."

He pulled down the last support and opened up the door to the bailey.

The door to Third Platoon's bastion was already open. Nobody was in sight, yet, but Julian figured they would be coming out as soon as Captain Pahner gave the word. Second Platoon's door was just . . . gone. He didn't want to think about what it must be like inside that tower.

He looked out over the rubble where the gatehouse had been. From the elevated "porch" in front of the keep, he could just make out the distant army that Pahner had spotted, and it looked formidable indeed. He dialed up the magnification on his helmet, and his jaw tightened. Most of the new force was armored, and if bronze armor wouldn't do the Mardukans much good against the rifles, it would let them hammer the Marines right under when it got down to hand-to-hand. And it would.

He jumped off the platform and onto the rubble in two long "bounces," then checked to be sure his chameleon system was engaged. The active system on the suits was more effective than that of the uniforms and made the armor virtually invisible, although the suits were "loud" both electronically and audibly, which gave advanced enemies many ways to target them. There were ways to counteract that as well, but not easily or when the suits were moving fast.

Not that it mattered in this case. The Mardukans weren't going to see anything but a flicker and bursts of bead fire punctuated with plasma bolts. It should seem like evil demons in their midst . . . as long as the juice lasted.

The original Kranolta force had moved around the shoulder of the hill and was preparing to hit Second Platoon again. He thought about triggering a burst of bead fire into them, but waited for orders.

They would be coming soon enough, and he saw Third Platoon filing out of its bastion even as the army by the jungle started up the long slope to the battleground. The scummy reinforcements were at least four or five thousand strong, and their banners flapped in the breeze. Their horns brayed again, and some of the survivors of the original Kranolta force turned and spotted them. They blared on their own horns, and waved their weapons in excitement as the newcomers hurried towards them.

"Who is that?" Danal Far asked.

"I don't know," his second in command replied, but he sounded uneasy. "It looks like . . . the host of Voitan."

"Hah!" It was the first good laugh Danal Far had had since this slaughter began. But they'd nearly taken the outer defenses, now. But for the damned fire-weapons, they would have already. The next push would see them in firm control of the bastion, and from there they could roll up these damned humans easily.

"Ghosts!" he scoffed. "No, it's some other tribe come to help us against these humans. Perhaps the Talna or the Boort."

"Nooo," Banty Kar said dubiously. "Neither use armor. The last time I saw such a host was in the fighting for T'an K'tass."

"Ghosts," the chieftain grunted again, but with a nervous edge. "All of those lands are ours, now. We took them, and we keep them. Even against these 'human' demons."

"Took them, yes," Kar said as he started toward the walls. "Keep them? Maybe."

"How's it going, Julian?" Pahner asked over the radio. Third Platoon—what remained of it—had gathered on the gatehouse rubble while Second and First pulled their dead and wounded out of the damaged bastion.

"Oh, fair, Sir. Looks like they're getting ready to come back."

"Very well." Pahner looked around at the pitiful remnants of his company, and shook his head. "Swing around to cover our front. Third Platoon, prepare to deploy over the rubble."

* * *

"It *is* T'an K'tass!" Banty Kar cried. The Kranolta second in command gestured at the flag that had just been unfurled atop one of the armored *flar-ta*. "That's the Spreading Tree!"

"Impossible!" Far shouted, refusing to believe his eyes. "We killed them all! We destroyed their warriors, and scattered their people to the winds."

"But we didn't kill their sons," his second grated in a voice of bleached, old bone, and a groan of despair went up from the Kranolta host as another banner was unfurled and the long-lost symbol of the Fire and the Iron soared over the battlefield.

"Nor all the sons of Voitan."

"Captain," Julian called, "you might want to hold up. Something just happened with the two forces. The new one just raised some flags. I don't know scummies real well, but I don't think the Kranolta are all that happy to see these new guys after all."

"Understood," Pahner replied. "Keep me advised," he finished just as the Kranolta broke into a chant.

"Do you hear that?!" T'Leen Targ demanded. "That's the sound I've waited to hear most of my life: the sound of the Kranolta Death Chant!" The big, old Mardukan hefted the battle ax attached to his stump and waved it high. "Suck on this, you barbarian bastards! *Voitan is back!*"

"Aye!" T'Kal Vlan shouted back. The last of the princes of T'an K'tass grunted in laughter as he listened to the mournful dirge. "It's time for T'an K'tass to collect a debt!"

Much of the force consisted of mercenaries, gathered from all over the lower city-states. But the core of the army were the sons and grandsons of the cities fallen before the Kranolta. Both Voitan and T'an K'tass had managed to evacuate not only noncombatants, but also funds. Those funds had been scattered in businesses ventures in multiple city-states, awaiting the day when Voitan could rise again.

And this day, the humans had cleared the way.

"Oh, the demons are feasting well this day!" Targ clapped his remaining true-hand to the ax in delight as he surveyed the mountainous piles of corpses. "Look at the souls these humans have sent on!"

"And it looks as if they're still holding out." Vlan gestured at the smoking citadel. "I think we should hurry." He turned to the force at his back. "Forward the Tree! Time to take back our own!"

"Forward the Tree!" the roar came back to him. "Forward the Flame!"

"Hammer those Kranolta bastards into *atul* food!" T'Leen Targ howled, waving his ax overhead.

"Forward the Tree! Forward the Flame!"

CHAPTER FORTY-THREE

Despreaux knelt beside the prince in the dim light.

The wounded had been gathered in a line on the ledge on the north side of the cavernous keep, and the bandaged and burnt Marines were mostly asleep, courtesy of Doc Dobrescu. Their wounds were horrible, even by modern standards. Most of the wounded seemed to be from First and Second platoon; despite the protection of their flame resistant chameleon suits, most of them looked like so many pieces of barbecued chicken, and she shook her head and turned away when she realized that the white thing sticking out of Kileti's uniform was his ulna.

Horrible though it was, the damage would heal. Even the severed limbs would regrow over time, and the nanites and regenerative retroviruses the Marines were pumped full of were already hard at work repairing the gross wounds. As skin grew over burns and muscles mended at impossible speeds, the limbs would start regrowing, as well.

There was a metabolic penalty, of course. For the next several days, the wounded would be able to do nothing but eat and sleep as the nanites worked feverishly to repair the wounds and combat infections. But in time—short or long, depending mostly on the *amount* of damage rather than its severity—the terrible wounds would reduce themselves to nothing but scars. In time, even those scars would fade. To be replaced by new ones, undoubtedly.

She touched the prince's face and picked up the diagnostic tag attached to his uniform. There were only a few of those, and she was surprised Dobrescu had used it on him. Or maybe she wasn't. There were more seriously wounded—the tag told her that immediately with its readout of his alpha rhythms, blood pressure, pulse, and oxygen—but there were none so precious.

She touched his face again, gently.

"He gets to you, doesn't he?" a gravelly voice asked.

She froze and looked up at the sergeant major.

"You look like a rabbit in a spotlight," Kosutic told her with a quiet chuckle. The senior NCO had propped herself up on her uninjured right arm to contemplate the squad leader with a quizzical smile.

"I was just checking on Third Platoon's wounded, Sergeant Major," Despreaux said guiltily . . . and almost truthfully. That *had* been her rationale for the visit, but she'd realized almost immediately what she was really after.

"Try to tell the Old Man that, girl—not me!" the sergeant major snapped, shifting her burnt and mangled left arm into a better position. Or, at least, one that was marginally less uncomfortable. "You haven't so much as looked at any of the other wounded. You've just been making cow eyes at Roger."

"Sergeant Major—" Despreaux began.

"Can it, I said! I know exactly what's going on. It was obvious even back on the ship, if you had eyes. And I do."

"But . . . I *hated* him back on the ship," the sergeant protested. "He was so . . . so. . . ."

"Snotty?" Kosutic suggested with a chuckle that cut off abruptly. "Shit, don't make me laugh, girl! Yeah. And you were making cow eyes at him, snotty attitude and all."

"I was *not* making cow eyes," Despreaux insisted firmly.

"Call it what you want, girl," the older woman said with a grin. "*I* call it cow eyes."

Despreaux looked around almost desperately, but all the other wounded seemed to be asleep. If they weren't, they were being incredibly disciplined in not laughing at her. Then she looked back at Kosutic.

"What are you going to do about it?"

"Nothing," the sergeant major said, and chuckled again at her look of surprise. "We've got bigger things to worry about, Sergeant. And so far he seems to be either oblivious or beating you off with a club. I'm not sure which."

"Neither am I," the squad leader admitted sadly.

"Look," Kosutic said, "when I'm not feeling like a pounded piece of liver, come talk to me about this. I don't know if I can do anything, but we can talk. No reports, no notes, no counseling. Just . . . girl talk. About boy problems."

"Girl talk," Despreaux repeated incredulously. She looked at the sergeant major, then down at the line of combat ribbons and the burnt and mangled arm. "You realize that that sounds . . . odd."

"Hey, you've got boy problems," the senior NCO said, pointing at the sleeping prince with her chin. "Think of me as your older sister."

"Okay," Despreaux said, shaking her head slowly from side to side. "If you say so. Girl talk."

"Later," the sergeant major agreed, lying back down. "When I don't feel like pounded liver."

The first thing Roger noticed was a raging thirst. Hard on the heels of the thirst, though, was a headache that put it to shame.

He groaned and tried moving his fingers and toes. Something seemed to happen, so next he tried opening his eyes.

Well, he thought, cataloging his sensory impressions, it was hot and close, and there was a rock roof overhead. There was also a distinct stench of *flar-ta* droppings, and he swore, as he gagged on the dreadful smell, that he would never complain about grumbly oil again. He'd found so many, many smells that were worse.

Starting with burnt pork.

He turned his head to the side and groaned again. He didn't know what had happened to the Marine, but it been bad. Bad enough that he wasn't too sure, right offhand, whether it was a man or a woman.

"Plasma blast," a voice said from his other side. Roger turned his head, slowly and carefully, and looked up into the ugly face of Doc

Dobrescu. "Only the bloom from it, actually. Not that that wasn't bad enough." The warrant officer gazed at his other patient for a moment, then back at Roger.

"Morning, Your Highness."

"My head," Roger croaked.

"Kinda hurts?" the medic asked cheerfully.

"Yeah."

The former Raider leaned forward and administered a stim shot to the prince's neck. In a moment, a wave of blessed relief flowed through him.

"Ooooh."

"Don't get used to it," the medic cautioned. "We've got lots of wounded. And on that subject, I need you to get your ass in gear, Your Highness. I've got other people to attend to."

Roger felt a hand on his shoulder, pulling him up, and looked back to discover that it belonged to Matsugae.

"Kostas?" he asked him blearily. He listened, but there was no crash of plasma cannon or crack of bead rifles. "What happened? Did we win?"

"Yes, Your Highness," the valet said, propping him up and handing him a cup of deliciously cool water. "Welcome back."

An image flashed suddenly across Roger's memory.

"Despreaux?" he said sharply.

"Sergeant Despreaux?" the valet asked with a puzzled expression. "She's fine. Why do you ask?"

Roger thought about explaining the memory of an upraised ax, but decided against it. He might also have to explain the strange, unsettled feeling that the image caused him.

"Never mind. What's the situation?"

"We won, as you surmised," the valet told him. "But things are complicated at the moment."

Roger looked around the fetid keep and blanched.

"How many?" he asked, gazing at the rows of wounded.

"Thirty-eight," Dobrescu replied, coming by checking monitors. "That aren't walking wounded. Twelve KIA . . . including Lieutenant Gulyas, I'm afraid."

"Oh, God." Roger's eyes returned to the burn patient next to him. So many of the wounded seemed to have terrible burns. "What happened?" he repeated.

"Plasma fire," Dobrescu said simply. "Things got . . . a little tight."

"We need to get them out of here," the prince said, waving a hand around in the stinking dimness. "This is no place to put a hospital."

"They're working on it, Your Highness," the medic told him. "We'll have them out of here by nightfall. In the meantime, it's the only roof we've got."

"Okay." Roger levered himself up with help from the valet. "Make sure of it."

The prince stumbled across the floor to the open doorway and stopped at the view that greeted him. The interior of the citadel was a scene from some demented vision of Hell.

The eastern bastion, Second Platoon's redoubt, was a blackened ruin. The curtain wall on that side was still covered in Mardukan dead, and the doors and spear slits were blasted, blackened, and broken.

The gatehouse was nothing but rubble, and half-fused, still-smoking rubble, at that. And the bailey was covered in Mardukan dead, piled five and six deep . . . where the piles weren't even deeper. Since the gate had been the only drain for the torrential Mardukan rains, the courtyard had started to fill with water. The line of natives who were working to clear the area already waded ankle deep in the noisome mess as they bent over the dead, and it was getting deeper.

Roger peered at the natives picking up bodies and bits of bodies in the gruesome, deepening soup.

"Are those who I think they are?"

"Kranolta," Kostas confirmed.

"They have weapons," Roger pointed out in a croak. He took another sip of water and shook his head. "What happened?" he asked for the third time.

"We won," the valet repeated. "Sort of. Forces from the other city-states showed up right at the end. They hit the Kranolta from the rear, and drove them back over the wall, where they finally took the eastern bastion. By then, Captain Pahner had evacuated it anyway, and it was the only cover they could find. Between the pressure of the new forces and having them pinned down, the Marines more or less wiped them out.

"But quite a few of them had withdrawn to their encampment before the city-state forces arrived. Only a handful of their original army, but enough that they could still have caused lots of problems, so Pahner arranged a cease-fire. The Kranolta that are left don't have any interest in facing Marines or the 'New Voitan' forces, but they'll fight if forced to. So the Captain and our new . . . allies agreed to let them keep their weapons and bury their dead."

"What a disaster," Roger whispered, looking over his shoulder back into the keep.

"It could have been worse, Sir."

"How?" Roger demanded bitterly.

"Well," the valet said as the rain began again, "we could have lost."

CHAPTER FORTY-FOUR

"If you hadn't come, we would have lost."

Roger took a sip of wine. The vintage was excellent, but then, all of the tent's appointments were excellent, from the finely tooled leather of its walls, to its hammered brass tables. The cushions on the floor were covered in a cloth the humans had never seen before, silky and utterly unlike the more common rough and wool-like material found in Q'Nkok. Obviously, T'Kal Vlan traveled in style.

"Perhaps so." The last ruler of T'an K'tass picked up a candied slice of kate fruit and nibbled it. "Yet even so, you would have destroyed the Kranolta. That's surely worth something even in the eyes of gods of the most distant land!"

Captain Pahner shook his head.

"I'm sorry, Your Highness, but it isn't. We come from an empire so vast that the Kranolta and all the valley of the Hurtan are an unnoticeable speck. I'm glad that you're glad, but the losses we took might mean the prince won't make it home." He grinned at the Mardukans. "And that would really disappoint his mother."

"Ah!" Roger exclaimed. "Not that! Not Mother angry! God forbid!"

"A formidable woman, eh?" T'Kal Vlan grunted a laugh.

"Rather," Roger told him with a shrug. "He has a point, though. I'm sure that if I died, Mother would visit me beyond the grave to chastise me for it."

"So, you see," Pahner continued, "I'm afraid I have to count this one as a straight loss."

"Not really, Captain," the prince said, swirling his wine gently. "We've cleared the way. One way or another, we had to get to the other side of this range of hills, and *none* of the choices were particularly good. There's no reason to second-guess this one. If we'd gone south, we would've been walking through a war, and we would undoubtedly have second-guessed ourselves then and said 'I bet those Kranolta pussies wouldn't have been *this* much trouble.'"

"Well, I for one thank you for clearing out most of those 'Kranolta pussies,'" T'Leen Targ said, with his own grunt of laughter. "Already, the ironworkers we brought with us are building the furnaces. We have gathered all the surviving masters of the art and their apprentices. Soon the lifeblood of Voitan will flow once more."

"Aye," T'Kal Vlan agreed. "And the sooner the better. My own treasury is flowing away like blood."

"You need to capitalize," O'Casey said. The chief of staff had been quietly sipping her wine and listening to the warriors' testosterone grunting with amusement. This, however, was her specialty.

"Agreed," Vlan said. "But the family has already liquidated most of its holdings to fund the expedition. Short of borrowing, at extortionate rates, I'm not sure how to raise more capital."

"Sell shares," O'Casey suggested. "Offer a partial ownership of the mines. Each share has a vote on management, and each gains equity and shares in the profits, if any. It would be a long-term investment, but not a particularly risky one if you're sufficiently capitalized. "

"I didn't understand all the words you just used," Vlan said, cocking his head. "What is this 'equity'?"

"Oh, my." O'Casey grinned widely. "We really must have a *long* conversation."

"Don't worry," Pahner told her with a shrug. "We're not going anywhere for a while."

Roger sat up in his tent, damp with sweat and panting and looked around him. All clear. Tent walls faintly billowing in the wind that had come up. Camp gear. Eyes.

"You should be resting, Your Highness," said Cord faintly.

"So should you, old snake," Roger said. "You don't heal as fast as we do." He sat up on the camp cot and took a deep breath. "It just, you know, comes back."

"Yes, it does," the Mardukan agreed.

"I wonder how . . ." The prince stopped and shook his head.

"How?" the shaman queried, lifting himself up with a grimace.

"You should be flat on your back, Cord," Roger said with another headshake.

"I grow weary of lying about like a worm," the Mardukan countered. "How, what?"

"Not one to be distracted, are you?" Roger smiled. "I was wondering how the Marines handle it. How they handle the fear and the death. Not just ours, God knows I got enough Marines killed here. But the Kranolta. We've ended them as a tribe, Cord. Piled them up against the wall as if they were a ramp. They . . . don't seem affected by that."

"Then you have not eyes, Young Prince," the shaman countered with a grunt. "Look at young Julian. Your people, too, have the laughing warrior who hides his pain with humor, as did our Denat, he who I lost to the *atul*. Always he faced danger with laughter, but it was a shield to the soul. I'm sure that he jested with the very *atul* as it ate him. Or young Despreaux. So young, so dangerous. I am told that she is beautiful for a human. I don't see it myself; she lacks . . . many things. Horns for one. And her shield is that face like a stone. She holds her pain in so hard it has turned her to a stone, I think."

Roger tilted his head to the side and played with a stray lock of hair. "What about . . . Pahner? Kosutic?"

"Ah," Cord grunted. "For one, you notice that though they are capable warriors, they control from afar. But mostly they have learned the tricks. The first trick is to know that you are not alone. While I was in the cavern still, Pahner came to visit, to see the wounded, and we talked. He is a font of wisdom, is your captain. We talked of many things but mostly we talked of . . . song. Of poetry."

"Poetry?" Roger laughed. "What in the hell would Pahner be doing talking about poetry?"

"There is poetry and poetry, my Prince," the shaman said with a grunt. "Ask him about 'The Grave of the Hundred Dead.' Or 'Recessional.' Or 'If.'" The shaman rolled over to find a more comfortable position. "But ask him in the morning."

"Poetry?" Roger said. "What in hell would I want with poetry?"

"Eleonora?" Roger asked. The chief of staff was on her way to another of the numerous meetings she had arranged with the Voitanese forces. She apparently considered herself a one-person social reengineering team, or at least the best equivalent available. She was determined that when she left, the Voitanese would have the strongest governmental structure available to the situation. Since that was probably a rational oligarchy, it fit in well with the Voitanese plans.

"Yes, Ro . . . Your Highness?" she asked hurriedly. Her pad was almost overloaded with notes, and there were only a few days left to get everything in place. Whatever Roger wanted had better be quick.

"Have you ever heard of a poem called 'The Grave of the Hundred Dead?'"

The chief of staff stopped and thought then consulted her toot. "The name is familiar, but I can't quite place it."

"Or 'Recessional.'" Roger's brow wrinkled but he couldn't think of the other. "Or something like 'If?'"

"Ah!" the historian's face cleared. "Yes. That one I have. Why?"

"Uh," Roger stopped, caught. "Would you believe Cord recommended it?"

O'Casey laughed merrily. It was a twinkling sound that Roger realized he had never heard. "Not without some sort of body transference, Your Highness."

"I think he heard of it from someone," Roger explained stiffly.

"Set your pad," she said with a smile and transferred the file.

There was a blip and Roger looked at the translation remark on his pad. "You keep it on your toot?" Roger asked, surprised.

"Oh, yes," O'Casey said as she started back down the path. "I love that poem. There are very few pre-space poets that have even one poem known. Kipling has to be right up there with the Earl of Oxford.

You might see Captain Pahner. I believe Eva said he has the collected works in his toot."

Warrant Officer Dobrescu tossed the chunk of reddish ore from hand to hand as he gazed up at the towering wall of red and black.

And, lo, the answers come clear, he thought.

The last two weeks had been good for the company. The troops had been given time to rest and get some separation from the terrible losses inflicted in the battle. Since Voitan was going to be held by "friendly" forces, Captain Pahner had decided to leave all of their dead. If they made it through alive, they would come back for them. If they fell along the way, these Marines, at least, would be honored.

The Voitanese had opened a vault in their own catacombs, which had been looted by the Kranolta. The sepulcher had been the resting place of the city's royal guards before its fall, and there were still a few of their bones moldering in the back. The Marines had been bagged but not burned and laid to rest along with their brethren. Sergeant Major Kosutic, as the only registered chaplain in the company, had performed the ceremony, and if any of the Marines had objected to their honored dead being prayed over by a High Priestess of Satan, they hadn't mentioned it.

The pause had also given the wounded time to recover, and a regimen of heavy eating and bed rest had done wonders. All but the most critically injured were back on their feet and training, and, from a purely selfish point of view, it had given Dobrescu time to scratch a few itches.

The first itch had to do with the local steel. The point had been made again and again that only the "water steels" made in Voitan were of the finest quality. That steels from other areas, even if processed in what they thought was the same way, did not possess the "spirit" of Voitan's Damascene steels.

The second itch had to do with the Mardukan biology. Something had been bugging him ever since they landed and ran into D'Nal Cord, and the downtime and necessity of working on Mardukan wounded, as well as human, had given him the opportunity to do a little studying. What he'd discovered would startle most of the company, but the warrant thought it was hilarious. He hated it when people made assumptions.

Time to go watch some people cringe, he thought with an evil smile.

"So the steel has a high percentage of impurities," O'Casey said. "So what?"

"It's not just that it has a high percentage," Dobrescu said, consulting his pad. "It's what the impurities are."

"I don't know what this 'impurity' is," Targ said.

"That's going to be difficult to explain," Eleanora said with a frown. "It involves molecular chemistry."

"I'll give it a shot," Roger said. "Targ, you know how when you first smelt the ore, you get 'black iron.' The brittle stuff, right?"

"Yes," T'Kal Vlan agreed. "It's what was given to Cord's tribe, that broke so easily."

"You have to remelt it," Cord put in. The wounded Mardukan was seated behind Roger, as was proper, but stretched out on cushions to save his ravaged legs. "Very hot. It's hard and expensive, which is why black iron is cheaper."

"Okay," Roger went on. "Then when you heat it in a crucible, 'very hot,' as Cord said, you get a material that's gray and very easy to work."

"Iron," Targ said. "So?"

"That's what we call 'wrought iron,' and it actually is almost pure iron. Iron is a molecule. Black iron is iron with carbon, which is what's in charcoal, mixed into it."

"What about steel?" T'Kal Vlan asked. "And why do I think we need an ironmaster here?"

"Somebody else can explain it later," Roger said with a laugh. "The point is that iron is a pure element, a kind of molecule. Is that sort of clear?"

"I hear the words," Targ replied, "but I don't know their meaning."

"That would be hard to really explain without teaching you basic chemistry first," Dobrescu said. "You're just going to have to take our word for most of this and I'm not sure how much you can do with it."

"The point is that steel is also iron with carbon in it," Roger said. "But less carbon, and heated to a much higher temperature."

"That much is well known to our master smiths," Targ said, with a human-style shrug. "Yet mere heat and tempering does not produce the water steel. Even in exile, our smiths have forged weapons far superior to those of other city-states, but never the water steel of Voitan."

"No, steel is complicated," Roger agreed. "Especially 'water steel'—what we call 'Damascene.' We—well, I—was really surprised you had it and of such quality. It's unusual at your technology level."

"I think it's driven by their pumping industry," O'Casey interjected. "They have quite a bit of refined technology dedicated to pumps. Once that starts to spread out a bit, look for an industrial revolution. I wish they were just a bit further along. If they were, I'd introduce the steam engine."

"Let's stick to the subject, if we can," Pahner suggested with a slight grin, "and reengineer their society when we can do it with a regiment at our back. Okay?"

"His Highness is right," Dobrescu went on to Targ, ignoring the captain's amusement. "Normal steel is specially formed iron with a bit of carbon and high temperature, but you need some other impurities, if you want *good* steel, which explains Voitan blades. The first thing to realize is that the local ore is what we call 'banded iron.'"

"I know," Roger said. "Geology, remember? It's formed by early oxygen-generating organisms. Prior to their evolution, atmospheres are mostly reducing, and iron can remain on the surface in a mostly pure state. But once the first green or blue-green organism occurs and starts producing oxygen, the iron rusts. Then the oxygen gets used up over millions of years, and there's a band of non-rusted ore, then another band of rusted ore. Right?"

"Right," the warrant officer agreed. "Which makes it some of the best possible taconite, so it's comparatively easy to work. But, even better, it's contaminated with vanadium, which is one of several possible hardening agents for steel. Molybdenum and chrome are a couple of others."

"Molybe—molby—?" Cord grimaced. "I can't pronounce that."

"Don't worry about it," Dobrescu said. "The point is, Targ, that it really *is* the local ore, and your know-how, that's special. And I ran a tap in on one of your main mines, and it's all laced with impurities: vanadium and molybdenum. In fact, I'd give odds that by the time you get back into full swing, you'll hit a vein that makes the best steel you've ever seen."

"Ah, good," Targ said. "We have long wondered what it was that made our water steel. That's part of it, surely."

"Hold on a minute," Roger said, frowning at Dobrescu. "Vanadium and molybdenum are important, yeah, but not really critical for *sword* steel, Doc." The warrant officer blinked at him in surprise, and the prince chuckled with a humor that was more than slightly sour. "I won't claim to be an expert on the topic," he said, "but no MacClintock can avoid learning at least a little about ancient weapons . . . no matter how hard he tries."

"Oh?" Dobrescu cocked an eyebrow, and Roger shrugged.

"Oh," he replied. "Vanadium helps produce a finer grain structure in heat-treated steel, which helps with the tempering process and eliminates some of the problems in overheating steel. And it helps prevent loss of temper in reheated metal, so steel with vanadium in it can withstand higher temperatures before losing its temper.

"Molybdenum does some of the same thing by helping to transmit the temperature deeper into the steel, and it also increases hardness some and helps reduce the fatigue factor. But carbon is the most critical element in hardening steel."

Both of Dobrescu's eyebrows had risen during the prince's explanation, and the warrant officer's surprise was not an isolated phenomenon. Even O'Casey was staring at her one-time student, and Roger shrugged.

"Hey, like I said, I'm a MacClintock," he told them.

"According to something I read years ago, though," Dobrescu said, "vanadium and molybdenum were what produced Damascene steel."

"Almost right," Roger told him. "The 'water pattern'—those white lines on the black background—are a crystalline damask that's largely the result of those sorts of impurities. But you can have that kind of pattern on a blade that really sucks. Good Damascene steel hits a carbon content of something like one and a half percent, if I remember correctly, but even then, the trick is in the tempering. There are some beautifully patterned blades in the Roger III Collection that were never properly heat treated. I think their Rockwell number was only thirty or so, which would make them pretty useless as real weapons. You need to hit a Rockwell of around fifty if you want something to cut through mail and bone like this baby." He touched the katana lying beside him even in T'Kal Vlan's tent.

"Really?" O'Casey asked, trying to hide her delight at hearing Roger—*her* Roger!—in professorial mode. Sort of.

"Yeah. There were different techniques for making the good stuff back on Old Earth," Roger told her. "Europeans did it with pattern welding, the Japanese used mechanical construction, but the Indians probably did it closest to the way Voitan smiths did it, judging from this." He touched the katana again. "They heated the steel in sealed clay crucibles that allowed the iron to soak up lots of carbon."

"That is, indeed, how our craftsmen work," Targ said, regarding Roger narrowly. "It is part of our closely held craft secrets," he added, and Roger grinned.

"Don't worry, Targ—I don't plan on telling anyone else. But the humans who used that technique produced something called 'wootz' steel that happened to have the very impurities the Doc here was talking about thanks to the local ores. And he's probably right that their presence helps account for at least some of your weapons' superiority, but don't let that distract you. The real secret's in the tempering and how well you judge temperatures and what quenching techniques you use. You might not get as pronounced a 'water' pattern using steels without the impurities, but your people would still be turning out some of the best weapon-grade steel in the world!"

"But it is the water steel which warriors associate with the superiority of our blades," Targ pointed out. "It shows the soul of the steel."

"And it's flat out beautiful, too," Roger agreed. "I'm not saying the nature of your ore isn't important, just that you shouldn't sell yourselves or your smiths short. The hardest thing of all in making a true master blade is the tempering, and you guys obviously have that down. For the rest—" He shrugged. "Now that you've got access to the right ores again, everyone else will see that the true 'water steel' is back. I imagine that's going to do good things for your income while you rebuild the city."

"True," T'Kal Vlan put in. "It is what warriors and merchants will look for when they judge the quality of our blades, and it is well to know what creates it. But where else do we find these ingredients? If we do start to have problems, we could mine them separately and add them, no?"

"Yes," Roger said with a frown. "The problem is finding them and separating them. I'd say that for the time being, you should probably just use what you have. I'll talk to a couple of your ironmasters if you want. Between us, Dobrescu and I might be able to explain it and point them in the right direction. If I recall clearly, chrome is actually easier to detect and separate."

"It is if you have an acid," Dobrescu agreed. "Less so, otherwise. And it's tricky to hit the right proportions and heat treatments. Humans didn't turn out good chromium steel until, oh, the last century and a half or so before space flight, I think. Of course, they didn't have anyone from the outside telling them how it worked, either."

"No, but they had more or less started figuring out chemistry on their own by then," O'Casey pointed out, and frowned thoughtfully. "I wonder if we could help them make that jump," she mused, and Pahner snorted.

"It sounds to me like we could probably spend a year or three just trying to remember what we don't remember about the processes," the Marine observed. "It would be better to just come back with a lander filled with science texts."

"Agreed." Roger chuckled. "Or, hell, a lander filled with a social reconstruct team. I don't want to crack Mardukan society; I like most of what I see. But I do want to bring them into the Empire."

"We can do that," O'Casey said. "God knows we've brought in enough devolved human societies without smashing their forms."

"Like Armagh?" Roger asked with a grin.

"Well," the chief of staff said, "there's something to be said for a planet full of battling Irishmen. Look at the Sergeant Major."

"True, true," Pahner said. "However, to bring back a Soc team, we need to get to the port. And to get to the port . . ."

"We just have to put one foot in front of the other," Roger said. "And that means breaking up this little party."

"Yep." Pahner nodded. "Targ, Vlan, thank you for coming."

"Not a problem," Vlan said. "We're at your disposal until you leave."

"Thank you," Pahner said, carefully not raising an eyebrow at the surreptitious signal Dobrescu flashed him. "I think we'll see you tomorrow. Until then?"

"Yes," Targ said. "Thank you. And good night."

Pahner waited until the Mardukans had left the tent, then turned to the medic.

"Yes, Mister Dobrescu? You had something to add without the Mardukans present?"

The warrant officer glanced at the shaman behind Roger.

"Yes, Sir. But I'm not sure about Cord."

"He stays," Roger said coldly. "Whatever you have to say, you can say in front of my *asi*."

"All righty, Your Highness," the medic said. "It's about the Mardukans. And about some assumptions we've been making."

"What assumptions?" Pahner asked warily.

"Oh, it doesn't relate to security, Captain," Dobrescu said with an evil grin. "I'm not sure it matters at all, actually. But, you see, we've got their genders confused."

"What?" O'Casey demanded. As the manager for the translation program it was her job to make sure that that sort of thing didn't happen, and she started to bristle indignantly. Then she remembered all the times the program had tried to switch gender, and looked at Cord, stretched out behind Roger.

"But . . ." she began, and blushed.

"What you're looking at, Ms. O'Casey," the medic told her with an even wider evil grin, "is an ovipositor."

"An ovi . . . What?" Roger asked, checking his impulse to turn around and look. Dealing with the habitually nude Mardukans had slowly inured the humans to the size of the natives' . . . members, but he wasn't about to turn around and get all depressed again.

"Gender is a slippery term when you start discussing xenobiology," the medic continued, pulling up a different entry on his pad. "But the current 'definitive' definition is that the 'male' gender is that which supplies numerous gametes to fertilize a single gamete. However that's done."

"I take it, then, that Cord and his 'gender' do not supply numerous gametes," Pahner said carefully. "They certainly look . . . capable of doing so."

"No, they don't, and yes, they do," Dobrescu responded. "The gender we've been calling 'male,' Cord's gender, that is . . . implants, is the correct term, between four and six gametes that are functional cells, with the exception of a matching set of chromosomes. Once these have been implanted, they're fertilized by free swimming zygotes resident in the egg pouches of what I suppose should technically be called 'brooder males.'" The medic pursed his lips. "There are a few terrestrial species of fish that use a similar method, and it's common on Ashivum in the native species."

"So, Cord is actually a female?" Pahner asked.

"Technically. However, there are sociological aspects that make the 'males' fill traditional female gender roles and vice versa. That and the physiology are what have been confusing the program."

"And me," O'Casey admitted, "but I'll bet you're right. We didn't have much of a language kernel to start with, and I never tried to get at its fundamental, underlying assumptions. Even if I'd thought about it, I wouldn't have known how to access them or what to do with them once I had. But given what Mr. Dobrescu just said about 'definitive' definitions, I'd guess that whoever prepared the kernel in the first place knew that Cord and his gender were *technically* 'female.' It tried to switch gender a couple of times, which is just the sort of literal-minded lunacy you might expect out of an AI with partial data, and I wouldn't let it."

"I am *not* a female," Cord stated definitively.

"Shaman Cord," Eleanora said, "we're having a problem with our translator. Try not to pay any attention to the flipping gender discussions."

"Very well," the shaman said. "I can understand problems with your machines. You have them all time. But I am *not* a female."

"What was the word he actually used there?" Dobrescu asked.

"'*Blec tule*'?" O'Casey consulted her pad. "The etymology looks to be something like 'one that holds.' 'One that holds the eggs'? 'One that broods'? I bet that's it."

"What about Dogzard?" Roger asked, looking at the faintly snoring lizard.

"Another interesting aspect of local biology," Dobrescu answered. "There are two dominant families in Mardukan terrestrial zoology. You can think of them as equivalent to reptiles and amphibians if you want. Cord is from the 'amphibian' type. So are damnbeasts and damcrocs and bigbeasts. They all have slimy skin and similar internal organ structures.

"But the feck beasts, the dogzards, and the *flar-ta* are completely different. They have a dry integument with some scaling and radically different internal structures. Different heart chambers, different stomachs, different kidney analogs."

"So is Dogzard a he or a she?" asked Roger in exasperation.

"She," Dobrescu answered. "The 'reptile' analogs are set up, sexually, much like terrestrial reptiles. So Dogzard will eventually have puppies. Well, eggs."

"So what do we do about the translator?" Roger asked.

"We don't do anything about it," Pahner said. "We inform the troops of the physical aspects, and explain to them that the Mardukans are flipped gender, but we'll continue with our current distinction. As Elenora just suggested, the difference is purely technical, and since none of us are xenobiologists, I think we can get away with ignoring it. I can't see that it matters one way or the other, anyway, and this way we keep from confusing the troops. And the software."

"Just make sure that they're aware," Cord said stiffly, "that I am *not* a brooder."

"He's a female?" Julian asked.

"Sort of." Roger laughed. "But just keep treating him like he's a male. And hope like hell the software doesn't slip up when you get a visualization miscue." The implant-based software had already miscued once, with Poertena and Denat. Fortunately, it was a minor wound. The Pinopan would heal quickly, and the tribesman had accepted the explanation.

"Oh, man," Julian said, shaking his head. "I cannot *wait* to get off this planet. I got so much culture shock I feel like my dick's stuck in a culture socket."

Roger touched PFC Gelert on his shoulder as he strode past. The Marine grinned back at him, and hefted the spear over his shoulder. He obviously still found it an odd item for a Marine to carry.

All the Marines were armed with Mardukan weaponry. There'd been thousands of ex-Kranolta weapons available to choose from, and the New Voitan forces had let no time pass getting the first forges lit. They weren't up to custom work yet, but they were able to modify most of the weapons to fit the smaller humans, so the company was now well armed with short swords—long daggers, to the Mardukans—and Mardukan-style round shields, as well as at least one spear or javelin per Marine.

During the three weeks of rest while the company recovered, the Marines had begun their training. They had nowhere near the ability of the Mardukans, who'd practically been born with weapons in their hands, but unlike the natives, they were *soldiers*, not warriors. All of their training emphasized teamwork and cooperation, not individual, uncoordinated prowess, and they only needed to be good enough for one platoon to hold a shield wall—which no Mardukan seemed ever to have heard of—while the other one got out the real weapons.

Roger grinned back at the private and jabbed a thumb to indicate the sword over his own shoulder. The entire company looked better for the rest, although a few of the most seriously wounded were still going to be riding *flar-ta.*

Roger tossed a salute toward Corporal D'Estrees. She'd been one of the worst burn cases, and Dobrescu had eventually been forced to remove her left arm from the elbow down. Now she waved in return with her pink stump and scratched at the growing bulb of regenerating tissue. It itched like mad, but in another month or so, she'd be back in gear.

Roger finally reached the pack beast assigned to Cord. The shaman gestured to the straps holding him in place.

"This is most undignified."

Roger shook his head and waved at the endless row of grave mounds along the woodline. Figures could be seen moving down there, cutting wood for the charcoal pits and clearing brush from the beds of former roads.

"Be glad you're not in one of those."

"Oh, I am," Cord said, with a grunt, "but it is still most undignified."

Roger shook his head again as Pahner approached from the opposite direction.

"Well, Captain, are we ready?"

"Looks that way, Your Highness," the captain answered as a delegation headed by T'Leen Targ and T'Kal Vlan approached.

"We're leaving a lot of good people behind," Roger murmured, his smile fading just a bit as he glanced at the entrance to the city catacombs.

"We are," Pahner agreed quietly. "But we're leaving them in good company. And to tell the truth, Your Highness, I think it's better this way. I know it's a Marine tradition to bring our dead out with us, but I've always thought a soldier should be buried where he fell." He shook his head, his own eyes just a bit unfocused as he, too, gazed at the catacomb entrance. "That's what I want if my time ever comes," he said softly. "To be buried where I fall, with my comrades . . . and my enemies."

Roger looked at the Marine's profile in surprise, but not as much of it as he might have felt before reading "If." Or the other dozen or so Kipling poems Elenora O'Casey's toot had contained. There were depths to the captain which the old prince had never suspected . . . and which the new one respected too deeply to mention out loud.

"Well," he said cheerfully, "I'll bear that in mind if the time comes, Captain. But don't go getting any ideas! You're strictly forbidden to die until you get my royal butt home where it belongs! Clear?"

"Aye, 'Colonel,'" Pahner agreed with a grin. "I'll bear that in mind."

"Good!" Roger said, and the two of them turned back towards the approaching delegation together.

"I'd say this is the farewell committee," Kosutic observed, coming around the pack beast. She gestured at the groups of soldiers gathering along the route out of the rebuilding city. "I think they're getting ready for the big sendoff." She scratched at her own pink skin.

"I'll put on a bigger hat," Roger said jokingly, and flicked at a bit of leaf on the front of his chameleon suit. The suit was indelibly stained in places, but it was still self-cleaning, to an extent, and was more or less intact. Many of the company's uniforms were in tatters from where they'd been cut off in the course of hasty first-aid.

"Well, if you can find one, you can wear it," Pahner said calmly.

"Why, thank you for that permission, Sir." The prince grinned. "Should I go look?"

"I wouldn't suggest it at the moment, Your Highness," O'Casey said tartly. The little chief of staff had snuck up behind them so quietly that her unexpected voice made Roger start. "I think we need to thank our benefactors."

"I suppose," Roger answered impishly. "Of course, they might have saved our bacon, but we wiped out the Kranolta for them," he pointed out, and Pahner smiled again as Targ approached.

"I suppose there is that," the captain agreed.

It took an hour, but the company finally broke free of its brothers in arms, after profuse expressions of eternal friendship and undying mutual fealty, and started back on the long trail to the sea.

Marching upcountry.

CHAPTER FORTY-FIVE

The messenger lay prostrate in front of the throne. He couldn't think of any bad news in what he had to convey, but that didn't really matter. If the king was in a bad mood, the messenger's life was forfeit, anyway, no matter how important he was.

"So, 'Scout,'" the king said with a grunt of humor, "you say that the humans will come out on the Pasule side of the river?"

"Yes, O King. They follow the old trade route from Voitan."

"Insure that they bypass Pasule." The monarch picked at the ornate intaglio of his throne. "They must come to Marshad first."

"Yes, O King," the messenger said. Now to figure out a way to do that.

"You may go, 'Scout,'" the king said. "Bring them here. Bring them to me, or kill yourself before We lay Our hands on you."

"It shall be done," the messenger said, wiggling backwards out of the king's presence. *Cheated death again*, he thought.

"Cheated death again." Julian sighed as the company broke through the final screen of trees into obviously civilized lands.

"Yeah," Despreaux said. "Damn, but I'm glad to be out of the jungle."

The passage over the hills from Voitan hadn't been terrible. In fact, they hadn't lost even one person to the jungle flora and fauna, although Kraft in Second Platoon had been badly mauled by a damnbeast.

The march from Voitan had also given them time to shake down into their new organization. The reduced company had separated into just two platoons, Second and Third, and they were getting used to all the empty files. Not happy about them, but adjusted.

All in all, they were probably in better shape both physically and in morale than at any time since leaving Q'Nkok, and the vista stretching out before them would help even more.

The region was obviously long and widely settled. Cultivated fields, interspersed with patches of woodland, spread for kilometers in every direction, and the river the old path had been following was flanked in the middle distance by two towns, one clearly larger than the other.

Captain Pahner waved for the column to hold up as it cleared the jungle completely. The bare track they'd been following for the last day had suddenly become a road. Not much of one these days, perhaps—weeds and even small trees thrust up through the roadbed's cracked, uneven flagstones—but it showed that this had once been an important route.

The company stopped by the ruins of a small building. The structure was set on a raised mound, one of many scattered across the floodplain, and its construction had been massive. It looked as if it had been a guardhouse or border station to receive the caravans from Voitan, and Pahner stepped up onto its two-meter-high mound to watch the caravan pull to a halt as the company deployed.

The Marines had been training hard with their new weapons, and it showed. Bead rifles and grenade launchers were still slung over their shoulders, but their primary weapons were clearly the short swords and spears they carried, and the small units spread out in a cigar perimeter, one swordsman to each spear carrier. Once Pahner had the shields designed, the formation would be quite different, but that was going to have to wait. The tower shield was another thing the Mardukans had apparently never discovered, so he would have to have them built somewhere.

And that somewhere would, hopefully, be here.

He made another gesture, and his "command team"—a grandiose term for a small group of battered Marines and civilians, but the only one he had—gathered about him. Sergeant Julian was filling in as Intel officer in the wake of Lieutenant Gulyas' death, but other than that, it was the same group he'd faced in Voitan.

"Okay," he said, gesturing to the two towns, "it looks pretty much the way the Voitan contingent said it would. This has to be the Hadur region." Heads nodded, and he wished—again—for an even half-way decent map. According to the Voitanese, the Hadur region took its name from the Hadur River, which had to be a truly major stream even for Marduk from the descriptions. He had no reason to doubt them, but he hated trying to fix his position without a reliable map. "If we're where we think we are," he went on with a crooked smile, "that larger town should be Marshad. And that," he pointed to the smaller town "must be Pasule."

Heads nodded again. Marshad had been the primary destination for caravans from over the hills before the fall of Voitan, which had made it a wealthy mercantile center. Pasule, on the other hand, was just a farming town, according to T'Leen Targ.

"I'd almost prefer to get our toes wet locally in Pasule before we tackle the big city," he went on, "but if we're going to get the shields and armor made, it will have to be in Marshad. On the other hand, we need resupply, too, and Pasule might be a better source for that."

As he spoke, he looked around the nearer fields, where peasants had stopped their work to gawk at the force coming out of the jungle. Most of the workers were breaking ground for another crop of barleyrice, but other laborers were harvesting the ubiquitous kate fruit. That was good. It meant that both the fruit and the previous barleyrice harvest would be fully available when it was time to buy.

"Yeah," Jasco agreed, with a grunting laugh that sounded almost Mardukan, as he, too, watched the workers, "these damn pack beasts go through some grain."

"Sergeant Major, I want you and Poertena to handle the resupply and procurement of the shields."

"Got it." The NCO made a note in her toot. They'd discussed the possibilities before, of course, but now that they were actually able to see the lay of the land, it seemed clear that Pasule would be a better, and probably cheaper, source for the food.

"We've seen that they can make laminated wood, plywood," said Roger, who'd been quietly listening. "We should have the shields made out of that."

"Plywood?" Jasco sounded incredulous, but, then, he hadn't been present to hear the prince discuss sword making with the Voitanese leaders. "You've got to be joking . . . Your Highness. *I'd* want something a little more solid than that!"

"No, he isn't joking." O'Casey shook her head. "The Roman shield was probably the most famous design ever to come out of Terran history, and *it* was made out of 'plywood.' The histories always call it 'laminated wood,' but that's what plywood *is*, and it's enormously tougher than an equivalent thickness of 'solid' wood."

"They have to have metal or leather rims to protect the edges," the prince continued, "but the bulk of the shield is plywood."

"Okay." Pahner nodded. "Kosutic, coordinate with Lieutenant MacClintock on the design of the shields." He looked around and shook his head. "I hope I don't have to remind anybody that we need to maintain as low a profile as possible. We can't afford another butt-kicking like Voitan. Hopefully, we'll be greeted as heroes for taking out the Kranolta and be able to pass on quickly. But if we get into a hassle, we have to think our way out of it. We're way too short on ammo to shoot our way out!"

Corporal Liszez trotted toward the command group with one of the locals. The Mardukan wore a haversack full of tools and appeared to be some sort of tinker.

"LT?" the corporal said as she approached Roger.

"Whatcha got, Liz?" the prince replied with a nod.

"This scummy's gabbling something, but the translator can't make anything of it."

"Oh, great," O'Casey sighed. "Dialect shift. Just what we needed."

"Get on it," Pahner said. "We have to be able to communicate with these people." The local was gesturing across the river at the distant city, obviously agitated about something. He either wanted the company to go there, or else he was warning them away. It could have been either, and Pahner nodded and gave him a closed-lip, Mardukan-style smile. "Yes, yes," he said, "we're going to Marshad."

Either the smile or the words seemed to calm the local. He gestured, as if offering to lead them, but Pahner shook his head.

"We'll be along," he said soothingly. "Thank you. I'm sure we can find our own way."

He smiled again and started to wave the still-gabbling local politely away, then paused and looked at O'Casey.

"Do you want to talk with him?"

"Yes." She sounded a bit absent, obviously because she was concentrating on the translation—or lack thereof—from her toot. "I'm starting to pick up a few words. Let him walk with us to the town, and I'm pretty sure I can have most of the language by the time we arrive."

"Okay," Pahner agreed. "I think that's about it. Questions? Comments? Concerns?"

There were none, so the company reassembled and moved on up the road.

The ancient high road became even more cracked and damaged-looking as it entered the planted areas, despite clear indications of repairs. Heavy deposits of silt had been thrown up to either side, obviously as the result of post-flood road clearing, which forced the company to move between low, brown walls. In places, the walls built up to true dikes to protect the barleyrice crops, and in places the dikes were planted with the tall kate trees.

The peasants harvesting the kate fruit dangled from ropes or perched on tall, single-pole ladders that were unpleasantly reminiscent of scaling ladders, but they paused in their labors to gape at the human contingent as it headed toward the distant city-state. Whether because of the humans' outlandish look, or the fact that they came on the road from dead Voitan, the locals' reaction to them was far different from reactions in Q'Nkok.

"You'd think they'd never seen a human before," Denat snorted.

"Buncha rubes," Tratan agreed with a grunt. "Ripe for the plucking." He looked down at the diminutive human striding along beside him under his huge rucksack. "What should we teach them first?"

"Poker," Poertena replied. "Always start wit' poker. Den, I dunno. Maybe acey-deucy. If they really stupid, cribbage."

"They pocked," Cranla said with a grunt of laughter. He waved at one of the harvesters. "Hello, you stupid peasants. We're going to pluck your merchants for all they're worth."

Julian pointed at the Mardukan tribesmen with his chin.

"They've taken quite a shine to Poertena," he said to Despreaux.

"Birds of a feather," the other squad leader responded absently. "Is it just me, or does this place look fairly run down?" she went on.

The company was approaching a fork in the road, where the travelers had to choose between Marshad or Pasule. There was another official-looking building on a mound where the roads diverged, but although it was in better repair, it had obviously been converted into an agricultural outbuilding.

"Yeah," Julian said, glancing at the structure. "I think the loss of the Voitan trade must have hit them hard."

The company took the left fork and headed for the river. The solid stone bridge which crossed it was the only structure they'd so far seen which appeared to have been properly kept up. In fact, there'd been some obvious renovations—the well-fortified guard posts on either bank looked like fairly recent additions.

The guards on the near bank gestured for the caravan to halt, and Julian looked around as the long train of *flar-ta* dragged to a stop. An outcropping of the underlying gneiss of the Hadur region rose steeply on the right side of the road, he noted. The oxbow river took a bend around it, and an extension of the outcropping acted as a firm base for the bridge.

The hill was surmounted by trees and what appeared to have once been a small park. A well-made road in very poor repair wound to the summit, but it was obvious that the track was rarely used anymore. Only a thin path cut through the layered silt and entangling undergrowth on its lower sections. Despreaux followed his eye, and shook her head as Captain Pahner argued with the guards on the bridge. They obviously felt that the travelers ought to keep themselves—and the business they represented—on this side of the river.

"This place has really been hammered," she observed.

"No shit," Julian agreed. "It looks like it used to be a pretty nice place, though. Maybe it'll get that way again with Voitan back in business."

"We'll see," Despreaux said. "The old Voitan wasn't built in a day."

"No," Julian acknowledged as the caravan lurched back into movement, "but that guy from T'an K'tass looked like he was going to try to do it pretty damned fast."

"That he did," Despreaux said, but her tone was a bit distracted, and she nodded at the sour looking guards on the bridge as they passed. "Those guys don't look happy."

"Probably pissed at all the money they're losing," Julian said. "We're about to pump a lot of cash into the local economy . . . on the other side of their bridge."

"We hope," she answered.

The approaching city-state was huge, much larger than Q'Nkok, but it had a seedy air. Once past the bridge area, the road was once again rutted and cracked from traffic and ill repair. In fact, it was in worse shape than it had been on the other side of the river, and the peasants plowing the fields to either side of the roadbed also seemed less interested in the passage of the company.

Flar-ta were useless as draft animals, because they were far too large to move effectively in the fields. That meant that the only way to plow was to use teams of Mardukans for traction, which was a remarkably inefficient method. It was also extremely hard work, but while the plowers on the far side of the river had taken the opportunity for a break while they watched the company march by, those on this side all kept their heads down, concentrating on their tasks. And while the majority crop had been barleyrice on the far side of the river, on this side most of the fields were being sown with legumes or a crop the humans didn't recognize. The Marines had encountered the legumes before, and promptly christened them bullybeans, but they'd never seen the other crop, and the locals seemed to be planting a lot of it. At least two-thirds of the fields they could see seemed to be dedicated to producing whatever it was.

"I wonder why there's a difference," Julian said, pointing it out to Despreaux, who shrugged and gestured across the wide expanse of fields. There was another hill barely visible in the distance, but it was apparent that the local city-state dominated a vast area.

"They've got plenty of room," she pointed out. "This is probably just their area for bullybeans and . . . whatever that other stuff is."

"I guess," the intel NCO said. "But that much change just from one side of the river to the other?" He shrugged. "I'm no farmer, but it seems kinda strange to me."

"I suppose we'll find out why they do it eventually," Despreaux said with a shrug of her own. "But I wonder what that other plant is?"

"*Dianda*," the itinerant tinker said to the chief of staff. "It is . . . *urdak* into *wosan* . . . like that," he finished, gesturing to the chameleon cloth uniform the civilian wore.

The local was named Kheder Bijan. It was obvious he expected some sort of reward from the company for guiding them to the clearly evident city which the ignorant foreigners could never have found on their own, but the chief of staff was happy to have him along, anyway. He'd been a good way to update the language program, and he was a mine of information about conditions around Pasule. He was strangely uninformative, however, about Marshad.

"Ah!" Eleanora said. "Something like flax or cotton!" The software had updated the local dialect well enough for Pahner to talk their way across the bridge. She was puzzled by the fact that the officials of Pasule had been more trouble than Marshad's. The local guards had simply stepped aside, almost as if the humans had been expected.

"Yes," the local said. He rubbed a horn in thought while he considered the best way to explain. "We make cloth from it for trade."

"A cash crop." The chief of staff nodded. "Where are the subsistence crops?" she asked, looking around. "I'd think you'd be planting more barleyrice than this."

"Well," Bijan said, fingering his horn again, "I don't really understand farming. I fix things." He gestured with his haversack. "I suppose there must be other farms around here somewhere."

"Who owns the land?" Eleanora had been pleasantly surprised to discover that in the Q'Nkok region the farmers owned their own land, for the most part. The farms were passed down through complicated cultural "rules" that moved them from generation to generation more or less intact. That denied inheritance to most of the "younger sons," but that was a common problem for agrarian societies the galaxy over, and the important thing was that the farms weren't broken into minuscule lots that were impossible to manage. Nor were they sold or lost in chunks to form giant latifundia. The Houses of Q'Nkok had been well on their way to the sort of backward agricultural "reform" which would strip the peasantry of land ownership, but hopefully the destruction of their power would stop that in its tracks. At this level of technology, small-scale "yeomanry" farming was as good as it got.

"I'm not sure who owns it," the tinker said, fingering his horn again. "I've never asked."

The chief of staff blinked, then smiled cheerfully. The "tinker" had blithely nattered on about the minutiae of the inner workings of the council of oligarchs who ruled Pasule, and the different groups of independents and sharecroppers who farmed the land on that side of the river. Now, on the side that he claimed he was from, he suddenly clammed up. She wouldn't have survived a day in the imperial court if *that* hadn't set off some alarm bells.

"That's interesting," she said with complete honesty. "I suppose a tinker wouldn't really care, would he?"

"Not really," Bijan said. "I just look forward to returning to my beautiful city!"

"Nice city," Kosutic said tugging at an earlobe.

"It's okay," Pahner replied.

Marshad was larger than Q'Nkok, but smaller than the former Voitan had been, with streets that wound up the hill from several gates in the curtain walls.

The gates were unusual. They were constructed of thick wood, well joined and even caulked, and their bottoms were lined with copper, which must have cost a fortune. There was also a base upon which they were, apparently, supposed to seat, but it was shattered, and any metal which might once have sheathed it was long since gone.

Much of the city appeared to be in the same dilapidated condition. The walls were higher than Voitan's, but in even worse shape. Numerous parapets had fallen to lie in rubble at the base of the main wall, leaving gaps like broken teeth in the battlements, and in places the outer stones had worked out, exposing the rubble interior fill. One section was so badly damaged that it might as well have been called a breach, and they discovered even more signs of neglect once they entered the city proper.

The area immediately inside the gate was clear, but beyond that the city reared up the hill in a maze of alleys and tunnels. The houses were mostly built of stone, pink granite and blinding white limestone, erected in a crazy quilt of warrens, with one house on top of another in a widely varying mixture of styles and quality.

The main thoroughfare was wide enough for the passage of the company, but only barely, and the boulevard was lined with wide gutters which were joined by thin streams leading out of the alleyways. This lower section clearly wasn't the best place to live: the noisome stew in the streams which obviously provided the entire city's drainage was a noxious compound of fecal matter and rot that was practically explosive.

As they continued inward, the road presented a graphic cross-section of the city. The lower slopes showed the best quality of work, with well cut blocks of feldspar and gneiss cunningly fitted, mostly without mortar. The surfaces had been coated in white plaster, and the lintels and trim still showed signs of colorful paints. But now the plaster was patched and fallen, with caved-in roofs and shattered corners, and the once bright paint was pathetically faded in the blazing gray light. There were signs of flooding, as well, with brown high-water marks well up the sides of the houses. Many of the buildings were deserted, but shadows moved in some of the wreckage—furtive inhabitants who clearly only showed their faces under the friendly cover of night.

The quality of the stonework fell as the procession headed up the hill, but the upkeep improved. More houses were inhabited above the level of the floods, and the warren became truly mazelike, with houses piled on houses and built across alleyways which their floors turned into tunnels.

Business was being conducted in this labyrinth, but with a definitely desultory air. A few vendors lined the road with sparse offerings of half-rotten fruits, moldy barleyrice, cheap and poorly-made jewelry, and assorted minor knickknacks. The obvious poverty of the area was crushing, and the stench of rotting garbage and uncleaned latrines hung in the air as young Mardukans sat in doorways, scratching listlessly at the dust in the street.

The slums ended abruptly in a large square. Its downhill side was lined with tall townhouses which had apparently been carved out of the warren beyond at some time in the past. They fronted on a broad, flat, open area that was partially natural and partially Mardukan-made. The centerpiece of the square was a large fountain around the statue of an armed Mardukan, while the upper side of the square was occupied by a large ornamental building. The building seemed to climb—without a break, but in a myriad of differing styles—up to the citadel at the hill's summit. It appeared to be one vast palace, and a ceremony was in progress at its entrance.

It was apparently a public audience. The ruler of the city-state sat in a resplendent throne set up at the front door of the palace. As with the throne in Q'Nkok, this was made of many different inlaid woods, but the local monarch's throne was also set with precious metals and gems. The entire edifice gleamed with gold and silver and the twinkle of the local sapphires and rubies in their rough "miner's" cut.

The king was the first Mardukan the company had seen wearing any significant clothing, and he was garbed in a light robe of lustrous saffron. The outfit was slit down the sides, gathering only at the ankles and trimmed in bright vermillion. Traceries of silver thread ran through it, and the collar was a lace of silver and gems.

The monarch's horns had also been inlaid with precious metals and gems and were joined by a complex web of jewel-strung gold chains that caught the gray light and refracted it in a dull rainbow. As if all of that weren't enough, he also wore a heavy chain of jeweled gold around his neck, dangling far down his chest.

Arrayed to either side of the king were persons who were probably advisers. They were unclothed, except for one obvious commander in armor, but their horns were also inlaid and gemmed. The display was an obvious indication of rank, for it grew less expensive and spectacular in direct proportion to the owner's distance from the monarch.

About six hundred guards lined the steps at the front of the palace, standing at parade rest in two ranks. They were more heavily armored than the guards in Q'Nkok, with metal thigh-guards and bracers in addition to breastplates shining gray-silver in the clouded light. They carried the same long spear as the Q'Nkok guards, but they also wore palmate swords, about a meter in length, and despite their carefully polished breastplates, their purpose was obviously more than merely ceremonial.

The crowd before the monarch was a mixed bag. Most of them seemed to be from the Mardukan "middle class," to the extent that the planet had one. They also had decorations on their horns, but the displays were generally simple and made of base metals or brass. A few of the poorest of the poor were mixed in here and there, and it was one of them who was currently making some plea to the refulgent monarch.

The petitioner was in full prostration before the king, all six limbs splayed out as he abased himself. Whatever he was saying was unintelligible at this distance, but it didn't really matter, since the king was sitting half across his throne and paying virtually no attention to him.

As the company watched, the suppliant apparently finished whatever he was saying, and the monarch picked a kate fruit off a platter and nibbled on it. Then he threw the fruit at the petitioner and gestured to a guard.

Before the first protest could leave the unfortunate Mardukan's mouth, the guards had seized him and cut off his head. The head rolled to the edge of the crowd as the stump spurted a red spray and the body of the serf slumped into a twitching heap.

There was not a sound from the gathered Marshadans.

"We may have a problem here," Pahner observed.

"Oh, my," O'Casey said. A few months earlier, she probably would have lost her breakfast, but after Voitan, she was going to have a hard time finding anything that truly shocked her. "I agree."

"Well, if we turn around and leave," Roger said, "which is my first instinct, we *will* have a problem."

"Agreed," the captain said. "Stick to the prepared speech, Your Highness. But I want the up squad right on you. Sergeant Major!"

"Captain?"

"Fall in the company in extended formation, Sergeant Major. I want a snappy movement. And drop the pig-stickers. Rifles and cannon front and center!"

The caravan devolved into an organized frenzy as the Marines prepared to "present" their noble lord to the local monarch. Roger, for his part, rehearsed his speech and checked his pistol, on the assumption that he was equally likely to need either of them.

"Credentials, credentials," O'Casey muttered, diving into the packs on the *flar-ta* called Bertha. Somewhere she had the now much travel-stained, vermillion-sealed documents of Roger's credibility, along with letters from the King of Q'Nkok and the new council of Voitan, but she hadn't expected to need them so soon. They'd assumed that they would have to deal first with a functionary just to find shelter, then the king—not the other way around.

"Snap it, snap it, snap it," Kosutic chanted subvocally. The change from a tactical formation to one intended for parade had to be made as cleanly and professionally as possible. Any trace of disorder would not only reflect poorly on the Regiment, but would create an opening. If you looked professional, it stopped nine out of ten fights before they started; the tenth, of course, was Voitan.

The post guide had found a mark, and the squad leaders fell in on her, with their squads in turn falling in behind them. On command, the company—less one squad, which was "tight" on the prince—deployed in a double line facing that of the local guards. The Marines were pitifully few in number, but soon enough the locals would know what that pitiful few had accomplished at a place called Voitan.

Then let them get ideas.

Roger looked behind him into the unsmiling blue eyes of Sergeant Nimashet Despreaux.

"We've got to quit meeting like this. People will talk," he told her, but her demeanor didn't change.

"I'm on post, Sir. I'm not supposed to carry on a conversation."

"Ah." Roger turned back to the front and tugged at his braid as Pahner and O'Casey walked up to find him. "Sorry. I'll put myself on report."

"Ready?" Pahner subvocalized over the com.

"Bravo in position," Lieutenant Jasco replied almost as quietly.

"Inner team in position." Despreaux's voice was the ghost of a whisper at the back of Roger's head.

"Documents," O'Casey said, handing them to the prince.

"Then let's do it, Captain," Roger said calmly, and hid a silent snort of mental laughter. The presentation ceremony they were about to use was the same one they'd planned and rehearsed for Net-Hauling on Leviathan. The only difference was that the survivors of the company were on a hair trigger, and if anything went wrong he was hitting the deck at about Mach 3. Fifty-eight weapons would turn the square into an abattoir at the slightest sign of threat, and anything he personally might have added to the carnage would be purely inconsequential.

The group started forward in a slow, hieratic half-step which was used for only two purposes: formal presentations, and funerals. Since Marines did a lot more of the latter than the former, they referred to it as "The Death March," which, in Roger's considered opinion, did not bode well in this circumstance.

The crowd before the throne parted to let them through. It was surprisingly silent; the only sound in the entire square was the slow tap of the humans' boots and the distant rumble of thunder.

Roger reached the sticky red stain where the previous petitioner had pled his case and stopped. He bowed deeply and held out the documents as the iron and shit smell of a fresh kill rose around him.

"Your Majesty, Great Ruler of Marshad and Voice of the People, I, Prince Roger Ramius Sergei Alexander Chiang MacClintock, of the House MacClintock, Heir Tertiary to the Throne of the Empire of Man, greet you in the name of my Imperial Mother, Her Majesty, Empress Alexandra MacClintock, Empress of Man, Queen of the Dawn, and Mistress of the Void."

Eleanora took the documents ceremoniously back from him and stepped forward and to the side. Dropping to both knees at the edge of the stairs, she held them out, hoping that one of these glittering idiots would figure out her purpose.

One of the advisers—a senior one, by the decoration of his horns—trotted down the steps and accepted the documents as Roger continued his speech about the magnificence of Marshad and its ruler, whose name he had yet to find out.

She backchecked the translation and winced. The program had reversed genders on Empress Alexandra, making her "Emperor Alexander," which was historically humorous but a pain otherwise. Eleanora locked that description in for this culture (they were never going to know the difference anyway), and checked the other gender settings. Sure enough, the program had reversed gender in the dialect. Fortunately, the translation glitch hadn't come up yet, so she suppressed a snarl and fixed it, then dumped the patch to the other toots and went back to listening to Roger's speech.

" . . . bring joyous news: Voitan is restored! The Kranolta in all their fury came against us when we entered the fallen city, but that was a grave mistake. Aided by the forces of New Voitan, we defeated them in a terrible battle and destroyed their war host utterly. Even now the foundries and forges of fabled Voitan ring once more with the sound of forming metal! Soon the caravans will come once more on a regular basis. We are the first, but we shall not be the last!"

The prince paused in a planned break for the expected applause, but there was only a quiet murmur, and even that was almost instantly hushed. Roger was clearly nonplussed by the lack of reaction, but he carried on gamely.

"We are foreign emissaries on a voyage of exploration, and we are to be met by ships on a distant shore to the northwest. Thus we ask the boon of permission to pass through these lands in peace. We also wish to rest and enjoy the hospitality of your city, and we have brought rich booty from the conquest of the Kranolta which we wish to trade for supplies to continue our journey."

He bowed again as the king sat up. The entire company tensed, although an outside observer might have been pardoned for not realizing that it had, as the saffron-clad monarch leaned forward and examined the documents. After a brief, whispered consultation with one of his advisers, concentrating on the letter from the King of Q'Nkok, the monarch clapped his hands in agreement and stood.

"Welcome, welcome, Your Highness, to the land of Marshad, you and all your brave warriors! We have heard of your exploits in defeating the Kranolta and raising Voitan to its ancient and honorable place! In Our name, Radj Hoomas, King of Marshad, Lord of the Land, We welcome you to Marshad. Rest here as long as you like. A place has been prepared for you and your great warriors, and there shall be a great feast in your honor tonight! So We declare! Let there be merriment and celebration, for the way to Voitan is open once more!"

CHAPTER FORTY-SIX

"I don't think I understand your reasoning, Sir." Lieutenant Jasco shook his head and gestured around the sumptuous quarters the officers had been given. "They;ve certainly been friendly enough."

"So is a spider, Lieutenant," Pahner replied. "Right before it eats a fly."

The room was paneled in blond wood, the pale grain cut to expose abstract swirls. The floor was covered in cushions a shade or two darker than the wood, most of them piled to one side, and the single window revealed a breathtaking view of the city and the river, with a glimpse of Pasule and the vast stretch of cultivated land beyond.

All in all, it was a pleasant place. Now if they could just decide whether or not it was a prison.

"We've been dealing with Mardukans for a while now," Roger said. "They're not the gentlest people in the galaxy, but they have more regard for life than we saw this morning."

"Roger is correct," O'Casey said. "This town, the whole local culture, appears atypical. And the focus of that would seem to be Radj Hoomas." She fingered the silken cover of the pillow on which she sat. "*Dianda*. Everywhere you look, you see this flaxsilk. All the fields, throughout the citadel. I bet if we peeked behind doorways, we'd find that everyone is weaving the stuff."

"Well, okay," Jasco said. "But that doesn't necessarily mean there's anything wrong. There have been plenty of societies where everyone was a weaver, or whatever. It doesn't make this culture evil."

"No, but it does make it dangerous," Pahner said definitively. "We need to back off from thinking like Marines and start thinking like bodyguards again."

Cord nodded in a gesture he'd picked up from the humans.

"A monarch like this Radj cares only about himself and his needs. And this *atul* has obviously been in power long enough to put his stamp on the entire kingdom."

Pahner nodded back at the shaman and looked at Kosutic.

"What are the major assassination methods?"

"You think he's going to try to assassinate Prince Roger, Sir?" Jasco asked. "Why?"

"Maybe not Roger," the sergeant major rasped, "but if he thinks there's some profit to be made from killing the guards and taking Roger hostage, he might try." She looked at the ceiling and began ticking methods off. "Poison, bomb, hand, knife, smart-bot, close-shot, long-shot, heavy weapon, weapons of mass destruction."

"This society has hand, poison, and knife," Pahner said. "So we need to concentrate on those."

"We already have analyzers," Roger pointed out, "they'll pick up poisons."

"If they come at us with swords, we respond with guns," Jasco said.

"And if they come at you with knives?" the sergeant major asked with a grim smile. "*En masse*, from every side? What then, Lieutenant?"

"Exactly." Pahner turned to O'Casey. "You're going to be handling point on the negotiations again. Make sure they're aware that Roger has to have," he paused and thought for a moment, "seven guards at all times. Seven is a mystic number to us humans. Not to be trifled with. So sorry if that's a problem."

"Okay," Eleanora said, making a note on her toot.

"I don't trust him as far as I could throw Patty," Roger said.

"Why not, Your Highness?" Jasco asked, perhaps just a trifle more dismissively than he really ought to have spoken to the Heir Tertiary to the Throne of Man. "They've given us everything we wanted on a silver platter, and no wonder. I mean, obviously, they're happy they'll be getting the Voitan trade back. Look at the slums we passed through on the way up."

"That's exactly why," Roger said quietly. "Look, I might have been a clotheshorse. Well, still am," he amended with a chuckle, looking down at his stained chameleon uniform. "But," he continued seriously, "it wasn't the same as this place. Right down the hill from us there's crushing poverty. In case you didn't notice, most of those kids were literally starving. And the guy who should be working on fixing that is sitting on his ass at the top of the heap, sucking on fruit, having his horns inlaid, and cutting peasants' heads off. And there are all these fields where food could be grown, but it isn't. They're being planted in flaxsilk. So the people are starving, and I don't think that that's the *farmers'* plan. I think it's the plan of the son-of-a-bitch we're about to have a 'Victory Dinner' with." The prince's jaw flexed in anger, and his nostrils twitched as if they'd scented something foul. "So that, Lieutenant, is why I don't trust that Borgia son-of-a-bitch."

"Seven guards, Chief of Staff, Sergeant Major," Pahner said emphatically. "Fully armed. Especially at this 'Victory Party.' And extra especially," he added dryly, "after all the trouble 'our friend' the monarch went to making sure we came here."

"Yeah," Roger said. "A 'tinker.'"

"You caught that, too?" Eleanora observed with a smile.

"I wonder what he really is?"

"You succeeded, Kheder Bijan," the king observed. He took a nibble out of a kate fruit and tossed the remainder on the floor. "Congratulations, 'Scout.'"

"Thank you, O King," the commander of the Royal Scouts replied. The Scouts actually did some scouting, especially when meeting with the informants they maintained among the surrounding tribes, but he was in fact the commander of the Marshad secret police.

"Once again you have avoided having your head lopped off," the monarch added with a grunt of humor. "One of these days, you won't be so lucky. That day will be a great pleasure to me. A day of comfort."

"I live to serve, O King." The spy knew he was on the edge of the knife, but that was what gave the role spice.

"Of course you do." The king gave a disbelieving chuckle. "It is a well-known fact, is it not?"

He turned to the commander of the Royal Guard. The commander had been nothing more than a common mercenary before being given his position, and the king had been careful to ensure that plenty of hatred was directed at him. It was one way to ensure the Guard's total loyalty, for if the king fell, so would the Guard.

"We will continue with the original plan."

"Yes, O King," the guard commander replied with a brief glance of fury at the spy. "The forces are at your command."

"Of course they are," he whispered. "And with Our mighty army and the power of these humans, We shall rule the world!"

Roger took another bite of the spiced meat. He'd run an analyzer over it and gotten all the usual warnings about alkaloids, but it wasn't poisonous. It just tasted that way.

The locals used a spice that tasted exactly like rancid fennel, and it was apparently wildly popular, because it was in every dish. Roger picked a bit of the purple leaf off the meat and checked. Yep, that was it. He surreptitiously spat, trying to get the rotten taste out of his mouth, then gave up. At least there were only fourteen more courses to go.

The diners were seated on cushions, arranged in pairs and trios around low, three-legged tables. The courses were borne in by silent servants, and the empty platters were borne back out picked over or finished off. Most of the diners were members of the Marshad court, but there were also some representatives from other city-states. They were neither exactly ambassadors nor simple visitors, but seemed to occupy some place in between.

Roger was seated with two such representatives near the king. He had initially engaged them in desultory conversation, but they'd rapidly dropped into a complex discussion of trading futures that drifted first out of Roger's interest, and eventually out of the local dialect. Since then, the prince had occupied himself picking at his food and observing the dinner party.

He looked over at Pahner. The captain was seated on a cushion, legs crossed as if he'd been born to this society, calmly chewing and swallowing the horrible food and nodding as if he actually heard every word his seat mate was saying. As always, the Marine was the perfect diplomat, and Roger sighed. He was *never* going to be that good.

Eleanora had stopped eating after only a couple of mouthfuls, but she could excuse that on the basis of the steady conversation she'd been maintaining with both her table mates. The chief of staff was doing her usual job of probing every nuance of the local culture, dissecting it as a biologist would dissect an invertebrate.

He didn't look over his shoulder, but he knew the Marines were standing at the ready. They lined the wall at his back, weapons at low port and ready for instant use if it dropped in the pot.

He felt mildly naked without the additional presence of Cord, but the shaman lacked the nanites of his human companions and was still recovering from the terrible shrapnel wounds he'd taken in Voitan. Whatever might happen, the shaman would have to ride it out from a pile of cushions in the visitors' quarters.

Everyone was still as nervous as cats in a roomful of float-chairs. Including, unless he was much mistaken, Radj Hoomas.

The king sat at the head of the room, with his back to the large double doors leading into one of his many throne rooms. He was surrounded, literally, by guards and hard to observe through the obscurement of the armored behemoths. From what Roger could see of him, however, he, too, was picking at his food, speaking occasionally with the armored commander seated beside him and glancing nervously around the room. It might be a victory party, but the host didn't look very victorious.

"The Prince isn't eating!" the king whispered angrily.

"He's eaten enough," Mirzal Pars responded. The old mercenary clapped his hands and grunted in humor. "They're so smart, but they don't even recognize *miz* poison. It may be tasteless, but you can see the leaves clearly. Everyone knows about it . . . except these *humans*." He grunted another laugh.

"But will it be enough?" Radj Hoomas demanded. The plan had to be executed flawlessly, for the power of these humans was terrifying to contemplate. Holding onto it would be like holding an *atul* by the tail.

"It will be enough. They've all eaten more than a large enough dose. If we withhold the antidote, they'll die within a day."

"And the guards are ready?"

"Assuredly," the commander chuckled. "They look forward to it."

CHAPTER FORTY-SEVEN

The celebration had moved into the throne room, where the king presided over the conversation swirling around him from his throne. Much of the court had excused itself after the dinner, pleading the excuse of work to complete, and the majority of the room was sparsely filled with the prince's party and the representatives from the surrounding city-states.

Eleanora sipped from a cup of warm, flat water and squinted at the representative from Pasule.

"The king is the *sole* landowner?" she asked incredulously. Even in the most despotic regimes in Earth's history, power had been more diffuse than that.

"Yes. Radj Hoomas owns not only the agricultural land, but all of the buildings of the town, and all of the houses of the Council outside the city wall." The representative, Jedal Vel, was short for a Mardukan, but he still towered over the chief of staff. She'd ended up talking exclusively to him after finding him a mine of information. The "simple trader" from Pasule was a student not only of commerce, but of government and history. He was, naturally, biased towards Pasule's oligarchical form of government, but having Marshad as a horrible counterexample would tend to do that.

"Two generations ago, in the chaos after the fall of Voitan, there was a great rebellion among the Houses of Marshad. Three of them were the most prominent, and the king of that time, Radj Kordan, Radj Hoomas' grandfather, allied with one of them against the other two. It was a terrible battle, but the king finally prevailed over all but his single surviving ally. Most unfortunately, he was, in turn, assassinated shortly after the end of the war by a son of one of the defeated Houses. He had intended simply to reduce their power, fine them heavily, and strip them of guards, but his son, Hoomas' father, killed every member of the defeated Houses. Then he forced a marriage with a daughter of the single surviving ally, and absorbed that House, leaving the House of Radj as the only power in Marshad."

The representative sipped his wine and gave a lower handclap, a Mardukan shrug.

"Pasule's actions in this were not the best. We supported both sides, trying to drag the war out and damage Marshad as much as possible. We've always seen the city as a rival, and since the fall of Voitan it's come to war more than once. But when Radj consolidated all the power under himself, it was clear we'd made a serious mistake. Since then, Radj has taken more and more power and treasure, and left less and less for others.

"The only thing that Marshad exports anymore is *dianda*, but it makes a tremendous profit on it. The crop is hard to grow, and takes up valuable land which might otherwise be used to grow food. Naturally, Radj Hoomas could care less. The land produces barely enough food to support the farmers; the city poor are left to starve and work the looms."

"It seems like a situation ripe for a revolution," O'Casey said. "Surely there's some group that might rise up?"

"Perhaps," Jedal Vel said carefully. "However, the profits from the *dianda* trade also permit him to support a large standing army. Most of it is composed of mercenaries, but they recognize that they need Radj in power as the only way to preserve their own positions. They've crushed the few attempted rebellions easily."

"I see," O'Casey said. *Take the army out of the picture though*, she mused silently, *and things might change.* She glanced at the guards lining every wall. Another, separate contingent formed a half-moon crescent around the throne, and the ostentatious display of force finally made sense to her.

"Millions for defense, not a penny for the poor. . . ." she murmured with a low chuckle.

"Pardon?" the Pasule asked, but it was only an absent courtesy, for he was looking towards the throne. Radj Hoomas had called over the guard commander, and it looked like he might finally be ready to make the announcement that would permit everyone to leave gracefully.

Pahner nodded to the prince as Roger walked up to him. The squad parted as the prince neared the captain, and the Marines expertly swallowed up both officers in a protective ring.

"Roger," the captain greeted him, and glanced at Despreaux. The Marines had been specifically tasked with eavesdropping on the king and his guard captain, but the sergeant shrugged her shoulders. Nothing clear to report.

"Radj is definitely planning something," the prince said, tucking a stray hair back into line. "But so far, so good."

"That's what the jumper said as he passed the thirtieth floor," Pahner pointed out. He looked at Despreaux again. "What?"

"Just something about the guards, Sir," the sergeant said. "Maybe something about poison, too, but that wasn't clear."

"Joy," the company CO said.

"I don't like being surrounded like this, Sir," she added. "We could take the king if it dropped in the pot, but I'm not sure we could keep the Prince alive."

"If that happens, Sergeant," Roger said quietly, "take the king. That's your primary mission. Understood?"

Despreaux glanced quickly at Pahner, but the captain only looked back at her without expression.

"Yes, Sir. Understood," she said.

"Let's be on our toes," Pahner suggested as conversation died down and the king climbed to his feet. "Looks like time to party."

"We are gathered here tonight," Radj Hoomas said, "to honor the brave warriors who crushed the Kranolta and reopened the road to Voitan. Puissant warriors, indeed," he said, and his voice echoed hollowly through the wood-paneled hall.

"Puissant warriors, indeed," he repeated, and glanced around at his own massed guards. "I ask you, Your Royal Highness, Prince Roger Ramius Sergei Alexander Chiang MacClintock, could your puissant warriors defeat all the guards in this room? Before you fell yourself?"

"Possibly," Roger replied calmly. "Quite probably. And I would be trying very hard to survive."

The king gazed at him for a moment, then glanced at one of his guards . . . who stepped forward, and, with a smooth motion, shoved his spear into the back of the representative from Pasule. Jedal Vel screamed in a froth of aspirated blood as the bitter steel spearhead emerged from his chest, but the guard only grinned cruelly and twisted his wrist as he jerked his weapon free once more and the envoy thudded to the floor.

"Are you so confident?" the king asked, grunting in humor.

"What?" Roger asked, with a smile he didn't feel, as O'Casey recoiled towards the Marines and away from the twitching corpse at her feet. "You think that the 'puissant warriors' who defeated the Kranolta have never seen blood?"

He booted up the assassin program he'd used in Q'Nkok, and as the aiming reticle appeared, superimposed on his vision, he dropped it onto the forehead of the laughter-grunting guard captain.

It required more than well-written software to be truly phenomenal with an assassin program. Even with hard encoding, it required smooth, practiced muscles that could handle the high twitch-rate strains placed upon them. But Roger *had* practiced, and the pistol came up with the blinding speed which had so surprised Pahner in the Q'Nkok banquet hall. The weapon simply *materialized* in his hand, and the supersonic crack of the bead's passage blended with a meaty thump as the decapitated guard captain hit the floor.

The king opened his mouth to shout, his face covered in the bright crimson spray of the captain's blood, then froze as he found himself looking down the barrel of the bead pistol.

"Now, there's an old term for this," Pahner said quietly, his own pistol out and trained as he transmitted furious orders to hold fast over his toot. The orders had to be in text, because the subvocalization equipment was part of the combat helmet he wasn't wearing at the moment, and his toot had to rebroadcast it through the systems of the bodyguards' helmets. That meant the orders were necessarily one-way, but he could imagine Kosutic's distant cursing just fine.

"It's called a 'Mexican standoff,'" he continued. "You try to kill us, and our company blows your little town to the ground. Not that you personally will care, Your Majesty, because you'll die right here, right now."

"I don't think so," the king said with a grunt as guards moved to interpose their bodies between him and Roger's weapon. "But I don't intend to kill any humans today. No, no. That was never my intent."

"You don't mind if we doubt your word, do you?" Roger asked, deflecting the pistol's point of aim to the ceiling as the tension eased slightly. "And, by the way," he added, nodding to the guards between him and Radj Hoomas, "we'll cut through those fucking bodies like they were so much cloth when we start. Bodies aren't going to stop us."

"But doing that would take time and prevent you from killing all the *other* guards that would be killing *you*," the king said. "But, again, that was never my intent."

"Ask him what his plan *is*," O'Casey hissed, now relatively safe between the bulks of Pahner and Roger. She was a fair negotiator, but these were not, in her opinion, optimal conditions. In fact, her mouth was dry with fear and her palms were sweating. She couldn't imagine how Roger and Pahner were staying so calm.

"All right, O King, what's your plan?" Roger asked, carefully not swallowing. If he did, it would be obvious his mouth was as dry as the lakebed they'd landed on.

"I have certain desires," the king said, with another grunt of laughter. "You have certain needs. I think we could come to mutually acceptable terms."

"All right," and Pahner said grimly. "I can see that. But why in hell did you choose to open negotiations like this?"

"Well," the king responded, with yet another grunt that this time turned into a belly laugh, "your need is food, supplies and weapons. Unfortunately, there is no great supply of either in Marshad. My desire, on the other hand, is to conquer Pasule, where it chances that both are readily available. I was fairly sure you wouldn't care to conquer Pasule for me, so it seemed advisable to discover an incentive to . . . *encourage* you."

"An incentive," Pahner repeated tonelessly.

"Precisely. I feel confident that your warband will take Pasule for me when I tell them it's a choice between that and the death of their leaders."

"Okay, okay," Kosutic said, waving for quiet. "Let's just stay cold here, people."

"We should extract them immediately," Jasco said. "I know those aren't our orders, but orders given under duress are invalid."

"Sure, Sir," Kosutic said. "Tell it to the Captain."

"Well . . ."

The conversation was taking place in the third-floor "officers' quarters" of the visitors' area. The pale yellow room where the prince had prepared for the fateful dinner party was now filled with the temporary command group.

"Lieutenant," Julian said, tapping his pad, "we have upwards of a battalion of scummies outside this building. They hold the high ground, and our pack beasts. We would have to fight our way out and up to the throne room."

"The Captain's right, Lieutenant Jasco," the sergeant major said. "We wait for the right moment, and play along in the meantime. We have to wait until the odds favor us, instead of the other way around. We have the time."

"This isn't right!" the exasperated officer said. "We should be taking down that throne room right now. This is a member of the *Imperial Family*!"

"Yep," Kosutic said equably. "Surely is. Dangerous one, too."

Roger listened calmly to the brand-new guard commander's bloodthirsty pronouncements about what would happen to any human who did not obey orders. The new, heavily-armored commander explained at considerable length, and when he finished, Roger bared his teeth in a smile.

"You're next," he said pleasantly.

The guard captain glared at the prince, but the Mardukan's eyes fell before Roger's did, and the scummy withdrew, closing the door behind him.

Roger turned from the door and looked around. The suite was large and airy, with several windows which overlooked the back side of the castle. The far curtain wall, he noticed, was covered with torch-bearing guards watching the shadows for any attempt to escape.

The floor was scattered with the ubiquitous pillows and low tables of the Hadur, and there were "chamber buckets" for relieving wastes. It was quite pleasant, all things considered.

"We have to get out of here," he muttered.

"And you propose to do that, how?" Pahner asked, handing Despreaux back her borrowed helmet. Unlike the prince, the captain was the very picture of sangfroid.

"Well, I feel like taking a rifle and killing a guard an hour until they either let us go or figure out to stay out of sight," Roger snarled, glaring at the guards manning the wall.

"Thereby suggesting retaliation," the captain said coolly. "Until we're actually in combat, we aren't decisively engaged. We should maneuver for room until then. Violence at this stage will only limit, rather than expand, our maneuver room."

"Do you have a plan?" O'Casey asked. "It sounds like you do."

"Not as such," Pahner said, glancing out the window. The lesser moon, Sharma, was rising, and its glimmer could be sensed rather than seen in the darkness beyond the windows. "On the other hand, I've often found that waiting for your opponent to move reveals the weakness in his own plans."

CHAPTER FORTY-EIGHT

Kostas Matsugae watched the line of stooped figures carrying in the sacks of barleyrice. These Mardukans were the first females, outside their mahouts' families, the company had seen since Q'Nkok, and they were clearly being used for this task because they were both nonthreatening and of subnormal intelligence. They were also thin as rails.

The valet nodded and looked around as the last sack of grain was carried in. The area where the food supplies were being piled was out of sight of the Mardukan guards stationed outside the visitors' quarters, and he quickly opened up a pot and gestured to the Mardukans.

"This is stew with some barleyrice in it." He gestured to a stack of small bowls. "You can each have a bowl. Only one, please."

After the almost pathetically grateful females had left, he looked up and noticed Julian watching him from the doorway. The alcove to one side of the entrance was technically a guard room, but since there were nothing *but* guards in the building, it had been converted to storage.

"Do you have a problem with my charity, Sergeant?" Matsugae picked up one of the sacks and headed for the doorway; it was time to start work on dinner.

"No." The Marine plucked the twenty-kilo sack easily from the slight valet's grip and tossed it over his own shoulder. "Charity seems to be in short supply in this town. Nothing wrong with changing that."

"This is the most detestable town it has ever been my displeasure to visit," Matsugae said. He shook his head and grimaced. "It defies belief."

"Well," the sergeant said with a grim smile, "it's bad—I'll grant that. But it's not the worst in the galaxy. You ever read anything about Saint 'recovery worlds'?"

"Not much," the valet admitted. "Rather, I've heard of them, but I don't really 'know' about them. On the other hand, I believe the overall concept that the Saints espouse has some justice. Many planets *have* been damaged beyond recovery by overzealous terraforming and unchecked mining. That doesn't make me a SaintSymp," he added hastily.

"Didn't think you were. You couldn't have made it past the loyalty tests if you were. Or, at least, I hope you couldn't have. But have you ever read any reports about 'recovery worlds'? Unbiased ones?"

"No," Matsugae replied as they reached the kitchen area. A blaze had already been started in the large fireplace at one end of the guard room, and a pot hung from a swing arm, ready to be put into the fire. The room was amazingly hot, like an entrance to Hell, and Matsugae started gathering the ingredients of the evening meal. "Should I have?"

"Maybe." The sergeant set the bag of grain on the floor. "You know the theory?"

"They're former colonized planets that the Saints are trying to return to 'pristine' condition," the valet said as he began measuring ingredients into the pot. "They're trying to erase any evidence of terrestrial life on them." He smiled and gestured at the pot. "It's stew and barleyrice tonight, for a change."

Julian snorted, but didn't smile.

"That's the theory, all right," he agreed. "But how are they actually doing it? How are they 'unterraforming' those worlds? And what worlds are they? And where are the colonists who lived on them?"

"Why the questions, Sergeant?" Matsugae asked. "Should I assume that you know the answers, whereas I don't?"

"Yeah." Julian gave a mildly angry nod. "I know the answers. Okay. How are they 'unterraforming' the planets? They started with the colonists. Dirt poor farmers, mostly—none of these are worlds that produce anything the Saints give a damn about. That's why they're willing to drop them. So they have these people rounded up and put to work undoing the 'damage' that a couple of generations have done to the planets. Since they were farmers and terraformers—or the descendants of farmers and terraformers, anyway—before they were picked up, they were, *de facto*, guilty of 'ecological mismanagement.'"

"But . . . ?" the valet began in a puzzled tone.

"Hang on." The sergeant held up a hand. "I think I'll answer your question in a bit. Anyway, they put them to work 'reversing' the process. Mostly with hand tools, 'to minimize the impact.' And since humans, just by their excretions, if nothing else, tend to change the environment around them, the 'Saints' have to make sure that any fresh damage is minimized. Which they do by reducing the food supplies of the workers to under one thousand calories per day."

"But that's—"

"About half the minimum necessary to sustain life?" the sergeant said with a vicious smile. "Really? Gee."

"Are you saying that they're starving their own colonists to death?" Matsugae asked in a disbelieving tone. "That's hard to believe. Where's the Human Rights Commission report?"

"These are planets near the center of the Saints' own empire," Julian pointed out. "HRC teams aren't let anywhere near the recovery planets. According to the Saints, they're completely abandoned and quarantined, so what interest could the HRC possibly have in them? Besides," he added bitterly, "they worked their way through the colonists years ago."

"My God, you're serious," the valet said quietly. He accepted the help of the obviously angry NCO to fill the pot with water and swung it over the fire. "That's insane!"

"'Insane' describes the Saints to a 'T,'" Julian snarled. "Of course, the job is never really 'complete,'" he added with a ghastly smile.

"Oh?" Matsugae said warily.

"Sure. I mean, there's always some damned humanocentric weed cropping up somewhere on these pristine beauties," the sergeant said lightly. "That's why they still have to send humans down there to root them out."

"And where do they get those humans?"

"Well, first there's political prisoners," Julian said, ticking off the groups on his fingers. "Then there are other 'environmental enemies,' such as smokers. And there are general prisoners that are just going to be a bother to keep around. Last, but most certainly not least, there are nationals from other political systems that have, in the opinion of the Saint higher-ups, no utility," he finished with a snarl.

"Like?" Matsugae asked even more warily.

"Raider insertion teams, for starters," the Marine said bitterly. "We've lost three in the last year, and all we get out of the Saints is 'we have no knowledge of them.'"

"Oh."

"The hell of it is, that there are all these rumors that NavInt knows where they are." The NCO sat down on one of the tri-legged tables and hung his head. "If they'd just tell us, we'd go in in an instant. Shit, we've put Raider teams on the planets and *documented* what's going on—that's how we lost our people in the first frigging place! I know we could get at least some of them out!"

"So these are *rumors*? That makes sense. I can't believe that sort of thing is going on in this day and age."

"Oh, get a fucking grip, Kostas!" Julian snapped. "I've seen the damned pictures from Calypso, and they look like one of the internment camps from the Dagger Years! A bunch of skeletons wandering around with wooden tools and digging at *dandelions*, for God's sake!"

The valet regarded him calmly.

"I believe that *you* believe this to be true. Would you mind if I tried to corroborate it?"

"Not at all," the NCO sighed. "Ask any of the senior Marines. Hell, ask O'Casey when we get her back. I'm sure she's up to speed on it. But the point is that, bad as this place is, humans do ten times worse to each other every day."

Poertena watched the Mardukans carefully. He'd long since stopped regretting his "cheating" demonstration. There wasn't much point in regret, since he couldn't put the genie back into the bottle whatever he did, but it turned out that four arms made for hellacious cardsharps.

He'd first noticed the problem shortly after his brief demonstration to his cronies on the march from Voitan. Suddenly, where he'd been winning fairly consistently at poker, he started losing. Since his play hadn't changed, it meant that his companions' play must have gotten better, but it wasn't until Cranla fumbled a transfer that he twigged to what was going on.

Even though the Mardukans' "false-hands" were relatively clumsy, it was easy enough for them to palm one or two critical cards, and then it was a simple matter of switching them off. He caught them once on the basis of an ace that was covered in slime; Denat, the tricky bastard, had figured out that he could embed a card in the mucous on his arm and even show that his "hands were empty."

So now, they played spades. There were still ways to cheat, but with all fifty-two cards in play, it was trickier. Which wasn't much consolation at the moment, he thought, as Tratan dropped an ace onto the current trick and cut the Pinopan's king.

"Be calm, Poertena," the big Mardukan snorted. "Next you'll think these brainless females are giving us tips!" He gestured at the nearest one, who was slowly shuffling along in a squat, sweeping the floor with nothing more than a handful of barleyrice straw while she crooned and murmured tunelessly to herself.

A group of the simpleminded peasant women had been sent in the previous day to clean and had stayed. Not surprisingly; they were treated better among the humans than anywhere else in the city. But in the short time they'd been there, while the company waited for word on what the king intended, the inoffensive little creatures had faded into the background.

Poertena looked up at Tratan's gesture, and snorted.

"I don't t'ink so," he said.

The small, retiring Mardukan noted their regard and ducked her head, raising the volume of her croon slightly, and Poertena grunted a laugh and started to look back at his cards, then paused as his toot's translation program started to cycle. The system had tried to react to his unconscious desire to listen to the words of the song and detected that it was in an unknown dialect. He started to disengage the translation protocol's furious cycling, but decided to let it finish the run when the first phrase to pop out was "stupid man."

He hid a chuckle and picked at the program. The tiny female, very little more than normal human height, was apparently cursing the three Mardukan tribesmen.

> "O, most stupid of men, am I not singing in
>   your language?
> "Look at me, just a glance is all I ask.
> "I dare not call attention, for there may be
>   spies among my fellows.
> "But I am the only one who knows
>   your language,
> "You stupid, foolish, gutless, idiotic men.
> "Will you not listen to me that your prince
>   might live?"

Poertena wasn't quite certain how he managed to keep a straight face as he shifted from humor to panic, but he was a long-experienced negotiator, and that experience wasn't limited to legal goods and services. Individuals had made clandestine contact with him in public places before, and as soon as he realized the song was an attempt to do just that, he probed the translation program.

The problem was that the female was *not* using language of The People. Nor was she using the dialect of Q'Nkok, which was very similar. Instead, she was using a third dialect which was significantly different, and between those differences and the fact that she was trying to avoid calling anyone *else's* attention to herself, the three tribesmen had been totally oblivious to her.

"The problem is you language, O silly female," Poertena said. The translator, noting who the target of the statement was, automatically used the odd dialect. "They do no' speak it. So, who is tee foolish one, I ask you?"

"Ah," she sang. "I had wondered how any three boys could be so stupid. It is the language of the city you have passed through, a city restored." The song was almost atonal and, sung in a whisper, it could have been a lullaby in an unknown language. No threat. Despite that, the contact shifted to a completely wordless hum as another female passed through carrying a tray of food. She let the other female draw out of earshot, then glanced up discreetly while she continued her aimless sweeping.

"Move it or lose it," Cranla said, thumping on the table, and Poertena jerked out of his reverie and threw a card without even looking at it.

"Hey, *partner*," Denat began with a snarl, "what—"

"No, no, no table talk," Tratan chuckled as he covered the king with a spade. "Gotcha."

"Su', su'," Poertena said quietly. "We jus' stopped playing anyway. We gonna continue to throw cards until t'is hand is done, then *we* done."

"Hey, it's not that bad . . ." Cranla started to say.

"I jus' got word t'at there's a problem," Poertena lied. "So, me, I'm not really pay attention to tee game. We need to stop. Soon."

"I can quit," Tratan said. There was half a hand left, but he flashed his cards. "We just throw them down, tot up the score like it's real, and deal a hand of poker. And pretend to play until you have to move." He looked casually around for any immediate threats. "We need to get our spears?"

"What?" Cranla said. "I don't—"

"Shut up," Denat said mildly. "Just do it."

"Oh." The young Mardukan finally caught the drift and tossed his cards into the middle of the table with a shrug. "Not a great hand, anyway."

"Yeah," Tratan said. "I think it was a lousy hand we were just dealt."

"Okay, Lady," Poertena said. "What you message?" He deliberately kept his eyes on the table and addressed the apparent nonsense syllables to Tratan.

"I think I caught a bit of that," the tribesman said in return, glancing involuntarily at the female and then down at the table. "So it wasn't one of your mystical radio communications?"

"There is one who needs to talk to your leaders," the female sang, dusting the walls beside the table now. "One who must meet with your leaders."

"T'at will be hard," Poertena said, but he glanced up at Cord's nephews. "Cranla, go get tee Sergeant Major?"

"Okay," the Mardukan said, using the actual Standard, and got up and trotted towards the stairs.

"I will meet you near the fireplace downstairs, in a little while," the female sang, sweeping her way towards the door. "In the time a candle takes to burn a finger's breadth."

Poertena thought about it but decided against trying to get her to stay put. She was obviously working to a game plan, and if the humans wanted to use it, they had to have some idea what it was.

"All right," he answered, picking up the poker hand. "A half-hour." He glanced at his cards and grimaced. "A full house on deal. Jus' my luck."

"Not really," Tratan said soothingly. "I just didn't want you to be distracted trying to decide what to draw."

CHAPTER FORTY-NINE

"You're sure about this, Poertena?" Lieutenant Jasco asked dubiously.

The blazing fireplace made the kitchen an inferno which was normally empty, but for Matsugae and the mahout's wives who helped him with meals. Now, however, it was crowded with the sergeant major, the lieutenant, Poertena, and Denat, along with Julian and one of his fire teams. Matsugae and his current assistant continued preparing the evening meal, stepping around the Marines and Mardukans crowding the room, but it wasn't exactly easy.

"T'is is where she said, Sir."

"She's late, then," the lieutenant said.

"The time is ambiguous," Pahner said over the radio. "A 'finger's breadth' on a candle. Human or Mardukan, and what kind of candle?" The captain, Roger, and O'Casey were attending the assembly through the suit cameras from Despreaux's squad.

"But it still should have been about half an hour, Sir," Jasco argued. "This is a fool's errand," he added with a glance at the armorer.

"So you think we should have dismissed it, Sir?" Kosutic asked.

"I think," the lieutenant replied as the wall behind him swung silently open, "that we should all get ready to be hit. We don't know what might be coming at us," he finished as the female menial, moving in a much less menial fashion and accompanied by a familiar face, stepped out of the secret passage.

"Shit," Kosutic said mildly, and flipped her helmet sensors to deep-sonar. The view of the "visitors' quarters" in that frequency was interesting. "Captain, we got us a honeycomb here."

Jasco looked at her very strangely, then noticed where everyone else was staring, looked over his shoulder, and jumped half out of his chameleon suit, then backed hastily over to join the other humans.

Julian wrinkled his nose and chuckled.

"Well, if it isn't the tinker!"

Kheder Bijan nodded as the female, no longer looking either meek or unintelligent, padded across the room to secure the door.

"Please pardon my deception on your approach. It was necessary to prevent your destruction."

"What do you mean?" Jasco's natural suspicions had not been particularly eased by having someone step out of a "solid" wall behind him. "Trust me, nobody would be destroying *us*, bucko!"

"You can be killed," Bijan replied. "You were badly hurt at Voitan. You lost, I believe, some thirty out of your total of ninety."

"Slightly off," Kosutic told him with a thin smile. "You must have had someone counting wounded they assumed would die, but we're tougher than that."

Bijan clapped his hands quietly in agreement.

"Yes, my own count showed that the numbers were off. Thank you for that explanation. Nonetheless, if you hadn't come to Marshad, you would have been destroyed on the road to Pasule. Even if Radj Hoomas had needed his entire army to accomplish it, you would have been destroyed."

"Why?" Jasco demanded. "What the hell did we do?"

"Not what we did, Sir," Julian said. "What we are. We're his ticket to power."

"Exactly." Bijan nodded at the sergeant. "You are his 'ticket' to control of the *Hadur*. Make no mistake, Pasule is but a stepping stone. After Pasule comes Turzan and then Dram. He'll use you until you're used up."

"That's more or less what we figured," Pahner said to Kosutic and Jasco. He was using a discrete frequency to avoid having the rest of the company listening in; this was not a morale-boosting conversation. "And we can't afford the time. He has a plan, so ask him what it is."

"What's the plan?" Kosutic asked, cutting Jasco off.

"Let Kosutic take the lead, Lieutenant," Pahner coached when the lieutenant looked sharply at the noncom. "It's customary to let a lower-level person take point. That way if you decide to hang somebody out to dry, it's the Sergeant Major, not you."

"You have to have a reason to contact us," the sergeant major continued, suppressing a smile. The captain would be hard pressed to ever "hang somebody out to dry," but it certainly made a good excuse to let the grown-ups do the planning.

"You have a schedule to keep," the spy told her with a Mardukan grunt of humor. "Yes, I know even that about you. You have to reach this far distant coast within a set time frame. You can't afford to spend a year here campaigning."

"How in the hell—!" Jasco exclaimed.

"Nice piece of information," Kosutic said. "But you still haven't mentioned the plan."

"There are those who don't look with favor upon Radj Hoomas, obviously," the tinker said. "There are many such in Marshad. Perhaps even more, at least among those with power and funds, in Pasule."

"And you are what? A friend of these people? A believer?"

"Call me a friend," the spy said. "Or a humble servant."

"Uh-huh. Okay, humble servant, what's the plan of this anonymous group of people?"

"They simply wish to change the status quo," the spy said unctuously. "To create a better Marshad for all its inhabitants. And, among those in the group who are from Pasule, to save themselves from conquest by a madman."

"And why should we help them?" Kosutic asked. "Given that we might be 'monarchy: like it or die' types."

"You aren't," Bijan replied calmly. "My conversation with O'Casey made that clear. She was very interested in the ownership of land, and pleased when I told her Pasule practiced free ownership by the farmers themselves. Furthermore, you're trapped; you must destroy the House of Radj or miss your rendezvous. Nor will your part be difficult. On the day of the battle, you will simply switch your allegiance. With the aid of your lightning weapons and the forces of Pasule, the local rebels will be able to overcome Radj Hoomas' forces, most of whom will be involved in the attack on Pasule in your support."

"And what about our commanders?" Kosutic could see that the plan was as full of holes as Swiss cheese, but she also suspected that those holes were traps for the humans. "How do they survive our 'switch in allegiance'?"

"There are partisans within the palace," Bijan replied easily. "Between them and your leaders' guards, the purely Radj forces can be overcome. Certainly they can secure your leaders' safety until either you arrive to relieve them or the palace is taken by the city partisans.

"However," he continued, with a hand slap of regret, "whether we can guarantee your leaders' security or not, you have little choice. If you don't assist us, you will be here a year hence, trapped, I suspect, in this horrible little backwater for the rest of your lives. Which, given that Radj intends to use you over and over again for shock troops, will probably be short ones."

Kosutic made sure her smile was broad and toothy; Mardukans didn't show teeth except in aggression.

"You've figured all the angles, haven't you?"

"You need our help," the spy said simply, "and we need yours. It's a simple meeting of needs. No more."

"Uh-huh." The sergeant major glanced over at the female. "Is that our contact?" she asked, gesturing with her chin.

"Yes," Bijan answered. "Her family was from Voitan and has . . . different customs. She's an excellent conduit."

"Nobody notices me," the diminutive female said, standing by the door with her broom and dusting idly. "Who would notice a brainless female? Even if she heard something, how could she remember it?"

The girl grunted evilly and Kosutic smiled, then nodded at the spy.

"Stay here. We need to go talk." She jerked her head at the

command group to precede her out of the kitchen's Stygian heat. They went as far as the second guardroom, where she made the "rally here" hand sign.

"Captain, you there?" she asked.

"Aye. We got it all, too," the CO said.

"Yeah," Roger chimed in. "Every goddamned bit of it."

"I want suggestions," Pahner went on. "Julian, you first."

"We need to go with the plan, Sir. At least at first. Like the guy said, right now I don't see a way around it."

"Don't worry about us," Roger said. "I don't know if Captain Pahner fully agrees, but I believe we'll be able to hold our own if most of the guards are involved in the assault."

Pahner's sigh was audible over the radio.

"I don't like it, but I more or less agree."

"We should be able to turn the tables on the ground," Jasco said, shaking his head. "But it's gonna be a helluva fight at the bridge, and then we'll be in a running battle all the way up to the palace."

"Actually, Sir," Kosutic said, thinking about the terrain, "the problem will be on this side."

"Correct," Pahner agreed. "If formed forces make it to the city, you'll be fighting every step of the way through that warren. That sort of fighting will whittle us down to nothing. If you have to fight street-to-street, we might as well surrender now."

"So you think that if the Marshad army is on the Pasule side of the river—and stays there—then the Company can relieve us?" Roger asked carefully.

"Yes," the Marine said after a moment's thought. "We'll still take some casualties. But if we can get some assurances that the Pasule forces will cover our retreat, we should be all right. However, we still face the problem of how to keep them from cross . . ." His voice trailed off. Then—"Are you thinking what I think you're thinking, Your Highness?" He asked carefully.

"Maybe. It depends on whether or not we can smuggle one of the Mardukans out of the visitors' quarters."

"Yeah," Julian and Kosutic said almost simultaneously. The two NCOs looked at each other and laughed.

"If we can get some armor for one of the Three Musketeers, I can rig a camera and radio," Julian said. "I've got the gear packed."

"I can coach him through the rigging, and Denat is fairly good with knots," Kosutic added rubbing her ear.

"What are we talking about?" Jasco asked.

The group trooped back into the stifling kitchen to confront the spies.

"We're in agreement," Kosutic said. "However, we have a few questions to ask and some requirements that must be met for us to be willing to proceed."

"Oh?" Bijan said. "And if I reject your demands?"

"We tell the king about your treason just before we tear this pathetic city to the ground," the sergeant major said quietly. "It will practically wipe us out to do it, but the 'not difficult' plan you just suggested will do the same thing. So are you going to listen? Or do we start now?"

The spy looked down at her for a moment, then grunted in laughter.

"Very well, Sergeant Major Kosutic. What are your demands?

"Questions first," the NCO said. "How secret are all these passages?"

"There's only one to this building," Bijan said, "which is why we came in here, but there are a few others in strategic spots throughout the city. As far as I know, Radj Hoomas doesn't know a thing about this one . . . or about any of the others, for that matter. This one was created during the construction of this building, which predated the rise of the House of Radj."

"Then how did you know of it?" Jasco asked, deciding that he had to get at least one word in.

"I showed him," the female spy replied. "My mother's family was involved in the construction. They were masons from Voitan, and my mother knew of it from her mother."

Kosutic was sorely tempted to ask why Voitan women seemed to be the only ones on Marduk with any freedom, but decided it was a side issue. Fixing the problems of the Company came first.

Although, she reflected, Roger's plan would certainly free up a few social constraints in Marshad.

"Okay," she said. "That has that covered. The reason we needed to know is that we need to smuggle one or two of our Mardukan allies out."

"Why?" Bijan demanded angrily. "This will make it much more likely that we'll be discovered! Those barbarians don't even speak the language!"

"What?" Julian snapped. "You have no barbarians in your city? No visitors whatsoever?"

"A few," Bijan admitted reluctantly. "But they're mainly from Kranolta tribes, and there are very few at the moment. They're mostly traders in hides and jungle medicines."

"Good," Kosutic said. "We have a mass of those we collected on the march, and he can take some with him as a cover. Also, before he goes, he'll need an armor apron and a helmet."

"No!" Bijan snarled. "No fighting. I don't know what your plan is, but he won't destroy all I've worked for! I'll wait for a better chance, if that's what it takes!"

"No, you won't," Kosutic told him with another toothy smile, "because if this goes wrong, I will follow you to Hell to spit on your soul. Do I make myself clear?"

They stared at one another for a long time, until, finally, the Mardukan clapped his hands reluctantly.

"Very well. *One* of them. I'll get appropriate armor and a helmet." He paused. "But if he gives away our preparations, on your head be it."

"He'll have a mission, which he'll divulge to you as he goes," the sergeant major said. "You will support it fully." She gestured with her head at the female spy. "And that one will be the primary control. Do you understand?"

"I'm in charge here—" Bijan started to say.

"No," Kosutic interrupted with a shake of her head. "Fate, chaos, and destruction are in charge here, *spy*. The faster you figure out how to ride the whirlwind, the better."

CHAPTER FIFTY

Denat padded through the trackless dark of nighttime Marshad, following the dimly perceived shape of the female in front of him.

The stench of the lower warrens was unbelievable, an effluvia of chemicals from dyes, rotting carcasses, shit, and misery. He'd visited Q'Nkok often, and although there had been many poor, it had never seemed as if the entire city was destitute. But in Marshad, he hadn't seen a single sign of relative wealth. It appeared that there were only king's advisers, and the penniless.

As his guide passed one of the tunnel-like alleys, a figure emerged from the deeper shadows and grabbed the little female by the arm.

Denat's orders had been to follow and, as much as possible, to avoid notice, so he stepped sideways into the deeper blackness along the alleyway, turning to put the heavy sack he carried against the wall. The little guide, Sena, had heartily endorsed the importance of his avoiding attention, and added an injunction against coming to her aid. She was confident of her own abilities. Or so she said.

Now Denat saw why. The confrontation was brief, and ended when the accoster suddenly flew into a wall. There was another flicker of movement as the two shapes merged, a horn flashed, and then the little female continued on, leaving a crumpled, life-oozing shape sprawled in the noisome alley.

Denat stepped around the growing, sticky puddle and followed his guide into the deeper blackness. There was just enough filtered light in the intersection for him to see that the thug's head was barely attached to his body. He'd heard of the *enat* techniques, but Sena was the first practitioner of the art he'd ever met, and he resolved to treat the guide with the greatest possible respect.

They took a fork away from the slightly wider alley they'd been following into a smelly path barely wide enough for the broad tribesman to pass. The alley's clay walls were intermittently coated in waterproofing, but much of it had worn away, exposing the walls to the rains. There were runnels in the material, and if it wasn't fixed soon, the houses to either side would collapse.

The narrow slit dropped into one of the tunnels that was a bit wider. It was impossible to see in the lightless passage, so the guide took the tribesman's hand and put it on her shoulder. The passage was half-flooded with a river of sludge—runoff from the evening's rains and rancid beyond compare—through which they were forced to wade. Denat steeled himself and refused to wonder what the things bumping against his legs or disintegrating beneath his feet might be.

That passage was blessedly short, however, and soon Sena led him up onto a slightly elevated platform and stopped. There was an almost unheard tapping, and the creak of a hinge, and then the guide stepped forward once more.

Denat started to follow . . . and slammed his nose into a lintel. He stifled a venomous curse, ducked through the doorway and stepped forward until he felt a hand on his chest. There was another creak behind him, a thump as a door closed, and the click of a bolt shooting. Then light flared from a tinderbox.

The candle that the tinder lit revealed a space which seemed too tiny for the group filling it. Besides his guide, there were three other females of about the same age, two older females, and half a dozen children. The only male in the room was obviously old, the lighter of the candle.

Two of the younger females cringed back at the sight of the armored tribesman in their midst, but the rest simply regarded Denat calmly.

"Unexpected visitors, Sena?" The old male sat creakily on a stool and gestured for the visitor to seat himself, addressing Denat's guide in the Voitan dialect which Denat, now that he was paying attention, could fuzzily understand.

"Yes," the guide agreed, wiping the filth of the sewer off her legs. "A requirement of the humans. They must have one of their own perform some mission. Also, we must smuggle communiqués to and from their commanders. They must have permission to help us."

She added something else in the dialect, speaking much too rapidly for Denat to follow.

"That was to be expected," one of the older females said, coming forward. "Welcome, tribesman. I am Selat, which my daughter would have told you, if she'd any manners."

"D'Nal Denat." The tribesman bowed. "I greet you in the name of The People." He hoped he'd gotten all the sounds right. Some of the words were the same, but accented so differently as to make them nearly unintelligible.

"Denat," Julian said over the earbud the intel NCO'd installed, "if you're having translation problems, ask me. I'll give you the right words. You just said 'I sneeze you in the name of The Idiots.'"

The Mardukan had been seeded with more listening devices than a Saint embassy, and the company now had a way out of the building. The sergeant major was hard at work tracing out the other hidden passageways, and if Denat truly needed help, it was possible the Marines could come to the rescue.

The locals looked at one another, and then the older female bowed slightly towards him.

"I . . . greet you in the name of our house. Won't you take a seat?"

Denat nodded as reassuringly as possible at the worried females in the corner, guarding the children, and sat on the floor. The walls of the room were well-set stone and the room itself was a snug, out-of-the-way burrow.

"I . . . have . . ."

"A mission," Julian prompted.

". . . a mission to put a human . . ."

". . . thing . . ."

". . . thing on the . . ."

". . . bridge . . ."

". . . *bridge*," the tribesman finished with a snarl and a triple cough, the agreed-upon code for: GO AWAY.

"Okay, okay," the NCO whispered. "Going into lurk mode."

"Are you quite well?" his host asked. The old Mardukan leaned forward in concern; if the contact became unwell, it would ruin all their plans.

"Yes," Denat answered. "I am well."

"What is this device?" the older female asked as she poured their visitor a drink of water and proffered the cup.

"I don't know," Denat lied easily. He'd quickly learned the expression Poertena called a "poker face," an apt description. "However, the humans say that it's vital to their plans."

"How large is it? How do you have to attach it? And where?" Sena clapped her hands in agitation. "It will be difficult to do. The bridge is well guarded."

"It has to be attached anywhere on the underside," Denat said.

" . . . underside," Julian corrected. "You just said anywhere on the 'butt.' Well, 'ass' is closer." The NCO chuckled.

"Underside," Denat amended.

"Ah," his host said. The old Mardukan male looked at the ceiling of the dwelling. "This is perhaps possible."

"How large is this package?" Sena asked, taking a seat as well.

Denat pulled the sack he'd been carrying around in front of him and opened it. Pulling out several hide-wrapped packages and partially prepared hides, he removed a final package covered in red leather. It was done up with thongs, which he untied to reveal a strange shape. It looked like a small box attached to a cube of clay the size of his hand.

"How do you attach it?" Sena asked, for there were no strings or ropes in evidence.

"They told me that if I pushed it on stone, it would stay." Denat tried it, and it adhered to the nearer wall, which was in easy arm's reach. He pulled at it, and it came away with difficulty.

"Like glue," Selat observed. The older female looked at the device curiously. "Very interesting. What does it do?"

"That I don't know," Denat lied again. He knew very well what it did, but he wasn't about to tell the locals. "I also need to be near the river on the day of the battle," he added.

"That won't be hard," Sena assured him. "Right on the river would be difficult, but there are several places on that edge of town where you'll be outside the walls and within easy running distance. Will that do?"

"Yes. Now, how do we get the item attached?"

"How well do you swim?" Sena asked with a handclap of humor.

"Well enough to swim that little puddle you call a river."

"There's a landing beneath the bridge," the little female said. "We can put you in the river upstream. You swim down to the bridge, climb up and attach your item, then swim downriver to another point, where someone will meet you to lead you back."

"Very well," Denat said with satisfaction. "Now, I suppose we wait."

"Indeed," Sena said. "And starve," she added sourly.

"Oh, it isn't that bad, dear," the host rebuked. "We have enough to share with our guest. The House of T'Leen is not so fallen as to be unable to provide hospitality!"

"T'Leen?" Denat repeated, startled. "Was that a common name in Voitan? Because I know a T'Leen Targ."

"T'Leen Targ?" The host sounded surprised. "I am T'Leen Sul. He's my cousin on my father's side! Where do you know him from?" he asked eagerly. "I haven't seen him since before the fall of S'Lenna! How is he?"

"He's well," Denat said, glad to be able to impart some happy news. "He was one of the leaders of the force that relieved us in Voitan. They're rebuilding the city, and he'll be one of the leaders of that, as well."

"Ah!" Sul clapped his hands in joy. "The shining city shall rise again!"

"Let it not be too late for us," his wife said quietly. "Would that we could go to it before our deaths."

"We shall," Sul said with quiet firmness. "We shall return to the shining city. We might have only our hands to offer, but it will be enough."

There was no doubt in his voice, but the whole group had lost its animation. Even if they returned to Voitan, it would be as beggars.

"I was surprised by your choice of messengers," Denat said, deliberately moving away from what was obviously a painful subject. "My people wouldn't have entrusted such a grave responsibility to a female."

"Because we're worthless and unintelligent?" Sena snorted. "Good only for birthing babies and cooking?"

"Yes," Denat said calmly. "I was surprised that the people of Voitan were so accepting of women working other than in the fields and home. You keep to the Voitan customs?"

"With difficulty," T'Leen Sul said. "Marshad doesn't agree with those customs. A female cannot own property and she must obey the orders of any male. Such are both customs and law in this land, so it's hard for one raised among the customs of Voitan to put up with. Females are common in weaving, but that's because it's work males don't want." The old male grunted in laughter. "But Sena was raised in the Voitan way, and she's proof that not all females are worthless and weak."

"So she is," Denat grunted. He looked at the little female out of the corner of his eye. "So she is." He gave himself a shake. "But returning to the matter of starvation." He reached back into his sack. "I brought some food. When that runs out, we'll have to see what we can think of."

"Well," Sena said, clapping her hands in resignation, "that means we can stay out of sight until we have to go to the bridge. Of course, staying out of sight means being stuck in the company of a smelly tribesman for all that time, but at least one part of the plan is working."

CHAPTER FIFTY-ONE

"This is going too smoothly," Pahner complained, shaking his head.

"Really?" Roger looked around the room and chuckled. "I suppose Voitan was your idea of just the right amount of friction?"

"Yes, Your Highness, it was." The captain turned dark eyes on the prince and nodded. "We survived." He shook his head again. "Something is bound to screw this up, and there's not much in the way of a backup."

"Blow the town down and take what we can?" Despreaux suggested.

"More or less." The CO straightened and kneaded the small of his back with both hands. "I'm getting too old for this shit."

"Seventy isn't *old*," Roger told him with a laugh. "Look at my grandfather. He lived to the ripe old age of one hundred and eighty-three senile years."

"Not a record I hope to beat, Your Highness." The captain smiled. "Time for bed. We'd better be on our toes tomorrow."

Roger nodded a good night to Pahner as he left the room, then looked over at O'Casey.

"You've been particularly quiet this evening, Eleanora," he observed, taking off the borrowed helmet he'd been using to monitor the operation.

"Just thinking about our host," the chief of staff replied with a smile. "And about universality."

"How so?" Roger asked, mopping at his sweaty forehead. The evening was unusually hot, even for Marduk. It usually cooled off a bit after nightfall, but not tonight, apparently.

"If you don't mind, Your Highness," Despreaux said, "I'm going to turn in as well. I have guard duty in a few hours."

"Take off, Nimashet." Roger waved one hand in a shooing gesture. "I think we can guard ourselves for a while."

The sergeant smiled at him and left the room behind the captain. Roger watched her go, and then turned back to O'Casey.

"You were saying?" he said, then noticed her slight smile. "What?"

"Nothing," his former tutor said. "I was talking about universality. It's not quite a given that fops aren't to be trusted, but rulers who pay more attention to their wardrobes than their subjects have a habit of coming to bad ends."

"Did you have anyone in mind?" Roger asked coldly.

"Oh," O'Casey chuckled, "that wasn't directed at you, Roger. Although, at one time it might have been," she added pensively. "But, frankly, son, there's not much of the peacock left in you."

"Don't be too sure of that." Roger gave her a wry smile now that he realized the comment wasn't directed at him. "I'm definitely looking forward to getting back into some civilized clothing."

"That's fair." O'Casey looked down at her own stained uniform. "So am I. But I wasn't speaking of you. I was actually thinking of Ceasare Borgia and your father."

"Now that's a comparison you don't often hear," Roger said tightly.

"Perhaps *you* don't," O'Casey acknowledged, "but before I was your tutor, I used it frequently in lectures. I suspect that was one of the reasons I was assigned to you in the first place. That and the follow-through, which is that, frankly, it's an insult to the Borgias. They never would've screwed up their plot the way New Madrid did."

"You know the whole story?" Roger asked in an odd voice. "I never realized that."

"I'm sorry, Roger," O'Casey said sadly. "I'm surprised you weren't aware of how widely it's studied. I only learned the details after becoming your tutor, of course, but the broad outline is used in political courses as a case study. It's right up there with the takeover of the Solarian Union by the Dagger Lords."

"Really?" Roger's eyes were wide. "Well, you never discussed it with *me*!"

"It's a sensitive subject, Roger." His chief of staff shrugged. "I didn't want to hurt your feelings, and I felt that you must have already learned any lessons it could teach long before I was named your tutor."

"Really," Roger repeated, sarcastically, this time, and leaned one elbow on the table and fixed her with a glare. "That's just absolutely fascinating, Eleanora, because I have *never* known what it was that got my father exiled from Court, which makes it rather difficult to *learn* anything from it, wouldn't you say?" He let out an exasperated hiss and shook his head. "I'm so glad that you were respectful of my feelings, *teacher*!"

"But . . ." O'Casey stared at him, her face white. "But what about your mother? Or Professor Earl?"

"Ms. O'Casey," Roger snarled, "I don't remember my mother from when I was a young child at all. Only a succession of nurses. From the time I started to know who she was, I have a general impression of seeing her—oh, once a week or so, whether I really needed to see her or not. She would comment on the reports from my tutors and nannies and tell me to be a good boy. I saw John and Alexa more than I ever saw my mother! And as for Professor Earl, I asked him once—just once—about my father. He told me to ask my mother when I was older." Roger shook his head. "The good doctor was a fair tutor, but he was never very good with the personal stuff."

It was O'Casey's turn to shake her head, and she pulled at a lock of hair.

"I'm sorry, Roger. I just assumed—Hell, *everybody* probably assumed." She grimaced in exasperation, then inhaled sharply.

"Okay. Where do you want me to begin?"

"Well," Roger said with a smile, "I had this tutor once who was always telling me—"

"To start at the beginning, and go through to the end," she finished with an answering smile. "This will take a long time, though," she said more seriously, and Roger gestured around the room.

"You may not have noticed, but I've got all night."

"Hmph. Okay, let me think about how to begin."

She gazed into an unseen distance for several seconds, then made a little moue of annoyance which was clearly directed at herself.

"You know, I never really covered recent history with you too well, did I? I just let that little detail slide. Renaissance or Byzantine politics, yes, but not what was going on right under your nose. Of course," she flashed a quick grin, "most of the time it was stuck so far up you'd never have noticed anyway."

"True, unfortunately." Roger chuckled ruefully. "But I have to get the story."

"New Madrid," she said, nodding. "As you know, there were few major military actions during your grandfather's reign. This is sometimes pointed at as an indication that he was a great emperor, but what was actually happening was that your grandfather was almost completely ineffectual. The Fleet and Marines were being slashed to the bone, and we lost several border systems to treaties we accepted out of weakness—or disinterest—or small actions that never got much press coverage back home. There weren't any *major* actions because no one was drawing any lines to stop the gradual erosion of the frontiers. And while they were crumbling, the Empire was self-destructing internally with plots and counterplots.

"New Madrid was part of that action, but not as a central player." She sighed and looked at the prince in the glow from the camp light. "Roger, you got almost all your brains from your mother, thank God. If you'd gotten your mother's looks and your father's brains, you would have been shit out of luck."

"That bad?" he asked with a chuckle. "He's as smart as Mom is good-looking?"

"Say rather that he's as good-looking as your mother is smart. Which is where you come in."

"What a line!" he observed.

"John Gaston, John and Alexa's father, died, as you know, in a light-flier accident. The Duke of New Madrid was part of the Court at that time, fairly recently arrived. He was, and is, a gorgeous man, and quite the ladies' man, as well. However, he was very circumspect at Court. He and your mother struck up an acquaintance shortly after the death of Count Gaston, and the acquaintance slowly changed to . . . um . . ."

"Me," Roger said with a raised eyebrow.

"Well, the 'proto' you. Empress Alexandra—Heir Apparent, at that time—might have been having a hard time, but she was no fool. She was more or less swept off her feet, which is why she wasn't on a contraceptive, but she landed back on them quickly. Especially when the head of the IBI brought her a report on New Madrid's contacts among factions known to be maneuvering to control the Empire.

"There'd never been a question of marriage, because she had to leave the way open for a dynastic alliance. With the IBI report in hand, though, she had to know if New Madrid's interests were from the heart or the scent of power. So she let herself appear to weaken."

Eleanora twisted her lock of hair again, and let a smile quirk.

"I understand New Madrid can be somewhat dominant, and he apparently found nothing odd in Alexandra's suddenly becoming compliant during her pregnancy. Which was when he tipped his hand. He began forcefully lobbying her for some of the precise policies that the Jackson Cabal had been promoting."

"Are you talking about Prince Jackson of Kellerman?" Roger asked. "He's one of the most important noblemen in the Senate!"

"Ummm-hummm. And doesn't he just know it?" O'Casey wrinkled her brow. "Towards the end of your grandfather's reign, it became apparent even to him that the Saints were becoming very expansionist. That caught him by surprise, since he'd felt that the Saints were . . . well, saints. Once he realized he was wrong, and possibly *because* he recognized that he had been and felt somehow 'betrayed' by them, he began giving a great deal of weight to the more militant factions in the House of Lords."

"And Jackson was one of those." Roger nodded. "He's always been one of the more, um, hawkish members."

"Indeed. However, your grandfather began making most of his

appointments on the basis of Jackson's advice. Many of them weren't appointments, whether to the House of Lords or to the imperial ministries, which Alexandra thought were wise. She had long argued against the military drawdown, but when it became apparent even to her father that the Empire was in trouble, he turned not to her, but to Prince Jackson.

"It might have appeared on the surface that there was little difference, since both she and Jackson supported many of the same policies. But even then, Alexandra was more interested in loyalty to the concept of the Empire of Man than in a specific cant. Worse, all of Jackson's choices for appointments were people he could depend upon to follow *his* lead.

"So when Alexandra found New Madrid spouting the Jackson line, after having been handed that damning report, she saw the situation with amazing clarity. One of the few things she managed to convince her father of in his waning years was to have New Madrid banished from Court."

"However . . ." The former tutor gave her former student a winsome smile.

"That left me," Roger said, his eyes wide. "I'm surprised she didn't . . ."

"Oh, it was contemplated. She'd already had the fetus, you," she pointed out with another smile, "transferred to a uterine replicator, so it would have been a simple matter of—"

"Turning a tap," Roger said woodenly.

"Sort of." O'Casey nodded. "For whatever reason, though, she didn't." She began twisting another lock of hair. "I understand that she spent quite a bit of time with you when you were an infant, Roger. It was only as you matured that she started spending more and more time away."

"As I began looking more like my father," he said in a deathly tone. It wasn't a question.

"And acting more like him, frankly," O'Casey confirmed. "There were other reasons. Things were getting very tense at Court as your grandfather began to fail, and Alexandra was desperately trying to line up partisans against the coup she could see in the offing. In the end, of course, she was able to. But even so she's spent the last decade trying to repair the damage to the Empire."

The chief of staff shook her head again.

"To be honest, I don't know if she ever will be able to truly repair all of it. Things were getting tense again before we left. Most of the Fleet has been pulled away from home systems towards the Saint sector, which is Jackson's sphere of influence, and she doesn't trust the Imperial Inspector's Corps. At least she can trust the chief of the Fleet and the IBI, but those are thin reeds with the Saints pressing the border and the House of Lords deadlocked most of the time.

"So," she finished, "that's the tale. Both the one that I used as a case study of blown political conspiracies, and the additional data I was made privy to as your tutor." She looked at the prince, who was staring at the far wall. "Questions?"

"A million," Roger said. "But one simple one first. Is this why no one has ever trusted me with anything important? Because of my *blood*?" he ended angrily.

"Partially," she admitted with a nod. "But more of it was, well . . . *you*, Roger. *I* certainly didn't realize you'd never been 'briefed,' so I'm guessing that, just like me, everyone else around you must have assumed that someone *else* had told you. They thought you knew. So if you knew the problems that had been associated with your father, and yet chose to emulate him in every way, then one logical conclusion was that you'd chosen *him* as your role model rather than your mother."

"Oh, shit," Roger said, shaking his head. "So all this time . . ."

"Captain Pahner asked me, early in the voyage, if you were a threat to the throne," Eleanora said quietly. "I had to tell him that, frankly, I didn't know." She looked the prince in the eye. "For that, I'm sorry, Roger. But I *didn't* know. And I doubt that *anyone*, except probably Kostas, was sure about you."

"Is that why we're here?" Roger asked, with a hand over his eyes. "Is that why we're stuck in this rathole?" he grated in an iron tone. "Because everyone thought I was in a conspiracy with Prince Jackson? To overthrow my own *mother*?"

"I prefer to believe you were being protected," the chief of staff said. "That your mother saw a gathering storm and chose to put you out of harm's way."

"On Leviathan." Roger dropped his hand and looked at her with tight eyes. "Where I'd be safe if it 'dropped in the pot,' as Julian likes to put it."

"Um," O'Casey said, thinking about the company's incredible battle to have reached even as far as Marshad. "Well, yes."

"Oh!" Roger began to laugh even as tears welled up in his eyes. "Thank God she didn't let me stick around for something *dangerous*! I'd hate to think what *Mother* might find *dangerous*! Maybe facing the Kranolta with a *knife*?!"

"Roger."

"*Aaaahhhhh!*" he screamed as the door burst open to admit a worried Marine sentry. Kyrou panned his bead rifle around the room, looking for the threat, as the prince slammed both fists down on the table. "Fuck, fuck, *fuck*! Pock, *pock it*, and pock *you*, Mother! Fuck you *and* your fucking paranoia, you secretive, Machiavellian, untrusting, coldhearted *bitch*!"

Kyrou stepped aside as Pahner slid through the door, pistol in a two-handed grip.

"What the hell is going *on* here?" the captain barked.

"*Out!*" Roger screamed. He picked O'Casey up by one biceps, and shoved her towards the door. "Out! All of you, *out*!" He pushed Kyrou so hard the heavyset private skittered backwards on his butt through the doorway. "If you're not out of here in *one fucking second*, I will fucking *kill* every fucking *one* of you!"

The solid door of the suite slammed shut with an ear-shattering boom, followed almost instantly by the sounds of complicated destruction.

"I think I could have handled that better," Eleanora said judiciously. "I'm not sure how, but I'm almost certain I could have."

"What just happened?" Kyrou said, lurching upright and looking around the main room of the suite, where the Marines were all staring at the door.

"Did he just say what I *think* he said?" Corporal Damdin asked, his eyes wide. "About the *Empress*?"

"Yes," Eleanora said calmly, "he did. But," she continued, raising her voice, "he just found out something very personal and unpleasant. He's very upset with the Empress, not as the Empress, but as his mother. I think that once he calms down," she suggested as the sound of breaking wood came through the door, "he'll be less—"

"Treasonous?" Pahner suggested lightly.

"He's angry at his *mother*, Captain—very angry, I might add, and not completely without reason—and, not at the Empress," the chief of staff said coldly. "There is, in this instance, a distinct difference. One you and I need to discuss."

Pahner looked at her, then glanced at the door as the sound of hacking came from the far side. The door shook to the pounding blows of the prince's sword.

"What did you *say* to him?" the captain asked incredulously.

"I told him the truth, Captain," the former tutor said tautly. "All of it."

"Oh," the Marine said. "You're right. We do need to talk." He looked around the room. "Kyrou, back on post. The rest of you—" He glanced at the door and winced at the sound of steel skittering on stone. Roger loved that sword; if he was willing to bang stones with it, his fury was even more towering than the captain had thought.

"The rest of you, go back to sleep," he said finally, and beckoned for O'Casey to follow him out of the room.

CHAPTER FIFTY-TWO

The next day passed quietly, especially in the hostages' suite.

Roger failed to emerge from his room even when a breakfast of barleyrice and vegetables was brought to the suite. The food no longer contained the obnoxious herb that had been so prevalent in the first dinner, but there was still a weird, bitter aftertaste. Despite that, Roger had been able to stomach it on the previous two days, but he obviously had no interest in it at all today.

An hour after the breakfast had been cleared, Pahner opened the door to make sure he was all right. Roger was sprawled on his camp bed, in the middle of a mass of broken fixtures, his forearm across his face. When the door opened, the prince simply glanced at the captain and resumed his position. Recognizing a deep funk that was in no mood for semi-parental bitching, the Marine shook his head and closed the door.

Back in the troop barracks, however, the mood was quiet but active. Rumors were still the only method of faster than light communication the military had discovered.

"I heard he called the Empress a whore!" St. John (M.) said.

"I heard it was just a bitch," St. John (J.) said. The older twin had often had to control the outbursts of his younger brother. "But still."

"It was a bitch," Kosutic confirmed, appearing as if by magic behind them. "To be precise, a 'paranoid bitch.' But," she added, "he was also referring to the Empress as his mother, not the Empress. It's a big difference."

"How?" St. John (M.) asked. "They're the same person, ain't they?"

"Yes," the sergeant major agreed. "But calling one of them a bitch is treason, and calling the other one a bitch is just being really, really pissed at your mother." She looked from twin to twin. "Either one of you ever been upset with your mother before?"

"Welll . . ." St. John (M.) said.

"He always calls her a damnsaint when he's mad at Momma," St. John (J.) said with a grin.

"Well so do you!" St. John (M.) protested.

"Sure, Mark. But not to her face!"

"The point is," the sergeant major said before the family feud could go any farther, "that he was mad at his mother. *Not* at Empress Alexandra."

"Well, why?" St. John (M.) asked in a puzzled tone. "I mean, Her Majesty's not exactly here to get mad *at.* I mean, I don't get mad at Momma back on New Miss just 'cause, well, she ain't here."

"You got mad at Momma just the other day 'cause she had twins," St. John (J.) said slyly.

"Well, the Prince ain't got no twin," his exasperated brother said, then he got a puzzled expression and turned back to the sergeant major. "He doesn't, does he? We'd a heard, right?"

Kosutic kept the smile off her face only with difficulty. She knew why the St. John brothers had made it into the Regiment; they were both very, very good soldiers with the protective instincts of Dobermans. But the younger twin was no Hawking.

"He doesn't have a twin," she said precisely. "However, he was told something yesterday about some of his mother's decisions that really upset him."

"What?" St. John (J.) asked.

"What it was is between him and his mother. And he really wants to talk to her about it. The thing for all of you to keep in mind is that our job is to make sure that that conversation takes place."

"Okay," St. John (J.) said with a snort. "Gotcha, Sergeant Major."

"Now, I want you guys to pass it on. What happened yesterday is between Roger and his mother. Our job is to make sure that he gets home to ask her why she's a paranoid bitch in person."

Roger emerged without a word just before dinner was delivered. There'd been sounds of movement for some time before that, and he carried a pile of crushed and broken fixtures from the room. He took them to the door to the suite, deposited them in the guarded hall beyond, and turned to Pahner.

"What's the status of the Company?" he asked coldly.

"Nominal," the CO replied in a neutral tone. He was seated on a cushion, tapping on a pad, and he cocked his head as he looked up at the prince. "They've been doing some training with the new weapons, and they're waiting for the word on when we move." He hesitated, then went on. "They got the word about last evening. The Sergeant Major has been spending most of the day quelling rumors."

Roger nodded in acknowledgment, but didn't respond directly to the last sentence.

"We have a problem, Captain," he said instead.

"And that is?"

"I don't think we have enough troops or ammunition to make it to the coast." The prince pulled up a pile of cushions beside the Marine and dropped down onto them, and Pahner regarded him calmly as O'Casey looked up from her own pad.

"To an extent, I agree, Your Highness. Do you have an answer?"

"Not directly." Roger picked up a canteen and took a sip. The water was tepid, but his chilled camel-bag was in the other room. "But I was thinking about Cord and his nephews. We need more Mardukan warriors attached to us, whether that be by cash or loyalty oaths."

"So we keep an eye out for a group of mercenaries to attach?" Pahner sounded dubious. "I'm not sure about using mercenaries to protect you, Your Highness."

"Let's not look too far down on mercenaries," Roger said with a bitter smile. "After all, we're about to take still another city so that we can get the gear to continue our journey. I don't think we should be calling the kettle black."

"That is a point, Your Highness," Pahner said ruefully. "However, it's not like we're doing it by our own choice."

"Let's go," Denat hissed. "It's not like we have a choice!"

The little female didn't even look around. She was totally focused on the path from the walls to the water, and a part of Denat wished he could match her total concentration.

Unfortunately, he couldn't. He didn't know what was happening back at the barracks, but whatever it was, it was making Julian nervous as hell, which hadn't done a great deal for Denat's state of mind, either. The good news was that the NCO had steadied down when the time to move arrived, and now he was monitoring the sensors scattered over the Mardukan's gear.

"Well," the earbud whispered. "There's nothing large moving between you and the water. By the way, I'm glad it's you and not me."

Denat wrinkled his nose but forbore to comment. The exit from the city was a sewer, and although the runoff stream was currently a mere trickle, the first hint of rain would transform it into a flash flood of obnoxious matter. It was high time to make a bolt for the river.

"Come *on*!" he hissed again.

"Great hunter," Sena said derisively, "I have learned not to move too fast. You have to know what the next step is. Otherwise, you find yourself paste between the toes of the *flar-ke*."

Denat shook his head and stepped forward.

"Julian," his subvocalized, "have you got anything?"

"Guards on the bridge," the human responded, detecting the movement at a hundred meters. "Other than that, there's no movement."

The tribesman tried to sniff the air for the musk of a hidden enemy, but the sewer stench overrode any other scent.

"Stay here," he whispered to Sena, removing the encumbering armor. When he was finished, he wore only his normal garb, a belt with a knife and a pouch. The pouch bulged with the human gift to the King of Marshad.

He stepped out of the sewer-stream and moved forward slowly but naturally. The bridge guards were using lanterns, which would destroy their night vision, so the two conspirators should be impossible to see at this distance.

He was confused by the little female's timidity. She'd been practically fearless up until this moment, and the change was baffling . . . until he suddenly realized that all the previous action had taken place within the confines of the city walls. Now, out in the open, the spy was no longer on familiar ground facing familiar threats.

Denat, on the other hand, was close to his element. He had grown up hunting the jungles of the east, and was one of the few of his tribe who was as willing to hunt the night as the day. The nighttime jungles were a pitch black mine of hazards, both inanimate and animate alike; from quagmires to *atul*, night was when death stalked the forests.

And was stalked in turn by D'Nal Denat.

Now he moved away from the stench of the sewer and let his senses roam. The way to move by night was without focus. Trying to concentrate, straining to see, fighting to hear—those were the ways to die. The way to live was the way of intuition. Place the feet just so, and the leaf did not stir. Open the eyes wide, but look at nothing; open the ears, but hear nothing; and breathe the air, but smell nothing. Become one with the night.

And because that was the way he moved, he was instantly aware when the faint sound out of harmony with its surroundings came to him. He stopped, motionless, like a darker hole in the night, as a furtive shape stole past him. The figure was short—a small male or a female—returning from the river and bent under a dripping pack, and the tribesman's stomach dropped as he realized there was smuggling across the river.

If there was smuggling, there might be patrols, and he paused for several seconds to consider the problem, then made a small gesture of resignation. The plan was the only one possible, so if there were patrols, he would simply have to avoid them. And from what he'd seen thus far of the locals, at least that shouldn't be difficult to do.

He continued his slow but steady movement, stopping occasionally and making a little natural noise, scuffing a foot, rattling a leaf. The noises blended into the natural night sounds, the sounds of little animals rustling in the *kur* grass for seeds and roots. If anyone was there to hear his slow passage, they would dismiss him as a *stap* or *basik*. Now if only no *insheck* pounced on him, everything would be fine. In the past, he'd been attacked by *insheck* or juvenile *atul* while moving this way because the diminutive predators had mistaken him for natural prey.

He reached the banks of the river without incident, however. The current was fast, but nothing to deter someone who'd been swimming in worse since he was a cub. The humans had assured him that the package was waterproof, so he lowered himself into the water, moving as carefully as if he were stalking an *atul-grack*.

The current caught him and swept him away from the low earthen bank. The water was warmer than the night, a soothing bath that washed away the stench of the city. He let the current swirl him like a bit of flotsam, keeping his head just above water and breathing through his nose while he kept an eye out for *asleem*. If he met one of those, the entire plan was forfeit . . . as was his life.

He approached the bridge quickly under the impetus of the current and ducked under to swim towards the bank. There was a danger in this—the danger of striking an underwater obstruction, as much as anything. But it was a calculated risk, for the guards might well be watching the water as much as the banks.

He surfaced carefully when his air ran out and found himself nearly to the bridge, with a guard directly above him, looking up the river. The guard was not, however, looking *down*, and the tribesman suppressed a grunt of laughter. These shit-sitters were as blind and stupid as *basik*.

He drove himself towards the edge, where the bridge's foundation shelf was clearly evident in the reflected light of the lamps. He grabbed the rock and held himself still, head out of the water, letting his senses adjust to conditions under the bridge.

The chuckling water echoed oddly in the arches of the structure, gurgling and sucking air into their watery vortices. He heard the echoing footsteps of guards overhead and smaller night sounds—the hissing calls of *feen* and the chittering cracks of water *slen*.

Finally, when he was sure he had all the sounds cataloged, he began to lift himself out of the water. The movement was painfully slow, but it allowed all the water to run off his body, leaving nothing to drip-drop-drip and betray him by the out-of-place sound.

He crept up the rock to the junction of the bridge and its foundation. The humans had been careful in their instructions on this point: the package must be in contact with the bridge, but out of sight. He placed the box against the cool stones of the arch, and spread some of the wiry *flir* grass that thrived in the shadow to cover it. Then he began his slow progress back down the slope.

With any luck at all, there really would be a guide on the downstream side.

"That's half the plan in place," Roger said, and Pahner nodded.

"Now if we can just be in place for the other half."

"About that—" Roger began, then paused as someone thumped on the door.

Despreaux stepped back with most of her squad, covering the door as Corporal Bebi jerked it opened.

The new commander of the Guard was revealed in the doorway, and looked at the leveled weapons evenly.

"I was sent by His Majesty. You are to write a message to your company. It will command them to follow my orders until you are reunited."

Roger looked at Pahner, then back at the visitor.

"How long do you want to be the new commander?" the prince asked. "I can cut that tenure short, if you'd like."

"If you kill me, another will take my place," the commander said in indifferent tones. "And if your company isn't given help in the battle, it will be wiped out. I'll be in command of the support forces. If you anger me, I guarantee that you'll have no soldiers left after the morrow."

"Ah," Roger said with a feral smile. "Nice to know we're all on the same sheet of music." He pulled a pad over, tapped on the interface for a moment, then threw it to the Mardukan. "Take that to them. It gives them all the orders they need."

"Very well," the Mardukan said, holding the pad upside down as he studied it. "Tomorrow morning, you will join my lord in observing our glorious battle." He grunted evilly, the first expression he'd made other than contempt. "To Victory!"

"Yeah," Roger said. "Whatever."

CHAPTER FIFTY-THREE

The day dawned bright and almost clear. The lower layer of clouds had pulled away, leaving only the permanent thin upper layer, which actually raised the temperature a few degrees.

The human troops gathered in front of the visitors' quarters, checking their gear, making sure their rucksacks rode well, and getting their mission faces on. The fight was looking to be short, sharp, and unpleasant. They were critically short of bead and grenade rounds and had no plasma rifles, so unless they got more support than they expected from the Marshadans, it would get down to hand-to-hand.

At least they had their swords, but they still didn't have the proper shields to go with them, and without the shield wall, the superior individual training of the Pasule forces would weigh against the humans. All in all, it looked to be a bad day.

Julian was running a whetstone over the blade of his sword when his helmet radio came to life on the general frequency.

"Mornin', Marines," Roger's voice said. "I thought you should understand something before we start the ball.

"I'm not going to get into my bitches about the way I was raised. We've all got complaints about our parents, and I'm no different from anyone else in that respect. But I want you to know that no matter how angry I was the other day, I love my mother, both as my mother and as my Empress.

"What happened was that I found out why we're really here. Sure, there was an assassination attempt, and that was the final cause that put us *here*, on Marduk. But the reason we were on the cruise, the reason we were in an assault ship and not a carrier, had to do with a personal problem between me and my mother. One I didn't even know existed.

"So I have a few things to apologize for. I'd like to apologize for causing any of you to wonder about my loyalty. We're just going to have to get in out of the cold and let me discuss it with my mother to straighten that one out. And I want to apologize for not forcing my mother to have that talk with me before we left. We could all be in Imperial City having a beer right now, if I had. So, last, I'd like to apologize for getting you stuck in this goddamned situation with me. And I pledge, on my word as a MacClintock, to do everything in my power to get each and every one of you home."

The prince paused, and Julian looked around at the company. Every Marine sat as still as he did himself, listening. It wasn't often that you heard a member of the Imperial Family open up his heart . . . and it was even rarer to hear one apologize.

"Now, you've got some things to do today," Roger went on after a moment. "And I'm not going to be there with you. But we all need to go home. We all need to get our asses back to Imperial City and have that beer together. Today, in my opinion, is the first step on the road home. So let's get it done.

"Roger, out."

The new commander of the Royal Guard walked over to the humans as they began to break out of their strange stasis.

"What are you doing?" he snapped. "Why have you stopped preparing? Get moving, you stupid *basik*!"

Lance Corporal Moseyev was closest to the spluttering Mardukan, and the Bravo Team Leader looked up at the native coldly.

"Shut your gob, asshole." He turned to his team and gestured at the folded up plasma cannon. "Jeno, give Gronningen a hand with that." He turned back to the Mardukan commander who had been spluttering at his back, and looked the taller native in the eye. "You can move out of our way, or you can die. Your choice."

"Move," Roger said coldly.

The Mardukan guard seemed disinclined to obey, but he stepped aside at a head gesture from the king, and Roger walked forward to the parapet and looked down. The balcony was located at one of the highest points in the hilltop castle and permitted a breathtaking view of the town laid out below. He could see the company moving through the local forces gathered around the gate and heading for the bridge.

Radj Hoomas stood a short distance down the balcony's low, stone wall, watching the same deployment. There were only a few guards between him and the humans, but at least fifty lined the back of the balcony, ready to fill the hostages full of javelins at his command.

The king looked over at Roger and grunted.

"I believe you and Oget Sar came to an understanding?"

"If you mean your new guard commander, yes," Roger said without a smile. "He'll use up my troops, and I'll try my best to kill him. We understand each other perfectly."

"Such a way to talk to your host," the king said crossly, clapping his cross hands in displeasure. "You need to learn better manners before someone gets hurt."

"I always have had that problem," Roger admitted as the company deployed across the fields along the river. "I guess it's my short temper."

"Everybody stay cool," Moseyev said. "We're almost at the deploy point."

In traveling configuration, the Marine plasma cannon was a meter and a half long, a half meter square, and nearly seventy kilos in weight, which made it marginally portable for one unarmored human. Fortunately, it also had a pair of handy carrying handles at either end, so two Marines could lug it for short distances without any problems. Except, of course, for the inevitable bitching.

"God," Macek said. "This is one heavy mother."

"You'll be glad to have this heavy mother along in a few minutes," Gronningen chuckled.

"Yeah," Macek admitted. "But that don't make it any lighter."

"Okay," Moseyev said, eyeing the bridge guardhouses. "This is a good angle. Set 'er up."

The two Marines dropped the featureless oblong in the half-grown flaxsilk, and Gronningen hit an inconspicuous button. A door opened, and he flipped the key switch within and stood back as the M-109 cannon deployed like a butterfly from a chrysalis.

The surrounding matrix was a set of memory plastic parts. The first part to open was the tripod, which pushed down a small pre-tripod to hold the weapon off the ground, then deployed the main supports. Once the main tripod legs had reached their maximum extent and done a pre-level, they deployed spikes into the ground with a susurrant hiss-thump. Then the tripod elevated the gun to its full extension, and the blast shield deployed.

The shield was, arguably, the most important feature of the support module. The thermal bloom when the cannon fired was immense, and without the shield, the firer would incinerate himself. That would have been enough to endear it to any gunner, but it also acted as armor against frontal fire. Now it opened like the ruff of a basilisk lizard or a *flar-ta's* head shield, deploying in a rectangle to either side. It offered ample vertical coverage above and below the weapon, but most of it spread to the sides in a shape largely governed by the expansion pattern of the plasma shot.

Gronningen tapped a control on top of the weapon and sat down cross-legged behind it. He looked at the bridge where the Mardukan soldiers in both guardhouses were watching the company deploy. None of them appeared to have noticed the team's preparations.

"We're up," he announced.

"Plasma cannon's up," Moseyev relayed over the com.

"Copy," Kosutic replied. "We're in position. Take the shot."

"Why haven't they jumped yet?" Kidard Pla snarled. The Pasulian watched the wings of the fearsome weapon deploy and fingered the stone rail of the bridge nervously.

"Maybe they weren't told?" his companion suggested.

The Pasulian guards had been specially detailed to the bridge because all of them could swim. They'd been informed of the plan just before they went on duty, and now they watched their Marshad counterparts, waiting for them to abandon their posts. The plasma weapons were supposed to sweep the Pasule defenders off the bridge, but they would kill or severely wound the Marshad guards as well, unless they got themselves safely out of the way. But none of them were moving. Either they hadn't been informed that their "allies'" weapons were dangerous to them, as well, or else they were playing a game of *basik*. Whichever it was, Kidard Pla wasn't playing along.

"I'm going to start yelling and pointing," he said. "Then we jump."

"Sounds good to me. Hurry."

"*Look!*" the guard leader called. "The human lightning weapons! *Everyone off the bridge!*"

He took his own advice without further ado and launched himself over the low wall of the bridge and into the water. He was *not* sticking around to see what happened next.

Gronningen had already started to depress the firing stud when he saw the Pasule contingent start pointing. He paused for only a moment, all the time it took the keyed-up guards to hit the water, and then fired.

The plasma charge traveled at nearly the speed of light and smote the nearer Pasule guardhouse in a flash of actinic light and a bellowing explosion. The Marshadan guards were swept effortlessly from the bridge by the thermal bloom, vanishing like gnats in a candle flame, and the plasma bolt carved a ruler-straight line of blazing vegetation across the fields between the cannon and the bridge. The center of that line was bare black to the soil, which steamed and smoked in the blazing gray light.

The Marines broke into a trot, heading straight for the bridge with bead rifles and grenade launchers at port arms, and the rest of the Marshad forces poured out of the city gates behind them.

Gronningen flipped the safety back on and hit the collapse key, and the fire team waited while the cannon reabsorbed itself, then looked at their leader.

"Mutabi," Moseyev said, slinging his bead rifle and taking one of the handles. "Let's go."

The team hefted their weapons and followed the rest of their company. Walking through the fire.

"Glorious! Glorious!" Radj Hoomas clapped all four hands in glee. "The bridge is clear! Pity their guards got away, though."

"You didn't inform your own guards?" Roger's tone was wooden.

"Why should I? If they'd panicked early, it might have given away our attack." The king looked towards the distant city. "Look, they still haven't even begun to issue forth. We've caught them completely by surprise. Glorious!"

"Yes," Roger agreed, as Pahner stepped up beside him, obviously to get a better view of Pasule. "It's going well so far."

Eleanora O'Casey nodded at the group of guards around the king, who waved for them to move aside. It was well known that the chief of staff was an academic, not a fighter, and so tiny a person hardly posed a threat to Radj Hoomas.

"What do you intend to do with them when you capture their city?" she asked, stepping up on the far side of the king from the prince and captain and gesturing at the other city.

"Well, the market for *dianda* is fully satisfied at the moment," the Mardukan said, rubbing his horns. "So after stripping the Houses, I will probably permit them to raise barleyrice. Well, that and use them to support my combined army as it conquers the rest of the city-states."

"And, of course," O'Casey said, "we'll be free to pass on our way."

"Of course. I will have no further need for you. With the combined force of Marshad and Pasule, I'll control the plains."

"Ah," the academic said. "Excellent."

The king grunted as the gates of the distant city opened at last. It was difficult to see much at this distance, but it was obvious that the city's forces were pouring out into the plain to defend their fields.

"I'd hoped they would take longer to respond," he grumped.

"Well," O'Casey smiled, "they say no plan survives contact with the enemy." She tried not to smile too broadly as she recalled Pahner's explanation of the sole exception to that rule—the first few moments of a surprise attack.

"Look." The king pointed to the struggling plasma cannon team. "Your lightning weapon is almost to the hill."

Moseyev's team had reached the parklike hill, and were toiling up the overgrown path, and Radj Hoomas pointed again, this time to a small group of his own forces which had separated from the main body.

"I hope no one minds, but I sent along some of my own troops." He grunted in laughter, looking down at the chief of staff. "Just in case your soldiers should meet up with stragglers or brigands. You can never be too careful, you know."

"Oh, I agree," the academic said with a slight frown. "War is a terrible business. One never knows what might go wrong."

"Okay," Gronningen said. "We've got nursemaids." The big Asgardian frowned. "This is going to fuck things up."

"I see 'em," Moseyev grunted. "Stay with the plan."

"There's nearly twenty of 'em," Macek's tone wasn't nervous, just professional.

"Yeah," Moseyev said, grunting again—this time under the combined weight of their overloaded packs and the plasma cannon. "And there's four of us, and we planned for this. When we get in place, put out the gear right away. Even *with* this heavy mother, we can make it to the top of the hill in plenty of time."

The king grunted in laughter as the Marshad forces came to a halt on the plain. The formation's wings were composed of standard mercenary companies, professionals who would stand and fight as long as they felt the battle was going for them, and not a second longer. They could be expected to lend weight to a successful attack, but only a fool would depend on them for more than that.

No, the critical point was in the center, where the strongest and deepest companies stood. The humans formed the front rank, "supported" by the majority of the Royal Guard immediately behind them, ready to cut them down if they attempted to flee or to exploit the expected breach the human weapons were about to rip through the Pasulians.

The Guards had stopped to dress their ranks before attacking . . . which gave the humans an opportunity to make one last communication.

"Fire it off, Julian," Lieutenant Jasco said.

"Yes, Sir." The NCO dug the star flare out of his cargo pocket and prepared it, then fired it into the air over the human forces—where both the Pasulian army and their Marshadan allies in the city could see it—with a thump.

"What was that?" the king demanded suspiciously as the green firework burst in midair.

"It's a human custom," O'Casey said indifferently. "It's a sign that the force is here for battle and that no parley will be accepted."

"Ah." The mollified monarch gave another grunting laugh. "You seem eager to enter battle."

"The sooner we finish, the sooner we can be on our way," O'Casey said with absolute sincerity.

"There's the signal," Denat whispered.

"You don't need to whisper," Sena said grumpily. "No one can hear us here."

They were back in their sewer tunnel, but Denat wasn't paying any attention to the smell this time. The two of them were too busy watching the humans who had just topped out on the small hill across the river.

"What's that they're setting up?" Sena asked. The activity could barely be seen at this range.

"A lightning weapon," Denat replied offhandedly. "One of their largest. It will cut through the enemy like a scythe."

"Ah," the spy said. "Good. It looks like they're ready."

* * *

"We're up, boss."

"Roger." Moseyev looked to where Macek and Mutabi were putting in the last of the crosslike stakes. The stakes ran in a semicircle ten meters back from where the plasma cannon was set up. "You set, Mutabi?"

"Yep." The grenadier dusted his hands. "Limit line's all set."

"Good, because here comes our company." The team leader raised a hand at the group of Mardukans struggling up the hill. "Hold it. Why are you here?"

The Mardukan in the lead swatted at his hand.

"We were sent to keep an eye on you, *basik*," he grunted. "Make sure you didn't scuttle off into the bush like the cowards you are."

"Did you see what this thing did to the bridge?" Moseyev snapped. "I could give a shit why you're here, frankly, but if you don't follow our instructions *exactly*, you're all going to be a pre-fried lunch for the crocs, got it?"

"We're going to do as we damned well please," the leader shot back angrily, but there was more than a hint of fear under his belligerence, and the troops behind him muttered nervously. "We'll stay out of the way, but only where we can watch you," he said in slightly more moderate tones. Clearly, he had no more interest in dying than the soldiers he commanded.

"Okay." Moseyev pointed to the line of stakes. "There's enough room behind the gun shield for the four of us, but no more, and we all have jobs to do so we can't put any of you behind it. The stakes are the limit line—you'll be safe enough as long as you stay behind it, but you'll be close enough so that if we try to run or do any other funny stuff you can fill us full of javelins."

The leader examined the situation and clapped his hands in agreement.

"Very good. But remember—we'll be watching you!"

"You just do that," Moseyev said, and turned back towards the gun so the idiot couldn't see his feral smile.

CHAPTER FIFTY-FOUR

"Captain, this is Lieutenant Jasco," the field commander said. He looked around at the bare platoon of soldiers and shook his head. "We're in place with the Marshad forces. The plasma gun is in place, with its line out. Denat and the package are in place. I would say we're a go."

"Roger," Pahner replied over the circuit. "Plasma team, you're the initiators. When the Pasule forces charge."

"Roger, Sir," Moseyev responded nervously. "We're ready."

"Pahner, out."

Moseyev looked over Gronningen's fire plan one last time. "Wait for my call," he said.

"Got it," the Asgardian grunted. "We're locked and cocked."

"Corporal," Macek whispered. "We've got movement."

"Let's get ready to rock and roll, people," Sergeant Major Kosutic said as a leader of the Pasule contingent stalked to the fore. The two armies had stopped just beyond javelin range from each other, and the Pasulian now waved his sword overhead, clearly exhorting his smaller force to attack. His words, probably fortunately for the humans, couldn't be discerned, but whatever he said worked, for the mass started into a trot behind him.

"Showtime."

"Fire," Moseyev whispered, and Gronningen tapped the fire button.

The plasma cannon spat out three carefully calculated bursts. One into each flank of the Marshad contingent, and the third directly into the rearmost ranks of the Royal Guard.

Pahner drew, turned, and fired three carefully aimed beads. The only three guards between him and the king went down like string-cut marionettes, and he sprinted forward.

The anticipated explosions roared behind them, and Bravo Company, Bronze Battalion, The Empress' Own, executed a perfect about-face and opened fire into the forces at their back.

Eleanora O'Casey hit the ground and covered her head.

Sergeant Despreaux dropped her bead rifle to hip level and followed her HUD aiming point as the grenadiers to either side of her went to continuous fire.

Corporal Moseyev pressed the hand unit detonator button, simultaneously firing the semicircle of stake-mounted directional mines and detonating the kilo charge of C-20 catalyst under the bridge. The charge was half the company's total supply . . . and sufficient to take down a three-story office building.

Pahner's first kick took Radj Hoomas in the groin. Anecdotal evidence had suggested that the area was nearly as vulnerable for Mardukans as for humans, which proved to be the case as the monarch doubled over in agony. The captain followed up with a spinning sidekick that intercepted the descending head on the temple. Mardukans, unlike humans, had thick bone there, but the impact still spun the king off his feet and stunned him.

The ruler of Marshad hit the balcony's stone floor and bounced, and Pahner grabbed the heavy Mardukan by one horn, yanked his head up, and shoved the muzzle of his bead pistol against it. Then he looked up, prepared to threaten the king's life to control the guards.

But there were no guards to control.

Those who had lined the back wall of the balcony had been reduced to so much paste by the impact of hundreds of beads and a dozen grenades in the confined space. Stickles was down, with a javelin in the side, but he would live, and that was the only casualty the humans had taken.

All eight of the guards who'd been directly around the king were dead. Most of them appeared to have been caught flat-footed, watching the plasma cannon, but one, at least, had apparently reacted to the captain's attack. That one had his sword out . . . and a bloody hole in his stomach. All the others had been hit in the head, neck, and upper chest.

Roger holstered his pistol and rotated his shoulder.

"I really have to find the guy who wrote that program and thank him when we get back."

Gronningen pounded rounds into the two flanks. The company was too intermixed with the Royal Guard now for him to fire into the center, but the flanks were fair game. He winced as he saw another Marine go down, but there was nothing he could do from here. Nothing but give covering fire and keep the flanking mercenaries off their backs.

Moseyev picked up one of the shredded guards' javelins. The directional mines had stripped away a few centimeters of the end, but aside from that—and the dripping gore—it was intact, and he tied the first line to its haft and waited.

Denat sprinted to the water's edge, then skipped aside as the javelin came scything through the air. The last rocks were still raining down from the demolished bridge when he picked the weapon up and threw it over the chosen tree limb. He motioned for slack and quickly tied a bowline slipknot in the rope and signaled complete. The rope twitched upward, and he smiled. Company was coming.

* * *

Roger heaved on his end, and the Mardukan he'd been sharing with Kyrou thumped soddenly into the pile against the door. He skipped aside and shook his head as Pahner and Surono came out with another.

"I've heard the expression before," he said, "but I never thought I'd do it."

"You see anything else to barricade the door with, Your Highness?" Pahner asked with a frown. "This is what war is all about: doing things you don't like to people you don't like even more."

"Sergeant Major," Julian said, jumping over a small mountain of Mardukans, "remind me never, ever to make that joke again."

"What's that?" Kosutic asked. She was simultaneously trying to walk sideways over the mounded bodies of the Royal Guard, tie a bandage on Pohm's neck, and make sure nobody was being left behind.

"Join the Marines . . ." Julian said.

"Travel to fascinating planets," Georgiadas chorused as he fired at one of the flankers who'd stopped to throw a javelin at them. The Marshad contingent's instinctive retreat to the city had come to a screeching halt when the bridge disintegrated in its face. Unable to fall back, it was beginning to reform south of the original battlefield, and even after the terrible pounding it had taken, the Marshadans were almost as numerous as the Pasulians.

"Meet exotic natives," Bernstein yelled, dropping a line of grenades across the line between the humans and the Marshadans.

"And kill them," Julian finished somberly as he shouldered the rolled up bag of ashes that was all that was left of Lieutenant Jasco. "Somehow, it's just not funny anymore."

"It never was, Julian." Kosutic finished the bandage and clapped the "repaired" private on the back. She looked around the battlefield and pointed to the marked assembly area. "*Assemble at the O-P!*" she yelled, then looked at the NCO who was jogging alongside her.

"So I should just shut up and soldier?"

"No. But you might wait until we're done with the mission," the sergeant major said, "and that will be a long time. Or at least wait to have your moral dilemma until the battle's over. In case you hadn't noticed, it isn't. And afterwards, you can drown your sorrows in wine, like the rest of us.

"I'm not saying that you have to be one of those guys who drinks from the skulls of dead enemies," she said as the company started to gather and tally off the dead and wounded. "But we have a few to pile yet. So wait until we're done to start the bitching."

"So you're just gonna leave me here, huh?"

Gronningen triggered another shot at the distant Marshadans. There were at least a thousand warriors in the mass, but it was nearly three thousand meters away. Maximum effective range for the cannon was only four thousand meters in atmosphere, due to energy bleed, so shots at this range were relatively ineffectual, but they still served to keep the Marshadan force off the backs of the rest of the Marines as they trotted steadily back towards his hilltop position. And, of course, the cannon would become increasingly effective if any of the Marshadans were stupid enough to come into shorter range.

"Bitch, bitch, bitch," Macek said nervously. Dozens of Mardukan soldiers had appeared at Marshad's gate, and more were coming from around the backside of the hill. If the main contingent didn't arrive soon, the bridgehead Denat had established across the river from them would be lost.

"Think of the poor bastards back in the barracks," Moseyev said. The word had come down that the first assault on the "guests' quarters" had been repulsed, but the group of walking wounded, mahouts, and tribesmen had been hard pressed.

"I'll think about them when I can quit thinking about myself," Mutabi said, hooking a clip onto the overhead rope. "I hate heights."

"Let's move out, people!" Kosutic snarled as she reached the foot of the hill and the plasma cannon atop it began firing across the river at Marshad. She glanced back at the stretcher teams toiling to keep up with her and shook her head. "Hooker!"

"Yes, Sergeant Major?" the corporal, who'd been promoted to team leader to replace Bilali after Voitan, responded.

"Your team stays with the stretcher bearers." There were three stretcher cases and four walking wounded, one of them in Hooker's team. "And St. John (J.), Kraft, and Willis," she added, naming off the other three walking wounded. "The rest, follow me," she finished, and went from the dog trot that they'd been maintaining to a loping run.

Macek ducked behind the tree as another flight of javelins rained down. There were only a few dozen Marshadans in the sewage ditch, but their last charge had nearly made it to the riverbank where the team crouched.

"This *sucks*!" he yelled.

"Oh, I don't know," Mutabi opined. "It could be worse."

"How?" Macek shouted back. "We're pinned down, the Company's not gonna get here in time, and there are more of them coming. How could it be *worse*?"

"Well," the grenadier said, pulling out his last belt of grenades. "We could be *completely* out of ammo."

"I can't get the angle into the ditch, Sergeant Major!" Gronningen reported furiously.

The senior NCO sucked in deep, cleansing breaths as she stepped to the edge of the hilltop to look the situation over.

"Grenadiers," she snapped, "flush those bastards. Gunny Lai!"

"Yes, Sergeant Major!"

"Your team first—go! Everybody else, lay down covering fire!"

Lai pulled the loop of rope out of her cargo pocket and hooked to the clip on the overhead line. She slung her bead rifle across her back and smiled.

"I always wondered why we did this in training." She laughed, and jumped off the cliff.

The company began to pour fire down on the scummy positions surrounding the sewage ditch bridgehead as the gunnery sergeant slid down the rope. The Marine gained speed rapidly as she felt another body hit the rope behind her, but there was an uplift at the bottom that slowed her. She let go near the top of the swing, and landed lightly a few meters from the riverbank.

"Ta-*Da*!" she said with a grin, and pulled the rifle off her back.

"Gunny," Macek told her, "you're a sight for sore eyes." He had a red-stained pressure bandage clamped on the side of Mutabi's neck, and there was a bloody javelin head next to the unconscious grenadier.

"Where's Moseyev and the scummy?" she asked as Pentzikis came off the rope, followed by St. John (M.). The latter had a rope trailing out of his rucksack and trotted off to the north, flipping it up and out of the river's current as he went.

"They're somewhere over there," Macek said, pointing south. "They're not responding anymore."

"Okay." The NCO looked around as more and more of the remnants of her platoon came down the rope. "Dokkum, Kileti, Gravdal—go find Moseyev and Denat." She waved to the south. "The rest of you, follow me!"

Roger's sword lopped the head off the spear as it thrust at him and opened up the scummy's chest on the backstroke. He spun in place to take the one grappling with Despreaux in the back, and then took the arm off of one fleeing towards the smashed-in door.

The wounded Mardukan slipped on the pool of blood which covered most of the floor and slid into the pile of bodies barricading the door. He started to scramble up again, but before he could, Captain Pahner took off his head with a single powerful blow of the broad, cleaverlike short sword he carried.

Roger straightened up, panting, and looked out over the city. The sounds of fighting carried clearly up to the balcony.

"We should have figured out how to smuggle in ropes. We could have gotten them in with the camping gear."

"No way." Despreaux disagreed, jerking hard to retrieve her own sword from the Mardukan in whose ribs it had wedged. "They were looking for stuff like that." She looked over at the remnants of the squad in one corner of the balcony. "How you doin'?"

"Oh, just fine, Sergeant," Kyrou said. He gestured at the securely trussed up king. "His Majesty's a bit put out, but we're fine."

"Right," Pahner said. "We may be low on ammunition, but that was too close. Next time we use the rifles and pistols as our primary weapons." He waved the remaining team to the door. "Your turn to cover."

Roger wiped at his face with a sleeve, trying to get some of the blood off, but his sleeve was even more sodden than his face.

"Anybody got a hankie?" he asked. "Yuck."

"Captain," Damdin shouted. "We've got movement!"

"Check-fire," the sergeant major called from the landing. She peeked around the corner until she had the corporal in sight, then stumped wearily up to the top of the stairs. "Check-fire, Damdin. The cavalry has arrived."

"Great," Roger said, looking at the sergeant major. She was just as blood-covered as he was. "So what took you so long?"

CHAPTER FIFTY-FIVE

Roger glanced at the fresh bloodstains on the floor as he approached the throne. Some things never seemed to change in Marshad, he reflected. Or not, at least, without a little nudge from the outside.

"Tinker!" He smiled at the throne's new occupant. "You seem to have come up in the world."

Kheder Bijan did not return his expression of pleasure.

"You are to bow to a ruler, Prince Roger," he said. "I would suggest that you get used to it."

"You know," Roger said, glancing at the full platoon of Marines behind him, "I can understand how Radj Hoomas made the mistake of underestimating us, but I'm surprised at you. Surely you don't think *you* can bully us? Although, if you really are that stupid, I imagine that explains why we haven't received any of our agreed-upon equipment yet. You were supposed to have the barleyrice, *dianda*, and shields to us three days ago, Bijan. Where are they?"

"You humans are so incredibly arrogant," the new ruler observed. "Do you think that we're simple provincials? That there was only one javelin in the quiver? Fools. You're all fools."

"Perhaps," Roger said with a thin smile. "But we're starting to be angry fools, Bijan. Where's our gear?"

"You're not getting any gear, human," the ruler snorted. "Nor are you going anywhere. I have far too much to do to lose my most important contingent of troops. Become accustomed to these walls."

Roger cocked his head and smiled quizzically.

"Okay, what neat trick do you have up your sleeve now, spy?" he asked brightly.

"You will address me as 'Your Majesty,' human! Or I will withhold the antidote to the *miz* poison you ate the first night you were here!"

"Unfortunately, we didn't have any poison," and Roger told him. "I'm fairly sure of that. For one thing, we're still alive."

"It was in your dishes at the banquet," the former spy scoffed. "It is visible as small flecks of leaf, but it's virtually tasteless. And it only takes one dose. Only a fool would have missed it, but you ate it nonetheless. Since then, we've been keeping you alive with the antidote. If you don't have it, you'll die, *basik*!"

"Hold it," and Roger said, thinking back. "Little green leaves? Taste like raw sewage?"

"They're tasteless," Bijan said. "But, yes, they would have been bright green."

"Uh-huh," and Roger said, trying not to smile. "And, let me guess—the antidote has been in all the food you've been giving us since, right?"

"Correct," Bijan sneered. "And if you don't have it, you'll die. It starts within a day, but it takes days of agony to end. So I suggest that you avoid it at all costs. But enough discussion of this, we must plan the next conquest and—"

"I don't think so," Roger interrupted with a chuckle. "Haven't you been keeping up with recent news, Bijan?"

"What are you talking about?" the new ruler asked. "I've been doing many things . . ." he continued suspiciously.

"But obviously not keeping up with who's been cooking my meals for the last few days," Roger purred like a smiling tiger.

Bijan gazed at him for a few seconds, then gestured to one of the guards standing by the throne. There was a brief, whispered discussion, and the guard left.

"Sir," Julian said, leaning forward behind Roger, "is this a good idea?"

"Yeah, it is." Roger never took his eyes off of Kheder Bijan. "In fact, send somebody to collect up T'Leen Sul. That seems like a capable family. Oh, and tell Captain Pahner that it looks like we're going to be staying a little longer then we'd planned."

He stopped talking as the guard returned to the throne room. The guardsman crossed to the new ruler and said a few words, and Roger had become sufficiently familiar with Mardukan body language to tell Bijan was suddenly one worried scummy.

The new king turned to the prince and placed his true-hands on the arms of the throne.

"Uh . . ."

"We're not Mardukans, Bijan," and Roger told him with a deliberately Mardukan laugh. "In fact, I'll tell you a little secret, Tinker. We're not from anywhere on this planet. We have no similarity to anything on it, we're not vulnerable to the same poisons you are, and we most especially aren't *basik*."

"Ah, Prince Roger, there seems—" the ruler began.

"Bijan?" Roger interrupted, as the door opened to admit Pahner.

"Yes?"

"Say goodbye, Bijan."

Including the representatives from Voitan and all the surrounding city-states, there must have been two or three hundred diplomats, alone, in Marshad. The exact number was open to some debate, since no one had ever gotten a definitive count, but there were certainly enough to make the goodbyes both long and fulsome. Roger smiled and shook hands, smiled and waved, smiled and bowed.

"He's getting good at this," Pahner said quietly. "I hope he doesn't get to liking it too much."

"I don't think he's a Caesar, Captain," Eleanora said, just as quietly. "Or even a Yavolov. Besides, he has Cord beside him muttering 'You, too, are mortal.'"

"I don't really think he is either," the Marine said, then grunted in laughter. "And you know what? I'm beginning to think that it wouldn't matter, anyway."

He surveyed the troops surrounding the prince. You always knew the ones who should be in the Regiment, even before RIP. They were the ones who always looked out. Even when they joked, they were the ones who watched others, and not just whoever they were talking to. The ones who saw their whole surroundings in one gulp. The ones who were human anti-assassin missiles.

Sometimes those weren't the ones who made it. Sometimes, rarely, you got those who were straight plodders. And sometimes even the missiles lost their edge. He'd felt that in the company before leaving Earth. Too many of the troops hadn't cared; it was only the prince, for God's sake.

Not now. The survivors were like a Voitan blade. They'd been tempered over and over, folded and refolded. And, at their core, it wasn't Pahner or even the sergeant major who'd given them their true temper. It was the prince—the trace element that made them hard and flexible. That was where their loyalty lay now. Wholly. Whether it had been his admission of fault, or his swift and decisive removal of the spy who, more than anyone, the company blamed for putting them in the noose of Marshad, or the realization that he'd removed Bijan not simply out of vengeance but because he'd finally learned the responsibility that came with power, as well, the captain didn't know. But whatever it was, it had worked. This was no longer the company of Captain Armand Pahner, escorting a useless prince; it was a detachment of Bronze Battalion, The Empress' Own, Colonel Roger MacClintock, commanding, and the captain smiled.

"Yours is the Earth and everything that's in it, *and—which is more—you'll be a Man, my son!*"

Roger thanked the representative from Sadan for his kind words. The broad, well-watered Hadur River valley was heavily settled, and the trade routes ran far and wide. And throughout that entire region the word had spread over the last several weeks that you didn't want to mess with the *basik*. Sadan was the city-state furthest along the route, and its representative had already promised that not only was the way open through his lands, but also in the lands beyond.

Roger looked up at the *flar-ta* loaded with wounded. The two beasts were crowded with stretchers, but most of the Marines in the stretchers were recovering from leg wounds. They'd be back on their feet in a week, and getting used to marching again, he thought, and smiled at one of the exceptions.

"Denat, you lazy bum. You just wanted to ride!"

"You just wait until I get out of this stretcher," the tribesman said. "I'll kick your butt."

"That's no way to address the Prince," Cord said severely, and Roger looked over his shoulder at his *asi*.

"He's permitted. By your laws, Moseyev would be *asi* to him, so I give him leave to be a lousy patient." The prince reached up to clap the towering shaman on the shoulder. "But it's good to have you behind me again. I missed you."

"And well you should have," Cord sniffed. "It's past time to begin your teaching again. But I had a fine time in the barracks. Great fun." The still-recovering Mardukan had emerged coated in red, as had Matsugae and Poertena.

"It's still good to have you back," Roger said, and passed up the line of *flar-ta* and Marines, touching an occasional arm, helping to adjust a shield or commenting on a recovery, until he reached the head of the column, where he smiled broadly at T'Leen Sul.

The Mardukan nodded to him. The human expression was accepted now throughout the Hadur region, and the new council head clapped his lower hands in resignation.

"It won't be the same here without you," he said.

"You'll do fine," Roger said. "The land distribution was more than equitable, although you and I both know there'll be complaints anyway. But the trade from Voitan will soon mean you can relieve the tax burden and still maintain the public works."

"Any other points I should remember, O Prince?" the Mardukan asked dryly. "Should I, perhaps, think about a fund to restart the forges? Reduce the crops of *dianda* and balance it with barleyrice? Remember to use my chamber bucket and not the floor?"

"Yeah," Roger chuckled. "Something like that." He looked back along the line, where the natives of Pasule were pressing forward to offer baskets of food to the Marines.

Roger looked up and smiled as the sergeant major walked up the line of packbeasts but the smile slid off his face at her expression.

"What?" the prince asked.

"D'Estrees picked up a transmission," said the sergeant major. "No direction and it was only a tiny snip of encryption. But it looks like somebody found the shuttles and reported them to the port."

"Grand," Roger snarled. He glared up at the clouds for a moment, then looked back at Kosutic. "You've told the Old Man?"

"Yep."

"And he said?"

"He said it may be a good thing you and Elenora talked him into telling our friends along the way the truth," the sergeant major said with a small, crooked smile. "Something about covering our back trail."

"That was the idea," Roger agreed, then sighed. "I just hope we don't really need it in the end."

"You and me both, Your Highness."

"All right, SMaj," the prince said, and punched her lightly on the shoulder. "Guess we'll just have to improvise, adapt, and overcome."

"Like always, Sir," Kosutic agreed, and moved off to complete her own final check.

Roger watched her go, then turned to look to the northeast, where the mountains which were probably their next major obstacle loomed. They were reported to be high, dry, frozen and impassable. Of course, that was the judgment of a species which would find the Amazon drought stricken.

"I guess it's time to get this train a-moving," he murmured, and grasped Patty's armored head glacis, stepped on her knee, and lifted himself onto her back. Another mahout had been killed, so somebody had to drive, and he plucked the mahout stick from his belt and lifted it.

The line of drivers behind him, Marine and Mardukan, lifted their sticks in response. Everyone was ready to go, and Roger looked to Captain Pahner, who waved in reply.

"Okay," the prince said to the pack beast. "Time to head upcountry."

"*Move 'em out!*" he shouted. He pressed the forked head of the stick into the tender flesh under the armored collar, and as the *flarta* lurched into motion, he looked up at the mountains once more.

They weren't going to be fun.

MARCH TO THE SEA

For "Uncle Steve" Griswold, USMC
The "barbarian" who taught me that
people are always responsible for their own actions,
but that sometimes good people have to take
the responsibility for fixing other people's mistakes.
You did . . . for thirty-one years. God Bless.

Dedicated to Charles Gonzalez:
The sort of person who would discuss quantum mechanics,
dialects of Amazonian tribes and garroting German
sentries with an impressionable twelve-year-old.

CHAPTER ONE

Sergeant Adib Julian, Third Platoon, Bravo Company of The Empress' Own, opened his eyes, looked around the inside of his cramped, one-man bivy tent, and frowned sleepily. Something was different, but he couldn't tell what. Whatever it was, it hadn't twanged his finely honed survival instincts, which at least suggested that no thundering hordes of Mardukan barbarians were likely to come charging through the sealed flaps at him, but that sense of change lingered. It poked at him, prodding him up out of the depths of slumber, and he checked his toot. The implanted computer told him that it wasn't quite dawn, and he yawned. There was still time to sleep, so he rolled over, pushing aside a pebble in the dirt, and shivered in the cold . . .

His eyes snapped wide, and he unsealed the tent opening and popped out into the predawn light like a Terran prairie dog.

"*It's cold!*" he shouted in glee.

Bravo Company had been marching uphill for the last several days. They had long since passed out of the valleys around the Hadur River, and the city-state of Marshad lay far behind them. In fact, they were beyond any of the surrounding cities that had the dubious pleasure of lying on the borders of the late, unlamented King Radj Hoomas' territory.

They'd made better time than they'd anticipated, yet despite the rigorous pace and steadily increasing upward slopes they faced, they had enjoyed a period of remarkable respite. Between the sale of the captured weapons gathered in Voitan, the remnant funds from Q'Nkok, and the lavish gifts T'Leen Sul and the new Council of Marshad had bestowed upon them, they had been able to purchase all their needs along the way.

In many cases, that had been unnecessary. Several towns had hosted them like visiting dignitaries . . . for more than one reason. The towns had been fearful of Radj Hoomas' ambition and avarice, and were delighted to do anything they could for the aliens who had put an end to them. They'd also been fascinated by the off-world visitors . . . and, in many cases, they'd wanted to get them out of town as quickly as possible.

The trader network in the Hadur had spread accounts of the destruction of the entire dreaded Kranolta barbarian federation at Voitan, the battle at Pasule, and the Marshad coup far and wide, and the message encapsulated in all the stories was clear. The humans were not to be molested. The few times they'd run into resistance—once from a group of particularly stupid bandits—they had successfully demonstrated the effectiveness of classical Roman short-sword-and-shield combat techniques against charging Mardukans without ever being forced to resort to bead rifles or plasma cannon. But thanks to the stories which had run before them, any potentially ill-intentioned locals had known that those terrifying off-world weapons lurked in reserve . . . and had no desire at all to see them any more closely than that.

The Bronze Barbarians of The Empress' Own, veterans all, were well aware of the advantages inherent in a fearsome reputation. This one had come with a higher price tag than they had ever wanted to pay, but it also meant that they'd been able to travel for several weeks with virtually no incidents. That happy state of affairs had given them time to lick their wounds and get ready for the next hurdle: the mountains.

Julian had been off guard duty the night before, but Nimashet Despreaux had had the last shift. Now, as he stood grinning hugely into the semi-dark, she smiled at him while groans sounded across the camp. The female sergeant bent over the fire, picked something up, and walked over to where he was dancing in delight.

"Hot coffee?" she offered, extending the cup with a grin. The company had practically given up the beverage; it was just too hot on Marduk in the morning.

"Oh, thank you, thank you, thank you," the NCO chortled. He took the cup and sipped the brew. "God, that tastes awful. I love it."

"It's bloody freezing," Corporal Kane grumped.

"How cold *is* it?" Julian asked, diving back into his bivy tent for his helmet.

"Twenty-three degrees," Despreaux told him with a fresh smile.

"Twenty-three?" Gronningen asked, furrowing his brow as he sniffed the cool air. "What's that in Fahrenheit?"

"Twenty-three!" Julian laughed. "Shit! I'd set my *air-conditioning* to twenty-three!"

"Something like seventy-three or seventy-four Fahrenheit," Despreaux said with a laugh of her own.

"This feels much colder," the big Asgardian said stoically. If he was cold, it wasn't showing. "Not *cold*, but a bit chilly."

"We've been out in over a forty-degree heat for the last two months," the squad leader pointed out. "That tends to adjust your perspective."

"Uh-oh," Julian said, looking around. "I wonder how the scummies are handling this?

"What's wrong with him, Doc?" Prince Roger had awoken, shivering, to find Cord seated cross-legged in the tent, still and motionless. Repeated attempts to get the six-limbed, grizzly bear-sized Mardukan shaman to wake up had resulted only in slow groans.

"He's cold, Sir." The medic shook his head. "Really cold." Warrant Dobrescu pulled the monitor back from the Mardukan and shook his head again, his expression worried. "I need to go check the mahouts. If Cord is in this bad a shape, they're going to be worse. Their cover isn't as good."

"Is he going to be okay?" the anxious prince asked.

"I don't know. I suspect that he's probably sort of hibernating, but it's possible that if they get too cold something will shut down and kill them." Dobrescu took another breath and shook his head. "I've been meaning to do a really thorough study of Mardukan body chemistry and physiology. It looks like I waited a bit too long."

"Well, we need—" the prince began, only to break off at the sound of shouting from outside the tent. "Now what the hell is that?"

"*Modderpockers, let me go!*" Poertena shouted. He snarled at the laughing Marines who were crawling out of their one-person tents to sniff at the morning air. "Gimme a pocking hand, damn it!"

"Okay, everybody," St. John (J.) said, slowly clapping. "Let's give him a hand."

"Now that," Roger said, "is a truly disgusting *menage a* . . . uh . . ."

"*Menage a cinq* is the term you're looking for," Doc Dobrescu said, laughing as he walked over to the pinned armorer and the four comatose Mardukans wrapped tightly about his diminutive form.

Roger shook his head and chuckled, but he also waved to the Marines.

"Some of you guys, help the Doc."

St. John (J.) grabbed one of Denat's inert arms and started trying to disengage it from the armorer.

"This really is gross, Poertena," the Marine said as he tried to pull one of the slime-covered arms off the armorer.

"You pocking telling *me?* I wake up, and it not'ing but arms and *slime!*"

Roger began to haul on Tratan as the Mardukan groaned and resisted the pulling Marines.

"They seem to like you, Poertena."

"Well," the armorer's response sounded mildly strangled, "they tryin' to kill me now! Leggo!"

"They like his heat," the warrant officer grunted as he helped Roger heave, then said something unprintable under his breath and gave up. The united efforts of three Marines had so far been unable to get Denat to release his grip, and the bear hug actually did threaten to kill the armorer. "Somebody build a fire. Maybe if we warm them up, they'll let go."

"And somebody help me get Cord," Roger said, then thought about the weight of the Mardukan. "Several somebodies." He looked over to the picket lines where the mahouts made their camp. "Did anybody notice that the packbeasts are missing?" he asked, bemusedly.

"We passed through a cold front," the medic said, shaking his head. "Or what passes for one on this screwy planet."

Captain Pahner had called a council of war to consider the night's events. The group sat near the edge of the camp, looking down on the forest of clouds that stretched into the distance from their foothills perch. Above them, the true mountains loomed trackless.

"What cold front?" Julian asked. "I didn't see any cold front."

"You remember that rain we had yesterday afternoon?" Dobrescu asked.

"Sure, but it rains all the time here," the NCO replied skeptically.

"But that one went on for a long time," Roger noted. "Usually, they just sort of hit in short spurts. That one rained, and rained, and rained."

"Right." The medic nodded. "And today, the air pressure is a few points higher than yesterday. Not much—this planet doesn't have much in the way of a weather system—but enough. Anyway, the cloud layer got suppressed," he gestured to the clouds, "the humidity fell, and the temperature . . ."

"Dropped like a rock," Pahner said. "We got that part. Can the locals handle it?"

The medic sighed and shrugged.

"That I don't know. Most terrestrial isothermic and posithermic creatures can survive to just above freezing temperatures as long as they don't stay that way too long. However, that's terrestrial." He shrugged again. "With Mardukans, Captain, your guess is probably as good as mine. I'm a doc, not an exobiologist."

He looked around at the camp, and especially at the *flar-ta*.

"The packbeasts, now, they seem to be better adapted. They

burrowed underground last night on first watch and stayed there till things warmed back up. And their skin is different from the Mardukans', scaled and dry where the Mardukans' is smooth and mucous-coated. So I think the *packbeasts* can make it, if we stay below the freezing line. But I don't know about the locals," he finished unhappily, gesturing at Cord and the lead mahout.

They had been speaking in the dialect of Q'Nkok so that the two Mardukan representatives could follow the conversation. Now Cord clapped his hands and leaned forward.

"I can withstand the conditions of last night with *dinshon* exercises. However," he waved a true-hand at D'Len Pah, "the mahouts are not trained in them. Nor are any of my nephews, except Denat, and he poorly. Also," he pointed to patches on his skin, "it is terribly dry up here. And it will only get worse, from what Shaman Dobrescu says."

"So," said Pahner. "We have a problem."

"Yes," D'Len Pah said. The old mahout looked terrible in the light of midmorning. Part of that was the same dry patches that affected Cord, but the greater part was bitter shame. "We cannot do this much longer, Lord Pahner, Prince Roger. This is a terrible, terrible place. There is no air to breathe. The wind is as dry as sand. The cold is fierce and terrible." He looked up from the scratches he'd been making on the ground with his mahout stick. "We . . . cannot go any farther."

Pahner looked over at Roger and cleared his throat.

"D'Len Pah, we must cross these mountains. We must reach the far coast, or we will surely die. And we cannot leave our gear." He looked up at the towering peaks. "Nor can we carry it over the mountains without the *flar-ta*. It's not like we can call Harendra Mukerji for a resupply."

The lead mahout looked around nervously. "Lord Pahner . . ."

"Calmly, D'Len," Roger said. "Calmly. We won't take them from you. We aren't brigands."

"I know that, Prince Roger." The mahout clapped his hands in agreement. "But . . . it is a fearsome thing."

"We could . . ." Despreaux started to say, then stopped. With the loss of most of the senior NCOs, she was being groomed for the Third Platoon platoon sergeant's position. This was the first time she'd been included in one of the staff meetings, so she was nervous about making her suggestion.

"Go ahead," Eleanora O'Casey said with a nod, and the sergeant gave the prince's chief of staff a brief glance of thanks.

"Well . . . we could . . ." She stopped again and turned to D'Len Pah. "Could we *buy* the packbeasts from you?" She looked at Captain Pahner, whose face had tightened at the suggestion and shrugged. "I'm not saying that we will, I'm asking if we *could*."

Roger looked at Pahner. "If we *can*, we *will*," he said, and the Marine looked back at him with a careful lack of expression.

His Royal Highness, Prince Roger Ramius Sergei Alexander Chiang MacClintock, Heir Tertiary to the Throne of Man, had changed immeasurably from the arrogant, conceited, self-centered, *whiny* spoiled brat he'd been before a barely bungled assassination by sabotage had shipwrecked him and his Marine bodyguards on the hellhole called Marduk. For the most part, Pahner was prepared to admit that those changes had been very good things, because Bronze Battalion of The Empress' Own had been less than fond of the aristocratic pain in the ass it had been charged with protecting, and with excellent reason.

Pahner supposed that discovering that a dangerously competent (and unknown) someone wanted you dead, and then coping with the need to march clear around an alien planet full of bloodthirsty barbarians in hopes of somehow taking that planet's sole space facility away from the traditional enemies of the Empire of Man who almost certainly controlled it, would have been enough to refocus anyone's thoughts. Given the unpromising nature of the preassassination-attempt Roger, that wasn't something Pahner would have cared to bet any money on, of course. And he more than suspected that he and the rest of Bravo Company owed a sizable debt of gratitude to D'Nal Cord. Roger's Mardukan *asi*—technically a slave, although anyone who made the mistake of confusing Cord with a menial probably wouldn't live long enough to realize he'd stopped breathing for some odd reason—was a deadly warrior who had become the prince's mentor, and not just where weapons were concerned. The native shaman was almost certainly the first individual ever to take Roger seriously as both prince and protégé, and the imprint of his personality was clear to see in the new Roger.

All of that was good. But it never would have occurred to the old, whiny Roger even to consider that such a thing as a debt of honor might exist between him and a troop of barbarian beast drovers on a backwoods planet of mud, swamp, and rain. Which, much as Pahner hated to admit it, would have been a far more convenient attitude on his part at this particular moment.

"Sir," he said tightly, "those funds will be needed for our expenses on the other side of the mountains. When we get out of here, we'll need to immediately resupply. That is *if* we don't run out on the way. Or have to turn back."

"Captain," Roger said steadily, sounding uncannily like his mother in deadly reasonable mode, "we have to have the *flar-ta*, and we will *not* take them from mahouts who have stood by us through thick and thin. You yourself said that we're not brigands, and shouldn't act like them. So, what's the answer?"

"We *can* improve things for them," Gunny Jin said. "Wrap them in cloths so that they don't lose so much moisture. Put them in a tent with a warming stove at night. That sort of thing."

D'Len clapped his hands in regret. "I do not think I can convince my people to continue on. It is too terrible up here."

"If you think we can continue," Cord said, "my nephews will do so. I, of course, am *asi*. I shall follow Roger wherever it leads."

"Let's put it to a vote," Roger said to Pahner. "I won't say that we'll go with it either way, but I'd like to see what everyone thinks."

"All right," the captain agreed reluctantly. "I think, though, that we're going to need all of our funds on the far side of the mountain. Desperately. Still," he added with a shrug. "Despreaux?"

The junior NCO cleared her throat. "It was my idea."

"So noted," Pahner said with a smile. "I won't hold it against you. I take it that was a 'buy the beasts' vote?"

"Yes, Sir, but D'Len Pah hasn't said he'll sell."

"Good point," Roger said. "D'Len? Can we buy them from you?"

The old Mardukan hesitated, drawing his circles on the stony ground.

"We must have at least one to make it back to the forests," he temporized.

"Granted," Roger said promptly.

"And . . . they aren't cheap," the mahout added.

"Would you rather bargain with Captain Pahner or Poertena?" the prince asked.

"*Poertena?*" The mahout looked around wildly. "Not Poertena!"

"We'll strike a fair bargain," Pahner said severely. "If we decide to buy them." He thought about it for a moment. "Oh, hell. When. There isn't a choice, is there?"

"Not really, Captain," Roger said. "Not if we're going to make it over the mountains."

"So," the commander said to the mahout. "Are you willing to bargain for them? In gems, gold, and *dianda?*"

The mahout clapped his lower hands in resignation.

"Yes. Yes, we will. The *flar-ta* are like children to us. But you have been good masters; you will treat our children well. We will bargain for their worth." He lowered his head and continued, firmly. "But not with Poertena."

"Good t'ing they didn't know I was coaching you over tee poc— tee radio, Sir," Poertena said as they waved to the mahouts, slowly making their way back downslope.

"Yep," Roger agreed. "How'd I do?"

"We got pock— We got screwed."

"Hey," Roger said defensively. "Those things are priceless up here!"

"Yeah," Poertena agreed. "But t'ey takin' tee money down t'ere. We prob'ly pay twice what they *flar-ta* is worth. T'at more money than t'ey ever see in t'eir po . . . in their lives."

"True," Roger said. "I'm glad that Cranla went with them. Maybe he can keep people from taking it before they buy their new mounts."

"Sure," the armorer complained. "But now I out a fourth for spades. What I gonna do 'bout t'at?"

"Spades?" Roger asked. "What's spades?"

"I can' believe I get taken by my own pocking prince," Poertena grumped much later as he and Denat watched Roger walk away, whistling cheerfully while he counted his winnings.

"Well," Cord's nephew told him with a remarkable lack of sympathy, "you keep telling us there's a new sucker born every minute. You just didn't get around to mentioning that you were one of them!"

Cord raised the flap of the cover as the *flar-ta* came to a halt. The three remaining Mardukans had ridden the big packbeasts for the last several days while the humans had searched for a path through the mountains. To avoid the cold and desiccating dryness, the three had huddled under one of the hide tents. There, in a nest of wet rags, they had spent the day, warmed by the sun on the dark tents.

But as the packbeasts continued to stand motionless, Cord decided to brave the outside conditions. Pushing aside one of the moistened clumps of *dianda*, the shaman slipped out from under the tent and began to walk towards the front of the column, and Roger looked up and smiled as he approached.

"We might have hit a bit of luck," the prince said, gesturing at a pile of rocks. The cairn was clearly artificial, a fairly large pile of stones at the mouth of one of three valleys diverging from the river they'd been following.

The humans had been hunting back and forth in the mountains for a week and a half, looking for a relatively low way across. Several promising valleys had so far yielded only impossibly steep ascents. This valley would not have been considered promising, since it narrowed abruptly up ahead and bent sharply to the south out of sight. However, the existence of the cairn was indisputable.

"Could be some traveler's idea of a practical joke," Kosutic said dubiously. The sergeant major shook her head, looking up the narrow track. "And it'll be a bitch getting the beasts through there."

"But it's the first indication we've had that there's ever been anybody up here," Roger said stubbornly. "Why would anyone lie about the path?"

Pahner looked up at the path the valley might take.

"Looks like there's a glacier up there," he said. He nodded to the stream roaring out of the valley. "See how white the water is, Your Highness?"

"Yes," Roger said. "Oh. Yeah. I've seen that before."

"Snowmelt?" Kosutic asked.

"Glacial runoff," Pahner corrected. "Dust particles from the glacier grinding the mountains. At least part of this stream has its origin in a glacier." He looked at Cord and then back at the *flar-ta*. "I don't see them being able to make it in glacial conditions."

"There is that," Roger admitted, looking up at the snowy caps. "But we still need to check it out."

"Not *we*," Pahner said. "Sergeant Major?"

"Gronningen," she said instantly. "He's from Asgard, so he could care less about cold." She paused and thought. "Dokkum is from New Tibet. He should know something about mountains. And I'll take Damdin, too."

"Do it," Pahner said. "We'll make a solid camp here in the meantime." He looked around at the coniferlike trees. "At least there's plenty of wood."

Kosutic looked around the narrow defile with critical eyes. In the week since they'd started up the valley, they had yet to find a spot the packbeasts couldn't negotiate, but this was pushing it.

"You think they can get through?" Dokkum asked. The little Nepalese was taking the slow, steady steps he'd taught the others when they tried to take off like jackrabbits. The simple method of one step per breath was the only way to move in serious mountains. Anything else would wear humans to the bone between the thin air and steep slopes.

Kosutic measured the defile with the range finder in her helmet and looked at the ground. "So far. Much worse and the answer would be no."

"Heya!" Gronningen shouted. "Heya! By Jesus-Thor!" The big Asgardian was perched at the top of the slope, shaking his rifle overhead in both hands.

"Well, I think we found our pass," Kosutic said with a breathy chuckle.

"Damn," Roger said, looking at the view spread out below the company.

The last of the *flar-ta* were scrambling up the defile as he stepped aside to get a better look. The broad, U-shaped valley at their feet was clearly glacial shaped, and in the center of the deep bowl directly below them was an immense tarn, an upper mountain lake.

The water of the lake, still several thousand meters below their current altitude, was a deep, intense blue, like liquid oxygen. And it looked just about as cold. Given their surroundings, that was hardly surprising. What was a surprise, was the city on its shore.

The town was large, nearly as large as Voitan once had been, and did not fit the usual huddled-on-a-hilltop pattern of every other Mardukan city the humans had yet seen. This town frankly sprawled around the shores of the lake and well up the valley slopes above it.

"It looks like Como," Roger said.

"Or Shrinagar," O'Casey added quietly.

"Whichever it is," Pahner said, stepping out of the way of the beasts as well, "we need to get down to it. We've got less than a hundred kilos of barleyrice left, and our diet supplementals get a little lower every day."

"You're always such an optimist, Captain," Roger observed.

"No, I'm a pessimist. That's what your mother pays me to be," the Marine added with a smile. The smile quickly turned to a frown, however. "We have a smidgen of gold and a few gems left after we paid the mahouts. Oh, and some *dianda*. We need barleyrice, some wine, fruits, vegetables—everything. And salt. We're almost out of salt."

"We'll figure it out, Captain," the prince said. "You always do."

"Thanks—I think," the commander said sourly. "I guess we'll have to." He patted a pocket, but his store of gum was long gone. "Maybe they chew tobacco down there."

"Is that why you chew gum?" Roger asked in surprise.

"Sort of. I used to smoke pseudonic a *long* time ago. It's surprising how hard it is to kick that habit." The last of the *flar-ta* was trotting by, and the captain looked at the line passing down the defile. "I think we'd better hurry to get in front of the band."

"Yep," Roger agreed, looking at the distant city. "I'm really looking forward to getting to civilization."

"Let's not go too fast," Pahner cautioned as he started forward. "This is liable to be a new experience. Different hazards, different customs. These mountains are a fairly effective barrier, especially for a bunch of cold-blooded Mardukans, so these folks may not take all that kindly to strangers. We need to take it slow and careful."

"Slow down," Kosutic called. "The city isn't going anywhere."

The company had been moving through the twisting mountain valleys towards the distant city for the last two days. It turned out that the pass they'd exited from was on a different watershed, which had required some backtracking. The delay meant that they'd run out of fodder for the packbeasts, who were becoming increasingly surly about life in general.

Fortunately, they'd recently entered a flatter terrain of moraines and alluvial wash. It was well forested, and by slowing down they'd been able to let the *flar-ta* forage. But that only worked if the point kept the pace down.

"Gotcha, Sergeant Major," Liszez replied over his helmet com, and slowed down, pausing for a moment to look around.

The path they were following was wide for a game trail, and well beaten. The vegetation was open on either side, and the lower limbs of the coniferlike evergreens had been stripped off by some forager, which permitted good sight distance . . . unlike the damn jungle.

He'd stopped at the edge of an open area. It looked like whatever had been eating on the trees had used the clearing for rooting, because the ground was torn up and turned over in every direction. It was also fairly smooth, however, and the path continued on the other side.

The morning was clear and cool, with the dew just coming off the bushes. This area was a blessed relief for the company, but they still wanted to keep moving. Not only did they look forward to a respite in the city, but the faster they went, the sooner they would reach the coast.

The coast was, of course, only an intermediate stop, but it had begun to loom large in the minds of the company. The coast was an end in itself now, and on maps it looked like they were nearly there. They weren't. At best, it was weeks away through the jungles on *this* side of the mountains, but at least it was getting closer and closer. And that was a damned good thing, Liszez told himself, because good as their nanites were at extracting usable nutrition from the most unlikely sources, there were limits in all things. The severe losses the company had taken at Voitan and Marshad "helped" a good bit, in a gruesomely ironic sort of way, because each dead Marine had been one less charge on the priceless cache of vitamin and protein supplements packed on the animals and on their own backs. Fewer mouths meant they could stretch their stores further, but once the stores were gone, they were gone . . . and the shipwrecked humans were dead. So the sooner they could get their butts aboard a ship and set sail, the better.

Liszez looked over his shoulder and decided the column had closed up enough. He reminded himself to keep the pace down, checked his surroundings for threats, and moved out. On his third step, the ground erupted.

Roger looked at the trees. The stripped bark reminded him of something, and he glanced at his *asi*.

"Cord, these trees . . ."

"Yes. *Flar-ke*. We need to be careful," the shaman said.

Pahner had finally convinced the prince that the lead packbeast was not a place for the commander to be, but Roger still insisted on driving Patty and covering the column with his big eleven-millimeter magnum hunting rifle. So far in the mountains the only hazards had been inanimate, but Marduk had taught them not to let their guards down, and the prince keyed his radio on the reserve command frequency.

"Captain, Cord says that this area is *flar-ke* territory. Like where we first met him."

Pahner didn't reply for a moment, and Roger remembered the Marine's incandescent rage on that long ago day. The prince never had explained to the captain that the company's free-flow com net had been so unfamiliar—and confusing—to him at the time that he genuinely hadn't heard the Marine's order not to fire at the *flar-ke* which had been pursuing Cord. It had been Roger's very first personal experience with a full-fledged tongue lashing, and Pahner's fury had been so intense that the prince had decided that anything which sounded like an excuse would have been considerably worse than useless.

At the same time, even if he *had* heard the order, he would have taken the shot anyway. He knew that. And he hadn't taken it to save Cord, either—no one had even known the shaman was there to be saved. No. He'd fired because he'd hunted more types of dangerous wild game than most people in the galaxy even realized existed, and he'd recognized the territorial strop markings on the trees in the area. Markings very like those which surrounded them now . . .

"I see," the captain said finally, and Roger knew the same memories had been passing through the older man's mind. They'd never discussed the episode again, and Roger sometimes wondered how much that owed to the fact that the *flar-ke* so closely resembled—physically at least—the *flar-ta* packbeasts with which the company had become intimately familiar. *Flar-ta* could be extremely dangerous in threat situations, but the huge herbivores were scarcely aggressive by nature, and a part of the captain had to have noted the relative passivity of the *flar-ta* and transposed it to the *flar-ke*, at least subconsciously, as proof that he'd been right to order his troops not to fire. The old Roger probably wouldn't even have considered that point, but the new one recognized that Pahner had no more taste for admitting he might have been wrong than anyone else. That was a very natural trait, but one which was an uncomfortable fit in a man like the captain, who had an acutely developed—one might almost say *overdeveloped*—sense of responsibility. Which was one reason Roger had never brought the matter up again. He'd learned not only to respect but to admire the Marine, and he was determined to let sleeping dogs lie rather than sound as if he were defending past actions . . . or trying to rub Pahner's nose in a possible error.

"He's really worried," Roger said diffidently into the fresh silence.

"I know he is," Pahner replied. "He's said often enough that however much they may look like *flar-ta*, they're completely different. I just wish I knew exactly how that worked."

"The closest parallel I can think of is probably the Cape buffalo back on Earth, Captain," Roger offered. "To someone who's not familiar with them, Cape buffaloes look an awful lot like regular water buffaloes. But water buffaloes aren't aggressive; Cape buffaloes *are*. In fact, kilo for kilo, they're probably the most aggressive and dangerous beasts on Terra. I kid you not—there are dozens of documented cases of Cape buffaloes actually turning the tables and hunting down the game hunters."

"Got it," Pahner said in a completely different tone, and switched to the company frequency. "Company, listen up—" he began, just in time for the first screams to interrupt him.

Kosutic never knew how she survived the first few seconds. The beast that erupted out of the ground caught Liszez with a tuskhorn and threw the grenadier through the air to land in a sodden, bone-shattered lump. The Marine didn't even bounce, and the animal couldn't have cared less. It was too busy charging straight at the sergeant major.

Somehow, she found herself propelled to one side of the beast by a muscle-tearing turn and dive that landed her on one shoulder, and she'd flipped the selector of the bead rifle to armor piercing even before she hit the ground.

The tungsten-cored beads penetrated the heavily armored scaled hide which the standard beads would only have cratered, and the creature screamed in rage. It pivoted on its axis, but the NCO had other problems to deal with—an entire herd of the giant beasts had burst out of the ground and was stampeding towards the company.

They were very similar in appearance to the packbeasts, but with months of Mardukan experience behind her, the differences were now obvious to the sergeant major. The *flar-ta* looked somewhat like a cross between a triceratops and a horned toad, but the armor on their forequarters was actually fairly light, their horned head shield did not extend much beyond the neck, and their fore and rear quarters were more or less balanced. These creatures were larger by at least a thousand kilos each, and their side armor was thicker than the cross section of a human forearm where it covered the shoulders and heart region. The head shield extended far enough up and back that a mahout would never have been able to see over the top, and their forequarters were immensely strong.

The sergeant major avoided a stamp from one of those sequoia-thick legs and spun again to dodge the flail of a tuskhorn. She straightened and put three more rounds into the head shield, and watched in disbelief as at least two of them bounced off the unbelievably refractory bone armor.

The corner of her eye caught a flicker that sent her flipping backwards in a maneuver she never could have made practicing, and the space she'd just been in was overrun by another of the giant horned toads. She dodged and rolled twice more as the herd thundered past, then flipped the bead rifle to burst and began hammering the one she'd been battling.

The beast charged at her, and she dodged again. But it had learned the first time and turned with her. The sergeant major knew she was dead and tried desperately to twist aside but she couldn't quite evade the tuskhorn that . . .

. . . suddenly rolled sideways as Patty plowed into the larger beast at full speed.

Roger pumped three fatal rounds into the exposed underbelly of the wounded beast, then leaned over to offer the sergeant major a hand.

"Come *on!*" he shouted, and jabbed the packbeast in the neck the instant the NCO's hand locked onto his wrist. "*Hiya!* Come on, you stupid bitch! Let's get out of here!"

The beast spun on its axis with a bellowing hiss and charged back towards the embattled company. Patty appeared to have forgotten that she was a *flar-ta*. She was on the warpath, and the mountains had better beware.

Pahner swore vilely as Roger's packbeast accelerated straight towards the stampeding giants.

"Action front!" he called over the company frequency. He saw a couple of javelins skitter off the armored front of the charging beasts and shook his head. Most of the company had one magazine of ammunition left. If they used that up, there was no way they could take the spaceport. But if they all died here, it wouldn't matter.

"Weapons free! Armor piercing—do it!" He dodged a milling packbeast as he pulled his own rifle off his shoulder. "Move the packbeasts forward! Use them as a wall!"

He had a brief flash of Roger hitting the avalanche of *flar-ke*. By some miracle, the boy was able to convince his mount to go through the charge rather than ramming one of them head-on. As they passed the head of the column there was a glimpse of the prince pumping fire into the stampede; then he disappeared into the dust.

The experienced CO knew a moment of despair. The charge had hit them from the front and come on, headfirst, down the long axis of the column. That meant the Marines could target only the head shields, which were the most heavily armored part of the attacking beasts, and the fire that was starting to pour into the charge was having negligible effect. He saw a single beast go down, but in another moment the company would be engulfed in a charge of elephants, because nothing was going to stop them.

The first grenades started to fall into the mass, but not even that was enough to turn them. And the only way to kill them was to hit them from the side. It took just a moment for a thought to percolate through his shock, and his sense of guilt for the lives that momentary delay cost would live with him the rest of his life.

"*On the packbeasts!*" he yelled, grabbing for a dangling strap on the *flar-ta* he'd been dodging and swinging himself frantically aboard. "*Everybody on the packbeasts!*"

The stampede hit like a meat and bone avalanche. From his precarious perch, Pahner saw dozens of the Marines go down under the feet and tusks of the giant lizards. But many—most—of the others were scrambling onto the company's mounts.

Even that wasn't the most secure situation, but at least it gave them a fighting chance as the enraged *flar-ke* charged clear through the company, then turned to charge right back. The good news was that they didn't seem to realize which was the greater danger and directed their fury at the packbeasts rather than the insignificant humans who were actually hurting them, and they slammed into the *flar-ta* like lethal, ancient locomotives. The thudding of massive impacts and screams and shrieks of animal rage and pain filled the universe, but the company's bead rifles were finally able to come into play in the melee. As one of the giant herbivores charged, massed fire from the Marines perched on its flank would smash into it from the side. They were using ammunition like water, but it was that or die.

The situation was a complete madhouse. The Marines, some surviving afoot, some perched on packbeasts, some even having attained the safety of the treetops, poured fire into the rampaging herd. At the same time, the *flar-ke* were charging and slashing at the company's packbeasts and the Marines who'd been dismounted.

Pahner spun from side to side, snapping orders for concentrations of fire where he could, then looked up just in time to see Roger come charging into the melee. Where and how the prince had learned to use a *flar-ta* as a war steed was a complete mystery, but he was the only member of the company who seemed at home in the maelstrom.

He'd apparently picked his target from outside the mass, and he and his mount charged in at full speed. The impact when the galloping Patty hit the larger beast was a carnal earthquake.

The target squealed in agony as the *flar-ta's* tuskhorns penetrated its side armor and slammed it down to its knees. As the sergeant major poured fire into the *flar-ke* to either side of them, Roger pumped rounds into the exposed underbelly of Patty's target. Then, using nothing more than words and thumping heels, he backed the packbeast off its victim and charged back out of the mass to wind up for another run.

Pahner slapped Aburia, who was driving his own beast, on the back of her head.

"Get us out of here! Try to line us up for a charge!"

"Yes, Sir!"

The corporal goaded the beast into a lumbering run, and dismounted Marines dashed in from either side as they cantered through the melee. Pahner snatched them up as they came alongside, snapping orders and passing over his own ammunition.

As he cleared the last embattled pair of behemoths he heard another thunder of flesh headed into the battle. Roger was back.

"I wish the mahouts were here," Berntsen said as he hacked at a ligament.

"Why?" Cathcart asked. The corporal wiped at his face with the shoulder of his uniform. Everything else was coated in blood.

"They used to do this."

The company had halted in the open area created by the burrowing beasts and set up defenses. With this much meat around, scavengers were bound to come swarming in, but the unit could go no further. The casualties had been brutal . . . again.

The friendly Nepalese, Dokkum, who'd taught them all about mountains, would never see New Tibet again. Ima Hooker would never make another joke about her name. Kameswaran and Cramer, Liszez and Eijken, the list went on and on.

"Tell you one thing," Cathcart said. "Rogo was right the first time. These motherfuckers are bad news."

"Yeah," the private admitted, pulling on the heavy skin of the dead beast. "He was right all along."

"You were right back on the plateau, Roger," Pahner said, shaking his head over the casualties laid out inside the perimeter. "These are not packbeasts."

"Like the difference between buffaloes," Roger repeated wearily.

He'd just finished sewing up Patty's wounds, using the kit the mahouts had left and a general antibiotic provided by Doc Dobrescu. He'd been forced to do the work himself, because no one else could get near the grumpy beast.

"Cape and water, you mean?" Dobrescu asked, walking up and sitting down on a splintered tree trunk.

"You were saying something about them just before it all fell into the crapper," Pahner said. "I'd never heard of them before."

"You're not from Earth," Roger pointed out. "Of course, most people on Earth never heard of them, either."

"They have in Africa," Dobrescu said with a bitterly ironic chuckle.

"So what are they?" Pahner asked, sitting down himself.

"They're a ton of mean is what they are," Roger said. "You go out after buffalo, and you take your life in your hand. If they scent you, they'll swing around behind and sneak up on you. Before you know it, you're dead."

"I thought buffaloes ate grass."

"That doesn't mean they're friendly," Roger told the captain tiredly. "'Herbivore' doesn't automatically equate to 'cowardly.'" He gestured at the mounded bodies of the *flar-ke*. "Capetoads," he snorted.

"What?" Pahner asked. There were a million things to do, but at the moment they were getting done. He was, for once, going to just let the camp run.

"They look like horned toads, but they're nasty as Cape buffalo." Roger shrugged. "Capetoads."

"Works for me," Pahner agreed. He sniffed at the smells coming from the cooking area. "And it appears that we're about to find out what they taste like."

"One guess," Dobrescu said, with a grunt of effort as he shoved himself to his feet.

As it turned out, they tasted very much like chicken.

CHAPTER TWO

"Now that's something you don't see every day," Julian said tiredly.

"I guess you do around here," Despreaux replied.

The beast looked like nothing so much as a bipedal dinosaur. A *large* bipedal dinosaur, with short forelimbs and extremely atrophied mid limbs . . . and a rider.

"Cool," Kyrou said. "Horse-ostriches."

The rider reined in in front of the company, said something in a loud voice, and raised a hand for them to stop. The reins, which led to a bridle arrangement much like that for a horse, were held with the false-hands, leaving the upper hands available for things like imperious gestures . . . or weapons, and Kosutic walked forward, holding up her own open hands.

"Ms. O'Casey to the front, please," she called over the company frequency. "I can't get a bit of what this guy is saying."

"On my way," the academic's voice replied, and Kosutic returned her attention to the mounted Mardukan. He was clearly a guardsman of some sort, for he was heavily armed and armored. Not that the arms and armor bore any resemblance at all to the equipment in common use on the far side of the mountains. He also looked like a tough customer who wasn't entirely pleased to see them, and the sergeant major clasped her hands before her in the nearest approximation to a Mardukan gesture of polite greeting a human's mere two arms could achieve.

"Our interpreter is on her way," the Marine said pleasantly in the trade tongue commonly used throughout the Hadur. There was no way in the world that the local was going to understand her, of course, but she hoped the tone and body language would get through, at least.

It seemed to work, for the guardsman gave her a Mardukan nod, lowered his raised hand, and settled back to wait. He still didn't seem overjoyed by her company, but his own body language indicated that he was willing to be patient . . . up to a point, at least.

The sergeant major took advantage of the delay to study her surroundings. She rather suspected that the locals had known they were coming at least a little in advance, for the mounted soldier had intercepted them just as they emerged from the dense tree cover higher up the mountain on the edge of their destination's cultivated fields.

The peasants tending those fields had looked up at the commotion, turning from their drudgery for a bit of distraction. They wore dark colored robes that covered them from head to foot. The rough, dark cloth was wet in patches, and as they stopped, several unstoppered water bags and wet themselves down. It was obvious how the locals dealt with the, for humans, pleasant dryness of the plateau.

The plants they were tending were thoroughly unfamiliar, however—some sort of low climbers, staked up on pole-and-string arbors. They were also in flower, and the heavy scent of the millions of flowers drifted across the company like a blanket.

In addition to their odd dress and plants, the locals had the first beasts of burden—other than *flar-ta*—the humans had seen in their entire time on Marduk. The elephant-sized packbeasts were unsuited to any sort of agricultural use, but some of the local peasants were plowing one of the nearby fields, and instead of the teams of natives which would have been pulling the plows on the far side of the mountains, they were using low, six-limbed beasts clearly related—distantly, at least—to the "horse-ostrich" ridden by the guard.

Kosutic looked away from the natives as Eleanora O'Casey walked up beside her and gave the local a closed-mouth smile and a double hand clap of greeting. The march had toughened the prince's chief of staff to a degree the little academic would have thought flatly impossible before she'd hit Marduk, and she'd become thin and wiry as a gnarly root, with knotlike muscles rippling up and down her forearms.

"We are travelers passing through your land," she said, using the same trade tongue Kosutic had used. "We wish to trade for supplies."

She knew the local wouldn't understand a word, but that was fine. The original, extremely limited Mardukan language kernel in the linguistics program she'd loaded into her toot had acquired a far wider database during their travels. It was much more capable than it had been, and if she could only get him to talk to her a bit, it would quickly begin finding points of commonality.

The guardsman gobbled back at her. His tone was stern, almost truculent, but the words still didn't mean a thing, and she concentrated on looking inoffensive as she nodded to encourage him to continue speaking while she studied him. His primary weapon was a long, slim lance, five or six meters long, with a wicked four-bladed head. The lance's point was oddly elongated, and the chief of staff finally decided that was probably to help it pierce the tough armor of the capetoads. It made sense. The giant herbivores were undoubtedly a major pest in the area.

In addition to the lance, the rider had a long, straight-bladed sword sheathed on his saddle. The weapon would have been the equivalent of a medieval two-handed sword, but since Mardukans were nearly twice the height of humans, this weapon was nearly three meters long.

The last two accouterments were the most startling. First, the rider was armored in chain mail with a back and breast cuirass and armored greaves on thighs, shins, and forearms. The overall covering of armor was in stark contrast to the leather and gabardine apron-armor of the Hadur and Hurtan.

Second—and even more interesting—was the large pistol or short carbine stuck in a holster on the saddle. The weapon was of the crudest possible design, but the workmanship was exquisite. It was clearly made from some sort of blued steel, rather than the simpler iron in near universal use on the far side of the mountains, and the brass of the butt was as pale as summer grass. Nor was it the matchlock arquebus she'd expected. Instead of a length of slow match which had to be lit ahead of time and then used to ignite the weapon's priming, this pistol clearly was fitted with the Mardukan equivalent of what had been called a wheel lock on Earth. No doubt that only made sense for a mounted warrior, but coupled with the armor, it clearly indicated a remarkably advanced metal-working industry.

No, they definitely weren't in Kansas anymore.

The soldier reached an apparent stopping point in whatever he was saying, jabbed a hand back the way the company had come, and asked a sharp-toned question.

"Sorry," she told him apologetically. "I'm afraid I still can't quite understand you, but I think we're making some progress."

In fact, the software was signaling a partial match, although it was still well short of true recognition or fluency. The local language appeared to be at least partly derivative of the language used by the natives living around the distant spaceport, but that didn't mean much. The software would have gotten the same similarity between Mandarin and Native American. It just showed that this area was divorced from the region—and language families—across the mountains behind the company. Still, she thought she had enough to make a start, at least.

"We come in peace," she repeated, using as many of the local words as possible and substituting those from the original kernel where local ones were unavailable. "We are simple traders." The last word was part of the language the soldier had been using. "Captain Pahner," she called over her radio, "could you have someone bring up a bolt of *dianda*? I want to show him that we're trading, not raiding. We probably look like an invasion force."

"Got it," Pahner replied, and a moment later Poertena came trotting forward with a bolt of their remaining *dianda*. The beautifully woven silk-flax had turned out to be an excellent trade good throughout the Hadur region, and she hoped it would be as well received here.

Poertena handed one end of the bolt to Kyrou, and the two of them spread it out, being careful to keep the cloth off the ground. The result was all that O'Casey could have hoped. The guard fell silent, then dropped the reins of his mount to the ground, seated the lance in a holder, and dismounted with the sort of casual grace which always struck a human as profoundly odd in someone the size of a Mardukan.

"... this ... cloth ... where?" he asked.

"From the area we just came from," O'Casey said, gesturing over her shoulder towards the mountains. "We have a large amount of it to trade, along with other goods."

"Bebi," Poertena said, guessing what would interest their greeter, "go get me one of t'ose swords we gots left from Voitan."

The corporal nodded and disappeared, returning a moment later with the weapon rolled in a chameleon cloth cover. Poertena unrolled it, and the ripple pattern of Damascene steel was clearly recognized by the Mardukan cavalryman, who exclaimed at the beauty of the blade. He glanced at O'Casey for permission, then picked up the weapon at her handclap of agreement. It had a broad, curved blade, somewhere between a saber and a scimitar, and he waved it back and forth, then grunted a word in laughter.

"What'd he say?" Poertena asked. "I t'ink it important."

"I don't know," O'Casey said.

The Mardukan saw their evident confusion and repeated the word, gesturing at the sky and the fields around them, at the mountains, and then at the sword in his true-hand.

"Well," O'Casey said, "two things. We now have the local word for 'beauty' and agree on definitions. I'm pretty sure he just said that it's as beautiful as the sky, as beautiful as the flowers of spring and the soaring mountains."

"Oh." Poertena chuckled. "I t'ink we gonna do okay tradin' here."

"Come meet our leader," Eleanora invited, gesturing for the rider to accompany her, and the guard gave the blade back to Bebi reluctantly as he turned to follow the chief of staff.

"I am Eleanora O'Casey," she said. "I did not catch your name."

"Sen KaKai," the Mardukan said. "A rider of Ran Tai. You apparently understand our language now?"

"We have a remarkable facility for learning other languages after listening for a bit," the chief of staff replied, putting enough of a grunt into her laugh to make it clear she was chuckling.

"So I see, indeed." The guard chuckled in response, but his eyes were busy as he examined the small force of humans. "You are . . . oddly armed," he commented, waving at their hybrid Roman-Mardukan weaponry.

"Conditions are very different on the far side of the mountains," O'Casey told him. "But that region isn't our original land, either. We come from very far away, and we were forced to adapt local equipment to our needs. None of these swords and spears are our customary weapons."

"Those would be the guns on your soldiers' backs," the guard guessed.

"Yes," the chief of staff replied briefly. She looked across at the heavily armored cavalryman. "Your armor is closer to what we're familiar with," she said, and he nodded.

"Your equipment is quite unusual," was his only comment, then his gaze sharpened as he saw the bulging skins lashed atop the packbeasts. "Are those *sin-ta* skins?" he asked in obvious surprise.

"Uh, yes. Or, at least, I imagine they are, although we call the beasts *flar-ke*, not *sin-ta*. We were attacked by a herd of them just up the valley." O'Casey paused. "I hope they weren't a . . . uh, protected herd."

"Hardly," Sen Kakai said, his eyes round as he noted the size and numbers of tuskhorns beside the skins. "That herd had just moved into the area. It was one of the reasons I was patrolling up here. I'm sorry about your greeting, by the way. We've been having some problems lately."

"Problems?" the chief of staff asked as they approached the command group. "What sorts?"

"It's been hard, lately," the guardsman replied. "Very hard times."

Eleanora thought about that as the introductions were made all around. She also thought about an ancient Chinese curse which she was beginning to think had been specifically created for Bravo Company. Even if it hadn't been, it was certainly an excellent fit, and speaking simply for herself, she was thoroughly tired of living "in interesting times."

The caravansary was set on the edge of the main market. The cries of the vendors carried over the walls of the large hotel and stable and all the way to the third-story room the command group occupied.

The open window looked out over the flat roofs of the city and the lake beyond. A constant wind blew from the lake and across the city, following the river that flowed down the slope to the distant jungles and carrying the scent of the spices for which the region was famous to the window.

The reason for Ran Tai's existence had become clear on the walk to the town—as clear as the broad, carefully cultivated fields of nearpeppers that spread in every direction. It turned out that the spice, an important component of many of the dishes that Matsugae fixed, could be raised only in high, dry environments. That made it extremely expensive on a planet whose sentient species required high humidity and temperatures, and its cultivation and preparation, along with a few other spices, was the basis of half of the region's income.

The other basis was mining. The mountains were a major source of gold, silver, and iron. There were also small concentrations of gems scattered through the hills around the city, most in alluvial deposits. The combination made Ran Tai a rich, if harsh, town.

But it was a town with a problem.

"Maybe there's been a change in the weather patterns," O'Casey said, shaking her head. "That's one of the few things I could think of that would explain invasions on the scale these people seem to be talking about."

"We don't want to have another set-to with the Kranolta," Roger said definitely.

"Oh, Satan, no," Kosutic agreed, rubbing the still-fresh scars on her arm. "I'd rather go toe-to-toe with a Saint strike force than face up to those Kranolta bastards again. The damned Saints at least know when they're beat."

"Well, these aren't like Kranolta, exactly," O'Casey told her. "Or not like *our* Kranolta, anyway. The Kranolta were a fading force by the time we met them. From the description, these seem to be more like the Kranolta when they first swarmed over Voitan."

"Oh, great!" Julian gave a slightly hysterical chuckle. "New, fresh Kranolta instead of tired, worn-out Kranolta!"

"This group," O'Casey went on, "is apparently coming from the same hill country up on the edge of the northern plains that the Kranolta spread from, but the Kranolta found a gap in the mountain barrier over here, where it flattens out to the east." She gestured at the low detail map, pointing at the far northern region of the huge continent they had been crossing and tracing the dividing mountain range Sen Kakai had called the Tarstens with a fingertip.

"These Boman are pretty much more of the same, but they seem to be distinct from them in several ways. The most obvious one, of course, is that they *haven't* found a way around the Tarstens—they seem to have hit the range and slid along it to the west, instead. They also seem to have started their migration somewhat later than the Kranolta, and their weaponry is significantly different. The Kranolta didn't have gunpowder, but at least some of these Boman use arquebuses, although I suppose they might have gotten them from trading with this area.

"Actually, the Boman—like the Kranolta—seem more like a loose confederation of tribes than anything we might call a unified force, and there appear to be varying levels of technology among different tribes. For example, the tribesmen who apparently act as the leading edge of their movement are considerably more primitively armed than what we might call the 'core' tribes who give their invasion its real weight, with traditional muscle-powered projectile weapons instead of firearms. You might think of them as, um . . . skirmishers, I suppose. Lightly armed and expendable, filtering forward like tentacles to feel out the local opposition and opportunities."

"Great," Pahner said with a dry chuckle. "More Fuzzy-Wuzzies and their shovel-headed spears. So what's driving them? Why have they begun their invasion now? When we're passing through?"

"I can't tell you that," the historian admitted, shaking her head.

"Certainly not with any degree of confidence. The motivations of barbarian expansions aren't always clear, but I wasn't joking when I said that there may have been a change of weather. On the other hand, it could be simply a matter of a particularly effective tribal leader looking to carve himself the local equivalent of a Mongol empire. Or it could be that a climate shift has permitted them a higher than normal reproductive rate, providing an expansion in military age manpower. Or it could be the converse—a weather shift which is putting a squeeze on their ability to feed their people where they are and fueling a survival-oriented migration." She shrugged. "Whatever's causing it, they're sweeping down through this region, crushing everything in their path and pushing other tribes ahead of them."

"Which is why the guard was so nervous," Roger said, taking a bite out of something the natives called a *targhas* and which seemed to fill the same niche the ubiquitous kate fruit had filled on the southern side of the Tarsten Mountains. The company had become very fond of the kate fruits, but the kiwi-dates seemed unknown in this region, as did *dianda*. Barleyrice, luckily, was common to both sides of the mountain range, but Roger already missed the kates. The *targhas* had a completely different taste and texture—more like a persimmon crossed with a hairy-skinned crab apple—and he wondered what the troops would dub this one. Persapples? Crabsimmons? Apsimons?

"They've probably got raiders coming up from the jungle as these new barbarians push in," he continued, "and eventually, the Boman themselves are liable to get down here, as well."

"We need to resupply." Pahner looked over at Poertena. "Is that going to be a problem?"

"I been checkin' prices in tee market." The armorer shook his head. "We can get good prices for tee *dianda*. Goood prices. But tee barleyrice is all brought up from tee jungle." He shook his head again. "Food 'round here is expensive."

"So we buy what we need to get to the jungles, then buy the rest down on the plains," Pahner said, then paused as the armorer shook his head. "No?"

"They harvests is po—messed up." The Pinopan shrugged. "Barleyrice is hard to find, even down on tee plain. We walkin' into another war, Cap'n. Food, it's gonna be hard to find."

"Wonderful." The captain sighed and looked at the ceiling. "Just once, could something go right?" he asked God.

"If it did, you'd figure there was a catch," Roger told him. "Okay, so the bottom line is that we need more cash?"

"We could use it, yes, Sir," the Pinopan said. "Tee barleyrice is gonna be expensive, and t'at don't count tee fruit or spices."

"I would like to get quite a bit of those," Matsugae said. Roger's valet usually attended these meetings, partly to make sure that everyone had refreshments, but also as the expedition's head cook and true logistics manager. "The nearpeppers in the markets around here are absolutely fabulous. Also, there are some other spices that I'd like to get a few dozen kilos of. I've already spotted some very good dishes that I want to try. And we should also think about hiring some camp help, even if they're not mahouts."

"That takes cash, Matsugae," Pahner said pessimistically. "If we hadn't had to buy the *flar-ta*, it would be one thing. But the treasury's pretty bare. We have enough for now, but there's no apparent source in the future."

"So we raise some cash." Roger shrugged. "We've been doing that all along."

"I hope we're not going to have to take any more towns," Gunnery Sergeant Lai said. "The last one was bad enough for me."

"No towns," Roger agreed. "But," he continued, sitting up, "we need money, and we're a top-notch combat unit. There's a massive migratory movement going on, and lots of fighting because of it. There should be a high-paying mission around here that we can do with minimal casualties."

"You're talking about becoming mercenaries," Pahner said incredulously.

"Captain, what else were we in Marshad? Or, for that matter, Q'Nkok?" the prince asked with a shrug.

"We were Bravo Company of the Bronze Battalion," the captain replied with a tight smile, "forced by circumstances to fight. Then taking payment for services rendered because it made sense to. We were not common goddamned mercenaries!"

"Well, Captain," Roger said quietly, "do *you* have a better alternative?"

The Marine started to open his mouth, then closed it with a snap. After a moment, he shook his head.

"No. But I don't think we've sunk low enough to be mercenaries."

"Poertena," Roger said. "Do we have the funds to buy enough barleyrice to make it to the coast?"

The armorer looked from the prince to his company commander wildly. "Hey, You' Highness, don' get me in t'is!"

"Yes, Roger," Pahner said tightly. "We do. But eventually we'll run out of cash. Of course, we can forage once we hit the jungles. That will eke out supplies a little longer."

"Which will double our travel time," Roger pointed out mildly, one eyebrow raised. "And wear down the *flar-ta*. And use up our dietary supplements. Not to mention that we'll undoubtedly be out of funds when we reach the coast . . . and need to charter or buy ships for the next stage."

"Captain," Kosutic said, and paused. "We . . . might have to think about this. There's more than just the barleyrice to consider. The troops need a break, and I don't mean sitting in the jungle. They could use some downtime in the city, drink a little wine, do a little shouting. And not having to forage would really speed up the march. It . . . might make sense to look around for a . . . job. But it would have to pay enough to matter."

Roger looked at Pahner and could see that he was thoroughly pissed by the situation. He smiled gently at the commander of his bodyguards and shook his head again.

"What was it you told me? 'Sometimes we have to do things we don't like.' I think this might be one of those times. And I also think that whatever we do to get me home is within the mission parameters. We need cash to do that, so this is within the parameters. And as a last point," he added with a broader smile, "if we don't get Kostas his nearpeppers and spices, he might go all sulky." He winked at his valet, who returned the look blandly.

Pahner regarded the tertiary heir to the throne of the Empire of Man darkly. It had been a vast relief when Roger finally accepted that there truly was nothing—literally nothing at all—more vital than returning him safely to the imperial court on Terra. The captain knew that it had been hard for the prince to come to grips with the notion that his life was that important, given the estrangement which had existed between himself and his mother, the empress, for as long as he could remember. The simple fact was that Roger had believed no one in the entire universe, with the sole exception of Kostas Matsugae, had given much of a good goddamn for him. Which, Pahner had to admit, had been true in many ways. Even, he had come to realize, in Roger's own case, for the prince hadn't much cared for the spoiled, petulant brat he'd seen in his own mirror each day. If anyone had ever sat down and explained to him the reason his father had been banished from court things might have been different, but it had become painfully clear that no one ever had. Personally, Pahner suspected that Eleanora O'Casey was right—everyone had simply assumed that someone *else* had explained his father's inept conspiracies against the throne to him.

No one had, however, and the fact that Roger was the very mirror image of his incredibly handsome, incredibly spoiled playboy father had made things immeasurably worse. Since everyone "knew" Roger was aware of the reasons for his father's disgrace, they'd assumed that the fact that he seemed bent on turning himself into a physical duplicate of that father represented some sort of declaration of defiance . . . or worse. Nobody except Matsugae had ever guessed how much of Roger's "spoiled brat" exterior had been the almost inevitable response of a little boy who had never understood why no one seemed to trust—or love—him to the pain of his loneliness. Certainly no one in Bravo Company had ever guessed just how much more there might be inside him before events in Voitan and Marshad.

But like the other changes in his personality, Roger's new awareness of the realities of the political instability which plagued the Empire of Man, and of the fact that the MacClintock Dynasty truly was the only glue holding that empire together, had proved to have a nasty double edge from the perspective of the commander of his personal security detachment. It meant that the prince had finally learned to accept that there truly was a reason he had to allow his bodyguards to die if that was what it took to keep *him* alive, and also that nothing could be allowed to stand in the way of his return home. But it had also brought the famous MacClintock ruthless practicality to the surface. If nothing could be allowed to stand in the way, then by the same token, there was nothing he was not prepared to do . . . including turning Pahner's beloved Bravo Company into raggedy-assed mercenaries on a planet full of barbarians.

The captain knew that, and the prince's reasonable and all too logical arguments didn't make him feel one bit better about it. He glowered at Roger for a moment longer, then turned to the two gunnery sergeants.

"What do you think?"

"I don't want to take any more casualties if we don't absolutely have to," Lai said immediately. "We've got quite a way to go and a battle at the end. We need to keep that in mind." But after a moment she shrugged. "Having said that, I have to side with His Highness. We do need the cash. And the downtime."

The captain nodded, then turned to the other gunny. "Jin?"

"Yeah," the Korean said. "I gotta go with the merc idea. But it's gotta pay." He looked up at his CO. "Sorry, Cap'n."

"Well," Pahner said, patting his breast pocket. "It looks like I'm outvoted."

"This isn't a democracy, as I believe you've pointed out once or twice," Roger said mildly, propping himself sideways. "If you say 'no,' the answer is no."

The Marine sighed. "I can't say 'no.' You're right. That doesn't mean I have to like it, though."

"Tell you what," the prince offered, sitting up straight. "We'll handle it. You just sit back and make sure we don't screw up. That way you can imagine it wasn't really Bravo Company that did it." He smiled to take away any sting in the words.

"We can do it 'incognito,'" he continued. "I won't be 'Prince Roger.' I shall be . . . 'Captain Sergei!' And it will be 'Sergei's Raiders' who perform the mission, not Bravo Company of Bronze Battalion." He chuckled at his own suggestion, but O'Casey raised an eyebrow.

"So you'll be incognito, Your Highness?" she said, smiling slightly. "With your *incognito* band of bodyguards?"

"Uh, yeah," he said suspiciously. "Why?"

"No reason," the historian told him. "No reason at all."

"Oh, whatever," Pahner sighed. "Okay, Roger, you take it. Find the mission, plan the mission, command the mission. Just make sure that it's as low risk and high pay as possible."

"Those are usually contradictions in terms," Jin said darkly.

"Maybe we'll come up lucky," Roger told him confidently.

CHAPTER THREE

"Well, I think we came up lucky for the downtime," Kosutic said, floating faceup in the lake. She sat up in her jury-rigged float chair and took a sip of wine. "And with the apsimons. Real lucky."

From the humans' perspective, Ran Tai was a pleasant change from the previous towns they'd visited . . . which meant it was Hell itself for the Mardukans who lived there. Not that they hadn't done their best to make their Hell as civilized and bearable as possible.

The town was wrapped around the stream which led from the lake, and every street had wide gutters that were washed from the same source. These gutters, or *chubes* in the language of the area, were used by street cleaners to keep the well-paved streets clear of manure from their bipedal mounts and packbeasts. In addition, the city had an aqueduct system to provide water that was used for drinking and also pumped throughout the city through clay pipes, and there were fountains and spigots everywhere, drained by the *chubes*. Ran Tai's infrequent—by Mardukan standards—rains made it the first city the humans had encountered where the need to provide water was even a consideration, but the aqueduct and lake between them made it widely available, despite the climate. That permitted the homes and taverns to spray the water across mats of grass specially grown for the purpose, which, in turn, increased the indoor humidity of the buildings to the point that it wasn't—quite—a trauma for the mucous-covered Mardukans.

But the very things which made the city's climate so unpleasant for its normal inhabitants were what made it a virtual paradise for the humans. The valley was above the lower cloud layer, so the sun was frequently visible. In fact, at the moment, it was near zenith and bathing them in pleasantly damaging UV. Not only that, the upper layer of clouds rarely produced rain, which was why the valley wasn't continuously pounded with monsoonlike downpours. The daytime temperature rarely got above thirty-two degrees Celsius, and the nighttime temperatures frequently fell into the twenties.

The waters of the lake were near perfection, as well. Since the lake was clear, cool, and untroubled by the large predators which seemed to infest every body of water in the planet's jungles, the humans had been able to go swimming on a daily basis—something that had been impossible on the march. In addition to swimming in it, they bathed in it, an almost forgotten luxury. The standard issue waterless cleaning cloths provided by the Imperial Marine Corps had continued to hold out to an extent, permitting the Marines to avoid the worst of hygiene problems, but the smooth waters of the lake and the improvised soaps that Matsugae had been able to create made the baths heavenly in comparison. Thus, most afternoons found the troops recovering from their morning sword drill by swimming and floating in the lake.

They'd been surprised to find Mardukans swimming alongside them, but only until they realized how much the locals preferred to be submerged in water rather than exposed to the dry air. The locals had problems with the cool lake temperatures; they had to get out from time to time and warm up. But practically the entire population of the city came down in the afternoons to take a swim.

There'd been a lot of curiosity about the humans at first. It was clear that they were different, but, as in other areas through which the company had traveled, the locals weren't as bothered by their lack of limbs as humans would have been if the situation had been reversed. After the first few days, many of the locals had become well-known to the company, and the humans were accepted as just another visiting caravan.

The Marines also followed the local custom of the afternoon

siesta. Pahner, with a few exceptions, had put the company on half-days. Mornings were spent in sword drill, maintaining their advanced weapons, and a thousand and one other minor items that had been neglected out of necessity on the march. The afternoons and evenings, though, were for the troops, and they'd been spending them, to a great extent, napping and soaking up the local culture. Which included its excellent wines.

The upland region supported large groves of apsimon trees from which the natives created a variety of preserves, candies, and wines. The troops had unanimously adopted Roger's suggested name for them, although several of them were of the opinion that the name was entirely too melodious for something so tart and astringent tasting. The natives, including Cord, loved their taste, but as far as Kosutic could determine, no one in the entire company actually liked the damned things. Which didn't keep the humans from gobbling them down by the kilo anyway, for the apsimon had one huge advantage over the much tastier kate fruit. It contained a vitamin analogue close enough to Vitamin C for the Marines'—and Roger's—nanites to actually make the conversion . . . which meant that the unpleasant tasting apsimon might literally be the difference between life and death for the company. Vitamin C wasn't the only dietary supplement humans required on this misbegotten planet, but it was probably the one whose absence would have the quickest consequences. Scurvy wasn't something the IMC normally had to worry about, but it was just as lethal as it had ever been for humans deprived of antiscorbutics.

Of course, O'Casey, Matsugae, and the Navy pilot officers the Marines were lugging around with Roger, didn't have the same sorts of nanite support. They couldn't process the Vitamin C out of the apsimons, but the Marines, who could, no longer required that particular supplement, which meant that *all* of their Vitamin C could be rationed out amongst the folks who still needed it. Better yet, Doc Dobrescu's discovery of the apsimon's unsuspected virtues had given them all a ray of hope. Their original sketchy data on the planet hadn't mentioned anything about apsimons—which was hardly surprising; they had only fragments of the original planetary survey data, and any planet was a *big* place, with lots of secrets tucked away—which suggested that there might be other things they didn't know about . . . including other native foodstuffs which truly could eke out the off-world nutritional items they required.

And which might even taste good enough that humans would enjoy eating them.

In addition to apsimon fruit, however, the area around Ran Tai also supported another tree whose fruit was remarkably similar to large grapes. Unlike the apsimon, the fruit of these greatgrapes, as the Marines had dubbed them, offered nothing in the way of desperately needed trace vitamins or proteins. On the other hand, the best wines of the region were prepared from their musky fruit, and the Marines had become quite addicted to the light but fruity vintages.

Kosutic sat up again and took a look around at the frolicking Marines. Gronningen was swimming endless laps. St. John (M.) had bet the Asgardian that he couldn't swim two laps across the five-kilometer lake and back. Which was a sucker bet: Gronningen was a machine at any physical activity. Another half hour, and St. John (M.) would be out a quarter-kilo of silver. Aburia looked miffed, though. The ebony corporal and the Asgardian had become an "item" in the last month, and she appeared rather pissed at her oversized boy-toy for spending so much time on something other than herself.

But however upset Aburia might be, things seemed to be going just fine for other members of the company. Stickles was making a hard, and so far successful, run at Briana Kane. The brunette plasma gunner was laughing at whatever the PFC had just said to her and didn't appear to need any rescuing. Gelert and Macek also appeared to have come to a mutual understanding and were leaving hand-in-hand. That was probably going to be tough luck on Gunny Jin, but she'd held his hand through other heartbreaks.

"You look like you could use a refill," Julian said.

The intel NCO had swum up behind her in total silence, but she suppressed her automatic start and nodded at the bottle he held out over her cup.

"Thanks."

"I managed to rig a chiller," he said, rolling onto his back and propping the bottle on his stomach. The image he presented, apparently unconsciously, was extremely phallic, she noted as she took a sip of the chilled wine and smiled. The vintage from a minor local winery was flavored with a hint of cinnamonlike spice. It also had a slightly higher than normal alcohol content, as well, and she savored it.

"And where did you scavenge a chiller from?" she asked.

"Russell's armor, of course," Julian replied. He rolled up to stand in the chest-deep water and took a much longer and deeper pull from the bottle.

There didn't seem to be much to say to that. There were a lot of conversations that stopped that way—a quick reference to one of the dead, and a change of topic.

"Any leads on a job?" the sergeant major asked. Because he was the company's intelligence specialist, Julian had been spending his mornings snooping for clues to a job. Along with Poertena, he'd been combing the city, visiting merchants and hanging out in taverns.

"No, and don't think I haven't heard the jokes about it," the NCO said sourly. "'When are Julian and Poertena going to find a job? When they're done tasting all the wines in the region.'"

"Are you sure?" Kosutic asked with a smile. "There's still all the beer to go."

"Oh, gee, thanks, Sergeant Major!" The squad leader grimaced and took another pull at the wine. "I have to admit that it's a good thing the locals don't distill."

"It's okay," the sergeant major said with a throaty chuckle. "When we get back, you can have your liver replaced."

"*If* we get back," Julian replied gloomily.

"Now, what kind of an attitude is that?" Kosutic rolled over to look at the squad leader, who paused for just a moment.

Since the Marines were drawn from a variety of planets with varying levels of body modesty, it was general practice to reach a minimum societal comfort level. Thus, the females in a unit, except under the exigencies of field conditions, tended to avoid open nudity in front of the males, and vice versa. That meant that the female

Bronze Barbarians wore the skin-tight, nearly indestructible undershirts and shorts that went with the chameleon suits while swimming, while the male Marines wore just the shorts. The clothing would have been a capital offense on Ramala, Damdin's home world, and utterly unacceptable on Asgard or Sossann. On the other hand, it would have been considered painfully overdressed for swimming on Earth or Vishnu.

All of which fascinating bits of cultural baggage were no doubt very interesting, but also beside the point. The sergeant major was as hard and flat as a battle tank. Constant exercise and the nanites that all Marines bore had reduced her body fat to the level of an Olympic athlete's. But her basic physiology leaned towards soft curves and relatively large breasts—which became obvious as her left breast slid ever so slightly downward under the V-neck, skin-tight T-shirt and formed the tiniest hint of cleavage.

And totally arrested whatever Julian had been about to say.

Kosutic looked at the squad leader and suppressed a laugh. He looked as if someone had just struck him between the eyes with a hammer, but that was certainly a better direction for his thoughts than where he had been going.

"Centicred for your thoughts?" she said, and Julian almost visibly shook himself. Then he smiled and poured a bit more of the wine into her cup.

"You don't have a centicred. And I don't have a death wish."

"Well, we could think about a trade in kind," the senior NCO told him with a smile. "And I know you don't have a death wish."

The prince was getting used to the local mounts. The *civan* "horse-ostriches" were omnivorous and occasionally vicious, but they were also a quicker way to get out to the mining site than walking, and he reined the beast in and slid off the high-backed saddle. The saddle was stirrupless but had a sort of cup for the thigh that helped a rider balance himself. Of course, it was scaled for a Mardukan and far too wide for a human, but there was nothing to do about that until the new saddles he and Poertena had designed and ordered became available.

He hit the ground with flexed knees, then looked over to watch

Cord dismount. The old Mardukan was slower than the prince, and unlike Roger, he'd had absolutely no prior experience with any riding beast other than the *flar-ta.* A lifetime of physical exertion and discipline stood him in good stead, however, and he climbed down carefully until he finally stood on level ground. Once there, he gave his own *civan* a look which clearly indicated that he would have preferred it for supper rather more than he did as a mount.

Roger tied both beasts to the hitching post set outside the low stone building. There were two other *civan* already tied to the same pillar, and the resident beasts snapped at the prince's mount.

When asked what sort of mount he preferred, Roger had sent Poertena to see the guard from their first encounter, and, after questioning the prince at length and trying him out on several potential beasts, Sen Kakai had settled on a proper war mount for him. The beast in question was slightly larger than the norm, and trained for combat duty. It was also extremely aggressive, and it hissed in response to the others' challenges and snapped a foot out. The wickedly clawed hind talons barely missed the closer beast, and were followed by a resounding, guillotinelike snap of impressive teeth. Both of the other *civan* recoiled ever so slightly, and Roger's mount snorted in satisfaction.

Protocol satisfied and hierarchy established, the three beasts settled down to a chorus of back and forth hissing while Cord's milder beast looked around for something to eat.

Roger waited until he was sure the precedence was settled, then glanced up at the two Marines who were still mounted. However much freedom Pahner was prepared to allow his charge in securing employment for "Sergei's Raiders," he wasn't about to relax his insistence that the prince be accompanied by suitable bodyguards at all times. Personally, Roger felt quite confident in his own ability to look after himself, especially with Cord at his side, but he also knew better than to argue. Not only would it have been fruitless, but harsh experience had taught him to understand exactly why no one in his right mind screwed around with the chain of command and authority in what was for all intents and purposes a single gigantic, planet-wide combat zone.

Which didn't mean that he wasn't prepared to *bend* that chain ever so slightly when it suited his purposes.

"You two mosey on over to the barracks, Moseyev," he told the senior Marine in Standard English. "Spread a little silver around in the bar, if they have one, and keep your ears open. I'd like to hear what the grunts have to say about this."

The corporal seemed inclined to argue for just a moment, but the moment passed. Moseyev had no doubt at all that Captain Pahner would remove wide, painful strips from his hide if the captain ever discovered that he'd allowed the prince to send him off on an errand. At the same time, like every other member of Bravo Company, he'd realized in Marshad that the strict letter of the regulations which had made Prince Roger the official colonel in chief of Bronze Battalion was no longer a legal fiction.

He glowered at Roger for a few seconds, wondering just how blithely Colonel MacClintock would have ignored Captain Pahner had the latter been physically present, but then he glanced at the small building awaiting Roger and shrugged. Orders were orders. Besides, every Bronze Barbarian knew that the prince was sudden death on two feet with the bead pistol holstered at his side, not to mention the sword across his back. And that didn't even consider Cord's well-proven lethality. There was no way in the world a building the size of their destination could hold enough scummies to pose a threat to *those* two.

"Right, Your Highness," the corporal said. "Of course, I hope you'll remember not to mention this in front of the wrong ears."

"Mention what?" Roger asked innocently, and Moseyev chuckled and sent his *civan* trotting off towards the barracks.

"That was undoubtedly foolish," Cord observed thoughtfully as he watched the Marines ride away. "In anyone other than yourself, I would probably say that it was *remarkably* foolish, in fact. In your own case, however, familiarity prevents me from feeling the least surprise."

"Yeah, sure." Roger grinned. "You don't like being shadowed everywhere you go any more than I do, you old reprobate!"

"I am not yet so feeble as to require a keeper," the shaman replied with awesome dignity, hefting the long, wickedly bladed spear he continued to carry everywhere. "I, on the other hand, am not the heir of a mighty ruler, either."

"Neither is 'Captain Sergei,'" Roger chuckled, and Cord snorted in resignation as the prince stepped up to the building and clapped his hands for permission to enter it.

The structure sat at the foot of a steep slope that led upward to the opening to a narrow gorge or valley. A series of walls had been thrown up across the opening, and a small army was entrenched before them. It was clear that they'd been there for a while, and were prepared for an extended stay.

"Come in," a voice called from the interior in reply to Roger's clap, and Roger slipped the door catch and stepped into the hutlike building's single room. It was occupied by a trio of guards and two unarmed Mardukans who'd clearly been in conversation when he arrived, and the larger of the civilians grunted in derisive laughter when Roger entered.

"I see the *basik* have heard of our plight," he half-sneered, but the other civilian sliced a true-hand across his chest in a gesture of negation.

"We're in no position to laugh," he said sternly. "You, especially, are not," he added in a pointed tone, and the larger Mardukan hissed sourly, although he made no other response. The smaller native turned to Roger. "I am Deb Tar. And you are?"

"Captain Sergei," Roger said with a slight bow. "At your service."

"And at yours," Deb Tar replied. "What can we do for you?"

"It's more what we can do for you," Roger told him with a smile. "I understand you have a problem."

"That we do," Deb Tar agreed with a handclap of emphasis. "But I doubt you'll be able to do anything about it."

"I don't know about that," Roger said. "We might surprise you."

"Some other time, *basik*," the other Mardukan grunted. "We're about to get the problem solved for us."

"Oh." Roger raised an eyebrow. "I take it there are competitors?"

"For a month's production from my mine?" Deb Tar's snort was perilously near to a snarl. "Of course there are—including my former mine manager," he continued with a distasteful gesture of a false-hand at the other civilian. "Nor Tob seems to feel that it should be easy to take the valley back. Since, after all, it was so easy to take away from him in the first place."

"It was not my fault," the former manager ground out. "Was *I* the guard commander?"

"No, you weren't," the owner agreed. "Otherwise your horns would be over my fireplace. There's still an empty space I could fit them into, though. I would have saved half the cost if you hadn't persuaded me to relocate the refinery there, as well!"

"You made money hand over hand from that!" the former manager shot back, then turned to Roger and Cord. "Come on, *basik*," he snarled. "Let us show you how *real* Mardukans deal with scum like this!"

"Oh, by all means, lead on," Roger invited, waving towards the door. "This I've got to see."

CHAPTER FOUR

"The valley's a fortress," Roger said, and took a sip of wine.

"So, what happened?" Julian asked.

"I've got the whole thing on helmet recording, but the short answer is that it was a farce."

"How?" Kosutic asked. She looked at the schematic of the valley entrance and shook her head. "I don't see anything particularly humorous about the situation. You could take that with a wave of Kranolta, but that's the only way to go over the wall that comes to mind."

"Yep," Roger agreed. "And that was more or less what our friend Nor Tob tried. He gathered up a few hundred out-of-work miners and half-assed mercenaries with a promise to divide the loot when they took the place and threw them straight at it."

He laughed and shook his head.

"They came at the wall with ladders, but it's so damned high that half the ladders broke under the weight of the climbers. Those that didn't got pushed down easily. Basically, they didn't get within five meters of the top."

"How many casualties?" Gunny Lai asked. The gunnery sergeant stood beside Kosutic, looking down at the map and rubbing the side of her nose.

"None," Roger said with another laugh. "Oh, there were a few broken arms and more bruised egos, but no military casualties. The barb mercenaries never even shot back. They just pushed the ladders down and threw stuff. Mostly smelly stuff, like their slop buckets."

"Contemptuous, were they?" the sergeant major asked as she panned the map out to get a look at the entire valley.

"Very," Roger told her. "These guys—they call themselves the Vasin—are apparently a tribe that got displaced by this Boman invasion. Either they were already mercenaries, or else they took up the trade after they got shoved off their homeland originally. Nobody's too sure about that, but whichever it was, it sounds to me like they were looking for work when they hit Ran Tai and they'd gone to the mine as a good place to trade some of their hides for raw gold and silver at refinery prices. As nearly as I can tell, they didn't have any intention of taking it before they got there and realized how wide open it was. No one seems to know exactly what started the ruckus, but they ended up in possession of the place, and according to the owner, Deb Tar, he had over two months of refined output bagged and crated for shipment when they moved in on him. He really, really wants that loot back, but they're not especially eager to hand it over, and since they grabbed it so easily, they're pretty contemptuous of all the locals. Even if they weren't, the city authorities aren't about to take the losses involved in throwing them out—especially when Deb Tar deliberately located his refining facilities right there at the minehead to avoid paying city taxes on them. The way the Council sees it, it's out of their jurisdiction, so good luck to him. And from some of the conversations we overheard, the Vasin have offered Deb Tar a price to get his property back . . . an even *three* months' production."

"Ouch!" Kosutic grimaced. "Still, I'd think giving up an extra month of output wouldn't sound all that unreasonable if it got the mines back for him. He can always dig more, after all."

"But they are bargaining?" Sergeant Jin asked. "That wasn't what we were told."

"Oh, yeah, they're ready enough to deal." Roger smiled broadly. "Deb Tar is just holding out for a better price, which is why he's looking so hard for someone who can kick them out without meeting their demands. Nor Tob was the first to actually try to take him up on it, but when he saw that his own valiant effort was going to be a bust, he decided to haul ass and headed out as soon as it was clear the assault was a failure."

"No wonder," Kosutic laughed. "I bet those miners were some pissed individuals. Anybody know where he went?"

"Nope," Julian said. "It looks like he's gone to ground somewhere. He hasn't left the area, but he hasn't been seen in his usual haunts, either."

"I been lookin' around," Poertena interjected. "T'is Deb Tar, he offering a full month's output to whoever get them out. T'at be something like thirty sedant in gold an' another ten in silver, an' a sedant's nearly half a kilo. Even with tee prices up here, we can load up ever't'ing we need for less t'an twenty sedant of gold." He shrugged. "Tee other gold an' silver be profit."

"So it's a worthwhile operation," Roger said. "If anyone can figure out a method to get in, at least."

"Oh, that's easy enough," Kosutic told him, looking up from the map display.

"Yeah. Getting in isn't a problem," Jin agreed. "The question is how we go about taking on a hundred scummy mercenaries after we do."

"Oh?" Roger looked over the sergeant major's shoulder at the map. "What are you planning?"

"Welll . . ." Kosutic drawled, and pointed at the map. "Your helmet imagery shows that there's a straight cliff at the entrance, right?"

"It widens out further in," Roger said. "But, yes, the entrance is a narrow gorge, nearly fifty meters high. There's a stream that comes out through a metal grate at the base of the wall. It's probably what cut the gorge in the first place."

"Yes, Sir," Gunny Lai said. "But if you get up on top of that plateau at the entrance, you can come around behind the wall and rappel right down on their heads."

"Oh." The prince tugged at a flyaway strand of hair and frowned. "What about getting up the face in the first place?"

"That we can do, Sir," Kosutic said. "But I want to know more about the scummies on the inside. What their pattern is, what sorts of guard posts they set—that sort of thing."

"All right," Roger said. "But we've got some competitors in this. Let's not let them have an edge or tip our own hand. Send a team up to the plateau to check out the route, but tell them to stay low and keep their heads down."

"Kosutic and her great ideas," Julian said sourly.

The windswept plateau was actively cold in the night wind, and the distant lights of the town didn't make him feel any better. If he and Poertena hadn't happened to hear about this job and pass the word to Roger, he could have been down there now, drinking on the prince's decicred.

"Hey, *I* think we lucked out again, Sergeant," Gronningen said quietly.

The big Asgardian was very good in the mountains. He moved like a mountain goat, just as surely and almost as silently. That was why Julian had included him on this little jaunt, and the NCO nodded in agreement with his observation as he took another look at the objective. The mercenaries weren't stupid, and they had guards on the wall against the possibility of a night attack. But they were very complacent, for there were no sentries actually patrolling the camp they'd established in the valley. Or maybe complacent wasn't exactly the right word for it, he conceded after a moment. No Mardukan raiding force could possibly have come after them through these temperature conditions, after all, even if it could have made the climb up the cliffs in the first place, which was questionable.

"This is going to be a cakewalk," he whispered.

"Something's bound to go wrong," the plasma gunner disagreed, getting up carefully to avoid sending a rock bouncing into the valley to give away their position.

The two Marines moved back to the bivouac the team had established. It was an overcast, moonless night, and without the vision systems of their helmets, they would have been stumbling along blind. As it was, the faint reflection of the fires of Ran Tai was enough to give them near daylight vision.

They rounded the small projection of stone that shielded their camp from view from the valley and squatted down by Macek. The private was heating a cup of soup with a resistance heater. Technically, that was a violation of doctrine, since they were supposed to be making a cold camp, but the resistance heater only radiated in infrared, and it wasn't like they had to worry about scummy scan teams picking it up.

"That looks good," Julian observed as he flopped down on his open bivy tent.

"Fix your own, then," the private suggested, and Gronningen chuckled and pulled out a piece of jerked capetoad. The meat from the animals had yielded several hundred kilos of jerky that some of the company relished.

Julian generally found it awful, but he was hungry enough to pull out a piece of his own and start gnawing on it.

"I can't believe that after all I've done for you, you begrudge me a little soup," he said in a whiny tone.

"Yeah? Like dragging me up a mountain to alternately freeze and bake?" the private asked, then chuckled. "Hell, I was making it for all of us," he admitted. "It's not much, just a little jerky and a few leftover pieces of tater."

"Sounds good," Gronningen said. "I'm ready to get off this hill, too," he admitted reluctantly. The Asgardian religion had some extremely stoic overtones.

"Me, too," Julian assured him. "I'm ready for some of Matsugae's cooking." He sighed. "Or even some of the stuff in the town. It's not too bad, you know."

"I want a bitok," Macek said. "That doesn't seem too much to ask."

"Oh, man," Julian said, smacking his lips. "You would have to say that. I want one, too. About an eighth of a kilo. With cheese and onions."

"Yah," Gronningen said, leaning back in his own bivy and masticating the shoe-leather jerky. "A bitok sounds good. Or my mutra's lutefisk." He sighed. "It's been a long time since I had my mutra's lutefisk."

"What's lutefisk?" Julian asked as he took the cup out of Macek's hand and sipped.

"Lutefisk?" The Asgardian frowned. "That is . . . hard to explain. It is a fish."

"Yeah?" Macek took a chew of his own jerky. "What's so special about a fish?"

The Asgardian thought for a moment about trying to explain the attraction of cod soaked in lye, then decided to give up.

"It is a family thing, I think," he said, and retreated into his normal reticent shell after that while Julian and Macek wrangled quietly over the quality of different bitok joints in Imperial City. Eventually, they both agreed that the only thing to do was get back to Earth and go on a bar-crawl to compare them properly.

They finished the soup, then divided up the watches and settled down for the night. One more day of alternately baking and frying on the plateau, and the company should be on its way.

Roger pulled himself over the lip of the plateau and stepped forward to let the next Marine up. The windy tabletop was beginning to fill up with the company, but the Marines stayed well away from the northern wall. One noisy, rolling rock could ruin the entire operation.

Roger nodded to Kosutic as she walked up. The flattened view in the night vision systems worked hand in hand with the helmet's face shields to make everyone anonymous, but the helmet systems threw up little tags as people came into view. The tags were effectively invisible, once you got used to them, unless you consciously concentrated on seeing them, but they provided a way for the user to distinguish who was who.

"How we doing, Sergeant Major?" the prince asked. He looked around as the last Marine hauled herself onto the plateau and checked his toot for the time. "I think we're a little ahead of schedule."

"That we are, Sir," the sergeant major replied. She glanced around and saw that the team leaders were getting their people into position. Everything was working out smoothly, exactly as planned.

Which made her very, very nervous.

CHAPTER FIVE

"Ah, finally something that's working out," Julian said quietly.

The two oversized squads which were all that remained of Bravo Company were lined up along the middle section of the gorge. The gorge snaked back from the entrance for nearly three hundred meters before opening into the mining area, where the majority of the barbarians were bivouacked, but the only guards were on the gates themselves. By landing between the barbarians' camp and the guards, the company could take the mercenaries by the throat . . . assuming everything worked as planned.

"Remember," Roger said over the company frequency, "minimum violence. I want them taken down, and taken down hard, but no killing if possible."

"But don't take unnecessary chances," Kosutic added.

"Right," the prince agreed. "Okay, you all have your targets," he said, clipping his drop line into place. "Let's do it."

The platoon dropped down into the darkness like the shadows of so many chameleon-cloth-covered spiders. The drop clips automatically slowed them as they approached the nearly invisible bottom, then detached as their feet hit the ground. Then the shadows split up, one squad heading valley-ward while the other headed for the gates.

* * *

Roger moved through the sleeping encampment and wanted to laugh. The barbarians were pretty clearly a nomadic cavalry outfit, since the recon teams had confirmed that they had their women and children with them, but their picket lines were well up the valley. The *civan* that would have warned them of the humans' approach were well out of sight from the tactical squad.

Julian and his team had determined which hut belonged to the leaders of the barbarians, and the prince had chosen it as his personal target. He hoped that if he took the leader, he could convince him to surrender. He'd been able to negotiate an agreement with Deb Tar and the city authorities of Ran Tai to let the barbarians go free if they surrendered, so he had that to bargain with. If the barbs wanted to fight, though, things could get messy. Whatever else these scummies might be, and however overconfident they might seem, they were also professional warriors, and unlike the Kranolta, they had firearms. As cavalry, they carried the big wheel lock pistol/carbines, not the heavier-caliber infantry arquebuses with their resin-coated slow matches. Developing reliable gunpowder and ignition systems for firearms on a planet with Marduk's predominately humid, one might almost say "saturated," climate must have been a nightmare. It had certainly required more ingenuity than had been the case back on Terra, and from what the humans had been able to discover so far, the several-times-a-day rains which were so much a part of the normal Mardukan weather experience were a major tactical factor in their use. Armies without arquebuses, or with fewer of them than their opponents, strove mightily to avoid battles under anything except rainy conditions, and no scummy in his right mind would have dreamed of building an army without plenty of old-fashioned, muscle-powered weaponry in reserve.

For himself, Roger suspected that he would never have bothered to try to overcome the all but insuperable difficulties involved with the use of loose-powder, muzzle-loading weapons on a planet like Marduk. But the locals had managed it, and he had no desire at all to see what a two-centimeter pistol ball would do to one of his people, so if it did come to a fight, he was determined that the company would have the upper hand from the start. That was why Aburia's team was busy planting explosives throughout the camp; if the barbarians didn't surrender, the plan was to back off and blow them in place.

Roger and his team froze as a figure stepped out of one of the huts. The small buildings of the mining facility were made of rock rubble from the mine shafts, but their doors were nothing more than hide flaps, and the Mardukan's exit had been silent. One moment, the street was empty—the next the scummy was in clear view. Despite the darkness, they would be spotted in an instant if he looked around, and the entire plan would be blown.

The barbarian scratched at a dried patch on his arm and snarled. Then he relieved himself on the side of the hut, and went back in.

Roger breathed a silent sigh of relief and continued onward. He detoured slightly to get away from the restless barbarian's hut and cut between two of the rough buildings.

His team ended up behind the hut of the mercenary leader and crept around to its front. Roger consulted his helmet systems and looked around. Aburia's team was nearly done placing their explosives, but not quite, so he held in place to give them a bit more time. The squad headed for the gates was already in position and hadn't been spotted as they set up for an ambush. Their only job was to make sure that the Mardukans at the gates didn't come to the aid of their compatriots when Roger's squad hit the main encampment. If the plan went off without a hitch, their presence would never even be noticed.

Roger consulted the demo schematic and his toot clock again. The charges were emplaced, and Aburia had pulled her team back to provide cover if the entry team needed it. And if that wasn't enough, Roger had a hole card.

He'd lost out on the argument over who went through the door first. Actually, it would have been fairer to say that there'd never been anything which might properly have been called an "argument" in the first place. Pahner might have delegated field command to "Captain Sergei," but there were definite limits to the freedom Roger was permitted in the risk-taking department, and so he waved Julian forward, instead.

The squad leader smiled and waved in turn to Gronningen, who stepped forward quietly and pushed the flap aside. Julian followed him through, and Roger entered behind the NCO. The hut was larger than most, and had a few appointments, including a writing desk, but it was still basically a hovel. Roger shook his head and stepped over to the still-sleeping scummy leader as the team fanned out to cover the other scummies in the room. Two of them were females, but the humans were taking no chances and made certain that *all* of the Mardukans were covered.

Once they were, Roger bent until his helmet was pointed at the barbarian's face, and triggered the helmet light.

Rastar Komas Ta'Norton of the Vasin, Prince of Therdan, stared up into the light, and all four hands filled with the knives that were his trademark. But he'd hardly moved when he encountered the hard shape of what could only be a gun barrel pressing into his chest. He wasn't sure, because the light in his eyes was the brightest he'd ever seen in his life, but it was unlikely to be anything else.

"Do you want to live?" a disembodied and very peculiar-sounding voice asked from beyond the light. "Or do you want to die, and have your entire tribe die with you?"

"What's the difference?" Rastar snarled. "You'll kill us all anyway. Or make us slaves. Kill us now. At least that's freedom, of a sort."

"Death is lighter than a feather, duty heavier than mountains," the voice, which sounded like no Mardukan Rastar had ever heard, said. "Yet we take up the burden of duty, do we not? I have been given permission to spare you and your tribe if you surrender and leave. You may even retain your weapons. You simply have to pack up and go, taking with you nothing but what you arrived with. If you are in the Vale of Ran Tai at sunset of this day, your lives are forfeit. Your call."

Rastar considered the knives. He was certain he could kill this one, but there were other lights, other guns, and he couldn't kill his women, his tribe. It was the last duty he had, and he could not drop it, even when death beckoned so seductively.

"We keep our weapons?" he asked suspiciously.

"Yes," said the voice. "However, if you try to double-cross us, we'll be forced to kill you all."

"No." The chieftain sighed and put his knives on the floor. "No, we won't double-cross you. Have this foul valley, and more power to you."

Things were still going too smoothly.

Roger watched the Vasin filing out of their huts and gathering in the central square. He had his own squad moving about in an intricate, flowing pattern that gave the impression he had forces everywhere, when the barbarians actually outnumbered him by three to one, in hopes of keeping things smooth. In fact, the mercenaries outnumbered the force that he had in the camp itself by nearly *ten* to one, and he congratulated himself, in a modest sort of way, on how well the op had gone down.

Of course, he admitted, it had nearly gone the other way. Roger had been terrified by the speed with which the Mardukan had reacted—those knives had seemed to teleport into the chieftain's hands, and he'd had them out and ready before Roger could even blink. If the Mardukan had decided to start the ball, the Empire would have been short one fortunately disposable prince. It had been a sobering experience.

The Vasin's equipment was much better made and finished than Roger had expected, but their nomad background was obvious, for they were packed before Roger had imagined they could even get started. Their *civan* were lined up to leave in less than ten minutes, and Roger approached the chief, Rastar, and nodded.

"It's better this way," he said.

"I hope you won't mind, but if we actually get out of this valley alive, we're planning on being out of the Vale before dawn," the Mardukan told him with a grunt of laughter.

"Not at all," Roger said. "You're not terribly popular. Just one question," he added. The Marines had watched the packing with an eagle eye, and he knew the Mardukans hadn't packed any large amounts of gold and silver. "Where's the shipment?"

"Your guess is as good as mine, *basik*," the chieftain told him.

"They keep talking about their 'shipment,' but we've never understood why. There's no large store of metals here." The chief gestured to a heavily built stone shack near a worked-out, abandoned mine shaft. "That's the storehouse. It was empty when we arrived."

"What?"

"Hah!" the chieftain grunted. "Let me guess—that was your pay."

"Yes!" the prince snarled. "What happened to it?"

"As I said," the barbarian said in a voice which held a sudden hint of dangerous ice, "it was gone when we arrived here. We don't know what happened to it."

"Sir," Sergeant Major Kosutic put in, "they didn't load it, and there's no way out of the valley, so they didn't carry it out after they got here. Either it left before they arrived, or else it's still here somewhere."

"Shit," Roger said. "Okay, Rastar, you can leave. Pick up your guards on the way out. If you try to come back, I might just get pissed."

"Not as pissed as I am, Lord Sergei," the Mardukan told him. "But for whatever comfort it's worth, I've always heard that the life of a mercenary generally consists of getting stuck with the sword of the paymaster far more often than with the swords of the enemy. From my own limited experience, that's putting it mildly."

He tossed his head in a Mardukan nod, walked over to his *civan*, and climbed into the saddle. In moments, the Vasin column was gone.

"All right, Sergeant Major," Roger sighed wearily. "Let's tear this place apart. Find our gold."

"Yes, Sir," the sergeant major said. But she already had a sinking feeling.

"No gold?" Armand Pahner's voice was admirably composed, but he kept his head turned slightly away to hide his incipient grin.

"Nope." Roger kicked one of the low tables. "None. We found a few kilos of silver—hardly enough to outfit us, but maybe if we scrimp . . ." He shook his head angrily. "We searched every mine, as far as we could with the way the groundwater's risen since Deb Tar's people's pumps shut down. Not a bit of gold anywhere."

"Oh, great," O'Casey said. "Stop kicking the table, Roger. We can't afford to break any furniture."

"The worst part is that I'm a laughingstock," Roger said bitterly. "Of course Deb Tar wasn't willing to pay us a red centicred, and the local courts won't touch it. Especially not after the way he kept accusing us of hiding the gold ourselves, as if that made any sense."

"Oh, it's not that bad," Kosutic said. "It was a good op. It went down exactly as planned, and nobody got hurt. Hell, it was basically a training exercise, and a good one. And nobody faults you, Sir. Everybody thought the gold was there, and Deb Tar is furious."

"But where did it go?" O'Casey asked.

"That's the million-credit question," the sergeant major replied, "and His Evilness only knows the answer. It was definitely in the storehouse when the Vasin slipped through the gates, and it's definitely not there now. And the Vasin did *not* carry it out. Unfortunately, none of that tells us what *did* happen to it, and where it went is a mystery. The storehouse was empty, and even the carts they kept the stuff in are gone."

"Carts?" the chief of staff repeated.

"Yeah. They load the stuff into carts to carry it to the storehouse from the refinery, and they just shove the carts into the storehouse to save themselves the trouble of unloading it just so they can load it again when the time comes to haul it down to the city. But the carts weren't there—and they weren't in the refinery or anywhere else, either. We looked just to see if they'd been hidden in the smelters or something."

"There's no way they could've gotten it out of the valley without taking it through the gate," Roger said despairingly. "Mardukans just can't climb that well."

"Well, Your Highness," Captain Pahner said with a smile, "I'm sure we'll think of something. But maybe you want to get some sleep, or even go hit the taverns. Go blow off some steam."

"With what? We're tapped!"

"We're not that tapped," the CO said. "Take the . . . platoon out and have a trooper blast. We can afford it, barely, and it's the best thing to do after a busted op."

"Okay." Roger shrugged. "If you say so."

"Go have some fun, Captain Sergei," the captain told him with a smile.

"That particular ancestor wasn't very lucky," Roger said, summoning a slight grin of his own in return. "I think I'll pick a different moniker."

Pahner chuckled in sympathy, and the prince turned and headed for the door. Behind him, Kosutic looked at the captain and lifted an eyebrow. He was planning something.

Roger was drunk. So was Nimashet Despreaux. And just at the moment, the prince was stone-cold positive that that was a Bad Thing.

The two of them had somehow ended up in a pool of silence in the middle of the roaringly successful party. The inn's owner had been only too happy to have the custom, but most of the Mardukan patrons had gone home early. The off-worlders were too drunk, too aggressive, and, by all means, too loud. A group of Marines in one corner was roaring out one of the dirtiest ditties Roger had ever heard in his life—something about "Three-Ball Pete"—and in another corner, in competition with their theoretically musical efforts, was an arm-wrestling match, complete with chanting cheerleaders. Neither group could have carried a tune if you'd given them a hundred buckets, but everyone was far too plastered to care.

So the little pool of privacy that had formed around him and the sergeant had a queasy setup feel to the high-flying prince's somewhat befuddled instincts. He could feel the little prods from the group even through his wine-induced haze, and, in a way, it was gratifying. Despreaux was by no means ugly, after all. And if the company had decided it was a good thing for them to "get together," it meant a form of acceptance. On the other hand . . .

Roger cleared his throat as Despreaux, apparently oblivious to the little nods, winks, and maneuvers around them, poured him some more wine.

"Nima-sh-sh-shet?" he asked.

"Hmmm?" Her smile was warm, and his resistance wavered for a moment. She was, in fact, quite beautiful. And he'd had that thought any number of times before, he reminded himself, so it wasn't the several bottles of wine he'd consumed at this point.

"I . . . don' ge' involved wi' . . . uh . . ."

What he wanted to say was that he didn't get sexually involved at all. The consequences and ramifications for someone in his position were simply too great, and the two times he'd made the mistake of forgetting that, the public discussion of his sex life had hammered the point mercilessly home. No one outside the Imperial Family could possibly conceive of the intensity with which a public microscope examined the behavior of all MacClintocks, and anyone who thought Roger or his siblings could conduct even the most discreet love affair without the newsies finding out had to be a drug addict. The last thing the dynasty's "bad boy" had needed was to hand the scandal faxes *that* kind of story!

That would have been more than sufficient reason for discretion on Roger's part, but he was honest enough—with himself, at least—to admit that there was another and much more personal reason. His mother had never married his father, and until Eleanora O'Casey had explained the actual train of events to him in Marshad, Roger had always believed deep in his heart that *he* must have been what had driven them apart and led to his father's banishment from court. Looked at logically, the notion that he could be to blame was ridiculous, but the wounded, lonely child to whom it had first occurred had scarcely been in a position to consider it rationally.

And one thing he was totally and bitterly certain of was that he would never put another child into the position of thinking the same thoughts and enduring the same pain. Oh, he knew perfectly well that the drugs and nanites that eliminated the monthly curse for the female Marines also eliminated any possibility of pregnancy, but engaging in a casual affair, especially under these conditions, was as impossible for the prince as it might have been for other scions of the "nobility" to resist banging the servants. And even if it hadn't been, there was no way that he would damage the unit's cohesion that way—no way that he was going to damage his companion-at-arms relationship with the sergeant, one he'd literally shed blood to create, for an evening's romp in the sack.

No matter how badly his inebriated body yearned to throw itself onto the highly trained Marine, rip her uniform off, and bury his face in her high, firm breasts.

But he'd never been able to explain any of his tangled feelings and rational analyses to anyone in his life. Not even to Matsugae, who was, in many ways, the closest thing Roger had ever known to a genuine "father." His personal . . . quirks had led to problems ever since upper school, and he'd still never been able to articulate them. Not even when the commander of his mother's bodyguard had been standing in his bedroom, trying to understand why the stark-naked and raving daughter of a grand duke was calling him a eunuch.

He couldn't think of the way to do it now, either, however hard he tried. And he *did* try. His fuddled brain searched for something—anything—to say to take the sting out of his rejection, but what dropped from his lips was " . . . associateatsh."

Nimashet Despreaux blinked twice and tried to focus on the prince, but all she could see was the target zone just above his Adam's apple.

"Di' you jus' say what I thin' you said?" she enunciated carefully.

"Look, call me weird," Roger said, gesturing with his cup. "But I don' fool around with . . . assoc . . . ass . . . aizoaceae . . . . Look, not tha' it wouldn' be fun. You' gorgeous. Bu' I won'."

"Wha' you mean is you don' fool 'round wi' the help. Tha's wha' you were gonna say, right?" the NCO demanded. "I s'pose a sergeant from a ass en' o' nowhere planet isn' good enough for you!"

"No, is no' *like* that!" the prince protested vehemently, leaning forward to give her a hug. "I like you, an' you're beau'ful, but it wouldn' be right!"

"Kee' you hands off me, you aris-aris . . . aristocratic *worm!*"

"Whaddid I say?" Roger asked in perplexity. "I guess maybe some'ay, but no' tonigh'."

"You're damn' right we won't," the sergeant hissed as she drew back to strike. "Thas' not somethin' you're ever, *ever* gonna worry abou' again."

* * *

"Oh, shit."

For no reason he could think of, Julian had decided to forego the party. Technically, he was off-duty and could've gotten as drunk as a skunk if he wanted to. Unlike Gronningen and Georgiadas, who were supposed to be covering Roger. But they, bless their stupid little hearts, had stepped far enough away to give Roger and his girlfriend some space, some privacy, just like everybody else who'd watched the two of them dance closer and closer all evening. The company was not a unit of voyeurs, but the pool had gone bust twice on when those two were finally going to do the beast with two backs, and if they didn't get it out of their systems soon, somebody was going to squeal to the Skipper.

At the moment, however, Julian was ready to call the pool off. Just as soon as he saved Roger's life—the ungrateful bastard . . .

The hard-driven slap slammed painfully into Julian's forearm as he blocked it.

"Despreaux!"

"Get out of my way, Julian!" the enraged bodyguard screamed. "I won't kill 'im! I'm just going to rip his balls off!"

"That *would* kill him, Nimashet," Julian protested as he blocked another swing. Fortunately, the inebriated Marine was still trying to hit the rapidly retreating Roger rather than deliberately aiming for her fellow noncom.

"No, it wouldn't." Warrant Officer Dobrescu sounded remarkably—and falsely—sober for a man stretched out under a nearby table, bottle in one hand and little black bag in the other. "I'd stop the bleeding. They'd even regrow with enough regen and enough time. I saw it once in a guy that had a bad accident on Shiva."

"See!" Despreaux yelled, trying to force her way past. Roger had retreated into the group of singers in the corner, but the tall, long-haired figure was still easily discernible. "It wouldn't kill him—just hurt. A lot! And it's not like *he'd* miss them!"

She tried for one more moment to shove past Julian, but then, suddenly, all the fury seemed to drain out of her. Her strength went with it, and she dropped back onto a bench and put her face in her hands.

"Oh, Julian, what the hell am I gonna *do?*"

"There, there," he said, patting her awkwardly on the back. The thought crossed his mind—briefly—that this was probably the best time ever to make his own play. But even *he* wasn't that evil a bastard. Probably. He'd have to think about it. He'd done things nearly as low to get laid. But not quite that low. Well, some that were. And, admittedly, some that were even lower. But not to a friend. Had he? "There, there."

"Oooooh." Despreaux groaned and took a long pull out of a bottle. "What the hell am I gonna do? I was willing to be the laughingstock of the company, but this is worse! I'm in love with a man who's unable to screw!"

"He isn't functionally incapable," Dobrescu said carefully. He sat up and slammed his forehead on the underside of his table. "Ouch. Damned low ceilings in this joint. As I was saying. He's functional as a male."

"Oooooh," Despreaux moaned again. "I just wanna crawl under a rock and *die!*"

"Don't tell me this is the first time you've ever been turned down," Julian joked. "You'll get over it. Everybody does."

"It's the first time I've ever *asked*, you idiot! I never *had* to before! And I didn't even get to ask—he just assumed I was going to suggest it! *Assumed!*"

"Were you?" Dobrescu asked, sticking his head out from between the table and the bench. "Damned odd architecture in this joint."

"Well, yes," Despreaux admitted. "But that's not the point! Did you hear what he said to me?"

"Yes," Julian said. "That was when I got the tranquilizer gun ready."

"Can you believe the *nerve!*" she spat so furiously that wine flew out in a spray over the other NCO.

"Yes," Dobrescu said. "I can. And since he turned you down, I don't suppose you could do with some comforting from a warrant officer? If, of course, you're thin enough to fit through the entrance to this cozy little room I seem to have lucked upon."

Gronningen, fortunately, was large enough to pull her off the warrant officer. Who complained, vociferously, that since he was the only medic in the company, there was no one else who could work on his wrenched back and bleeding nose.

The owner, the new manager, and the survey parties had left the valley. The long process of pumping out the mines and putting them back into production would start the following day, but for tonight the valley was deserted. Not even the guards had been replaced.

Which made the fact that three of the windmill-powered pumps were running all out at the moment more than a tiny bit peculiar. Their hoses snaked into the mouth of an abandoned mine shaft, and Armand Pahner parked himself just outside its entrance and clicked on his helmet light as a Mardukan emerged from the opening.

"Why, hello, Nor Tob."

The Mardukan froze in the opening, pinned by the brilliant glare of light. He clutched a chest between his false-hands, while one true-hand carried an uncocked cavalry pistol.

"It was the carts that got me thinking," the Marine continued cheerfully. "If somebody thought really fast and worked quickly, he could wheel quite a bit of this stuff away in just a few minutes. But he couldn't get far with it."

"So he asked me what was right near the storehouse," the sergeant major said from her perch above the entrance behind the Mardukan. "Ah, ah, let's keep those true-hands away from the pistol flint, shall we?" She chuckled. "I nearly kicked myself. Tell me something, did you have them dig this shaft just for this reason?"

"I've slaved in this mine for *years!*" the former manager said. "It was my *right!*"

"And when the Vasin came through the gates, you saw a chance to take your 'right' in the confusion," Pahner observed. "Or did you arrange that, too?"

"No, that was mere chance," the Mardukan said. "But I took that chance when I saw it! Look, I can . . . share this with you. Nobody ever needs to know. You two can have half of it. Hell, forget that foolish child—there are cities on the plains where this much gold will allow you to live like a king for the rest of your life!"

"I don't think so," Pahner said quietly. "I don't like thieves, Nor Tob, and I don't like traitors even more. I think you ought to just go." The captain judged the weight of the chest the former manager was carrying. "You can take that with you, and nobody has to know any different, as you said. But that's it. Time to get on your *civan* and leave."

"This is my *right*," the former mine manager snarled. "It's *mine!*"

"Look," Pahner said reasonably, "you can leave vertical, or horizontal. It really doesn't matter to me. But you're not leaving with more than what you're carrying right now."

"That's what you think!" the Mardukan shouted, and grabbed the cocking arm of his pistol.

"I'm feeling kind of ambiguous about this," Pahner said as the shaft started to fill again.

"Don't," Kosutic said. "His Evilness knows he's no loss."

"Oh, no," the CO said, walking back up the shaft with her. "Not that. It's Roger. How are we going to tell him?"

"I'd suggest that we just pretend there's a magic bag somewhere with more money," Kosutic said. "I mean, he never has to know, right?"

"But what about Poertena?" Pahner asked as he threw one of the cases onto a *turom*. The local draft animals were, indeed, some sort of distant cousin of the *civan*, but they had far more placid dispositions, and this one only whuffled with mournful resignation under the weight.

"What about him?" The sergeant major lashed a bag to a second *turom*. "We tell *him* there's no cash at all; it just brings out his creative side."

"We don't want him getting too creative," the captain pointed out. He paused, trying to judge whether or not the *turom* was overloaded on one side.

"That's always been your problem, Armand," the NCO told him as she picked up another of the heavy cases and loaded it onto her beast. "You're too kindhearted."

"True, true." Pahner gathered up the reins of his *civan*, swung into the saddle (now equipped with human-style stirrups), and made sure he had a firm grip on his *turom*'s lead. "I need to get over that, I suppose."

"It'll get you killed some day, I swear," the sergeant major said as she mounted in turn. "Take it from me," she added as they headed down the track to town.

Behind them, the water rose over the last of the rock pile at the bottom of the shaft.

CHAPTER SIX

"You know, I really didn't miss this," Roger said as he slid down off of Patty.

"To be terribly honest, Your Highness," Pahner replied, wiping the sweat off his brow, "neither did I."

The first day of travel had been uneventful as the company followed one of the regular caravan trails down out of the mountains. Within a few hours of leaving Ran Tai, however, they'd hit the enveloping, sweltering clouds of the jungle-covered lowlands and passed once more from the region of relative cool back into Marduk's standard steambath.

Cord and the other Mardukans had, of course, been delighted.

There were quite a few of those "other Mardukans," now, including the recently hired mahout who climbed up on Patty and guided her to the picket lines. The mahout and his fellows were only a few of the "camp followers" the company had attached, however. Their stated destination, Diaspra, had been avoided by caravans for the last several months as the advance of the Boman barbarians made travel out of Ran Tai's high valley increasingly problematical. The riverport city lay on the Chasten River where it broke over the edge of the Diaspran Plateau, and the Chasten drained directly into the vast gulf or inland sea they'd identified from their rough, deplorably undetailed maps as their next objective. The locals called it the

K'Vaernian Sea; the humans called it the shortest path to the open ocean which lay between them and their ultimate goal. That made Diaspra their only logical intermediate objective, and their departure had been delayed repeatedly as caravan masters solicited their services for protection on the trip.

All of which explained why the Marines and their beasts were accompanied by two caravans of *flar-ta* and *turom*, along with another two dozen *civan*-riding guardsmen. Between the Marines' heavy weapons and unusual tactics and the additional guards, they might be able to beat off a few attacks.

Roger looked around as the rest of the caravan came to an untidy stop and the Mardukan guards straggled out to assist the Marines. One of Pahner's requirements had been that the guards be willing to follow his orders, even the strange ones, and now the Mardukans began digging foxholes while the Marines laid out mono-wire and directional mines. As always, however, the majority of both groups were on guard, and the work parties hadn't hesitated to conscript liberally from the chaotic mob which wasn't attached to any particular caravan but had simply followed the departing party.

"I don't know about this," the prince said, shaking his head. "There are too many for us to cover, and not enough to really help."

"It'll be all right," Pahner said. "There's a reason the Marines stay around you. They're obviously the best armed and most dangerous of the bunch, so any attacker in his right mind is going to hit the rest of the caravan first."

Pahner patted his breast pocket absently for a moment, then extracted a piece of *bisti* root, sliced off a thin strip, and popped it into his mouth. He replaced the rest in his pocket, and his eyes considered the river that the caravan route followed while he chewed.

"The Boman are also still reported to be on the north side of the Chasten, not our side. But you're right—we still need more guards. I wish we'd been able to hire that group of mercenaries you tangled with. They might have been a tad incompetent, but we could have fixed that quickly enough."

"Well," Roger said with a chuckle, "I understand they had to get out of town pretty quick." He shook his head again at the thought, then frowned. "And I don't know how we could afford a company of mercs, anyway. We're tapped. Remember, Captain?"

"Oh, I don't know," Pahner said with a faint smile as he masticated the mildly stimulating sweet root. "I'm sure something could have been worked out."

"Don't worry, Rastar," Honal said. "We can work something out."

The Vasin prince looked at the strip of overcooked *atul* meat, then out at the encampment. Many of the women had only a scrap of root or bark in their hands, but they were tearing at that avidly, and there was a faint underlying whimper from the young who had already finished their scraps.

"We're just about at our end, Honal," he said quietly, and gestured at the encampment. "We have three times as many women as men, and many of the men aren't warrior bred." He clapped his false-hands in despair. "We might have made it on our trade in Ran Tai. Now . . . I don't know. If we can make it to Diaspra we might be okay. But we couldn't make it the last time."

"I'm sorry about Ran Tai," Honal said. The younger Mardukan looked as if he would like to die. "It was just . . . Those guards were so stupid. And if the gold had been there like everyone said—"

"What?" his cousin asked. "We would have taken it? Are we Boman? Are we bandits, cousin? Or are we Vasin, the last of the war bands of Therdan and Sheffan? The Warriors of the North? The Free Lords? Which, cousin? Warriors or bandits?"

The younger Mardukan didn't answer. He only retreated into his own misery, and Rastar took a nibble of the leathery meat, then stood and walked into the camp. He squatted down in the midst of the nearest group of females, pulled out of one of his knives, and began cutting the strip into very small pieces.

The women remained sitting, looking in shame at their hands as the last Prince of the North shared his meal with the starving younglings.

"That was wonderful, Kostas," Roger said, and took another bite of the succulent drumstick. "What was it?"

"Ah, that was wine-basted *basik*, Your Highness," the valet-cum-chef replied, and Roger looked at him sharply. The only times the prince had heard the term before had been in reference to humans . . . and it hadn't been very complimentary.

"Huh?" he remarked suspiciously and glanced around at the other members of the dinner party.

Cord was doing his best to look inscrutable, but the company had been around Mardukans long enough to recognize suppressed mirth. O'Casey had set down her morsel uneaten as she raised an eyebrow at the cook, but Kosutic—after a look around—ostentatiously popped her next bite into her mouth and chewed with obvious relish.

"What did you say it was?" the sergeant major asked innocently.

"I finally found out what '*basik*' meant when I was shopping in the market," the valet told her with a puckish grin. "It's the Mardukan version of a rabbit. It's apparently shy and somewhat stupid, and it's generally herded into a circle and killed with clubs."

"Hah!" Roger laughed. He raised his glass of the local sweet wine and took a drink. "To the *basik!*"

"Hear, hear," Kosutic agreed, clearing her own full mouth. "And to more *basik*, too!" she added, looking poignantly at the empty serving platter.

"Oh, I imagine something can be done about that," Matsugae told her with a smile, and bowed himself out of the tent to a spatter of applause.

"While we're waiting for the Sergeant Major's *basik*," Pahner said, "I think we need to discuss tomorrow's march."

"You think we'll get hit, Sir?" Gunny Jin asked. The NCO popped a roll of sweetened barleyrice into his mouth and shrugged. "If it happens, what else is there to do? We rally around the prince and form a square."

"Maybe, and maybe not," Pahner said. "We're about out of ammunition for the light weapons, but we have the full loadout, almost, for the heavy weapons. I've been thinking that there should be a way to get them into action quickly."

"Not one that I see immediately, Captain," Gunny Lai said. She leaned back and looked at the ceiling of the tent. "We can't keep the armor going without wearing out the power packs; the little skimp of energy we've been collecting with the solar sheets isn't enough to recharge with. And without the armor, the heavies are pretty impossible to use in a close-contact fight."

"I was wondering," Roger said diffidently. "Do you think that there's a way to mount one on a *flar-ta*? Not a plasma cannon, obviously, but maybe one of the stutter cannons?"

"Uh." Gunny Jin frowned, considering with obvious care. "One of those things has a hell of a recoil, even with the buffers. How are we going to secure it?"

"I don't know," Pahner said. "But that's the sort of thing I was thinking of, and we certainly need to find a way to use the firepower we have left. I'm not sure we'll make it to the coast if we don't."

"We could try it with Patty," Roger said with growing enthusiasm. "Mount it behind the mahout's spot. The driver will just have to keep his head down. I've fired just about everything else off her back by now; firing a cannon shouldn't be all that much worse."

"I don't know about that," Kosutic said with a shake of her head. "There's a whole order of difference between firing a grenade launcher or that old smoke pole of yours and firing a stutter gun offhand."

"You thinking of Old Man Kenny?" Jin asked her with a chuckle.

"Yeah," Kosutic said with a laugh of her own. "That was more or less what I was thinking about."

"Old Man Kenny?" Roger asked. He picked up a sliver of candied apsimon (which didn't taste a lot better to human tastebuds than *un*candied apsimon) and raised an eyebrow. "Care to enlighten us poor mortals?"

"No big story, Your Highness," Pahner told him. "Retired Sergeant Major Kenny is an instructor in the Heavy Weapons advanced course at Camp DeSarge. There've always been war stories about people firing plasma cannons and bead cannons 'offhand' or without them being properly mounted, so he decided to try it and see if there was really anything to them. He's a big guy," the CO added parenthetically.

"Did it work?"

"Well, sort of," Kosutic said.

"He hit the target, Your Highness," Pahner said with a slight smile and another sip of wine. "But he ended up about ten meters from where he started with a couple of cracked ribs and a dislocated shoulder. He wouldn't have been able to hit the next one."

"Hmmm." Roger took a sip of his own wine. "So the straps had better be strong and tight."

"At the least," Pahner agreed. "The gun is going to convey a kick like a *civan* to the packbeast. I don't know what the damned thing is going to do then."

"Damnthings live on a different planet, Captain Pahner," Roger said with a grin. "I know; I've hunted them."

"Nonetheless, Your Highness," the Marine told him, "when we try it out it won't be with Patty and with you as the mahout. We'll have one of the professionals handle Betty, who's a bit more . . . biddable than Patty. And you won't be at the controls of the cannon, either. That's a job for a private."

"Oh, all right," Roger agreed with a small chuckle. "You undoubtedly know best."

"Uh-huh," Kosutic said as one of the mahouts followed Matsugae back into the tent with a huge platter of *basik* legs. "He does. He really does."

"I hope you know what you're about, cousin." Honal looked towards the sound of distant booms and the occasional bugle of a *pagee* in distress. "It doesn't sound good over there."

"These 'humans' should have nothing against us," Rastar said as he mounted his own *civan*. The beasts showed the effects of deprivation almost as badly as their riders did; the pride of his father's stables had become as gaunt as a cheap hack. "And they can undoubtedly do with some additional guards . . . particularly judging from *that*." He drew the first of his pistols and inserted the winding key to test the tension on the wheel lock drive spring. It was ready, and he grunted in satisfaction, opened the sealed pan, positioned the flint striker against the serrated wheel, and then jerked his head in the direction of the sounds of combat while he reached for a second weapon. “If we bargain well, they may not even realize that they can get us for the cost of a barrel of *fredar!*”

Honal slapped the sides of his head in agitation, then sighed.

“All right! Lead on. And this time, I’ll make sure not to try to take them over!”

CHAPTER SEVEN

Roger's head jerked up as the first line of scummies burst from the undergrowth. The tribesmen had been hidden in the jungle to one side of the beaten-down path between the two city-states, and their charge had caught the caravan by surprise, perfectly positioned in a narrow channel between the jungle and the Chasten River, with no room to evade them.

The prince checked his immediate impulse to order the mahout to countercharge with the aggressive *flar-ta* and threw his rifle to his shoulder instead. He caught one of the better dressed scummy barbarians in his sights and squeezed just as the ragged line came to a momentary halt and hurled its throwing axes.

It was the first time the company had dealt with that particular threat, but they were ready for it. The Marines on the ground lifted their Roman-style shields (design courtesy of one Roger MacClintock), and the rain of small axes scattered off of them like hail. It was sharp hail, however, as a yelp of pain from one of the riflemen proved. The wounded private hobbled backwards, his calf a bloody mess, and his place was taken by one of the second rank.

The humans were badly outnumbered, and the scummies hit them at the run, but the shield wall stopped them cold. The barbarians had never encountered the technique, and the bristle of spears from the rear rank, coupled with the stabbing short swords of the front rank, baffled them.

They paused, uncertain how to respond, and that momentary check was their doom. The stalled line of tribesmen was perfect meat for a tactic so antiquated to the humans that it was practically prehistoric. The sergeant major barked a command, and the Marines showed that perfect drill for which they were justly famous, jabbing their swords forward in unison and stepping forward to drive the tribesmen back from the vulnerable mounts.

The disciplined dike of shields and swords had also bought time for the single *flar-ta*-mounted bead cannon to be brought into action. Betty had finally been convinced that the noisy thing wasn't going to hurt her, barring some painful strap bruises, and she stood still as a statue while Berntsen and Stickles serviced the cannon. They walked the huge beads across the stalled crowd, killing half a dozen scummies with each shot, and the undisciplined tribesmen, totally unprepared for slaughter on such a scale, could stand the fire for only a few rounds. The rear ranks started to peel away and run back to the jungle almost instantly, quickly followed by the rest, and the less fleet footed of them fell under a brutal avalanche of javelins ordered by the irate sergeant major.

As Captain Pahner had anticipated, however, the majority of the attack had been directed at the remainder of the convoy, not Bravo Company, and things had gone far less well there. The noncombatants had fled to the river, some of them even diving in to escape the attacking tribesmen, while the majority of the guards, fighting as individuals against knots of tribesmen, had been quickly overrun and dragged from their mounts to be butchered despite their armor.

"Julian!" Pahner snapped. "Armor up your team. Bravo Company, prepare to wheel!"

Cord and two of the members of Julian's squad whose powered armor was off-line scrambled up on Patty as Roger rolled her into position behind the thin line of humans. The Mardukan settled into place behind Roger and prepared to wield his long spear while the Marines lifted their shields to cover the prince. Bodyguards or not, they had clearly accepted that his participation was a given.

There was still some fighting going on in the caravan, where armed drovers struggled desperately to hold onto their lives and their livelihoods, but many of the barbarians had already fallen to looting as the short platoon which was all that remained of Bravo Company of the Empress' Own countermarched to the rear.

Roger directed Patty's mahout to a position on the Marines' jungle flank as the cannon-armed packbeast fell in behind the tiny force. The Marines paused again, pulling fresh javelins from the quivers over their left shoulders. Then the sergeant major snapped a command, and they hurled the weapons at the rampaging tribesmen and charged forward with the deep, guttural yell which had been part of the Marine tradition for well over fifteen hundred years.

The tribesmen suddenly found themselves under attack from the flank. The flight of javelins was bad enough, but the bead cannon punching lines of death through their ranks was terrible. They tried to rally to face the charging attackers, but the humans were totally unlike the other caravan guards. Those guards, however courageous or skilled with their personal weapons they might have been, had fought as individual warriors, but the Marines weren't "warriors" in the Homeric tradition. They were *soldiers* who fought not as individuals, but as a deadly, trained and disciplined team, and they'd maintained their interval and dress despite their charge.

They slammed into the scummy force like a hammer hitting glass.

Dozens of the much larger tribesmen were simply bowled over and slaughtered by the charge, falling under the Marines' boots to be finished off by a slash or stab. The few who managed to survive the humans' passage and started to regain their feet were coldly dispatched by the line of mahouts, following the Marines for a chance to loot the dead.

The remainder of the barbarians were pushed to the sides, some of them spilling towards the milling *flar-ta* of the caravan and the Chasten, and others to the jungle side. The flankers on the river side had to contend with now thoroughly confused and angry packbeasts, who trampled several of them underfoot, but the ones on the jungle side were in even worse straits.

Roger and Patty had become a well-oiled machine, expert at the business of slaughter. There were a few ways to attack a *flar-ta* from the front, but most of them required the attacker to stand still to accurately throw a weapon at the beast's eyes or to brace a long spear, and those knots of stillness attracted Roger's attention. When he saw a tribesman ready himself to attack, the prince took him out with a single well-aimed round, but aside from that and an occasional shot at a notably better armed or dressed scummy, he let Patty carry the battle.

The *flar-ta* obviously had a thick strain of capetoad genes. She was not only aggressive, she was *nasty*. She spent no time lingering over kills—she simply spitted and gored enemies on the run, then charged on to the next group. She seemed to live for battle, and it was a terrifying thing to watch . . . so terrible that as she cleared the line of embattled Marines and emerged on its flank, most of the remaining scummies broke off their attack on the company and concentrated on the rampaging *flar-ta* out of simple self-preservation.

It started with a gathering hail of throwing axes. Most of them were poorly hurled, but the constant increase in the sheer volume of projectiles forced the two shield-bearing Marines to intercept them instead of attacking themselves. Next, the barbarians tried to circle the beast, dashing this way and that to get past its deadly horns. The Boman's main close-combat weapon was a long battle ax, and those tribesmen who managed to get in close wielded their broad-bladed axes to good effect, inflicting terrible wounds upon the prince's mount.

Roger slid his rifle into its scabbard and drew his pistol, picking off the tribesmen as they rushed in to attack Patty. But there were simply too many of them for one pistol to stop, even in the hand of someone with his skill and enhancements. Patty bellowed in enraged pain as the first axes bit into her thick hide, but retreat was not an option. They were effectively holding the flank of the entire company, and if they fell back, the scummies would pour past them and take the line of Marines in the rear.

The battle hung indecisively in that bloody stalemate which characterizes most hard-fought actions. There was no longer room for maneuver, or tactics; it was stand or die, until one side or the other finally broke and ran.

* * *

"Howahah, cousin!" Honal shouted as he threaded his *civan* through the trees. "Maybe this wasn't such a bad idea after all!"

"We'll see," Rastar snorted, dropping his reins and controlling the *civan* with legs alone as he drew four of his dozen pistols. "If we survive."

Honal looked around at the cavalry troop. Most of its men were from his household, since virtually all of Rastar's troop had been killed in the escape from Therdan, and he gestured to either side.

"Deploy when we clear the damned trees!" he shouted. "One volley, then in with sword and lance!"

The heavily armored troopers' answering shout was hungry and edged with hot anticipation. They'd crossed sword and ax with the Boman many times before, and the technique was simple: blast them with one shot from each of your pistols, then charge in knee to knee. Sometimes, they broke and ran. Sometimes, they stood and dragged your comrades off their mounts. But whichever it was, it was always going to be someone *else* dying.

There were nearly a hundred and fifty in the company, including the few survivors of Rastar's guard, and as they came into the open area along the Chasten their column spread expertly to either side and their worn steeds rose to the challenge of battle as usual. The omnivorous *civan* knew a good battle always meant a good feed afterwards, and these *civan* were getting hungry enough to eat their own riders, much less fallen enemies.

Rastar looked to either side as the company took its dress.

"Are you ready, cousin?" Honal asked, true-hands taking up his lance while he held his reins in his lower false-hands.

"As always," the prince replied, and let his eyes sweep the mounted line. "Let's stick it to these barbarian bastards!" he shouted, and an angry snarl answered him. The few Boman killed today would never repay the loss of Therdan and the League of the North. But it would be a start.

"Volley!"

Roger whipped his leg out of the way as the battle ax sank into

Patty's shoulder right where his ankle had been. He finally got the recalcitrant magazine to seat, and shot the scummy in his screaming face as he tried to work the broad ax back out of the wound. The range was close enough for the ritual scars on the scummy's forehead to be clearly visible, and the blood splashing back from the bead impact coated Roger's forearm.

Patty streamed blood from dozens of wounds. Individually, none were immediately dangerous to something her size, but all were deep and painful, and she was becoming increasingly frantic in her attacks, occasionally spinning in place to bring her tail into play. But the Boman had become more expert at avoiding her, or perhaps only those who'd already been experts survived on the blood-soaked ground around her. Whatever the explanation, the mass swarming in on her was mostly dodging her lunges and spins, charging in whenever she paused and dealing steadily mounting damage to her unprotected flanks.

Roger, Cord, and the two Marines had managed to limit even those attacks, but it was becoming increasingly difficult, and more and more of the scummies made it through on every rush. As the intensity of their private battle mounted, the *flar-ta*, her riders, and the scummies attacking her had become so totally focused on the area around her that none of them even saw the deploying cavalry until the first volley hammered into the Boman in front of the Marines. The heavy pistol balls smashed through the packed mass of raiders, driving in against the hard-pressed shield wall, and the tribesmen found themselves once again faced by a flank attack—this one coming straight into their backs from their main direction of retreat.

The bead cannon was still plowing its dreadful holes through their ranks, the rampaging beast on their left flank had laid low dozens of their finest warriors, and the cheating bastards to their front refused to come out from behind their cowardly shields. It was just too much, and the tribesmen turned away from the Marine line and ran up the trail to escape the cavalry charge.

But that wasn't going to happen. The Northern riders slammed into them like an avalanche, firing pistols and spitting them on lances.

Rastar's charge carried his troopers through the caravan, where their ranks were broken by the still-milling packbeasts. Then they turned around and charged back into the fray, dropping their lances and drawing their swords for the best part of any cavalry skirmish. Nor had the Marines been sitting on their hands. As soon as the tribesmen broke, the company began to move forward, cutting down any resistance. The remaining clots of tribesmen in front of them were easily dealt with, and the Marines charged over their bodies to hit the Boman around the engaged cavalry force.

That cavalry was now bogged down, but it didn't seem to care. The mounted Mardukans were hacking at their enemies, seemingly intent on nothing other than killing them. Even as the tribesmen pulled members of the troop off their mounts, the leaders refused to retreat. They'd come to kill Boman, and they went about the business with grim ferocity.

Patty's assigned mahout had survived the first part of the battle by the skin of his horns, and he knew it. So when Roger ordered him to charge to the aid of the embattled cavalry, the Mardukan decided that nothing was worth heading back into *that*, and slid silently off the packbeast.

Roger snarled in exasperation and climbed into his old, accustomed place and patted the beast on the soft spot under its armored shield.

"Come on, Patty!" he yelled. "Time to get some of our own back!"

The tired but willing *flar-ta* snorted at the familiar touch, and rumbled into a blood-streaming trot. Six tons of mad were about to hit the engaged tribesmen and let the chips fall where they might.

Rastar kneed his *civan*, and the beast did a hopping kick that killed the Boman trying to hamstring it.

The prince, however, was having less luck. The charge had broken through the damned Boman, but it hadn't managed to shatter them cleanly, and barbarians seemed to be everywhere. Worse, they were still fighting hard, despite having been caught between two sets of enemies. Oh, many of them had fled, but others—lured by the obvious wealth of the caravan—had stayed, and the holdouts were intent on killing his men.

Like any cavalrymen, Rastar and his troopers knew that their greatest assets were shock and mobility. Standing cavalry sacrificed almost all of its advantages over infantry, but Honal's force was too bogged down to retreat. Unable to break free and reorganize for a fresh charge, they could only stand and fight, trying to cover their occasional unseated brothers and hoping against hope that the stupid barbarians would realize they were *beaten*.

The prince spun his *civan* in place again, taking the face off of one of the barbarians trying to pull him off from the side. There were two others on the far side, but he was one of those incredibly rare and gifted Mardukans who were quad-dexterous, and that had stood him in good stead in many engagements like this one, where the ability to cover his *civan* was paramount. He whipped all four sabers around himself in a complex and lethal pattern . . . then looked up in half-stunned amazement as a *pagee* thundered through the middle of the battle, bugling like a *pagathar*.

Three humans and a tribesman of some sort were on its back, but they were letting the *pagee* do most of the fighting, and Rastar could see why. The beast tore into the Boman like the poor at a holiday feast, attacking with all the ferocity of a *pagathar* as it gored and trampled its way through the barbarians.

It seemed to be able to distinguish friend from foe as it stepped delicately across a fallen Northerner, somehow managing to avoid crushing him in the press. Or perhaps it was the driver. He seemed to be controlling the beast with knees and voice alone, shouting commands in some sort of gibberish and laying down a heavy fire from a pistol which widened the prince's eyes even in the midst of battle. Rastar loved pistols, especially since he could fire virtually simultaneously with all four hands. But the problem with them was that they had only one shot per barrel. He had twelve double-barreled pistols scattered about his harness and gear, and, at the moment, every one of them had been discharged.

This pistol, however, was spitting shot after shot. Its ammunition seemed limitless, but then he saw the rider pause momentarily, replace a container in the grip, and then start firing again. So easily! In an instant, the weapon was reloaded. With a pistol like that, he could plow through the Boman like a scythe through barleyrice!

He killed another of the barbarians almost absentmindedly, leaning to the side to scissor the bastard's neck with the two razor-sharp sabers in his false-hands. He might as well not even have bothered; the Boman were running.

He waved to Honal, who lifted a bloody saber in response and ordered his company into pursuit. The *civan*-mounted force would harry the enemy into the ground; if a hand of the Boman remained alive by dark, it would be a surprise.

Now to go bargain with these "humans." Despite his confident words to Honal, Rastar was far from certain that a bargain really could be struck, but at least now he could haggle with references in hand instead of a begging bowl.

Armand Pahner gave the Mardukan cavalryman a closed-mouth smile.

"We appreciate the help," he said as the big scummy swung down from his bipedal mount. "Especially since I think you're the folks we chased out of Ran Tai."

"I would like to say that we came to aid you because we're honorable warriors and couldn't just watch the barbarians destroy your caravan." Rastar removed his helmet and rubbed his horns. "Unfortunately, the fact is that we need a job. We'd like to hire on as caravan guards, and you—" he gestured at the carnage about them and the handful of survivors from the original force of caravan guardsmen "—clearly need more of them."

"Ah." Pahner cocked his head and contemplated the Mardukan for a moment and felt temptation stir. These people were the first Mardukan troops he'd yet seen who'd actually fought as a cohesive, organized force rather than a collection of individualists. They obviously had rough edges, by human standards, but they were head and shoulders above their nearest native competition.

"You're right," he said after a moment, "but there was no gold in the mine. We're as low on cash as you must be."

"We're not expensive," the prince said with a rueful grunt. "And there will be great profit to this caravan when it reaches Diaspra. *If* it reaches Diaspra. We can be paid then."

"How much?" Pahner asked. "When we reach Diaspra?"

"For the rest of the trip?" The prince rubbed the crest of his helmet with one finger. "Board and tack during the trip. Two gold K'Vaernian astar per trooper at completion. Three for each one lost. Five for the commander, and ten for myself." He looked at the pistol at the human's belt. "Although I would personally consider trading quite a bit of that for one of those pistols," he added with a grunt of laughter.

Pahner pulled out his *bisti* root and shaved off a sliver. He offered the leader a slice, but it was refused, so he put the remaining root away while he contemplated the offer. The K'Vaernian coin was about thirty grams in weight. They had more than enough hidden in the packs to meet the Mardukan's price, but he hadn't been born yesterday. Nobody ever went for the first offer.

"One gold astar each, two for the fallen, three for the commander, five for you, and you handle the board," he retorted.

The Mardukan drew himself up and appeared ready to snarl some curse, but paused. It seemed to Pahner that he wasn't used to haggling, which didn't make much sense for a mercenary, but finally he made a hand gesture of negation.

"I agree to the coin, but you must handle board. One sedant of grain per day per trooper. Five sedant per *civan*. An additional ten for our followers, and five for the commander and ten for myself. And it is not negotiable; we'll have to find another employer if we can't have the board."

Now it was Pahner's turn to be taken back. He wasn't sure they had enough barleyrice to support that all the way to Diaspra, and he chewed his *bisti* for a few moments, then shrugged.

"We didn't bring that much chow. And I don't know a way around that. If the damned Boman are on this side of the Chasten now, we can't afford to go back to Ran Tai."

"You might have to," the cavalryman told him soberly. "These are only the outriders, not the main horde, but they swarm like maggots as they advance. The way might be impassable."

"If I have to, I'll unload the armor," the captain said with a feral grin. "I've got enough power and spares for two uses of it. This might be one of them . . . and if I unass our powered armor, don't tell me about 'impassable'!"

The Mardukan regarded him levelly, then clapped hands in resignation.

"I have never heard of 'powered' armor, but you humans have many things we've never heard of, so perhaps you *can* fight your way through. Yet from what I've seen of the rest of your weapons, it still seems clear to me that you will require the aid of a force of guards who fight with discipline and order, and that is what we of the Vasin are. So, what can you afford for board? We wish to go to Diaspra also, mainly because we know they'll be hiring. But . . . we're out of food. Completely. We have nothing to bring to the table."

Pahner held the native's eyes, chewing steadily on his *bisti* root, then nodded finally.

"Okay, we can work with that. We'll share as available, and strip the caravan if we have to. Keeping the fighters in shape is the priority, but nobody starves. How's that?"

The Mardukan commander clapped hands in agreement and held one out, palm outward.

"Agreed. Everyone to share; no one to starve."

"To a long and fruitful alliance, then," Pahner said with a smile, matching the gesture of agreement. Then he chuckled grimly. "Now comes the fun part."

CHAPTER EIGHT

Roger slid off of Patty's back and caught one end of the plasma cannon as it dropped, then handed it off to Gronningen as the plasma gunner jumped to the ground and the mahout moved the packbeast back. The *flar-ta* still hadn't recovered fully from her wounds, and more had been added in the last three weeks, so the prince was keeping her back from this little skirmish.

He waved to the mahouts as the rest of the convoy pounded past towards one of the ubiquitous cities of the lowlands in the near distance. This one sat on a high promontory by the river where the now broad and powerful Chasten descended a series of cascades before reaching the coastal plains, and unless he was sorely mistaken, it must be Diaspra itself. The city was enormous in comparison to the towns of the Hurtan and Hadur regions and sprawled off the promontory and down onto the plains, with its outer portions protected from floods by its massive walls, flood control canals, and sturdy dikes.

It obviously looked good to the packbeast drovers. They were goading their mounts into a clumsy canter, and the Mardukan children packed on the backs of the beasts looked at Roger oddly as he waved. A few waved back, but with an almost puzzled air, for it was not a Mardukan custom.

The Marines had peeled off from the caravan as well, and now they aligned themselves on the road with a handful of their own, steadier *flar-ta* at their backs. Their chosen location was a narrow way between two thick groves of trees about a thousand meters from the wall, presumably left to provide firewood when the other approaches to the city were brushed back. The pursuing barbarians would be forced to face the Marine line or try flanking it through the heavy wood. No doubt the flank would eventually be turned, but by then the noncombatants would be through the gates of the city and the Marines would be able to *really* maneuver. With the aid of their *flar-ta*, the human force would be able to play hard to get all the way to the walls.

Pahner paced slowly up and down behind his line, gently masticating his *bisti* root, and nodded to Roger. He'd wanted the prince to accompany the noncombatants into the city, but he hadn't bothered to say so. Whether he liked it or not, he'd finally resigned himself to the fact that if there was a fight, Roger would be in the thick of it. As a matter of fact, he *didn't* like it one bit, but that was the bodyguard in him. The Marine in him had to admit (very privately, where Roger would never hear it) that it was far more satisfying to guard someone who refused to hide behind the bodies and lives of other people . . . however difficult that made it to protect the insufferable, headstrong, and often *irritating* someone in question.

Roger himself trotted forward to the line with Cord and Denat in hot pursuit. The two Mardukans had spent the last three weeks learning how to use the large shields the humans had introduced, and the reason was apparent as a storm of throwing axes descended on the human line. The two four-armed Mardukans threw up a double set of shields: one for themselves, and the other for the heedless prince who was carefully judging the approach of the barbarian forces. Roger nodded his thanks to Cord, and looked over at the sergeant major.

"About two hundred or so, don't you think, Sergeant Major?"

"About that, Sir," the NCO replied. "I'm still trying to divide my arm count by four."

Roger smiled and dialed up the magnification of his helmet display, then called up his combat program and put a crosshair on the head of the apparent leader.

"Your call, Smaj."

"Bravo Company will hurl javelins!" the sergeant major announced in a voice which would have carried through the teeth of a hurricane. "*Draw!* Take aim! *Throw!* Out swords!"

The hail of throwing spears didn't stop the barbarians, but it did break up their ranks, and Roger accompanied the javelin volley with three shots from his bead pistol. Like all the rest of the ammunition, pistol ammo was in too short a supply to waste, but Roger very seldom "wasted" ammunition, and his three carefully placed rounds dropped the barbarians' leaders in their tracks. Whether that was good or bad remained to be seen, of course. The company had already discovered that Boman warriors were altogether too prone to a sort of berserk fighting madness once combat began, and sometimes it was only the leaders who would—or could—call for a retreat.

This scummy force had a few arquebuses, and since it wasn't raining (at the moment), the gunners came to the fore as the force approached the humans. There were only six of them, but the rest of the band halted as they laboriously adjusted their waxy, smoking matches and aimed in the general direction of the human company. Three of the firearms, obviously captured from more civilized original owners, were beautifully made, with fancy brass inlay work which had seen better days, but all of them looked incredibly clumsy to a modern Marine. Which didn't necessarily mean they were ineffective . . . assuming that they actually hit something.

The gunners blew on the ends of their matches until the glowing embers satisfied them, then popped open the hermetically sealed priming pans which Marduk's humid climate made essential. They glanced at the priming powder, then grasped the leverlike triggers which would pivot the serpentine metal arms which held the slow matches and dip their glowing ends into the powder.

The weapons were scarcely accurate at anything beyond point-blank range. Of course, this *was* point-blank range, but the Marines were utterly contemptuous of the threat. Cord and Denat ducked behind the humans' line, but the Marines shouted insults at the Boman and actually pulled their shields out of line to expose their bodies to fire.

The reason for their contempt became apparent after the volley.

The blast from the relatively few weapons filled the space between the Mardukan and human lines with thick smoke, but it was clear that only a single Marine had been hit. One fatality out of six wasn't a bad average for a Mardukan arquebus volley, so the gunners' fellows shouted approvingly and sprang into a charge. But they checked when the single trooper who'd gone down heaved herself to her feet, swearing, and readied her shield once more.

"Now, now, Briana," Roger admonished Corporal Kane. "I'm sure that their mothers at least *knew* their fathers."

"Yes, Sir," the corporal said, bringing her shield back around to the front. "If you say so. But I still say I'm gonna gut that stupid bastard. Those damned bullets *smart*."

Roger had to agree. Mardukan arquebuses were wildly outsized compared to any human-scaled weapon, man-packed cannon that fired quarter-kilo balls. The projectiles' velocity was high at short range (which was to say, at any range at which a hit could realistically be anticipated), as well, which imparted a tremendous kick when one hit the kinetic reactive armor of the chameleon suits. But that velocity was what made the chameleon suits effective against them, for the Marines' uniforms were designed for protection against modern, high-speed projectiles. They were relatively ineffective against *low*-speed weapons, like spears, swords, or throwing axes, but arquebus balls were something else. The suits not only "hardened" when struck by the rounds, but distributed the kinetic energy across their entire surface and even around the back. Despite her understandable outrage, the impact was spread widely enough that the most the corporal would suffer was a few bruises.

The Mardukans checked for a moment at the sight of the unexpected resurrection, then charged forward anyway, screaming their battle cries and swinging their battle axes. Many of the barbarians used two axes at a time, and they came windmilling into the human line like four-armed juggernauts.

The Marines were ready for them. Over the last few weeks, they'd fought off repeated small attacks by the roaming tribes who formed the vanguard of the Boman. This was the largest one yet, but it would prove no more of a challenge than the others.

The plasma cannon rolled forward a few steps, placing its barrel just beyond the Marine line as the troopers to either side moved back to give it room, and fired point blank. The belch of ions scorched the fronts of the Marines' wood and iron shields, but otherwise left them unaffected. The same could not be said for the Mardukans.

The plasma cannon had been set at relatively low power, both to conserve energy in its power pack and also because its targets were too frail to require anything more energetic. It was still powerful enough to knock out a modern tank, however, and it tore through the mass of tribesmen like a fusion-powered brimstone battering ram. A ten-meter-wide gap appeared as if by magic straight through the center of their formation. There weren't even any bodies—only a smoking hell-hole bordered by blackened, half-consumed skeletons and screaming barbarians, writhing and twisting insanely with the agony of the flash burns seared across their bodies.

There was no time for a second shot . . . or for the howling tribesmen to break off their attack. They were moving too quickly, and the range was too short, for them to change their minds. They had no choice but to carry through with their charge, which actually was the best thing they could have done. At least it got them in close enough to prevent the hell weapon from effortlessly incinerating all of them!

Unfortunately, the fact that closing with their enemies was their "best" option didn't necessarily make it a *good* one.

The plasma cannon pulled back and its flankers closed ranks once more with perfect timing just as the remnants of the shattered formation hit the human shield wall and the Boman learned another lesson: a disciplined wall of shields shrugs off windmilling axes like rain.

Bravo Company was the product of an extremely advanced, high-tech society, but the Marines had been taught in a brutal school since their arrival on Marduk. Only a few of them had really been anything close to what a Mardukan might consider proficient with edged steel upon their arrival here, but those few had passed on all the tricks they knew. Other techniques had been learned the hard way, and Armand Pahner and Eva Kosutic had planned their tactics and training with the fundamentals firmly in mind: keep the shield up, and stab low.

Even as the thundering axes struck downward onto their hard-held shields, the Marines stabbed forward through the narrow gaps between them, aiming for the bellies and gonads of their enemies. The Mardukans had a tremendous reach advantage over the humans, but they were forced to step in close to hack down at the Marines' defensive barrier, and when they did, they also stepped directly into the sweep of the humans' weapons.

The result was a slaughter. The Mardukans, faced by a radically new approach to fighting and unable to find a way through the shield wall, found themselves slipping in the spilled intestines of their own front line instead. Kosutic watched the entire battle dispassionately. She'd become expert at gauging Mardukan morale over the last few weeks, and she saw the point of balance when the barbarians began to waver.

She glanced at Captain Pahner, who nodded. Time to finish this.

"*Bravo Company will advance!*" she called. She looked to the woods to her right, where there was a flash of metal. "Prepare to advance on cadence. *In step! HUT!*"

The company moved forward, calling the time, short swords and spears stabbing with every step, and the Mardukan tribesmen found themselves driven back. The alternative to retreat was to spit themselves on those dreadful knives the humans wielded.

The plasma cannon had killed perhaps twenty percent of the total Boman force, but the remaining barbarians still outnumbered the Marines by three-to-one, and despite the efficiency of the humans' combat technique, they hadn't really taken many casualties yet in hand-to-hand. They'd still suffered more than the Marines, who'd taken *no* casualties, but the battle was effectively a stalemate, with the edge in quality on Bravo Company's side, and quantity overwhelmingly on the Boman's side.

It came down to attrition and morale . . . but that was easy enough to change. Kosutic looked over at the captain once more, and Pahner nodded in response and keyed his radio.

"Now would be good, Rastar," the communicator clipped to the Mardukan's harness said, and the Therdan prince carefully depressed the talking switch.

"Right-oh," he responded in Standard English. Roger had started using the expression around him a good bit, and Rastar knew it was some sort of joke, but he liked it anyway. He looked over at Honal and wrinkled the skin over one eye in another human expression. "Shall we, cousin?"

The guard commander grunted in laughter and gave a tooth-showing human-style grin.

"Yes, cousin. Let's." He looked at his force and drew his saber. "*Sheffan!*" he cried, slapping the flank of his *civan* with the flat of his blade. Time to show these barbarian bastards what it meant to get in the way of the riders of the North.

The one worry the travelers had had, that the city might not open its gates to them, turned out to be moot. The square beyond those gates was lined with cheering townsfolk, and the guardsmen manning them waved the Marines and their Mardukan allies enthusiastically through.

In fact, the humans found themselves forced to form a perimeter around their packbeasts to hold back the cheering crowds. After a few moments' struggle, the Northern cavalry pushed through to join them, using their occasionally snapping *civan* to open up a space around the human contingent and their animals. It was as well that they had, for the shouts and high-pitched whistles of the ecstatic Mardukans bounced back and forth between the stone curtain wall and the city's structures. The enclosure trapped the bedlam, turning it into a hot, close maelstrom in which all sanity seemed to have been lost as the city guards slammed the gates behind the new arrivals.

The boom of the closing gates could barely be heard over the thunder of the locals, but it still startled Patty, and the overwrought *flar-ta* let out a low rumble and slapped her feet up and down on the cobbles, waving her horns back and forth at the pressing crowd.

"Ho, girl!" Roger yelled over the frenzied uproar, scratching her under her armored shield and patting her on the shoulder. "Steady!"

The huge beast uttered a half-furious, half-querulous bugle, but it was obvious that she hovered on the brink of a berserk response. In another moment she would charge the crowd like a six-ton bull in a china shop, and Pahner shook his head and keyed his helmet.

"Roger, try to keep her under control!" he said quickly, and patted his pockets until he came up with a flash grenade, set the timer for a three-second delay, and threw it straight up in the air.

The tremendous flash and crack of the human weapon had become normal to the packbeasts, who paid no attention to it. But the intense report, magnified by the echoing walls, shocked the crowd into momentary silence broken only by the low rumble of Patty's prebattle fury.

In the hush that followed, a group of guards clad in chain mail and plate pushed their way through the crowd, escorting a pair of elderly Mardukans. At their appearance, the crowd began to fall reluctantly back from the caravan. A few still cheered, but were quickly hushed into silence by their fellows.

Roger waited for several moments, until he was confident that Patty had calmed down at least some, then waved for the head mahout to relieve him on her back and slid to the ground. He walked across to where Pahner stood awaiting the delegation and smiled at the Marine.

"I think they're happy to see us."

"Too happy," the captain replied sourly. "Nobody is that pleased to see the Corps unless their ass is caught in a crack."

"Which means ours is, as well," Roger said. "Right?"

"What else is pocking new?" Poertena muttered, then looked up at his glowering CO and swallowed hastily. "Sir?"

The captain glowered at the armorer for another long moment, but finally relented.

"Nothing, Poertena," he said, shaking his head. "Nothing new in that at all. In fact . . ."

". . . it's getting really old," Roger finished.

"Yep," the company commander said as the delegation finally made it through the cordon of shield-wielding Marines. "Real old," he added, holding out his hand palm up in Mardukan greeting.

The delegation looked terribly pleased to see them.

Terribly.

CHAPTER NINE

Gratar, the priest-king of Diaspra, rolled up the document in front of him and crumpled it in his true-hands as he looked at the human visitors. They did not seem happy at the news he'd just imparted.

"So there's no way to the sea?" Roger asked, just to be sure that the information wasn't getting garbled.

"None that is clear." The answer came from the local guard commander, Bogess. The old Mardukan was technically one of the two water priests who held seats on the city council (the other council members were all merchants), but he wore chain mail and the back and breast from the heavy plate armor that was his normal gear. "The Boman swept down within the last ten-day and have encircled the city. Even before then, we had word that the city of Bastar, the port at the mouth of the Chasten, had fallen. Even if you could win down the river, there would be nothing there for you."

Pahner grunted.

"I don't care what city we get to, but we have to cross the ocean. Our destination is on the far side, and the K'Vaernian Sea is our shortest way to the ocean."

The locals at the table traded looks.

"There is nothing on the other side of the water," King Gratar said carefully. "The ocean is an eternal expanse of demon-filled water, placed there by the God to guard the shores of the World Island."

The priest-king's concern for their safety—or perhaps it was for their sanity—was obvious. The local prelate seemed determined to be friendly, despite their heretical notions about just what an ocean was, and the company's appearance immediately after the city's aqueduct had been cut had already been hailed as a sign from their god.

Pahner opened his mouth to reply, but O'Casey laid a warning hand on his arm.

"Perhaps we'll deal with that problem when we reach the sea," she said calmly. "Are there *any* cities on the sea that have held out against the Boman?"

"K'Vaern's Cove," Rastar said instantly. "It could hold out for the rest of eternity."

"You only hope that," Bogess said. "Surely K'Vaern's Cove fell with the rest of the Northern states?"

"It hadn't when we headed this way," the leader of the Northern mercenaries replied.

He'd been looking better since arriving in the city. Once the humans had gotten to know him and his troopers, they'd figured out fairly quickly that the Vasin certainly weren't barbarians, whatever the denizens of Ran Tai might have thought. And once they'd reached Diaspra, they'd found out just how true that was, for it turned out that several thousand troopers from Therdan, Sheffan, and the other city-states of the League of the North had straggled into Diaspra, where they'd reinforced the local forces. Those troopers had been almost pitifully glad to see Rastar alive, and even more so to see how many women and children he and Honal's guardsmen had gotten out. As soon as they'd learned the Prince of Therdan was in the city, the survivors had transferred their allegiance, giving him a quite respectable force and his seat at the table.

"Furthermore," Rastar went on now, "many of the troopers from the League cities have told me that K'Vaern's Cove holds out still. It has enormous granaries—big enough, it's said, to withstand siege for three or even four years if it must—and if that's not enough, it can hold out indefinitely by importing food by sea. More, the peninsula is protected as much by the sea about it as by its walls, and the Boman aren't going to be able to defeat the K'Vaernian Navy. No, K'Vaern's Cove is still there," he finished.

"Well, our granaries are *not* full," the priest-king said, crumpling the damning report once more. "We were unable to get in the harvest before the Boman struck, nor are we a well-prepared border city whose storerooms are kept filled in anticipation of war. Our fighters, especially with the help of the Northern forces, have held out so far, but we have only a few months' food, and the Boman squat on our fields. If we cannot harvest, we will starve, and they know it."

"They're awaiting the Hompag Rains," Bogess said gloomily. "They should start any day now. Once the rains abate and the land dries, they'll return. And that will be the end of Diaspra."

"Okay, okay," Pahner said, shaking his head. He wasn't sure what the Hompag Rains were, but first things first. "Let's not get negative. First of all, I don't know how familiar you are with sieges. Have you taken control of the granaries?" he asked the guard commander.

"No," Bogess said sourly. "The granaries are privately owned. We can't control them, and the price of barleyrice has already gotten out of hand."

Pahner shook his head again. "Okay, we need to talk about that." He looked around at the small counsel. "Are any of you familiar with sieges?"

"Not really," Grath Chain replied. He was one of the junior council members, one of its many merchants, and his expression was sour as he made a sign of negation. "We've usually managed to avoid wars."

"Usually by swindling the other side," Honal said in a stage whisper.

"It wasn't we who swindled the Boman and started this whole mess!" Bogess snapped. The old warrior's face twitched like a rat in a fury. "It was not *we* who brought this pestilence down upon us!"

"No, it was another scum-sucking Southerner!" the Northern cavalry commander shot back hotly. "Or have you forgotten Sindi?"

"Wait!" Pahner barked as the entire council chamber began to erupt in argument. "We only need to decide one thing at this council: do we want to survive, or do we want to die?"

He glared around the room, and most of the Mardukans turned aside from the heat of his fury.

"That's the only thing we need to know," he went on in a grating voice. "If we want to live, we're going to put aside these arguments and forget the niceties of normal business and do the things we need to do to survive." He turned to the king. "Now, Your Excellency, do you want to live?"

"Of course I do," the priest-king replied. "What's your point?"

"My point is that what I'm hearing is 'I can't,' 'we can't,' and 'it's not my fault,'" the Marine captain told him. "What we need to *start* hearing is 'we can' and 'can do.' Attitude is nearly half the battle in a situation like this."

"What do you mean by 'the niceties of normal business'?" Grath Chain asked suspiciously. "Would one of those things be seizing the privately owned grain?"

"Not at all. But we are going to have to make plenty of decisions that aren't going to be liked, and we can't hold a meeting for every decision and come to a group consensus. You have a problem here, and we have it also. There's no way out of the city, and you don't have enough food for an extended siege. That means we're going to have to bring the barbarians to a decisive battle."

"They won't attack the city," Bogess said wearily. "We've tried and tried to get them to do so. No chance."

"Then we'll have to leave the city with a large enough force to bring them to battle and pin them down," the Marine said. "If we take out a large force, will they attack it?"

"Yes," the king said. "But they'll also destroy it. We've lost half our army trying to fight them for the fields. They'll attack mercilessly as soon as they can concentrate on you outside the walls."

"So we won't have to chase them down?" Kosutic asked in surprise. "I thought we'd have to chase them all over Hell and gone to pin them down."

"Not this group," Rastar said with a grimace. "The Southerners call them all Boman, but this is really the Wespar tribe. You can tell by the tribal markings. The Wespar are uncivilized, even in comparison to the other Boman, and their tribal leader is Speer Mon, a pure idiot even by the standards of *his* tribe. All you'd have to do is say 'meet me here,' and he would."

"Well, they've been smart enough to avoid the walls of the city," Bogess said defensively.

"That's because we bled them white in the north," Rastar said with a grimace. "They learned to feint and hold the fields against us by bitter experience. If we'd had our full grain rations, we'd be holding out still."

"And what happened there, O Prince of the North?" Grath Chain sneered. "What happened to your vaunted stores? The stores that your precious League used as an excuse for its extortionate tolls?"

Rastar was quiet for a long moment. The moment was long enough for the Council to become uncomfortable, and some of them shifted on the cushions scattered around the low table. Finally, the Mardukan prince looked up from his hands at the councilor.

"If you wish to live out the day," he said very calmly, "keep a civil tongue."

"That's no answer, and I'll have you know that no northern barbar—" the councilor started, then froze as he realized he was looking down the barrels of five pistols.

"Put it down, Roger," Rastar said with a harsh chuckle, then stabbed Grath Chain with an eye as cold as the muzzles of his own pistols. "Here is the answer, *feck*-beast. The stores were poisoned. Probably by agents from Sindi; we too had 'offended' that thrice-accursed prince.

"But," he added with a human tooth-showing grin as he put his pistols away, "someone brought that agent to our city. It wasn't a trader from Sindi, for they'd been banned from all the cities of the Northern League." He grinned again at the councilor. "When I find out who it was that brought that agent to my city, I will kill that person. I will do it without asking any permission, or giving any warning. I will do it on the slightest thread of evidence. So I would suggest that you make sure your accounts are in order, *feck*-beast."

The shaken councilor looked to the king.

"I shouldn't have to put up with this from northern barbarians!"

"Your Excellency," Roger said, standing up, "we need to come to an understanding."

The king hesitated, but nodded for him to continue.

"We're in a 'war to the knife,'" the prince said. "What does that mean?" He gestured at Rastar. "Your Northern comrades have told you already. The Boman are here to stay. They'll continue to bleed you until you fall like a hamstrung *pagee*, and then they'll swarm over you like *atul*."

He looked around the council, daring one of them to meet his eye.

"Now, we can win against them. My people have been in wars like this many, many times, and we have a great deal of expertise to offer you. But it has to be a partnership. We'll tell you what we think you need to do. If you do it, we, all of us, might survive. If you don't, we, all of us, will die. And your women and children as well." He looked over at Rastar. "Correct?"

"Oh, yes," the Northerner said bleakly. "The Wespar have no use for 'shit-sitters.'" He looked over at Cord, sitting silently behind the prince, and the tribesman returned the look blandly.

Grath Chain began to sputter something, but the priest-king gestured the angry councilor to silence.

"What do you suggest?" he asked.

"Captain?" Roger invited, resuming his seat.

"Put guards on all the granaries," Pahner said crisply. "Dole out bulk foodstuffs in prescribed portions at fixed prices. This will not only prevent price gouging but prevent hoarding and stretch the available supply. Begin training not only the regular forces but all able-bodied males in new fighting techniques to be used against the tribesmen. Force an engagement at a time and place of our choosing, and destroy the bulk of the barbarian force."

"Where do we get the soldiers?" Bogess asked. "It takes years of training with the sword to make a warrior, and even then better than half are lost in the first battle, if it's a fierce one," he said grimly, and Pahner shrugged.

"I won't say that our methods can make warriors out of them, but we can make soldiers in a few months. It's mostly a matter of training them to obey orders unquestioningly and to stand. If they do those two things, the way we fight can be taught in less than a month."

"Impossible," Grath Chain scoffed. "No one can train a warrior in a month!"

"I didn't say anything about warriors," Pahner told the merchant coldly. "We'll be training *soldiers*, and that's a hell of a lot more dangerous than warriors are. The only thing we need is able bodies." He turned to Bogess. "Can you find several thousand able-bodied men? Ones that can walk two hours with a heavy weight? Other than that, six limbs and a quarter brain is all we need."

Bogess grunted in laughter.

"That we can find, I believe." He turned to the priest-king. "Your Excellency? May we have the Laborers of God?"

Gratar looked pensive.

"The Hompag Rains come soon, and the damage is already extensive. Who will repair the dikes and canals? Who will clean the face of the God?"

Bogess turned to the humans, who were clearly confused.

"The Laborers of God are simple men, common folk. They labor on the Works of God, the canals, dikes, and temples of our city. There are many of them—they far outnumber the small Guard of God—and they're strong-backed laborers. Would they do?"

"Perfectly," Pahner said with a note of enthusiasm. "I assume they already have some sort of structure? That they're broken down into different divisions or companies or something?"

"Yes, they're separated by districts and responsibility," the cleric seated beside Gratar said. The heavyset Mardukan had remained silent throughout the entire discussion so far, but now he leaned forward to meet Pahner's gaze. "I am Rus From, the Bishop of Artificers. The groups are irregular in size, depending on what their responsibilities are."

"And what of those responsibilities?" Grath Chain snapped. "Who will repair the dikes and canals? Who will insure that the face of the God is clean?"

"Your Excellency," Roger responded quietly, "who will do those things if the Boman lay you waste? This is an evil time for your city, one in which you must choose between lesser and greater evils if you are to survive. Yes, repairing and maintaining your city and its temples is important, but you built those artifacts once. You can build them once again . . . if you—and your city—live."

"I suppose," the priest-king mused, then drew a deep breath. "Once again, your truths win through, Prince Roger. Very well. General Bogess, you are authorized to take command of the Laborers of God and turn them into Warriors of God. I suggest that you put the leadership of the Laborers under Sol Ta for this. Chan Roy will understand. Chan is getting old, and Sol Ta has much fire. And may the Lord of Water be with us."

"Thank you, Your Excellency," Captain Pahner said quietly. "We'll do our best to save your beautiful city."

"Hmmm," an older councilor said, rubbing his horns. "I was about to suggest that you'd contradicted yourself on the seizure of grain, Captain. But you didn't. You danced a fine line instead, didn't you? You said you wouldn't seize the granaries, but you didn't say anything about putting guards on them."

"The merchants will still make a profit, just not as large a profit as they thought they were going to. However, it will stretch out the resources and allow us time to train up a force."

"Two months," the old councilor said after a moment. "That's how long until the peasants must begin bringing in the harvest. If we wait longer than that, we might as well all cut our own throats."

"Two months should be more than enough time," Pahner said.

"Good." The councilor nodded at the human, then touched his own chest. "Gessram Kar. I'm one of those shifty merchants you're about to fleece. One of the largest ones, I might add."

"Glad to hear it," Pahner said with a broad smile. "If you don't object, no one else should."

"Perhaps," the merchant grunted. "But I wonder who you'll find to enforce this edict, hmmm?"

"T'ey pocking t'ieves, Sir," Poertena said looking at his pad. "Look, up in Ran Tai, where t'ey can' even *grow* barleyrice, it go for two K'Vaernian copper a kusul."

"At least now we know where all this reference to K'Vaern comes from," Roger observed, then grimaced. "Sorry, Poertena. You were saying?"

"T'ey pocking t'ieves is what I sayin', Sir," the Pinopan repeated. "I find t'ree prices on barleyrice. T'ey between fifteen copper and two *silver!*"

"That would be twenty-to-one on the high end, right?" Pahner asked.

"Yes, Sir. I t'ink t'ey should be around tee same cost as at Ran Tai. Reason is, Ran Tai already got a shortage, so inflation index be about right."

"Inflation index?" Roger repeated with a chuckle.

"Yes, Sir. It tee adjusted cost o' materials in a situation o' limited supply." Poertena glanced at the so far silent chief of staff who gave him a quick and unnoticed wink.

"I know what it is," Roger said. "It's just . . . uh . . ."

"What?" the Pinopan asked.

"Never mind. So, the price should be fixed at about two coppers a kusul? What about other foodstuffs?"

"I got some numbers from Ran Tai, Sir," Poertena said, gesturing at his pad. "Most of t'em're already inflationary, except tee spice. An' most of tee bulk supply for t'at in tee city is on our caravan. I figure out somet'ing for t'at."

"I picked up some information on that from our fellow travelers in the caravan," O'Casey offered. The now whipcord thin chief of staff glanced at her notes. "I think you can use it with the kusul of barleyrice as a base."

"Well, groups of guards have moved to secure all the bulk vendors' supplies," Pahner said. "We'll need to take an inventory and set up a rationing scheme. And I'll also want you to take charge of arming the militia we'll be raising, Poertena."

"Yes, Sir," the armorer replied, his face getting longer and longer.

"Sorry, Poertena," Roger told him with a grin. "We'll have to cut back on the poker games."

"Yes, Sir," the Pinopan said yet again. "But we gonna have problems wit' tee weapons. T'is ain't really a production center. It's a transshipmen' point. Tee caravans come here and load t'eir supplies on barges to send t'em downriver."

It took Pahner a moment to translate that. Then he frowned.

"So if it's not in a warehouse, we probably can't get it?"

"Pretty much, Sir," the armorer said, shaking his head. "We can' no' get steel armor made. T'ere ain't a armory in tee whole town."

"Then we'll have to make do with the shields, assegais, and pikes for the time being," the captain said. "We can have those made up quickly enough to do some good, unlike firearms. And even if we could get them made in time, I'm not about to rely on something as temperamental as a muzzle-loading matchlock in this kind of climate!"

The last sentence woke nods all around. Diaspra's Guard of God had several companies of arquebusiers, but they were essentially a defensive force. Like the huge, multiton hooped bombards made from welded iron bars which dotted the city's walls, their massed fire could be devastating from prepared positions (with overhead cover against the elements) along the city's fortified approaches, but a field battle under typical Mardukan conditions would be something else again. As a matter of fact, Pahner was already eying those arquebusiers as a potential source for the shield-and-assegai-armed companies of flankers his new army was going to require.

"As soon as we get somewhere that has a decent industry, though," the captain went on after a moment, "we're damned well going to see about having some breech-loading percussion rifles made."

"Is that going to be possible?" Roger asked. "I mean, there are a lot of steps between a matchlock arquebus and a breechloader. Spring steel comes to mind."

"Like the spring steel in Rastar's wheel locks?" Pahner asked, smiling faintly. "And have you looked at their pumps?" the Marine went on as the prince's expression turned suddenly thoughtful.

"Not in any depth," Roger admitted. "They have quite a few of them, and they seem pretty damned efficient. I noticed that much."

"Well, I *have* been noticing them, Your Highness—particularly since Eleanora commented on them back at Voitan. I even took one apart when you were running around in Ran Tai. These people have impeller pumps, and the ones in Deb Tar's mines were pneumatically driven."

"You mentioned that before," Roger agreed. "But what does it mean?"

"An impeller pump requires tight tolerances, Your Highness," O'Casey replied before Pahner could. "You have to be able to lathe, which they do with foot-pedal lathes. It also requires spring material—spring steel in most cases, here on Marduk, although that corrodes faster than the alloys we would use in the Empire. However, every basic technology you need for advanced black powder weapons is found in their pump industry. For that matter, as the captain just suggested, anyone who can build wheel locks can build more advanced lock mechanisms. What we call a 'flintlock' is actually a much less complicated device than a wheel lock. In fact, its advantage, and the thing that made it so important when it was introduced on Earth, was that its simplicity made it cheap enough that armies could afford to convert their infantry to it from the even simpler matchlock. Before that, only cavalry units carried wheel locks for exactly the same reason that Rastar and his troopers do—a matchlock is impractical for a mounted man to manage, and cavalry was considered important and prestigious enough to justify the purchase of specialized and expensive weapons for it."

"So we need to go where t'ey make tee pumps, Sir?" Poertena asked.

"That or one of the armories where the gunsmiths make wheel locks," Pahner agreed, then grinned and nodded at O'Casey. "On the other hand, the gunsmiths seem to guard their 'secrets' pretty zealously . . . and they make the pumps everywhere. They have to, with their climate. And I'd rather go somewhere where they have some genuine large-scale manufacturing industry. From what Rastar says, the local gunsmiths are both extremely expensive and pretty damned slow. The ones who make wheel locks spend a lot of time and effort on things like inlay work and decoration—just take a look at Rastar's toys! What we need is someone used to the practical requirements of mass production, or as close to it as anyone on this planet is going to come. When we find him, we'll give him a design for a rifle for the troops and have it produced in quantity. For Rastar's people, too."

"And let me guess," Roger said with a grimace. "That someone wouldn't happen to live in this K'Vaern's Cove, would he?"

"From what I've heard, he probably does, Your Highness," O'Casey said. "Diaspra is a theocracy, and for all that it's also a trading city, it seems fairly typical of the 'mañana attitude' we've seen everywhere else but New Voitan. That's why the Diasprans aren't going to be able to supply us with what we need. But to hear them tell it, this K'Vaern's Cove is the secular center of their known universe. I seem to be picking up a lot of respect for the K'Vaernians, even from the large number of people—mostly clerics—who obviously don't like them. But the Diasprans clearly regard them as not simply heathens, but very peculiar heathens, with all sorts of outrageous notions, including some sort of obsession with more efficient ways to do things, which is absolute anathema to something as inherently conservative as a theocratic priest-king's government. So, yes, the logical place to look for the sort of person the captain wants would have to be K'Vaern's Cove."

"Which means he's also right in the middle of this invasion," Roger pointed out. "How are we going to get there to talk to him?"

"Well, first we build us a little army here, then we head upcountry again," Pahner said. "Quickly." He grunted a laugh.

"You got anyt'ing more for me, Sir?" Poertena asked.

"No, Sarge. Thanks for your time," the prince said.

"It's corporal, Your Highness," the Pinopan reminded him. "But t'anks."

"Not any more," Roger said. "I think between the Captain and me, we probably have the juice to get a promotion approved."

"T'ank you, Sir," the armorer said, getting to his feet. "T'anks. I'm gonna turn in."

"Take off, Poertena," Pahner replied.

"Good night, Sirs," the little sergeant said, and headed out the door.

"That was well done, Roger," the Marine CO said when the door had closed.

"He's done a good job," the prince pointed out. "He's been working every night on getting our gear back in shape, and he and Kostas between them have been keeping track of all our supplies, as well. And now this job, without complaint. Well," he corrected himself with a smile, "not any *serious* complaints."

"Agreed," the captain said, then leaned back and scratched the tip of his nose thoughtfully.

"Getting back to the subject at hand," he went on after a moment, "this is a rich city, despite all of the Council's moaning, and this Laborers of God labor force looks top-notch so far. There's over four thousand of them, too." He shook his head. "I don't understand how any city can just set aside twenty percent of its productive male population as a labor force like this, either. Usually, societies like this use farmers in their off time for any required community labor."

"Eleanora?" Roger asked. "Got any suggestions?"

"It's the barleyrice production, of course," the chief of staff said. "Always look to basic production in societies like this, Roger."

"But there wasn't this labor surplus on the far side of the mountains," the prince replied. "Marshad had a fairly normal ratio, and so did Q'Nkok. And Ran Tai, for that matter."

"Ah, but Marshad and Q'Nkok didn't have draft animals like the *turom*. Aside from caravan use, the *flar-ta* might as well not exist as beasts of burden, but that's all they have on the far side of the Tarstens. And Ran Tai—as Poertena pointed out to us at the time—effectively imports all of its barleyrice," O'Casey reminded him with a smile. "I'd say that this place would probably be the center of a Mardukan Renaissance if it weren't locked up tight by the local theocracy."

She glanced at her notes and shook her head.

"The agriculture in this area is phenomenal. The *turom* gives them a remarkable advantage over Q'Nkok and Marshad, and what with the continuously mild weather, an efficient distribution system for nitrates, and excellent crop rotation, they have *five crops* of barleyrice every year. Five. And nearly as many crops of nearchicks and taters, not to mention three of apsimons. Each individual farmer is tremendously productive, which is why all those extra laborers are employed by the temple—they'd be out of work otherwise."

"But that condition has to have existed for some time," Roger said, shaking his head. "Shouldn't they have been pulled into other production areas by now? That's the normal reaction to technological improvement; one group is left performing the original function more efficiently, and within a generation the rest of the labor force is switched to other markets, usually new ones that become possible because of the freed labor."

"True." Eleanora smiled. "In fact, I'm delighted to see that you remember my lectures so well. In Diaspra's case, however, the society clearly reacted by taxing the farmers still on the land to establish a . . . well, call it a welfare system, and putting the out-of-work ones to work on temple projects. I suspect that if we had a time machine, we'd find that that reaction marked the beginning of the growth of the temple's secular power. And it was probably considered a 'temporary measure,' too."

"Aaargh," Roger groaned. "The only thing more permanent than a 'temporary measure' is 'stopgap spending.' But surely even here they must eventually have the labor shift to new technologies?"

"Not necessarily." The chief of staff waved her hands in a gesture that included the entire planet. "Marduk is a remarkably stable world. There's very little reason for technological improvement. Frankly, I'm surprised that they ever domesticated animals in the first place."

"There's a real lack of wheels," Pahner said in agreement. "There are wheeled carts near the cities, but that's about it. They have the concept—there are all sorts of wheels used in their pumping technology—but they don't use it for transport."

"It's all of a piece," O'Casey said with a quirky smile. "There's very little to drive improvements in this society, and the late Raj Hoomas notwithstanding, most of the city-states—the inland ones, at least—very rarely have major territorial competitions. Wars, yes—lots of those—but by human standards, those wars are pretty small potatoes. And they're not really what we'd call wars of conquest, either. Most of the city-states maintain professional armies to handle the fighting—and do the dying—which tends to insulate the general population from the consequences of combat. And the squabbles between cities are usually over caravan routes, mining sites, and that sort of thing, not over what you might call true life-or-death issues or because some local potentate suddenly got bitten by the notion of building himself some sort of empire. Their climate is fairly constant, too, so they don't have many times when large-scale weather patterns cause big migrations or force technological change. It's a very static society, so any major change probably gets swallowed up by the stasis. Which is probably a large part of the explanation for how devastating a large migration—like the Kranolta or the Boman—is when it finally comes along."

"What about the other cities in this area?" Roger asked.

"We'll have to see," O'Casey replied. "My guess from inference is that the states of Rastar's 'League of the North' were more or less parasitic defensive states. They protected the southern cities from the Boman and their fellow barbarians, and in return, they drew off the excess production from the city-states behind their shield. The next tier of states to the north, like this Sindi place, appear to have been secular despotisms, where the excess labor was involved in glorification of the leadership. I suppose that sort of mind-set might help fuel a potential Caesar or Alexander's ambitions, but so far I just don't know enough to hazard a guess as to whether or not it has, although some of the things Rastar's said about Sindi itself sound fairly ominous. And I don't know a thing about the societal types to the south of Diaspra."

"And K'Vaern's Cove?" Pahner asked. "That's the one I'm interested in."

"Me, too," the chief of staff admitted. "The more I hear about it, the more fascinated I get. If we think of the K'Vaernian Sea as analogous to Earth's Mediterranean, then the K'Vaernians themselves appear to be the local Carthaginians, or possibly Venetians. Their city is not only *the* major seapower in the K'Vaernian, but it's also the only one which appears to have reacted classically to technological innovation, although even it doesn't seem to have advanced very far by our standards. But I think we can change that. In fact, I wish we were building this army there."

"So do I," Pahner said, chewing his *bisti* root in deep thought. "As it is, winning this war—putting this force together, for that matter—is going to require everyone in the Company to pitch in. And the additional delay makes me really glad we happened across the apsimon. Anything new from Dobrescu on other substitutes?"

"Not yet," Kosutic told him, and the captain grunted. The fortuitous discovery of the apsimon had caused Pahner to reconsider their earlier acceptance of the survey report's insistence that nothing in the local ecosystem could supply their trace nutritional needs. He was still mentally kicking himself for having overlooked the possibility that such a cursory survey, of which they had only fragments, could have been inconclusive, and Warrant Officer Dobrescu had found himself with a new, extra assignment: running every new potential food source through his analyzers with fanatic attention to detail.

"Tell him to keep on it," the Marine CO said now. "He will, of course, but we're going to be too busy training Diasprans to look over his shoulder while he does it."

"And I think I'll just leave that training in your capable hands," Roger told him with a smile. "It's a job for an experienced captain, not a novice colonel."

"More like a job for Sergeant Whatsisname," the Marine responded with a laugh, and Roger smiled with sudden, wicked amusement. As far as the prince could tell, he'd managed to keep his mentor from figuring out that he'd been looking up some of the ancient poetry Pahner so commonly quoted.

"Indeed, 'not a prince, nor an earl nor yet a viscount,'" he said with a butter-won't-melt-in-my-mouth expression, and Pahner looked at the prince sideways and cocked his head.

"'Just a man in khaki kit . . .'" the captain said, ending on a slightly questioning note.

"'Who could handle men a bit,'" Roger responded with a chuckle. "'With his kit bag labelled "Sergeant Whatsisname." ' " His smile grew still broader, then faded a little around the edges. "It doesn't seem to change much, does it, Captain?" he said quietly.

"No, it doesn't, Sir," the Marine agreed, with a faint smile of his own. "It never does seem to change. And whether you intend to sit it out or not, I think we'll all have to become Sergeant Whatsisname."

CHAPTER TEN

Krindi Fain wasn't certain exactly why he was standing at the front of a milling group of Diasprans in the dawn rain while three of the odd-looking humans discussed something at the far edge of the courtyard. He was sure that it had something to do with that nice human in the tavern, and he could vaguely remember shouting about teaching the Boman to respect Diasprans and the God. Or something like that. There'd been a lot of shouting. And a *lot* of beer.

But now, just thinking about the shouting hurt his head. He felt as if someone had wrapped thorns around his horn sockets, and from the yelling in the distance, he was afraid there was more coming his way.

There hadn't been any shouting when they were first dragged out into the large square by the chuckling temple guardsmen. They'd been counted off into groups and then given a speech by one of the high priests. The priest had explained that they'd all volunteered for the new forces that were going to be fighting the Boman. That they were the bedrock of the army of the God, and that they would wash over the Boman like a wave. That the barbarians would be as sand before the dreadful tide of their righteous wrath.

Then he'd rattled off the rules under which they would now live. Fortunately for all of the new recruits, keeping track of the punishment for any given offense would be child's play itself . . . since *all* of the rules ended in "guilty party shall be put to death."

The three humans finished their conference, and turned his way. Suddenly, they didn't look nearly as friendly as they had the night before.

"God save me for a drunkard and a fool," Julian said, looking at the crowd of Mardukans.

"You qualify on both counts, Adib." Roger clapped him on the shoulder. "You'll be fine. You've got your notes?"

"Macek does," the squad leader said. "I'm going to give them a few choice words, then turn them over to Gronningen and Mutabi to wear them out."

"That'll work," the prince said, and turned to the crowd of young Mardukans. "Listen up! You men—and I use that term lightly—don't know why you're here or what's coming. Some of you think you do, but you're wrong. If you listen to Sergeant Julian here, and the veterans with him, you might just survive the battle with the Boman! If you don't, I guarantee that you'll end up in an unmarked grave, unpitied victims of a contemptible struggle! So pay attention! Follow orders! And may the God defend the right!"

He glowered at them for a moment longer, then clapped Julian on the shoulder, nodded briskly in the general direction of the thoroughly wretched and confused recruits, and strode off.

Julian considered the group like a farmer picking out just the right chicken for supper. Then he pointed to four of the largest or, in one case, most intelligent looking, of them.

"You, you, you, and you." He pointed to marks on the square's cobblestones. Next to each mark was a thirty-meter line. "Here, here, here, and here," he said, and propped his hands on his hips, tapping his toe impatiently until he had the four bewildered nascent squad leaders in place. Then he turned to the rest.

"What the hell are you *waiting* for? *Breakfast?!* On the lines, now, *now, NOW!*"

Between them, he and Moseyev's Alpha Team got the milling crowd lined up. It happened neither easily, quickly, nor neatly, and Julian favored the more or less formation with a ferocious glare.

"When I say, '*Fall In,*' you will fall in, just like this, on the line, with these four on the marks!" He strode up to the first squad leader and looked him up and down. "*Is that any sort of position of attention?!*" he screamed.

"I, uh . . ." Krindi Fain said.

"When you answer a question, there are *three* possible answers! They are: '*Yes*, Sir!' '*No*, Sir!' and '*Clear*, Sir!' *Is that clear?*"

"Uh, yes," the miserable and hungover Diaspran said. If this little *basik* didn't quit shouting at him, he was definitely going to have to do something about it. What, he wasn't sure, since one of those rules had covered the penalties for hitting their superiors. He didn't really feel inferior to this *basik*, but, on the other hand, he didn't want to feel the God's embrace *that* much.

"Yes, *WHAT?*" the human screamed at him.

"Sir," Gronningen mouthed silently behind Julian's back.

"*Yes, SIR!*" Fain shouted as loudly as physically possible, and the Marine noncom glared at him for a moment, then spun in place.

"Gronningen! Ten *Hut!*"

The plasma gunner snapped to attention, and Julian stalked over to him, then turned to face his new recruits again.

"This is the position of attention. Chest out! Stomach in! Heels together! Hands half-cupped and thumbs along . . ."

His mouth clicked shut, and he glared at the Mardukans for a moment in despair as his familiar, well-practiced lecture hit a pothole. Normally, it would have been "thumbs along the seam of the trousers." But that assumed that the sentient in question had only two arms, both of which reached to his thighs . . . and that the aforesaid sentient wore trousers.

"Macek?!"

". . . thumbs of the false-hands aligned with the middle of the outer thigh and true-hands aligned above false-hands," Macek supplied instantly, and Julian grunted in approval and strode back over to the poor squad leader-to-be.

"Got that, four-arms?" He poked the Mardukan in the stomach with his sheathed short sword. The Mardukans had a solar plexus much similar to that of a human, although larger and, if anything, more vulnerable, and the Diaspran partially doubled over, so Julian tapped him on the chin with the hilt of the sword. "Stomach in! Chin back! Chest out! False-hands half-cupped! Thumbs aligned along the thigh! *Do it!*"

So Fain did it. And then, without any ceremony or warning, he threw up all over the little *basik*. He really, really hoped that didn't count as hitting.

Poertena was trying to watch twelve pairs of hands at once, and it just wasn't working.

The group was too large to play spades, so they'd settled on poker. After some initial wrangling about what kind, they'd further decided on dealer's choice, although the initial decision by Chal Thai to start with five-card stud had been greeted with universal suspicion. The local Mardukan factor, who'd become their most prominent supplier of finished pike and spearheads was infamous for bottom-dealing, palming, and that notorious, Mardukan-only technique, "sticking."

It didn't seem to affect the quality of the materials he supplied. The perennially friendly merchant had been on time with every shipment, which had been hard in a city as busy as Diaspra.

The city had been in a night-and-day fever for the last two weeks. After some token resistance from the senior merchant families, the bulk of the populace, the guilds, and the church had thrown themselves wholeheartedly into the preparations. There was no time to build the kind of armaments the humans would have preferred for the struggle: mobile cannon and flintlocks, as a start. So Pahner, after a series of roundtable discussions, had settled on a modification of their own "Roman" approach.

Since the Boman—and especially their outriders, like the Wespar tribe—had relatively few arquebuses, designing a force to fight arquebuses would hardly have made sense, anyway. Instead, the army the captain envisioned would be designed to handle the threats it did face: the hail of throwing axes which continued to provide the bulk of the Boman missile assault, and their foot charge.

The first tier of what O'Casey had dubbed the "New Model Army of Diaspra" would consist of shieldmen armed with assegais, most of whom would come out of the regulars from the surviving Guard of God (and, oh, but the reassigned arquebusiers had been *livid* about that one!). The second tier would be the pikemen Julian and his henchmen were busy creating out of the recruits from the Laborers of God. Pikes required at least as much discipline but less individual training than assegais would, and just as no one on this planet had ever heard of Roman tactics, none had ever heard of hoplites or classic pike phalanxes. And the third tier would be the *civan*-mounted cavalry Rastar and Honal were teaching a whole new concept of "combined arms" operations.

The short assegais required less metalworking than short swords for much the same utility, plus they could be thrown, in a real emergency, and their broad heads had been readily supplied by the smiling merchant who usually had at least four aces stuck somewhere on his body's mucous covering. Chal Thai was also the main supplier for the needle-sharp awl pikeheads, and he was managing—barely—to keep deliveries ahead of the pike shafts being turned out by dozens of small shops throughout the city. Javelins were another matter. There weren't going to be nearly as many of them as Pahner could have wished, but the hand-to-hand weapons were even more important, so he was concentrating on them and the shields to protect the troops using them.

Those shields were being supplied by the other civilian Mardukan at the table. Med Non had been a minor supplier of custom woodworking and laminated tables until it became apparent that he was the only woodworker in the city with a firm grasp of how to increase production rapidly. Thereafter, he'd become the central manager of the suddenly roaring shield industry in Diaspra. His abrupt elevation and prominence had caused a brief mutiny on the part of one of the larger merchant houses, but Med Non had quashed that quickly by pointing out that none of the changes were going to affect the wealthier merchant's core business, and that his drive to rationalize and speed production gave the other's house many of his own "business secrets," instead. When asked about losing his own business after the emergency was over, he just laughed.

Poertena could understand why; the relatively small Mardukan ran rings around his more established competitors. Accustomed as he was to rapid turnaround of orders—something almost unthinkable to the hidebound leaders of the larger houses—there was no chance that he would lose any business to those larger houses. Indeed, it would be the larger houses who would have to keep an eye on their rearview cameras.

He also appeared—bizarrely, for a Mardukan—to have no interest in cheating at cards. He'd been raised and trained in a business which required him to calculate lengths and volumes in his head, and he played a conservative game that stuck strictly to the averages. While, of course, watching his opponents' hands.

He was currently peering at the Mardukan in half-armor across from him. Sol Ta, the commander of one of the newly raised assegai regiments, had just laid down a handful of jacks and started to scoop in the pot.

"Card check," Non said, throwing down his cards face up and raising all four hands above his head.

The purely Mardukan variant of poker, which would have made the professionals of New Vegas choke if they ever saw it, said that any player could call a check of all the cards once per game. The rule also required that all the Mardukans at the table throw all of their cards *on* the table and raise their hands above their heads.

"What?" Sol Ta said, then looked at the single jack sitting faceup in the other Mardukan's hand. "Oh." The guardsman raised his hands with the rest as Poertena got up and started checking.

The Pinopan had found that the locals had become downright fiendish about where they hid their cards. One of these days, he half expected to find one with a hollowed out horn, and he looked at Honal, the fourth Mardukan at the table, and raised an eyebrow.

"You wanna 'fess up now?"

The young cavalry commander was notorious, even by Mardukan standards, but he only wrinkled his brow and grinned in the human style.

"I have nothing to hide," he stated, wiggling all eighteen fingers.

Poertena sighed and started with the backs of his hands, then worked his way down. In fact, he was pretty sure the cavalryman wasn't holding—this time—but poker rules were poker rules.

Roger kicked back and laughed silently while he watched. The locals had the oddest approach to cheating he'd ever heard of. If you weren't cheating, they considered you stupid. But if you got caught, they considered you a gross incompetent. As soon as they'd started figuring out the ways they could cheat at cards, they'd leapt in with abandon. Spades and the other whist derivative games were the only ones where they couldn't hide cards, but even then they bottom-dealt, cross-dealt, and stacked decks so cold they froze. And yet they still played for money.

Poertena stood back and shook his head. The cavalryman's harness and tabard were clean. Nothing in his holsters, nothing in his scabbards. The Pinopan knew from experience that it was entirely possible that he'd missed a card somewhere, but he let the Mardukan lower his hands anyway.

Next, he started on Sol Ta. The Diaspra infantry commander wasn't as heavily armed as Rastar's cousin. He had a broad spatha kicked out under the table, and his harness sported only a single wheel lock pistol, but lack of hiding places didn't prevent him from regularly managing to fool them anyway. After a close search, the human stepped back and shook his head, then turned to Chal Thai. The other merchant sat patiently, with an air of benign amusement, while Poertena searched him minutely . . . and without success.

"I gots not'ing," he told Med Non with a shrug, and the merchant looked over at the last Mardukan present as Matsugae quietly entered with fresh drinks. The room was buried deep in the local palace-cum-temple, and had actually been provided by the last player.

Rus From waved the water-colored scarf that was his badge of office.

"What? Surely you don't believe that a humble cleric would introduce a jack into the deck? What possible reason could I have?"

Roger smiled again as he took a glass of cool wine off the tray. He winked at Matsugae, who rolled his eyes in return. The Mardukans seemed to spend better than half their time arguing about who was the more clever at cheating. And the other half denying—purely for the record, of course—that they themselves would ever even *consider* something that dishonest.

"Oh, I don't doubt for a moment that you'd do so," Ta said suspiciously. "I just wonder what involved plot it's a part of."

"I?" the cleric asked, spreading his hands in front of him. "I am but a simple cleric," he added ingenuously. "What would I know of involved plots?"

All five of the others laughed as Poertena carefully counted the cards. The complex hydraulic engineering that was the hallmark of the Diaspra priesthood was managed, almost wholly, by this "simple cleric." There were higher posts to be found in the local theocracy, but "Bishop of Artificers" was arguably the most powerful. And the most technical. This "simple cleric" had the local equivalent of a couple of doctorates in hydraulic engineering.

"Besides," he added, as Poertena silently held up the spare jack from the pile, "I don't understand this human fascination with simple adjustments. Isn't it your own Sergeant Major who says 'If you aren't cheating, you aren't trying'?"

"You cheat you own side, you gonna screw you'self," Poertena said, discarding the jack, sitting back down, and shuffling. As he dealt, he had to stop periodically to unstick cards.

"But we're not exactly cheating, are we?" Sol Ta replied, looking at his hole card. "We're just . . . trying for an advantage."

"Whatever." Poertena shrugged.

"No, seriously," From said. "I'm wondering where you got this odd attachment to 'fairness.' It has very little purpose, and is so very easily used against you. It seems to be a weakness."

"Maybe so," Poertena said with another shrug. He finished dealing and tossed a silver piece on the pile. After a moment, he looked around and realized that they weren't going to let him get away without answering.

He thought about it for a minute. He knew the answer, but he'd never had to explain it to anyone, and he was far from certain how to do so. From his point of view, you either understood it, or you didn't, but he decided to give it a try.

"Okay. Chal, you 'member the firs' time you come and offered you price for spears?"

"Sure," the Mardukan said, tossing a small raise onto the pot.

"You remember what I give back?" the Pinopan asked.

"Sure." The merchant grunted in laughter. "My sales gift."

"Right," Poertena said, and looked at the others. "He hand me a bag of silver an' a nice little statue. An' what I say?"

"'No thank you, and I won't say it twice.' I thought you were hinting that I should offer something a bit larger, but then I realized what you really meant," the merchant said, setting down his cards and picking up the cup of wine Matsugae had left. "So I took the cost off the bid I gave you."

"I had Fri Tar give me a gif' prob'ly ten time as nice as you," the Pinopan told him. "If I made tee call on tee basis of tee gifts, we'd be tryin' to get our gear outta pocking Fri Tar."

"Good luck," Sol Ta snorted. "I've been trying to get him to complete a set of swords for the past six months."

"Right." Poertena picked his cards back up. "That's you answer."

"But how did you decide on Chal, then?" Roger asked, taking a hand in the discussion as he saw the natives' continued puzzlement. "If not by the size of his gift, I mean?"

"He was tee only one take tee cost of tee gif' back out of tee bid, You Highness," the Pinopan said, and Roger nodded and smiled, then looked at the other players.

"I know you Mardukans think this is a quaint custom," he said, "but it's the only way to really build a society."

"We got 'sale gift' some places, too," Poertena said. "It call 'baksheesh.' But if tee size of tee baksheesh is mos' of a salary, people stop workin' for t'eir pay and start workin' for baksheesh."

"And then you have the goddamn plasma rifles," Roger growled. "An excellent example of why you *don't* want your procurement people taking little gifts."

"What's that?" Rus From asked, looking at the up cards, then grimaced. "Fold."

"We discovered that we . . . had a problem with one of our main weapons," Roger said, tossing in his own cards. "It would have helped us out several times. In fact, we'd probably have twice the people we do now—if we'd only been able to use it reliably."

"But t'ey blow tee pock up," Poertena said bitterly. "Sorry, You Highness."

"Not at all, Poertena," Roger told him, and looked at the Mardukans. "As he said, they blow the pock up when we try to use them."

"Well," Ta said with a wave of one true-hand, "guns always tend to blow up. But . . . most people survive." He waved his hand again in the local equivalent of polite amusement. Arquebuses were notorious for blowing up, as were the local pistols.

"If one of these were to blow up, it would take out this wing of the palace," Roger said, taking a bite out of an apsimon fruit.

"Oh." The guardsman looked suddenly thoughtful and took another sip of his wine before he tossed in a silver piece to stay in the game.

"Now a situation like that occurs for one of two reasons," Roger went on, leaning back and looking at the ceiling. "Either somebody's been incompetent, or, more commonly, somebody is cutting corners. Usually, cutting corners happens because somebody got greedy. And it usually means that at least one person has had his palm greased."

"'Palm greased'?" Honal asked, raising the stake by a couple of silvers, and Poertena pointed at the pot with his chin and rubbed his fingers together.

"Money," he said bluntly. "Somebody got paid off."

"Ah." Thai gazed at the young cavalryman speculatively, then folded and turned his attention fully to Roger. "That's why you explained in our first game that the next time you caught me cheating in your favor, you could no longer play."

"Right," the prince said. "It's a really strange concept, but it's all about playing fair with your own side. If you don't, since we're all interconnected, you inevitably pock yourself."

"But what about what Sergeant Major Kosutic says?" Honal asked, scooping in the pot without ever showing his hole cards, since everyone had folded rather than stay in the game.

"Ah," Roger said, pulling out a strip of *bisti*. "That's a bit different, you see. The Boman aren't our side. And in that case, 'if you ain't cheating, you ain't trying.'"

Despreaux slid into the spider hole and nodded to Kileti.

"Tell them we've found their main base," she whispered.

The small hole was on a slight elevation, twenty-five kilometers northeast of Diaspra. It was crowded and close with four Marines and the gear for two more. The team from First Squad was one of three sent out to find the main enemy concentration, and Despreaux was pretty sure she knew why she was here. Since her pissing match with Roger back in Ran Tai, Kosutic and Pahner had been going out of their ways to keep her separated from the prince. Since she was a squad leader, that meant keeping her squad separated from the prince. And in this case, it meant putting them out on the sharp end . . . all because His Highness was a stuck up, aristocratic prick.

She pulled out a leather pouch and dumped out the bleeding head of a killerpillar.

"It nearly got me," she said while her quick fingers extracted the valuable poison glands and dropped them into a plastic bottle. Both the neurotoxin and the flesh-dissolver were much sought after by the local apothecaries. Harvesting the bounty of the forests was one of the ways the individual troopers made their drinking money, so patrols had become a privilege rather than a task.

PFC Sealdin picked up his own translucent bottle and shook it.

"One of the mamas came by a few hours ago," he told her cheerfully. The vampire moths had stopped being a danger as soon as the Marines learned to sleep in their sealed personal shelters, but with the invention of a sticky trap, they'd become another source of funds. The anesthetic they produced was one of the most effective available for the Mardukans.

PFC Kileti picked up a plug and jacked it into his helmet com. The microscopic wire attached to the plug ran out of the chameleon cover over their hole and up a nearby tree, from the top of which a small transmitter sent short, directional burst transmissions and bounced them off of the micro meteors that skipped into the atmosphere on a regular basis.

Report complete, the PFC sent a command to his toot, and nodded at the team leader.

"On the way," he said, and the leader, St. John (J.), nodded.

"Okay, Macek and Bebi are going to keep an eye on them for now. We'll switch out tomorrow. In the meantime," he continued, digging into his rucksack and pulling out a strip of jerky, "we wait."

CHAPTER ELEVEN

"You know," Roger said as he hurried from one meeting to another, "they say that the waiting is the hardest part. Does 'waiting' include the preparation, too?"

"Yes, it does, Your Highness," Pahner replied, matching his rapid stride. "You'd do better to quit playing cards all night."

They were passing through one of the outer sections of the vast palace/temple complex, down a cobbled walkway the size of a small street but unoccupied except for themselves. The low wall to their right looked out over one of the city's innumerable canals, and beyond that to the eastern fields. This section used a pumped-out dry canal as a flood preventative, instead of the more normal dikes or walls, and there was a clear view of the vista of fields and trees leading to the purple mountains in the distance. A few farmers could be seen moving in the closer fields with a protective escort of Northerner cavalry.

"Ah, it's not slowing me down," Roger said. "I don't sleep much. It used to drive the teachers at boarding school nuts. I'd be up in the middle of the night, trying to get other kids to play with me."

"You spent a fair amount of time in your cabin aboard the *DeGlopper*," Pahner noted dryly.

"Yeah, well," Roger said with a grin, "I was sulking, not sleeping. Big difference."

They reached the end of the path and started to ascend a series of steps that stretched up and to the left around the central hill. Although the steps were quite shallow for the locals, they were anything but for the far shorter humans, but by now Roger and Pahner had grown accustomed to that, and the prince admired the palace architecture yet again while they climbed. Like most Mardukan structures, the city had started out atop a hill, but over time it had sprawled down to the flatlands, and the Diasprans, as water worshipers, had taken a different approach to the regular flooding to which all of Marduk was prone. Their technique was to work with the water, accepting and controlling it with strategically placed channels, holding pools, and canals rather than fighting it with unbroken lines of dikes. Oh, there *were* dikes—some of them more massive than any others the humans had yet seen—but they were placed more to divert water into other channels than to stand like a fortress in its path. Only the truly critical areas of the city and the areas most vulnerable to flooding had the sort of impervious barriers other cities routinely erected, although Diaspra's were constructed on a far vaster scale where they existed at all.

That relative sparseness of the dikes and coffer dams which served other Mardukan city-states as a sort of additional set of fortified outworks had almost been the Diasprans' downfall when the Boman assault arrived. Fortunately, they'd been able to slow the initial rush of the barbarians by selectively flooding their fields and occasionally artificially inducing flash floods to catch groups of raiders.

In the meantime, the priesthood, accustomed as it was to large-scale public works, had organized vast labor gangs to link the dikes and canals which already existed into one continuous defensive circuit. It wasn't perfect, but the walls, dikes, and canals had combined to stop the barbarians' second, more concerted rush.

It was in the interval after that second assault, when the Wespar had withdrawn to lick their wounds and prepare for a third attempt, that the humans had arrived. And that was also when the barbarians had cut the most prominent and religiously important public work of the entire city-state: the Diaspra Aqueduct.

Roger and Pahner passed under one of the flying buttresses of the massive aqueduct as they continued up the hill, and the prince looked up at it and shook his head in something very like awe, for the aqueduct was a structure fit to make any Roman proud. Normally, it carried water from a reservoir at the foot of the mountains to another reservoir within the city itself, from which it was pumped still further up the hill. At the very summit of the small mountain upon which Diaspra sat was the final reservoir of the city, the source of all its water for use and worship.

The reservoir had originally been a small cluster of very high output volcanic springs which fed a bowl-like lake whose temperature was high even for Marduk. The most ancient part of the city clustered around the lake, and its venerable structures—the oldest the humans had yet seen anywhere—had been carefully preserved. The ancient springs were the focus from which the locals had spread their worship of water, whether it came from the ground, or the rivers, or the sky. They had studied its movement and nature, trying to glean an understanding of their changeable god, and in the process, their understanding of hydraulics had become astounding.

The larger, cooler reservoir below the original lake was tapped for many different purposes. There were public drinking fountains throughout the city, where people came to draw fresh, clean water and make offerings to their god. In addition, there were thousands of decorative fountains, ranging from tiny carvings of Mardukan piscines that spat water a meter or two to a couple of giant structures that fired compressed water jets tens of meters into the sky. There were misting fountains, and playing fountains, and fountains that danced. There were wading pools, and swimming pools, and hundreds of canals.

Or there had been, for all the fountains were dry, now. The Boman had cut the aqueduct at its source, and for the first time in local history, water had to be drawn from the many canals. There was no chance of any Mardukan city running out of water—not with the daily cascades of rain—but for a people who worshiped water, the loss had been devastating.

"I wish there were a way to use water as a weapon," Roger said with a sigh, running his hand over a small fountain carved like a *civan.* "The way these people work with it, the Wespar would be screwed if we could come up with a way to use it."

"I'd considered it," Pahner said, stepping forward to open one of the heavy doors into the temple proper. The temple was a graceful structure over all, comprised of arches, curving lines, and narrow domes like the miters of bishops, but its doors were just as heavy—and Mardukan-sized—as any others. "But aside from the use of strategically placed inundations, which the locals already understand perfectly well, nothing really suggested itself to me."

"So we're still going to have to fight this out with weapons from the Dark Ages," Roger said, entering the dim corridor beyond the door. The passage was lit at intervals by light wells on the outer side, and although the wells were sloped to prevent water from coming in, it was obvious that another heavy rain had started.

"Well," Pahner told him with a dry chuckle, "it would seem to me that fighting a Mardukan with water would be like fighting a Marine by shooting beer at him."

"Today," Julian told the assembled platoon of Mardukans, "you graduate from your first phase of basic training! And everyone gets a beer."

The recruits had shaped up to a remarkable degree. Despite a disastrous start, Krindi Fain had even turned out to have a head on his shoulders. All four shoulders. The squad leader was, whether he knew it or not, in line for the platoon sergeant position, and his promotion would arrive sooner than he could possibly have expected, for there was a severe shortage of NCOs.

The recruits had learned to make their own tents and even gotten to sleep in them for a day or two. They'd been issued boiled leather and had cut and sewn their own armor. Then they'd marched in it.

All of them—even Erkum Pol, who appeared to have had a lobotomy as a child—had mastered the arts of standing at the various positions, marching in straight lines, and simple column movements. But that had been without weapons in their hands.

Now it was "calculus" time, and from the expressions on their faces (and even more so on their instructors' faces) it was obvious that despite all they had learned so far, the recruits once again had not a single clue. Each of the students held a four-meter wooden shaft in his upper two hands, and a three-meter-square plywood shield in the lower two. And it was abundantly clear that they didn't know what the *hell* to do with either one. Much less both of them.

"But that's for this evening!" Julian continued. "Today, we will begin your real training. Today, you'll be issued your pikes. And the pike simulators you have in your hands. Because if you think we're going to trust you four-armed monstrosities with *real* pikes, you've got another think coming. Until you learn what it means to be a *soldier*, you can just look at them and long for the day you get to hold them! In the meantime, we will begin study of the manual of arms!"

Gronningen stepped forward and began to demonstrate the first movement of the manual of arms, as rewritten for four-armed Mardukans and pikes and demonstrated by two-armed humans. The recruits watched with both intensity and anxiety, and as they did, the blunted pike shaft slipped out of Erkum Pol's nervously sliming hands and hit a second squad team leader on the head. The team leader responded by turning in place and laying out the slightly "slow" recruit with his own four-meter shaft of hardwood. At that point, things . . . devolved.

Somewhere, in the distance, there was the melodious chanting of priests going about their daily rounds. From the city stables came the lowing of *civan* and *turom*, and from the work gangs still laboring on city projects came the sound of deep-voiced work chanties. But the only sounds from the training square were those of wooden pike shafts hitting wooden shields and the coarse bellowing of foul-mouthed Marines.

The line of supplicants approached one by one, each kneeling in turn before the high priest to receive the blessing of their god. Gratar stood before an altar which consisted of a square marble base with a hollow, liquid-filled top. Crystal-clear water flowed up from below through the base, spilling over the edges of the top in a perpetually renewed, glass-smooth cascade that rippled like a living creature as it slid endlessly into the gold and gem-ornamented catcher basin at the altar's foot. Four additional fountains flanked the priest, pouring water into basins of polished lapis, where it was sucked away to join the rest of the underground flows. Spreading his arms to either side, the priest-king chanted as he scooped water from the fountains in a complex ritual and cast the handfuls over the worshiper kneeling at his feet.

The benediction over, the supplicant walked out through a fine shower, signifying that he had been purified, and the next worshiper came forward.

"We should have taken our time," Roger whispered.

"They say the waiting is the hardest part, Your Highness," Pahner joked.

The captain looked across the room and out to the northwest. The audience chamber was at the summit of the hill, a broad theater surrounded by columns and covered only above the stage where the priest-king performed his ritual. Behind him was that holiest of holies, the springs from whose bosom the entire religion had issued. The water from the springs filled the ancient lake and then flowed across natural rock to spill down into the reservoir and away to the north along its endless path to the Chasten River.

The large open area in front of the stage was filled with worshipers and other supplicants, including a delegation of merchants there to protest the rationing plan the temple had imposed. Dozens of the locals stood in the pouring rain, another sign of blessing from their god, patiently awaiting their turn for a moment with the priest-king. The narrow roofs of the surrounding pillars channeled the water into innumerable sprays which interacted with the pounding rainfall to wash down over the worshipers in abundant cascades of shimmering silver.

Roger and Pahner, on the other hand, stood in pride of place under the limited cover at the end of the stage behind the priest-king. Roger noticed that the Marine was distracted, and turned his head to look in the same direction. The rain, like every Mardukan rain, was heavy, but even through the downpour it was possible to see the swollen, dark charcoal clouds blotting the skies to the northwest. Despite their drenching power, it appeared that the current heavy showers were no more than a dress rehearsal for the true deluge to come.

"Usually this would be lightening up by now," Pahner said, "but it looks like we're in for a long one."

The last of the worshipers passed through the spraying water, and Gratar stepped away from the liquid altar.

"Hear now, hear now!" the master of ceremonies bellowed. "His Most Holy Excellency Gratar, High Priest of the Waters, Lord of Diaspra, Chosen of the God, will now hear petitions and grievances."

The stentorian bellow had to compete with the hammering rain and the rumble of overhead thunder. It won the contest, but it was a near thing.

"This reminds me of a Slaker concert," Roger said with a chuckle. He didn't bother to lower his voice, since nothing but a bellow could possibly have been heard more than a meter away over the sound of the storm.

"One of the ones where they use a weather generator to make a hurricane?" Pahner asked. "Ever been to one?"

"Just once," the prince said. "Once was enough. Their groupies all look like drowned sailors."

The two humans stood as patiently as they could. Both of them had better things to do, but they had no real choice but to wait for the petitioners for relief from the rationing. Technically, Poertena could and should have answered any questions which the complainants might pose. Eventually, however, it would inevitably have reached their level anyway, so it made more sense to just get it over with now.

"I wish we could have bugged all the merchant houses," Pahner said. "I feel like we're flailing around without any intel at all."

Roger frowned. While he shared the captain's frustration at the holes in what they knew, he had begun to question the wisdom of depending on eavesdropping for all their decision-making.

"We might as well start getting used to not having that intel," he replied after a moment. "It's not like we could get away with planting bugs everywhere on Earth. For that matter, I'm not even sure it was legal in Q'Nkok and Marshad. This is a Trust World of the Empire, after all."

"True, Your Highness." Pahner smiled faintly. "Believe it or not, I considered that when we first hit Q'Nkok. But the planet is also currently controlled—as much as anyone really 'controls' it—by the Saints, which means that we're in a *de facto* state of war."

"Oh." Roger furrowed his brow, trying to dredge up long-forgotten legal clauses O'Casey and his other teachers had tried to drum into him while he'd paid as little attention as possible. "So we're operating in a wartime condition in a combat zone?"

"Yes, Your Highness." The Marine's grin widened slightly. "So your mother shouldn't have a problem with it," he said, and Roger grinned back.

"Actually, I wasn't thinking about Mother. I was thinking that when we get back, I'm bound to end up somewhere in government. I might as well start learning not to cut corners now."

"I sort of agree, Your Highness. But let's get you off the planet alive before we get *too* ethical, okay?"

"Okay by me," Roger agreed, but then his grin faded. Gratar had dealt rapidly with the first two petitioners—some arguments about dike and canal maintenance. Now it was time for the main event.

The merchants' spokesman was Grath Chain, naturally. He'd remained a thorn in the side of the defense preparations throughout, and his constant carping and complaining were getting worse, not better. It seemed likely that the relatively low-ranked councilman was being used as a tool by the more senior merchant houses—certainly something gave him the confidence to oppose his ruler's decisions, and the only two possibilities which suggested themselves to Roger were truly invincible stupidity or the knowledge that he possessed powerful backers of his own.

Which made him all the more dangerous.

"Your Excellency," the councilor said when Gratar gave him permission to state his grievance, "I come before you as a humble petitioner. I hope that you will deign to listen to my just grievance—a grievance which you alone are able to remedy.

"A month ago, these foreign mercenaries came to our city. They antagonized the Boman beyond the walls and provoked a fresh attack upon the city. They physically threatened me before the entire

Council. They have forced upon us the most grievous of measures, whereby the poor starve and the wealthy are impoverished. They have taken the men from the just Works of the God and instructed them in foreign and unfamiliar ways of fighting.

"All of this they do in the name of defending our city against the Boman. But need we make these hasty preparations? The great Works of the God, His dikes and canals, falter beneath the rains, and soon the Hompag Rains will come. Perhaps they are already upon us." He gestured at the sky, where the downpour continued unabated. "With the men 'training' and the women preparing the barbaric materials of war, who then shall repair the ravages of the God?

"And is this even truly necessary? Have we explored alternatives? Surely, if permitting unnecessary ravages to the Works of the God was an act of apostasy in previous Rains, it must also be apostasy now. And surely this is a time to *avoid* apostasy, not to embrace it! Yet have we explored all other possibilities to avoid angering and outraging the God? No, we have not."

He paused for effect and gestured around at the temple.

"We are a great and rich city, but our strength has never rested in weapons or warlike preparations. Our strength has always been in our riches, and the love of our God, the one running from the other. Our treasury overflows with gold and silver. Certainly, this was offered to the God, but the God calls for sacrifices to serve His greater purposes, and now His temple's walls fall while its treasury is fat. Surely, if a small portion of that treasury were offered to the Boman, they would leave us to plunder other cities. Then the Laborers of God could return to their accustomed duties, preventing the fall of the Works of God."

"Oh, shit," Roger said quietly.

"Yeah," Pahner responded. "Actually, I'm surprised nobody suggested it before. Real surprised."

"Why now?" the prince asked, thinking furiously.

"Probably somebody had a rush of inspiration. Maybe they've even made contact with the barbs already. Who knows?"

Gratar regarded the councilman with obvious disgust but signed official acceptance of his petition.

"Your statement is understandable and has merit," he said, not sounding particularly as if he believed his own words. "However, what you suggest is too important to be decided in haste. It shall be considered by the full Council of the city and the temple."

"Your Excellency," the councilor interrupted in a terrible breach of protocol, "there's scarcely time to consider. Surely we must quickly contact the barbarian host, lest they come upon us by surprise and the opportunity be lost."

"You should learn your place, Grath Chain," the priest-king retorted sharply. "Your place is to bring forward petitions and argue their merits. *Mine* is to choose the time and place for them to be debated. Do I make myself clear?"

"You do, Your Excellency," the councilman agreed quickly, lowering his eyes and head in chagrin.

"The Hompag Rains are upon us," Gratar continued, gesturing at the skies. "There is no way for the Boman host to move in the floods of the Hompag, and so we have until the rains pass and the ways dry to make our decision. We shall deal with this petition expeditiously, but without unseemly haste. Yet before that, I wonder if our visitors have anything to say upon this matter?"

The local ruler gestured at the humans standing under the sheltering portico, and the two Terrans barely managed to conceal their surprise. Gratar had obviously had at least some prior information about the petition and its content when he'd asked them to attend the ceremony, but he hadn't shared that information with them. Or not fully, at any rate. His message had made it clear that he would want to hear their responses to any specific complaints the grain merchants raised, but it had never suggested that they might be required to respond to a formal petition to completely abandon military preparations! Certainly no one had suggested they would have to do so in an open forum before Gratar himself reached a decision, and so neither was prepared to make any public statement about it. It was a decidedly awkward situation, which the king seemed to have arranged specifically for their public humiliation.

Roger cleared his throat and stepped forward into the rain. The slight dais at the end of the temple made a satisfactory stage, and he'd been trained since birth in public speaking, but he usually had a script to work from and time to prepare his delivery. This time, he had neither, and he thought furiously for a moment about the proposal and its implications while he gave mental thanks to Eleanora O'Casey for drumming at least some history into his head. Then he looked at Chain and his supporters and smiled. Broadly.

"We have a saying in my country, Your Excellency. 'Once you pay the Danegeld, you will never be rid of the Dane.'

"What does that mean? Like the history of your own home, beautiful, water-washed Diaspra, our history goes back for thousands of years. But unlike the peaceful history of your city, ours is a history drenched in blood. This invasion which is so unusual for you, which makes your skin dry in fear, would be no more than a single bad day in the distant history of my country. Many, many times we have had to face the depredations and devastation of barbarian invasions—so often that our priests once created special prayers for deliverance from specific barbarian tribes. Like the Danes.

"The Danes, like the Boman, were raiders from the North. But they came in lightning-fast boats along the seashore, not by land, and they swooped down upon the coastal villages, killing and enslaving the locals and despoiling their temples. They had particularly gruesome ways of butchering the priests, and mocked them as they died, for they had called upon their god and been greeted only with silence.

"So, in desperation, one of the lands they raided offered up its gold and silver objects, even the reliquaries which had been created to show its people's love for their god, as Danegeld. As a bribe to the Danes, a desperate effort to buy immunity for their own land and people. Lords from all across their land contributed to the goods offered to the Danes in hopes that they might stay far from their shores.

"But their hopes failed. Instead, the Danes, finding that they were offered such tempting wealth without even a fight, moved in. They took lands about the area and became the permanent overlords and imposed *their* gods and *their* laws upon the people they'd conquered. All that society, that beautiful shining land of abbeys and monasteries, of towns and cities, fell into darkness and is forgotten. Of all their great works and art and beauty, only a few scattered remnants have come down to us over the years, preserved from the Danes. Preserved not by the Danegeld, but by the few lords who stood up to the Danes and defended their lands with the cold, keen steel of their swords rather than soft gold and silver and so preserved their people, their gods, and their relics.

"So if you wish to gather your own Danegeld, gather it well. But don't expect to be rid of the Dane."

Gratar considered the prince levelly for a moment, then turned back to the petitioners.

"This measure will be considered by the full Council in ten days. And this audience is now closed."

With that, he turned away from the petitioners and the humans alike, and left the temple by a side entrance, followed by his guards.

"Captain," Roger said as they watched the petitioners begin to file out of the temple, "you remember what I just said about intelligence and eavesdropping?"

"Julian's pretty busy drilling the troops," the captain replied thoughtfully as he pulled out a slice of *bisti* root.

"He couldn't get in to see the councilmen, anyway," Roger said. "But I know who can."

CHAPTER TWELVE

"Seriously, Your Councilship," Poertena said, leaning forward to point out the details of the design, "you can get a much better return from you ores. An' it would be easy to do with you technology. I surprised you don't do it already."

The molecular circuitry fleabug slid down the armorer's finger and across the desk to nestle into a crevice in the wood. It could hear every sound in the room, but detecting it would have required top-of-the-line modern sweeper technology. *Only four more to do*, Poertena thought.

"What's in it for you?" the council member asked suspiciously.

"Well, we not goin' to be back t'rough here. I'd t'ought about some cash up front."

"I thought you couldn't be bought," the Mardukan grunted, leaning back and looking at the water-driven trip hammers in the drawing.

"Well, t'is isn't a materials contract," the armorer told him with a grin. "It off tee books."

Of course, that wasn't, unfortunately, the truth, but the thought of helping to subsidize the company's coffers with bribes from the scummies he was bugging tickled the Pinopan's sense of humor immensely.

* * *

"How'd you get Grath Chain bugged?" Roger asked as he watched Julian flipping through conversations. The intelligence AI searched for indexed terms, but sometimes a human could still pull a nugget it had missed out of the sand.

"It wasn't easy, Your Highness." The intel NCO rubbed a blackened eye and winced. "He's refusing to have anything to do with anyone associated with 'the abominations.' He's not even letting most of the water priests in, but Denat finally suggested something that worked."

"What?" Pahner asked. So far they hadn't found anyone pulling Chain's strings, but the puppet master was out there somewhere, and the captain wanted to find him. Badly.

"We used a woman, Sir. Or a brooder-male—whatever. One of the mahouts' women."

"Well, it must've worked," Roger said, pointing at the conversation texts displayed on Julian's pad. Chain was definitely discussing his antipathy for the humans. In fact, he'd discussed it in private with just about every member of the Council. But so far they'd found no meetings in which he was taking orders. Nor, for that matter, was his suggestion of bribing the Boman being well received. He was pitching it as an arrangement in which the church would pay the tribute, but all of his fellow merchants knew where the money would actually come from in the end.

"Huh," Julian said, looking at the index list. "He's been to solicit everyone on the Council except the priests and Gessram Kar."

"Why not Kar?" O'Casey asked. Since the problem they faced was almost purely political, Pahner and Roger were leaning on her to untie whatever knot was threatening to strangle them. "He's in our corner, but so is Welan Gor, and Chain visited him."

"I've been thinking about that, Ma'am," Julian said. "The only explanation I can come up with is that the communication must already have been made before our bugs came online. Either Chain got a firm no, or . . . not."

"You mean that Kar could be conspiring against the throne?" Pahner asked.

"I submit that it's a possibility we can't afford to overlook, Sir," the intel NCO replied.

"We actually seem to have two different things going on here," the sergeant continued, pointing to the transcripts. "We have a debate taking place behind closed doors about the most effective method to deal with the Boman. Don't get these locals wrong; they all seem to think that they're doing the right thing. There are so many good intentions around here that you could mark a superskyway to Hell with them. Even Grath Chain is well intentioned, in his own—you should pardon the expression—scummy, self-centered, underhanded, devious, and treacherous sort of way. Oh, he's also upset about some economic losses and his loss of privilege, but mostly he just wants things to be back to normal. That means putting him back into the catbird seat, of course, but it also means a return to a situation in which the Boman aren't a threat to Diaspra, which isn't exactly a 'bad' thing."

"I'm perfectly willing to accept that all the parties involved have the best possible motives for everything they're doing," Roger told him. "Given the mess we're in, though, what does that have to do with anything?"

"Maybe not a lot, Your Highness, but then there's this other conversation going on in the shadows."

"What other conversation?" O'Casey asked.

"Here's an example. Welan Gor to Fan Pola. 'I think Grath's plan is an interference. We should use the humans for the Great Plan.' The caps are mine to reflect the emphasis all of them seem to be placing on it," Julian said.

"What's the 'Great Plan'?" Roger asked.

"That's a very good question, Your Highness. There's not much confusion about what it means among the five or six, Gessram Kar included, who apparently know about it. But if they ever get together to discuss the details of whatever it is, they haven't done it anywhere that we have monitored." Julian looked around the ring of puzzled and slightly worried faces. "Any ideas?"

"Have our bugs just missed it because of bad luck in their placement, or does there seem to be a particularly high level of security consciousness where this 'Great Plan' is involved?" O'Casey asked.

"Security consciousness is *definitely* high on this one," the sergeant said promptly. "At one point, a council member wanted to discuss something peripheral to it with Gessram Kar, and Kar got very upset. He said that not only was the conversation finished, but that such discussions could only take place 'at the times and places so designated.' Security's very tight on whatever it is. About the only thing I can tell you for sure is that whoever is orchestrating the 'Great Plan' is always called the 'Creator'."

"'Creator'?" Roger repeated, then chuckled sourly. "Well, that certainly has a fine godlike ring to it, doesn't it?"

"Yes, it does, and that means it's probably something targeted at the hierarchy," O'Casey said with a nod. "I'll need to look at all the relevant conversations. Maybe I can pick something out."

"What do we do about Chain?" Roger asked. "That was the original point of this meeting, if I remember correctly."

"So far, he doesn't appear to be a viable threat, Your Highness," Pahner said. "Until he reaches the level of a viable threat, let's not do anything which would foreclose any of our options."

"Agreed," Roger said. "I think we ought to talk to Gratar again, though. Get a feel for what he thinks."

"About Grath Chain, or about the 'Great Plan'?" O'Casey wondered.

"About Chain . . . and whether or not he realizes there's anything else going on," Pahner replied grimly.

Honal waved his hand, and the hornsman trumpeted the call which brought the unit of *civan* to a stop.

"Damn it, Sol Ta! You were supposed to open out!"

"We're trying!" the infantry commander shouted back. "It's not as easy as it looks!"

"Yeah? Well, you ought to try pulling a thousand *civan* to an unexpected stop before they stomp all over your infantry allies!"

"Enough!" Bogess shook his head as he trotted his own *civan* over to where the two leaders were arguing. "Enough," he repeated more calmly. "It's the timing, Honal. And training. That's why we're out here, in case you didn't notice."

"Oh, I've noticed, all right," Honal said sharply, then drew a deep breath and waved over his shoulder at his troopers. "But my cavalry doesn't need training in basic movement orders. So we're going to cut back to just the minimum—myself and a company of about a hundred. Something that can stop unexpectedly if it has to without turning into this sort of confused mess . . . or walking on our allies."

"Fine." Bogess gave a handclap of agreement. "But this is important. I can see the humans' point about a charge at the end, rather than the beginning, but can you keep your cavalry under control? Wait for the order?"

"Easily," Honal grunted. "The ones who weren't with us on the trek down from the mountains might have been a problem before we got hold of them, but not now. Those humans know what they're talking about, and their tactics have never failed. As long as we can hold up our end, everything will be fine."

"Good," Sol Ta said. "But for that to happen, we have to get this maneuver right. And that means—"

"Back to training," Bogess finished for him. "In the meantime, I'm going to see how it's going with the recruit forces. If we're having this much fun, you can just imagine what training them must be like!"

"On the square!"

Krindi Fain groaned and stumbled wearily to his feet. For three endless weeks from hell, they had assembled on this accursed square at the edge of the city and practiced the simple drills of how to stand and march as squads and platoons. Then they'd been issued their sticks in lieu of pikes and taught to march and stand with their sticks and shields. And then they'd learned more complex countermarches, company and battalion formations, and how to form and break. How to move at a trot with pike and shield in hand. How to do the approved Mardukan pikeman squats. How to live, eat, sleep, and defecate while carrying a pike and shield.

For every endless hour of each long Mardukan day, they'd trained for fifty minutes with a single ten-minute break. Then, at night, they'd been mercilessly hounded by the human demons into cleaning their encampment and gear. Finally, in the middle of the night, they'd been permitted to get some rest . . . only to be awakened before dawn and chivvied back onto the square.

He gave Bail Crom a hand to his feet.

"Don't worry, Bail," the squad leader said with mock cheerfulness. "Just think—a couple more weeks of live pike training, and then, when it's all over, we get to fight the Boman."

"Good," the former tinker grumped. "At least I'll get to kill something."

"We're going to kill something anyway," Erkum Pol said nervously.

"What do you mean?" Fain asked as he led them to their places. If you didn't make it to your mark before the humans, there was punishment drill: trotting around the square with lead weights on your pike and shield while chanting "I am a slow-ass! I want to kill my buddies!"

"Somebody told me we gotta kill something to graduate," Pol said sadly.

"What?" Bail Crom asked. "A *civan*? A *turom*?"

"No," the simpleminded private said with an expression of great woe. "We have to kill a member of our family."

"What?" Fain stared at him. "Who told you that?"

"Somebody," the private said. "One of the other squad leaders."

"From our platoon? Who?"

"No," Pol said. "Just . . . somebody."

The squad leader looked around the mass of troops on the square and shook his head in a gesture he'd picked up from their human instructors.

"Well, I don't care if it was another squad leader, or Sergeant Julian, or Colonel MacClintock himself. We are *not* going to have to kill a member of our own family."

He reached his position just as Corporal Beckley came up to take over the formation.

"Are you sure?" the private asked, his confused face still a mask of woe.

"Positive," the squad leader hissed out of the corner of his mouth. "We'll talk about it later."

Frankly, he sort of wished the job of squad leader was someone else's. This leadership stuff was for the *atul.*

Roger stepped through the door at a gesture from the guard, then stopped in surprise. He knew that this wasn't a throne room, but he was shocked by the informality of the setting. The priest-king of Diaspra was invariably surrounded by dozens of attendants and lesser priests, but this room, although large, was virtually empty. There were five guards along the inner wall, but Gratar stood alone by a northeastern window, looking out at the rain.

The room echoed to the rumble of thunder. The Hompag Rains had come, and the city had been buried under the deluge for two days. The rain gurgled in the gutters, chuckled in the *chubes*, and filled the flood canals. Sheets of water wrestled with the dikes and threatened to overwhelm the defenses of the fields at every turn. The Chasten, once a clear blue-green from its mountain origin, now ran swollen and brown with the silt of the forests and plains, and everywhere the rains poured down and down and down.

After a glance at the guards, Roger walked to the window and stared out at the downpour beside the priest-king. The room was on the highest level of the citadel, and on a good day, the mountains were clearly visible from its heights. Now, the view was cloaked with rain.

The gray torrent gave patchy views of the fields to the east and of the dikes which protected them. That area was the drier upland of Diaspra's territory and should have been more or less immune to flooding, but beyond the dikes a sheet of water at least a meter deep—two meters, in places—washed across the landscape, hurrying to plunge over the cliffs and into the rivers and thence to the distant sea. That swirling sheet seemed not so much to spread from the river as to *be* a river a hundred kilometers wide; the actual Chasten was just an incidentally deeper channel of it.

The bluff line that created the normal Falls of Diaspra was now a hundred-kilometer-wide Niagara, clearly visible to the north. The mist from that incredible cascade should have filled the skies, but it was beaten down by the rain, and that same curtain muted the rumble of the plunging tons of water. The sight was both impressive and terrifying, and the prince suspected that that was the reason for having the audience here.

After a moment, the king gestured out the window without looking at the prince.

"This is the True God. This is the God all Diasprans fear—the God of the Torrent. We worship the placid God of the Spring, and the loving God of the gentle Rains, but it is the God of the Torrent we fear. This is the God we strive to placate with our dikes and canals, and so far, that has always worked, but only with unceasing toil.

"Your preparations for war take our workers from that toil. Already, the walls of the canals crumble, and the weirs are not turned in their proper times. Already, the slopes of the dikes erode, and the pumps fail for lack of maintenance.

"This, then, is our God, and our worship is a battle against Him." The king turned at last to look at the prince. "So, which enemy do we face? The Boman, who can be bought off with a few coins and pretties? Or our God, who can only be fought through toil and preparation?"

Roger stared out at the brown flood and the yellow lacework of its foam and understood the trouble in the priest's heart. It was only too easy to imagine how quickly the first Mardukan to look out at that sight must have gotten religion. Even as he watched, in the distance one of the massive forest giants slowly toppled and was swept over the cliffs. It looked like a toothpick in the distance, and was pounded into fragments that size in moments.

It was impressive and terrifying, yes. But a look to the east told a different story. The inhabitants of Diaspra had spent generations expanding their fields and making preparations for the annual rains, and it showed. There were dozens of flood canals between the city and the edge of the fields, with dikes interspersed between them. The primary purpose of the dikes was to break the force of the flooding water so that the weakened waters could be gathered by the canals and drained to the north and south. To the south, they drained into the swollen Chasten; to the north, they drained into an even more impressive native-made river, which, in turn, drained over the bluffs and into the lowlands.

A concentric set of three dikes protected the fields themselves. All of them led back to the city upland, and between each was a flood canal that led to an enormous storage basin which was kept pumped dry during the "dry" season, when it only rained four or five hours a day, not thirty-six. During the Hompag, however, the inflow outpaced the pumps, although not by much. The level of the reservoirs rose by only a handful of centimeters per day, and there was little likelihood that they were going to be overwhelmed before the end of rains.

Given that everyone had been commenting on how intense this season's Hompag Rains were, it looked to Roger as if the city could have made do quite handily with about half the defenses against flooding that it actually had. But trying to tell Gratar that was probably futile, so . . .

"There are several aspects to consider, Your Excellency," he said delicately, after a moment. "I've already referred to one: once you pay the Danegeld, you're never rid of the Dane. The Boman will take your treasure until you can't pay anymore, then they'll wipe you out anyway and plunder what they can from your ruins. And that treasure is what pays for all of this." The prince gestured sweepingly at the flood defenses. "If you're forced to give it to the Boman, there will be no funds to maintain all of this, anyway.

"But there's another issue which must be faced, Your Excellency. A delicate one which I've been reluctant, as a foreigner, to address." The prince continued to gaze out over the foam-streaked brown and amber torrents, but he no longer truly saw them. "Perhaps, though, it's time that I speak of it and tell you the story of Angkor Wat."

"Angkor Wat?" the priest-king repeated. "Who is he?"

"What, not who, Your Excellency," Roger said with a sad smile. "Angkor Wat was a city long, long ago on my . . . in my land. It was, and is, one of the most beautiful cities ever to exist—a paradise of gorgeous, ornate temples and lovely public buildings.

"It, too, was ruled by a priest class which worshiped water, and it was filled with magnificent canals and bridges. As you know, no doubt better than anyone else, such things take manpower to maintain, and in addition, the temples needed to be kept clean and the public buildings needed to be kept clear of greenery, as well. But the priests accepted that, and they dedicated themselves and their treasury—and their people—to the tasks of building and maintaining their magnificent city, and thus they lived for many, many years.

"They were a shining gem among lesser cultures, a splendid and beautiful vision, but there came a day when one of their neighboring rulers joined a group of fractious tribes. That neighbor saw the richness of Angkor Wat and was jealous. He had no fear of the wrath of their god, for he had his own gods, nor did he fear the people of Angkor Wat, for they were priests and temple workers, and Angkor Wat had few warriors.

"And so that shining gem fell before those barbarian invaders and its treacherous neighbor and was lost in the depths of time. So complete was its fall that its barbarian conquerors even forgot where it was. For thousands of years, it was no more than a rumor—a city of fables, not reality—until, finally, it was found again at last, and our searchers for antiquities cleaned the ruins. The labor required was immense, but they did the work gladly, out of the sheer joy of uncovering and restoring the beauty and magnificence which once had been and then had been destroyed.

"In the end, they made the entire city into a museum, a showcase of splendid temples and public buildings, and I went there, once. I was forced to go by a tutor to see the architecture. But I didn't come away with a love of the beauty of the buildings . . . I came away with a bitter contempt for the leaders of that people."

Roger turned and faced the priest-king squarely.

"Those leaders weren't just priests of a god. They were also the leaders of their people—a people who were slaughtered and enslaved by barbarians, despite the tribute that they paid and the battles they fought to build and preserve their city. They were butchered because their leaders, the leaders charged with keeping them safe, refused to face reality, for the reality was that their world had changed . . . and that they were unwilling to change with it."

The prince turned back to the window and the flood beyond.

"You can prepare for the water if you wish, Your Excellency. But if that's the enemy you choose to face, the Boman will kill you—and all of your people—before the next Hompag Rains come. The choice is yours."

The priest-king clapped his hands in agreement. "It is indeed *my* choice."

"The Council doesn't have a say?" Roger asked. O'Casey had been of two minds about that, and it wasn't as if there were a written constitution she could refer to for guidance. Not in a society which was based entirely upon tradition and laws of the God, which mostly bore on small group interaction and maintaining the dikes.

"Not really. They may advise, and if I discount their advice too many times and my decisions are shown to have been in error, I could be removed. It has happened, although rarely. But, ultimately, it is my choice."

The king rubbed his hands in distress, which was something to see in a four-armed Mardukan.

"There is a festival at the end of the rains," he said finally. "A celebration of rejoicing that the God has chosen to allow us to break ground again. I will make my announcement at that time, either to fight the Boman or to pay them tribute."

The monarch regarded the prince levelly.

"I have valued your advice, Prince Roger, and that of your adviser, the invaluable O'Casey. Yet I also understand your bias. You still must travel to the sea, and if we do not fight the Boman for you, that trek will be impossible. The Boman will never let you pass after your actions against them."

Roger's eyes rested once again upon the distant, thundering cascade. He said nothing for several moments, then he shrugged.

"Perhaps it *will* be impossible, but if you think the tales from the north are terrible, you never want to see the Empress' Own in true fury." He turned his head and smiled at the monarch. "You really, really don't, Your Excellency . . . and neither do the Boman. Better to face the wrath of your God of the Torrent armed only with belief, because when He's done, those of you who survive will still have silt in which to plant. When the Empress' Own are done, there will be no one to care."

CHAPTER THIRTEEN

"Today is your first taste of war."

Julian pointed to the four-armed dummies set up on the frames. They were the simplest possible effigies of a Mardukan: a head, two horns, four arms, and two legs, all connected by a long, dangling tube. Ropes ran to the tops and bottoms of the frames so that they would stay in place, and two more ropes ran to either side. The sergeant watched the recruits regard the dummies with perplexed and very cautious eyes and grinned ferociously.

"Now we get to have the fun of good training!" he told them loudly. "Fain! Front and center."

The Mardukan squad leader marched up to the human and came to a position of order arms with his pike. It was the real thing now, wicked meter-long steel head and all.

"You've been instructed in the use of the pike, correct, Squad Leader?" Julian asked as St. John (M.) and Kane gripped the ropes attached to either side of the center dummy.

"Yes, Sir, Sergeant Julian!"

"You are now going to demonstrate your proficiency. On command, your job is to advance at a steady pace and drive your pike through the dummy, just as you will in combat against the Boman enemy. Can you do that?"

Fain didn't even look.

"Yes, Sir, Sergeant Julian!"

"Very good. Now, I will be behind the dummy. If it makes it easier for you to stick it all the way through by thinking that you might get me, too, you can feel free to envision that. Clear?"

"Clear, Sir!"

Julian stepped around behind the dummy and waved to Corporal Beckley.

"Take it," he said.

"Private Fain! Order arms! Private Fain, advance arms."

The Mardukan automatically dropped the butt of the weapon to the ground at the first command, then pointed the weapon at the target on the second.

"Private Fain will advance with determination at my command. Advance by half-step! Two, three, hut, hut, hut . . ."

The private stepped forward at the slow, balanced advance of the pike regiment until the pike was in contact with the dummy. Despite the simplicity of its construction, it was difficult to drive the weapon into it, and realistic enough to make him feel as if he were committing murder, but he put his weight behind the slow-moving weapon and tried to press it into the thick leather of the dummy's "body."

At the first hard thrust of the pike, the two Marines began to yank on the ropes while Julian, out of sight behind the dummy, set up a horrible, heart-wrenching wail as if from a soul in Hell.

The Mardukan private, horrified by the dummy's "reaction," flinched backward. And—inevitably—the instant he did, he found the diminutive Corporal Beckley at his side, screaming as loudly as Julian.

"What the fuck do you think you're doing, you four-armed *freak?!*" she shouted. "We told you to *kill* that bastard! You *will* advance with determination! *Advance*, two, three . . . !"

The shaken Mardukan grasped the pike firmly in two sliming true-hands and raised his shield as he advanced. This time, he expected the reaction of the team behind the dummy and drove forward despite it as the dummy apparently died in shrieking agony. For his pains, as the pike penetrated, a concealed sack of blood burst and went spurting out on the ground.

That red flood was enough to send him stepping back again, only to be verbally assaulted from behind. He drove forward once more, and this time, with a final, desperate thrust, he stabbed the razor-sharp pike all the way through the target.

Julian's screaming ended . . . so abruptly that Fain was afraid he'd actually skewered the squad leader. His momentary fear, followed by elation that he might truly have killed the sadistic little two-armed shrimp, was short-lived as the sergeant came around the blood-drenched dummy.

"Listen up!" the Marine barked. "What we've just demonstrated here is the training technique you will all use. Two of you will pull on the ropes while a third stands behind—well behind—and simulates the sounds of a person dying. This will prepare you, as well as we can, for actually doing it. We will be participating in other training to prepare you, as well.

"This may seem hard, but hard training saves lives—*your* lives. And if you think that this is hard, wait until you actually face someone with a weapon in his hands, trying as hard as he can to stick it into you before you stick yours into *him*.

"You won't like it, because killing a person with steel, up close and personal . . . well, that really sucks."

"Their drill sucks," Honal groused as he waved for his company to wheel to the left and take the opposition cavalry in the flank.

The other contingent, also from the Northern League but from Shrimtan in the far east of the Ranar Mountains, tried to react to the flanking maneuver, but the ill-led mass of *civan* became tangled in its own feet and reins. The leader of the troop, who'd been a very junior officer when he led his own band of refugees south looking for any shelter from the Boman storm, waved his battle flag to call for a halt.

"True," Rastar said. "But we'll change that, won't we?"

"We'd better," the Therdan cavalry leader grunted. "From what I've been hearing in the city, it might be just us and the humans in the end."

"May the gods forfend," Rastar said with a grimace. "We've taken their gold and their food, and I would be bound to our agreements. But I truly wouldn't care to try for K'Vaern's Cove with the Wespar between us and the hills."

"Aye," Honal said as he spurred forward to "explain" to the other Northern lordling that "drill" meant doing things in a certain way, at a certain time, the same way, every time. And beyond the hills? The rest of the fucking barbs—including the true Boman.

CHAPTER FOURTEEN

"What are you guys so enthused about?" Roger asked.

There'd been little change in the week since his inconclusive meeting with Gratar. Training went on, and the inexperienced workmen were slowly turning into drilled units under the tutelage of the Northerners and the Marines, but other than that, things seemed to be coming slowly but inexorably apart.

More and more of the Council had begun siding with Grath as the floodwaters rose and dikes washed away without workmen to maintain them. From all reports, these were normal events precipitated by heavier rains than usual, yet each fresh inroad was another nail in the coffin of the policy of using the laborers as a military force. The calls to have them out in the rain working on the failing flood controls had already become clamorous, and every sign said that it was only going to become still worse.

At no point were the city, its inhabitants, or even the fields seriously threatened by the water, but that didn't seem to matter. The combination of the endless, enervating rains and a constant drumbeat of pressure from the cabal of carefully orchestrated tribute proponents eroded the confidence of the Council further with every failing dike, however inconsequential.

At the same time, the company's bugs provided constant tidbits of information about the second cabal working on its unknown

"Great Plan." Whatever that plan was, it was large, for Julian had already identified no less than ten Council members, including several on the tribute side, among the conspirators. Whoever the Creator was, he'd amassed a sizable following and had excellent operational security, and so far no one who might have been in the know had used his actual name where the bugs might have overheard it. One of the reasons for that, apparently, was a suspicion that the humans might have listening devices like those they were, in fact, actually employing. All of which made the pleased expressions on everyone's faces seem particularly out of place to the gloomy prince.

"We think we intercepted a message to the Creator," Julian said, tapping at his pad. The handheld device was attached to the top of the all-purpose tactical intel computer the NCO had packed along, a helmet-sized, half-kilo device which contained fifteen terabytes of multiuse memory and a host of Military Intelligence software.

"What? It had an address on it?"

"No, Sir," Kosutic said. The sergeant major and Poertena were watching the intel NCO as if he were a woman giving birth to their first child. "We had an intercept that said a message was going to be passed, and we decided to have Denat stake out the pass in hopes of seeing who got it. But they used a dead drop, so Denat went ahead and picked it up."

"Won't that tip them off?"

"Dead drops go missing," Pahner said with a shrug, chewing calmly on a *bisti* root slice and pointedly ignoring the intel NCO. "Often. But one of the Council members who's involved in the Great Plan called this 'a very important message,' which seems to be a code phrase for messages directly to and from the leader. So Denat followed the messenger until the guy dropped the tube with the message in it into a *chube*. When I realized it could be going anywhere, I told Denat to pick it up. I doubt that we could have rolled up the whole line to the Creator no matter what happened; as crafty as this guy has been, there were probably a half dozen links in the chain. Not to mention that it would have been obvious that we were onto them with Denat trying to trot after it watching it float along."

"What's running?" Roger asked, watching the cavorting critters on the tiny screen of Julian's handheld. The device was running a query program, and the NCO had replaced the ubiquitous purple sundial of most programs with the graphics from a popular game program. The spinning and dancing hedgehogs formed into lines, and once all of them were in place, they blew up. There looked to be only about five or six explosions to go, which suggested the program was nearing the end of its run.

"Pocker was in code," Poertena said.

"I had to load the local written language before we could do anything else," Julian added. "We'd never gotten around to doing that. Then I scanned in the message, and now we see if it decodes it." The intel NCO beamed. "And it seems that it does," he added as the hedgehogs performed a final unnatural act and then exploded. "God, I love that game."

"B-T-H was a favorite of mine when I was a kid, too," Kosutic agreed. "Which I suppose says something about my childhood. So, what does it say?"

"Hmmm," Julian murmured. "Flowery for a secret message. 'Estimable Leader. Attempts to suborn human Marines have thus far failed. It is recommended that direct contact with their senior officers be made at the soonest possible moment. Aid in the Plan from the humans would be useful. Their resistance to the Plan might be disastrous.' "

"Well," Pahner said, climbing to his feet and beginning to pace in the small room, "that was refreshingly cryptic. What attempts to suborn our Marines? Sergeant Major?"

"Nothing reported to me," Kosutic said, pursing her lips.

"Maybe tee people tryin' to pay me off?" Poertena asked.

"Maybe," Julian said. "Anybody in particular come to mind?"

"Nah," the armorer replied with a shrug. "T'ey all try to give me gif's. I said 'no.' "

"Maybe he should have said 'yes,' " Roger suggested.

"For that to work, he would have had to do it from the beginning," Pahner disagreed with a frown, "and we didn't know we were going to have these problems when we started here. Twenty-twenty hindsight."

"Something we need to think about as an operating procedure for the future, though," Roger said. "Maybe the order should be 'Take the bribe and report it so we can find out where the string leads.'"

"The standing orders of the Empress' Own already call for anyone who's 'tapped' for an intel request to report it," Pahner told him, still frowning. "But the Sergeant Major says no such reports were made. Right?"

"Right," Kosutic confirmed. "I'll ask around and make sure." She got to her feet. "Keep me updated, Julian."

"Bet on it, Smaj," the NCO said. "I want to know what they mean by 'direct contact.'"

Roger stood by his window, watching the pike units forming up and drilling, and frowned. The morning of Drying had dawned unusually hot and steamy, but the newly minted soldiers appeared unaffected by the heat or humidity.

The units were colorful. They'd scared up enough leather to make a short leather cuirass of sorts for each soldier, and the Leathermakers' Guild had dyed them in the colors of the different companies. The company shields matched, turning the gathering forces into a panoply of colors as the companies wheeled and formed like a huge kaleidoscope. The casual observer might have concluded that all that martial color was simply to make a splendid show, but Roger had enjoyed more personal experience than he'd ever wanted of just how difficult it was to keep track of who was who in the howling bedlam of combat. Identification of who was a friendly and who a hostile was always difficult from inside the furball, even for the humans with their sophisticated helmet sensor systems. For Mardukans fighting other Mardukans and equipped only with Mark One Eyeball scanners, it would be even worse, but the strong visual cues of the company colors ought to help greatly. Or that was the idea, at any rate.

The new troops' drill was excellent, he reflected. The days of pounding rain had rung to the sound of marching formations as the Marines first drilled the original cadre and then acted as advisors as the cadre trained the next layer of units. Roger had participated in that as well, while trying to run down support and supplies and figure out what cabals they faced. All in all, it had been a good time, despite the unrelenting workload and the sense that, apsimons or no, their supply of diet supplements was steadily dwindling, but now it was time to find out if the new companies and regiments would be used as planned, or if it had all been for naught.

For that matter, there still had been no contact from the cabal of the Creator, and the prince wondered if he would ever know whether that was because their interception had prevented the critical message which might have initiated that contact from reaching the Creator, or because follow-up messages suggesting the same thing had gotten through only to be ignored.

He turned from the window and started preparing for the ceremony. There would be a parade to start, then an invocation of the God of Water by the high priest, followed by any number of other ceremonies. The festivities were to continue through the night, and he'd been invited to over sixty separate parties. He would be attending about five; the rest had been farmed out to O'Casey and various Marines.

He buckled on his pistol belt and had just checked the chamber when there was a knock on the door.

"Enter," he called, holstering the pistol.

PFC Willis stuck her head in the door.

"Sir, Bishop From is out here. He requests a moment of your time."

Roger frowned and tugged at the front of his tunic. It was one of the *dianda* outfits Matsugae had had made for him in Marshad, and its light, lustrous saffron complemented his golden hair and the intense tan he'd developed.

"Show him in," he said, and turned as the artisan-priest entered and looked around the small and spartan room.

"Pardon my intrusion, Your Highness," Rus said, smiling and gesturing in self-deprecation. "It was but a small matter. I believe that you wish to have conversation with the Creator?"

Roger froze in shock. Of all the people who might have contacted him from the cabal of the "Great Plan," the second or third highest ranking priest in the temple was not who he would have picked as most likely.

"We wish to speak to you, and there is not very much time at all," the cleric continued. "You may bring two guards. Or you can continue in blissful ignorance. 'Your choice,' as you would say."

Roger thought very hard for a moment, then nodded.

"We'll go. Let me get the guards and brief them."

He stepped out into the hall, and the two Marines guarding his door looked at him in surprise as he pulled his bead pistol back out to check the charge. Roger wasn't sure if the meaning of his action was plain to Rus From, but he knew it would communicate his own seriousness to the Marines. He looked at the power indicator, then nodded, holstered the weapon once more, and looked at the troopers.

"We're going to a surprise meeting. Just me, you two, and the priest. And we're leaving now."

"Sir," Georgiadas said, "shouldn't we inform Captain Pahner?"

"I don't have time to call him, Spyros," Roger said, with a very slight emphasis on the first-person pronoun. "We have to go now."

"Yes, Sir," the grenadier replied. "Let's do it, then."

"After you, Bishop From," the prince invited, gesturing down the corridor.

"This should be interesting," Willis muttered as they left their post and accompanied the prince on his latest harebrained excursion.

"Yeah," Georgiadas whispered back as he used his toot to key his communicator for a subvocal message. "Like the Chinese curse."

"Roger just left for an unspecified location with Rus From!" Pahner snapped, as he slammed open the sergeant major's door.

"Shit," Kosutic responded, throwing on her tunic. Unlike the prince, the rest of them had to wear their battle-worn chameleon suits, but they'd finally had the time to really attack the stains and tears. There were also spares available from the wounded and the dead, and they'd been put to good use. The final patchwork suits had clearly seen hard usage, but they were no longer the stained rags they had been.

"Not good, Sir," Julian added from the other side of the camp bed.

The intel NCO pulled on his boots and sealed them to his uniform, then picked up his bead rifle and checked the chamber. "Do we go after him?"

"And does he have any guards at all?" Kosutic demanded harshly.

Pahner looked from one to the other and not quite visibly shook himself. It wasn't that seeing two Marines together was unusual, but the Regs were very specific about relationships between two people in the same direct chain of command. There were, in Pahner's opinion, very good reasons for that regulation, given that Marines were still people and that favoritism—or the need to keep one's loved ones out of harm's way—remained an ineradicable part of the human condition. And whether the captain agreed with them or not, the Regs made any such relationship a "crash and burn" offense. If two people in the same chain of command wanted to marry or become lovers, that was just fine with The Book . . . as long as one of them transferred out of that chain of command.

But there was nowhere on Marduk for anyone to transfer *to*, and Pahner felt a moment of absolute fury at Kosutic for allowing such a thing to happen. The sergeant major was his right hand. It was part of her job to make sure that *other* people weren't in violation of military law, not to go around violating it herself! Besides, she was forty years older than Julian—not, Pahner had to admit, that she looked it.

And Julian . . . Julian was an experienced troop who'd been around the block a few dozen times. He damned well knew as well as Kosutic did just how far out of line they were and what a dilemma their actions were going to create for one Armand Pahner!

But even as those thoughts flashed through his mind, the captain knew it wasn't that simple or cut and dried. What were people supposed to do with themselves, with their emotions and their sex drives? Turn them off? Pretend they didn't exist? The Regs had never envisioned a situation in which a unit this small would be this isolated for so long, and what were two people to do when there was no place either of them could transfer to? And even if that hadn't been so, what was he supposed to do in this specific case? Oh, sure, Kosutic and Julian were both supposed to be setting examples to their subordinates, which meant holding their conduct to a higher standard, but how could he justify lowering the boom on them when he knew that *they* knew that he knew there were plenty of other similar relationships cooking away out there. Christ, there was even Despreaux and the prince to think about! God only knew where *that* mess was headed, and what was Pahner supposed to do if the two of them decided that the solution was to give in and do what they both so obviously *wanted* to do? Order them to behave—like that would do any good at all? Charge a member of the Imperial Family with violation of the Regs? Court-martial just Despreaux?

Besides, he thought as his initial, shock-born fury faded just a bit, he couldn't think of a single person less likely than Kosutic to let anything that was happening in her bed affect her decisions and actions in the field. Or, for that matter, less likely than Julian, despite the intel NCO's well-earned reputation for bending the rules. So if it wasn't going to have any negative side effects on the way they did their jobs, and if making a point out of jumping all over them was only going to unsettle his command structure and force him to take note of other, potentially even stickier relationships, then shouldn't he just keep his mouth shut and pretend he hadn't seen a thing?

"Derail your train of thought there, Armand?" the sergeant major chuckled.

"He has two guards," Pahner replied somewhat coldly. It was the first time Kosutic had ever addressed him by his given name in front of another member of the company, but the comment had been as effective a way to restart his mental processes as a slap to the face. Which was what the NCO had intended, he was sure. This whole situation was just going to have to wait, he decided firmly. Like maybe for the next ten standard years or so.

"Willis and Georgiadas, Sir?" Julian asked, apparently (and falsely, Pahner felt certain) unaware that there was any particular reason he ought to be sweating bullets. Or maybe he just had his mind totally focused on the job in hand. He was buckled up and ready to go, waiting only to be told where, so maybe that was all he was thinking about.

Yeah. *Sure* it was.

"Right. Georgiadas called it in," the captain said after only the briefest of cold-eyed pauses. "Rus From was the contact from the cabal," he added.

"Oh, my." Kosutic sat back down on the camp bed with a thump.

"So, no, we're not going in guns blazing," the captain continued. "We need to know what's going on before we make any decisions."

"We need to get Eleanora," the sergeant major said. "This is her area of expertise. And we'll need to crossfeed from Spyros to Roger."

"Julian," the NCO said.

"I'm on it, Sir," the intel sergeant replied, keying his helmet communicator. "I'll get her headed for the command post."

"Let's get to it, people," Pahner said, and stepped back out the door. Once it was safely closed against observation, he stopped and shook his head. Julian and Kosutic. He snorted. God. Like he had time to think about that right now.

CHAPTER FIFTEEN

Rus From led the prince and his bodyguards to a back corridor of the temple/palace and an inconspicuous door that revealed a long spiral staircase which appeared to have been hammered from the bare rock of the Diaspra outcrop. The dank, Mardukan-sized stone steps were both steep and slippery with condensation, and as the party descended, the temperature dropped precipitously.

The stairs seemed to spiral downward forever, but they finally reached bottom at last and emerged into a dark, soot-streaked room illuminated only by a few sputtering torches. The cleric led them from there down a curving hallway/tunnel that was at least partially natural. There were chisel marks in places, but most of the walls seemed to be natural, water-worn limestone.

Then they turned a curve, and the priest paused as the passageway disappeared ahead of them into a curtain of plunging water.

"I must ask your warriors to leave their helmets at this point," he said.

"May I ask why?" Roger asked, eying the curtain of water dubiously. "And am I to take it that we have to pass through that waterfall?"

"Yes, we do," From said. "There are two reasons to do so. We are about to enter one of the most holy of the Secrets of the God. Beyond that Curtain of the God is His other self: the Dark Mirror of the springs above.

"We chose to use this place as a meeting ground for that reason, but also for the same reason you must first remove your helmets then pass through the curtain. It is believed that this will disable your 'transmission devices.' They are, I believe, susceptible to damage from water, yes?"

"Yes," Roger said with a sinking feeling in the pit of his stomach.

"Georgiadas!" Pahner snapped. "Tell the Prince to agree. Then set your helmet on retrans and we'll monitor the feed from your toots."

"Sir," Georgiadas said with a swallow, "it would probably be best to go with the priest's suggestion. That's what my . . . intuition says, anyway."

Roger looked at the lance corporal, then at his helmet.

"Right. Georgiadas, Willis, off helmets." He looked down at his practically new suit and winced. "Kostas is going to kill me."

"We can monitor, Sir," Julian said as he manually adjusted the gain on the video, "but we can't send them audio."

Pahner nodded in understanding. The toots pulled video and audio off of the appropriate nerves and rebroadcast them, but while the broadcast could be picked up and boosted by the helmet systems, the Marines' toots were not designed to *receive* audio and video. Marines were fighters, not intelligence agents. As such, they were supposed to have their helmets on whenever it might be necessary for them to receive anything like that. Roger's toot could both send and receive audio and video, but he couldn't retransmit through the Marine helmets, largely as a consequence of the enormously redundant security features built into the implant hardware of any member of the Imperial Family.

"We can send them text if we need to," the captain told the sergeant. "Bounce it through the helmets, then to the guards' toots, then to Roger. Input isn't that big a deal; I think Roger's going to be walking out of that meeting unmolested, and I've got the rest of your squad armoring up in case he doesn't."

"I hope it doesn't come to that," O'Casey said pensively. "If Rus

From is being used as a messenger, we can assume that the group behind this plot is even larger and more powerful than we'd thought. If we have to use force, it will gut Diaspra at exactly the moment it most needs solidarity."

"If we know that, then *they* know that," the NCO said stolidly. "They have to, and they won't do anything to jeopardize the preparations."

"Let's hope so," Kosutic said, then smiled. "But, take it from me—His Evilness knows partisans aren't always reasonable."

"Well, that was refreshing."

Roger shook the droplets from his fingers and wrung out his hair, then looked around the torch lit room at the circle of hooded, lantern-carrying figures and fought down a smile.

The room was part-cavern and part-construct. The back wall had been mined out to enlarge a natural grotto, but the far wall was mostly natural, and a small spring welled up at the base of a wall of sculpted limestone. It was surrounded by stalagmites and stalactites, and the light of the lanterns shone through the stone and water with a hollow translucence. Behind the spring was a small, natural ledge, the edge of a dry waterfall. It had been scrubbed immaculately clean, but fine discolorations indicated that something other than water flowed over it from time to time.

The site was probably as secret as they came. And it was still lousy tradecraft.

"This is the Dark Mirror," Rus From said, stepping up to the spring. "It is the brother of the God of the Sky." He nodded at the gathered figures and waved his lower hands in a gesture of deprecating humor. "And this is the dark mirror of the Council."

"Unless I'm much mistaken," Roger said dryly, glancing around the gathered figures in turn, "it *is* most of the Council."

"Whether it is or not, is beside the question," one of the robes replied.

"Chal Thai," Julian said. The voice print recognition was almost instantaneous. "Shit."

★ ★ ★

"We represent the dark mirror of the surface," the robed figure continued. "On the surface all is agreement, but in the shadows there are questions."

"We seek to change the society of our city," From clarified. "To break it of its dependence on the temple."

Roger blinked.

"But . . . you're a *priest*," he blurted.

"Yes," the cleric replied with a gesture of resignation. "So I am. But what I am more than anything else is an artisan. An . . . artist. I create things with my hands, things that move and work, and that is my true calling. But to do that?" He made the gesture of resignation again, this time with a negative emphasis. "To be a creator of things in Diaspra, I must be a priest."

"The Creator," Julian said.

"*Nicht scheisse*," Pahner responded. "Send a message to Roger. Do not agree to anything, but don't turn them down flat, either."

"Yes, Sir."

"So why am I here?" Roger asked.

"We feel there is a need for change," another figure said. "The power of the temple has grown too great. It is . . . choking us. We could be a great city, a city as powerful and well-regarded as K'Vaern's Cove, but we have this great choking beast of the temple on our backs."

"We don't hate the God," another voice chimed in. "But we feel that it's time and past time for the power of the temple to be reduced."

"Gessram Kar and Velaum Gar," Julian read the voice print identifications aloud as he hit the "send" button.

"Hail, hail, the gang's all here," Kosutic whispered.

"Yes," Eleanora said with a note of desperation. "It's a 'quorum of the Senate of Rome.'"

"What?" Pahner asked.

"One of the arguments for Caesar's assassination having been legal was that the conspirators who effectively signed his death warrant constituted 'a quorum of the Senate,'" the history professor said.

"Oh," Pahner said. Then, "*Oh.*"

Roger read the text message received by his toot and tried, again, not to smile. They must be having gibbering fits at the command post.

"To an extent, I agree," Roger said carefully. "And I'm sure—" actually, he was positive "—that my advisor on such things, Ms. O'Casey, also agrees."

"She does," From said. "Eleanora and I have had long discussions about the local political situation and your human political history. Our conversations and the points she raised were what convinced us to arrange this meeting. They gave us hope that you would . . . assist us in this endeavor."

Pahner's head turned like a tracking tank turret. His eyes nailed the chief of staff, who shrugged and held her hands out, palms up.

"How was I to know?" she asked.

"You didn't happen to give them a copy of Machiavelli or Permuster while you were about it, did you?" the Marine growled.

"The . . . precautions that we took on the way in were, of course, to defeat your 'electronic' transmitters," the priest/technician continued. "Conversations with your Marines indicated that they were susceptible to water damage. I presumed that your helmets were sealed, however, which meant they would have been unaffected by the Curtain."

By now, Roger was familiar enough with Mardukan expressions and body language to easily recognize smugness when he saw it. The question was whether he ought to pop the bubble or permit blissful ignorance, and he decided to go with ignorance for the time being.

"This is all very interesting," he said, "but you still haven't indicated what you want us to do."

"Isn't it obvious?" another voice practically hissed from the shadows. "This 'New Model Army' looks up to you. The people see you as saviors sent from the God. If you were to overthrow the temple, it would be over without the slightest bloodshed. Over in an instant."

"Grath Chain," Julian said in a surprise.

"No way!" Kosutic said, then glanced over his shoulder at the voice print labels and shook her head. "But . . . he couldn't have been in on the plot from the beginning, could he?"

"A recent and ill regarded addition, unless I miss my guess," Eleanora told her. "Note the distance between him and the others, his position in the group, and Rus' body posture. Not well regarded at all, at all."

"It's a bit more complicated than that," From said with a quelling glance at his fellow conspirator. "Gratar is a revered figure, what your chief of staff would call a 'saint,' although we have no such designation. Overthrowing him will be *hard*, but because he's so well-regarded and because he's so deeply and genuinely devoted to the God, he's doing more damage than any ten previous prelates."

"The taxes required to create and maintain the public works of this madman are choking us," the figure identified as Gessram Kar said.

"And whatever the taxes," From put in, "the lack of innovation is stifling us. The temple has always been conservative, which is death on the habits of thought which produce innovation. That's bad enough, but its narrow focus on the Works of God reduces ambition, as well. It's almost impossible to get capable young people to take up the crafts these days. Why should they, when they know they're going to do nothing but spend their days building and repairing pumps . . . and that many of those pumps are no more than backups to the backups to the backups? Pumps which will never be used?"

The cleric gestured at Roger and his two silent bodyguards angrily.

"And all of this when it is so clear that there's so much more to learn and to do and build! Those tiny, tiny transmitting devices we found in Gessram's office. The weapons you bear. The 'simple' devices that your Captain Pahner has described to me. There's an entire world of inventions there to be made; a world of learning to be drunk from! And what do we do? *Pumps!*"

"Oooo, that's got to be frustrating," Kosutic said.

"Obviously," Pahner said, with a shake his head.

"No," she said. "I don't think you've quite got it yet, Sir. I've got the feeling that this guy is like a Taketi or a da Vinci . . . stuck fixing pumps."

"Oh." Pahner rubbed his chin, then nodded. "Oh, yeah."

"And let's not forget the security aspects," another figure said. "Had you not arrived, there's no way we could have gotten the Laborers of God released to bolster the Guard of God, yet with the Northern states overrun, we can expect other waves of barbarians to follow this one like plagues. Without you, we would already have lost to the Wespar; unless we change the direction of the city, we *will* lose to the next wave."

"You don't have to tell me," Pahner said sadly. "Bogess. I recognized his voice."

"That tears it," O'Casey said. "The only major figure not there is Sol Ta."

"Who could just be one of the quiet ones, or not in the conspiracy because of his relatively low rank before we arrived," Pahner responded. "It really doesn't matter. If it weren't for the position Gratar holds in the eyes of the populace, they would've already moved. Damn."

"And they want us to counterbalance his prestige," O'Casey agreed. "What do we do?"

"Normally, I'd say 'tell them to at least wait until we leave,'" the Marine said, rubbing his chin once more.

"But Gratar is on the fence about fighting the Boman," Kosutic said with a raised eyebrow.

"If they kick off a civil war now," Julian put in, "we have serious problems. We'll be forced to choose sides."

"Teach your grandmother to suck eggs, Julian!" Kosutic snapped, then inhaled sharply. "Sorry, Sergeant," she said contritely.

"Not a problem, Sergeant Major, but it's so much more complex than that."

"Yep," Pahner agreed. "We'd be absolutely against it under almost any other circumstances, but . . ."

"Yes, 'but,'" O'Casey said. "But we don't know if Gratar's going to support fighting the Boman."

"We don't know, for sure, that this cabal is going to support fighting them, either," Kosutic pointed out. "Not if it includes Chain."

"We need clarification," Pahner said, but Roger had given up waiting for a message.

"Rus From, the rest of you," the prince said, smoothing back his hair, "you're under a few false impressions.

"We're not here to cure all of this world's ills. We weren't here to fight the Kranolta. We didn't come here to put down a coup in Q'Nkok, nor to install a rational regime in Marshad. We especially aren't here to interfere in internal Diaspran politics.

"We're wrecked here, and just trying to get home. And, frankly, kicking off a coup just before a major battle against an external enemy is *not* an action that favors that."

"Gratar doesn't favor fighting the Boman," the figure the computer—and Pahner—had identified as Bogess said.

"Neither does Grath over there!" Roger snapped. "What? You thought I wouldn't recognize his voice, Bogess?"

There was a moment of silence, and then Bogess threw back his hood and made a gesture of resignation.

"You humans all sound alike to us. We assumed you wouldn't be able to distinguish *our* voices."

"He cannot be allowed to talk!" Chain squeaked furiously. "We've come too far; we're too exposed."

"And what would you have us do, merchant?" the war leader asked with a grunting laugh. "Kill him? Have you seen those weapons of theirs in action?"

"I wouldn't suggest trying it," Willis said, unprompted. "I really, really would not."

"Yes," From agreed. "We are exposed. And that's the point. We've advanced our timetable on the basis of our hope that you would intervene."

"Well, that was certainly silly," Roger said. "Until the battle's over, we're not about to interfere."

"But *we* must," Bogess told him. "Other cities had begun eyeing us with greed even before the Boman advanced upon us. With the damage we're certain to take from the Boman, they'll surely take advantage of us."

"Yeah," Roger said. "But not until after the battle. And they might not, even then. If we beat the Boman soundly—which is possible, if we're not fighting a damned civil war at the same time—it will give them pause."

"And continue to leave businesses stagnant, if there's no change within the city," Gessram Kar said, still without lowering his hood.

"And our technology," From agreed. "Not to mention the fact that we who have sought to change things will undoubtedly be sent to visit the God."

"Guys, I don't know the answer to that," Roger said. "All I can say is, let's get the battle done. Then we can try to work something out. But until we get rid of the Boman threat, a civil war is out of the question."

"What if Gratar says we won't fight the Boman?" Bogess asked. "What then? As you've pointed out, we will have them as an *astain* on our necks for the rest of eternity."

"Oh, not that long," Roger said with a chuckle. "Just until they drain you dry and decide to finish overrunning you."

"But if Gratar decides to appease the Boman?" Kar asked.

"Then . . . we'll see," Roger said. "There are some ways we might be able to make a fast strike through to K'Vaern's Cove. We might not have to fight the Boman at all. And we'll know Gratar's decision soon enough," he added, directing a thought at his toot. "In fact, if we don't hurry, we'll all be conspicuously missing from his speech."

"If he says 'no,'" Chain hissed, "you'd better hope the Boman give you time to escape!"

"Captain Pahner, Sir," Private Kraft said from the door of the intel room. "Sir, St. John (J.)'s team has been trying to get hold of you, Sir. It looks like the Boman are moving."

CHAPTER SIXTEEN

"What've you got, Despreaux?"

The Drying Ceremony was about to start, and virtually everyone who was anyone wasn't going to be there on time. Pahner shook his head at the black humor of the situation, wondering what, if anything, Gratar was going to think when half his Council and all of his alien advisers arrived late from every direction, out of breath, and clearly disturbed. The fact that the long-awaited Boman offensive could actually be used to cover domestic shenanigans which should never see the light of day appealed to the captain's sense of irony.

Which, unfortunately, didn't necessarily make that offensive good news.

"Captain, we've got loads of trouble," the sergeant responded over her com. "I sent Bebi and Kileti out to eyeball the encampment just as soon as it started to dry out at all. They'd just gotten into position—they hadn't even had time to start a proper hide—when the Boman started pouring out of their camps on the hills."

"Tell them to pull back," Pahner snapped as the headquarters group turned the last corner to the court where the audience was to take place. The solid wall of Mardukans in front of them forced them to pause briefly, and he could hear the intonations of the opening ceremony on the other side. Things weren't quite out of hand yet. If

Gratar decided against engaging the Boman, though, it would be a near run thing.

"I did, but they're stuck. They were setting up on a little ridge leading to that group of hills the Boman are on. Now the barbs are using the ridge to stay out of the muck down in the lows. They're headed right for Bebi and Kileti, and they both say if they move it would give them away. They're stuck, Sir."

"Right." The captain had been in enough screwed-up situations to know exactly what his Marines were thinking, and he agreed. If they were even slightly hidden, it would be better for them to stay still than to try to move. "What about you?"

"We're not on their direct line to Diaspra, Sir," the sergeant replied. "Right now it looks like they're going to bypass us. If they don't, well, we'll see what happens."

"Okay," Pahner said as the Marines began to push their way through the throng of scummies. "Get a movement estimate and count, then report back. Patch it to the Sergeant Major, though. I'm going to be kinda busy."

"Aye, Sir," the patrol leader said. "But I can already tell you, the count is 'a shitload.'"

"There's a shitload of 'em," PFC Kileti whispered.

"I know, Chio," Bebi whispered back. "Now shut up."

The team had just reached the observation point when they spotted the oncoming Boman horde. The barbarians flowed without any semblance of order, a vast mass of walking Mardukans that seemed to move in extended family groups. A senior male or two and several younger males would be accompanied by nearly as many females and a gaggle of young from "snot-sucker" infants up to preadolescents. There were some purely male groupings, and a few of unescorted younger females, but, by and large, the horde was centered around the familial groups.

They appeared to be carrying all of their worldly possessions on their backs. The males all supported large bundles—personal goods and loot from earlier conquests—while the females carried children and smaller bundles. There didn't seem to be any groups of "slaves," nor did they use many beasts of burden. There were pack *civan* scattered through the group, and *turom*, but they were few and far between.

The reconnaissance team wore not only their hard-used chameleon suits, but also an ancient invention called a gill suit. The genesis of the gill suit was lost in the mists of time, but in its simplest form—which these were—it was a net tied through with strips of cloth. The local cloth used for sacks had turned out to have all the properties the humans were looking for; the strips broke up the human outline, making it almost invisible in any sort of cover. The projectors of the combat armor did the same thing, but the recon team didn't *have* armor . . . and gill suits didn't require batteries.

Captain Pahner nodded to Roger as the prince slid into position beside him. Roger had taken time to slip back to his room and change clothes, replacing his ruined saffron outfit with a black one, and Pahner hoped the color wasn't an omen.

"We have another problem," the CO whispered.

"Julian told me," Roger replied, his nostrils flaring wide and white. "What the hell are we going to do, Armand? We can't fight the Boman by ourselves."

"We'll do whatever we have to, Your Highness," the Marine commander told him flatly. "If we have to fight the Boman with just ourselves and Rastar's troops, we will. And we'll win."

"How?" Roger asked hopelessly.

"'Our strength is as the strength of ten,' Your Highness," the captain said with a slight, sad smile. "We'll win because if we don't, we'll never know it. That world won't exist for us, and that's a form of winning, if you look at it from just the right angle."

"Go out in a blaze of glory?" the prince asked. "'Death is lighter than a feather'? That's not your style, Captain."

"And the alternative is?" The Marine grunted. "Your Highness, we *will* get you home . . . or die trying. Because whether it's death from lack of supplements because we didn't get home in time, or death from an alien spear on some battlefield, our swords will still lie in the heather. There's no other possible outcome if Gratar chooses not to fight."

"We can work the conspiracy angle," Roger said.

"Eleanora and I discussed that," Pahner replied. "But if the conspirators start their coup just after Gratar calls for an offering of tribute, it will appear as if the whole purpose of the rebellion is simply to avoid the cost that will fall on the merchant class."

"Ouch. I hadn't considered that."

"Nor had I, until Eleanora pointed it out," the CO said with a smile. "And as she also pointed out, that would make it seem as if all the rebels are really after is simply to shift the monetary loss from the rich merchants to a far higher cost from the poor soldiers. If Gratar doesn't come up with that line of reasoning, I'm sure someone—Chain perhaps—will adduce it."

"And that would really kill the coup," Roger grunted. "The largest single military force would be on Gratar's side, and so would moral supremacy."

"'God favors the side with the most cannon,'" Pahner agreed. "But, of course, in this case, just who has the most 'cannon' might be a debatable matter. I've got the platoon standing by. Julian and everybody else in his squad is in armor; the replacement circuits are ready to put in place as soon as I pass the word."

"You're going to back them?" Roger asked, eyeing him askance.

"If it's that or face the Boman in our skivvies, hell yes!" the Marine said, turning to look at the prince. "You think I'm crazy? If Gratar says no, it's our only shot . . . even if it won't work."

"Well, I guess it's blaze of glory time, then," Roger said with a wince. His own death he could face calmly, but the continued loss of Marines was something else, and he found himself wondering if getting as close to them as he had was for the best after all. When they'd started this long journey, they'd been mere faceless automatons; now each and every member of the dwindled company was a face and a soul, and the loss of each of them was a wrenching pain. Even as he and Pahner discussed the loss of the rest of the company, he was fretting for the two Marines in the reconnaissance patrol, pinned down by the passing Boman. And he continued to fret as the annual and extremely long Drying Ceremony, with its distribution of grain and blessings upon the fields, continued through the endless Mardukan day.

Between the out-of-the-way position of their hide and their gill suits, the two cowering Marines had managed to remain unseen as the tide of barbarians passed them. And it was a tide, indeed—a flow that continued through the morning and long into the afternoon. There were a couple of times, as groups used the lee in which the humans sheltered for a pause, when it seemed that they must be detected. One time, a warrior walked up to the bush they lay under and peed on the side of its trunk. The urine splashed off of the root and onto Bebi, but still they managed to avoid detection.

Their helmets automatically processed targets seen and heard, using that for max/min estimates of hostiles. The processors had some problems separating the noncombatant females from the male combatants, but even the most conservative estimate was overwhelming.

"Over twelve thousand warriors," the team leader subvocalized with a slight shake of his head. The comment was picked up by his throat mike and transmitted to his companion.

The flood was beginning to trickle off as stragglers wrestled with the churned path the army had created. Those stragglers were mostly individuals: older females, and wounded who'd been cast out as unfit. There were some younger Mardukans, as well—orphans who hadn't been absorbed by other families and weren't old enough to fight for space in one of the bachelor groups. Yet, varied as they were, all of these scavenging stragglers had one thing in common; they survived solely on the leavings of the family groups . . . and no one else in the tribe gave a single, solitary damn what happened to them.

"What a fucked-up society," Bebi whispered. "Look at those poor people."

"Not so unusual," St. John (J.) radioed back from the base camp. "Until it was brought into the Empire, Yattaha practiced the tradition of casting out the old just as their ancestors did. Once he was no longer useful to the community, it was customary for an old person to voluntarily take himself away somewhere and starve himself to death. That was the tradition, anyway. What actually happened was that they got tossed out of the house and wandered around the camp until the winter killed them."

"That's barbaric," the Mausean protested.

"That's why they call 'em 'barbs,' Bebi," St. John (J.) retorted. "People like the Saints make like barbarism and tribes and living hand-to-mouth is so great. Until they look at what that actually means, anyway. Then half the time they don't pay attention to what they're seeing, 'cause if they *did* pay attention, it'd knock all their pretty dreams right on the head. Living like this is just living in Hell for everybody in the society every single day, whether they know it's Hell or not."

There was silence over the communications link, and then St. John (J.) inhaled deeply.

"Time to call it in. Looks like upwards of twelve, fifteen thousand hostiles. Sounds like Voitan all over again."

"And this time with a shitload of poor, noncombatant sad sacks added," the PFC said, shaking his head again as an emaciated Mardukan with only one arm sat wearily down in view and rolled over on his side. The pink scars on the new-made corpse clearly indicated that he'd been a warrior until recently.

"They're all sad sacks, Bebi," the team leader said. "Just some worse off than others."

Gratar completed the last ritual blessing of the barleyrice and ascended the dais through the crowd of lesser priests to stand by the liquid altar and dancing fountains. He remained there, silent, head bowed, as the crowd patiently awaited his pronouncement. Despite the tension in the air, the vast square was silent but for the hushed susurrus of thousands of lungs breathing the humid atmosphere and the occasional shuffle of feet.

For Roger, it was a moment of odd transcendence. It was as if he were perched on a precipice, without any control over his immediate future. He felt as if he were leaning into a strong wind, storming up the cliff into his face to support him. It was a mighty wind . . . but at some point, it would fail, and he would fall. That was inevitable, beyond his control, and whether he fell to death or to victory would depend on the words about to be said by someone else.

Finally, the prelate turned from his devotions and looked out over the crowd. He raised his arms as if to call for even deeper silence, and when he spoke, the exquisite acoustics of the temple square carried his voice clearly to the farthest ear.

"We are the People of the Water. The People of the Water are ancient beyond memory. When the first prospectors came to the Nashtor Hills, the People of the Water were here. We remember."

"We remember," the gathered priests chorused.

"We remember the Autean Empire. We remember when the Auteans, consumed by the pride of their own power, threw off the strictures of the God and spread their crops to the farthest distance, the better to extend their might. We remember how they built their roads and leveled mountains. How they dammed and bridged the rivers.

"We remember how the long, dry times that allowed them to flourish ended in eternal rains, and how the Auteans fell before the Wrath of the God. How their cities and crops flooded, their roads washed away, their fortresses sank into the mire. In time, northern barbarians drifted down upon them, driven by hunger. They found the ruins of the Auteans, conquered their scattered survivors, and founded their own cities where once the proud Auteans ruled.

"Thus was born the Northern League . . . and we remember."

"We remember," the crowd responded somberly.

"We remember when K'Vaern's Cove was nothing more than a barren place of temporary respite for fishermen from distant ports. No more than a rocky, unusable place where fishermen would gather to ride out the storms . . . until a clumsy fisherman named K'Vaern wrecked his boat on the rocks and, being bereft of support, charged fees from other boats who wanted to tie up to his wreck that their crews might come ashore and stretch their legs. And in time, on the ruins of that wreck, he built a dock, and a shelter from the storms. Then an inn. Then a city. We remember."

"We remember."

"Through it all, the People of the Water remember. We remember when Sindi was founded, and when the Auteans themselves came from the north. The founding of Ran Tai, and the wars of the south. Through it all, the People of the Water have watched, and remembered, and been true to themselves. We worship our God, and teach the ways of worship to all and sundry, and that has been enough.

"Now come the Boman, the latest in the unending river of time, and we are threatened by them, as has happened before in our long history. First, by the early Auteans. Then by the Sartan, dread riders of the *civan* they brought with them, who, in time, became the Vasin of the League of the North. And now, by the Boman.

"The Auteans never pressed upon us. They found civilization, something they had never seen, and in time they founded their own cities and became contemptuous of us. But we survived when they perished by staying true to the worship of our God.

"The Sartan came down from the north in their shrieking thousands, wielding long spears and mounted upon their fierce *civan*. The Sartan we fought, and kept from our lands until they finally returned to the north to found their own cities. And, in time, they, too, became contemptuous and forgot the God, to their shame."

"To their shame," rumbled back from the crowd.

"Now come the Boman. Many say that we should take the Laborers of God, now recreated into the Warriors of God, and face the Boman in battle. That we should throw them back to the northern wastes through our power and knowledge and faith in the God.

"Others say that we should set our Laborers of God to the tasks of the God, rebuilding our Works of God, that our God may not turn His face from us, or, worse, come upon us with the Eternal Wrath that destroyed Autea. That we should pay the Boman from the monies that are set aside for the temple and from additional taxes upon our merchants. That the Boman will turn aside if we give them gold without battle."

"This, then, is the dilemma. Shall we be a nation of Warriors of God, who go forth and crush the enemy while the Works of God waste away? Or a nation of Laborers of God, making and maintaining the Works of God, while an enemy threatens us with destruction of all the God holds sacred?

"Whatever my decision, there will be misery. If I decide for tribute, the monies taken from the merchants will mean mouths that go unfed and crops that are never planted. Money is the lifeblood of a city, and giving it to the Boman in an amount that will appease them will cripple us as a people. And however much we give, still it may not prevent the destruction of all we hold dear.

"Yet fighting the Boman will not be bloodless. We will certainly lose sons to the fury of battle, with all the misery and grief that will bring upon us. We will lose sons who have grown up in our midst, and will be sorely missed. And if we fight, we might yet lose, and then all would be lost to no avail."

"If he doesn't make up his mind, we're kicking off anyway," Julian said, rattling his armored fingers on the helmet on his knees.

"You're a fine one to bitch," Cathcart said. "You got any fucking idea how hot this shit is when it's shut down?" The plasma gunner looked like a gray statue with a sweating, animated head. His plasma cannon was pointed up over his back, as if threatening the ceiling with terminal prejudice unless it surrendered.

"And you know the fucking plumbing doesn't work, right?" Pentzikis snapped. "I've gotta pee like a *flar-ta!*"

"You shoulda gone before you suited up," Poertena said. He fingered the baggies of capacitors nervously, waiting for Pahner's orders to open the bags which were the components' only protection from the destructive humidity and molds of Marduk. Without them, only the four suits of armor with the old-style capacitors—the ones fortunate enough to have escaped the last "upgrade" cycle—were operable. But if the little armorer was forced to install them, their serviceable lifetime could be counted in days, or weeks at most. Certainly, they would never last long enough to retake the planetary spaceport from the SaintSymps who controlled it.

"If we gotta use tee armor, it'll be peein' time for sure, anyway," he added grimly.

"I'm still gonna kill the old fart if he doesn't get this over with," Julian snarled.

"There is a third way," Gratar intoned. "We could send emissaries to the Boman with gifts. Lesser gifts than the Boman might like, but followed by the Warriors of God. We could try to buy peace with them at a lesser price even while we dissuade them from war with the might of our army and the power of our God.

"Yet this would leave the Boman, and ourselves, unsure. Incomplete. Waiting to discover what ultimate resolution awaits us both if the tribute should be demanded a second time. Or a third. In the long run, it would be no more than the first choice—to maintain the Laborers and hope for peace rather than to accept the burden of war.

"The God tells us many things about the world. He tells us that there are ways of greater and lesser resistance. That all is change, even if it appears eternally the same on the surface. That rocks come and rocks go, but eddies are eternal.

"And above all else, our God tells us that when we are faced with a challenge, we must understand it and confront it squarely, then do whatever is necessary to meet the challenge, no matter the cost.

"When a flood comes, one does not ask for it to go away. One might pray to the God for it to be lessened, but even that is usually in vain. The God calls for us, as a people, to build the Works that are necessary to meet his Wrath, and thus we have always done.

"And today, we have built a new Work of God, one called the Army of God. . . ."

CHAPTER SEVENTEEN

Roger pulled Patty to a stop and nodded to Captain Pahner and General Bogess.

The two commanders stood on a tall mound at the center of a solid redoubt. One nice thing about using the Laborers of God for their core force was that the Mardukans had, by and large, been digging ditches and building levees one shovelful at a time for their entire working lives. Constructing a fortification was simply a matter of laying it out and letting them get to work; a Warrior of God was never happier than when he had a shovel in his four hands.

The commanders had put that willingness to good use. Once the battleground—a shallow valley at the edge of the sprawling fields of Diaspra—had been determined, construction had begun. The New Model Army had built a central bastion to hold the Marine reaction force and some of the *civan* cavalry, and then the Warriors had gotten to work on their own lines.

A hedge of stakes, pointed forward, had been set up in front of the pike regiments. The sharpened stakes ranged from one to two meters in length, and created a prickly forest in front of the Diaspran regiments.

There were regular breaks in the hedge. Blocks of Northern cavalry waited at their ease behind the pike regiments, resting their *civan* yet ready to sally through the lines. The stakes were spaced widely enough for the *civan* to squeeze through them going out at almost any point, but the openings in the hedge were the only gaps through which the cavalry might come back. Which was why the steadiest of the pike companies, flanked by the shield and assegai-armed regulars from the pre-Marine Guard of God, had been stationed to cover those openings.

One end of the battle line was anchored on a canal, while the other abutted the forest. Although the Boman could conceivably flank them from that direction, it was unlikely. The ground was rough, the forest was thick, and the Wespar were not well known for fancy battlefield maneuvers. They were lucky if they could all arrive at the same battle on the same day, and even in a worst-case scenario, any movement to flank the Diaspran line should be obvious, and the Marines or Northerners could beat it off.

"It looks good," Roger said as Dogzard slid down off the flank of the packbeast. Although he'd made great strides in mastering the art of *civan*-riding, Roger had also firmly grasped that pearl of veteran wisdom: stick with what you *know* works in combat. He and the *flar-ta* had worked out the rules for a lethal partnership he had no intention of breaking up. Besides, the dog-lizard could ride behind the *flar-ta*'s saddle, a practice which no *civan* would tolerate, and the prince's pet—now a veritable giant for her species—refused to be separated from him. Not that her devotion or increased size had made her any less importunate, and Roger watched her sidle up to Bogess and accept a treat from him as her due.

"It could be better," Pahner replied. "I'd prefer more ranged weapons, but even if we had more arquebuses . . ." He waved a choppy gesture at the drizzling rain. The Hompag had passed, but "dry season" was a purely relative term on sunny Marduk, and at the moment, the relationship was distant, indeed. "If the Boman are smart," the Marine went on, "they'll stand off and pound us with those damned hatchets."

"We've got the javelins," Roger pointed out, frowning at Dogzard. She finished off Bogess' treat, licked her chops, and jumped back onto the *flar-ta*, which snorted its own disgust.

"Yes," Bogess said, absently wiping his fingers on his armor. "But only one or two per soldier. The Boman carry several axes each."

"It's not that big a deal," the prince insisted. "The pikes have their shields, and if they really do stand off like that, we can hammer them with plasma fire."

"Some of the companies could be steadier," Pahner commented pessimistically.

"Jesus, Armand," Roger laughed. "You'd bitch if they hanged you with a golden rope!"

"Only if it were tied wrong," the captain told him with a slight smile. "Seriously, Roger. We're outnumbered three-to-one, and don't think the Diasprans don't know that. It will affect them, and the Boman are bogey men to them. They're all . . . six meters tall. I was going to say three meters, except that that's about the height of a normal Mardukan. But that ingrained fear is something we have to be prepared for."

"Well," Roger said, waving as he prepared to ride down the line, "that, as you've told me, is what leadership is for."

"When they going to come, Corp?" Bail Crom asked.

Krindi Fain tried to keep his expression calm as he surreptitiously wiped one hand on his cuirass. It wouldn't do for the troops to see that his palms were sliming.

The pikes stood at rest on the battle line, awaiting the arrival of the Boman. They'd been there since just after dawn. They'd prepared the defenses well into the night and then gotten back up after only a brief rest for a sketchy breakfast. Now, between the up and down stresses and the physical labor of marching to the battle site and digging in, the entire New Model Army was adrift in a hazy, semi-hallucinatory condition, the mixture of physical fatigue and sleep deprivation that was the normal state of infantry.

"If I knew that, I'd be up in the castle, wouldn't I?" he snapped.

The drums from the Boman encampment just over the ridge had been beating since dawn. Now it was moving into late morning, and their enemies' refusal to appear was making the Diaspran noncom far more anxious than he cared to appear.

"I was just wondering," Crom said almost humbly. The normally confident private was a sorry sight to see in the morning light.

"Don't worry about it, Bail," Fain said more calmly. "They'll come when they come. And we'll be fine."

"There's supposed to be fifty thousand of them," Pol said. "And they're all five hastongs tall."

"That's just the usual bullshit, Erkum," Fain said firmly. "You can't listen to rumors; they're always wrong."

"How many *are* there?" Crom asked.

"Bail, you keep asking me these questions," Fain said with a grunt of laughter. "How in the Dry Hells am I supposed to know?"

"Well, I was just wondering," the private repeated . . . just as a burst of intense drumming echoed from the opposite ridge line.

"And I think you're about to find out," Fain told him.

"Quite an interesting formation," Pahner remarked as he dialed up the magnification on his visor.

The Boman force was at least fifteen thousand strong, yet it didn't stretch as wide as the smaller Diaspran army. Its narrowness would have invited a devastating flanking movement if he'd had the forces for it, but he didn't, and if it wasn't as wide as the Diaspran battle line, it was *far* deeper. It flowed and flowed across the ridge, a seemingly unending glacier of barbarians, and it was obvious that the New Model Army was badly outnumbered. The captain watched them come for several more moments, then keyed his communicator.

"Okay, Marines. Here's where we earn our pay. These scummies have to stand."

"There's a million of 'em!" Pol wailed, and started to back up.

"*Pol!*" the squad leader barked. "Attention!"

The days and weeks of merciless training took hold, and the private froze momentarily—just long enough for the squad leader to get control.

"There are *not* a million of them! And even if there were, it wouldn't matter. They all have to come past your pike, and my pike, and Bail's! Stand and prepare to receive! Stand your ground!"

The private in front of Bail Crom started to turn around—then froze as a chilly voice behind them echoed through the thunder of the drums.

"Sheel Tar, I will shoot you dead if you don't turn back around," Lance Corporal Briana Kane said with a deadly calm far more terrifying than any enraged shout. The private hesitated, and despite the drums and the approaching shouts of the Boman, despite the odd, visceral sound of thousands of feet pounding down a far slope, the sound of the Marine's bead rifle cycling was clear.

Sheel Tar turned back toward the onrushing enemy, but Fain could see him shuddering in fear. The mass of enemies advancing towards them was horrifying. It seemed impossible that anything could stop that living tide of steel and fury.

Pahner saw the occasional flicker of a face turned towards the bastion. It was a nervous reaction he was used to, yet this time was different. He was a Marine, accustomed to the lethal, high-tech combat of the Empire of Man and its enemies. Prior to his arrival on Marduk, he had *not* been accustomed to the ultimate in low-tech combat—the combat of edged steel, pikes, and brute muscle power. Yet for all of that, he knew precisely what he had to do now. An ancient general had once said that the only thing a general in a battle needed to do was to remain still and steady as stone. Another adage, less elegant, perhaps, but no less accurate, summed it up another way: "Never let them see you sweat." It all came down to the same thing; if he gave a single whiff of nervousness, it would be communicated to the regiments in an instant . . . and the Diaspran line would dissolve.

So he would show no anxiety, despite the Boman's unpleasant numerical superiority. Even with the arguably superior technique of the phalanx and shield wall, and the advantage of the stake hedge, the battle would be a close run thing indeed.

And like so many close run battles, in the end, it would come down to a single, all-important quality: nerve.

Roger sat on Patty, eleven-millimeter propped upright on one knee, his hand resting on the armored shield of the *flar-ta*, and watched the oncoming barbarians. He knew as well as the captain that he should be presenting a calm front for the soldiers of the regiment he was parked behind, but for the life of him, he couldn't. He was just too angry.

He was tired of this endless battle. He was tired of the stress and the horror. He was tired of facing one warrior band after another, each intent on preventing him from getting home. And more than anything else in the universe, he was tired of watching Marines who had become *people* to him die, one by one, even as he learned how very precious each of them was to him.

He wished he could pull the Boman aside and say, "Look, all we want to do is get back to Earth, so if you'll leave us the hell alone, we'll leave *you* alone!"

But he couldn't. All he and the Marines could do was kill them, and it was at times like this that the rage started to consume him. It had started at the first battle on the far side of this Hell-begotten planet, and just seemed to build and build. At the moment, it was a fury so great, so bottomless, that it seemed it must consume the world in fire.

And he was especially angry that Despreaux was out there somewhere. Most of the Marines were as safe as they could be in a battle on this misbegotten world. They were standing at the back of the formations, providing "leadership," and if the enemy broke through the lines, they had a better than even chance of escape. Losing the battle might well mean starvation would kill them all slowly in the end, but not today.

But Nimashet was out there, somewhere, with her team. Cut off, with nowhere to run. All she could do was hide and wait for her orders, and Roger knew what those were going to be and wished—wished as if his soul were flying out of his body—that their positions could be reversed. Despite what had happened in Ran Tai, he'd realized that he had to face the fact that he was madly smitten with one of his bodyguards. He had no idea whether that was only because he'd been beside her in good times and bad for the last few awful months or whether it was something that would inevitably have happened under any conditions, nor did it matter. Right now, all that mattered was that he wanted to kill every stinking Boman bastard before they could put a slimy hand upon his love.

Frightened Mardukan pikemen who knew human expressions, looking over their shoulders for reassurance from their leaders, took one look at Prince Roger Ramius Sergei Alexander Chiang MacClintock and turned instantly back to face their foes, for even the Boman in their fury were less frightening than the face of their human commander.

"Don't mind us!" Honal called out to the nervous Diasprans as their hands shifted on their pikes and their anxious faces turned to the rear. "We're just here as observers, after all! Still, we're glad you're here, too . . . and we definitely prefer for you to stay right where you are."

The muttered, grunting laughter of a hundred heavily armed cavalry rose hungrily behind him, and the wavering faces turned back to the storm.

Bogess watched the surges of uncertainty ripple through the pike regiments. He was totally confident in the steadiness of his assegai-armed regulars. Despite their earlier losses to the Boman, they had demonstrated their determination often enough even before the humans had taught them their new tactics and discipline. Now they truly believed what the human Pahner had been telling them for weeks—that no organized force of *soldiers* was ever truly outnumbered by any horde of barbarians.

Nor did the Diaspran general harbor any fears about Rastar and his cavalry. No one had ever called a Northern cavalryman a coward more than once, and these Northerners had a score to settle with the Boman. Like his own men, they were supremely confident in their own leaders and the humans' tactics, but even if they hadn't been, the only way the Boman would have taken this field from them would be to kill them all.

But the new regiments . . . They were the complete unknown at the very heart of the "New Model Army." The human Marines had accomplished a miracle Bogess hadn't truly believed was possible just by bringing the ex-Laborers of God this far, but there was only one true test for how any army would stand the stress of battle, and that test was about to be applied.

Assuming that his regulars, Rastar's cavalry, and the Marines could make the regiments stand in place long enough.

He looked over at Pahner, who nodded.

"I'd say it's time, General," the human said, and Bogess gestured to the drummer by his side and looked back out over the field.

The drum command sent an electric shock through the standing ranks of the pike force. The first thunderous rumble brought them to attention, and the second fierce tattoo lowered their forest of pikes into fighting position.

Suddenly, the charging Boman were faced with a wall of steel and shields, and that thundering charge ground unevenly to a stop just out of throwing ax range. A few individuals came forward and tossed the odd ax at the wall of shields, but the light hatchets rattled off uselessly, demonstrating the efficiency of the simple, ancient design. Insults followed the throwing axes, but the regiments stood in disciplined silence, and the Boman seemed confused by the lack of response. Then one of them, a chieftain of note, to judge by his ritual scars and necklace of horns, came out of the mass and shouted his own incomprehensible diatribe at the motionless wall of pikes.

Roger had had all he could take. He slid the eleven-millimeter into its scabbard, pulled out a whistle, and kneed Patty into a trot.

"Roger!" Cord called from where he stood at the *flar-ta*'s side, startled out of his calm assessment of the incipient battle. "Roger, where are you going?"

"Stay here, *asi*." For the first time since he'd saved Cord's life, it wasn't a request. It was an order, and he also snapped his fingers abruptly for Dogzard to unload. "I'm going to go teach these barbs a lesson in manners."

"Oh, shit!" Julian said. "Captain!"

"Roger," Captain Pahner called calmly, calmly. "Where do you think you're going?"

Even as he spoke, he saw the prince remove his radio-equipped helmet and sling it from the *flar-ta*'s harness.

"I'm going to kill him," Pahner whispered, maintaining a calm, calm, outward demeanor. "See if I don't."

The ranks in front of the packbeast parted at the shrill whistle to let the behemoth through, and Roger trotted towards the still-shouting chieftain, slowly raising the gait to a canter as the ancient Voitan steel blade whispered from its sheath. His rage against the obstacles of the long journey had gone icy cold. All the world had narrowed to the blade, the *flar-ta*, and the target.

As Patty neared the Boman lines, he kneed for her to turn, and rolled off her back. Hitting the ground at that speed was risky, but he was far too focused to worry about something as minor as a broken ankle, and it brought him to his target in a full charge.

The three-meter native was armed with a broad iron battle-ax which had seen long and hard service. The scars on the barbarian's body and the condition of his ax told his story as well as any chanted saga might have. This was a chieftain who'd conquered half a world and smashed the finest fighters in the Western Realms to dust.

And Prince Roger MacClintock could have cared less.

The Mardukan was fast. The first, furious slash of the prince's katanalike blade was parried by the heavy iron ax. The razor-sharp steel sword sliced a handspan-thick chunk out of its relatively soft iron, but the blow was blocked.

The second, backhand blow, was not.

The Mardukan was as good as dead, with a cut halfway through his torso, but that wasn't enough for the prince. As the body crumpled, slowly, oh so slowly to its knees, the sword whistled back up and around in a perfectly timed slash, driven by all the power of his shoulders and back, that intersected the native's tree trunk-thick neck with the sound of a woodsman's ax in oak. That single, meaty impact was clearly, dreadfully, audible in the sudden hush which had enveloped the entire battlefield. And then the Boman chieftain's head leapt from his shoulders in a geyser of blood and thudded to the ground.

Roger recovered to a guard position, then looked at the thousands of barbarian warriors standing motionless in the drizzle a mere stone's throw away, and spat. He gave a single flick of his blade, spattering the blood of their late chieftain halfway to their lines, then turned his back on them contemptuously and started back to his own lines in near utter silence . . . which erupted in a sudden, thunderous cheer.

"I'm *still* gonna kill him," Pahner muttered through his own forced smile. "Or make him write out 'Arithmetic on the Frontier' until his fingers bleed."

Beside him, Bogess grunted in laughter.

It took another fifteen minutes for the Boman to work themselves back into a frenzy once more. Other chieftains stepped to the fore and harangued the stolid Diaspran lines. Many of them waved the bloody souvenirs of past conquests at the pikemen, while others spat or urinated in their direction. But the ones who cast nervous glances at Roger, once more sitting atop Patty and glowering at the barbarian swarm, weren't much help to their cause.

Eventually, the barbarians began to move forward once more, in a creeping, Brownian fashion. A few axes arced out and thudded down, a few warriors charged forward and menaced the pikes, and then, finally, when some magic proximity had been reached, the entire mob flashed over into a howling fury and charged forward, shrieking defiance and hurling axes.

A storm front of javelins answered them. The New Model Army's javelin supply was severely limited, because there simply hadn't been time—or resources—to manufacture them in anything like the numbers Pahner could have wished for. Not if the artisans of Diaspra were going to provide the pikes and assegai he needed even more desperately, at any rate. There was only a single javelin for each pikeman, and three for each assegai-armed regular, but they did their job. The avalanche of weapons, hurled in a single, massed launch at the shrieking mob, ripped the charge into broken blocks. Given the numerical disparity between the two sides, the effect was actually more psychological than anything else. In absolute terms, the Boman's numbers were more than sufficient to soak up the javelins and close, but the holes torn in the front of the charge proved to the pikemen that they *could* kill the barbarians, and the object lesson worked. The pikes held their ground as the enemy charged forward . . . and was stopped again.

It was deadly simple: there was no way for the Boman to make their way through the thicket of pikes. The weapons were layers deep, jutting through every interstice. Stakes could be pulled up or knocked down, even if that meant stopping long enough for the shit-sitters to try to kill one, but those pikeheads were another thing entirely. Pushing one of *them* aside was no more than a temporary solution . . . and only left another to drive into an attacker's vitals, anyway. That became horribly obvious very quickly, yet some of the barbarian horde tried anyway. Some even succeeded . . . for a time.

Fain wasn't sure who'd started the chant. It wasn't he, but it was a good chant, as such things went, and it was simple—which was even better. "Ro-*Ger!*" with a poke of the spear on the "Ger!"

"Ro-*Ger!* Ro-*Ger!*"

The whole force, or at least the regiment he was a tiny part of, was chanting the prince's name. And it seemed to be working. The ferocious Boman, who'd been a source of such terror before the battle, weren't so terrible, after all. What *was* terrible was killing them.

Fain's regiment was one of the ones guarding the openings deliberately left in the hedge of stakes. Had he considered it, he might have realized that their position was a form of backhanded compliment, a decision based on the fact that their commanders considered his regiment steady enough to be entrusted with responsibility for holding such an exposed and critical position. At the moment, however, the squad leader wasn't thinking about compliments; he was thinking about how the absence of any stakes in front of them seemed to have drawn the attention of every demon-cursed Boman in creation . . . all of whom were running straight at *him*.

Which meant that the only way for him to live was for *them* to die.

When the barbarians had first charged forward, that hadn't been a problem. Given his place in the front ranks of his pike company,

Fain had been too busy getting his own pike into fighting position and keeping an eye on the rest of his squad to worry about throwing any javelins. That had been the job of the ranks behind them, and of General Bogess' regulars. Despite his own hatred for and fear of the Boman, it had been ghastly to watch the savage storm of javelins rip into them, but at least *he* hadn't had to throw one. And those of the barbarians who'd survived and kept coming had balked when they first confronted the leveled wall of pikeheads. Clearly, they hadn't had the least notion of how to proceed, but the pressure from behind them had been too great for them to stop and figure out what to do next. That pressure had driven them forward . . . and Fain had been forced to kill them.

The experience had been far worse than the simulation. The first Boman who'd been spitted on his pike had been young, barely old enough to sire sons. He'd clearly been trying to claw his way to the rear, anything to avoid the wall of pikes. But the young barbarian had lacked the strength to force his way through the seething mass behind him, and that mass had driven him remorselessly onto Fain's spear.

The Mardukan noncom's true-hands had tightened on his pike shaft like talons, yet they'd seemed weak, so weak, as if the frantic contortions of the shrieking Boman transfixed on the wicked head of his pike must wrench the quivering shaft from them. In that unique, private instant of hell, Krindi Fain was all alone with the young warrior, who dropped his weapons and seized the steel-headed wooden shaft driving into his guts with all four hands and tried desperately to wrench himself off of its agonizing sharpness.

But then the training came to the fore. Fain put a wall of disbelief up around his senses. The shrieking on the other end of his pike became a teammate, playacting in the background. The frantic shudders transmitted up the spear were just two of his friends, pulling on the ropes that suspended the training dummy. With the spear well and truly stuck in, the squad leader could turn aside and not see the bulging eyes or the lolling tongue as the barely scarred young barbarian gasped out his life on the end of the wickedly sharp spear.

Then, for the first time in his life, he blessed Julian and all the other Marine bastards who'd trained him. And as he looked around at the other members of his squad, he knew that they all had to do the same, or his own killing would be for nothing.

"Stick it in!" he shouted. "You just have to *get it stuck in!*"

Pahner flipped up his visor and nodded.

"Pikes are like bayonets. They're terror weapons. The Boman can't force themselves onto the pikes to drive forward far enough to reach the pike*men*. We're not really killing that many of them, but we have them well and truly stopped."

"But we *will* kill many of them if the ones behind keep pushing the ones in front forward," Bogess demurred. "They don't have anywhere else to go, and in time, they'll push the spears down by the sheer weight of dead bodies. And when that happens, they'll walk over the corpses and kill us all."

"And not everyone can stand it from *our* side, either," Pahner agreed harshly.

"No!" a private in the front rank cried. "No, *no!*"

The Diaspran was shuddering as he dropped his pike and turned to the rear. The dropped weapon, coupled with the way his flight knocked the men to either side of him out of their own positions, opened a momentary gap into which a Boman inserted himself. The warrior was well-nigh crazed with fear, surrounded by a wall of sharp steel and the smell of death, but the only escape from his own terror seemed to be up the suddenly opened path before him.

The path that led straight to Bail Crom.

The private blocked the first hack of the Boman's ax with his shield, but the second frantic slash licked over the shield's upper edge. It bit into his lower shoulder, severing the muscles that lifted the lifesaving piece of plywood, and after that, it was all over. Half a dozen pikes stabbed forward to fill the gap, thrusting at the crazed Boman, impaling him even as he hacked and hacked at the body of the private, but the fact that the barbarian joined him in death was lost on the happy-go-lucky Crom.

"Bail?" Pol called hesitantly. The simpleminded private tried to look around the intervening squad members. "Bail?"

"Stand your ground, Erkum!" Fain shouted. The humans had a mechanism for sadness and grief. They "cried." The liquid of the God Himself flowed from their eyes in moments like this. Strange that people who did not worship the God should be given such a gift.

"Stand your ground and get it stuck in, Erkum Pol!"

But not everyone was a Krindi Fain, and not everyone could stand.

"Captain, we've got ourselves a situation here!" Kosutic called.

Pahner spotted the sergeant major's icon on his HUD and looked off to the left. Some of the brighter Boman had realized that their best chance was to go around the hedge of pikes, since they couldn't get *through* it. Most of their flanking efforts had been defeated by Bogess' regulars, wielding their assegais with deadly effect. Whether Crassus or Shaka would have approved more strongly of them was difficult to say, but any barbarian who had expected it to be "easy" to get past their shorter weapons quickly discovered that he'd been dead wrong.

Yet for all their skill, the regulars lacked the standoff reach of the conscripted pikemen. The Boman were paying at three or four to one for each spearman they managed to hack down, but here and there they managed to batter their way through, however extortionate the cost. An isolated squad of regulars suddenly found itself under overwhelming assault and went down under a blizzard of throwing axes and the thundering blows of battle-axes. Its fall opened a brief but deadly hole in the line, and dozens of howling barbarians lunged through it and flung themselves onto the flank of a pike regiment.

The pikemen, already dazed and bewildered, despite their training, by the howling holocaust of battle, were taken at a deadly disadvantage. It was impossible for them to swing their long, heavy weapons around to confront their attackers in time, and the sudden onslaught was too much for them.

They broke.

The sergeant major's radioed warning turned Pahner's attention to the regiment just as it shattered like crystal under a hammer. The ground was suddenly scattered with the pikemen's shields and weapons. And bodies. As was always the case before the advent of artillery, the majority of casualties were inflicted when one side finally turned its back and tried to run.

Bogess followed the direction of Pahner's gaze, and then looked at the captain.

"Cavalry?"

"Not yet." The laconic Marine shook his head. "Let the armor handle it." He keyed his communicator. "Sergeant Julian, left wing, please."

The four fully functional suits of armor were already moving when the command came in. As they swung past the bastion, it was clear that the Boman were well and truly into the rear areas, and Julian couldn't understand why Pahner was so calm about it.

The Marines to either side of the breach were down, although it looked like they were only wounded, not dead, and the pike regiments to either side of the breakthrough, stiffened by a reserve of Bogess' regulars, had re-formed to protect their own flanks. But all they could do was hold their ground and cling to their own positions, and the flood of barbarians pouring through the seventy-meter-wide hole swept past the formed units and threatened to fan out and take still other regiments from the rear. And if that happened . . .

Clearly, it was time to show the locals what "peace through superior firepower" meant.

The four armored Marines spaced themselves across the salient with the two plasma cannon in the center, since they had the worst secondary effects, and opened fire.

The ten-millimeter bead cannon were loaded with flechette rounds. Each shot pumped out a half dozen narrow darts with moly-blade edges instead of a single normal bead, and the darts cut through the packed barbarians facing the four armored suits like horizontal buzz saws. Their molecule-wide edges would have cut through chain mail and steel plate, and they shredded the totally unarmored natives effortlessly into so much constituent offal . . . which the plasma cannon flash fried.

The fire wasn't widespread enough to stop all of the barbarians, but it ripped straight down the center of the breakthrough, and the hammer of it was a shock that sent the majority of those to either side—those who survived—into screaming, terrified flight. They turned and clawed and fought, not to advance, but to run from the Hell-spawned demons who had appeared in their very midst. The few warriors who'd been forward of the main damage, and out of the zone of effect of the plasma rounds, continued their charge, because there was nothing else they *could* do, only to find that iron was no match at all for ChromSten.

Julian casually backhanded a barbarian half again his own height who was obscuring his vision, crushing the unfortunate native's skull like an eggshell, and shifted the team's fire.

"Captain, we have the hole closed again, but we can't really keep it plugged. Can we get some cavalry over here to handle the leakers?"

"Will do," Pahner responded as he prepared to call Rastar on another channel. "Good job, Julian."

"Just another glorious day in the Corps," the squad leader replied stonily, tracking his flechettes back across the shrieking barbarians. "Every day's a holiday."

"Yes," said the captain sadly. "Welcome to the Widow's Party."

"Still a stalemate," Bogess said. "We hold, and they do not quit. We could be here day after day."

"Oh, I think not," Pahner said dryly. "Roger obviously doesn't have the patience today for us to squat here in a game of chicken." He glanced at his pad, nodded, and keyed his communicator once again. "Okay, Despreaux. It's about time."

The team had crept past the lightly defended encampment and down the reverse slope of the ridge. If anyone had looked hard for them, they would have been obvious, but none of the Boman were watching their own rear. Why should they? All of their enemies were in front of them, and so the Marines were overlooked, just a few more odd bits of flotsam left by the passing horde.

Until, that was, they calmly stood up at Pahner's command, took off their camouflage, and opened fire into the backs of the entire Boman force.

At first, their efforts were almost unnoticed. But then, as more and more of the barbarians pushing towards the front fell under their fire, some of the Mardukans looked over their shoulders . . . especially when the grenades began to land.

"*Yes,*" Pahner whispered as the rear of the enemy formation started to peel away.

"They're running?" Bogess asked. "Why?"

"They aren't running from their perspective," Pahner replied. "Not that of their rear ranks, at any rate. They're chasing the Marines behind them. But from the point of view of the ones in the front rank, they *are* running, and we're not going to disabuse them of that notion." He turned to the drummer. "Order a general advance of pike units. First, we drive them out of position, then we harry them into the ground.

"But they haven't broken," Bogess protested.

"No? Just watch them," Pahner said. "'And then along comes the Regiment, and shoves the heathen out.'"

Fain heard the drum command with disbelief, but he passed it on verbally, as he had been trained to do, to ensure that the punch-drunk soldiers had the orders.

"*Prepare to advance!*" he bawled wearily.

His arms felt like stones from holding the pike for what seemed like all day, poking it into the screaming, twitching dummies—or so his mind told him. And now the command to advance. Madness. The enemy was as thick as a wall; there was nowhere to advance *to.*

The New Model Army's losses had been incredibly light. The front rank of his company had only lost a handful, the next rank less. Of his own squad, only Bail Crom had fallen, but to advance on the enemy, who'd stood their ground the entire day, was impossible.

He knew that, and nonetheless he took his pike firmly in hand and prepared to step forward to the beat. It was all that was left in his world—the Pavlovian training the human sadists had put them all through.

* * *

"You know, Boss," Kileti gasped, slithering down the slope toward the distant canal, "I used to wonder why we were always running in training."

"Yeah? Well, as long as we don't twist an ankle in our court shoes," Despreaux managed to chuckle grimly.

It seemed that all the hounds of Hell were on their trail as they approached the canal. But the rope bridge—the blessed, blessed rope bridge—was in place as promised, with a grinning Poertena already starting across to the other side. Denat was there, too, and saluted Marine-style as they approached.

"Permission to get the hell out of here, Sir?" the Mardukan called as the Marines thundered towards him.

"Just don't get in my fucking way," St. John (J.) yelled, leaping for the ropes as the rest of the team clambered on behind him.

"Not a problem," Denat said, inserting himself into the midst of the team. The team had split into two groups and taken opposite sides of the two-rope bridge, each group leaning out to balance the other side. The much more massive Mardukan was a bit of a hassle, but not too terribly so.

"What's to keep them from crossing the canal?" Kileti asked. "I mean, we cut the rope once we're on the other side, sure. But, hell, it's not that wide. You can swim the damn thing."

"Well, Yutang and his little plasma cannon, for one thing," Denat said with a grunt. "Heavy bastard, too. But he promised me I could try to fire it 'off-hand' if I agreed to carry it for him. And, of course, Tratan brought Berntsen's bead cannon."

"You're kidding," Despreaux said. "Right?"

"About Tratan carrying the bead cannon? Why should I kid? He's not all that weak," the Mardukan said with another grunt of laughter. "Seriously, I've wanted to try it for some time. And what time could be better?"

"This is gonna be fun," Macek said.

"Are we having fun yet?" Julian asked. The rear of the Boman force might have run off in pursuit of the recon team, but a solid core of the front ranks had stood against the advance of the pikes so far. He was fairly sure what Pahner would use to break the stalemate.

"Julian," his communicator crackled. "Get in there and convince them that they don't want to stand there."

The four armored figures advanced through the open salient toward the Boman force to their front. That area already had a slice cut out of it, a line written in blood on the ground, beyond which only the most stupid and aggressive barbarian passed. Briefly.

Now the Marines opened that hole wider, firing their weapons in careful, ammunition-conserving bursts. The dreadful fusillade cleared a zone deep enough for them to actually pass the front of their own forces and step onto ground held by the Boman.

The friable soil was greasy with body fluids blasted from the Marines' previous targets, and their path was choked with the results. But the powered armor made little of such minor nuisances, crunching through the hideous carnage until the four turned the corner and pivoted to face the flank of the Boman still massed before the Diaspran pikes.

Once again, the armor burped plasma and darts, soaking the ground in blood and turning the churned field of the watershed into an abattoir.

"You know," Pahner mused as the cavalry sallied out in pursuit of the Boman force, "if that pike regiment hadn't broken, it would've been a lot harder to get the armor into the middle of the Boman. That's a case of the fog of war working *for* you."

"So now what?" Bogess asked.

"The force that took off after the recon team will be pinned against the canal. Detail about half the pikes to keep them pinned in place, and we'll pound them with plasma from the far side of the canal until they surrender. As for the rest—"

He gestured in the direction of the pursuing cavalry.

"We'll put in a pursuit. They'll break up in the face of the *civan* forces; they don't have polearms of their own, so they'll have to. We'll follow up with the rest of the pikes, and any groups the cavalry can't hammer into *feck*-shit, we'll hit with the pikes and armor. Next week, the Wespar Boman will be a memory."

Bogess looked out over the field strewn with corpses. There was an obscenely straight line of them where the two forces had grappled throughout the long day. They were piled in blood-oozing windrows, yet there weren't really that many bodies for a fight which had lasted so many hours. But the field *beyond* that line more than compensated. The ground there was littered with them where the Northern cavalry had ruthlessly cut down the fleeing barbarians.

"Why don't I feel happy about that?" he asked.

"Because you're still human," Pahner replied, and the native general turned to him with a quizzical expression.

"You mean Mardukan, don't you?"

"Yeah," Pahner said, watching the prince's *flar-ta* disappear over the crest of the far ridge with the Northerners. "Whatever."

CHAPTER EIGHTEEN

"You asked to see me, Your Excellency?" Captain Pahner asked.

From Roger's description, the room was the same one in which he'd met with Gratar during the Hompag. The previous meeting, however, hadn't included Grath Chain, who stood by the far wall. Mardukans didn't go in much for facial expressions, but the councilor looked like a three-meter cat who'd just swallowed a two-meter canary . . . or *basik*.

"Yes, Captain," the priest-king said, stepping away from the window and walking to the small throne on the far side of the room. His guards eyed Pahner nervously; obviously, something was up.

Gratar sat on the throne and rubbed one gem-encrusted horn thoughtfully as he looked at the floor. Then he raised his eyes to the human and clasped his hands before him.

"I have been given unpleasant news by Grath Chain," he said.

"I could play dumb," the Marine responded, "but there wouldn't be much point."

"Then you admit that you were—are—aware that there is a plot to overthrow the Throne of God?" the king asked very quietly.

"We were, and are. And if you hadn't decided to fight the Boman, we would have supported it," the captain told him. "My armored platoon was prepared to assault the Drying Ceremony, with orders to seize you and terminate Sol Ta and Grath Chain with prejudice."

The king clasped his hands again and lowered his head in regret.

"I have come to know and trust you, Captain, and as for the traitors of whose actions Grath has informed me . . . Many of them are men I know and trust and, yes, love as brothers." The king raised his head and looked at the human with sorrow, reproach . . . and building anger. "How could you be so disloyal?"

"I'm not disloyal, Your Excellency," Pahner told him levelly. "Nor, however, am I a Diaspran. My loyalty is to my mission, and my mission, as we explained to you on our arrival, and to the conspirators when they finally approached us, is to deliver Roger, alive and sane, to his mother. Any action we have to take to secure that reunion is an act of loyalty on our part. *Any* action, Your Excellency, no matter how personally repugnant it may be."

"So you would have overthrown the Throne of God?" the king snapped. "I should have your head for this! And I *will* have the heads of every member of this cabal!"

"The head of your recently victorious war leader?" Pahner asked with a raised eyebrow. "And of your second in command, the architect of so many of your favorite Works? The heads of the leaders of the Warriors of God? The head of your own guard force? Most of the members of your Council, all of whom manage businesses or farms that are the lifeblood of this city?"

"I—" Gratar paused. "Tell me the rot isn't so deep," he said despairingly.

"What rot, Your Excellency?" Pahner asked.

"The hatred of the Throne of God!" the priest snapped. "And through that, the hatred of the God, Himself!"

"Who said they hated the Throne of God?" the Marine inquired with a slight smile, pulling out a length of *bisti* root. "And who said that they hate the one who sits on the Throne of God? Do they chafe at the restrictions imposed by your defenses against the Wrath? Yes. Do they think those defenses are far more extensive and costly, in both time and effort, than they need to be? Yes. But they all swore to the depth of their admiration for you, personally, and not one of them has mentioned hatred of the God."

"Then why do they seek to overthrow me?" Gratar asked in confusion.

"I suppose I have to ask another question to answer that," Pahner said, popping a slice of the *bisti* root into his mouth. "How many canals and dikes does the God want?"

"Listen to him not, Your Excellency!" Chain exclaimed. "He but seeks to blind you with the false words of his people!"

"Shut up, Grath. Or I'll feed you your left horn through your butt-hole," Pahner said mildly. "You've obviously had your say. Now it's time for somebody else to talk."

Gratar seemed to pay the interplay little attention. He only waved vaguely at Chain, and his eyes were fixed on the human.

"How many dikes?" he asked. "As many as necessary to secure the city against the Wrath. We were lucky in the Hompag and lost only the outermost defenses, despite our inattention. But we must not depend upon 'luck' or forget the lesson of the Auteans."

"Lucky?" Pahner shook his head. "Your Excellency, I was under the impression that these rains were particularly fierce. That it had been twenty rains since last they were this heavy, and that only two rains in all of your recorded history have exceeded their intensity."

"Yes, but we were given a reprieve by the God," the priest returned. "We fought the Boman in His name, and so he forgave us for our inattention and chose not to overwhelm us as He could have. He might not always be so forgiving."

"Or, possibly," Pahner said carefully, "the outer defenses were sufficient against the threat. Isn't it possible that the God was satisfied with just them?"

The priest-king leaned back and clasped all four hands once more.

"Is this the crux of their argument? That there are too many Works to the Glory of the God? That we should follow the path of Aut and spread ourselves to the winds?"

Pahner looked that one over carefully before he replied.

"I'd say that that *is* the crux of the argument, more or less, of those who are honest in what they say," he admitted after a moment. "There are some," he gestured with his chin at Chain, "who were in it only for power or profit, no question; there are those among the conspirators that are the Sons of Mary to be sure. But even some or all of those believed that Diaspra would be a greater city if there were fewer Laborers of God and more . . . 'Laborers of Diaspra,' I guess you could put it. Laborers free to find their own work. Artisans free to work on something besides 'pumps, pumps, pumps that are never used.'"

"Rus From," Gratar sighed. "My oldest and, I thought, best friend. I'd heard his complaints before, but I thought them nothing more than . . . mild blasphemies."

"Rus *is* your friend, Your Excellency," Pahner said seriously, "and he certainly worships the God. True, he worships the art of technology, as well, but there's no real need for the one to exclude the other. It's just that he needs a greater challenge than, well, 'pumps, pumps, pumps.'"

"What shall I do?" the priest-king asked in a near wail. "My Council is against me, most of my soldiers are against me, the merchants are against me. . . . My back is to the wall, Captain Pahner!"

"Not quite," the Marine said. "Sol Ta supports you."

"Grath tells me otherwise," Gratar said, looking at the Council member.

"The human lies," Chain said. "Sol Ta has professed his hatred for you. He seeks your overthrow, that he might keep command of this accursed 'New Model Army,' and Bogess has promised it to him for his support."

Pahner gazed at him speculatively for a few seconds, then shrugged.

"That's the first I've heard of this, Your Excellency, and once we figured out what was going on we used some of our devices to infiltrate the cabal pretty thoroughly. We knew almost everything that was happening, I think, and all we've heard says that Sol wasn't even approached because he thinks darkness comes and goes at your command. Which was why, despite the feelings of the conspirators, he had to go to the wall right away. I can't, of course, explain why the testimony of such a selfless and trustworthy soul as Grath Chain might contradict that of every single other person involved, but perhaps some explanation for that might occur to *you*."

He and Gratar gazed into one another's eyes, and the beleaguered priest-king actually grunted a ghost of a laugh, but then the human continued.

"If you want a serious suggestion about what you should do, though, I have one. Several actually."

"I'll listen," Gratar said. "I've always found your advice to be, I believed, honest and well thought out."

"That's my job," Pahner told him, and clasped his hands behind him.

"Whatever happens, things are going to change," he began. "You took four thousand menial workers and turned them into pretty fair soldiers, and when the wounded heal, there will still be well over three thousand of them left. Some are going to be willing, even eager, to go back to their old jobs, but many others will be discontented. They'll feel that since they and their mates saved the city, the city owes them a living from here on."

"That isn't a logical conclusion," Gratar interrupted. "They saved the city because otherwise they themselves would have been killed when the city fell."

"But it's a conclusion they'll reach," Pahner said flatly. "In fact, some will already have reached it. It's common, almost inevitable, among veterans, and however illogical, it's still something you'll have to deal with. They've . . . changed. They've seen the high and the wide, and they can't go back to just rolling the lawn for the abbott."

"This is a nightmare," Gratar muttered, shaking his head.

"Don't think of it that way, Your Excellency," the Marine advised. "Instead, regard it as a test—one like the Wrath. You must put dikes where they're needed to stem the flow of change, and canals where *they're* needed to divert it into other channels. And, of course, you must learn to embrace change even as you embrace Water, recognizing both its light side and its dark."

The priest-king gazed at him, his body language arrested, and Pahner smiled.

"The other issue, of course, is the cabal and their feelings about the Works of God. Now, there's a saying in my land, that 'when you have one problem, you have a problem; but when you have a bunch of problems, sometimes they solve each other.' You're going to have to do *something* with your veterans. Many societies, placed in a similar pressure cooker, end up with an army they have to use, and so they proceed to go out and conquer everything in sight until stopped. For example, you realize that you could take over Chasten's Mouth and most of the other broken city-states rather easily?"

"We could," Gratar agreed with distaste, "but we wouldn't. The God is not a god of battle."

"From what I've seen and learned of your people, that would be my observation, as well, Your Excellency," Pahner said, then shrugged. "But if some other, less honest priest deposed you, he might not be so honorable, and a dishonorable priest can achieve terrible things by manipulating a people through cynical misuse of their faith. 'The God demands worshipers. These heathen cities have suffered at the hands of the Boman as His punishment for their worship of false gods. It's our duty to bring them to an understanding of the true God, if only to save them from His further just and terrible Wrath. And if they refuse to embrace the true God, then it's our duty to send them to their false gods!'"

"Is that a quote?" Gratar asked.

"More like a mosaic of quotes," Pahner admitted. "We humans have a . . . more varied palette to draw upon then you do."

"I couldn't see Rus doing that," Gratar objected. "He's no more a believer in conversion by the sword than I am."

"Oh, I agree, Your Excellency. But it's rare for the original revolutionaries to get to enjoy their revolution. Often they're too focused on fixing the things they see as 'wrong' to manage and maintain the structure and organization their societies require, and everything collapses into chaos for a period. In other cases, the idealism which got them to act in the first place makes them vulnerable to betrayal in turn. In either case, the *feck*-beasts any society contains generally pull them down and install one of their own."

The human very pointedly did not look at Chain.

"So are you saying we should go forth and conquer to keep our army out of mischief at home?" Gratar asked curiously.

"No. I said it's sometimes done. Raiden-Winterhowe in my

own . . . land is an excellent example. They were a peaceful people until they were invaded by barbarians, much as you were by the Boman. And, like you, they had to learn war, fast. In fact, they were much more damaged by their attackers before they learned their lessons than you've been, but they learned them well in the end. In fact, they got much better at it than their enemies, and they won. Now they're aggressively expansionist . . . and a real pain in the ass to their neighbors. They know it, too, but they've established a tradition of expansion, and they can't stop. To them, the only question is how much air they can blow into their divers' air bladders."

"One could make an argument there," Gratar said slowly, rubbing a horn in thought. "We could blow up quite a large bladder at the moment, and without requiring our new subjects to embrace the God. I would never force them to convert to a faith they don't truly hold, but the payment of some tithes, now . . ."

"The problem," Pahner said with a grim smile, "is that you have no administrative structure for it. Question: Who administers the cities you conquer? Local officials, or a governor appointed from here? And how do you choose the governors? Is Grath here one? And what about military forces? Some of the locals, the ones with a degree of power, especially, are going to object to your control. Do you raise forces there to keep their opposition suppressed? Or do you raise forces here, or from your other conquests, and send them to keep the peace? And if you raise forces there, and keep them there, and the governor is from there, how do you convince them to send you tithes?"

"Ah . . . These are . . . interesting points."

"Interesting or not, the logic of empire would require you to answer them, Your Excellency," the Marine said. "And don't even get me started on roads. One of the reasons you guys don't have empires is because you can't move your forces over large distances or support them logistically on field operations, and you won't be able to without decent roads."

"There are many problems with roads," Gratar said. "As I suggested in my sermon, the God does not, apparently, favor them."

"Given your climate, Your Excellency, I'd have to call that a fairly drastic understatement." The human shook his head. "But without roads, forget empire. I doubt you could make it work. Hell, I don't think *I* could make it work on Marduk, and even if someone *could* hammer an empire together, it wouldn't last more than a generation. Transportation is simply too tough. No, you need another way."

"And you have a suggestion?" the priest-king asked. "Or are you just going to ask impossible questions?"

"Yes, I have a suggestion," Pahner told him. "But I wanted you to have a feel for your constraints before I put it to you.

"Some of your veterans are going to want to go back to their old jobs. Take them back. Repair the dikes and canals. Drain the overflow lakes. Fix the washouts on the roads.

"But some of them *won't* want their old jobs. They'll want to continue their new career. Some of them will have developed a taste for it. Soldiering isn't a career for the weak of heart, but some have a mentality—which isn't, mind you, a bad thing for society as a whole—that finds soldiering better than digging ditches. We Marines are going from here to K'Vaern's Cove, and there are Boman yet to be engaged on the far side of the Nashtor Hills. Send the veterans who don't want to leave the army with us as an 'Expeditionary Force' to help us relieve K'Vaern's Cove. That gets them out of the city while you work on some of the other problems, and it also raises your profile with your neighbors as an ally, instead of a threat. Or a potential victim. There will be other city-states who use the Boman and their defeat as an opportunity for expansion, and convincing them not to expand in your direction ought to be high on your list of priorities.

"Now, rather than sending Sol Ta with these forces, send Bogess. That gets the most sticky military threat off the board without kicking off a revolution by killing him. And send Rus From, as well. We're planning on giving the people of K'Vaern's Cove the designs for a variety of weapons. We would prefer to avoid engaging the Boman ourselves, if we can help it, but the secrets of those weapons should be worth the price of the trip across the ocean to the people who have no choice but to fight the barbarians. However, creating those weapons, especially in quantity, will be difficult, and tinkering with those problems will give Rus a chance for something other than 'pumps, pumps, pumps.'"

"You would have me *reward* them for their treachery?" Gratar demanded angrily.

"What reward? Do you think they love this city any less than you do? What I'm proposing is, effectively, exile from their home—the home in whose interests, as they saw them, at least, they were willing to risk traitors' deaths. Or would you rather try to fight them in a civil war? Bogess is no slouch as a military commander, and in a war in the city, I could see Rus From being remarkably dangerous. Whatever happened, it would be bloody and nasty, not to mention expensive. And without Bogess or Rus on your side, you'd probably lose."

"But without the Laborers of God . . ."

"And that's my final point, Your Excellency," Pahner said quietly. "You *have* to pull back on the Works of God. They were beautiful symbols during the time of stasis you've just been through, but this invasion is going to shake things up, and you're going to need those workers in other areas. You'll need them as soldiers, and as artisans working on things you don't even know yet that you have to produce. Even with your climate, we should have been able to fight this war with muskets or rifles, not pikes!

"You know now, if you think of what the God has told you, the extent of the Wrath of the God. Consult your temple's records, Your Excellency. Compare the worst ravages of the Wrath to the Hompag Rains which have just passed and judge what is the very worst flooding your God will send upon you, then design your dikes and canals to resist that degree of Wrath. That's what your God is asking for, no less and, probably, no more. But surely He doesn't expect you simply to go on building redundant dikes, digging redundant canals, and manufacturing redundant pumps forever when there are so many other things that His people also require."

"Now he presumes to speak for the God!" Chain snapped. "Haven't you heard enough treason and blasphemy yet, Your Excellency?"

"Grath," Gratar said mildly, "if you say one more word without my asking, I will have a guard . . . what was it? Ah, yes—'feed you your left horn through your butt-hole.'" He gazed at the council member coldly for several seconds, and Grath Chain seemed to shrink in upon himself. Then the priest-king turned back to Pahner.

"And what of the Council?" he asked.

"The Council is a snake pit," Pahner admitted. "But without Bogess and Rus From to give them legitimacy, they're a snake pit which will fang itself to death. Dump the problem of the displaced Laborers of God on them and watch them scramble for cover."

"Make the Council's members responsible, individually, for their maintenance?" Gratar mused. "How very . . . elegant."

"So long as you insure that it doesn't become a form of slavery," the Marine cautioned. "But, yes, that should work. This sort of thing is more O'Casey's area of expertise than mine, and I would certainly advise you to discuss the details with her, but I believe that the points I've laid out will defuse almost all the major problems. It won't be an easy time with all the region recovering from the Boman, whatever you do. But if you treat the changes as a challenge to be worked with, it should also be a profitable time. For the city and for the God."

"And Grath?" Gratar asked, looking once more at the conspirator standing by the wall.

"Do what you will," Pahner replied. "If it were up to me, I'd say give him a thankless job and all the worst people to do it with, and impose severe penalties for failure. But he's really a treasure if you use him properly. For example, you'll probably be threatened by another city-state soon, whatever you do. If that happens, send him there with some funds to destabilize it. If he succeeds, reward him. If he's found out, disown him and swear that whatever he did, it was never by your orders."

"But he has done me a service in warning of the coup," Gratar said. "Surely I owe him something for that."

"Okay," Pahner agreed. "Give him thirty pieces of silver."

"This way is probably for the best," Bogess said, gazing out over the canals and dikes in the first, faint light of dawn. "However early it is."

"Well, we need to be to the Nashtor Hills by nightfall," Rastar pointed out with a shrug. "Better to be hit there by the scattered tribes rather than caught out in the open."

"And how much of this precipitous departure is to prevent the people from seeing half their army and two of their leaders hustled off into the wilderness?" Rus From demanded with a growl.

The cleric shifted the unfamiliar weight of the sword baldric on his shoulder as he stood between the general and the Northerner prince and looked upon the flood-control works. He wondered if he would ever again see the Bastar Canal. It was the first project he'd worked upon as a young engineer under that old taskmaster, Bes Clan.

"The Boman are no threat to Diaspra; we made sure of that," Rastar replied, and it was true. The Northern cavalry, with the pillage and destruction of their own cities fresh in their collective memory, had been merciless to the retreating foe. If a thousand Wespar ever made it to their distant cousins, it would be astonishing.

"I had plans," From half-snarled.

"And now you'll have new ones!" the Therdan prince snapped. "You're the one complaining about nothing new. Haven't you heard the plans of the humans? Rapidly firing guns? Giant ships? Light, wheeled cannon? A 'combined arms force'? What do you have to complain about?"

The artisan turned slowly to look at the prince.

"What would you give to see Therdan or Sheffan once more? See them shining in the morning light as the *tankett* calls? See their people going about their business in peace and plenty through your actions?"

Rastar turned away from the cleric's hot gaze and looked out into the growing light.

"I see it every night in my dreams, priest. But I cannot return to my home; it's no longer there." He shrugged, the gesture picked up from the humans, and fingered the communicator on his harness. "Perhaps, in time, things will change and for some there will be a homecoming."

"Centicred for your thoughts?" Kosutic's voice was quiet, for Roger was definitely looking grim.

The prince leaned into the armored head of the *flar-ta* as his memory replayed again and again the sights and sounds and smells of the pursuit. It had been necessary. He knew that. But it had also been hideous . . . and the pleasure he'd taken in it as he poured out his anger and fear and frustration upon an enemy who'd really had nothing to do with creating his predicament in the first place had been still worse. There were dark places in his own soul which he'd never before realized were there, and he didn't like the look at them he'd just been given.

There was no one else in hearing distance. The Marines and Mardukans were engaged in final preparations for the fast march to the Nashtor Hills, and he turned his head to meet the sergeant major's eyes.

"I wanna go home, Top," he whispered. "I just want to go home."

"Yeah," the sergeant major sighed. "Me, too, Boss. Me, too." She gave Pahner a thumbs-up as the captain looked down the long line of march. All the mahouts and cavalry leaders gave the same signal, and she inhaled deeply. It was time to move out.

"The only way to get there is to put one foot in front of the other," she said, "and I guess it's that time." She looked up at the somber prince with a shrug and a crooked smile.

"Time and high time to be trekkin' again, eh?" the prince said. "Well, here's to the last march. To the sea."

CHAPTER NINETEEN

Dergal Starg waved at the bartender.

"Give me another, Tarl. Nothing better to do."

It was the fifth time he'd said that, and Tarl was probably getting tired of hearing it. Not that the bartender was going to say anything.

Ownership of the Nashtor mines had been disputed between three different city-states right up until they and the armies they'd kept glowering at one another might actually have been some use. Right up until the Boman had smashed two of the city-states into rubble and cut the mines off from K'Vaern's Cove, the only one of the three which had ever been worth a solitary damn. But none of those cities had ever believed they could *control* Nashtor, whoever might officially claim ownership. Those mines were the province of one Dergal Starg. Merchants could merch, warriors could war. But it took a by-the-gods miner to mine, and in all the lands of the Chasten and Tam, in all the Nashtor Hills, there was no miner to match Dergal Starg.

Which was what made the present situation so bitterly ironic, of course. Because what was needed right now was one of those iron-head Northern war princes. Or a K'Vaernian guardsman. Or even an idiotic war priest from Diaspra. Because no matter how good a miner you were, a mine without markets was just a hole in the ground that you poured money into.

Sure, a few hundred miners and a group of engineers had been able to create defenses the Boman avoided. Sure, they were able to keep mining, even with the occasional probing foray by the barbarians. But even though the sounds of the surrounding mines and smelters continued to echo through the tavern, they weren't quite right. At any other time, he would have been down Shaft Five in a heartbeat, for example. He could tell the lazy bastards were lying down on the job down there, but what was the point of working yourself to death, of building inventories, when there were no buyers?

There was none, of course, but Dergal Starg still ran the mines and smelters. And the miners were, by the gods, going to keep on mining right until the mines ran out of food, new picks, and the thousand and one other things they got from the stupid, cheating merchants.

And the bartenders were, by the gods, going to tend, which was why he glared at Tarl when his mug of wine wasn't immediately refilled. But then he noticed that the bartender was staring over his shoulder with wide eyes and all four hands thrown outward in a gesture of surprise.

Starg turned around to see what the nincompoop was staring at, and froze. The crew which had just walked under the roof of the wall-less structure was a flatly amazing sight, and not just because the mines were sealed off from everyone else in the entire world by the Boman, yet he'd never laid eyes on a single one of them before.

Four of them were obviously Northerner iron heads, two of them wearing some of the nicest ironwork it had ever been his pleasure to admire. The fluting on one of the cuirasses followed the new trend coming out of K'Vaern, picked up apparently from some outlandish place which had never heard of steel on steel. No doubt it reduced the weight of the armor by a good bit, but traditionalists—and Starg, by the gods, put himself in that category—thought it was likely to backfire. The damned stuff was bound to catch the point of a weapon or crack under any heavy pounding, although he had to admit that this armor was as hacked about as any he'd ever seen, and it seemed to have stood the test well. From the look of the wearer, it would probably be a better idea not to make any sarcastic remarks about it, either.

But the ironmongery, however impressive, wasn't the most interesting thing about the group. One of the iron heads' companions was a lightly armed, gods-be-damned *priest*. One of the damned water boys, no less, unless he was mistaken, and a senior one by his gear. Starg had seen a couple of water boy missionaries in his time, but most of them had been youngsters. This fellow was anything but, and the wrench he wore on the golden chain about his neck made him an *artisan* priest. Artisan priests were like *legends*; you never saw one outside Diaspra. But that still wasn't the most interesting thing about the group—that had to be the *basik* in the middle.

It couldn't be an actual *basik*. For one thing, it was too gods-be-damned big, but it sure as the gods *looked* like a *basik*. No horns, no claws, no armor—just soft and pink all over. Well, it was wearing some sort of covering, and its skin had an ugly dry look, like a *feck*-beast's. But other than that . . . and the helmet . . . it certainly looked like a *basik*.

The iron head in the fluted cuirass held out one hand, palm up to indicate friendship.

"You are Dergal Starg?" he asked.

"Yeah," the miner snarled. "Who by the gods wants to know?"

"Ah," the Northerner said with a weird facial grimace that exposed his teeth. "The famous Starg personality. Let me introduce myself. I'm Rastar Komas Ta'Norton, Prince of Therdan. King, I suppose now. I believe you once met my uncle under better circumstances."

Starg slumped suddenly, even his belligerence temporarily muted. Kantar T'Norl had been one of the only damned outsiders who hadn't been totally, by the gods, idiotic. Unlike all too many others, Kantar had always been a voice of reason in the region.

"I'm sorry, Rastar Komas Ta'Norton. I shouldn't have been so abrupt. The loss of your uncle was a terrible blow to the Valley of the Tam."

"He died as well as could be permitted," the Northern prince said, "leading a charge to cover our retreat. We were able to get many of the women and children out of Therdan and Sheffan because of his sacrifice and the willing sacrifice of his house warriors."

"It's still a great loss," the miner growled, taking a sip from his now refilled mug.

"Yes, and hardly the way he would have preferred to leave us," the prince agreed with another of those odd grimaces. "I suspect that he would have preferred drowning in a wine vat," he said, and Starg grunted in laughter for the first time.

"Yes, he was a bit of a drinker. It's a recent vice on my own part, of course."

"Not according to my uncle," Rastar disagreed. "He said you could drink a *pagee* under the table."

"High praise, indeed," Starg said. "And now that we've covered the pleasantries, where did you come from? The trails are swarming with Boman."

"The ones to the north may be," the thing that looked like a *basik* said, "but the ones to the south are . . . clearer."

"Who's the *basik*?" Starg asked, gesturing at the odd creature.

"This is Captain Armand Pahner of the Empress' Own," Rastar said with yet another of those odd grimaces. "And calling him a *basik* to his face could be a mistake of cosmic proportions. A *brief* mistake."

"Captain Pahner and his 'Imperial Marines' are the reason that there no longer *are* any Boman to the south," the cleric put in, and extended one palm-up true-hand of his own in greeting. "Rus From, at your service," he said, administering the mining engineer's second intense shock of the day.

"*The* Rus From? The Rus From who created the two-cycle pump system? The secondary aortal injector? The Rus From who designed the God's Lake runoff entrapment system? That was a thing of beauty! I used a modification of it in our Number Nine shaft trap."

"Um," the momentarily nonplused cleric said. Then, "Yes, I suppose that was I."

"So you came up from the south?" Starg asked. "What happened to the Boman?"

"Wespar, actually," Rastar said, and clapped hands in a shrug. "We killed them."

"That's a somewhat simplistic explanation," From noted reprovingly.

"Accurate, nonetheless," Rastar argued. "They don't have enough left to burn their dead."

"They don't burn them, anyway," Starg said distastefully. "They *bury* them."

"True," From said. "A terrible use of land. Can you imagine what would happen if *everyone* buried their dead? Before long, all the dry land would be overrun with dead bodies!"

"Could we debate social customs at some other time?" the maybe-not-*basik* asked with a grimace which, allowing for the differences in shape and form, was remarkably like the one Rastar had been making, and Starg finally remembered where he'd seen it before. It was the exact expression a *basik* made when you had it cornered and were just about to club it. Like it was trying to talk you out of it or something.

"Indeed," Rus From said. "We brought a caravan through with us. It includes some of the items you ordered from the merchants of Diaspra before the Boman closed the roads."

"We appreciated that last shipment of pig iron, by the way," the maybe-not-*basik* said. "It would have been tough to do everything we had to without it."

"Yeah, well, normally we do most of our trading with K'Vaern's Cove," Starg said. "But they were cut off by then. We just had to hope a caravan would make it back from Diaspra, instead."

"And indeed it did," From said. "I'm afraid that few of the mining implements you ordered are included, however. Most of the ones that were complete were converted into weapons. We do have a goodly load of food and wines, spices, and so forth, though."

"That's all well and good," Starg protested. "But we're going to need those tools soon."

"And they'll be completed in time," From said dryly. "With all the weapons we recovered from the Wespar, there's much more than sufficient iron to replace the material we commandeered."

"And with any luck, we'll be able to get the Boman's attention so centered on us that they won't be a problem between here and K'Vaern's Cove much longer, either," Rastar added. "There were none on the south side of the hills. Where are they?"

"Mostly still gorging on the corpse of Sindi," Starg said. "But there are many bands just wandering around, some of them quite large. You'll find it difficult to pass through to the Cove, if that's your target."

"Oh, I don't know about that," said the maybe-not-*basik*. "I think we might just give them pause."

"You see," Rastar said, "we're not *exactly* a caravan."

The forces from Diaspra sprawled everywhere around the mines. Most of them were inside the hasty walls the miners had thrown up against the Boman under Starg's direction. Those of them who were not, lightly armored figures carrying incredibly long spears or lances, were busy erecting another camp adjacent to the mining area. They dug with incredible energy and precision, as if they'd been doing it their entire lives.

"What, by all the gods, is this?" Starg asked, rubbing a horn furiously.

"Well," the maybe-not-*basik*, Pahner, said, "I'm afraid we weren't quite sure who held the mines, so we took the liberty of securing your guards until we were sure. They're unharmed," the not-*basik* added hastily.

"So you just snuck in and took over?" the mine manager demanded, wondering whether he was angrier at the newcomers or at the guards who were supposed to have prevented such things from happening.

"It's . . . something of a specialty of ours," the not-*basik* said with another of those strange grimaces.

"They did it to us once," Rastar confirmed with a weird move of both shoulder sets.

"So now what?" Starg asked. "You can't do any good here; the Boman just avoid us."

"We may leave a few groups of our soldiers with you," Rus From replied. "Some of our Diasprans haven't taken as well to conditions on the march as they thought they might. That doesn't make them poor soldiers, though, and they can be helpful training and supporting your miners. The rest of us are going to K'Vaern's Cove."

"You'll never make it," the mine manager warned. "You might have made it on a straight shot from the south, but it's different between here and the Cove."

"Yes, it is," the not-*basik* agreed with one of those weird grimaces. Suddenly, he looked much less like a *basik* than an *atul*. A hungry *atul*. "There's a road."

"We'll be moving very fast," Rastar added. "You might have noticed that we have a large number of *turom* and *civan* along with the *pagee*. The humans have shown us that an infantry force can move much faster than we ever believed possible if the spear-carriers take occasional rests by holding onto the packs of the *turom* and *civan*. Also, many of them, and all our wounded, ride on the *pagee*. I wouldn't have believed it before they proved it, but we can travel nearly as fast as *civan* cavalry."

"We should get through without problems as long as we can avoid their main force," the "human" noted. "You said that they're in and around Sindi. I've seen that on a map, and it's well out of the way of the direct route to K'Vaern's Cove. How sure are you of their location, and where do you get your information?"

"Some woodsmen still move among the Boman," Starg replied. "Charcoal burners and the like who simply give them whatever they want and survive as best they can. We help them out with whatever we can spare, and in return they keep us fairly well informed on where the barbs are and what they're up to. Also, Sindi is the largest and richest city they've conquered. They aren't done looting it even yet."

The humans shared a look with the Northern prince, but Rastar seemed to agree.

"They would know, Armand," the Northerner said. "The woods are filled with half-wild workers, and I doubt that they'd care much for the Boman. Their lives are never easy, but they must be truly impossible in the midst of this invasion."

"Then we need to factor them into our next move," said the not-*basik*, Pahner. "Intelligence cuts two ways."

"What?" Starg asked. "They're not particularly smart—"

"He means that they could talk to the Boman as well as to you,"

Rastar translated. "It's a human term meaning all that you know about your enemy."

"We don't want our axis of advance communicated to the Boman," Pahner added.

"I doubt that they'll be talking to the Boman," Rastar demurred. "They're insular even under normal conditions, and I'm sure they're staying as far away from the invaders as they can."

"That's truth," Starg said. "We've traded tools and weapons to them for food and other supplies. Otherwise, they'd have nothing to do with us, either."

"Tools," Pahner said. "That we're not in need of. But how much refined iron do you have on-site?"

"Why?" Starg asked suspiciously.

"Because we're taking it all with us to K'Vaern," Pahner said, looking out over the building Diaspran camp. "K'Vaern's Cove will need it if they're going to survive, and we need them happy with us. It's why we came this way, really."

"Oh, you are, are you?" Starg said angrily. "Just how are you going to pay for it? It's not like you even brought all that was already owed!"

The not-*basik*'s head turned towards Starg like a machine. The human was scarcely half the miner's size, and Starg had been in more fights as a youngster than his old bones cared to remember. But at that moment, he was as sure as the gods had made him that he did not want to test the human commander.

"Worry not," Rus From said calmly. "I'll guarantee payment for the material from the temple."

"Oh," Starg said, his hostility disappearing abruptly. "In that case, I suppose it will be all right. And in answer to your question, there are several tons waiting to go. We've been smelting most of the time."

"Pig iron, or wrought?" Rastar asked.

"Pig," the miner said with a shrug. "I've got a puddling forge, but I don't have the charcoal to make it worthwhile to run it."

"We can make steel from this?" Pahner asked. "That's important."

"You can," Starg said shortly. "At least they can in K'Vaern's Cove . . . if you get it there."

"Great," Pahner said, nodding as he slipped a slice of *bisti* root into his mouth. "Give him a chit or whatever, Rus, and let's get loading. I want to be able to pull right out in the morning."

Dergal Starg stood watching the receding column in the morning light. The humans and half the *civan* cavalry had left earlier to sweep the path of the caravan, and about a third of the "pikemen" were holding onto straps dangling from the pack *turom* and *civan*. The rest were spread out to either side and in front, screening the caravan as it headed for the broad, stone road to K'Vaern's Cove.

The head of the miner guard force walked up to Starg as he stood by the rough rock wall guarding the entrance to the mine.

"I'm sorry about yesterday, Dergal. We just weren't vigilant enough. It won't happen again."

"Hmmm?" the manager said, then shook himself. "Oh, don't worry about that, T'an—it's the least of our worries. I just got scammed by a human who spent half his time talking about pits, or pocks, or something. He also taught me an interesting game of chance, and I now owe him about four days' output. In addition to that, we've just sent all the metal we've processed since the invasion into the very midst of the Boman solely on a promise of payment from a priest who, I have since discovered, left home under . . . less than auspicious circumstances. And we can only collect it if we manage to get word back to Diaspra that they owe it to us. And if a caravan makes it back through to us, of course."

"Oh," said T'an. Then, "This isn't good, is it?"

"By the gods, I don't know," Starg said, with a grunt of humor. "But I *think* it's grand."

"Is Gratar going to pay?" Pahner asked. "We would've gone ahead and loaded the iron whether he would or not, but will he?"

"Yes," From said. "He will, and he'll know that I knew that he would. I regard it as it is— What's that phrase you humans use? 'A parting shot'?"

"And a nice one, despite Poertena's best efforts," the Marine agreed.

"Yes, it is," the priest said with a note of obvious satisfaction as he visualized the priest-king's reaction to the bill Dergal Starg was about to present to him. "But what matters is that we have the iron, which should be well-received in K'Vaern's Cove. Now all we have to do is get through with it."

"Oh, we'll get through," Pahner said. "Even if I've got to break out the armor, we'll get through. It's after we get through that it gets interesting."

CHAPTER TWENTY

"Where's the city?" the sergeant major asked. All she could see from the top of the *flar-ta* was walls and hills.

"Beyond the hills," Rastar said. "This is just the outer wall."

The city was on a peninsula between the ocean and a broad bay, and the peninsula narrowed to a low, very narrow neck where the wall closed it off before spreading out once more beyond it. If it hadn't been for a breakwater and some low dunes, the half-hearted waves on their left would have been washing over the road.

A fresh, onshore wind blew in from the sea, carrying away the scent of rot from the bay to their right. The shoreline on that side edged almost imperceptibly into a salt marsh, over which four-winged avians croaked and hissed. The salt marsh blended in turn into a small delta from the Selke River—more of a creek, really—which the road had paralleled all the way from the Nashtor Hills.

The wall itself was immense, the largest Kosutic had seen since Voitan. It stood at least ten meters tall and was nearly that broad. The gateway was a massive, double-turreted affair, with a dogleg and clearly evident murder holes, and massive bombards loomed from the walls at regular intervals. Either K'Vaern's Cove had common everyday enemies in plenty, or else it had entirely too much money and had needed something expensive to use it up on.

The ends of the wall were anchored by bastions, studded with more bombards, where it met the sea and the marsh, respectively. The seaward bastions apparently served double duty as lighthouses, and the wall continued back along both coasts until the land rose and became rocky enough to make a landing difficult or impossible.

"Bloody serious defenses," Kosutic muttered.

"K'Vaern's Cove has participated in numerous wars in the region, at one time or another," the Northerner prince told her. "Sometimes in alliance with the League, at other times in opposition. It's never been interested in conquest, though. Most of its wars have had to do with maintaining freedom of trade . . . or pressing for it."

"Was Sindi one of the ones it fought?" the sergeant major asked. "And what is the story there? You keep referring to it, but you've never explained."

"I assume that your Ms. O'Casey is familiar with the story by now, but, in short, Tor Cant, the Despot of Sindi, was a bloated *feck*-beast. He was also a fool whose desires far outweighed his vision or ability, and the foremost of those desires was to be the ruler of all the land around the Tam and Chasten.

"He began his efforts by moving against the League of the North. Since we were the greatest military threat to his plans, he attempted to cause trouble between our cities in the hope that we would turn on one another and destroy ourselves for him. Then, when that plot was revealed and even he realized it was a complete failure, he sent embassies to the Boman. After much placation, some of their senior chiefs agreed to come meet with him, and he also gathered representatives from many of the Southern states who chafed at our trade taxes. The official reason for the meeting was to negotiate a treaty with the Boman, because if the Boman were no longer a threat, then the League would no longer be required. And if that happened, he reasoned, all the lands of the South would unite to rise up against our taxes.

"It became clear, however, that he had no intention of negotiating in good faith with the Boman. I said that his desires outweighed his vision, and that was probably overgenerous of me. The Boman are barbarians, but Tor Cant *treated* them like barbarians . . . and not very important ones, either. Instead of offering concessions, he put forward demands which anyone, not just the Boman, would have considered insulting. And when the Boman chiefs rejected them, he completed his idiocy by throwing a fit and ordering them killed in his very throne room, in front of the Southern ambassadors.

"It was, I've heard, quite a scene. His guards were Southern weaklings, so the Boman chiefs and their guards nearly cut their way to the throne, despite having been taken completely by surprise. Unfortunately, they didn't quite reach it, and when word of what had happened reached the northern clans, they swore blood feud against all the 'shit-sitters' in the cities.

"They came upon the League first, and all of us had been sabotaged, one way or another, undoubtedly by agents of Sindi. In Therdan it was poison in the grain stores. Sheffan had its water supply fouled. Others had mysterious fires in their granaries, or found the fodder for their *civan* poisoned.

"The intent, probably, was for the League and the Boman to destroy each other. Then Sindi would move against both, coming as a savior to what remained of the League and destroying the Boman. Then the League would have been absorbed, and the warriors who were left would have been used against the other cities."

"But that's not what happened," Kosutic said.

"No," the native prince responded very quietly, gazing at the approaching walls. "Tor Cant was a fool, and he underestimated the Boman. He obviously expected them to attack us as they always had before, clan by clan and tribe by tribe, and he reasoned that, even crippled by his treachery, our cities would be able to hold long enough to bleed the barbarians and weaken them fatally before they could move further south. But the Boman were united, and their strategy was far better than it had ever been before. They came upon Therdan in a wave, for we were the chief city of the North, and their new leaders realized that if we fell, it would not only open the way south but dishearten the rest of the League, as well. They besieged us for barely a month and a half, and we took good measure of them. So long as we were able to man our defenses, we killed many of them for every warrior we lost. But in the end, we were starving, and before we lost the flower of our *civan*, my father had me fight my way out, with as many of the women and children as we felt we could take.

"My uncle, whom Dergal Starg spoke of . . . He and his household opened the way, and we went forth over the carpet of their bodies. The youngest of the cavalry, on the best *civan*, with the women and children clinging to us as we ran."

"We didn't bother going to Sindi; it would have been pointless. Instead, we struck for Bastar, thinking that we might find aid there. But the Boman were before us, and behind us. We could only flee before them.

"And so, in the end, you found us. A starving band of ragged fugitives, washed up as flotsam in the mountains."

"And Therdan?" the sergeant major asked softly.

"It fell shortly afterward. And Sheffan, and Tarhal, and Crin. And D'Sley and Torth. And Sindi."

"But not, apparently, K'Vaern's Cove."

"No," the Mardukan agreed. "The Cove is impregnable."

Bistem Kar peered through the telescope at the approaching column. There had been more than sufficient time to make his way from the Citadel to the wall, for the column had been sighted before First Bell by the sentinels, but he still didn't have a clue as to who this was. It clearly wasn't the Boman horde, as he'd first assumed. In fact, the lead units appeared to be Northern League cavalry, but just what the rest of the ragtag and bobtail might be was another question. And the matter of what its purpose here might be was yet another. Assuming that those glittering points were on the ends of extremely long spears, this force was far too large and well armed to be a mere supply caravan, and, by the same token, probably wasn't another column of refugees.

He slid the device shut and made a gesture of frustration.

"It makes no sense."

"More refugees?" Tor Flain asked. The second in command of the K'Vaern Company of the Guard glanced sidelong at his commander. Kar was called "The Kren," not just for his immense size, but for his speed and cunning, as well. The *kren* was a water beast, but the commander had proved that its tactics worked just as well on land.

Kar had turned out in his habitual wear—the armored jerkin and harness of a Guardsman private, without the glittering emblems of rank to which he was entitled. It was a uniform he'd worn for many seasons, and one he was comfortable in. He would wear it to all but the most formal meetings, and in all but the most pitched battles, for it was a badge to him, and one that the Guard appreciated. Many was the time that he'd proved himself a guardsman to the very heart, fighting for the resources to keep the Company in top form, whatever it took. And everyone knew that it was only his regular, unceasing battles for a decent budget which had permitted the Guard to repulse the first assault of the Boman.

But the Boman had sworn that no city of the south would remain standing after that stupid bastard in Sindi's actions, and the fact that none of the other cities had had anything to do with Tor Cant's massacre didn't seem to matter. So now it was up to the Guard, and the rest of the capable citizenry, to make that barbarian oath fail, and the odds against that were heavy.

Kar opened the telescope back up and looked through it once more, and Tor Flain took a moment to admire the device. Dell Mir was a wizard with contraptions, but the war against the Boman had seemed to bring out the genius in him. From the device that squirted burning coal oil to changes in the smelters that had steel coming out of their ears (when they could lay their hands on raw materials, at least), the quirky inventor had proved a priceless resource to the defenses. Another example of the sort of genius the Cove seemed to produce almost spontaneously.

Tor Flain loved his city, although he, like many others, had not been born here. His parents had moved from D'Sley when he was young and started a small fish-processing business. He'd grown up with the K'Vaernian bells in his ears and worked long hours as a child and teen, gutting the daily catches and running the results from Great House to Great House. His father was a good salesman, but it was his mother who'd really run things. She'd had an eye for the best fish, and the best way to do things—what some were now calling "efficiency"—and it was the efficiency of the House of Flain which had permitted them to rise from a tiny processor, one among hundreds, to a noted provider of luxury goods. They weren't a major house, by any means, but they were no longer living in a shack on the docks, either.

And as a result of that, their daughters had married well and their sons had spread into many major positions throughout the city and its varied businesses. Positions such as that of second in command of the Company. That hadn't seemed such a good move once; now, Tor Flain's position was arguably among the ten most important ones in the entire city. And while he wasn't about to use his influence to give business to the family, it wasn't really necessary for him to. Anyone who wanted to deal with the Guard assumed that while dealing with the House of Flain wasn't a requirement, it couldn't hurt, either.

Genius inventor from apprentice smith, commander of the Guard from simple guardsman, second in command from a family of fish-gutters. That was K'Vaern's Cove . . . and it was why he would willingly lay down his life for it.

Kar slid the telescope closed again and tapped it on one true-hand, his lower arms crossed in thought.

"It's a relief column," he said.

"Damned small one, then," Flain responded. "Barely three thousand."

"But what three thousand?" Kar mused. "The Northerners' lead banner is that of Therdan."

"Impossible," Flain scoffed. "It was overrun in the first wave!"

"True. But there were rumors that some of them had escaped. And the banner next to it is Sheffan's. They're all supposed to be dead, too, you know. But the really interesting thing is the banner at the head of those spearmen." Tor looked a question at him, and Kar grunted a chuckle. "It's the River."

"Diaspra?" Flain said in astonishment. "But . . . they would *never*. They don't involve themselves in wars at all."

"This war is different," Kar pointed out. "But what I don't understand are all the *turom* and *pagee*. There seem to be an awful lot of them for a relief column that size. It's almost more like a giant caravan, and there are some figures out there—strange ones that look a bit like women but are obviously something else. Many of them are on the *pagee*, too."

He opened the telescope yet again, peered through it for long, thoughtful minutes. Then, suddenly, he gave a whoop of delight.

"*That's* what they're packing!"

"What?" Flain asked.

"Iron, by Krin! Those beasts are loaded with iron bars!"

"They must've come by way of Nashtor," the second in command mused. "Somebody was using his head for something besides holding up his horns."

"Send out a rider," Kar said. "Let's find out what we have here. I think we're going to like it."

The Mardukan who greeted them was the biggest damned scummy—with the possible exception of Erkum Pol—Roger had ever seen. Which, given the size of normal Mardukan males, was saying something. Not only was this one damned near four meters tall, he was disproportionately broad even for that towering height and looked as if he could bench press a *flar-ta*.

"Bistem Kar," Rastar said with obvious relief. "You live."

"Yes, Prince Rastar," the monster responded in a deep, rumbling grunt of laughter. "And as amazed as you are to see me, I'm ten times as amazed to see the heir of Therdan at the door."

"We tried to win through to you when first we fled, but there were too many Boman," Rastar admitted. "And, as the gods would have it, perhaps that was for the best." He turned from the K'Vaernian commander and gestured to Roger. "Bistem Kar, Captain of K'Vaern's Cove, may I introduce His Royal Highness, Prince Roger MacClintock of the Terran Empire."

"I greet you, Prince MacClintock, in the name of the Council of K'Vaern's Cove," the Mardukan responded, admirably restraining his obvious curiosity about just what in hell a "Terran Empire" might be. "And I greet your loads with even greater happiness," he added.

"That's why we stopped by Nashtor," Roger said. "And may I

introduce my senior commander, Captain Armand Pahner, who was the one who insisted on retrieving the metal."

"I greet you as well, Captain Pahner," the Guard commander said, casting a close eye over the human. He looked from the chameleon-clad CO to the similarly clad Marines spreading out to either side of the caravan and suppressed an audible grunt of pleased laughter. "Welcome to K'Vaern's Cove."

"K'Vaern's Cove," Rus From said with more enthusiasm than he'd shown since leaving Diaspra. "We're here."

"Wonderful," Bogess responded in a much grumpier tone. "Another city, another battle. Just wonderful."

The area between the inner and outer defenses was given over to agriculture. There were crops of barleyrice and apsimon fruit, mostly clustered on the bay side of the narrow neck of land. On the seaward side there were fruit vines, the famous sea-plums of the coastal region that produced sea-plum wine.

"But this is *K'Vaern's Cove!*" the priest said. "K'Vaern of the Bells! All the world meets in K'Vaern's Cove! This is where over half the devices in the entire Chasten Valley come from. This is where the impeller pump system was *invented*. There's no other city like it!"

"Uh-huh," the general scoffed. "And all the streets are paved with gold. It's still just another city and just another battle."

"Well, we'll see," the cleric replied, refusing to be suppressed by the pessimistic soldier.

"And another new way of doing battle," Bogess continued. "It's not as if we can just teach them pikes and be done with it. No, we have to create these 'muskets' and 'mobile cannon.' Then we have to learn how to use them ourselves."

"Not quite," From corrected as the two representatives from Diaspra were called forward. "In fact, you'll have to, somehow, learn how to use them while they're still being created. And without the help of the humans."

"Podder mocker," Poertena muttered as the column rounded the first hill.

The basis of the city's name was immediately clear. Far below them lay a perfect natural harbor—a cove cut off from the worst effects of weather by hills on either side. All of the hills were extremely steep, with sheer-sided inlets or fjords between several of them, and the bay and the inlets had been linked to create a sheltered, multipart port. Clearly, some of the smaller side harbors could support only small craft, but there were hundreds of those circulating around the city.

The deep-water portions of the port were packed with ships. The most common was a single-masted, square-rigged, round-hulled design very similar in most respects to a medieval Terran cog. There were differences—the beam-to-length ratio was a bit better—but generally, the resemblance was remarkable. Most of them were about twenty meters from stem to stern, but a few larger ones ran to a bit over thirty, and one of the larger ones was being towed out by a galley, assisted by the slight puffs of the land wind coming over the hills.

One of the side-harbors seemed to be given over to military vessels, of which there appeared to be two basic types. At least two-thirds of them were sleek, low, needle-slim galleys armed with rams, but with no apparent sign of seagoing artillery. The remaining warships were larger, heavier, and clumsier looking. Like the galleys (and unlike most of the merchantmen in the harbor), they carried both oars and masts, but their main armament was obviously the batteries of heavy guns bristling from their heavily built forecastles above their long-beaked rams. Their banks of oars precluded any sort of broadside-mounted artillery, but they were clearly designed to lay down a heavy forward fire as they closed in on their enemies, and there was something very peculiar about those guns. Poertena dialed up the magnification on his helmet and grunted in sudden understanding and surprise, for the guns he could see weren't the built-up, welded-together bombards they'd seen on Diaspra's walls. These guns were *cast*, by God!

The four major hills around the port were part of a series of hills that ran for kilometers to the north, and all of them were covered by interlocked buildings. Houses were built on warehouses were built on shops, until virtually all the open spaces were filled with places of work or living, and often both simultaneously in the same structure.

And everywhere the eye looked, there were bell towers.

Sergeant Julian stood beside the little Pinopan and shook his head in bemusement. It surprised him a bit to realize that nowhere else in all their weary trek had he seen a single Mardukan bell. Not one. But now there were dozens—scores—of bell towers in sight from his single vantage point. God only knew how many there were in the city as a whole . . . or what it must sound like if they all tolled at once. He could see little bells, like carillons, in some of the towers, but there were also medium bells, big bells, and one great big giant bell which must have weighed as much as eight or nine tons in a massive tower near the center of the city, and he wondered why there were so many of them.

Roads twisted through the architectural crazy-quilt, packed with Mardukans. Everywhere Julian and Poertena looked in the city, there were Mardukans selling and buying and going about their business. From the edge of the sheltering hills, the city looked like a kicked anthill.

But anyone who actually wanted to kick this anthill had his work cut out for him. The city was encircled by another immense wall, much larger and stronger than the outer defense work and crowned with artillery which probably threw nine- to twelve-kilo roundshot, with bastions every sixty meters or so. The harbor mouth itself was protected by immense citadels, each liberally supplied with its own cannon, and those guns were massive. In fact, they looked big enough to throw seventy-five- to eighty-kilo shot, although Julian hated to think about the appetite for gunpowder those monsters must have. The only open space in the entire city was a large formation area on the inner side of the wall, which extended the full length of the fortifications' circuit. The area outside the wall had also been cleared, although there were some temporary buildings in that space now, especially near the water and around the main gate, where a virtual shanty town had sprung up.

The wall extended upward on the highest hill, bisecting the city, and connected to another massive citadel, a many-tiered fortress, obviously carved out of the mountain it sat upon. The stones of its exterior portions blended into the background rock so cleverly that it was difficult to tell where the fortress started and the mountain ended, and it, too, boasted a soaring bell tower, this one crowned with an elaborate gilded weathervane in the shape of a ship with all sail set.

"I can see why everybody thinks this place is impossible to take," Julian said.

"Yeah," Poertena said, then thought about it. "But, you know, you gotta wonder. Where's tee supplies?"

"Huh?" Gronningen asked. The stolid Asgardian seemed unaffected by the immensity of the city.

"Well, as long as you can be supplied by sea . . ." the intel NCO said.

"Sure, but where tee supplies gonna come from?" the Pinopan asked. "T'ere's no place to grow food for all t'ese people on t'is peninsula, even wit' all the fish they prob'ly catch. My guess is t'ey used to get most of t'eir food from t'is Sindi place or some such. Where's it comin' from now?"

"Ah," Julian said. "I see your point. And it's not coming from the next city downriver from Sindi, because that one's been overrun, too."

"So t'ey shipping t'eir supplies from where? A hundred kilometers? Two hundred? A t'ousand?"

"Yeah."

"Instead of just barging it downriver an' across tee bay. And t'at goes for all tee other stuff t'at isn't luxury stuff, stuff you usually get from nearby. Wood, leather, metal, stuff like t'at. And what you gonna bet most of t'eir trade used to be with t'ose cities tee Boman took?"

"But you can depend on distant supply sources and get away with it," Julian argued. "San Francisco did back in the old, old, old days on Earth. And everything it needed mostly came in on ships, not overland."

"Sure," the Pinopan agreed. "New Manila's not'ing but a seaport and a starport, an' it's as big as it gets on Pinopa. T'ey gets ever't'ing but fish from tee ass-end of nowhere. But two t'ings. You see t'ose ships?" He pointed at the oversized cog making its cumbersome way out of port.

"Yes," Julian said. "So?"

"T'at's tee worst pocking ship I ever see. Any kinda deep-water blow, an' it's gonna roll right over an' sink like a flooded rock. An' it's gonna be slow as shit, an' if it slow, it cost more money to run, an' t'at means tee grain gonna be expensive. And t'at means in tee end t'ey starve unless t'ey gots some big source o' pocking income. Which is what leads to tee other t'ing, which is t'ey not'ing but a market. Sure, t'ey might make some stuff here. T'ey might be a reg'lar New Dresden, but it's gonna be not'ing compared to tee stuff t'at's just waiting to ship to somwheres else. An' if not'ing coming down tee Chasten *or* tee Tam, t'en t'ey gots not'ing to sell. An' if t'ey gots not'ing to sell, t'en t'ey gonna starve."

"How are you supplied?" Pahner asked. "If you don't mind my asking."

The relief column had attracted remarkably little attention as it passed through the large shanty town around the gate and the outer wall. If a war threatening their very survival was going on, the people of K'Vaern's Cove seemed not to have noticed.

The main thoroughfare on which they were traveling was packed. Only the force of guardsmen calling for way and physically pushing blockages aside permitted the caravan to keep moving, and the side streets were just as crowded, with carts or kiosks set up every few meters selling a mixture of products from food to weapons.

The city was packed onto the slopes surrounding the cove, and the surrounding hills virtually stopped the sea winds, which turned the city into a sweltering, breathless sauna even hotter than the Mardukan norm. The still air also trapped the scent of the streets, and it closed in on the column as it passed through the gate. The effluvia was a combination of the cooking and spices of the side streets and the normal dung smell of all Mardukan cities, subtly flavored with a hint of clear salt air and the rot smell which was common to every harbor in the known universe.

Most of the buildings, aside from the soaring bell towers, were low and made from stone or packed mud, with plaster walls which ranged from blinding white to a glaring clash of painted colors. It was the first place the humans had seen where extensive use had been made of pastels, and the combination of riotous colors, furnace heat, and heady smells dazed some of the Marines.

Single doorways fronted directly onto the street, and children darted out into traffic without heed. One particularly reckless youngster was almost turned into paste by Patty, but the *flar-ta* made a weird five-legged hop and somehow avoided treading on the scrambling waif.

The corners of the buildings all sported elaborate downspouts that led to large rainwater containers. Some of those had markings on them, and Pahner watched as a person dipped from one of them and dropped a metal coin into it. Clearly, someone had just made a sale, and he wondered for a moment why, of all the cities they'd visited, only K'Vaern's Cove seemed to have some sort of water rationing.

The same emphasis on providing water was apparent in the occasional larger pools they passed. The pools, slightly raised above the level of the street and about two meters across and a meter deep, ranged from five to ten meters in length and collected water from the larger buildings' downspouts. They were covered with half-lids and clearly were kept scrupulously clean, for the water in them was as clear as any spring, and they, too, had copper and silver coins on their bottoms.

"Supplied?" Kar turned to look at the human, then gave the handclap of a Mardukan shrug. "Poorly, in all fairness. And, no, I don't mind your asking. Gods know we've crossed swords with the League before, but I don't think they're less than allies now."

"Indeed," Rastar said. The Northern cavalryman grunted in harsh laughter. "Many's the war which we waged against the Cove, or the Cove against us, over its control of the Tam Mouth, or our control of the Northern trade. But that's all past, now. The League is no more, nor will it arise once again in any strength in our lifetime. We're all in this together.

"But tell me," he continued, "why are you short? Don't you have nearly unlimited storage under the Citadel?"

"Yes," the K'Vaernian general agreed. "But we don't keep the granaries filled to capacity in peacetime, because stock—"

A sudden, deep, rumbling sound, like the tolling of bronze-throated thunder, interrupted the Guard commander. All of the bells, in all of the towers, sang simultaneously, in an overwhelming outpouring of deep, pounding sound that swept over the city—and the astounded column—like an earthquake of music. But it was no wild, exuberant cacophony, for the bells rang with a measured, rolling grandeur, every one of them giving voice in the same instant. Four times they tolled, and then, as suddenly as they had begun to speak, they were silent.

The humans looked at one another, stunned as much by the abrupt cessation as by the sheer volume of the sound, and their companions from Diaspra seemed only a little less affected. Rastar and his Northern fellows had taken it in stride, however, and the native K'Vaernians seemed scarcely even to have noticed, but then Bistem Kar grunted a chuckling laugh.

"Forgive me, Prince Roger, Captain Pahner. It didn't occur to me to warn you."

"What *was* that?" Roger asked, digging an index finger into his right ear, where the echo of the bells seemed to linger.

"It's Fourth Bell, Your Highness," Kar told him.

"Fourth Bell?" Roger repeated.

"Yes. Our day is divided into thirty bells, or segments of time, and Fourth Bell has just passed."

"You mean you get *that*—" Roger waved a hand at the bell towers "—thirty times a day?!"

"No," Kar said in a tone the humans had learned by now to recognize as tongue-in-cheek, "only eighteen times. The bells don't chime at night. Why?"

Roger stared at him, and it was Rastar's turn to laugh.

"Bistem Kar is— What is that phrase of yours? Ah, yes! He's 'pulling your leg,' Roger. Yes, the bells sound to mark each day segment, but usually only the ones in the buildings actually owned by the city, not all of them!"

"True," Kar admitted, with the handclap which served Mardukans for an amused shrug, but then the titanic guardsman sobered. "We are at war, Prince Roger, and until that war is over, all of Krin's Bells will sound in His name over His city at the passing of each bell."

Roger and Pahner looked at one another expressionlessly, and Kar chuckled once more.

"Don't worry, my friends. You may not believe it, but you'll become accustomed more quickly than you can imagine. And at least—" he gave Rus From a sly look "—we won't be constantly pouring water over you!"

The cleric-artificer chuckled along with the others, and Kar returned his attention to the humans.

"But before the bells interrupted us, I believe, I was about to explain to you that we don't keep the granaries fully filled during peacetime because stockpiling like that hurts the grain trade, and we normally have sufficient warning of a war to purchase ample supplies in time. But this time the Boman came too quickly, and we were having the same problems with Sindi everyone else was. That bastard Tor Cant actually started stockpiling last season, which makes me wonder if his murder of the Boman chiefs was really as spontaneous as he wanted us to think. But he wasn't interested in sharing any of his surpluses, and he went as far as putting a hold on all grain shipments out of Sindi 'for the duration of the emergency.' We got in some additional stores from other sources before Chasten's Mouth was overrun, but not much. There's no real shortage, yet, but it will come. Many of the merchants are rubbing their hands in anticipation."

"What of Bastar?" Rastar asked, gesturing to the north. "I've heard nothing of their people."

"Almost all of them escaped to us when it was clear they couldn't hold against the Boman." Bistem Kar made a gesture of resignation and frustration. "Another drain on our supplies, both of grain and of water, but not one that we could in good conscience reject. And we'd had our problems with D'Sley, as well as all the other cities, but again . . ."

"One for all, and all for one," Pahner said.

"Indeed," the general agreed, and turned his attention back to the human. "But what is your place in all of this? I'm told that these long spears are your innovation, and the large shields. I can see their usefulness against the Boman axes. But why are you here? And involving yourselves in our plight?"

"It's not out of the goodness of our hearts," Roger said. "The full story is long and complicated, but the short answer is that we have to cross that—" he pointed to the sea beyond the harbor "—to reach the ocean, and then cross *that* to get back to our home."

"That's a problem," Kar said forebodingly. "Oh, you can get passage from here to the Straits of Tharazh if you must. It will be expensive, but it can be arranged. But no one will take you beyond the Straits to cross the Western Ocean. The winds would be against you, and no one who's ever tried to cross the ocean has returned. Some people—" the K'Vaernian glanced sideways at Rus From "—believe that the demons which fill the ocean to guard the shores of the world island are to blame, but whatever the cause, no ship has ever succeeded in crossing it and returning to us. There's an ancient tale of one ship having arrived from the *other* side—a wreck, rather, for it had been torn to pieces by something. According to the tale, there was a lone, crazed survivor who babbled in an unknown tongue, but he didn't live long, and no one was ever able to determine what had destroyed the ship."

"Storm?" Pahner asked.

"No, not according to the tale," the general said. "Of course, it might be a fable, but there's an ancient log in one of the museums here. It's in a tongue no one I know of can read, but it's accompanied by what purports to be a partial translation—almost as old as the log itself—and you might find it interesting. The translation seems to describe monsters of some sort, and the tales of the ship's arrival here are very specific in saying that it had been bitten and torn by something."

"Goodness," From murmured provocatively. "You don't suppose it might have been one of those mythological demons, do you?"

"I don't know what it might have been," Kar admitted cheerfully. "Except that whatever it was, it must have been large. And unfriendly. Either of which would be enough to convince *me* to stay well clear of it, by Krin!"

"You know that there's something on the other side, though?" Roger asked.

"Oh, yes," the K'Vaernian replied. "Of course. The world is round, after all; the mathematicians have demonstrated that clearly enough, though not without argument from some of our, ah, more conservative religions. That means that eventually you must come back here, but the distance is immense. And in all honesty, there's never been much incentive for anyone to go mucking about in the open ocean. Quite aside from wind, wave, and possible sea monsters," he grinned at From, who chuckled back at him, "there's the problem of navigation. How does a seaman know where he is unless he can close the shore every so often and compare local landmarks to his charts? And what merchant would go voyaging beyond Tharazh? We know of no cities or peoples to trade with there, and we have—had, at least—all the trade we can service right here in the K'Vaernian Sea. As to what's happened to the one or two lunatics who *have* tried to cross it, no one truly knows, so it's a fertile subject for, um . . . imaginative speculation."

"Well, we'd heard that you're unable to sail across it," Pahner said, "but we've done quite a few things on this world that no one has ever done before."

"They crossed the Tarsten Mountains," Rastar interjected.

"No! Really?" Kar laughed. "And is the land beyond really filled with giant cannibals?"

"I think not," Cord said. The old shaman had a strong gift for languages, but without a toot of his own, he lacked the translator support the humans enjoyed, and the K'Vaernian general looked at him sharply at the sound of his pronounced and highly unusual accent.

"D'nal Cord is my *asi*," Roger said, "my, um, sworn companion and shield mate. He's from the People, who live in the Hurtan Valley. It's not only beyond the Tarsten Mountains, it's actually farther from the Tarstens than they are from here."

"Pretty close to a fourth of the way around the world from the Tarstens," Pahner agreed. "And the people on the far side of the Tarstens didn't look much different from you. No *civan* or *turom*, though."

"Truly, we live in a time of wonders," Kar said. "And I meant no offense to your people, D'nal Cord."

"And I took none," the *asi* said haltingly. "Far we have come, and much have I seen. Much is the same from one side to the other." He glanced around for a moment. "Although this is by far the largest city I've ever seen. Voitan was just as . . . alive before its fall, but it wasn't *this* large."

"Voitan?" Kar asked.

"A long tale," Roger said. "And a cautionary one."

"Aye," Cord agreed with a handclap of emphasis, and looked at the K'Vaernian levelly. "Voitan, as everyone knew, was invincible. Until the Kranolta."

CHAPTER TWENTY-ONE

Roger looked around the room and nodded in satisfaction. The space was relatively small but comfortable, placed on the seaward side of the citadel and looking out over the blue K'Vaernian Sea, and the sea breeze that blew in from the windows on that side blew back out through inner windows which overlooked a courtyard on the other side. The citadel's bell tower was less than fifty meters from those windows, and the prince winced inwardly at the thought of what it would be like whenever the K'Vaernians' "clocks" went off, but he was willing to accept that as the price of the windows. There wasn't anyplace in the entire city where he could realistically have hoped to escape the bells, anyway, and the breeze wafting through the room felt almost unbelievably good after the sweltering steambath of the city streets.

The chamber contained the ubiquitous low cushions and tables, but Matsugae had already set up his camp bed and acquired a taller table from somewhere. Together with his folding chair, it made for a comfortable place from which to contemplate their next steps.

The plan was simple. They would show the K'Vaern's Cove people some of the military technologies from humanity's bloody past which would be within reach of their current capabilities in return for a trip across the ocean. It had sounded reasonable when they worked it all out before leaving Diaspra, but Poertena had already given his opinion of the seaworthiness of the local boats, and it wasn't good. Roger's head was ringing with such phrases as "deck stiffness," "freeboard," and "jib sails," most of which he already knew from his own yachting days. Poertena, however, seemed to be a veritable mine of information on practical, sail-powered work boats, and that mine was saying "No Way."

So it looked like simply putting a better sail plan on one of the local boats might be out, which would mean months of time spent building new boats. Or at least refitting one of the local boats from the keel up.

The rest of the plan was beginning to look iffy, as well. They hadn't yet met with the local council, but Bistem Kar clearly felt that K'Vaern's Cove wasn't as unconquerable as Rastar and Honal had believed. If his attitude was shared by the Council in general, simply saying "Hey, here's a few tricks. Have fun, and we're out of here," might not work.

All of which sounded as if it might mean yet another battle, and Roger wasn't sure he was ready for that.

He gazed out over the sea and sighed. He'd spent most of his seventeenth summer blue-water sailing off of Bermuda, where, unlike Pinopa, sailing was the recreational province of the rich rather than a matter of economic survival. The blue-water races in the Atlantic were comradely competitions between members of the monetary elite and their handpicked crews, and the yachts used bore as little resemblance to what was needed here as a race-flyer bore to a hover-truck, but given the choice between sailing a cargo sloop through a Mid-Atlantic gale and battling the Boman, Roger was sure what his answer would be. Even with the possibility of sea monsters thrown in for good measure.

Someone knocked on the door, and he turned towards it. The guard outside was Despreaux, and she refused to meet his eye when she opened the door to let Matsugae enter. The incident in Ran Tai still lay between them like a minefield, and he had to get past it. Ran Tai had proven that it wasn't smart to get *too* close to the troops, but it was even less smart to have a bodyguard who was poisonously angry with you. And it wasn't as if Despreaux could ask for a transfer, so, sooner or later, he had to talk to her about it and try to smooth the waters.

Besides which, he was still deeply confused about his feelings for her.

He sighed at the thought, then smiled again as he heard Matsugae puttering around behind him. The little clucks as the valet straightened the eternal mess were soothing.

"Are you glad to be out of the kitchens, Kostas?"

"It was a very interesting experience, Your Highness," the valet replied, "but, all things considered, yes, I'm quite glad. I can always go back and putter there if the mood takes me, and it's not as if I'm really still needed at this point." With over five thousand total persons, human and Mardukan, with the column, cooks were easy enough to find.

"But we'll all miss your *atul* stew," Roger joked.

"I'm afraid you'll just have to suffer, Your Highness," Matsugae responded. "It's funny, really. I gave that recipe to one of the Diasprans, and he just stared at me in shock. I suppose it's the equivalent of Bengal tiger stew to humans. Not what they'd consider normal fare."

"'Skin one Bengal tiger . . .'" Roger murmured with a chuckle.

"Exactly, Your Highness. Or perhaps, 'First, fillet the Tyrannosaurus.'"

"I can just imagine Julian's stories about this little jaunt once we get home," the prince said.

"Perhaps, but the jaunt isn't over yet," the servant retorted. "And on that subject, you have the meeting this afternoon with the K'Vaernian Council. I obtained some cloth in Diaspra. It's not as fine as *dianda*—the threads are somewhat coarser, and the weave isn't as tight. However, it made an admirable suit, and I found enough *dianda* to line it and provide two or three *dianda* shirts to go with it."

Roger glanced at the proffered garments and nodded, but he also cocked one eyebrow quizzically.

"Black? I thought you always said black was only for weddings and funerals."

"So I did, but it was the best dye Diaspra had available." The valet looked uncomfortable for a moment, then shrugged. "It's what they make their better priestly vestments from."

"Works for me," Roger responded with a smile. "You know, you really have been a tremendous boon throughout this entire hike, Kostas. I don't know what we would've done without you."

"Oh, you would've made do," the valet said uncomfortably.

"No doubt we would have, but that doesn't mean we would have made do as well as we have."

"I suppose it *is* fortunate that I learned a little something from all of the safaris on which I've accompanied you," Matsugae conceded.

"A vast understatement, Kosie," the prince said fondly, and the valet smiled.

"I'll go make sure the arrangements for this afternoon are in place," he said.

"Very good," Roger said, turning back to the window and allowing Matsugae his space. "And pass the word for Cord, Eleanora, and Captain Pahner, if you would. We need to have our positions clear before the meeting."

"Yes, Your Highness," the valet replied with a small smile. The Roger who'd taken off from Earth would never have given that order with such certainty, assuming that the need to worry about preplanning would have occurred to him at all. Which it wouldn't have. At least this "little jaunt" had been good for something.

The council chamber was rather smaller than Roger had expected. The long room at the foot of the city's central and tallest bell tower was low-ceilinged (for Mardukans) and filled to capacity by a cross-section of the city. The actual Council—fifteen representatives of various groups within the city—sat at one end, but the other end was a public gallery, open to any voting citizen of K'Vaern's Cove, and there wasn't enough room to sneeze at that end.

The city-state was a limited republic, with the franchise restricted to those who paid a vote tax, which amounted to ten percent of a person's yearly income. It was the only direct tax levied upon the citizenry, but there were no exceptions from it and no exemptions for the poor. If you wanted to vote, you had to pay the tax, but even the poorest of the poor could come up with that much if they were frugal. It was obvious to Roger that although the vote tax provided a goodly chunk of income for the city, it was really intended primarily to limit the vote to those willing to make a genuine sacrifice to exercise their franchise. Other taxes and duties levied on warehouses, imports, and port usage by ships not registered to a K'Vaernian citizen provided the majority of the city's operating capital. Which, of course, raised interesting questions about future budgets now that the Boman had managed to eliminate at least two-thirds of the Cove's usual trading partners.

The Council was elected "at large," with the whole body of citizenry voting for all council members. In effect, however, each represented the particular social group from which he came. Some were guild representatives, while others represented the entrepreneur class that was the economic lifeblood of the city. Still others represented the class of hereditary wealth, and a few were even representatives of the poorest of the city's multitudes.

All of which meant that the Council was a diverse and—to Roger's eye—fairly hostile bunch as it greeted the human and Diaspran representatives.

The spectators behind the visitors were an even more diverse lot . . . and considerably more lively. The public gallery was open to all voters on a first-come, first-served basis, and while there were tricks the rich could use to pack the chamber if they really wanted to, the current audience seemed to be a pretty good cross-section of the city. And a raucous lot they'd been as the Diasprans began their presentation.

Bogess had started with a precise report on the Battle of Diaspra, complete with a long discussion of the preparations, including some of the more controversial training methods introduced by the humans. Those preparations had occasioned some loud and derisive commentary from the crowd of onlookers, but it was his description of the battle which had drawn the most responses. As seemed to be the case for the entire planet, the K'Vaernians had never heard of the concept of combined arms or, with the sole exception of the League cavalry, disciplined mass formations. Bogess' description of the effectiveness of the shield wall had been scoffed at so loudly by the raucous crowd that the chairman of the Council had been forced to call for order. His description of the effect of the Marines' powered armor, however, had drawn the loudest response. At first, his account had been greeted with stunned silence, but that had quickly given way to loud derision and the mockery of disbelief.

"They are very noisy," Cord commented to Roger.

"Democracy is like that, Cord," the prince responded. "Every yammerhead who thinks he has two brain cells to rub together gets his say." As he spoke, he noted that there were many Mardukan women in the group. They were just as vociferously involved in the debate as any of their male counterparts, and he decided that that was probably a good sign. It was certainly unlike anything they'd seen elsewhere on Marduk, with the sole exception of the reconstituted government of Marshad.

"I must say," the old shaman grumped, "that I would prefer some less noisy method of doing business."

"So would I," Roger agreed, "and the Empire is a bit less wide open and raucous than these people are. We're a constitutional monarchy with a hereditary aristocracy, not a direct democracy, so I guess you could say we're more representative than democratic. Then again, direct democracy wouldn't work very well for something the size of the Empire of Man, and all of Mother's subjects get to vote for their local representatives in the Commons. Every citizen is absolutely guaranteed the rights of freedom of speech, public assembly, and the vote, too, which means sometimes we get just as loud and noisy as these folks are . . . or even worse."

"Then you should make changes. Much *quieter* changes," Cord sniffed.

"Funny, a lot of people keep saying that . . . whatever form of government they have. The only problem is, if you tell the yammerheads to shut their gobs, you don't have real representation anymore. If everyone isn't free to speak his mind, then, ultimately, *no one* is, and in the end, that will come home and bite everyone involved on the ass. Noise and disagreement are part of the price you pay for freedom."

"The People are free," Cord said. "And they aren't noisy."

"Cord, I hate to break this to you, but the People *aren't* free," Roger disagreed. "The People are locked into a system in which there are two choices: be a hunter, or be a shaman. Well, three, since you can choose to be neither and starve to death, instead. Freedom entails the making of choices, and if you only have two choices, you aren't free. For that matter, the People's lives are no picnic. Doc Dobrescu's determined that the tribal clans have an average life span two-thirds as long as the townsmen. They also have twice the death rate among their young. That isn't freedom, Cord. Or, to the extent that it is, it's the freedom of misery."

"We're not miserable," the shaman argued. "Quite the opposite."

"Yes, but that's because you don't know, as a group, any other way to live. And, let's face it, the People are very tradition-bound. All cultures at that tech level have a tendency to be that way, and traditions and customs help restrict your choices and inhibit change. Look at your own case. You studied in Voitan before the Kranolta wiped out the original city, and you came home a scholar and a sage, but you also came home still a shaman of the People. I don't doubt for a minute that you loved your life and your tribe, however many worthwhile things you may have found during your stay in Voitan. And I certainly agree that the 'shit-sitters' in the People's neck of the woods weren't exactly shining beacons of the very best that civilization—and democracy—can offer. But the traditions which brought you home again may also have blinded you to the fact that the People as a whole simply have no concept of how much better their lives—or their children's lives—could be."

Roger shrugged.

"There are some humans—like the Saints—who think it's always best to let native peoples continue in their native conditions without 'corrupting' them by suggesting any sort of alternative. Despite the death rates, despite the pain and suffering they experience in day-to-day life, it's better to let them 'seek their own paths' and 'retain their cultural integrity.' Well, the Empire disagrees. And so do I. We don't want to come in and force any culture to embrace social forms which are anathema to its values or to impose some 'one size fits all' cultural template by force, but we have a moral responsibility to at least make them aware of the alternatives. There are many problems with our modern human society, but dying of malnutrition or an impacted tooth isn't one of them, and no other sentient should have to die of them, either."

"So it's better to have this?" the shaman asked, gesturing to the screaming matches at the back of the room. Bailiffs had been busy while Roger spoke, breaking up the handful of fistfights which had broken out. Now they were in the process of throwing out the terminally vociferous and combative, but it was still a noisy lot.

"Yes, Cord, this is better than life in the tribes," Roger said. "Most of the people in this room saw all of their littermates survive. Most of them are going to live twenty to thirty years beyond your own relatively long life span. Very few of them go to bed hungry at night because the hunters failed to find game, and very few of them have suffered from scurvy, or rickets, or lost teeth, or been reduced in stature because they were hungry all the time as children. Yes, Cord. This is a better life than the tribe's."

"I don't think so," Cord said with a gesture of disagreement.

"Well, see?" Roger grinned. "We've got a disagreement. Welcome to democracy."

"If this 'democracy' is so splendid," the shaman said, "why is it that Captain Pahner does whatever *he* feels is right without constantly calling for discussion and votes?"

"Ah. That's a bit different," Roger said with a shrug. "Democracies need militaries to protect them, but no effective military is a democracy."

"Oh, I see. It is yet another internal human contradiction," Cord remarked with a certain undeniable edge of satisfaction. "Why didn't you simply say so at the beginning?"

"Order! We're going to have order here!" Turl Kam banged his heavy staff of office on the floor. The burly ex-fisherman had been a minor boat owner until a clumsily run line had removed his lower leg. He might have been able to continue with the peg which had replaced it, but he'd opted to sell the boat and go into politics, instead.

After years of wheeling and dealing, he had attained the pinnacle of power as head of the Council, only to have the Boman invade on his watch. It was very frustrating. His constituency was the local fishermen and short-haul cargo sailors, and there was little or no good to be extracted from the situation for them. There was, however, a great deal of ill to be expected from it, which was why they were so restive at the moment, but that was no reason for them to take it out on him.

"There's been a bunch of stuff said by the folks from Diaspra that's hard to believe," he agreed, "but—" One of his own constituents jumped to his feet and started yelling, but the chairman stared him down. "The next one of you lengths of fish-bait spouts off, I'm gonna eject you. And the guard's gonna dip you in the bay for good measure! Now, I got the floor, so everybody just shut the hell up and stop interrupting the speakers! We're gonna give our visitors their say, by Krin!"

Someone else began a shouted objection—which ended abruptly as Turl Kam nodded and two of the bailiffs booted the loudmouth out of the chamber. One or two others looked as if they were contemplating saying something, but mouths closed all around at the chairman's glare, and he snorted in satisfaction.

"As I was saying, what they're saying is hard to believe. But it's also gonna be easy to prove or disprove, and when the time comes, we'll get some proofs. But now isn't the time or place.

"And, furthermore, there ain't no reason for them to be lying. They got nothing to gain by coming here—K'Vaern's Cove is less important than spit to Diaspra, so you just keep that in mind when they speak.

"Now it's the turn of the Cleric-Artisan Rus From. Rus From, if you would give us your words?"

From stepped forward and bowed to the Council, but instead of speaking to them, as Bogess had, he turned to the common citizens packing the chamber.

"You wonder at the statements General Bogess has made, and that's hardly surprising. We speak of miraculous-sounding events—of walking walls of spears and shields that broke the Boman like a twig. We speak of the very lightnings of heaven striking the enemy from the weapons of our human companions, and you wonder and doubt.

"Some of you know my name, and if you've heard aught of my own small achievements as an artisan, I ask you to remember that when I speak to you now of wonders beyond wonders. These visitors, these 'humans,' bring marvel after marvel. Their own devices and weapons are as miracles to us, yet in many ways, what they can tell us about our own crafts and technologies is even more miraculous. We cannot duplicate their lightning weapons, or the devices which allow them to speak and act as one over vast distances, but they've brought us new methods of doing, new methods of thinking, and new methods of making other things which we *can* duplicate and use. And by showing us the thinking behind those other things, they have opened up, for me, at least, a vast panorama of new ideas and new inventions. Ideas and inventions that will change our way of life forever.

"Many of these ideas and inventions would not have been well regarded in my own land. The Boman invasion has shaken up my city, but you know it well. It's a city of priests, where the responsibility of new thought is rigorously maintained. One is absolutely required to have a new thought once in one's life. No more, and no less."

He waited for the audience's grunting laughter to die, then continued.

"So when I was told 'Go to K'Vaern's Cove,' I was awash with excitement, for of all the cities between the mountains and the sea, surely K'Vaern's Cove would be the one where the reality of these new ideas and new devices could reach its fullest flower. Surely, in K'Vaern's Cove the people of Krin of the Bells would greet new ways of sailing and learning and manufacturing with the same enthusiasm I did! Surely, in K'Vaern's Cove, if anywhere, I could find thinkers and doers to rival my own thinking and doing! Surely, in K'Vaern's Cove, if anywhere, I could find people ready and eager to accept the challenge put before them! For the people of K'Vaern's Cove have never quailed before any challenge, and surely they would not quail before this one."

He paused and looked around at the assembled group.

"And now I am in K'Vaern's Cove, and what do I find? I find disbelief," he gestured at one of the more vocal locals, "derision," he gestured at another, "and mockery." He gestured at a third, and clapped hands in a gesture of grief and surprise.

"Was I, a foreigner, wrong in my opinion of your city? Is it in fact the case that K'Vaern's Cove, as noted for its acceptance and open-mindedness as for the majesty of its bells, is unwilling or unable to accept new ideas? New ways? Is K'Vaern's Cove unwilling to face new challenges? Has it fallen into the slothful trap of the lesser cities—the traps of fear, insularity, and complacency? Or is K'Vaern's Cove still the shining beacon that it seemed to be from distant Diaspra?

"The answer is up to you," he said, pointing at individuals in the audience. "It's up to you, and you, and you. For K'Vaern's Cove is not ruled by an oligarchy, as Bastar. It isn't ruled by a priest, as Diaspra, or by a despot, as Sindi. It is ruled by the people, and the question is, what are the people of K'Vaern's Cove? Fearful *basik?* Or courageous *atul-grak*?

"The answer is up to you."

He folded all four arms and gazed levelly at the suddenly much more thoughtful audience for several long moments, then turned to the Council and gave a very human shrug.

"For my own presentation, I have only this to add. The humans have given me designs for weapons which can fire bullets farther and straighter than you can imagine. They can also be reloaded far more quickly than any arquebus or wheel lock, and, perhaps even more importantly, they can be fired even in a rain to rival the Hompag and strike targets accurately from as much as an *ulong* away. They've showed me how to reduce the size of our bombards to such an extent that they can be pulled by *civan* or *turom* and be used against the Boman at short range in the open field of battle. I don't say that producing these weapons will be easy or fast, for we lack the skills and the techniques which the humans would employ in their own homeland, but I do say that they can be produced using our own artisans and our own resources. Given all of that and the support of the people of this glorious city, we can *destroy* the Boman, not simply defeat them. Or you can huddle here like *basik* until your grain runs out and the Boman come and take your horns.

"It is up to you."

"And what does Diaspra gain from this war against these invaders?" one of the Council members asked skeptically.

"Not much," Rus From admitted. "Everyone is fairly certain that the Boman are uninterested in the lands south of the Nashtor Hills. Once they've reduced K'Vaern's Cove, most of them will return to the North. Others will settle in these lands. Eventually, we might have to settle the Nashtor Hills with fortified cities against them, as the Northern League once protected the cities north of the hills, but that would be a far day in the future. Soon enough, we would be able to negotiate the reopening of Chasten Mouth, which would give us our sea trade back. Actually, without the competition of K'Vaern's Cove, we'd be the center for trade from the Tarsten Mountains and the Nashtor Hills. Financially, we would be well set.

"On the other hand, without your landward trade, there's little use for K'Vaern's Cove. In time, the trading ships will stop coming, and you will dwindle. Even if you reach an accommodation with the Boman and survive, you are bereft without the downriver trade of the Tam through D'Sley. In time, you will be nothing but a ruin and memory."

"Well, that's all the reasons you *shouldn't* be here," Turl Kam ground out between clenched teeth. For all of the K'Vaernians' legendary volubility, no one, not even Bistem Kar, had been so brutally honest about their predicament. "So why *are* you here?"

"I'm here because my master sent me," From replied. "I was happy to come in many ways, but I must admit that I also had projects and plans which would have kept me fully occupied in Diaspra." He chose—tactfully, Roger thought—not to go into exactly what all those projects and plans had been. "But Gratar had other ideas, and I'm here at his orders," the cleric finished.

"And what was his purpose?" the Council member who'd spoken earlier asked, and From remembered his name. He was Wes Til, a representative of some of the richer merchant houses. *Anything to get me out of town*, the priest almost replied, then thought better of excessive candor.

"I think that the words the humans gave me fit best," he said instead. "'In the face of evil, good persons must band together lest they fall one by one, unpitied sacrifices of a contemptible struggle.' Certainly, we could make an accommodation with the Boman. But that doesn't mean such an accommodation would be just, or right, in the long run or the short. And even leaving the question of justice aside, that accommodation might or might not hold. If it doesn't, and we've allowed those we should have aided—and who might have aided us in our need—to fall through our inaction, then whatever disaster comes upon us will be no more than we deserve.

"And so we bring iron, purchased from Nashtor by the guarantee of Diaspra's temple, and we ask only that its purchase be repaid after the war. However, I also come with two thousand infantry which must be kept and maintained, and we brought no great sums of treasure beside the iron. If, after the war is over, you have supported our 'Expeditionary Force' with food and goods sufficient to pay for the iron, then the account will be considered balanced by Diaspra.

"Thus we bring you your much-needed iron and a force to aid you, and effectively ask only for maintenance.

"Personally, I think Gratar is insane to be so generous in such a time of peril for us all. But then, I'm not as nice as he is."

"You sure are blunt, Rus From," Turl Kam said, rubbing his hands in worry.

"I'm a priest, not a politician," the cleric responded. "Worse, I'm an artisan, and you know what they're like."

"Indeed," Wes Til grunted in a laugh shared by the citizens behind the priest. "But where are these wonder weapons of the 'humans'? And what of the humans themselves? They have yet to speak."

"Yes," Kam agreed. "Who's gonna speak for the humans?"

Roger recognized his cue and stepped forward with a gracious nod to From as the priest relinquished the floor to him.

"Members of the Council," the prince said, half-bowing to that group, "and citizens of K'Vaern's Cove," he added, turning to give the crowd of spectators the same bow, "I speak for the humans."

"Why are you humans here?" Kam asked bluntly. The Council had already been informed of the humans' plans, in general terms, at least, but only informally.

"We aren't from around here, and we want to go home," Roger said. "That may sound fatuous, but it's important to understanding our needs and objectives. In order for us to return home, it's necessary for us to reach a city in a land which lies beyond the Western Ocean, and our time, frankly, is running out. Because of that, it's our intention to purchase passage—or ships, if necessary—and depart for that distant land as soon as possible. Our ship expert is of two minds about how best to proceed. He's of the opinion that the local ships aren't well designed for blue-water sailing, despite their excellent construction, and he's uncertain whether or not we could convert them to our needs. If he decides that we can't, and I believe he's inclining in that direction, then it will be necessary for us to build ships from the keel up."

"That will take time," Til said. "Time you said you don't have. And the cost will be substantial, especially in time of war."

"We have funds," Roger said, and managed—with difficulty—not to glare at Armand Pahner, who'd finally gotten around that very morning to revealing the true fruits of Ran Tai to him. "I'm sure," the prince went on, "that we can afford the construction or modification."

"Maybe you can, and maybe you can't," Kam said. "There's a shortage of building materials, and our navy had a short and nasty fight with the Boman out on the Bay after D'Sley fell. The stupid bastards seemed to think they could get through from D'Sley using rafts and canoes. We taught 'em better, but however dumb they may be once you get them on the water, they don't have a lot of give up in their nature. We took some pretty heavy damage of our own, and most all our timber, especially for masts, comes down the Tam. There aren't masts to be had for love or money, and there won't be none until we retake the lands where the cutting is done."

"We'll manage," Roger said with determined confidence despite a severe sinking sensation. "We've crossed half this world. We've fought our way across rivers in the face of an army of *atul-grak*. We've destroyed tribes almost as numerous as the Boman without support. We've crossed unscalable mountains. We've driven paths through the burning deserts. One stinking little ocean isn't going to stop us."

"The sea's a lady, but that lady's a bitch," Kam told him reflectively. "I turned my back on that bitch just once and lost a leg to her."

"You turned your back more than once, you old drunk!" one of the crowd shouted.

"I ought to have you ejected for that, Pa Kathor," Kam said with a grunt of laughter. "But it's almost true. I wasn't drunk—I was hung over. But the point is that the sea *is* a bitch, and a mean one when the mood strikes her, and the ocean's worse. Lots worse. You might want to bear that in mind, Prince Roger."

"We're aware of the difficulties and dangers, Turl Kam," Roger replied. "And we don't underestimate her. But whatever her mood, we must cross her, and we have many things going for us. For one thing, we have a technology, a simple rigging innovation, which permits us to sail far closer to the wind than your own ships can."

"What?" Wes Til asked in the suddenly silent room. "How?"

"It isn't difficult," Roger told him, "although it would be easier to demonstrate than to explain. But it permits a ship to sail within thirty or forty degrees into the wind."

"How?" Turl Kam took up Til's question. "That's impossible. No one can sail closer than fifty degrees to the wind!"

"No, it isn't, but as I say, it's something better demonstrated than explained, and we will demonstrate it. We'll teach your sailors and your shipwrights how it's done while we prepare for our own voyage, but that's only one of our advantages. Another is that we have much better navigational arts than you, and we know where we're going. We know approximately where we are on a map, we know where our destination lies, and we know how to keep track of our position while we sail towards it, so when we set out, we'll be heading for a specific destination on a course we can plot reliably, rather than making a blind voyage of discovery."

"And this destination lies across the ocean, does it?" Til mused aloud.

"Yes. It's a large island or small continent, a piece of land the size of the lands between the mountains and the sea."

"So you'll be building a ship . . . ?"

"Or ships," Roger corrected. "Precisely how many will depend on their sizes and the quantity of supplies or pack animals we must take with us."

"Or ships," the Council member accepted the correction. "But you're going to build them, then sail across the ocean to this other continent. And once you get there, you'll find a port waiting for you. And then what?"

"We'll probably sell the ships. Our eventual tar—destination is in the interior."

"Ah," Til said. "So you won't need the ships on the far side. So if someone were to participate in building the ships, perhaps pay for it entirely, and then give you passage for a nominal fee . . . ?"

"Someone wouldn't be thinking about getting a lock on a new market, would someone?" Kam asked through the scattered laughter.

"I'm sure that something could be worked out with someone," Roger said with a closed-lipped, Mardukan smile. "Which is an example of what I meant by not letting things get in our way. We have much to offer, but we also have priorities which, however much we might like to vary our plans, call for us to proceed on our way without delays."

"But you could stay and fight?" Til persisted.

"If we did, it would change several equations," Roger replied cautiously. "A delay to fight here would mean we would have to make a faster passage, which would require different ships. And we wouldn't be fighting directly, because there are too few of us to matter against a foe as numerous and geographically dispersed as the Boman. What we could do would be to act as trainers and leaders for your own forces, as we did in Diaspra. And although we're too few in numbers ourselves to fight the war *for* you, perhaps we could act as shock troops in one or two critical battles, again, as we did in Diaspra.

"But that isn't our intention. If K'Vaern's Cove throws its weight into the battle against the Boman, you should win, even in an open field battle, without us. And if you *don't* throw your full weight into the fight, it would hardly be in our interest to support a half-hearted war."

"But with your aid, would our casualties be lighter?" Til pressed.

Roger opened his mouth to reply, and stopped. He thought for a moment and almost turned to look at Pahner for an answer, but he already knew what the answer was.

"If we threw our full effort into it, your casualties would be lighter. We've described the new weapons to Rus From, but their construction is complicated, and we weren't able to tell him exactly how to solve all of the problems he would face in building them. Not because we deliberately chose to conceal or withhold information, but because we're simply not fully familiar with your manufacturing capabilities. Our own land has many technologies and machines which yours doesn't, and we don't know the best and most efficient way to adapt your own capabilities to solving the problems.

"To be honest, we didn't worry about that aspect. Rus From's reputation is well known, even here in K'Vaern's Cove, and from our own observation in Diaspra, that reputation is well-deserved. We were confident that he would be able to overcome any difficulties in time, and, unlike us, time is something which he—and you—possess. Not as much as we thought before we learned the true state of your supplies, perhaps, but still longer than *we* have if we're to reach our destination alive. Even without us, Rus From—and your own artisans, of course—would almost certainly be able to produce sufficient of the new weapons to defeat the Boman before lack of supplies defeats *you*.

"If, on the other hand, we remained in K'Vaern's Cove, our own artisans would be available to help with that production. We'd be able to learn what we don't currently know about your capabilities, and with that knowledge we could probably save a great deal of time in putting those weapons into your warriors' true-hands. Also, at the risk of sounding conceited, our Marines would be far better trainers than the Diasprans. We have an institutional memory to draw on, and a degree of personal experience which they lack. As an analogy, the Diasprans would be apprentices teaching unskilled people to be apprentices, while our Marines would be master craftsmen teaching others to be journeymen."

"How would you go about the actual fighting?" Til asked. "Would you go to some point and dare the Boman to attack you? Or would you try to draw them forward against our own defenses? Would you attack Sindi?"

"I can't answer those questions," Roger said, "because we haven't discussed the matter among ourselves. As I've repeatedly stressed, we aren't here to fight the Boman. We need to cross the ocean. Having said that, if we did take the field against them, we would probably begin by recapturing D'Sley to use as a base of supply. Trying to supply around the Bay would open you up to interdiction."

"Uh," Turl Kam said. "What was that last word?"

"Sorry." Roger realized he'd used the Standard English word and pulled up the translation software on his toot, then grimaced when he discovered that there *was* no translation. "You don't seem to have a word for it, so I was forced to use our own. Let's just say that packing stuff all the way around the Bay opens you up to having your supply line cut. Interior lines of supply are always better."

"So you'd want to retake D'Sley as a start," Til said, rubbing his horns. "What then?"

"Any moves after that would depend on what intelligence we'd gathered."

"What . . . thinking you'd brought together?" Kam said carefully. "Are you saying it would depend on what you decided as a group?"

"No," the prince said. "Look, this is getting complicated. What I meant was that when we knew where the Boman were and how they were moving, or *if* they were moving, then we could think about what strategy to use. But we're not going to be doing any of those things because—"

"Because you have to cross the ocean," Kam said. "Right. We got that. So what we've got is some soldiers of dubious worth and some half smelted iron from Diaspra. We're supposedly going to get some new toys—but not the *best* toys—from you humans by way of the Diasprans. And with these gifts, we're supposed to go out and beat up on the Boman. Because if we don't, Rus From tells us, the Cove is going to die on the vine."

"Don't know when I've ever heard it put more clearly," Wes Til said. "Krin knows, we've clearly died on the vine in every other war we've been involved in! So I guess that just about sums it up."

"Yes, it does," Roger said, grinning widely and this time letting a mouthful of pearly teeth show. "Now, as I was saying. Since from what you just said you guys are clearly having *no* problems with the Boman, perhaps you can tell me where I could buy a dozen masts?"

CHAPTER TWENTY-TWO

"Okay, Poertena, what've you got?" Roger asked.

The council meeting had adjourned without reaching any decisions, so the humans were continuing with their plan to modify or build a ship and the Diasprans were in limbo. If the K'Vaernians decided that fighting the Boman wasn't worth what it would cost, the Diasprans' trip would have been in vain, but Roger had a gut feeling that that wasn't what would happen.

"I went down tee harbor wit' Tratan, Sir. Just nosin' aroun'," the Pinopan said, and pulled out his pad. "We gots problems."

"There's a materials shortage," Pahner said. "We got that much at the council meeting. How bad is it?"

"Say t'at t'ere ain't no materials, an' you closer, Cap'n," the sergeant replied. "'Specially masts and spars. I see t'ree, four shipyards—t'ey shut down: no wood. Tee two I see working, t'ey workin' slow, just killin' time."

"Worse than I thought," O'Casey muttered. "The city didn't look all that depressed on the way in."

"Oh, tee parts we come t'rough, t'ey busy. It's tee docks t'at's idle. You go down tee docks, you gots lots o' people jus' hangin' around. Lots of tee porters, normally unload tee ships, t'ey just hangin' around. Lots of tee guys work in tee warehouses. And tee sailors. Hell, even tee taverns is shut down—no business."

"And the docks have got to be the linchpin of this economy," O'Casey said. "It's not like they produce much."

"I don't know about that," Julian said. "I was nosing around, too, and there's a large industrial sector beyond the first set of hills. The entire peninsula is short on ground water—that's why they've got all those catcher cisterns—but they've got some pretty good powered equipment running over there. A lot of it's wind-powered, but they use some water-driven machinery that draws on really big cisterns. Hell, I even saw one shop that uses tidal catcher basins to drive wheels with the outflow—they've got two moons, and that makes for some hellacious tides even on an inland sea like the K'Vaernian. But for all the equipment they've got, things seemed slow," he admitted. "Lots of people around, and all the foundries were active, but . . . slow. I think the city's probably a 'value added' economy. They get raw materials, work them into goods, and sell the goods. But there aren't any materials to rework right now, and more than half their markets are gone."

"Can we buy a ship and cross the ocean?" Pahner asked.

"No, Sir," the Pinopan answered promptly. "We can buy a ship, no problem. But we no can cross tee ocean in one of t'ese tubs. We might make it, an' we might not. You wanna take a maybe-maybe not chance with tee Prince?"

"No," Pahner said with a grimace. "So what's the alternative?"

"We can buy a ship, strip it to tee keel, an' use tee timbers to build a new one," the Pinopan told him. "T'at sound like a good idea, but it make it nearly twice as long to build t'an if we starts fresh, an' we ain't got an infinite supply of supplements."

"Is it just the masts that are in short supply?" Julian asked.

"No. Oh, tee masts're tee worst part, but ever't'ing's short. You build ships out o' wood, you needs seasoned timber. You can use green, but t'ey ain't gonna last very long. T'at's maybe not a problem for us, but t'ere ain't *no* timber in tee city—not where anyone gonna sell it to us, anyways."

"And there won't be any from their internal resources, either," O'Casey said grimly. "It's a classic problem for any seapower based on wooden hulls. Once you cut down all of the usable timber in your immediate vicinity, you become dependent on an overseas supply for your shipyards. And the overseas suppliers K'Vaern's Cove has depended on just got hammered under by the Boman."

"T'at's right," Poertena agreed. "Oh, I t'ink we can maybe pry loose 'nough timber for one ship, but no more."

"Well, can't the platoon fit on just one?" Julian asked, wincing as he used the term for the surviving Marines. Mostly because "platoon" was exactly what Bravo Company had become.

"Yeah," the Pinopan answered with a sideways glance at the captain. "But is t'at all we taking?"

"Captain Pahner?" Roger glanced at the CO. "Is there something I should know?"

"I've been talking with Rastar," Pahner said quietly. "The Boman didn't just sack Therdan and Sheffan—they razed them to the ground, and the surviving League forces are generally uninterested in returning to rebuild. There's nothing there *to* rebuild, and I think there's also an aspect of not wanting to see their dead in it. If they don't see them, don't see the ruins with their own eyes, they can remain in denial deep down inside. And the *civan* unit has also bonded well to us and, to an extent, to your person as a leadership figure. In addition, Bogess has mentioned that some of his forces aren't interested in returning to Diaspra. Again, for some of them it's that they've developed an interest in learning and seeing new things, and for others it's a basic change of allegiance."

"You're thinking of taking some of the Northern and Diaspran forces with us?" The prince chuckled. "Her Majesty's Own Mardukan Sepoys?"

"I cannot secure your person with thirty-six Marines, Your Highness," the captain said in a much more formal tone than usual, meeting the prince's gaze levelly. "Certainly not in this environment. I could barely manage with a full company . . . and I don't have a company anymore. As Sergeant Julian just said, I have a platoon. That simply isn't enough, and that means I have to do it through some other means."

Roger's chuckle died, and he nodded soberly.

"I hadn't intended to make light of your predicament, Sir. Or your losses. I was simply anticipating Mother's reaction."

"Indeed," Pahner said, and shook his head with a sudden grunting Mardukan-style chuckle of his own. "I can see our return now. Her Majesty will be most . . . amused."

"Her Majesty," O'Casey said, "after she reads the reports, will be most . . . amazed. There's never been a saga to equal this one, Captain. At the least, you've placed your name in the military history books."

"Only if I get him back to Her Majesty," Pahner pointed out. "Which requires crossing the ocean, making our way through whatever political zone we hit on the far side, and recapturing the spaceport with only thirty-six Marines and a half dozen suits of problematical powered armor. And that's why I would like to take a unit of *civan* cavalry and another of Diaspran pikemen, or riflemen or musketeers, whichever it turns out, with us."

"Which means how many ships?" Roger asked.

"Six," the Pinopan answered. "Six thirty, thirty-five-meter schooners. Lots of sail area, pretty good cargo volume, good sea legs, an' weatherly. Maybe topsail schooners. Square sails on tee main an' fore won' help much on tee trip over, but t'ey be good for tee trip back wit' tee prevailing winds behind you."

"You can build one of t'ose—those?" Pahner asked.

"Wit' a little help. T'ey gots most of tee techniques we need, they jus' use 'em all wrong. T'ese ships t'ey make are tubs—not all t'at bad for what t'ey does, but t'ey don' do much. Never sail out o' sight o' land, run for shore whenever a storm blow up, t'ings like t'at. T'at's why I don't t'ink nobody's gonna make it 'cross tee ocean in one o' t'ese toy boats. But smooth out tee lines, give some deadrise an' some more dept' of hull, lower tee freeboard fore an' aft an' bring it up some in between, an' you gots you'self a real tiddly ship. On'y real problem is, t'ey don' use buildin' drafts—t'ey designs by eye an' uses half-models to fair tee lines."

"Do you have any idea at all what he's talking about?" Roger asked O'Casey plaintively, and the chief of staff laughed.

"No, but it certainly sounds like *he* does," she said.

"It not so dif'rent from some o' tee little yards back home," the Pinopan said, "on'y we use 'puter wire drawings, instead. You build you'self a model—tee scummies, t'ey do it out o' wood, 'cause t'ey gots no computers—an' t'en you takes tee lines direct from tee model to tee finished ship wit'out detailed plans. 'Course, tee scummies, t'ey don' know nothin' 'bout displacement an' stability calc'lations, an' t'eir mouldin' lofts suck, but I can handle t'at no sweat."

"All of which means?" Pahner pressed.

"I wanna make a half-scale model to test my numbers," Poertena told him. "T'at take about a month. T'en, if it good an ever't'ing go smooth, t'ree months for tee rest."

"*Four* months?" Roger demanded, aghast.

"Can't do it no faster, Sir," the sergeant said apologetically. "T'at's as fast as we can go, an' t'at's after we gets tee materials. I can start on tee model as soon as I gets some funds. Talked to a pretty good shipbuilder today, an' I t'ink we can work wit' him. But we gotta get timbers, an' more important, we gotta get a dozen or so masts—an' spare masts an' spars, too, an' sails, now I t'ink about it—from somewheres."

"You were prophetic, Your Highness," Pahner said sourly. "This shipbuilder, Poertena—he didn't happen to have anything to do with a fellow named Wes Til, did he?"

"Don' know, Sir. Is t'at important?"

"Maybe, but not for the model, I think. Okay, you're authorized to draw funds as necessary. If it isn't terribly expensive, buy a small craft to unstep the mast for the model. And get that shipyard to work. I want the model completed in three weeks."

"I try, Sir," the Pinopan said mournfully, "but I don' t'ink it gonna happen in t'ree weeks. I only say a mont' 'cause I know you not gonna let me have two. But I try."

A quiet knock at the door interrupted the discussion, and PFC Kyrou poked his head into the room.

"Captain Pahner, Sir, we have two Mardukan gentlemen out here with what I think are dinner invitations."

Pahner raised one eyebrow and made a pointing gesture with the index finger and cocked thumb of his gun hand. The private shook his head in reply, indicating that neither seemed to be armed, and the captain nodded to let them in.

Both of the Mardukans wore enough jewelry to open a shop, but to Pahner's admittedly inexpert eye, it didn't appear to be of very high quality.

"I'm Captain Pahner. And you are?"

"I am Des Dar," the first said, bowing slightly in the local fashion with clenched fists brought into shoulders. "I bring Prince Roger an invitation to a personal dinner with my employer, Wes Til." The messenger proffered a tied and sealed scroll. "The location and time are within. May I tell my employer that you accept?"

"*My* name is Tal Fer," the second Mardukan interrupted quickly, proffering an equally ornate scroll, "and I am sent from Turl Kam with an invitation to Prince Roger to join *him* for dinner. May I tell him you accept?"

Kyrou saw three more functionaries, scrolls in hand, approaching the prince's room and judiciously turned off his toot's translator function. Then he leaned back in through the door and caught Captain Pahner's eye.

"Three more scummy flunkies inbound, Sir."

Cord, who'd learned enough English to recognize the untranslated human term for the locals, turned a grunt of laughter into a cough.

"Sorry," he said when Des Dar and Tal Fer looked at him. "Age is catching up with these old lungs."

Pahner frowned at the private and gave the old shaman a very speaking glance, then turned back to the first two messengers.

"Sirs, please convey to your employers our delight at their invitations and—"

He stopped, out of both polite phrases and his depth, and looked appealingly at Roger's chief of staff. O'Casey's eyes creased in a smile as she looked back at him, but she took over smoothly.

"However, we are unable to respond immediately," she told the messengers. "Please convey that to your employers, along with the fact that we will reply to them as soon as possible."

The messengers jockeyed for position as they handed their scrolls to the chief of staff. She took them smoothly, with a courteous refusal to give either precedence, then gave the same message to the trio

Kyrou had spotted when they arrived. Two more turned up after those, and at that point Pahner ordered Kyrou to repeat the mantra for O'Casey and closed the door. Firmly.

"We need some local input on these," O'Casey said, as she perused the documents. The text was readable, thanks to her toot, and the invitations were not only from Council members, but also from major merchants. She suspected that some of those might be more important in the long run than the Council members themselves.

"Cord, could you pass the word for Rastar, please?" Roger said. "We're going to need to get his input on these invitations and some sort of stronger feel for whether or not his forces really intend to accompany us overseas."

"Yes, My Lord," the shaman said obsequiously, and climbed to his feet. "Your *asi* lives only to obey, no matter what the dangers he must face. I will brave the hordes of messengers for you, although my heart quails within me at the very thought."

"It *is* your duty, now that I think about it," Roger said with a grin, then touched the Mardukan on a lower shoulder. "Seriously, I'm not sure I dare go out there at the moment."

"Not a problem," the *asi* said. "After all, I'm not the one they long to entice into their power."

"'Yea, though I walk through the valley of the shadow of death, I will fear no evil,'" Roger quoted with another grin. "I'll meet you at the room after this madhouse subsides."

"I'll see you then," Cord agreed, and opened the door and forced his way into the crowd of shouting messengers.

"And tell Kosutic to send some spare guards down!" Pahner yelled to Kyrou as the door closed, then looked at Roger with a crooked smile. "Ah, the joys of civilization."

CHAPTER TWENTY-THREE

Rastar shook his head over the invitations laid out on the floor.

"Some of these I can only guess at, but you're right. Whether or not we get any support is going to depend more on these invitations than any Council meeting."

"Am I reading these right?" Roger asked. "Do they really say something like 'and bring a date'?"

"Yes." Rastar chuckled. "The local custom, decadent in the eyes of my people, is to have men and women at the same dinner. The women are supposedly there to lend an air of grace to the proceedings. I think the idea is for them to keep us from spitting on the floor."

"Bloody hell," Roger said. "Do they realize that one of my main advisers is a woman? And one of my senior officers, as well, for that matter?"

"I'm not sure," Rastar said. "But it's going to be very important for you to attend at least three of these if you hope to achieve anything here in the city. How you divide them up is going to be . . . interesting."

"Eleanora . . . ?" the prince said plaintively.

"I'll do my best," the chief of staff sighed. "I wish I understood the position of women in this society better, though. I'm getting this queasy feeling that we've arrived in the middle of the suffrage movement, which means that any time a female opens her mouth in a definitive manner, as I tend to, it's going to be taken as a political statement."

"Well, let's go on as we intend to end," Roger told her. "We're a mixed unit from a mixed society, and I don't intend to convey anything else, whatever the societal norms. Also, there's this story of a woman who organized the evacuation of D'Sley."

"There are three invitations from D'Sley nobles," Rastar noted. "But none from a woman."

"Julian," Pahner said. "Track down that story and get us some clear intel on it."

"You think it's important?" Roger asked.

"If we have to stay and fight, it will be," the captain said. "If she can organize a sealift one way, she can organize one the other way."

"Ah." The prince smiled. "Rastar, I get the feeling that D'Sley wasn't a democracy?"

"No," the Northerner said. "It was controlled by a council of nobles and a weak king. From what I've heard, the king is dead, and many of the nobles as well, but many of the commoners escaped, especially the women."

"And they're clogging the city," Julian added. "That's one of the sore points at the moment—all the D'Sley refugees."

"Just once," Roger said, shaking his head. "Just damned once, I would like *something* to go smoothly *somewhere* on this planet."

"There is a sense of *déjà vu* here, isn't there?" O'Casey laughed. "I'll set about divvying up these invitations with Rastar. You go discuss clothes with Matsugae. I'm going to need a clean and presentable dress or suit, as are several of the Marines. We can . . . elevate their social importance for the evening."

"Oh, Lord," Roger said, grabbing his head. "Just once. Please God, just *once*." He shuddered. "Poertena. At a formal dinner? The mind boggles."

Kostas Matsugae shook his head and grimaced.

"You really don't appreciate me enough," he said.

"Probably not," Roger agreed wryly. "But we need dresses or suits for myself, Pahner, O'Casey, Kosutic, and some of the other Marines."

"Why here? They seemed to do just fine with chameleon suits everywhere else."

"The locals are a bit more sophisticated in K'Vaern's Cove," Roger said. "They deal with so many different cultures that they're more likely to notice the . . . poor condition of the uniforms, even if they don't wear clothes themselves. Unfortunately, we can't afford to create anything but the very best impression, because we need something from these guys, like a fleet of ships, so Armand wants you to coordinate with Eleanora to see to it that any appearance we present is a good one."

"Oh, very well," the valet said with a sudden twinkle. "I'll think of something. There are a couple of bolts of *dianda* left, and I'm sure the locals have some of that serge-like material I found at Diaspra, if nothing else. And I've already seen some very nice wall hangings and tapestries here, so if I look really hard . . ."

His voice trailed off thoughtfully, and Roger stood.

"Right, well, I'll leave you to it," he said.

"Hmmm," Matsugae said with an absentminded nod, but then his eyes sharpened. "Do we know who's going to be attending these events? And when are they?"

"Uh, no," Roger said as casually as possible. "We're not quite certain yet who's on the guest list from our side. But the dinners are mostly tomorrow evening," he finished brightly.

"Tomorrow!"

"I guess I'd better get going now," Roger said, beating a hasty retreat.

"Tomorrow?!"

"Have a good time, Kostas. Use whatever funds you need," the prince said, and disappeared out the door like smoke.

The valet stood staring at the closed door, jaw still half-dropped, for several fulminating seconds, but then he began to smile.

"Whatever funds I need, hmmm?" he murmured. "And coordinate with Eleanora, is it?" He chuckled evilly. "*This* one you're going to pay for, Roger," he promised the absent prince. "In fact, I think it's two-birds-with-one-stone time, young man!"

Eleanora O'Casey glanced up as Matsugae walked into her office, took one look at his expression, and chortled. Then she gestured at the scrolls scattered over the floor around her.

"Look at this before you complain to me about *your* problems," she warned him.

"Oh, I wasn't going to complain," he said with a decidedly wicked grin. "I was only wondering if you'd decided on who was escorting whom?"

"Well, we've got a minimum of two separate categories of meetings going on, and probably at least three. The first category consists of the ones which are going to be crucial to getting overall political support, so those are the most critical and I'm assigning senior officers and in some cases some of our more . . . polished NCOs to them."

"All right. And the others?"

"The second category are the dinners where I can reasonably expect the majority of the conversation to revolve around military-technical issues. Bistem Kar is hosting one of those, for example. For those, I feel comfortable sending experienced but slightly less polished NCOs. Then there's a dinner invitation from a shipyard associated with Councilor Wes Til. In fact, Til is hosting the banquet."

"So he'll be there in person?"

"Yes, and I'm not entirely certain whether that one ought to be considered overall political or military-technical . . . or possibly in a third category all its own. Call it, um, logistical. Or maybe financial. Whatever, I'm assigning it the same priority as category one. Particularly since Tor Flain, the local Guard's second in command, is also going to be present."

"So who's going to that one?"

"Oh, Roger. Technically, the Council chairman is higher in rank than Til, but given the fact that we're going to have to build our own ships, the combination of economic and military aspects make this the more important meeting, I think. And if military questions arise, I'm sure Roger can field them."

"And who's he going to be escorting?"

"I haven't decided yet. Given its importance, I suppose I should go with him, but there's another that fascinates me more. One of the other Council members, who's nearly as wealthy as Til, has arranged for a dinner to which a D'Sley nobleman will be bringing the female who arranged the D'Sley sealift."

"That does sound fascinating," the valet said. "Have you decided who'll be escorting you to it?"

"No, I hadn't," she said, then looked up and raised an eyebrow at his expression. "Really?"

"I would truly like to meet the . . . formidable lady who organized that evacuation," Matsugae said honestly. "And I believe my calendar is open."

"Okay," she agreed, pulling out an invitation scroll and making a note on it. "That's that one filled."

"Excellent. And, if I may, I believe I might have an appropriate suggestion for Roger's companion, as well."

"Christ on a crutch," Roger grumbled as he tossed his helmet on the bed the following afternoon. "I just came back from the harbor, and I see what Poertena means about tubs—those things must roll in a bathtub!"

"Well, some of us weren't able to go gallivanting about the city," Matsugae sniffed, and Roger smiled as he took in the valet's appearance. Matsugae wore a suit of dark blue velvet that was both extremely handsome and much too heavy for the local weather, and the glittering MacClintock crest of a palace servitor in personal service to the Imperial Family sparkled brightly on his breast for the first time since they'd arrived on Marduk. Its brilliance would have been sadly out of place on a chameleon suit, but it was also a proud award very few could claim, and the valet brushed it absently with his fingers as he returned the prince's regard.

"Nice outfit, Kosie! I take it Eleanora shanghaied you for the guest list, too?"

"I would scarcely choose the term 'shanghaied,'" Matsugae said primly, "but, yes, I will be attending one of the dinners tonight. In fact, Eleanora and I will be going together, thank you."

Roger's smile turned into a grin, and Matsugae sniffed again.

"It's certainly an evening out which I've earned," he said, pointedly. "While you were out playing in the harbor, I've had half the platoon cycling through my own private tailor's shop." Roger's eyebrows rose in surprise, and Matsugae gave him a triumphant smile. "I am—justifiably, I feel—quite proud of it, since I created it in a single day. And it's undoubtedly the largest tailor's shop I've ever seen, since I had to buy an entire idled sailmaker's loft to put it in!"

"Good work, Kostas! I knew we could count on you. Now all we have to do is replicate your outfit a few dozen times over, and we'll be able to attend all the boring dinners we have to to save our own buns and K'Vaern's Cove both! When am I scheduled for a fitting?"

"You will no doubt be happy to know that you won't require a fitting, despite the fact that you chose to spend the entire day playing hooky down at the harbor instead of assisting with the preparations. As it turns out, the St. John twins are both very nearly your size and build, so I was able to use one of them as a breathing manikin. You now have a new suit. Congratulations."

"Man, you were really upset at getting this dumped on you, weren't you?"

"Not as much as it might seem. You are, I believe, attending the small dinner party with Wes Til?"

"And Tor Flain," Roger agreed, unbraiding his hair and stripping off his chameleon suit. "I don't suppose there's time for a bath?"

"One has been drawn, Your Highness," Matsugae assured him. "And who are you taking to the party?"

"Eleanora, I'd presume," Roger said with a suddenly wary expression, one foot still in his trousers as something about the valet's tone sounded warning signals. "But you said you were going with her, didn't you?" he asked suspiciously.

"Actually, I did. The two of us are going to meet with Sam Tre and Fullea Li'it, the lady who arranged the D'Sley sealift."

"Oh." Roger finished stepping out of the uniform. "Kosutic, then?"

"Being accompanied by Sergeant Julian to a meeting with Bistem Kar, I believe."

"That should be interesting," Roger observed. "Too bad I didn't draw that one. So if not Kosutic, who? Gunny Lai?"

"Accompanying Captain Pahner to his dinner with Turl Kam."

"Okay," Roger said, turning to face him and planting his hands on his hips. "Spit it out, Kosie. Who?"

"Actually, I believe Sergeant Despreaux is the next most senior female Marine," the valet said with a bland expression.

"*Oh*," Roger oofed, his expression remarkably like that of a poleaxed steer. Then he shook himself. "Oh, Kostas Matsugae, I had no concept of the depths of wickedness lurking in your soul. You are an evil, evil person!"

"*Moi?* Well, perhaps. I can state without fear of contradiction, however, that she cleans up pretty. For one of the 'help.'"

"Such an evil person," Roger whispered to himself as Despreaux came through the door.

The sergeant's blouse was a lovely shade of off-white. The sleeveless and collarless garment was made of an opaque, white linenlike material that was almost paper thin but had an odd translucence, like mother-of-pearl. The base fiber was something called *halkha*, and it came from the pods of a hemplike plant unknown on the east side of the Tarsten range. The locals used it very much as Terrans had used cotton in the days when there were no synthetic fibers, for everything from wall hangings, to sacks and coarse-woven bags used to hold tubers and grains, to sailcloth. There was, however, an enormous difference between those rough, sturdy utilitarian fabrics and the fine threads and tight weaves required to make such lovely cloth, and Roger wondered where Matsugae had found enough, on no notice, to create several outfits.

Rather than buttoning up the front, the blouse was sealed with soft, beautifully tanned leather ties up the sides and at the shoulders. Roger supposed that was because it had been impossible even for Matsugae to introduce buttons and buttonholes to the generally unclothed Mardukans in the time available to him, but the ties lent the outfit an air of barbarism that was somehow in keeping with the whole crazy affair.

The simple peasant skirt that accompanied the blouse was also white, although a shade darker than the blouse. Its pleats swirled around her long legs, and Roger winced as he looked at her footwear.

"Court shoes? Where in the hell did he find court shoes?"

"Is that all you have to say, Your Highness?" the sergeant snapped, fiddling with the unfamiliar weight of the skirt. It was the first time in months that she'd worn anything but her uniform and skivvies.

"Uh," Roger replied, suddenly tongue-tied.

"I hope your 'associate' meets with your approval," Despreaux said in tones of deadly sweetness, and Roger grimaced.

"Look, I wasn't at my very best that evening, and that wasn't the word I really wanted. But neither was 'servant,' 'help,' or 'slave.' Sometime, maybe, I can explain what I did mean to say, and why. But right now, we have a mission. If it helps, I didn't ask for this, either."

Despreaux's eyes flashed, and she threw her hands up in the air.

"Oh, sure, that makes me *really* happy, 'Milord'! Now I'm not just stuck with *you* all night, I'm stuck with somebody who doesn't want his 'associate' to sully the evening!"

Roger grabbed his hair and started to pull it, then drew a deep breath and shoved the disarranged strands back into place.

"Sergeant Despreaux. Truce, okay? I'm sorry. Does that help? I'm sorry for offending you. I'm even sorry for not taking you up on your implication, or at least seeing if what I *thought* was an implication was, in fact, an implication at all. I am very attracted to you. Was, am, and will be. I was that night. I am tonight. I will be at some future date when perhaps we can sit down and discuss the . . . problems of one Roger MacClintock and why they cause him to keep making an ass out of himself in front of beautiful women."

He drew another breath and held a hand up before Despreaux could get a word in edgewise.

"But tonight, we have a mission to complete. A very important one. And that requires that we not be clearly at odds for the entire evening. Now, can we manage to *act* like we like each other? A little? For a few hours?"

Despreaux closed her mouth and let out her gathered breath through flaring nostrils, then nodded.

"Yes, Sir. We can."

"Very well. In that case, I think it's time." Roger started towards the door, only to be blocked by the sergeant's automatic reflex action—the Empress' Own *always* went through a door before its principal.

The prince looked at her and smiled. He also noticed that the court shoes, whose high heels had come into fashion once again, made her nearly as tall as he was. He still didn't have a clue how Matsugae had managed to find shoes, but he discovered that it was distinctly pleasant to have Nimashet Despreaux's eyes on a level with his own.

"Sergeant," he said, "tonight you aren't a bodyguard. Tonight, I'm your escort to dinner, and, as such, it's my job to open the door for *you.*"

Despreaux smiled back and let him open it. Then she went through first, automatically scanning from side to side.

That's what you think, she thought. And where did the Sergeant Major get that holster? Try to get between these thighs tonight, Your Highness, and you've got a hell of a surprise coming!

It took her a moment to realize that she assumed both that he would try . . . and that she would let him succeed.

Oh, Nimashet, you've got it bad.

CHAPTER TWENTY-FOUR

The restaurant at which Roger and his "date" arrived after a long journey from the Citadel appeared to be little more than a shack right on the edge of the water on the seaward side of the city's peninsula. North of the main portion of the city, the location was a perfect half-moon bay, partially sheltered from storms by a reef of rock clearly demarcated by the swirl of luminescence where marine organisms glowed in the gentle swell washing over it. The bay, with its strip of rock and sand beach at the foot of the high limestone cliffs soaring up to the city wall, was quite pretty, if a trifle exposed. The haphazardly built structure of gray, weathered wood perched out over the water on piles driven into the rocky shore, open on the bay side and with two small fishing boats tied up in the shelving water beside it.

Roger slid down from their *howt'e* and turned to give Despreaux a hand down. The Triceratops-like beast was a smaller version of the *flar-ta* that stood "only" two meters at the shoulder, which was still amply large to make it just a *tad* ostentatious as a mode of transport through the streets of K'Vaern's Cove. Fortunately, like most *flar-ta*, *howt'e* were remarkably placid. But they were also expensive, and the fact that Wes Til had sent one to collect his human guests was both a statement of his wealth and—Roger hoped—a deliberate gesture of respect.

Despreaux would normally have handled unloading from the

beast with athletic grace, but the fifty-millimeter heels the valet had somehow cobbled together got in the way of easy dismounts from Triceratops look-alikes.

Roger smiled at the thought, then smiled again as his squad of guards spread out around him and a team went in ahead to sweep the restaurant. He found the dichotomy odd. In battle, and even on the march, Pahner and the rest of the Marines had become accustomed to letting him risk his life alongside the lowliest private. They might not like it, but they'd finally accepted that it was going to happen. Get him into a "normal" situation, though, and their reflex protectiveness clamped down like armor.

The point team returned and nodded approval, and the remainder of his guards deigned to allow him and Despreaux to enter the restaurant themselves.

The interior of the shack was far superior to its inauspicious exterior. The building was broken into several smaller rooms, separated by simple woven walls that permitted the fresh sea breeze free run of the building. There were at least two dozen Mardukans in the first section, gathered around long, low tables, picking at trays of food and sipping from bulbous containers.

Roger's nose was assaulted by the scent of cooking as he entered, and he knew immediately that whatever else happened that evening, he was about to have a superior gustatory experience.

"Smells good," the sergeant whispered.

"Now I wish we'd brought Kostas," Roger said, as a jewel-bedecked Mardukan female approached.

"He's eating with Eleanora, remember?"

"That's what I meant."

"Welcome, gentle sir and madam, to Bullur's." The speaker seemed young to Roger, possibly the equivalent of a Terran teenager. "Did you make a reservation?"

"We're here with the Wes Til party," Roger said, handing over his invitation. He was moderately surprised by the fact that their greeter was female. It was the first time since Marshad that he'd spoken to a Mardukan woman, aside from exchanging a few words from time to time with one of the mahouts' women, although his observations in the markets and at the Council meeting had already confirmed that O'Casey was right in at least one respect. Here in K'Vaern's Cove, women clearly enjoyed at least some status.

"Very good, sir," the young lady said after a glance at the scroll. Her examination of it had been long enough, and purposeful enough, to indicate that she could read the angular script. "If you'll follow me?"

"Where are we going?" Despreaux asked, planting a restraining hand on Roger's forearm before he could move.

"Through here," the hostess replied in a slightly questioning tone.

"St. John," the sergeant said, and pointed with her chin.

"On it, Nimashet," the big Marine said, following the hostess with a grin. "Why don't you just let your hair down for the evening?"

"I don't think so," the NCO said primly as she and Roger followed St. John (J.) across the restaurant at a more leisurely pace, giving him time to check out the other room without being any more obvious about it than they had to.

"I think that would be an excellent idea," Beckley put in from behind the prince. "Letting your hair down, that is. Although, come to think of it, letting down *his* hair might be even more fun."

Roger drew a deep breath and bit his tongue rather firmly, but Despreaux's head whipped around and she gave the corporal a look like a solar prominence.

"I don't recall asking for your opinion, Reneb," she said in a dangerous tone, and the corporal chuckled.

"Nope, but them as needs help are usually the last to realize it. Just think of it as a friend trying to help you out."

"Reneb!" Despreaux began in a voice of mingled wrath and amusement, but she clamped her jaw when Roger put a hand on her forearm.

"It's not like she's the only one who thinks we're both being idiots, Nimashet." He sighed. "And the hell of it is, they're probably right! But," a wicked gleam entered his eyes, "if you won't tell them the deep dark secret of what passed between us in Q'Nkok, *I* won't!"

They reached the door opening into the last section of the building as he spoke, and St. John reappeared to nod that the room was clear just in time to see Sergeant Despreaux turn an interesting shade of crimson.

"My, my, my!" Beckley said in interested tones. "Whatever *did* happen in Q'Nkok, Nimashet?"

"Never you mind!" Despreaux snapped. "I mean, nothing happened in Q'Nkok! I—"

"*Nimashet!*" Roger's tone was one of shocked reproach. "How could you possibly have forgotten that wonderful morning?"

"There *wasn't* any wonderful morning!" Despreaux snarled, and then, as Beckley burst out laughing, the sergeant closed her eyes, drew a deep breath, and smiled in spite of herself. "Damn you, Roger," she half-chuckled. "I was willing to let you live for Ran Tai, but for that . . . ?"

She looked around the private room, the bodyguard reflex making personally certain that the room was indeed cleared, then relaxed ever so slightly. The area took up about a quarter of the interior of the restaurant, and it was occupied solely by the Councilman, his invited guests, and a few flunkies.

"Hey, you gotta catch me first," Roger told her with a wink as the Councilman and the K'Vaernian Guard's second in command came to their feet. "And kicking off those heels will give me at least a second's head start."

"Prince Roger Ramius Sergei Alexander Chiang MacClintock," Wes Til said, giving a shallow bow, "I believe that you've already met Tor Flain. May I introduce my life-mate, Teel Sla'at?" The woman beside him bowed at the waist and gave a gesture of greeting. She wore something Roger had never seen before, a magnificently worked harness of gold and lapis lazuli, and he returned her bow gracefully.

"Teel Sla'at, I greet you. And you as well, Wes Til. Well met."

"And may I introduce *my* life-mate, See Tra'an?" Tor Flain added. The guardsman had doffed his armor and instead was heavily bejeweled, with at least five necklaces, and bracelets on all four arms. His lady was even more heavily jeweled, with enough assorted metals and gems to be considered half armored. About half the total outfit consisted of a single sort of pearly gemstones, most of them greenish in cast and skillfully set in a pattern which emphasized the subtle gradations in their coloration. It made her look like some sort of Mardukan mermaid, and Roger wondered if the locals had that myth.

"I greet you, See Tra'an, Tor Flain," he said. The humans hadn't worked out the protocol for introductions at these dinners, although Eleanora had been sweating blood trying to figure it out. The biggest question was whether or not the women, who in virtually every other Mardukan society they'd encountered had been voiceless pseudo-slaves, should be greeted or even acknowledged. So far, none of the K'Vaernians had reacted with shock or outrage, and the female greeter and the conversations in the rest of the restaurant, which had involved mixed genders, also suggested that he'd hit just about the right note.

"And may I introduce Sergeant Nimashet Despreaux," he went on, gesturing to the sergeant . . . who, to his amazement, dropped a very creditable curtsy.

There was a momentary awkward pause, and then Teel Sla'at made a hand gesture of humor.

"Could you, perhaps, enlighten us as to your relationship to the 'sergeant'?" she asked politely.

Roger's eyebrows rose in a combination of surprise and dismay. Surprise because, despite the conversations that had gone on in the other rooms, he'd somehow assumed that the women would be along as a sort of window dressing. Dismay because he now had to explain his relationship to Despreaux, and even he wasn't sure what it was.

"Prince Roger and I are trying to determine if we're compatible to mate," Despreaux answered while he was still grappling with the question.

"And you have a choice?" Til asked. His tone indicated interest rather than distaste or shock, and Despreaux smiled as Roger chuckled ruefully.

"Oh, yeah, we sure do," the prince answered.

"Please, be seated," Til invited.

"'Compatible to mate,'" See Tra'an repeated. "I understand that you humans are capable of mating at any time. Is that true?"

"Yes," Roger said uncomfortably, as he and Despreaux stretched out on the pillows scattered around the low tables. The escorting Marines took positions around the room, and Cord dropped into a lotus position behind Roger. "We can."

"Pseudo-mating is a form of social interaction and even recreation among us," Despreaux added. "On the other hand, it's a taboo subject in several of our subcultures."

"Is that a hint to drop the subject?" Teel Sla'at asked. The Councilor's mate slid a platter of thin, cooked slices of something in front of Despreaux and followed the motion by popping a slice from a similar platter into Wes Til's mouth.

The sergeant looked at the platter in front of her, then picked up one of the slices and ostentatiously ate it herself.

"Not at all. Neither Roger nor I are from one of those subcultures." She paused and picked up another slice. "This is good."

"Calan," Tor Flain said. "A shell-covered species that lives on the rocks. Preparation is laborious, but the result is excellent. How does one tell the difference between human males and females? You and R—the Prince are almost the same size."

Roger smiled as Despreaux fell momentarily silent. He picked up one of the slices and offered to feed it to her, and his smile became a grin despite himself as she glared silently at him.

"The easiest way to tell is to look for protuberances on the chest," he told the K'Vaernian guardsman. "There are other clues, but they're difficult to explain."

"Protuberances?" Flain repeated. "What are they? Or is that a taboo subject, as well?"

It was Despreaux's turn to laugh at the prince as his face flushed, and she kept her mouth shut, waiting to see how he would answer.

"It's a taboo to some people, but not to me," the prince said determinedly. "They are . . . similar in purpose to the heavier secretions on the backs of your females. They secrete a thin substance that's consumed for sustenance by human young."

"May we see them?" See Tra'an asked.

Roger rolled his eyes, and Despreaux smiled sweetly at him.

"Certainly," she said, and undid the ties at her shoulders.

"Hmmm." Til leaned forward and prodded the exposed breasts

gently with his finger. "And you say these are used to produce food for your young? Is that their only purpose?"

"That and turning men into babies," Despreaux said with a silvery laugh as she did the ties back up, and Tor Flain looked at the prince.

"Your face has changed colors. Does that mean you and Sergeant Despreaux are going to mate?"

"*No!*" Roger said as Despreaux started laughing uncontrollably. "Oh, shut up, Nimashet."

"Is that a command, Your Highness?" the sergeant asked with a throaty chuckle.

"No, just a desperate attempt to steer the conversation onto less sensitive ground, I suspect," the councilor observed. "Unless I miss my guess, it seems that we've offended our guests."

"Only the more important one," Flain said. "Quick work. This is why I think inviting women to sensitive negotiations is insanity."

"Ah, my fine D'Sley import!" his mate said with a grunt of laughter. "You are so up-to-date."

"Well, it's true. You women are just too flighty."

"I wouldn't advise telling that to Eleanora," Roger said, taking another bite of the calan.

"She's your, what is the term, 'chief of staff'?" Til asked.

"Yes. She's my senior political adviser, as opposed to Captain Pahner, who's my senior military adviser."

"And a woman?" Flain asked.

"A woman," Roger agreed. "She's meeting with Lord Sam Tre and Madame Fullea Li'it this evening. And the person who's 'escorting' her isn't a senior adviser."

"So she'll be the one carrying the weight of the discussion?" Til asked.

"And any actual negotiations, political or financial, that might come up," Roger agreed, and didn't notice the looks that passed between the K'Vaernians at the word "negotiations" as he offered another bite to Despreaux. She accepted unthinkingly, and then they both froze as she nipped the slice off just short of his fingers.

"Ah, look," Tor Flain said. "He's turning red again. I say they're going to mate."

"I hope they can wait until after dinner," See Tra'an added. "I've heard wonderful things about the grilled *coll.*"

Roger cleared his throat.

"We are *not* going to mate."

"Certainly not here, that is," Despreaux corrected.

"This is an interesting restaurant," Roger said, managing not to sound—quite—desperate as he changed subjects.

"One of my family's," Flain said, accepting the change. "Most of the employees are cousins."

"It's not much to look at on the outside," Despreaux said. "I take it that was deliberate?"

"Part of its charm," Teel Sla'at agreed. "If you don't know about it, you don't come here."

"It has excellent food, though," Til added. "Tor Flain's family is well known for their fish."

"It's what we do," the soldier said with a gesture of agreement. "Father started off small, concentrating on quality. He was sure there was a market for much more expensive and higher quality products than are usually available, and there was."

"And you, Wes Til? What's your background?" Roger asked.

"The Til are one of the oldest families in the city," the councilman's mate answered.

"We bought K'Vaern's dock from him the second time he went bust," the councilor said with a grunt of laughter. "And we've managed to keep a grip on our properties. Unlike most families."

"And didn't fade away," Roger said with a nod. "That's unusual over more than three or four generations. On the other hand, we're having a hard time getting much of the feel for time with you guys."

"And you, Prince Roger?" See Tra'an asked. "You're part of a politically powerful family? How long has it been in power?"

"The MacClintocks have been the Imperial Family for nearly a thousand years now," Despreaux answered for him. "However, we're long-lived, so that's only—" She paused.

"Twelve generations," Roger concluded. "Our family can be traced back for many more generations before that, with various members holding positions of power, but there was no Empire, which meant no emperors."

"So you grew up with the exercise of power," Til said. "Interesting."

"Yes and no," Roger replied as a group of servants entered bearing steaming platters. The centerpiece was a large fish with a broad, flattened head resembling a stonefish. The head was intact, but the body had been gutted and skinned and the entire fish had been grilled with some sort of glazing.

"I'm the youngest child," Roger continued as the platters were scattered around the low tables. "I have two very competent older siblings to manage the family affairs."

"Ah," Flain said, carving a section off of the fish as the servants moved around placing small bowls of side dishes by each diner. "So you became a military commander? That's what happened to me. There was nowhere in the family that fitted my interests, so I joined the Guard."

"Not really," Roger said. "The Marines are my bodyguards. I'm their ceremonial commander, but Pahner is the actual military professional."

"You've improved," Despreaux said, taking a bite of a sliced orange root. "Yow! That's hot."

"Thanks, but I'm still not a real commander," Roger pointed out. "Just because the Marines will obey me doesn't mean I'm a Marine."

"They no longer obey you for reasons of coercion," Cord said. "You are a commander in fact, whether the law supports you or not."

"Whatever," Roger said uncomfortably. "But my 'career' isn't yet set."

"You're a sailor, as well?" Til asked.

"Only a dabbler," the prince responded, taking a slice of orange root of his own. "Wow! That *is* hot. But sweet, too." He took a sip of wine to reduce the burn, and shrugged. "I've sailed with people for whom it's a hobby, but one of our junior personnel who's meeting with your shipyard manager and the owner of the boatyard that's producing our model comes from a land of professional seamen. He's our real expert, and he worked for some years in a shipyard in his land while he was attending school, but I can talk about seafaring generalities, which is one of the reasons I'm meeting with you."

"It's a tradition among our people to assure that if any decisions are to be made at a meeting, no one there knows what they're talking about," Despreaux said. "Do your people have the same tradition?"

Roger choked on his wine, and Til grunted.

"I take it that that's a joke," the laughing councilman said.

"Unfortunately, it has a measure of truth to it," Flain said. "An inefficiency that my father expertly exploited."

"We will be making no decisions tonight," Roger said after swallowing more wine to clear his throat. "We might discuss some of the things that need to be worked out, but no decisions are going to be made."

"It isn't our tradition to make decisions over food," Teel Sla'at pointed out.

"But you do discuss things of importance?" Despreaux asked. She took a bite of the flaky fish and raised her eyebrows. "That's excellent. What's that glaze?"

"It's made from the same orange root," Flain said. "Ground very fine and mixed with wine, sea-plum juice, and some other spices which are a family secret."

"If you really want the recipe, I can get it," See Tra'an offered. "All it takes is scratching at the special place at the base of his horns."

"Is the fish a bottom feeder?" Roger asked, glancing at the centerpiece. He knew a good time to help someone by drawing fire when he heard one.

"Somewhat," Flain said quickly. "They lie on or near the bottom in large schools and rise to herd bait fish and clicker schools. They're generally caught on lines, although they can sometimes be netted with drift nets, and care is required in their preparation. They have a gland which must be removed before cooking, since it produces an oil which is quite poisonous."

Despreaux looked up quickly at that, and Roger chuckled at her expression.

"We have a similar fish in our own land," he assured the guardsman. "Some of our people actually prefer to sample small doses of the toxin it produces, though, and I gather from your tone that that's not the case here?"

"Hardly," Tor said with a grim chuckle. "'Quite poisonous' is a slight understatement, I'm afraid. 'Instantly fatal' would probably be better."

"I see." Despreaux swallowed a mouthful, her expression uneasy, and Roger took pity on her.

"Remember Marshad and Radj Hoomis' cooking, Nimashet," he told her, and she glanced at him, then visibly relaxed at the reminder of the inept Marshadan monarch's attempt to poison his "guests" . . . without any notion of how alien their physiology truly was.

"Please, feel no concern," Flain said earnestly. "I assure you, our people—and especially my own family—have been preparing coll for many, many years. Care is required, but the preparation process is relatively straightforward, and no one has actually been poisoned in as long as I can recall."

"I'm sure we'll be fine, Tor," Roger said, and smiled encouragingly at Despreaux as the sergeant gamely helped herself to another generous bite of the fish.

"Yes. In the meantime," the guardsman went on with the air of someone once again seeking a deliberate subject change, "I'm fascinated by these ships you envision. Triangular sails?"

"We'll have a model built fairly quickly," Roger told him. "We could do one on a smaller scale as a demonstrator, I suppose. I was down at the harbor earlier, watching some of your shipping, and I saw that you already know how to beat to windward."

"'Beat to windward'?" Til repeated.

"Sorry. A human term for tacking back and forth across the wind."

"Ah. Yes, we know how to tack, but it's a laborious process, and in light winds, especially, our ships often get caught in irons."

"'In irons'?" It was Despreaux's turn to repeat a phrase, and Roger nodded.

"He means their ships lose way before they can carry across the eye of the wind onto the opposite tack. Actually, I was a bit surprised that they tack instead of wearing ship." The sergeant rolled her eyes, and he grinned. "More sailorese, Nimashet. It means turning away from the wind in a near circle instead of turning *across* it when you change tack."

"And why should that be a surprise?"

"Because they use square headsails instead of the fore-and-aft jibs we use, and those are a pain to manage," Roger told her.

"Indeed they can be," Til agreed. "And you're quite right. At least half the time, our captains do prefer to wear rather than tacking. It takes more time, but especially in light breezes, it's often the only way to be sure you get clear around. But you have a new sail plan to allow us to avoid such difficulties?"

"I wouldn't go quite that far," the prince said, "but it should certainly make tacking a lot easier. You'll be able to sail much closer to the wind, too, so you won't have to tack as often, either. It'll still be easier to sail *with* the wind, but this ought to simplify things for you. A lot."

"So you can sail across the sea," Flain said.

"If there are any materials to build your ships," Til added.

Roger took another bite of *coll*. "Poertena believes we can purchase and cannibalize some of the local ships for parts."

"Still, that seems unnecessarily complex," Flain said, swallowing a bite of barleyrice. "It also will take some time."

"True," Roger agreed. "But there doesn't seem to be an alternative."

"Well, if the Boman weren't squatting on the forests, you could get all the masts and lumber you wanted," Wes Til pointed out. "For that matter, there's a huge stockpile in D'Sley. We've sent small raids over to recover raw materials, but the Boman are onto us now. They don't want to destroy the naval supplies, either—they may be barbarians, but they understand the decadent concept of money, and they intend to sell them at some point, no doubt. But taking any more would require an army."

"Hmmm," Roger said. "We weren't aware of that. It must be making the discussion with Eleanora interesting."

"Indeed," Flain agreed. "What are they discussing, do you know?"

"Eleanora wanted to meet the person who organized the D'Sley sealift."

"Ayeiii!" Til said. "When you mentioned that they were meeting with Fullea Li'it I hoped you were jesting."

"Why?" Despreaux asked. "Is there something wrong with her?"

"She's just—" The councilor paused, searching for a word.

"She is very direct," Teel Sla'at said with a laugh. "She speaks her mind. And D'Sley wasn't nearly so open with their women as we are, so a D'Sley woman speaking her mind is . . . unusual."

"She's also stubborn as a *turom*," Til put in.

"Then that ought to be an interesting meeting," Roger said with a smile.

"Fullea will press for your support in retaking D'Sley," Til said.

"There's no need for us to participate in that," Despreaux said. "We've done our fighting already."

"You have Bogess and Rus From to lead you," Roger pointed out, picking up another slice of orange root. "How does this do if you sauté it?"

"Quite well, actually," Flain answered. "But it's more piquant with the *coll* fish if it's raw. The problem is that no one trusts Bogess' understanding of the weapons or the tactics. Not like they trust you and Captain Pahner."

"Ha!" Roger laughed. "You'd trust unknown aliens over a known general?"

"We would when that's the reaction of the general's own army," Til said quietly. "And the reaction of the general himself. I doubt that the Council is going to be willing to leave the safety of the walls without the support of you Marines, your commander, and your 'powered armor.'"

"Bloody hell." Roger shook his head. "We're not here to fight your wars for you."

"Oh, I think we could fight our own wars, thank you," Flain said just a bit tartly, but then he paused and gave the Mardukan equivalent of a sigh. "Or we could, if we could build the support for it," he admitted unhappily, "and it will require some impetus to convince the populace that leaving the safety of the walls is the best plan. Which it is, since hiding behind the walls is a death sentence for the city, whether it comes by starvation or assault."

"Hmmm," Roger said, finishing off his fish. "Convincing populaces is one of Eleanora's specialties."

"That it is," Despreaux said. "I think that the meeting with the D'Sley contingent is going to be interesting."

CHAPTER TWENTY-FIVE

"So you are a female." Sam Tre's tone made the statement a question, and a fairly tentative one, at that. Despite his role as escort to the redoubtable Fullea Li'it, the D'Sley nobleman seemed confused at finding himself carrying on a serious conversation with a human woman, especially one who'd been represented as one of Prince Roger's senior officers.

"Yes," O'Casey said sweetly. "I am."

"And the 'Chief of Staff,'" the D'Sley female reclining on both left elbows across the low table said. "Fascinating."

"And your companion? Kostas, you are a senior officer also?" Tre asked.

"I don't think so," the valet replied with a smile.

"He's one of our logistics and supply experts," O'Casey said tactfully.

"That's one way of putting it," Matsugae said, picking at his rubbery *basik*. "Tastes like chicken and twice as many ways to prepare it," he muttered, then looked back up at his host with a slightly apologetic smile. "Excuse me. I can't help noticing the food, which is fair enough I suppose. For want of a better explanation, I'm the cook for this expedition."

"He's in charge of support for the Marines," O'Casey corrected. "He was Roger's body servant, and was pressed into service for his present job. Which, I might add, he's performed admirably."

"Ah," Fullea said. "So we have a D'Sley nobleman, a female chief of staff, a D'Sley fisherman's widow, and a human cook." She grunted in laughter until Eleanora was afraid she would choke. "This is quite a party."

"I wish you had cooked, Kostas Matsugae," Tre said. "You're correct—there are many good ways to do *basik*, and this isn't one of them."

"I fear I made a poor choice of restaurants," Fullea admitted ruefully. "I'm learning as fast as I can, but hosting important dinners in foreign cities wasn't part of the station to which I was born."

"You're a fisherman's wife?" O'Casey asked.

"I was," the D'Sley woman replied. "Not a poor fisherman; he owned his own boat and shares in his brother's cargo barge. But not . . . rich. Not a noble by any stretch, nor a man of means."

"And he was killed by the Boman?" Matsugae asked.

"Earlier, actually," the widow said. She made a gesture of resignation. "Swept off the deck by a line. Never found the body."

"'. . . The men who go down to the sea in ships,'" O'Casey quoted softly. "I'm sorry."

"The sea gives and takes away," Fullea said. "But the problem was his brother. Tareim felt he should take over the business. I was, after all, just a woman, even if I had been advising my husband for years. In fact, he'd far surpassed Tareim in gain, and it wasn't because my husband was an astute businessman. But Tareim didn't want to hear that. He didn't want to hear anything which might have made him 'subservient' to a mere woman, and the law favored him. There was little I could do, when he took over, except watch everything start coming apart, and things kept right on going from bad to worse until I . . . persuaded him to let me advise him. After which the business recovered."

"Our device translated that as 'persuaded,'" the chief of staff observed, toying with her wineglass. She supposed, given the restaurant's obviously costly fixtures and the jewelry of the other patrons, that the wine must be an expensive vintage, but it was also thin and tasteless as vinegar. "Would that be an accurate translation?"

"The term she actually used has overtones of gentle persuasion,"

Tre agreed. "However, in the context, it can be assumed that the reverse was true."

"I had two thugs accost him and threaten to break both his false-arms if he didn't put me back in control." The widow made a dismissive gesture. "Of course, they never said they were working for me. In fact, they didn't know they were. I'd hired them through a friend of my husband's, and they believed they were from a moneyman Tareim owed money to. Since part of the arrangement that put me back in charge also put me in direct contact with the moneyman and left me controlling all of Tareim's payments to him, no one was ever the wiser."

She chuckled softly, and the humans joined her.

"A neat solution to the problem," O'Casey said. "But what did this have to do with the sealift?"

"I'd built up a small fleet of ships by the time the Boman swept down from the north. When Therdan was surrounded and I realized the barbarians had no intention of stopping with the cities of the League, I decided that it would be good to move my base of operations, so I'd already arranged to shift everything to the Cove." Fullea picked at her dinner for a moment. "At first, when the Boman surrounded D'Sley in turn, there was a great deal of money to be made from ferrying rich nobles to the Cove. But then all of those who could pay to go were gone, and there were still all those people left."

She made another gesture of resignation.

"She organized the fishermen," Tre took up the story. "And the cargo barges. Begged, bullied—whatever it took—and started moving anyone who turned up at the docks across to K'Vaern's Cove."

"Not able-bodied men," the widow countered. "Not until the Seven tried to leave, anyway."

"Yes," the nobleman agreed with a grimace of distaste. "The Council tried to flee in the middle of Fullea's evacuation—on private boats, and without telling the military commanders, most of whom were mercenaries, anyway."

"That's when it all came apart," Fullea sighed. "We still refused to take soldiers if there were women and children, but more and more of the soldiers turned up. Then they started seizing the boats and not coming back. Finally, we called it off."

"You could see where the Boman were by the burning houses," the nobleman said quietly. "It was raining, hard, so the flames didn't spread from house to house—not on their own . . . but you could see the fires marking their line of advance."

"You were there," Kostas said.

"Sam held the rearguard for quite a time," Fullea responded. "But then he was wounded, and some of his men brought him down to the docks and loaded him on one of the ships. It was almost the last one out."

The nobleman clapped his hands in a Mardukan shrug. "After that, it got very bad. The final ships out . . . what they saw wasn't good."

"Sacks of heavily defended cities are like that," O'Casey said. "Fortunately, we humans, as a society, are pretty much past that. We had a bad period about a thousand years ago—the Dagger Years that caused the formation of the Empire. But since then, we haven't experienced organized pillaging. Not of major cities, at any rate."

The chief of staff toyed with the limp vegetables of a side dish.

"Are you going to go back?" she asked. "When the Boman settle down or move back north?"

The nobleman made a gesture of uncertainty.

"The Boman have vowed to remain on the southern lands until all of the cities of the south are destroyed, including K'Vaern's Cove," he said. "So we can only return if the Cove survives, and even if the Boman don't overwhelm the city walls, the Cove is weakening day by day while they squat on the timber and ore and fields. When the Boman leave, there may not be any reason to return."

"For me, I don't know," Fullea said. "I lost everything in the ferry efforts and the Battle of the Bay." She pointed at the two small necklaces she wore. "Would I wear a pair of simple *coll* pearl necklaces if I had more left? No bracelets, no rings. No ships, no funds. For me, it's all to do over." She made another gesture of regret. "I'm old. I'm not sure it's in me to start over again."

"There's also a labor problem," Tre pointed out. "We lost much of our population fighting the Boman. At least, much of our labor force. All we have left are . . ."

"Women and children," O'Casey said with a glance at Matsugae.

"Yes," the nobleman confirmed.

"And then there's the whole sticky political question," the widow added with a grunt of laughter, and the nobleman sighed.

"Too true. The Council lost all its political capital when its members tried to flee, and all the noble houses are now stained with the same reputation."

"But the nobles had portable funds," Fullea pointed out, "so they're the only ones with the money to rebuild the city."

"And no one trusts them to rebuild it and stay the course?" the valet murmured. "I can think of half a dozen ways to fix that."

"So can I," O'Casey said. "More, of course, but I think your half dozen are probably the same as the ones on my shortlist. Just one would be to offer shares in ownership to K'Vaernian interests. That's your funding problem solved right there. Offer lesser shares and a small stipend to volunteers from K'Vaern's Cove interested in rebuilding the city. Things like that. You'd end up with a limited corporation managing the city. However, it would be an economic vassal of K'Vaern's Cove."

"That's the weirdest thing I've ever heard of," Tre said. "Who's in charge?"

"The chief executive, strictly limited by a binding charter," Matsugae said, and glanced at O'Casey. "Therean Five?"

"Something along those lines, anyway," the chief of staff replied, taking an absentminded bite of limp vegetables. "But, in general, societies like that are lousy in wartime. Therean Five was a special case of a homogenous militaristic agrarian society." She paused and chuckled. "With a really funny charter, if you're a history buff."

"'And this time, we really, really mean it,'" Matsugae quoted. "And the majority and minority opinions of the framers are required for every amendment."

"Right," O'Casey agreed, then turned back to Fullea and Tre. "But if that wouldn't work here, you could try a limited monarchy, like the Empire. The nobles get an upper house with specific powers, the commoners get a lower house with specific powers, and there's a hereditary executive that must be approved by both houses. Various other restrictions and controls have to be cranked in as well, of course. The judicial branch, for example. And it's very important for long-term success to provide for ongoing periodic replenishment of the upper house. Like I said, lots of details, but that's the broad outline."

"Do you *know* all the details?" Fullea asked after a moment's pause.

"You could say I have a firm academic grasp of them," O'Casey replied with a smile. "One point about it—whatever system you use, you really need to have either unlimited suffrage or citizenship through service. Muzzling half your population won't work as technology advances."

"You're speaking of giving women political power," Tre said.

"Yep."

The nobleman glanced over at his dinner partner, his body language clearly troubled.

"While there are certainly *individuals* . . ."

"Oh, shut up, Sam," the widow said tartly. "There was no reason—outside of some truly stupid laws written by *men*—why Tareim should have inherited, and he squandered it all until I forced him to give it back. And there are other women who could do just as well as I did—possibly better."

"But few are prepared for it, or able for that matter," the nobleman argued.

"How do you know until you try?" O'Casey asked. "I've heard this argument throughout this entire journey, but look at K'Vaern's Cove."

"Well, the Cove isn't necessarily what we'd want to become," Fullea said. "But it *is* a good argument and case in point."

"You're going to need them as a work force," Matsugae told the nobleman. "And I think they'd probably surprise you. I've worked with women from many of your people's societies on this trek, and almost all of them were more than their men were willing to admit. Even the 'open-minded' ones," he added.

"Ayiee. I get your point." Tre picked up one of the overcooked tubers. "But I'm definitely choosing the restaurant next time."

"All of this is extremely interesting, and probably valuable, but doing anything about it depends on retaking D'Sley," Fullea pointed out.

"What we don't have is the funds to hire enough mercenaries to do that," Tre said with a sigh. "Even if there were enough mercenaries in the entire world."

"So you have to convince K'Vaern's Cove that it's vital to them," O'Casey countered. "Everyone seems to agree that if the Boman squat on the resources, K'Vaern's Cove is going to wither away. So why aren't they taking the fight to the Boman?"

"Because the Boman have smashed every army that's dared to face them." Tre made a gesture of resignation. "They far outnumber the K'Vaernian Guard, and this branch, at least, is ably led. Leaving the walls would be suicide."

"And you don't have the traditions, techniques, or tactics for conscript armies, so there's no structure to allow for rapidly increasing the size of the Guard," O'Casey said, nodding in understanding.

"But all of those are easy enough to get," Matsugae put in. "Right?"

"If you're willing to pay the political cost," the historian agreed. "But for that to happen, someone with a significant political base has to see the light."

"I think that you'll find it difficult to have ships commissioned under the current conditions," Fullea said. "And *you* have some political capital."

"No," O'Casey corrected gently. "Rus From and Bogess have some political capital, and we've given them sufficient information to be able to take the fight to the Boman. Perhaps the wrong people are having this dinner?"

"No," Fullea retorted flatly. "Neither Bogess nor Rus From show a clear understanding of the techniques and technologies you've given them. It's unfortunately clear that they're still feeling their own way into adapting to these new ways of war, and because it is, the

K'Vaernians are understandably reluctant to depend on them. They won't follow the direction of Bogess in the field the way that they would your Captain Pahner, who Bogess has told them is a military genius."

"Captain Pahner is very good," O'Casey said with a smile, "but not a genius. He does have that ability to stay calm in a crisis which is critical in a military commander, but generally he draws on historical background to fight his battles. 'Genius' implies innovation."

"But Bogess doesn't know the same history," Tre observed shrewdly. "Does he?"

"No."

"There you go."

"Fullea, Sam Tre," O'Casey said, "I understand your desire, but we have a schedule to keep. We *must* keep that schedule, and we're already far behind where we need to be. We can't dally in K'Vaern's Cove to help you fight your battles, and we most especially are not going to fight the Boman for you. We're not mercenaries."

"What would it take to convince you to help?" Fullea asked. "Besides a decent dinner, of course."

Eleanora smiled faintly. "I'm not the person who makes those decisions, and if I told you anything it would be the minimum requirements for us to *consider* assisting."

"Understood," Tre told her. "And those minimum requirements are?"

"We'd require more information about the Boman, their location, and numbers. We'd require a real plan, and the wholehearted support of K'Vaern's Cove, and that would have to include full support for the building of our ships and the outfitting of the army. We'd need to ride roughshod over some of the largest businesses in the city, and they'd have to take it and smile."

Tre winced and sat back, but Fullea remained leaning forward, all four hands clasped, as still and calm as a Vedic statue.

"And if all those requirements were met?"

"Impossible!" Tre exclaimed. "The K'Vaernians just aren't like that!"

"And if all those requirements were met?" the widow repeated.

"If all of them were met, Pahner would consider it," Matsugae said. "Especially if the campaign took no longer than building the ships did."

"There's no way to guarantee that," Tre said firmly.

"No, but by the time the ships were finished he'd have been able to train someone else and help them develop the experience and knowledge to take over," O'Casey pointed out. "And by then either the Boman would've been pretty well shattered or else they'd be at the walls."

"So we have to get the whole Council behind it?" the widow asked. "I can see getting *most* of them . . ."

"Even more important, you have to get the whole body of the citizenry behind it," O'Casey clarified. "Not because they control the Council, but because they'd have to work willingly for the cause."

"Do you have any ideas about that?" Fullea asked, taking a sip of wine.

It's not going to be a short dinner, is it? O'Casey thought.

CHAPTER TWENTY-SIX

Roger slumped onto the pillow and nodded to Despreaux. The sergeant had arrived early, and she looked up from her own pillow to nod back. At least her stiff acknowledgment was no longer actively hostile, but it wasn't exactly brimming over with joyous welcome, either, he reflected. Sooner or later, they were going to have to sit down and iron out their problems . . . assuming they ever managed to find the time to.

His *asi* settled quietly behind him as Julian and Tratan entered. They were followed by the rest of the staff and senior commanders, until the spacious room was rather full. Fortunately, it had large windows open on two sides to the sea breezes, so it wasn't stuffy even with the gathered staff.

Pahner arrived last, accompanied by Rastar and Rus From, who quickly took their seats.

"All right, we have to make some decisions," the Marine CO said. "Or, rather, *I* have to make some decisions. But we all need to know the parameters, so I want everyone to present what they've learned as succinctly as possible. Then we'll decide what we're going to do.

"Poertena, you start."

"*Si*, Cap'n." The Pinopan checked his pad. "I'm gonna say t'is one more time: we don' wanna cross no blue water in t'ose tubs. We could convert one o' t'em to a schooner sail plan in about a mont', but it'd turn turtle in tee first good wind, no matter what we do."

"Can you explain that for us nonsailors?" Julian asked. "They sail them just fine now, right?"

"Sure, but t'ey only sail in t'is little millpond," Poertena replied, gesturing out the window at the K'Vaernian Sea, "an' t'ey don' get out o' sight o' land, either. T'ey can't, even if t'ey wanted to, 'cause t'ey gots no way to navigate. What t'ey gonna use for noon sights on t'is planet?" This time his gesture took in the solid gray overcast. "So t'eir ships're buil' for shoal water an' what t'ey calls 'Mediterranean conditions' back on Terra."

"Mediterranean?" Kosutic repeated, and the Pinopan shrugged.

"You see any surf on t'ose rocks?" he asked, pointing to the rocky coastline far below the citadel. "No? T'at's cause t'is little puddle of a K'Vaernian Sea ain't big enough for real swells to build—not wide enough for tee wind to build a good, heavy sea. Oh, shallow water like t'is, it can blow up nasty quick when a heavy wind does come 'long, but t'at's not what tee normal conditions are, an' if t'ey sees a blow comin' up, t'ey heads for shore or drops anchor an' lies to to ride it out. 'Cording to all t'eir hist'ries, t'at's how come K'Vaern's Cove ever got settled in tee first place, an' I believe it. But you ain't gonna be able to do t'at out on no ocean, Smaj."

"Um." The sergeant major nodded slowly, and Poertena shrugged again.

"T'ese ships is shoal built," he went on. "T'ey gots no depth of keel an' t'ey flat-floored as hell—t'at's partly so's t'ey can beach t'em jus' 'bout anywheres t'ey wants to—an' t'ey still figurin' out how sail plans work. Frankly, I surprised t'ey uses square sails an' not a lateen rig, and t'at's part o' tee problem."

"'Lateen'?" Julian repeated plaintively, and O'Casey chuckled.

"Sailor technospeak is much older than your kind of jargon, Sergeant," she said, not unkindly but with a wicked glint in her eye. "Sailors have had thousands of years to develop it, so you're just going to have to ride it out."

"But what does it *mean?*" the intel NCO pressed, and the chief of staff glanced at Poertena.

"I don't know the nuts and bolts as well as you do, Poertena, but perhaps I can help establish a context for what you're telling us?" The

Pinopan nodded for her to continue, and she turned her attention back to Julian.

"Back on Earth, two different types of ship designs evolved before the emergence of steam power and propellers. Think of them as the 'Mediterranean type' and the 'Atlantic type.' The Mediterranean is very much like the K'Vaernian: essentially landlocked, shallow, and with very moderate normal wind and wave conditions. The Atlantic is a much rougher body of water, and typical mid-Atlantic conditions would be extremely dangerous for a ship designed to survive only in Mediterranean conditions.

"So the Mediterranean powers developed galleys and, later, galleases—light, shoal-draft, low-freeboard vessels, very like the K'Vaernians'—and with sail plans which utilized what was called a lateen rig, a single, loose-footed sail on a yard set across the mast at a fairly sharp angle.

"The Atlantic type evolved as a much deeper-hulled ship, to provide the sort of stability a vessel would require under typical conditions there, with more freeboard to move the deck higher to keep it clear of normal wave conditions. And unlike the Mediterranean sail plans, the Atlantic type gradually evolved a multimasted rig with two or three square sails on each mast and triangular fore-and-aft headsails—the 'jibs' Poertena and Roger keep talking about. It was a much more powerful arrangement, allowing the Atlantic type to depend primarily upon wind power rather than muscle power delivered by way of the oars, which also meant that they could be built bigger, heavier, and sturdier. Not to mention freeing up the sides of the ships to mount heavy batteries of cannon once the oar banks were out of the way."

She considered what she'd just said for a moment, then shrugged.

"It's not really my area of expertise, so I'm sure I didn't get it all right, and I've probably left out a good bit, but that may give you some idea of the kind of design incompatibilities Poertena has to overcome."

"Yep," the diminutive armorer agreed. "Even t'eir merchies, t'ey too shallow draf' for blue-water conditions, an' as for t'eir warships—!" He rolled his eyes. "Forget it. You gets a good blow, an' t'ey goin' over, no matter what you do. An' t'ey ain't never heard o' jibs or foresails—all t'ey gots is t'ose big pock—I mean, all t'ey gots is t'ose square spritsails t'ey sets under tee bowsprit. T'ose help some beatin' to windward, but not a lot. An' t'ey gots no drivers—no fore-and-aft sails on tee stern to help t'ere, neither. Nope, t'eir sail plans, t'ey suck for blue-water. T'at's why t'is design go 'way on Eart' after t'ey learn tee jib sail."

"So we teach them." Julian shrugged.

"Mebbe," Poertena conceded. "But we gots to do it pretty quick if we gonna get t'ese ships built. An' even if we do, I been down to tee local museum and took a look at tee log from t'at one ship t'ey say crossed tee ocean from tee ot'er side. We not only gots to worry 'bout building somet'ing can handle blue-water, we gots to build somet'ing can stand up to whatever ripped up t'at ship, too."

"Ripped it up with what?" Roger asked. "Tentacles? Claws?"

"Seem like a big fish, You' Highness," Poertena said. "You gotta remember, I didn' read it direct, only tee partial translation tee locals worked out, an' tee guy writin' tee log was half outta his mind even t'en."

"Great," Julian said. "So even if we make the ships in time, we have to fight sea monsters?"

"More arguments for a fast ship," Roger said with a crooked smile. "But was this sailor sure it wasn't a submerged reef, Poertena? You can get those in what looks like open water."

"I know, You' Highness, but it real specific. 'As a grea' jaw, tearin' tee craft asunder, a demon o' tee dept's,' an' like t'at."

"Bloody hell," Kosutic said mildly. "And I thought *atul-grak* were interesting."

"So we'll have to build," Pahner said, pulling the conversation firmly back into focus. "And that's going to take at least three months. Where does that put us in terms of rations and supplements?"

"It puts us in trouble, Captain," Matsugae replied quietly, and all eyes turned to the valet. "The apsimons are helping a lot, but we're still running shorter and shorter. Warrant Officer Dobrescu is checking everything we come across in hopes of finding additional substitutes, but if he can't, we've got about four months, four and a half at the most, before we begin facing very serious dietary deficiencies."

"Time to cross the ocean once we get the ships built?" Pahner asked, turning back to Poertena.

"Hard to say for sure," the Pinopan replied. "I t'ink we prob'ly lookin' at at least a mont', t'ough, Sir."

There was complete silence as everyone in the room digested those figures. Assuming that Poertena's estimates were as accurate as everyone there knew they were, then even if everything went perfectly, with no delays at all, their supplies would run out the moment they reached their final objective. And the one thing they'd all learned here on Marduk was that things were not going to go perfectly.

"Okay," Pahner said after a moment, "we have a look at our transportation and supplements constraints. I think the term to use is 'narrow.' Rus, how do the K'Vaernians look from the point of view of large-scale weapons production?"

"There's good news and bad," the Diaspran bishop told the humans. "The good news is that the K'Vaernians are much more capable metalworkers than we of Diaspra. Much of that may be due to their worship of Krin, for just as we've learned to work with the God's water, they've learned to cast the bells which give Krin his voice. Also, their reliance upon seapower has inclined them in different directions. We of Diaspra use bombards and arquebuses mainly as defensive weapons from our fortifications, but their heavier warships rely upon artillery, and even their light galleys carry many arquebusiers and light, swivel-mounted bombards along their rails, because they use the fire from those weapons to decimate enemy crews before they board. Thus, even though the K'Vaernian Guard isn't huge, the city has great store of arquebuses aboard its ships, and great experience in the casting of naval artillery.

"Their navy depends upon privately owned merchant ships to serve as auxiliaries and to support their regular warships in battle, and so many of those merchant vessels also carry artillery and arquebuses. The bombards and arquebuses of their warships, however, are all provided by the city government, and all are built to common calibers, which isn't true of the privately purchased small arms aboard the merchantmen.

"According to the figures Bistem Kar has been able to provide to us, there are some eleven thousand arquebuses between the Navy and the Guard. All of these are of the same caliber, and 'rifling' them as you've shown us wouldn't be difficult. There are more than sufficient skilled craftsmen in the city to deal with that part of the problem. There's a large stock of wrought iron and steel on hand, as well, and although much of it has already been made into weapons and armor, it could be handily converted by the city's foundries.

"Spring steel for the mechanisms will be somewhat more difficult to produce, but not impossibly so. The breech mechanisms which you've described to us will present much graver difficulties, however. Producing them in quantity shouldn't be overly complicated, but it will take time to develop a design suited to our capabilities, to produce the machine tools required to manufacture them, and to turn them out in large numbers.

"I've discussed the problem with some of the local artisans, and in particular with Dell Mir, however, and I believe an alternative solution can be worked out. Manufacture of 'percussion caps' will actually be much simpler than the production of a suitable breech mechanism. The city's alchemists are quite familiar with quicksilver, which is also used by some of the local physicians, and there's rather more of it in K'Vaern's Cove than I'd feared would be the case. No one here fully understands the production of the 'fulminate of mercury' you've described, but Sergeant Despreaux assures us that she can teach us how to make it, and the local mint will be able to produce the caps in very large numbers, although much care will be required in actually making them.

"Frankly, the greatest problem lies in the provision of rifle ammunition. We must design new bullet dies and get them into production, but that's only a part of the problem. If we're able to put eleven thousand rifles into the true-hands of our soldiers, and if we issue sixty rounds of ammunition to each, that will require us to provide *six hundred and sixty* thousand rounds of ammunition, and I see no way we can produce that many 'cartridges' in the time available to us. I'm considering possible ways around the problem, but so far I've been unable to think of one. Of course, we could always issue muzzle-loading rifles, which would both avoid the problems of machining breech mechanisms and alleviate much of the pressure in the area of cartridge production, but it would also cost us much of the advantage in rate of fire which we'll require to face the Boman's numbers in the field.

"There's also the question of gunpowder supplies. Because the K'Vaernian Navy uses bombards and arquebuses in such quantity, and because the shore batteries use such heavy bombards, there are much greater stores of powder in K'Vaern's Cove than there were in Diaspra. Unfortunately, no one in the known world has ever contemplated the expenditures of ammunition which would be required by an army like the one we propose to build. Bistem Kar is still inventorying the contents of the city's magazines, but it seems likely that we'll be unable to meet all of our needs out of current supplies. The powder mills stand ready, and, in fact, continue to produce small additional quantities of powder even as we speak, but the raw materials—in particular the sulfur—are all imported, and the Boman have already overrun the customary sources of supply. Alternative sources exist, but it will take time to develop them and transport the needed resources to the city.

"The best news may well be that because their metalsmiths already understand the casting of bombards—and bells—they will be able to produce your new 'horse artillery' much more rapidly than I'd believed would be possible. Their gun foundries already understand the mysteries of sandcasting and other techniques you described to me, and they have much more capacity than I'd dreamed, primarily because the Cove has long since become the major supplier of artillery to all of the navies of the K'Vaernian. None of them have ever considered the innovations you've suggested, however, and their master gunsmith had something very like a religious experience when my sketches demonstrated the idea of trunnions to him. That innovation by itself would have completely transformed the use of bombards, but the addition of percussion locks for the guns and the idea of mobile land artillery has thrown the entire gun casting industry of K'Vaern's Cove into a furor. My best estimate is that there is sufficient metal already here in the city to produce two hundred bronze and iron pieces to throw six to twelve-*sedant* shot—say three to six of your 'kilos'—although doing so will require the navy to sacrifice many of its existing larger bombards to provide the required metal.

"Once again, however, the problem is time. Not so much for the Cove, as for your own timetable. The actual casting of the pieces could be accomplished within one and a half or two of your months, but boring and reaming them will take considerably longer. They have the technology, but they don't normally produce weapons in the caliber ranges we need, nor do they normally have to work under such tight time constraints, and boring a gun is a long, painstaking process."

"We can help there," Julian grunted. The Diaspran looked at him and wrinkled the skin above one eye, and the intel sergeant chuckled. "All we need is to set up a 'Field Expedient Post Hole Cutter,'" he said, and Kosutic and Pahner startled everyone else present by bursting into laughter.

"Satan, yes!" the sergeant major chortled, and laughed even harder when Roger and O'Casey stared at her in obvious perplexity. She managed to get herself under control relatively quickly, however, and shook her head as she wiped her eyes.

"Sorry, Your Highness. It's just that Julian's absolutely right. All we need is our bayonets, and we've got plenty of those."

"Bayonets?" Roger blinked, and Kosutic nodded.

"Sure, Sir. They issue us with those nice memory plastic bayonets . . . you know, the ones with the same molecular edge they put on the boma knives."

"Oh." Roger sat back on his cushion, his eyes suddenly thoughtful, and Kosutic nodded again, harder.

"Absolutely, Sir. Those things'll cut *anything*, which is damned handy, since we use them a lot more for tools around camp than we do for sticking people close up and personal. But the point Julian's making is that the field manuals tell us exactly how to build 'post hole cutters' that'll cut nice, perfectly circular post holes in anything from clay and dirt to polished obsidian. We can sure as Satan set them up to bore and cut anything the locals can cast, and they'll do the job in hours, not days or weeks."

"Smaj's right, Sir," Julian said. "Give us a couple of days to get set up, and we can bore out the barrels one hell of a lot faster than the foundries can cast them!"

"That would be wonderful news," From said enthusiastically. "It would allow us to build up a much heavier artillery train than I'd believed possible, and that should help enormously. But even if that's possible, we still aren't going to be able to field the sort of rifles-only army you want, Captain Pahner. Not in the time available. Because we can't supply the quantities of ammunition required in the time available, Bogess and I have discussed with Bistem Kar the necessity of raising additional pike regiments to make up the required fighting force. There are more than sufficient metalworkers here in the city to manufacture pikeheads and javelins in very large numbers. Indeed, from what Bistem Kar has told us, it seems very likely that we'll run out of able-bodied soldiers well before we run out of the ability to equip them with pikes, assegais, javelins, and the new shields.

"Taking everything together, then, I believe that given two months with which to work—and the sergeant's 'post hole cutter'—the foundries and artisans of K'Vaern's Cove could equip a field army with some four to five thousand breech-loading rifles, assuming that we use Dell Mir's suggested design alternative, with sufficient ammunition, supported by two hundred pieces of artillery and ten to fifteen thousand pikemen and spearmen. Allowing for gunners, engineers, and other support troops, that would come to something on the order of thirty-six thousand troops. K'Vaern's Cove is a large and populous city, but that number probably represents the maximum force which the city can muster, even assuming that the entire manpower of the Navy is brought ashore and pressed into service with the Guard and that all of the refugees here in the city capable of military service are also placed under arms. There might be a few more able-bodied men available, but larger numbers cannot realistically be removed from the city labor force without catastrophic dislocation."

"Good God," Roger said, turning to Pahner. "Did you come up with all of that?"

"Yes," the Marine said. "If we have to stay and fight, I want to do it with the best possible equipment and the best possible field force. I'd hoped that we could put more riflemen and fewer pikemen into the field, but it sounds to me as if Rus, Bogess, and Bistem Kar have probably come up with the best practical mix of weapons and manpower numbers."

"How do you intend to train anyone on all those new weapons when none of them even exist yet?" O'Casey asked.

"I still don't *intend* to train them," Pahner said. "But the way it would be done if we ended up with no choice but to do it would be with simple wooden mock-ups until the real thing became available. Again, from the grunt's eye view, it would be primarily a matter of instilling the discipline the troops need and giving them confidence in their new equipment. For the officers, it would be a matter of a lot of sand table exercises to make them familiar with the capabilities—and weaknesses—of their new army. The real problem is that this would be a much larger battle to administer than Diaspra was, which means we'd be spread accordingly thinner and that a more comprehensive organizational infrastructure would be required."

"I'm very impressed with Kar," Rastar said. "And with Bogess, of course. But I'm not sure that they can both develop an understanding of the tactics and simultaneously manage the training, particularly in the time available. For that matter, this whole concept of a 'staff' is very odd."

"All right," the captain said. "There's sufficient production to create the weaponry to equip a small field army. We don't have a fixed number on the enemy at this time. The time required to create the weapons would be approximately the same as the time to train the individuals in their use, but doing either or both of those things would narrow our window to reach the spaceport before the supplements run out. Sergeant Julian, could you give us your report on the political situation in K'Vaern's Cove?"

Julian pulled out his own pad, keyed it alive, and scratched his chin.

"It's a pretty open democracy, so the political situation is complex, Sir. There are about fourteen major positions on the matrix, and most have a party of adherents prepared to support them at the expense of their competitors. However, the majority parties are pretty well represented by Wes Til and Turl Kam. Til represents old money, shipyards, and land-based mercantile interests in general, while Kam represents the labor groups and the actual sailing community.

"Tratan," the intel NCO continued, nodding at the Mardukan, "has spent some time on the streets, feeling out the attitudes and opinions here in the city. I'll let him talk about it."

"It's amazing what people talk about around a dumb barb," Cord's nephew said. "My only problem has been keeping up with the local dialects. You humans aren't able to really hear it because of however those 'toots' of yours do the translating, or so I understand from Julian, but the locals speak a very fast pidgin of several of the coastal languages. I didn't know any of them before we arrived in Diaspra, and I only speak one of them with any real fluency, even now, so talking to these people has been . . . interesting.

"In the long run, though, I think that the fact that I don't speak the local language very well probably helped, because it contributed to the 'dumb barb' image and let me eavesdrop on a lot of conversations without anyone really thinking about the fact that I was there.

"What I can tell you is that the city is *very* worried. In the abstract, everyone is hostile towards the notion of taking in all the refugees from the mainland, too. The reason I say in the abstract, is that most of the refugees are staying with distant relatives, acquaintances, or what have you, and everyone thinks that *their* refugees are just fine. It's all the *other* refugees they want to run out of town."

"It's a branch of Turl Kam's party that's agitating against the refugees," Julian said. "A splinter party, really; I haven't seen any sign that he personally supports the agitation."

"True, but everyone is also extremely worried about the Boman," Tratan continued. "Because of the stories from all the refugees, they have a clear picture of what having the Boman come over the wall will mean, and no one wants to see that here in K'Vaern's Cove. Most people aren't willing to admit that they don't really buy into the idea that the Cove isn't an impregnable fortress, but the nervousness is growing, and when the food begins to run out, I think it's likely to turn into panic. At the same time, though, there's a significant voice—a very quiet one, but persistent and very widespread—that wants full-scale war against the Boman as the best way to keep them away from the city walls in the first place."

"Does it have any spokespeople?" Kosutic asked intently.

"No," Julian and Tratan replied simultaneously, and the Mardukan shrugged and gestured for Julian to continue.

"None of the arguments in favor of all-out war have a spokesperson because the idea itself seems to cross party lines," the sergeant said. "It's like an undercurrent, a strong one, that keeps turning up in all discussions of the Boman crisis. 'If only someone would face them . . . We can face them . . . We could use our might to destroy them, but . . .' That sort of thing. *Anytime* you discuss the Boman, it comes up, and the few who I've talked to who were against taking the offense were pretty defensive about their opposition."

"Same here," Tratan agreed. "This land blockade is strangling the city, and everyone knows it. They're blaming the refugees for their problems, but they really know it's the Boman."

"Also, D'Sley might or might not have the resources we need to build the ships," Julian noted. "There were significant stockpiles of raw materials there that hadn't been shipped at the beginning of the war, including seasoned wood and masts. No one's positive that the Boman haven't destroyed them since, but the consensus seems to be that they haven't because they recognize the value the stockpiles represent."

"We got that, too," Roger said.

"Tor Flain and Wes Til were very careful to point it out," Despreaux added.

"Yes," O'Casey said. "Our couple were careful to make the point, too. But they were also careful to point out that getting access to those supplies would require more than a raid."

"That depends on your definition of 'raid,'" Pahner said, "but I agree in general."

"And if there aren't sufficient materials here in K'Vaern's Cove," Roger added, "cutting the needed timber upriver from the city would require a military covering force to keep the Boman off the woodcutters, and managing that would be almost as difficult as taking and holding D'Sley in the first place."

"Let me make one thing clear," Pahner said. "In my opinion, there's no way to face the Boman with Marines and Northern cavalry alone. Any kind of confrontation in the field would require the backing, at the absolute minimum, of the K'Vaern's Cove Guard and everyone we could pry loose from their Navy, and that would be a dangerously slim field army, with virtually no margin for any sort of losses. It would take a fully mobilized citizenry to field the much larger army Rus is talking about building, and, frankly, even that would be none too heavy a force to go up against someone as tough as the main Boman horde sounds to be."

"We actually put it that way in our conversation with Sam Tre and Fullea Li'it," O'Casey said. "No support without a fully mobilized citizenry."

"You think we could take them . . . if we had to, that is?" Roger asked.

"With artillery and breech-loading percussion cap rifles added to the pike and assegai regiments?" Pahner nodded. "Yes."

"Excuse me, Sir," Kosutic said, "but are you suggesting that we stay and fight?"

"I'm suggesting that we consider it," the CO said. "Tratan, what do you think?"

"Fight." The Mardukan shrugged. "You need the willing support of the K'Vaernians to build your ships, and their construction requires materials that are on the other side of the Bay, underneath the Boman. Also, I think kicking their barb asses would be a good idea on general principles."

"Poertena?"

"Fight, Sir," the Pinopan said. "We need tee pocking timber."

"Sergeant Despreaux?"

"Fight, Sir," the NCO responded. "We're going to be here, either way you look at it, when the Cove goes head-to-head with them.

However it looks *now*, I don't think we'd get away with sailing off into the sunset *then*."

"Julian?"

"Fight, Sir. All the other reasons, and I've developed a real case of the ass about barbs, Sir."

"Let's cut this short. Anyone against?"

"Not against, really," Kosutic said, "but the troops are getting worn close to the ragged, Captain. Nothing against the boys and girls, but we saw a lot of overreaction in Diaspra. It's something to keep an eye on."

"Noted," the CO said. "But that's not an objection?"

"No, Sir," the sergeant major said, and the captain leaned back on his pillows and looked around.

"All right. If the Council can build a consensus for all-out war against the Boman, elements of the Empress' Own will participate as cadre trainers and advisers in return for full-scale support in building a fleet of fast, blue-water ships. Preproduction of the ships should begin at the earliest possible moment."

"We need intel," Roger said. "We don't really know what the barbs' main force is doing. We think it's sitting in Sindi, but we don't really know that for sure."

"Absolutely," Pahner agreed. "And when we know where it is, we'll start to plan. Right now, however, the basic plan is to start from D'Sley. Retaking that will be the first step however the intel stacks up; after that we can work the rest out."

"Recon teams?" the sergeant major asked.

"Yes. Use Second Squad and send Gunny Jin out to coordinate it. Keep Despreaux here, though; we need her to work with the alchemists." Pahner leaned back and his eyes went unfocused. "And add shovels to that list of vital materials."

"And maps," Roger said. "And axes. And we probably need to get Poertena or Julian involved with Rus and Bistem Kar to be sure their projected numbers for raw materials are accurate. No offense, Rus, but we're talking about a production scale like nothing that's ever been done around here before."

"No offense taken, Your Highness," the Diaspran assured him.

"Having someone double-check our estimates would make both of us feel much better, actually."

"A thousand and one questions, people," Pahner said, picking up his pad. "Including how to get the K'Vaernian in the street solidly behind the war. We need them all answered. Sergeant Major, get the reconnaissance out. Don't just use the squad. There's too much area to cover, so use local woodsmen and some of Rastar's cavalry, too, and pass out all the communicators you can scrounge. Eleanora, get to work on a propaganda program to get these K'Vaern's Cove people fighting mad. Poertena, we need you on the ships, so that leaves you, Julian, as our premier armorer."

"Joy," the NCO said with a grin.

"That's 'Joy, Sir,'" the captain told him, eyes on his pad as he entered notes. "Look over the materials numbers and production estimates with Rus, then work with Rus and this Dell Mir on designs. I suggest that you get His Highness involved in that, as well, and I'll be looking over both of your shoulders."

He made another entry on his pad, then looked up and raised an eyebrow.

"Why are you all still sitting here?" he asked mildly, and various people found themselves pushing to their feet almost before they realized they were moving. The Marine smiled wryly as they began filing out, but then he raised one hand.

"Stay a moment, Roger," he said.

"Have you been naughty again?" Julian whispered as he passed the prince on his way to the door. Roger only smiled and shook his head, then walked back to the company commander.

"Yes, Captain?"

"Sit down," Pahner said, pouring a cup of wine. "I want to discuss a couple of things with you."

Roger accepted the wine warily.

"I made up with Despreaux . . . sort of," he said. "Or, I think I have, at least. In a way. Kind of."

"That's not the point of this discussion," Pahner told him with a frown, "although we do need to discuss that sometime, too. But this is a 'professional development' counseling session."

"Professional development as a prince?" Roger asked with a grin. "Or as a Marine."

"Both," the captain said, and Roger's grin faded as the Marine's somber expression registered. "I want to talk you about your actions since . . . Marshad, basically."

"I've been holding up my end," Roger said in a quieter voice. "I . . . think I've even gotten most of the troops to like me."

"Oh, you've done that, all right," Pahner said. "In fact, you're a fine leader, from an officer point of view. You don't undercut your NCOs, you lead from the front, all that stuff. But one of those good qualities is also a hell of a problem."

"Would that be leading from the front?" Roger asked.

"In a way." Pahner took a sip of his wine. "Let me tell you a little story. Call it 'This Is No Shit,' since it's a space story. Once upon a time, there was a Marine sergeant. He'd seen a few engagements, but one day he did a drop on a planet after a pirate raid had been through."

The captain took another, much deeper sip of wine, and Roger suddenly realized he'd never seen the Marine really drink. Until today.

"It wasn't pleasant. I think Despreaux talked to you once about coming in behind pirates. We seem to do it too often, and you only have to do it once to get real excited about pirate hunting.

"So, after that, the sergeant in our little story did just that—he got *real* excited about pirate hunting. In fact, the sergeant got so excited that one time he took a bunch of buddies and raided a ship that they just *knew* was a pirate at a neutral station.

"And it was one—a pirate, that is. But so, it turned out, were about half the spacestation's permanent personnel, and the cruiser the sergeant and his buddies were assigned to ended up having to fight its way off the station and nearly took a shitload of casualties. All because a sergeant couldn't figure out when it was appropriate to go hunting pirates, and when it wasn't."

Roger watched the captain take yet another drink of wine.

"What happened to the sergeant?"

"Well, all sorts of things went wrong at that spacestation. Among other things, the commander of the cruiser hadn't really been supposed to dock there in the first place. So nothing, officially, happened to the sergeant. But it took him a while to make gunny. Quite a while. And even longer to make captain."

"So I should quit chasing barbs," Roger said flatly.

"Yep," the captain said. "There's too many of them for the few you kill to matter a hill of beans. And when you're killing barbs, Cord and the platoon are trying to keep you alive . . . and having a damned hard time of it.

"But that's not all I'm getting at, either. Another reason that sergeant went on a private expedition was that he'd been on combat ops too long. After a point, you start trying too hard, not caring about what happens, whether you live or die. I think most of the platoon is there right now, Roger. That's what the Smaj was getting at a few minutes ago. But, frankly, son, you're showing the worst signs of all."

"And I'm the worst one to be showing them," Roger said very quietly.

"Yep," the Marine said again. "Want to talk about it?"

"Not if I can avoid it." Roger sipped his own wine and was silent for several seconds. Then he shrugged minutely. "Let's just say that I feel somewhat responsible for the entire situation."

"Let's just say that you feel *very* responsible for the situation," the captain told him. "Which is bullshit, but telling you that doesn't help, does it? And now you see the Marines as people—*your* people—and even the new, native troops to an extent, and every one of them you lose is like a piece of skin ripped off your body."

"Yeah," Roger half-whispered, peering down into his wine.

"Didn't they have a class about that—several, actually—at the Academy?"

"Yes, Captain, they did. But I'm afraid I didn't pay as much attention as I should have," the prince answered, "and I'm having a difficult time applying the lessons."

"I'm not surprised," the Marine told him almost gently, and Roger looked up quickly. Pahner smiled at him. "Roger, don't take this wrong, but part of the problem is that at heart, you're a barbarian yourself."

"I'm what?" Roger blinked in surprise.

"A barbarian," Pahner told him. "Mind you, being a barbarian isn't always such a terrible thing. There are barbarians . . . and barbarians, you know, and you don't have to be a butchering maniac like the Kranolta or the Boman to have what the Empire thinks of as 'barbarian' qualities. Just like some of the most 'civilized' people you're ever going to meet would cut your throat for a decicred if they thought they could get away with it. The thing is, the Empire has gone all civilized these days, and the qualities of a barbarian warrior aren't exactly the ones your lady mother's better classes of subjects want to see when they invite someone over for a high tea. But the qualities the people at those teas denigrate as barbaric are the ones the soldiers who keep them safe have to have. Courage, determination, discipline, loyalty, passion for your beliefs, and the willingness to lay it all on the line—and lose it, if you have to—out of a concept of honor and responsibility, rather than looking for compromise and consensus because 'violence never settled anything.' The military has always been out of step with the mainstream culture in most wealthy societies which enshrine individual liberty and freedom, Roger. It has to be, because those sorts of societies don't have the natural 'antibodies' against foreign and domestic enemies that more militaristic ones do. By and large, I think that's a very good thing, even if I do sometimes wind up thinking that most civilians are over-protected, under-educated drones. But the reason I think of them that way is that *I'm* a barbarian by their standards, and they keep me around because they need someone with barbaric qualities to keep them safe in their beds at night. I don't imagine you ever really realized that you had those qualities, too, before we hit Marduk, and I hope you won't be offended if I say that no one else realized that either. Except for Cord, maybe."

The captain sipped from his cup once again, his expression thoughtful.

"I hadn't really thought about it before, but you and he are almost mirror images, in a way. You come from the most protected place in the most powerful and civilized empire in the known galaxy, and at the moment you find yourself on a barbarian planet at the ass end of nowhere, and in some ways it's like you were born to be here. Cord comes from a bunch of ragged ass barbarians in the middle of a godforsaken jungle full of *flar-ke*, *atul-grak*, and killerpillars, but he was educated at Voitan, and there's a sage and a philosopher down inside him, as well. There's some sort of weird resonance there, one I don't imagine anyone outside the two of you really understands, but it's certainly real. Maybe that resonance is why he slipped so easily into the mentor role for you. Or maybe it was just that, unlike any of the rest of us, he had no preconceptions where you were concerned, which let him see you more clearly than the rest of us did.

"But whatever it is, Roger, you need to be aware of what you really are. You can't afford not to be, because of *who* you are. I'm not just talking about the situation we're in here on Marduk and your place in the chain of command, either. You're the Heir Tertiary to the Throne, and somehow I don't think you're just going to fade into the woodwork again when we get you home. But you're going to be up against some operators who are used to manipulating people with a lot more life experience than you have, and if they have a better read than you do on who you are and how you think, you're screwed."

"I don't guess I ever thought that far ahead," Roger said slowly.

"I'd be surprised if you had. However you got here, you're in the position that every junior officer worth a flying fuck finds himself in sooner or later, Roger. To work with your troops, you almost have to love them. If you don't give a damn about them, that comes across, and not caring is like an acid that corrodes whatever you have inside that's worth keeping. But you also have to be willing to let them go. People die, son. Especially Marines, because we're the ones who volunteer to be at the sharp end of the stick. That's what we do, and sometimes we crap out, and sometimes the mission means that we have to die or, worse, we have to let our *people* die . . . or choose which of them are going someplace we know some of them won't be coming back from and which of them aren't buying a ticket this time. Either way, Roger, when it's time, it's time."

Roger crossed his arms and looked away, his mouth a stubborn line, and despite his own sincerity the captain almost laughed at how hard the onetime royal brat was fighting against accepting what he knew was true. There was nothing at all humorous about it of course, and Roger would never have forgiven him for even the driest chuckle, yet the irony was almost overwhelming as the captain reflected on how the mighty had fallen . . . and how much Roger had discovered that losing *his* people hurt.

"Roger, here's the bottom line. If you stick yourself out on a limb, everybody else climbs out there with you, and now it's less because they have to than because they *want* to follow you into whatever desperate situation you've managed to find. There are times when that's good, but only when things are *already* desperate. So quit climbing out on the limb, okay? It might make you feel a little better, because you're sharing the danger, but it just gets more troops killed in the end."

"Okay."

"For what it's worth, you seem to be a natural born leader, and it's not just your hair. The Marines are bad enough, but the Diasprans seem to think you shit gold. It's an unusual commander who can cross species like that. I can't. They respect my judgment, but they don't think I walk on water."

Roger inhaled deeply, then nodded.

"So what you're saying is that if I go out and do something stupid, it's not just the Marines I'll imperil."

"No, it isn't," the captain agreed. "So start letting other people take point, all right? We all know you care, so put down the rifle."

"Okay," the prince said again, then met the Marine's eye. "How does this affect my command?"

"Like I said before, it's going to be a reserve. If I need you, I'll use you, and you'll go out with the scouts if everything works out right. But *behind* the scouts, right?"

"Right," Roger said. "Behind the scouts."

"Take care, Your Highness," Pahner said, nodding in dismissal, and Roger set aside his wine and rose.

"Good night, Captain."

CHAPTER TWENTY-SEVEN

"It worked," Wes Til said as he swept into the room, and Turl Kam looked up from the letter he was drafting.

"They agreed?"

"They're willing to agree, with some tremendous qualifiers—the most serious of which is that we have to demonstrate our willingness to fight a 'war to the knife,' as Prince Roger puts it. He seems awfully fond of that phrase . . . I wonder if it could be the motto of his House?" The councilor thought for a moment, then made a throwing-away gesture. "At any rate, that's what they demand—that we throw the entire power of the city into the war. No faction fighting, no politicization of the commands, and no graft."

"That won't be simple," Kam said, sitting back. "To get agreements, we're going to have to make promises, give favorable contracts, that sort of thing."

"As long as it doesn't have any negative effects, I think anything goes." Til sat on a cushion. "They also require us to throw our support behind building these ships of theirs. They want them completed while the campaign is actually underway."

"Where do they expect us to get the materials?" the Council chairman demanded in exasperation.

"Well, they've already said that the first stage has to be the retaking of D'Sley to use as a base, so the materials will be available.

And let's be honest, Turl. Sure, materials are tight here in the Cove, but they're not as tight as we've been telling them. The Navy is still sitting on its minimum stockpiles, and if the Council officially agrees to help build their ships, you and I can pry at least the keels and ribs out of old Admiral Gusahm if we have to."

Kam grabbed his horns and pulled at them.

"Krin! I *hate* trying to get things out of Gusahm. He seems to think he invented the entire concept of navies and that everything that floats is his own private property!"

The chairman stared into space, trying to suppress a shudder as he pictured the looming confrontation with Gusahm, yet he knew Til was right. Eventually, Gusahm would yield, however gracelessly, to the direct orders of his civilian superiors. The real problem was going to be lining up the political support to meet the *rest* of the humans' demands.

"Can you swing your faction? I *think* I can convince the fishing contingent, and the trade faction is already screaming for me to do something."

"We need to do more than convince them," Til said. "We need to get them enthusiastic. To raise an army the size of the one the humans insist is necessary, we're going to need every able-bodied sailor from the Navy, and we're going to have to triple the Guard, as well, and that will require volunteers."

"Our citizens are very civic minded, but I'm not sure we can get all the volunteers we need with a straight appeal to civic duty. You have any suggestions?" the former fisherman asked. "Because I'm not sure those kinds of numbers are possible."

"Yes, I do have a suggestion. Or rather, O'Casey had some," the merchant said. "Very good ones, at that. That human is tricky."

"Suggestions such as what?" the chairman asked skeptically.

"You know," the councilor said pensively, "the Cove has a reputation for pinching coins till they squeal. I'm certain a lot of that reputation comes from jealousy among other cities that can't seem to pinch quite as tightly as we do, but there may be a little truth to it. So what we have to ask ourselves is what one factor could convince our mercenary countrymen that taking on the Boman would be a good thing?"

★ ★ ★

"So are we going to fight, or not?" Chem Prit asked as the squad of New Model pikemen navigated the streets of the city.

"I don't know, Chem," Krindi Fain said. This was the first evening their company had had off, and he didn't really care one way or the other about what the high command was thinking. He and Erkum Pol had a pouch of silver each, and he was far more interested in the fact that somewhere up the street was a tavern that served soldiers. "When Bogess tells us to fight, we fight. Until then, we wait."

"I hate waiting," Prit complained.

The private was a replacement, and not much of one, for Bail Crom. He'd been at the Battle of Diaspra, but not with Fain's squad, and he wasn't fitting in well.

"You hate everything," Fain responded. His tone was absent, for he'd spotted the tavern he'd been told about. Most of the drinking places in the town had prominent signs denying entry to thieves, itinerant singers, and soldiers. Unless they wanted to go all the way down to the docks, this was one of the few taverns available.

"Keep your hand on your cash," the corporal said as they approached the open door. "I hear a singer."

The dirt-floored room was long and low. Something about the setup made Fain sure it had been a stable at one time, but if there was any remnant of the stable smell it was overwhelmed by the stench of urine and rotting beer. Drinkers lounged on piles of barleyrice straw, their drinks and food propped on low tables that were no more than heavy planks set on split logs, and listened to the crack-throated singer in the middle of the room.

The bar, such as it was, was at the far end—a broad plank laid on a set of upended kegs. The corporal led the half-dozen pikemen through the gloom, stepping over and around vomit and less identifiable substances, until they reached their objective.

"What've you got?" Fain asked the barkeep, turning sideways to the bar to keep an eye on the scene behind him. With itinerant singers around, there were bound to be thieves, as well.

"Beer or channy leaf," the bartender replied. "There's a mite of plum wine, but I doubt you've the pocket for it."

"How much is the beer?" Prit asked.

"Three silver a mug."

"*Three silver?* That's outrageous!" the replacement snapped. "By the God, I never should've left Diaspra! These damned K'Vaernians are all thieves!"

"Shut up, Chem." The corporal backhanded the loudmouth on the ear. "Pay no attention to the idiot," he told the barkeep. "He hasn't got the wet out from behind his horns."

"You need to keep him muzzled, then," the bartender said, setting down something heavy and pulling his false-hand out from under the plank. "In case you Diaspra fuckheads hadn't heard, we've been cut off from most of our supply for fucking months. He'd better be glad there's beer to be had at all. And another shitass remark like that, and I'll have you out the door."

Prit started to open his mouth, and Fain backhanded the private again before the retort got out.

"We only have bar silver," he told the bartender.

"I've the weights," the barman said, opening a lockbox.

"You don't mind if I take your measure, do you?" the corporal asked. "Not that anything would be off, of course."

"Not if yours are right, there wouldn't be," the bartender replied with a grunt of laughter.

Fain pulled a sculpture of finely carved sandstone out of his pouch and compared it to the silver-piece weight on the K'Vaernian's scales. The two pans balanced almost perfectly, and the corporal grunted in satisfaction at the proof that the bartender was fairly honest in his scale and base measure.

"There's a law against illegal measures in the city," the barkeep said as he measured out the silver in the corporal's pouch. "I'll give you a hair over standard measure on the silver if you want to change it all for coin," he added.

"Why? Because you love our faces?" Prit asked.

"By Krin, you really are a walking invitation to have your face smashed, aren't you?"

"All the same, he's got a point," the corporal said. "Why give us better than standard measure?"

"My littermate's a silversmith. A bit over standard is still better than he has to pay for bar silver."

"Done," the corporal said. "I'd rather have it in coin, anyway."

"Where'd you come up with all this?" the barkeep asked, serving out mugs as he weighed and changed the contents of their pouches. The bulk silver was in irregularly shaped thumb-sized nuggets that looked like shiny knucklebones.

"Them Boman was rolling in it," Prit said. "We just got our pay from that last fight."

"Thought so," the barkeep said. "You Diaspra guys are the only silver we've seen in a while. Surprised to see infantry with cash, is all."

"It's why I came in with these twerps," the private told him. "I'm for some more loot, loot, loot! These Boman took Sindi, they're going to be shitting gold."

"You'll be shitting yourself when you finally see them, you gutless infantry bastard," a Northern cavalryman said, looming out of the darkness. "Give me some more channy leaf, you K'Vaernian thief."

"You'll be keeping a civil tongue in your head, or you'll be chewing with one side," the bartender snapped. "Five silver."

"It was two before," the cavalryman snarled.

"The price goes up with the aggravation," was the reply. "Make that seven."

"Why, you pissant thief!" The cavalryman's hand dropped to his sword.

"Let's not get carried away here," Fain said, looking to see if there were any cavalry NCOs in the joint.

"Fuck off, you infantry maggot," the cavalryman slurred, spinning on the slightly smaller junior NCO. "It wasn't for you fucking Southerners, we wouldn't be in this mess."

"Hey, forker, we're all soldiers together," the corporal said with a grunt of laughter. "Let me stake you to a round of beer."

"I don't need any of your damned silver, either!" The Northerner slapped the corporal's hand and sent the freshly counted coins, more than an infantryman's pay for a month, spinning into the gloom. "Short, leg bastards. Do nothing but slow us up."

"Corp," Pol said slowly. "He knocked . . ."

"I know, Erkum," the corporal said calmly. "Look, fellow, that was uncalled for. Now, I know you've got problems—"

"*I* don't have any problems," the cavalryman growled, picking the junior noncom up by his harness. "You do!"

The corporal hit the low table sideways, spilling beer and less mentionable products of the local economy across the revelers. He rolled away from the group as it surged to its feet and tried to come back upright himself, only to run into another set of backs instead.

"*DIASPRA!*" Prit yelled, and plowed into the cavalryman, all four arms windmilling.

Fain took a kick to the ribs and flipped the kicker onto his back, then came vertical with a twist and a heave, but by the time he regained his feet, the bar had turned into a giant free-for-all. A club hit him in the side of the face, and he felt a hand pulling at his pouch.

"God bedamned minstrels!" he snarled, and grabbed the itinerant singer by the horns and spun the thieving bastard off into the melee. He ducked another swinging club, catching it on his own horns, and kicked the club swinger in the balls. His assailant went down . . . and he suddenly found himself faced by the Northerner and three of his larger friends.

"It's time to clean up this bar," the original troublemaker snarled.

"Let's be sensible about this, folks," the infantry corporal said, although sense seemed to be in short supply. "Nobody wants to get hurt."

"And nobody's gonna get hurt," another of the cavalrymen said. "Except you."

"Leave my friend alone." Erkum Pol's voice was so quiet it was almost inaudible through the tavern's bedlam, but the order was accompanied by a whistling sound.

"Why?" the original cavalryman scoffed, never looking away from Fain while he raised a large chunk of wood purposefully overhead.

If there was a verbal answer from the simpleminded soldier, it wasn't audible over the sodden thump and the crunch of bones as the hard-driven plank crashed into the foursome.

Fain stepped back as the cavalrymen hit the ground, then grabbed the tabletop before the improvised battering ram could be drawn back for another swing.

"Good job, Erkum. Now, eet's time to pocking leaf."

"But I never got a beer," the private complained.

"Take one," the proprietor said from behind his pile of kegs. "Take a keg. Just get out of here before the Guard arrives."

"They destroy our taverns and inns, carousing day and night," Dersal Quan complained. The Council member twisted his rings in frustrated exasperation. "And the stench!"

"Yes, and that's another thing. What with the shortages and all, we don't need all these soldiers waving their money around. It's just driving up prices and leaving the penniless . . ."

Sual Dal, the representative for the cloth merchant's guild, paused, trying to find the word he wanted.

"Pennilesser?" Wes Til suggested. "Yes, yes. It's a terrible thing. People having money to spend is quite awful. Fortunately, that's not much of a problem in a city like K'Vaern's Cove just now."

"Don't take this so damned lightly, Til!" the guildsman snapped. "I don't see any of these folks buying sails or any of their silver lining the pockets of my guild. It's all going for beer and channy leaf."

"And fish," Til countered. "And whatever other consumables can be found in the city. For that matter, there was a large purchase of fine woven materials lately, wasn't there?"

"It was all material bound for Sindi," the guildsman said with a gesture of resignation. "We practically took a loss."

"Practically and actually are two different things," Til replied. "The problem isn't the soldiers from Diaspra. Nor is it the Northerners. Or even the refugees. The problem is the Boman, and until we get rid of them, we're all going to be taking a loss."

"That's all well and good to say, Til, but it's not so easy to do," Quan said, twisting his rings again.

"No," Til agreed. "It won't be easy, and it won't be cheap, but until it's done, we're all going to do nothing but lose money. Sooner or later, it's going to catch up with us. I'm set pretty well, but I understand that you, Quan, had already paid for a large shipment of copper ore coming out of Sindi. Yes?"

"Yes," the businessman growled.

"And are you ever going to get that shipment?"

"No."

"And how are the rest of your investments doing? Well?" He paused, but there was no answer. "Thought not. As for sails, I don't see *any* ships being built, do you, Sual?"

"No," the guildmaster admitted.

"On the other hand, the humans are planning at least six very large ships with a *brand-new design of sail.* A very special kind of sail whose new shape and size will, I'm sure, require only the best of weavers and sailmakers."

"Ah?" the guildmaster grunted. "Really? That's . . . interesting news."

"But to build those ships, they need materials—*lots* of materials. They were going to just buy some of the ships that had been laid up and take them apart, but if we could retake D'Sley and get the materials from there, it would be much better for them. And, of course, that would mean that they wouldn't be cutting up the already available sails from the ships they'd purchase to make their new, special sails."

"Ah."

"And as for you, Quan, they're discussing a radical new version of arquebus and a new-style bombard. All of them will have to be made somewhere, and if I recall correctly, your foundries aren't doing a lot of business just this minute, are they?"

"Ah." The industrialist thought about that for a moment. "Where's the money for all of this going to come from?"

"Where did the money all these soldiers have been throwing around come from?"

Wes Til leaned back and watched as the concept settled into their minds. Oh, yes, that Eleanora O'Casey was a sly one. Better to do anything to get her on her way before she decided to just go ahead and take over K'Vaern's Cove lock, stock, and barrel! But for now, at least, they were all headed the same way, and O'Casey's shrewd contributions were pushing the ship along nicely.

CHAPTER TWENTY-EIGHT

Krindi Fain stood braced outside the company commander's office and willed his heart to stop. It had been three days since the fight in the bar, but he was certain the Guard had finally tracked them down. He'd heard through the grapevine that the cavalry shits were still in the hospital—one of them had been touch and go, according to the scuttlebutt—and two guardsmen had been in with the CO since early morning. That could only mean one thing, and when the summons had come, he'd nearly run for it. K'Vaern's Cove was an easy city to get lost in, after all, but he'd finally decided it was better to face his punishment.

"Fain. Come!" the CO called.

The commander was a regular, a young officer who'd been a sergeant in the Guard of God before the humans turned up. He'd initially resented being placed with the pikes, until it became clear that the New Model Army was where everything was happening. He had, however, already had quite a career before his posting to the regiment, including a brawl in the distant past with some Northerner cavalry that had left him with only one horn and blind in one eye. Maybe that would mitigate the punishment.

"This who you're looking for?" the commander asked one of the guardsmen with a head jerk in Fain's direction.

"You Krindi Fain?" the guardsman asked.

The corporal knew he was in trouble now. It wasn't just a couple of guardsmen, but one of the Guard's underofficers.

"Yes, I am," he answered. Best to keep it simple. The more you said, the more likely you were to make a mistake.

"Good," the underofficer said. "Little thing, aren't you? Sergeant Julian made it sound like you were five hurtongs high and breathed fire."

"I don't know how I'm possibly going to run a company if my best people keep getting pulled out from under me," the CO groused.

"So this isn't—" Fain stopped and backed up before an over-active mouth could get him in the trouble he might just have skated out of after all. "What is this about? Captain?"

"We're going to change weapons again—you knew that, right?" the company commander asked.

"Yes, Captain. Muskets, or some word like that."

"Well, that's been changed again," the Guard underofficer said. "The weapon's still being designed, but it's going to be something else—something called a 'rifle.'" He snorted. "Arquebuses may be all very well for those pussies in the Navy, but they've never worked half the time in the field, so I don't see these 'rifles' working any better. But you're one of the ones pointed out by the humans as a good person to participate in what they call 'weapons development.'"

"Oh," Fain said faintly.

"You're to take one other member of your squad, as well," the CO informed him. "Who?"

The young NCO hesitated for only a moment.

"Erkum," he said.

"Are you sure?" the CO asked with a laugh.

"Yes, Captain," Fain replied. "I know it sounds funny. But I also know I'll take care of him, and I don't know that about my replacement."

"Good enough." The officer stood up behind his low desk and offered his true-hand, human fashion. "Good luck, and do the Regiment proud."

"I will, Captain." The NCO turned to the guardsmen and made a gesture of question. "What now?"

"Get your gear loaded up," the underofficer said, and jerked a true-hand's thumb at his fellow guardsman. "Tarson here will escort you to your new quarters." The officer grunted a laugh. "Congratulations, you're moving down in the world."

The workshop was deep beneath the Citadel, a natural cavern filled with the whisper of winds flowing through ancient limestone passages. Besides a long, deep light well, at least partially manmade, the room was also lit by torches, candles, and lanterns until it was nearly as bright as day. All, apparently, to support the eyes of one Mardukan.

That person was standing in front of a large wall of limestone which had been smoothed to the consistency of glass. The white wall was heavily overlaid with black charcoal scribbles, and those scribbles were getting thicker as the ancient Mardukan covered the wall in meandering doodles like a cave painter of old.

Most of the scribbler's constant mutter was directed at Rus From, who was following him around with a bemused expression. Other than that, Fain recognized a couple of other members of the pike regiment. And, especially, a couple of the humans.

Pol followed him like a shadow as he walked up behind sergeant Julian.

"Pardon me, Sergeant," he whispered. "Do you perhaps remember me?"

Julian turned and gave him one of those strange human tooth-baring smiles.

"Fain, glad you could come," the human whispered back. "Hell, yes, I remember you. I was the one who suggested you for this."

The sergeant turned back to the show and waved at the gathering around the white wall.

"Look at that guy, will you? Amazing."

"Who is it?" the corporal asked. He knew better than to ask why he was here; the humans would tell him that when they were ready.

"Dell Mir. The local equivalent of Rus From, except that that's like comparing a hand grenade and an antimatter missile." The Marine shook his head again. "Rus From had barely started showing him a couple of outlines of what we were talking about, and he just took off, dropping ideas like rain."

"So is he going to make all the stuff they're talking about?"

"Nah. See the people following him around?" The sergeant pointed to a group of Mardukans with scrolls and tablets trailing along behind the two mechanical geniuses.

"Priests?"

"Nah. More like technicians, or maybe mechanical engineers. This guy, Wes Til, apparently set this up. Dell Mir spouts ideas all day long, and those guys write them all down and then go see how well they really work."

"Cool," Fain said. It was a human expression that meant "interesting" and "unusual" and several other things. Like "okay," it was such a good expression that it had been adopted by the entire New Model Army, and Julian gave a grunt of laughter when he heard it.

"We're going to be on the trigger team. Once the design is finalized, we'll be working with the job shops that are going to make the trigger mechanisms."

"I don't know anything about triggers or mechanisms at all," the Diaspran confessed. "Just because I'm from Diaspra doesn't mean *I'm* some sort of mechanical genius."

"Don't worry," Julian replied. "I'll handle all that. You're going to be a gofer."

"Gopher?" the Mardukan asked in some confusion. The human translating device sometimes used words that were just as alien as the humans themselves, but it was odd the way that even the strangest word seemed to carry hints of other meanings. "Some sort of *basik?*"

"No, a 'go-fer,'" Julian corrected. "'Krindi, go-fer coffee. Krindi, go-fer lunch.'"

"Oh," the corporal said with a laugh. "Okay."

"Don't worry, it'll be more than that. In fact, we'll probably be bumping you up to sergeant to give you a bit more weight dealing with the locals. We'll be making sure the shops are supplying quality parts and that assembly shops are using only the specified materials. Everything's going to be standardized with interchangeable parts, so we can produce it in quantity."

"Big . . . ummm," the Diaspran struggled for a word.

"'Project' would be the human term. Like building a dam or a major dike. Yeah, it is, and a rush one, too. We're about out of time."

The Marine broke off as Captain Pahner stepped to the front. The Marine CO looked at the sketches on the wall and shook his head.

"Simpler, Rus, Dell. Simpler. This thing has too many parts. Every one of them will tend to break in the field, and every one has to be made, adding to cost and time. So look at something like this and say to yourself 'How can I get rid of parts?'"

The slight K'Vaernian with the piece of charcoal in his true-hand turned and looked at the Marine with his head cocked to one side.

"But your techniques of industry and mass production will cut the production time, surely?"

"True," Pahner said, "but they're not magic, and there's something called lead time to allow for. The more time we spend here, working out potential bugs in the designs, the less time we spend working them out in the foundries, and the fewer we get into the field. Don't forget, 'mass production' requires us to design and set up the production lines before we get to the 'mass' part of the equation, and the more parts we have to make, the more setup time we'll need. So cut down on the complexity and find some way to get rid of parts. You did a good job of that with the new breech design, so I know you can do it here, too. Let me show you what I'm thinking about."

The captain stepped forward, took the charcoal from the Mardukan's unresisting hand, and began marking on the wall.

"See this? You've got a double set of springs *here*. But if you move the lever to *here*, you can eliminate one spring entirely."

"Yes!" the K'Vaernian said, taking the charcoal back. "And eliminate this—what did you call it? Sear? Take this one out, and extend *this* lever . . ."

"As you can see," Julian whispered again, "we have our work cut out for us."

"Sergeant, how are we going to train on these if they're not even produced yet? And how long are we going to have? I mean, the Boman could move out at any time."

"That's somebody else's problem," the Marine said with an evil grin. "You concentrate on ours."

The long, low boat grounded on the mud of the riverbank, and D'Estrees slipped over the side and into the underbrush.

Gunnery Sergeant Lamasara Jin consulted his pad as he checked position before he inserted the last team. There were five more two-person teams scattered along the line of advance from D'Sley to Sindi, where the Boman main host supposedly was. This team was the furthest forward, and along with some local woodsmen, would probe still further forward until they reached Sindi or made contact with the Boman force.

Personally, the gunny really doubted that *all* of the Boman could be at Sindi, whatever the locals thought. The best premassacre population estimate Julian and O'Casey had been able to put together for Sindi gave the city a total population of only around seventy thousand. Which, Jin was willing to admit, was a really huge number, even allowing for the efficiency of Mardukan farmers, for a society which made virtually zero use of the wheel. It might not seem like much for the Empire, where that entire population could have been put into a single pair of residential towers in downtown Imperial City, but for a barb planet like Marduk, it was huge.

And it was also no more than a third of the total numbers people kept throwing around for the Boman.

Jin hoped like hell that the enemy force estimates were excessive, but he didn't really think they could be off by too much. Like all the Marines, he'd developed a pronounced respect for Rastar and Honal, neither of whom seemed at all inclined to inflate enemy numbers to excuse their own defeats, and they both insisted that the combined clans of the Boman could put at least a hundred thousand *warriors* into the field . . . which suggested a total population, including women and children, of at least half a million. And given that, like the Wespar, all of the Boman clans brought their women and children along rather than leaving them at home and undefended while the men were away, that meant one hell of a lot of scummies had descended on what used to be the League of the North and the other cities on the northern shore of the K'Vaernian Sea.

According to all reports, those scummies had been sitting more or less motionless for at least three or four months since taking Sindi, and that many mouths would have eaten the countryside around a city Sindi's size clean in far less time than that. Not to mention the fact that a city of seventy thousand could never provide even minimal housing for six or seven times that many invaders.

All of which suggested to the veteran noncom that—as always seemed to be the case—he and the rest of the company were about to find out that the backroom intelligence pukes had screwed up again. Fortunately, the captain had been a Marine long enough to be very cautious about how much trust he put in intelligence his own people hadn't confirmed. *Un*fortunately, there was only one way to confirm this intelligence.

Jin tapped the pad off and stepped ashore as D'Estrees reappeared and gave a thumbs-up. Normally, as Bravo Team leader, D'Estrees would have been teamed with Dalton, the team's plasma gunner. The only problem with that was that Dalton was now . . . dating Geno. If Jin put the gunner out on the point of the spear, everybody was going to think he was trying to kill his rival for Geno's affections. So instead, the plasma gunner was nice and safe and in the center of the deployment of the recon teams . . . and the overall commander of the insertion was taking point. Which, when Captain Pahner found out, would bring up words like stupid and suicidal. Instead of favoritism.

Damned if you do, and damned if you don't. But nobody was going to accuse Mamma Jin's boy of favoritism. Stupidity, though, okay, maybe.

But somewhere out there was the target, and right now he didn't care if that target was Saints or pirates or Boman. Because sooner or later, he was going to get a chance to kill something, and the closer he was to the action, the more likely that was to happen. And if he didn't kill something else soon, he just might start on one too-good-looking plasma gunner.

Two klicks to the track that ran from D'Sley to Sindi. It paralleled the river, so it never saw much traffic, since barges made so much more sense than land transport. But it was there, and if the Boman came to play, it would be along that track.

And if they didn't come out to play on their own, then they were just going to have to be called.

"I don't care if you do think it's a waste of time," Bistem Kar told the skeptical underofficer in a deceptively calm tone. General Bogess stood beside the K'Vaernian CO, but the Diaspran was being very careful not to involve himself in the conversation. "I don't even care if your *men* think it's a waste of time. *I* don't think it is, and this—" he tapped the ruby-set hilt of the sword at his side, the one only the commanding officer of the Guard Company was permitted to wear "—means that what I think is all that matters, now doesn't it?"

The underofficer closed his mouth and straightened both sets of shoulders. The thought of being ordered around by Diaspran "soldiers" so new they still had canal mud on their feet was enough to infuriate anyone, and he sympathized perfectly with his men. And even if the idea of being instructed by jumped-up common laborers hadn't been hard to swallow, the sheer stupidity of what they were supposed to be learning was almost intolerable. Damn it, they *knew* how to do their jobs, and they'd done them well enough for decades to make K'Vaern's Cove the most powerful city-state on the entire K'Vaernian Sea! And they hadn't done it by hiding behind any silly shields and refusing to come out and fight like men!

Even granting the incontestable truth of all of that, however, Kar's tone of voice had just forcibly reminded him that there were other considerations, as well. "The Kren" was a guardsman's guardsman, always willing to listen—to a point at least—to the opinions and concerns of his men, but anyone who'd ever been stupid enough to think that that mild tone was an invitation to further discussion never made the same mistake twice.

Kar gazed at him for a moment, clearly waiting to see if he'd finally found someone stupid enough to keep pushing. He hadn't, and after waiting a bit longer to be sure the point had been adequately made, he allowed his own manner to ease.

"I admit it seems a bit . . . bizarre," he conceded then, "but I've watched the Diasprans drilling. I've never seen anything like it, either—not for infantry. But much as I hate to admit it, now that I've seen the humans' notions of how infantry should drill and maneuver, I can't understand why the same ideas never occurred to us."

"Sir, it just seems . . . wrong," the underofficer said in a carefully dispassionate tone, and Kar grunted a chuckle.

"It isn't the way our sires did it, or our grandsires, or *their* sires," the Guard commander agreed, "and I suppose it's inevitable for us to feel some sort of, um, emotional attachment for the way things have always been. But it's worth thinking about that the League, which spent the most time fighting the Boman instead of other civilized sorts of armies, already used tactics a lot closer to these new ones of the humans than ours. Now that *we're* the ones up against the barbs, maybe it's time we considered the fact that we can't take them on one by one. Even if they were willing to play by the old rules, there are so many of the bastards that we'd run out of bodies before they did, no matter how good we are. But these new tactics—all this teamwork with these 'rifles' and 'pikes' and 'assegais,' and those big shields the humans have invented—are going to change all that *if* we can figure out what in Krin's name we're doing with them. The problem is, we don't have a whole lot of time, and we're going to have to *un*learn almost as much as we have to learn.

"So I don't have a lot of time to spend arguing with my underofficers," Kar went on in a slightly harder tone. "We're all going to be much too busy listening to General Bogess here. And we're also going to be busy making sure that our noncoms understand that they're going to be listening to the Diaspran training cadre. I don't care if most of the Diasprans *were* dam builders and canal diggers four months ago. What they are *now* are soldiers. More than that, they're combat veterans who've done something none of us ever have: met the Boman bastards in the field and kicked their miserable asses all the way into whatever Krin-forsaken afterlife they believe in.

"So you *will* go back to your unit, and you *will* tell them that they really, really don't want me to come explain all of this to them in person. Is that clear?"

"Yes, Sir!" the underofficer said quickly. "Perfectly clear, Sir!"

"Good." The Guard commander gazed at him once more, then nodded dismissal. "I'm glad we had time for this little conversation," he told the underofficer. "Now go back and get that mess straightened out."

"Yes, Sir! At once, Sir!"

"We're going to train them *how?*"

St. John (J.) would much rather have been out in the field probing for the Boman camps. Anything but trying to explain the captain's brainstorm to this evil-looking scummy.

"The weapons are going to be something like an arquebus, Sir," the Marine answered. "But they're going to need to be aimed, not just volley-fired in the target's general direction, and Marines know all about teaching aiming. The most important part is breath and trigger control."

He picked up the contraption which had been leaning against the wall, brought it to his shoulder, and pointed it.

"We teach them about sight picture, then we put a K'Vaernian copper piece on this carved sight mockup and have them practice squeezing the trigger. When they can do it time after time without the copper falling off, they'll be halfway there."

The company commander picked up the wooden carving of the rifle and tried to point it while balancing the copper piece on the narrow width of the sight. The coin chimed musically as it promptly hit the stone floor, and the Mardukan snarled in frustration.

"This is madness. Is this supposed to be war?"

"Oh, yeah," the Marine breathed. "You have no idea. Just wait until you see the cannon."

"You want them to what?"

"Your company is going to be cadre for the artillery corps, Sir," Kosutic told the Mardukan who stood looking at her incredulously with all four arms crossed. Until that very morning, the scummy had been the executive officer of the *Sword of Krin*, the galleass flagship of the K'Vaernian Navy, and he didn't seem particularly delighted by his new assignment.

"This is ridiculous," the naval officer grunted. "Bombards are shipboard weapons—they're too heavy, too slow, and eat too damned much powder and shot to be practical for any damned mudpounder to use!"

"Sir, I understand why you feel that way, but I assure you that these 'bombards' aren't anything like the ones you're familiar with."

The Mardukan made a skeptical sound, and Kosutic drew a deep breath. She was the only member of the company besides Captain Pahner himself who had been through crew-served heavy weapons training. In Pahner's eyes, that made her the logical senior trainer for the envisioned artillery. The fact that, unlike this dubious scummy, she'd never fired a muzzle-loading, black powder artillery piece in her life was apparently beside the point. And, in a way, it was, because no one on this miserable mudball of a planet—including the four-armed pain in the ass glowering at her—had ever heard of the concept of field artillery.

"Sir," she went on after a moment, "the main reason you were assigned to this duty is that unlike the Guard officers, you do have experience with artillery. But you have to realize that the bombards you're used to aboard your ships are very different from the field guns we're going to be producing."

"Bombards are bombards," the Mardukan said flatly, and Kosutic bit her tongue firmly.

Part of the problem, she knew, was that K'Vaern's Cove was accustomed to being the supplier of the finest artillery around, and the K'Vaernian Navy was even more accustomed to considering its gunners to be the best in the world. Which meant that none of them were very happy to be told that the smart-ass humans were going to show them how artillery *ought* to be made and used.

That reaction was inevitable, at least initially, and not simply among scummies. Human military types through the ages had reacted negatively to suggestions that what they knew had worked in the past might not still be the best technique or weapons available in the present. The big problem here was that they simply didn't have time to bring people around gradually, which meant that Turl Kam and Bistem Kar had been fairly direct and brutal in laying down the law to their more doubtful subordinates. And that meant that a certain degree of tact was absolutely required.

"Sir," she began diplomatically, "I wouldn't know where to begin to tell you how to go about fighting a naval battle. Frankly, I don't know shit about that particular subject, but I understand that your standard tactics for heavy bombards are to row directly at your target and to fire a single, close-range salvo from all of your guns just before you ram and board them. Is that about correct?"

"In general terms, yes," the Mardukan said grudgingly.

"And why is it that you don't fire more than one shot per gun, Sir?"

"Because it takes seven chimes to reload them," the naval officer told her with exaggerated patience. A chime, Kosutic knew, was a K'Vaernian time measurement equal to about forty-five seconds, so the scummy was talking about a five-minute reload time. "And," the officer went on, "because relaying the guns for a second shot would take even longer."

"Yes, Sir, it would," the sergeant major agreed. "But the guns that we're going to be using can be reloaded much more quickly than that. In fact, using bagged charges and fixed antipersonnel you'll be able to fire them once per chime—maybe even a little more rapidly—under maximum rate conditions at short range."

The Mardukan stared at her incredulously, and she showed her teeth in a thin smile and continued.

"In addition, the new carriages we're going to be building, coupled with how much lighter the cannon themselves are going to be, will make them a lot more mobile than any bombard you've ever seen. We figure a single pair of *turom* should be able to haul even the bigger ones around without much trouble. And this new feature here—" she tapped the trunnions of the wooden mock-up someone from ancient Earth might have recognized as remarkably similar to something which had once been called a "twelve-pounder Napoleon" "—will actually let you make changes in elevation between shots."

The Mardukan uncrossed his lower arms and leaned closer. It was apparent that he was truly looking at the new weapon for the first time, and Kosutic hid a smile as some of his truculent skepticism seemed to fade. If they could just get the scummies to really *see* the advantages, three quarters of the job would be done.

The K'Vaernian Navy's bombards were very well made from the standpoint of their metallurgy and casting techniques, but as practical artillery pieces they left a lot to be desired. In fact, they were simply huge bronze or iron tubes which were strapped to heavy wooden timbers and then chained or roped to the deck of a ship. They looked more like big, clumsy rifles than they did anything a human would have called an artillery piece, and it was impossible to adjust their elevation in any way. As for recoil, the K'Vaernian gunners simply stood as far to one side as they could and touched off the priming. The heavy hawsers which fastened the bombards to the deck and bulwarks kept the gun from jumping clear overboard, and the friction between the wheelless "carriage" and deck acted as an extremely crude recoil damper. Hauling the guns back into position for the next shot without any sort of wheels under them was a backbreaking process, of course, but they accepted that as the price of doing business because that was the way it had always been done before.

The new guns, on the other hand, were a very different proposition. Their carriages, with large spoked wheels with extra-wide rims, and lighter weight, would give them a degree of mobility no Mardukan had ever dreamed was possible, and the introduction of trunnions and elevating screws would completely change their tactical flexibility, both afloat and ashore. With the addition of premeasured, bagged charges and fixed rounds of grapeshot and canister, their rate of fire would also be enormously increased. If the team working on ammunition actually managed to get the bugs out of a decent shrapnel round in the time available, the guns would be even more effective, but the sergeant major had no intention of holding her breath while she waited. In fact, she had a pretty shrewd notion that the more optimistic visions of explosive filler for cast-iron shells were doomed to disappointment. The rocket batteries were a different matter entirely, of course, but no one really knew how well that project was going to work out either. And in the meantime . . .

"Sir, as you know much better than any of the Guard officers, the important thing with crew-served weapons like this is for everyone to perform their jobs precisely according to a standard drill. What we're going to add to what you already know is speed, because it will be possible to load and fire the new guns much more quickly . . . if the crews are properly trained.

"You know what your bombards do to the hulls of enemy ships. Try to picture what a weapon like this will do to a mob of Boman. Each shot will punch right through them and kill anyone who gets in its way, and when dozens of these guns are massed, there's nothing like them. In our society, artillery was called 'The King of Battle,' but for the guns to be effective, their crews must be drilled to exhaustion. They have to be able to clear, load, and fire the weapon under the most extreme circumstances, then limber up, move on, and do it again. So you learn the steps, then you practice them again and again.

"That means that there's no need, initially, for the cannon themselves. A training mock-up, or even a few marks on the ground to show its outline, will do in a pinch, because it's how you move around the gun that really matters. The trick is to teach the gunners how to do it right before they ever *see* a real cannon—teach them never to stand behind it once it's loaded, to do their jobs in a certain sequence, and to do them *fast*.

"So we're going to show you how. You and your people were chosen because you're already familiar with artillery. Whether you realize it or not, you already have most of the basic knowledge you need, and all we have to do is to teach you to see that knowledge a little differently and adjust to a whole new tempo. So once we've shown you that, your people will show others, and those people will show still others, and so on. And when we're finished, we'll have ourselves a tiddly little artillery corps that will pile up Boman like barleyrice."

The skeptical naval officer was listening much more closely now, and she hid another smile as she turned to the six Marines standing around the carved wooden model. The end of the barrel was slightly scorched, because it had just finished double duty as a model for the mold and been left a bit too close to a furnace afterward.

"These fine young Marines, who just spent the last few hours learning what to do, are going to demonstrate," she continued. "What they can't demonstrate is that there are some things you Mardukans can do, with four arms, that they can't do with just two. We'll have to work that out, with your assistance, as we go along."

She drew a deep breath, and nodded to the senior Marine.

"Squad!" she barked. "Prepare to place the gun into action! Gun in action . . . Move!"

And the six Terran Empire Marines, born on planets circling five different stars, began the ritual of service to the artillery—a ritual which had been old before the first rockets lifted beyond the atmosphere of Terra and looked to be going on when the last star cooled.

Some things just never seemed to change.

CHAPTER TWENTY-NINE

Something hard and circular socketed instantly into Fain's temple as he trotted through the doorway, with Erkum hard on his heels, and ran straight into the human prince.

The newly promoted sergeant heard a deep rumble of displeasure behind him and reached back to very carefully put a restraining hand against Pol's chest until Roger could reach out and push the bead rifle muzzle aside.

"It's all right, Geno. He's one of ours," the prince said, then tapped the sergeant on his mid-shoulder. "Krindi Fain, isn't it? You did well at the Battle. Held your squad together admirably."

"Thank you, Your Highness," Fain said, braced to attention and trying not to show his relief *too* plainly.

"Not so formal, Sergeant—we're all old soldiers here. Sergeant Julian making sure you're getting fed, right? I can't promise sleep; none of us are getting much of that."

"Yes, Your Highness."

"Good. Remember to take care of your troops, and they'll take care of you." The human turned to the sergeant's shadow and craned his neck to peer up at the towering giant. "And the inimitable Erkum Pol, I see. How are you, Erkum?"

"Yes, Your Highness," the private said.

"I'll take that as 'doing well,'" Roger said with a smile. Apparently he knew about the soldier's simplemindedness. "And, Erkum, next time use a smaller plank, right? I need all the cavalry I can get."

"Yes, Your Highness," Fain heard himself say.

"Carry on," the prince said, striding off with a wave, followed by his bodyguards, and the Diasprans braced back to attention.

"Lots smaller plank," the last Marine guard whispered with a human-style wink as he passed Fain. "Fuckers are *still* in the hospital."

Roger shook his head as he turned the corner to the training ground. That lad Krindi was going to go far . . . assuming he could keep Pol from killing someone at an inopportune moment.

He chuckled, then turned his attention to the company of riflemen-to-be. The ranks were lined up in an open formation, with each soldier holding a wooden mock-up of the final rifle design. As the prince entered the area, the cadence of fire was being called.

"Open. Load. Close. Cock. Cap. Aim. Fire."

The bull-throated Mardukan giving the orders saluted as Roger went past. Another veteran of the New Model pike regiments, the Diaspran, like most of that force, had been broken off for cadre for the new units.

The numbers for those new units were looking much better than Roger had feared they might, if not quite as good as he could have wished in an ideal world. The core of the new and improved K'Vaernian army would be the veterans of the Guard, their less than enthusiastic fellow citizens temporarily reassigned from the Navy, Rastar's Northern cavalrymen, and the Diaspran pikemen. But that would account for little more than a third of the total numbers they needed, and volunteer levels had been gratifyingly high. Some of the local volunteers were in it only for the expected loot, which, however mercenary, was certainly understandable. The Boman on this side of the Nashtor Hills had conquered the northern cities and Sindi, all of which had been wealthy and powerful states, so it was only to be expected that they would be swimming in treasure as a result of their victories. Other volunteers had come forward because they perceived the Boman as a threat to their own city, and some had volunteered because they were refugees from other cities who wanted some of their own back.

Whatever their reasons for joining, the troops were being formed into a tidy little army. Now if they could only get some weapons for it.

And maybe they were doing something about that, he thought, looking up to see Rastar grinning as he waved something and trotted towards him from the other side of the square.

"First production unit out of the Tendel foundry," the Northerner said as he reached the prince, and handed him a massive rifle.

The weapon was gigantic and starkly utilitarian. The twenty-five-millimeter bore made his own eleven-millimeter look like a toy, and the breech was the size of a plasma cannon firing chamber.

The final design was very different from the one the Marines and Rus From had sketched out before leaving Diaspra, and almost equally different from the new, improved cartridge version Pahner had wanted to produce once they actually got to K'Vaern's Cove. The original design had been very similar to the old Sharps breechloader from the ancient American Civil War, with a moving breech block that clipped the end off of a linen cartridge when the breech was closed to expose the powder charge to flash from a priming cap. Although gas leakage would probably have been a problem, just as it had been with the original, From and Pahner had rather doubted that it would seriously inconvenience anyone already accustomed to the godawful priming flash of a Mardukan arquebus.

The much more advanced design Pahner had wanted once he decided to stay and fight, on the other hand, would have used either a brass cartridge case or a composite brass and paper case, either of which would have been a centerfire percussion design with a metallic base to provide an excellent, flash-proof seal at the breech. One look at the manufacturing complexity and lead time required to produce that ammunition in quantity had knocked that idea on the head, however, and everyone had gone looking for some workable compromise solution. One had been found—and finally put into production—in a design which had been suggested by Dell Mir and owed more to local expertise with pumps than even Pahner had believed might be the case.

The prince gripped the protruding bolt handle, which looked very similar to that of his own hunting rifle when it wasn't configured for semi-auto fire, and raised it, turning the bolt through a half rotation. K'Vaern's Cove's pump makers had developed a standard fixture for use as an inspection/cleaning port for their pumps, which was closed by what was in effect a big, coarse-threaded bolt with a washer at one end. Mardukans spent a lot of time doing maintenance on their flood control pumps, even in a place like K'Vaern's Cove, where the steepness of the slopes (which promoted very rapid runoff) and the absence of a readily tapped aquifer made potable water scarce, and the inspection port had been designed for ease and speed of access. It was fitted with a crank-style handle on one end, and moved in a cam-mounted sleeve, so that when the bolt was run out of the threads, the entire plug pivoted downwards and hung from the underside of the pipe it normally closed.

Mir, with an eye to practical adaptation which explained much of his reputation for genius, had seen no reason not to use a perfectly sound existing design rather than get bogged down in esoteric new concepts. Of course, there had been some changes. The two biggest ones had been to convert the fittings from bronze to steel and his decision to cut away the threads on two sides of the threaded bolt plug and to interrupt the threads that the plug seated into so that only a half turn was required to engage and disengage the threads. He'd also made some other minor changes, including moving the bolt handle to the side (an idea he'd borrowed from Roger's eleven-millimeter) and machining a guide onto the rifle bolt to ensure that it followed the proper mechanical path, but the overall effect had been to take a simple plumbing fixture and use it to manufacture the most deadly weapon K'Vaern's Cove had ever seen.

The cartridge design had also been simplified. There wasn't much question that the K'Vaernians would have been able to produce Pahner's brass cartridges . . . eventually. Certainly, their tech base and metallurgy were capable of making the jump to manufacture the captain's design, but setting up to produce it and experimenting to come up with exactly the right alloy for the cases would have taken considerably longer than K'Vaern's Cove—or its human visitors, at least—had. So instead, Dell Mir had turned to a local plant.

The Mardukans called it *shonash*, but after one demonstration of its properties, the Marines had instantly christened it the flashplant, because on any planet without Marduk's daily rains, it would have been a deadly fire hazard. The K'Vaernians crushed its stems to extract a fine, clear, hot-burning oil, which they used in industry and as lamp fuel, and the large, flat leaves were sometimes used to wrap packages where wetness was an even greater than usual danger. They were so heavily impregnated with volatile oils that they remained tough and flexible even after they'd been "dried" and were almost totally impervious to water. That was good, but, unfortunately, they were also extremely combustible, which made it somewhat dangerous to use them for packaging in conditions which wouldn't keep them fairly wet.

Dell Mir had recognized instantly that those very qualities made flashplant leaves almost ideal as a cartridge paper substitute. A little experimentation had quickly demonstrated that the flash from one of Despreaux's early percussion caps would burn straight through a double layer of leaf almost instantaneously. So the K'Vaernian inventor had produced a design in which one of the new hollow-based bullets and its propellant were wrapped together in a flashplant leaf cartridge. The base of the cartridge was a thick, disklike, heavily greased felt patch, and when the rifle bolt was driven forward and engaged in its threads, the explosion of the cartridge drove the felt back against the face of the bolt to complete the seal and prevent any gas leakage. The next round loaded pushed the remnant of the previous round's patch forward and out of the way, and the rifle was ready to fire again. The final product of his efforts adhered very closely to Pahner's drive to reduce the number of parts, yet worked with a robust simplicity Roger had to admire. There was still plenty of room for improvement, but this design had the three most important virtues of all: it worked, it would be hard for even a soldier to break, and it could be produced quickly.

The workshops of K'Vaern's Cove had sprouted rifling benches like toadstools, and the Guard and Navy's arquebuses had been hauled in and handed over to the machinists for modification. The rear ends of their barrels had been sliced off, they'd been rifled, the exterior of the back end of the barrels had been run through thread-cutting dies, the modified pump inspection ports had been screwed on, and a redesigned trigger mechanism taken from the existing wheel lock pistols had been modified to control a side-mounted hammer for a percussion lock. And that had been that. Well, aside from the provision of bayonet lugs on the ends of the barrels.

Now the prince finished opening the breech and flipped the rifle up to his shoulder to take a good look at the breech mechanism and the barrel. Although there were a few burrs on the exterior from the hurried work of the shops, the interior was beautifully machined and the bolt's threads engaged and disengaged with smooth precision.

"Very nice," he said. "The only thing that would make it better would be proper metallic cartridge cases, but this will more than do the job."

Despite what Rus From had told them, the volume of production that was in the pipeline still amazed Roger. The effective blockade of the city from the land side had idled hundreds of small foundries and shops throughout the peninsula on which K'Vaern's Cove sat. All of them, it seemed, wanted in on the new government contracts, which had given the designers some leeway to stray from the "simpler, simpler, simpler" mantra. They hadn't wandered far, but the provision of a proper bayonet had been one of the "frills" Pahner had been prepared to forego. The K'Vaernians, on the other hand, found the notion of parking a sixty-centimeter blade on the end of their new rifles *very* attractive. One of the great disadvantages of the arquebus had always been that it was essentially little more than a clumsily shaped club if the arquebusier found himself forced into a melee. Now each of the new riflemen would be able to look after himself in the furball if he had to, which had proven extremely reassuring to soldiers who were still none too sure about the effectiveness of all these newfangled ideas. Roger was a strong supporter of the bayonet, but he personally found the ladder sight even more useful, and the butt-mounted cleaning kit was nothing to sneer at, either.

The logistics bottleneck, as From had predicted, lay far less in the rifles than in the manufacture of their ammunition. There was plenty of lead for bullets, and the new bullet dies hadn't been a problem, but actually putting the cartridges together—even using Dell Mir's flashplant design—was a delicate, time-consuming, hand labor task, and not one that could be trusted to off-the-street casual labor. Even if simple assembly hadn't been a problem, no one in K'Vaern's Cove had ever imagined the rate of ammunition expenditure Pahner was projecting. An arquebusier did well to fire one shot every two minutes, and under normal circumstances probably wouldn't fire more than five to ten rounds in any engagement. Pahner was talking about issuing sixty rounds per day as the new riflemen's standard unit of fire, and he wanted a reserve of no less than four units of fire for the entire army before committing to action, and that didn't even consider the rounds they were simply going to have to expend in training. While each individual cartridge used very little gunpowder, hundreds of thousands of them used tons of the stuff, and given the competing needs of the artillery, the claymores, and the new rocket batteries, there simply wasn't enough powder to provide ammunition for the numbers of rifles which could, in theory, have been produced.

But what they *could* produce, Roger thought with a wicked smile, was going to be more than enough to give the Boman serious problems.

"And look at this," Rastar told him with an even more wicked grin of his own as he brought another weapon around from behind his back . . . then froze when three bead rifles instantly snapped up to cover him.

"Hey, come on!" he said. "It's me, Rastar."

"Yeah," Roger said, taking the pistol from the cavalryman, "but we've had another death threat. And the attempted assassination of Rus From. So they're a little twitchy." He looked the weapon over and smiled. "Again, very nice."

The weapon was a revolver, very similar in appearance to what had once been known as a Colt Dragoon, but much larger and with some significant design peculiarities to fit the Mardukan hand. It was lighter than the rifles—with no more than a mere twenty-millimeter bore—and it was also a seven-shot weapon, not a six-shooter. The rear of the cylinder had nipples for the copper percussion caps the alchemists' guild was producing in quantity under Despreaux's direction, but the biggest differences (besides an odd indent in the grip so that it could be held more easily with a false-hand) were the fact that it was double action, not single, and that it was a swing-out cylinder design. Obviously, the firer was supposed to swing the cylinder out and slide more of Dell Mir's flashplant-bagged cartridges into place from the front, base end first, then cap the chambers, and lock the cylinder back into place, which would make it much quicker to reload than the cap-and-ball revolvers of ancient Earth.

"Really nice," Roger said, handing it back. "Of course, it would break my wrist if I tried to fire it."

"It's not my fault you're a wimp," the Northerner said, taking his prize back.

"Ha! We'll see who's a wimp in a month's time," Roger replied. "How many of these are we producing?"

"As many as possible," Rastar said with a gesture of dismissal. "The machining is more complicated than for the rifles, and we can't just convert existing arquebus barrels, and there are some problems with about a quarter of them—they break for some reason, after a couple of shots. I got the first four."

"Of course," Roger said. Rastar was not only the commander of the Northern cavalry but also far and away the most dangerous pistoleer, himself included, the prince had ever seen. "I suppose we should thank goodness for pumps, pumps, and more pumps. Those industries are certainly coming in handy. Are you scheduled for the exercise this afternoon?"

"Yes," the Northerner replied with a grimace. "Maps, maps, and more maps."

"It's good for the soul," Roger said with a grin.

"So is killing Boman," Rastar said. "Although, at this point, anyone would do."

"I think we're going to have to kill somebody, Sergeant," Fain said.

"Why?" Julian asked, looking up from the meal on the low table.

He couldn't wait to get back to someplace that had decent chairs. Hell, he couldn't wait to get back to someplace that had decent food.

"Show him, Erkum," the Diaspran noncom replied.

The huge private held up a spring to show it to the Marine, then started to stretch it. The heavy spring resisted at first, then began stretching outward . . . until it snapped with a brittle sound.

"Skimping on the springs again, huh?" Julian said, dropping his fork and picking up his sword. "You'd think they'd learn."

"Yeah, but this foundry's owned by one of the members of the Council," Fain said. "Which was very carefully pointed out when I saw the shop foreman about this."

"How much did he offer?" the Marine asked, taking out his pad and punching a message into it.

"A kusul of silver," the Diaspran replied with a shrug. "It was insulting."

"Damn straight," Julian laughed. "Maybe up front, or weekly, but a one-time offer after they'd already been caught? Jesus."

"So what are you going to do?"

"I guess we're just going to have to explain to him what the words 'quality process improvement' mean. You, me, Erkum, and a squad from the New Model. Get it set up."

"Who is," Julian ostentatiously consulted the scrap of paper in his hand, "Tistum Path?"

"I am," said a heavyset Mardukan, appearing out of the gloom of the foundry.

The forging room was hot. Unbelievably hot, like a circle of Hell. Julian could have sworn that water left on any surface would start to boil in a second. There were two ceramic furnaces where steel—spring steel, in this case—was being formed over forced-air coke fires, and the fierce flames and bubbling steel contributed to a choking atmosphere that must have been nearly lethal to the Mardukans working in it. Which wasn't going to dissuade Julian one bit from his appointed duty.

"Ah, good. Pleased to meet you," the sergeant said cheerfully, walking up to the foundry manager . . . and kicked him in the groin.

The squad of riflemen behind him were all from the New Model Army's Bastar Battalion of pikes. As the workers in the foundry grabbed various implements, the Diasprans' brand-new rifles came up and the percussion hammers clicked ominously as they were cocked and leveled at the workers. There had been enough demonstrations of the weapons by now that the workers froze.

The mastoid analogue behind a Mardukan's ear wasn't quite as susceptible as the same point on a human, but it would do. The hardwood bludgeon bounced off it nicely as the shop manager was driven to his knees.

Julian ran a length of chain around the stunned foreman's ankles and gave a thumbs-up to Fain, who began hauling on the pulley arrangement. The sliding crane was designed for lifting multi-ton crucibles of boiling steel, and it made short work of lifting the three-meter Mardukan into the air. As the manager recovered, Julian threw a rope about his horns and used it to drag him along until he was suspended in the flaring heat over one of the furnaces.

"Here's the deal!" the Marine shouted to the head-down Mardukan. "Springs are very *important* in weapons, and *you*, Tistum Path, are very important in the manufacture of *springs*. This is a *vital* position you hold, and one that I *hope* you are worthy of! Because if you're not—" the human hawked and spat into the furnace, but the glob of mucus exploded before it hit the surface of the bubbling steel "—it would just be a *senseless* waste of Mardukan life."

"You can't do this to me!" the Mardukan screamed, coughing and squirming frantically in the fumes blasting up from the furnace. "Don't you know who *owns* this place?"

"Of course we do, and we're going to be visiting him next. He's going to be *terribly* disappointed to learn that one of his employees misunderstood his orders to produce the best quality material, and damn the cost. Don't you think?"

"That's not what he said!"

"I know *that*." The Marine shook his head. "But there's no way he's going to admit that he told you to cut the cost, no matter what kind of shit you produced. So we're going to explain to him, in a gentle way, that while profits are the lifeblood of any economy, the contract he signed was supposed to include a reasonable profit margin *without* cheating. And we're already paying top dollar, so since we can't figure out which springs are shit and which ones aren't, he's going to be taking them *all* back. And replacing them. With good ones."

"Impossible! Who's going to pay for it?"

"Your boss," the Marine hissed, stepping into the blazing heat from the furnace. The red light of the boiling steel turned his angular face into a painting of Satan gloating over a new-caught sinner. "And the next time I have to come back here, both of you are going to be nothing but trace elements in the steel. *Is that perfectly clear?*"

"These humans are insane!" the councilor complained hotly.

"All the more reason to support getting them on their way," Wes Til replied, rolling a bit of spring in his fingers.

"They threatened me—*me!* They said they'd melt me in my own steel! I want their heads!"

"Hmmm?" Til looked up from the spring. "Wouldn't have anything to do with cracked revolver frames, broken springs, and exploding barrels, would it?"

"Those aren't my fault," the other Mardukan sniffed. "Just because a few of my workers were cutting corners, probably to line their own pockets—"

"Oh, be quiet!" Til snapped. "You signed contracts. From the point of view of the humans, you're responsible, and you know as well as I do that the courts would back them up if there was time for that. But there *isn't* time, and they don't really seem to be very interested in half-measures, now do they? So, under the circumstances, I suggest that you do exactly as they say, unless you want your heir to be the one who does it."

"Is that a threat?"

"No, it's more on the order of a statement. They seem to have the most remarkable intelligence system. For example, they've already tracked down the person who ordered the attack on Rus From. Or so I would guess. You notice that Ges Stin hasn't been gracing us with his presence lately?"

"Yes. You know something?"

"No. However, it's lately become common knowledge that it was Ges Stin who ordered the attack. It's even common knowledge who planned the attack at his orders and actually paid those unfortunate assassins. None of them, however, are anywhere to be found."

"Ges Stin has many shipping interests. He could be in the southern states by now."

"Hmmm. Perhaps."

"What does Turl Kam think of this?"

"He thinks that he's down one competitor for the fisherman's guild vote," the merchant said with a grunt of laughter.

"I will not be intimidated," the other councilor declared defiantly.

"The sliming on your forehead gives you the lie. But you don't need to be," Til replied. "Just make sure your shops produce what they promised. Instead of weak crap." The spring he'd been flexing broke with a pop. "You really don't want a few thousand people with rifles in their true-hands . . . discussing the problem with you. Do you?"

CHAPTER THIRTY

Dersal Quan stood on the foundry floor and watched in disbelief as the human-designed device sliced through his best bronze as if it were *qwanshu* wood. He'd had even more doubts than he'd cared to express to Wes Til when he discovered just how many pieces of artillery the insane humans and their Diaspran henchmen expected to cast in the ridiculously short time limit they'd imposed. Now it looked to him as if they might actually manage to meet their preposterous production schedule.

The Quan foundries had been among the largest and wealthiest in K'Vaern's Cove for generations. They'd provided over half the Navy's total bombards since Quan's father's time, and at least a third of the bells hung in the Cove's towers to the glory of Krin also bore the Quan founder's stamp. Quan had never doubted that his modelers and patternmakers could produce the forms or that his casters could pour the guns, but pouring bronze wasn't like pouring concrete. It had to be done right, and there were no corners that could be cut unless one really liked bombards which were honeycombed with flaws and failed when proofed . . . or blew up in combat, always at the most inopportune time possible. And even after that time requirement had been allowed for, the need to bore out the guns was the single most time-consuming element of the entire process.

The true secret to a bombard of superior accuracy lay in the care taken in the preparation of its bore and the shot it would fire, although it had taken the gunners generations to realize how critical things like windage and uniform bores truly were. In fact, Quan's own father had begun his apprenticeship in the family business manufacturing cannonballs out of *stone*, and the art of cutting and reaming bores properly had been practically invented by one of Quan's uncles. It was a multistage process which required days for each piece, and no one had ever imagined that someone would demand so many guns in so short a time period, which meant that no one had the machinery to bore out more than a half dozen or so guns simultaneously. Not only that, but the crazy humans had insisted on a shot size which no one in K'Vaern's Cove had ever used, which meant that none of the boring equipment which already existed was the right size, and that the foundries also found themselves forced to produce new shot molds even as they cast the gun tubes themselves.

But the humans had insisted that there were ways around the problems, and so Quan had accepted their contracts, trusting Krin to prove the diminutive foreign lunatics knew what they were talking about. And trusting in the Cove's courts to absolve him of legal responsibility for failure when it turned out that they didn't.

As it happened, they *had* known what they were talking about, and now he watched in lingering disbelief as the ebony-skinned human called Aburia switched off her device and pushed the transparent goggles up on her forehead while one of her K'Vaernian assistants spun the handcrank which retracted the boring head from the new piece.

"What did you say this is called?" Quan asked, waving a true-hand at the device.

"I don't know that it really has a name," Aburia told him with one of the "shrugs" humans seemed so fond of. "It's sort of a bastardized field expedient, actually. The cutting head is only three of our bayonet blades, and Julian and Poertena made the shaft by welding a couple of broke-down plasma rifle barrels together and then splicing in a powerplant from Russell's powered armor. Your own people put together the rack-and-pinion system to move it, and your shop foreman and I worked out the clamps and brackets to hold everything still while we drill."

She shrugged again, and Quan clapped hands in a gesture of profound respect, tinged with surprise.

"I didn't believe you could really do this," he admitted. "Even watching you, I'm not sure I believe it now! Seeing a shaft that thin"—he gestured at the slender rod, no thicker than a human finger, which Julian and Poertena had welded together with something called a laser kit—"take that sort of load without even flexing isn't just impossible, it's preposterous! It ought to be wobbling all over the place, especially since you had to piece it together in the first place out of hollow tubing. There's certainly not any way that it should be allowing you to cut such uniformly true bores! And I've never heard of any knife blade that could pare away bronze like so much soft cheese and never even need sharpening."

"Well, sir," the human said with one of those teeth-showing smiles Quan still found mildly disturbing, "we haven't used bronze for something like this in close to two thousand of our years. We've got a lot better alloys now, and a blade with an edge a single molecule wide will cut just about anything without dulling down so's anyone would notice!"

"So your Julian said," Quan agreed, "although I'm still not very certain just what these 'molecules' you keep talking about might be. Not that I suppose it really matters all that much as long as your wizards' spells keep working as promised."

"The Regiment usually manages to hold up its end, sir," Aburia assured him. "Especially when we've got a member of the Imperial Family with his ass in a crack!"

"How about the rocket batteries?" Pahner asked.

He, Rus From, and Bistem Kar stood on a catwalk watching Dersal Quan talk to Corporal Aburia.

"They are progressing better than I'd anticipated," From told him. "The Cove's pump artificers have set up to machine the 'venturis' in quantity, and the test rockets have performed well. The biggest problem, of course, is that they consume even more gunpowder than the new artillery will."

"Price of doing business if we want a decent bursting charge at the terminal end of the flight," Pahner said with a shrug.

"That's understood," Kar rumbled in his subterranean voice, "and I've been most impressed by the weapons' effectiveness. Yet that doesn't change Rus's point. We have only so much powder, and at the moment we have at least three different things to use every *sedant* of it on. We're doing our best to get production levels back up, but even if we had every powder plant working at full capacity, we would still feel a serious pinch." He shook his head in one of the gestures the K'Vaernians had already picked up from their human visitors. "You humans may be the most deadly fighters anyone has ever seen, but the strains your way of fighting put on the quartermaster are enormous."

"You only think they are," Pahner replied with a chuckle. "Actually, the logistics for an army equipped with such simple weapons as this are child's play compared to the supply problems we normally have to deal with. You folks are the most advanced and innovative society we've come across yet on our journey, but you're only really getting started on what we call the 'Industrial Revolution.' Trust me, by the time you hit your stride, you'll look back on this as a relatively minor effort!"

"Assuming that we survive the Boman, of course," Kar pointed out.

"Oh, I feel confident that you'll survive them," Pahner said. "Whether we succeed in crushing them in a single campaign or not, we're going to do so much damage to them—and you guys are going to learn so much in the process—that their poor barbarian butts are pocked in the long run, whatever happens."

"Perhaps," Kar agreed. "Yet for that to happen, we must do enough damage and give our people enough confidence in the final outcome for them to see the wisdom in sustaining the struggle to that point."

"Which is where we come in," Pahner said with a nod. "Believe me, Bistem, we've figured that out. Don't worry. We'll give you and your people the basic skills and tools you'll need, and we'll play the 'Krin-sent champions' to get your army into the field in the first place. But don't sell yourself or the Guard short. Between you, Bogess, and the Diaspran cadre, you'll be able to hold up your end without us just fine if you have to after we leave."

"But what do they *want* all these wagons for?" Thars Kilna demanded in the tone of a person who knew no one could answer his question.

"Do you know, I think they forgot to tell me," Miln Sahna told him sarcastically. "I'm sure it was only an inadvertent oversight though. Here—you put the wheel on this end of the shaft, and I'll run ask Bistem Kar. When he explains it to me, I'll come right back and tell *you*."

"Very funny," Kilna growled. "You keep right on telling yourself you're a wit, Miln—at least you're *half* right. In the meantime, I still want to know why in Krin's name they need so many wagons! It just doesn't make sense."

"Um." Sahna grunted sourly, but he had to admit his fellow apprentice had a point. Not that either of them was complaining, precisely. The cart-makers' guild usually had orders to fill in a place like K'Vaern's Cove, but they were seldom as busy as they would have liked. Carts and wagons were very useful within the confines of a city, but they weren't a lot of use anywhere else, given what weather tended to do to roads on Marduk. Once you got off a paved surface, it made much more sense to rely on pack *turom* or *pagee* than to drag a wheeled vehicle through hub-deep mud. The fact that wheels would let a single beast pull a far heavier load than it could actually carry when paved surfaces were available was beside the point when those surfaces *weren't* available . . . which was virtually all the time.

Of course, the new wheels the humans had designed were different from the heavy, solid ones Kilna and Sahna had been learning to make before their arrival. Like the wheels for the new gun carriages, their spoked design was both stronger and far lighter, and if their steel rims were preposterously expensive, they should also make them last much longer. Not to mention that those rims were almost three times as wide as the rest of the wheel, which offered a huge decrease in ground pressure and should make them at least a little less inclined to sink into soft ground than traditional ones. But still . . .

"I don't know what they want with them," Sahna admitted finally. "All I know is that they told us they were important, they're paying us to make them, and we're learning new techniques no one else ever heard of." He gave the handclap of a Mardukan shrug. "Aside from that, all I can tell you is that they must have a lot of stuff they want to haul somewhere!"

Krindi Fain looked on with interest as Prince Roger examined the rifle. It was a tiny thing, compared to the weapons equipping the new rifle battalions, but the native sergeant had been around humans long enough not to nurture any foolish theories about "small" meaning "not lethal."

"Nice work, Julian," Roger said, trying the balance of the rifle. Unlike the Mardukan-scaled weapons, this one hadn't been made by converting existing arquebus barrels, which meant it represented far more man hours than one of the mass-produced weapons. On the other hand, the rifle shops had produced only forty of them.

The prince shouldered the rifle, checking the weld between cheek and buttstock, and grunted in satisfaction. It wasn't the custom-fitted stock of his hunting rifle, but it was excellent for a one-size-fits-all military weapon, and he lowered it once more to open the bolt.

There were distinct differences between that bolt and those of the Mardukan-scale rifles. In fact, aside from the fact that it was made out of old-fashioned steel and had no provision for conversion to semi-auto mode, it was effectively identical to the bolt of Roger's own rifle, complete to the small electronic contact on the bolt face, and he laughed.

"Remember that little bet beside the river, Adib?" he asked, and Julian chuckled just a bit sourly as he recalled the day he and Roger had perched in adjacent treetops, posted to cover the troops swimming a Mardukan river against the voracious predators who called that river home.

"Yes, Sir, I do," he said. "Cost me quite a few push-ups when I lost, as I recall."

"Yep," the prince said with a grin, closing the bolt and admiring the smoothness of the action. "But what I was thinking about was your suggestion that I should get myself a bead rifle because of its magazine capacity. Seems to me there's just a smidgeon of ironic humor in the situation now."

Julian snorted, but he also had to nod in agreement, and it was hard not to chuckle himself as he remembered all the times Captain Pahner—and Sergeant Adib Julian, for that matter—had groused about the way the prince's old-fashioned, nonstandard "smoke pole" complicated the ammunition supply problem. The fact that the prince would be unable to fire military bead rounds out of it when he ran out of chemical-powered ammo had been a big part of it, but so had the sheer grunt work involved in lugging along the cases of ammunition the prince (still in original, patented, pain-in-the-ass mode) had insisted on bringing down to the planet. It hadn't been all that bad once they got pack animals to take the weight instead of carting it on their own backs, but Roger had brought over nine thousand rounds down with him, which had represented a pretty severe case of overkill . . . at least until the company discovered just how nasty Mardukan jungle fauna truly was.

Most of the Marines had been prepared to forgive Roger his foibles when it turned out that his big magnum was the most effective antipredator armament they had, particularly in his skilled hands, but there'd still been the odd grumble over his habit of policing up his brass. Modern military weapons left no cartridge cases to worry about, but Roger's personal cannon littered the ground with thumb-thick brass cases every time he used it, and he'd flatly insisted on picking up after himself.

Most of it, Julian was certain, went back to the fact that even the old Roger had always taken his responsibilities seriously when in the field on safari, whether anyone else had realized it or not. But there'd been another reason, although no one had known it, since no one had bothered to ask the prince about his motives.

The Parkins and Spencer was the crown jewel of big game rifles, and Roger's cherished weapon had probably cost more than most luxury aircars. But it was also intended to be taken on safari in places so far out back of beyond that ammunition shops might be few and far between, and because of that, its ammunition had been designed for reuse and ease in reloading. The electronic igniter built into the base of each case was certified for a minimum of one hundred discharges without replacement, and although the cases themselves were still called "brass," they were actually a much more advanced alloy which could be reloaded almost infinitely without deforming, cracking, or splitting.

Which meant, given Roger's mania for cleaning up his shooting stands, that the company still had well over eight thousand perfectly serviceable rounds of ammunition, once they were reloaded with black powder. True, they wouldn't generate the velocity and kinetic energy the same rounds had when filled with the considerably more sophisticated propellant they'd been designed to use, but the cases were strong enough to take maximum capacity loads of black powder, which still produced something no one in his right mind wanted hitting him. And a kick like an irritated *flar-ta* . . . not to mention a smoke cloud from Hell.

Still and all, that ammo's existence had certainly justified manufacturing forty custom rifles to provide each surviving human with one, plus spares. It gave the company around two hundred rounds per rifle, too—more like three hundred and fifty for each of the surviving riflemen. That wasn't a spit in a hurricane compared to the sort of ammunition expenditures bead rifles used up on full auto, or even in three-round burst mode, but it was a hell of a lot for a bolt action rifle. Not to mention the fact that at the moment the company had a total of exactly one hundred and eleven bead rifle rounds.

And Julian knew *exactly* how much it amused the prince to see the entire surviving company carrying around *his* ammo after all the grief the Marines had given him over his choice of weapon.

"I still say it's a pain in the ass," the sergeant said after a moment. "Yeah, yeah—I know all about 'field expedients.' But the projectile drop on these things is a bitch!"

"That's because you Marine pussies are spoiled," Roger told him smugly as he handed the weapon back over. "The muzzle velocities on those bead rifles of yours are so high they've got about the same ballistic profile as a laser over their effective sight range. This kind of weapon takes a *real* marksman!"

"Oh, yeah?" Julian challenged. "In that case, let's see you fire some of these black powder monsters out of something besides that Parkins and Spencer of yours!"

"A petty thought, Sergeant," Roger said loftily. "Very petty."

Both of them grinned at that, because unlike the rifles the K'Vaernians were making up for the humans, Roger's big magnum had a built in system to measure projectile velocities without a chronograph. Better still, it automatically fed the information on the last round fired to the rifle's holographic sight unit, which, in turn, automatically adjusted the sight's point of aim. Just knowing exactly where to aim wasn't enough to make a crack shot out of anyone who hadn't mastered the techniques to make sure the bullet actually went there, but it did help to explain some of Roger's uncanny ability to make the really long-range shots.

"Well, I never thought I'd admit it," Julian said, "but I guess I really am glad you brought that smoke pole along. Mind you, I'd still prefer a bead rifle—or to have the damned plasma rifles on-line!—but if I can't have that, this is a pretty damned good substitute. Thanks, Your Highness."

"Don't mention it, Sarge," Roger said, clapping him on the shoulder. "Remember, it's my imperial ass, too, if we come up short against the Boman."

Julian nodded, and the prince smacked his shoulder again, nodded briskly, and strode off, followed by Cord and his assigned bodyguards.

"Sure it is," the NCO said, so quietly that Fain could barely hear him. "Sure it is . . . and the only thing you're worried about, too, I bet!"

The human laughed, shook his head, and turned back to the native sergeant.

"Now, Krindi, about those bayonets—"

★ ★ ★

Poertena stood beside the building ways and watched the swarming K'Vaernian shipwrights at their work.

There was no real possibility of completing the vessels the humans would require for their transoceanic voyage out of the resources currently available in K'Vaern's Cove. But there was enough seasoned timber to begin laying down the keels and frames, and the fairing battens were already in place. The light planking ran over the frames Poertena had selected to establish the lines of the hull, and the local shipwrights were busily setting up the intermediate frames within the template so established. All in all, the little Pinopan was more than satisfied with how quickly his teams were working. And they *were* "his" teams.

Once the Council had committed to full-bore support for the shipbuilding project, that carefully hoarded, officially "nonexistent" timber had started falling out of certain artfully concealed stockpiles, and the shipwrights' guild had turned out hundreds of trained shipbuilders. At first, enthusiasm had been limited, despite the Council's insistence and financial support. However, even the grumpiest and most conservative of the workers had been delighted to have work at all, given the current besieged state of the city, and there'd been a certain excitement over building such large ships to such a novel design. And what Poertena had been able to show them about molding lines and lofting hulls properly had been devoured with a burning passion. But for all that, there'd also been a great deal of skepticism, for no one had ever suggested the hull form and, particularly, the rig Poertena had designed.

Most of that skepticism had disappeared once he got his "technology demonstrator" into the water, however. Given the support of the Council, he'd been able to get the ten-meter test vehicle built and launched considerably more quickly than he'd anticipated. In fact, he'd managed it almost as quickly as Captain Pahner had demanded, and he was justifiably pleased with himself for the accomplishment.

He was also deeply satisfied with how well the new craft had performed. Some adjustments had been required, but the basic hull form was a well established and thoroughly proven one, used all over

Pinopa and virtually identical to what had once been called a "Baltimore clipper" on Earth. Although Poertena had worked for almost four standard years in his uncle's yard on Pinopa to help defray his college expenses, this was the first time in decades that he'd turned his hand to any sort of design work, and he was actually a bit surprised that he'd gotten it as close to right as he had. He'd been forced to move the mainmast of his twin-masted design about one meter aft, and there was a little more hoist to the big gaff foresail, which was actually the primary sail for this rig, than there really ought to have been, as well. Like most Pinopans, all of whom had a certain mania for fast ships, Poertena had a tendency to over-spar his designs. Unlike some of his fellows, though, he also recognized that he did, and he'd modified his sail plan accordingly.

Despite those minor flaws, however, the demonstrator had been a complete success, particularly when it came to laying the doubts of the local maritime community to rest. The expressions and consternation of the Cove's grizzled captains as they watched the half-sized topsail schooner go bounding across the dark blue of the K'Vaernian Sea, leaving a ruler-straight wake of creamy white as she sailed almost twenty degrees closer to the wind than any other ship in the world could have, had been priceless. And well they should have been. The ability to sail a single compass point—just a hair over eleven degrees—closer to the wind than another ship meant that the more weatherly vessel would be almost four minutes ahead, all other things being equal, after sailing a mere thirty kilometers. Beating dead to windward, a ship which could sail no closer than fifty degrees to the wind (which was better than any of the locally produced designs could manage) would have to travel fifty-two kilometers to make good thirty-two, whereas Poertena's new design would have to travel only forty-two kilometers, or only eighty percent of the same run. That was an advantage, over a voyage of many hundred kilometers, which no merchant skipper could fail to appreciate, and it didn't even consider the fact that being able to sail closer to the wind than a pursuer could would provide an invaluable insurance policy against pirates . . . or that the new rig required a much smaller crew of sail-handlers. Those thoughts had suggested themselves almost instantly to the captains watching Poertena's design go through her paces, and when she spun on her heel, shooting neatly across the wind to settle on the opposite tack and go racing onward at a speed no other ship could have sustained, those same captains had been ready to kill for ships of their own like her.

To the Mardukans, Poertena's little ship was pure magic, and they regarded him with the sort of awe which was the just due of any irascible wizard. There might be questions about the humans' endless store of innovations in some quarters, but aside from two or three dyed-in-the-wool reactionaries, there were no longer any in the shipbuilding community. And while the Cove's seamen still had enormous reservations about the wisdom—or sanity—of any attempt to cross the ocean, they were thoroughly prepared to embrace the new rigging concept and hull form, and Poertena had used their desire to master the new techniques unscrupulously. He was perfectly willing to teach them to anyone . . . as long as his students agreed to sign on for the voyage. More than a few would-be students disappeared into the woodwork when he explained his conditions, but a much larger number agreed. Not without trepidation, and not—he was certain—without comforting themselves in many cases with the belief that the voyage might never happen, but they agreed.

He suspected that Wes Til's strong backing had more than a little to do with that. As Til had half suggested he might at the first Council meeting, the canny merchant had agreed to subsidize the cost of building the new ships in return for Pahner's promise that the ships and crews would be his once the humans were delivered to the far side of the ocean. The fact that the Council had also agreed to pick up a third of the construction cost, and that his shipyards were building them (and thus acquiring an enormous headstart on his competition where the new techniques and technology were concerned *and* recouping a good chunk of his own outlays) had been a factor as well, of course, but Poertena had no problems with that. Even with the Council's contribution to the cost, Til was picking up the tab on an enormously expensive project, and he certainly deserved to show a handsome return on the risk he was running. Besides, his contacts in the seafaring community, especially with Turl Kam's backing, had been essential to recruiting the sailors which the expedition would require.

Now the Pinopan stood in the dockyard, watching the work progress, and hoped that the campaign Captain Pahner and the Mardukan commanders were putting together would come off as planned.

If it didn't, he was going to run out of timber in about another two weeks.

Roger was devoutly thankful for his ear plugs as he walked behind the line of firing Mardukans with Cord. The concussion from each shot was chest-compressing, which was hardly surprising, since the "rifles" would have been considered light artillery by most humans.

Each firing pit held a firer, a trainee coach, and a human or Diaspran safety coach. The targets were outlines of a Boman warrior, including an outline of an upraised ax. Many of the axes had been blown away by an avalanche of bullets over the last few weeks, but the system still worked. When a recessed metal plate in the primary target zone was struck, the target would fall, then rise back up a moment later. Hits anywhere else, even in the head, wouldn't drop the target.

Roger saw a spark on the head of the target in front of him and lay down on the ground behind the firer. It gave him a better perspective on the shooting while he listened to the safety coach.

"Get your barrel lower." The trainee coach was a Diaspran, a former Laborer of God, to judge from the muscles in his shoulders and back, with a deep, powerful voice which managed to carry through the thunder of rifle fire. "Shoot that barbarian bastard in the gut! It hurts them worse."

"Also," Roger put in from behind the pit, "a bullet shot low will tend to hit *something* even if you miss your target. One that goes flying overhead does nothing but let that barbarian bastard through to kill you. And your buddies."

"Excuse me, Sir!" The Diaspran started to scramble to his feet. "I didn't realize you were back there."

Roger waved all three back down.

"Continue what you're doing. We don't have time for all that saluting and scraping and bowing. We pull out for D'Sley in three days, and every one of us had better be ready." He turned to the K'Vaernian private in the fox hole. "A few days—a week—and you're going to be in one of these facing *real* Boman. Barbarians with axes that have no purpose in life but to kill you. Every single time you squeeze that trigger, I want you to keep that in mind. Got it?"

"Yes, Your Highness," the K'Vaernian said.

From his looks, the rifleman had been a fisherman until a month and a half ago, with nothing to worry about but whether his boat's nets would bring in enough fish to keep the wolf from the door, or whether a sudden storm would send the boat to the bottom, like so many before it. Now he was faced with radically different stresses, like the possibility that someone he'd never met, and had never hurt, would try to kill him, and the question of whether or not he could kill in return. Roger could see the confusion in his face, and produced a smile.

"Just keep your aim low, and follow the orders of your officers, Troop," he said with a chuckle. "And if your officers are dead, and your sergeants look white, remember, it's ruin to run. Just lay down and hold your ground and wait for supports, like a soldier."

"Yes, Sir, Your Highness!"

Roger pushed himself to his feet, nodded to the other two, and continued down the line with his *asi*.

"There was something suspiciously polished about that last statement, 'Your Highness,'" Cord observed, and Roger smiled.

"More of the Captain's Kipling," he said, "I ran across it in a book at the Academy, but I'd almost completely forgotten about it. It's called 'The Half-Made Recruit.' 'Just take open order, lie down and sit tight, and wait for supports like a soldier. Wait, wait, wait like a soldier. Soldier of the Queen.'"

"Ah," the shaman said. "A good sentiment for them, then. And it sounds familiar."

"Really?" the prince looked up at his *asi*, wondering just how much Kipling Pahner had shared with the old shaman, but refrained from repeating the last stanza of the poem:

When you're wounded and left on Afghanistan's plains,
And the women come out to cut up what remains,
Just roll to your rifle and blow out your brains,
And go to your God like a soldier.
Go, go, go like a soldier.
Soldier of the Queen.

Turl Kam copied the posture of the humans around him, standing with his foot and peg not too far apart and all four hands clasped behind his back. The blocks of fresh-minted soldiers striding by were impressive. He had to admit that, yet he wished that he was as inwardly confident as his outward appearance proclaimed.

"We've poured out money and political capital like water," the one-legged ex-fisherman said. "I've bullied friends, tormented enemies, and lied to everyone but my wife—and the only reason I didn't lie to *her* was because she agreed with me and was busy helping me lie to everyone else. So tell me one more time that you're going to be able to do something with this army."

Captain Pahner looked at the ranks of four-armed natives, brand-new harnesses polished, their freshly made pikes, assegais, or rifles gleaming under the bright pewter sky.

"There are no guarantees in war, Sir. The troops have trained hard in the time they've had, we've picked the best officers we could find, and we've got pretty damn good initial intelligence on the enemy. That puts us in the best position we could realistically expect, but all I can absolutely promise is that we'll try. Hard."

"Your plan is complex," the chairman grumped. "Too complex."

"It is," Pahner agreed. "Especially for a green army. But if we're going to take the field with you, we've got to come up with a way to hit them hard and do it fast, and at least there are three bullets in our gun. Any one of them could—probably would—kill the Boman. Certainly we should eliminate them as a threat for the remainder of this year if even one of them works properly. If all three work, then we should eliminate the Boman threat permanently . . . and reduce our own casualties enormously."

"I suppose that will have to be good enough," the chairman said, sighing.

"I will tell you this," Pahner said, after a moment. "You, and your society, will never be the same again. Once the genie's out of the bottle, you can't put him back."

"Excuse me?" Kam looked at the human in perplexity, and Pahner shrugged.

"Sorry. It's an expression my own people use. What it means is that once a new idea or a new invention is turned loose, it takes on a life of its own, and you can't get rid of it. These weapons won't just go away, and using any new weapon just gets easier and easier . . . especially if they let you kick the shit out of your enemies on the cheap."

"I suppose so," the chairman said. "But perhaps this will be the last war. Surely we'll learn from this, put away these toys, and become a society devoted to peaceful trade."

The Marine looked up at the towering Mardukan, and it was his turn to sigh.

"Let's talk about this after the battle, okay?"

"Bravo Company?" Fain stepped up to the sergeant assembling the riflemen.

"Yes, Sir," the K'Vaernian NCO said, and snapped to attention.

The docks behind the group of K'Vaernian riflemen were a picture of frenzied activity. Hundreds of watercraft, from barges barely fit to navigate across the Bay to grain ships that normally plied their trade along the coast, were lined up, disgorging soldiers and cargo. As Fain watched, a column of pikes formed up and marched inland. Beyond them, one of the new bronze "field pieces" was being swayed out of a grain ship's hold and down to the dock, where its limber and team of draft *turom* were already waiting for it.

D'Sley's whole lifeblood had been trade. Located in the swamps created by the Tam River as it neared the sea, the city had controlled the estuary of that vital waterway. Since the estuary was relatively shallow, most seacraft had unloaded their cargo on these docks and cross loaded it to barges designed for river trade. Most of the latter had been destroyed or stolen by the Boman, but there had been numerous shipyards and stockpiles of building materials scattered around the city, most of which hadn't been lost, stolen, or burned.

"Don't call me 'Sir'!" the Diaspran sergeant snapped. "I work for a living. This is your guide. You know where you're supposed to go?"

"Southwest wall," the K'Vaernian NCO said, and nodded to the D'Sley woman who was to guide them to their positions.

"You don't have a problem with following a woman, do you?" Fain asked. There damn well would have been problems for a Diaspran unit, and he knew it, but these K'Vaernians didn't seem to mind.

"Not at all," the K'Vaernian said.

"Okay, move out when you have eight out of ten of your people. We'll round up the stragglers back here and send them along."

"We're ready to go now, then," the other NCO said. "Except I don't know where our captain is."

"He'll be along. Most of the officers are in officer's call at the moment." Fain handed the other sergeant a hastily prepared map. "Here. There's been some damage to the city. This should help, if you get lost. Move out."

"Yes, Si—Sergeant," the K'Vaernian said as he took the map, then turned to the company of riflemen. "Okay, you maggots! Fall in and get ready to move! Act like you've got a pair!"

"You're ready?" Fain asked the guide, who kept her eyes on the ground but made a gesture of agreement.

"Yes, Lord."

"Don't call me— Oh, never mind. Just don't let anyone bully you, and guide them well, all right?"

"Yes, Lord," the woman said. "I won't fail you."

"Don't fail *yourself*," the Diaspran responded. "Good luck."

The infantry marched off on the guide's heels, merging with the swarm of pikemen and spearmen funneling into the city, and Fain looked over his shoulder as the first troop of cavalry pounded past towards the distant, shattered gate. Someone in the next regiment raised a cheer, and the officer at the head of the cantering troop flourished his sword until they were out of sight in the ruined city.

"And good luck to you, you poor bastards," the sergeant said softly.

Roger looked out at the city through the open flap of the command tent. D'Sley had been much smaller than K'Vaern's Cove, but it had, by all reports, been quite beautiful in its heyday. The construction of the city on a rise in the middle of the tree-filled swamp had run heavily to wood, however, and when the Boman horde washed over its low walls, not even the Mardukan climate had been able to prevent the fires from getting out of hand.

Some of the piles of corpses near the docks, most of which were, thankfully, done decomposing, showed clear signs of having been heated to the point where bone burned. It must have been a veritable firestorm, so there wasn't much to be found in the way of sights. Just scattered chimneys, blackened stubs of pillars, and the curtain walls. Most of the lumber and shipyards, though, had been *outside* the walls, fortunately.

"It looks like the city was stripped before being burned," Julian was saying. "There are no signs of grain in the ruins of the granaries, and all the worked materials are gone from the ironworks. All the ore that should be there is, though."

"So did they use boats, or carry it out by land?" Pahner asked.

"Land," Rus From said. "The trail to Sindi is badly damaged from heavy traffic, and there are no indications of barge construction. I'd say everything left by land."

"What's available in the shipyards?" the Marine CO asked, swiveling his head to look at Poertena.

"Ever't'ing we need," the Pinopan said with a huge grin. "We can get to work shippin' it back home to tee Cove right away."

"Do it," the captain said, and turned to Fullea Li'it. "How's the transfer going?"

"Well," the widow answered, consulting a scroll of notes. "All of your infantry regiments are across. The cannon and rockets are all unloaded, and most of the provisions are across. We're cross loading to the barges, and that will be completed by tomorrow."

"Tor?"

"We're still pushing the field force through," the Guard's second in command and designated CO for the D'Sley garrison said. "My people will be coming ashore starting tomorrow. Don't worry, Captain. Whatever happens at Sindi, D'Sley is going to stay firmly in our hands."

"Rastar?"

"We had to take the long road around the end of the Bay," the pistol-covered Northerner said, taking a sip of wine, "but we're all here. We didn't run into anyone on the way, either, and we'll be ready to move out again in the morning."

"Get used to long days in the saddle; there are lots more to come," Pahner told him, and looked back to Julian. "The Boman haven't moved?"

"No, Sir. Not *en masse*. Parties of them have come and gone from the city, some of them quite large, but the main force there is sitting tight, and those nodal forces of theirs are sitting just as tight on what used to be other cities."

"I still don't understand that," Bistem Kar admitted candidly. "It's not like them at all."

"We already knew the bastards had learned not to throw themselves straight at fortified walls at Therdan," Rastar told him with bleak pride. "Obviously, they're sitting in place and waiting for starvation to weaken the Cove before they hit it."

"Oh, that part we understand," Tor Flain assured him. "They've never been smart and patient enough to try it before, but there can't be much doubt that that's exactly what they're doing. But it's the way they're deployed while they wait that bothers me."

"There could be several reasons for it, Tor," Bogess suggested. "For one thing, Julian was right about the additional security it offers their women and children."

Bistem Kar gave a hand-clap of conditional agreement, but he still looked decidedly unhappy, and Pahner didn't really blame him. The comfortable belief that all of the Boman were clustered in and around Sindi had turned out to be somewhat less than accurate once Gunny Jin and his LURPs got into position. Actually, smaller forces of a "mere" ten to fifteen thousand warriors each had been deployed to the sites of several of the other conquered League and non-League city-states . . . all of them on the far side of Sindi from D'Sley. But so far as Jin and his human and Mardukan scouts had been able to determine, those satellite forces had only a relative handful of women and children as supporting camp followers. At least half of all the Boman dependents were packed into Sindi with "only" thirty or forty thousand warriors to keep them company. What was more, the women and children in the city apparently came from every Boman clan and tribe, not just from those of the warriors deployed there.

"No doubt the sergeant is correct, at least in part," Kar told Bogess after a moment. "Certainly Sindi had the best fortifications of any of the states outside the League, and from all reports, they took the city—and its walls—pretty much intact. So, yes, it probably *is* the best and most easily defended place from which to protect their families. But Boman clans *always* stay together, and they trust no one—not even tribes of the same clan—to protect their women and children." He shook his head in a human-style gesture. "We've seen entirely too many innovations from the Boman to make me happy, and this strikes me as another. I would be much happier if I understood precisely what it's intended to accomplish."

"We're trying to figure that out, Sir," Julian told him, "but we haven't been able to get any of our listening devices actually into the city . . . yet. From what the shotgun mikes have picked up from the troops' bull sessions, though, it's pretty clear that this Kny Camsan has a whole bunch of new ideas, and this seems to be one of them. Lot of the troops aren't too crazy about some of his notions, either, but Camsan's the one who took over after Therdan, and he's kicked so much ass since then that he's almost like God. Or he was right after they took Sindi, anyway. It looks like some of the shine may be starting to wear off from the troops' perspective—kind of a 'but what have you done for us lately' sort of attitude."

The intel NCO gazed down at the map on the table for a few moments, then shrugged.

"Whatever he's up to, at least we know where the bastard is, and the whole Boman position is still pretty much a holding one. Mostly, they seem to be busy foraging around the cities, and I imagine they'll sit right where they are until they finish eating the countryside bare and don't have any choice but to move on out. In the meantime, though, we know where they are and, so far as we can tell, they *don't* know where *we* are.

"The scout teams report that the maps are fairly accurate," he continued. "There've been some changes—like the damage the roads have taken from the Boman's use, like the track from here to Sindi. But in general, the cavalry should be able to trust them."

"Good," Pahner said. "Better than I could've hoped. Rus, is the damage to the track going to slow up your work crews' transit?"

"Not appreciably." The cleric took a bite of apsimon. "They'll be mainly foot traffic, and they can keep to the shoulders if they have to. By the time we're ready for the caravans, we should have all the road repair gangs in place."

"You need to make the timetable," the Marine said warningly. "If you don't, that whole part of the plan is out the window."

The cleric shrugged all four shoulders.

"It's in the hands of the God, quite literally. Heavy storms will prevent us, but other than that, I see no reason to fear. We'll make the schedule, Captain Pahner, unless the God very specifically prevents."

"Fullea?"

"We'll be waiting," the D'Sley matron said. "We're already repairing the dock facilities, and things will go much quicker once we get some decent cranes back in action. We'll make *our* timetable."

"Rastar?"

"Hmmm? Oh, timetable. Not a problem. Just a ride in the country."

"I swear, you're getting as bad as Honal," Roger said with a chuckle.

"Ah, it's these beautiful pistols you gave me!" the Northerner prince enthused. "With such weapons, how can we fail?"

"You're not to become decisively engaged," Pahner warned.

"Not a chance, Captain," the Northerner promised much more seriously. "We've fought this battle before, and we didn't have any friends waiting for us that time. Don't worry; we aren't planning on leaving our horns on their mantels. Besides, I want to see what cannon do to them, and we won't have any of our own along."

"Bistem? Bogess?"

"It will be interesting," the K'Vaernian said. "Very interesting."

"A masterly understatement, but accurate," the Diaspran agreed.

"Interesting is fine, but are you ready?" Roger asked. "Some of the units still seem pretty scrambled."

"They'll be ready by tomorrow morning," Kar assured him, and Tor Flain nodded in agreement.

"All right," Pahner said, looking at the tent roof. "We'll transfer the bulk of the cavalry tomorrow. Once they're off, we'll embark the infantry. As we're doing all of that, we'll also push out aggressive patrols on this side of the river to screen our advance. Starting tomorrow."

He gazed up at the roof for a few more seconds, obviously running through a mental checklist, then looked at Roger.

"One small change," he said. "Roger, I want you to take over the Carnan Battalion of the New Model. That and one troop of cavalry—Rastar, you choose which."

"Yes, Captain." The Mardukan nodded.

"They're going to be moving with the infantry. Roger will command the combined force as a strategic reserve. Roger, look at putting *turom* under all the infantry."

"If you're thinking of a mobile infantry battalion, *civan* would be better," Roger said. "Also, aren't we going to need the *turom* elsewhere?"

"We'll see. If you can get them on *turom* in the next three days, they'll go upriver behind the cavalry screen. If you can't, they'll go with the infantry."

"Yes, Sir," the prince responded.

"Okay," the captain concluded. "Get as much rest as you can tonight. There won't be much from here on out."

CHAPTER THIRTY-ONE

The gentle current of the river was barely enough to make the barge bob, but the war *civan* was having none of it.

"Get *on* there, you son of a bitch!" Honal snarled, but the *civan* was remarkably impervious to his rider's gentle encouragement. Finally, the cavalry commander gave up. "Get some ropes!"

Enough lines on the horse-ostrich and enough hands on the lines finally managed to drag the recalcitrant beast onto the barge.

"Last one, Rastar!"

"Good, we're already behind schedule," the Northern prince replied, and turned to look over his shoulder as something moved up behind him.

"Good luck, you two," Roger said. The prince was riding his huge war *pagee* again, with that weird creature from the far lands and his war slave up on her back. It was fortunate indeed, Rastar reflected, that the captain's plan didn't require Roger to cross the river. Getting that huge beast on a barge would have been far worse than unpleasant.

The last prince of fallen Therdan looked past the human and his odd companions to the troop of cavalry following along behind the *pagee*. Chim Pri, the troop leader, was a cousin of sorts, a distant one, but he'd shown great promise on the retreat and in Diaspra. He also worshiped the ground Roger strode on, so detailing his troop as bodyguards—whatever the captain might call it—had been an easy decision.

Rastar was hard put not to grunt in laughter at the sight of the brand-new banner snapping in the breeze beside Patty. It had been Honal's idea to have the thing made, but Rastar had gotten behind and pushed once his cousin suggested it. It hadn't been easy to get it made without Roger's discovering that they were up to something, but the expression on the prince's face when it was formally presented had made all of the secrecy and skulking about eminently worthwhile. Rastar hadn't been certain whether Roger wanted to laugh or shoot them on the spot, which was more or less what he'd expected. What he hadn't expected was the fierce pride the prince's new personal cavalry troop took in their banner.

Rastar watched the stiff breeze blow the *dianda* standard straight out to display the *basik* head. Of course, it didn't depict *quite* a standard *basik*. This one lacked the timidly inoffensive and stupid expression of the original, and the mouthful of needle-sharp fangs—clearly exposed in a particularly nasty-looking human-style grin—were hardly part of the issue equipment of the garden-variety *basik*.

On the other hand, they went very well with the incredibly deadly *basik* who commanded the cavalry riding under it.

"Good luck yourself," Rastar told him now. "And try not to get killed. Captain Pahner would do all manner of incredibly painful things to me if you did something that stupid."

"Coward," Roger said, and Rastar shook a playful fist up at him.

"Just make sure you're ready when we come scampering back," Honal put in with a grunt of laughter.

"We will be," Roger said. "I swear it."

Rastar stuck out a true-hand, and Roger leaned down to take it.

"Keep your powder dry," the human said in a voice which was only half-teasing.

"We will." The Northern prince spurred his war *civan*, and the beast easily trotted down the planks onto the barge beside Honal's recalcitrant mount. "See you in Sindi."

* * *

"*No!*" Kny Camsan, paramount war leader of the Boman, slammed a fisted true-hand onto the table hard enough to send half the cups flying into the air and spill wine everywhere. Not that it mattered particularly, for the floor of the former throne room was well over a centimeter deep in food and other debris. The once splendid chamber reeked like a midden, but the barbarians lying on mats of straw atop the mire paid no more attention to the muck than they did to the stench.

"We have those K'Vaernian bastards right where we want them," the war leader continued in grating tones, "and I, for one, have no intention of throwing myself at their walls until they're a hell of a lot weaker than they are right now. I am *not* letting anyone repeat Therdan."

There was a mutter of agreement at that. The war leader who'd decided that Therdan could simply be overrun with enough bodies had died in the second wave, but Boman in fighting frenzy weren't precisely noted for tactical flexibility, and the waves had continued while the tribal leaders argued over who would replace him. And while they argued, nearly a tenth part of the combined clans had died.

"K'Vaern's Cove isn't Therdan," Knitz De'n argued. "And they're just sitting there like *knivet* in a burrow. They obviously aren't going to send forces out, and if they won't come out to fight, we should strike them now. Instead, we sit in our own shit in this foul city when we should be on the trail to war, not hiding behind walls!"

"He has a point," Mnb Trag said mildly. The old chieftain was Camsan's closest adviser, but he was also smart enough to appear receptive to the suggestions and demands of others. It was, as he'd shown Camsan, one of the most effective ways to *defuse* those demands. Unfortunately, it worked better for an adviser or the chieftain of a single clan than it did for a paramount war leader, and Camsan glowered at De'n.

"Let the damned shit-sitters break *their* teeth on walls for a change!" he shot back. "If you want to attack K'Vaern's Cove, go ahead, but I shall remain here until they're on their knees. And when they're weak enough, then we'll destroy *that* city and return to our homes. That's what we swore—that's what *you* swore—to do. To remain as long as it took to destroy the Southerners once and for all."

"And that's what we want to do!" Knitz De'n snapped. "Let the shit-sitters hide inside their walls if they want—*we* are the warriors of the Boman!"

The women came out with new cups of wine and more cooked meat. The herds of *turom* and *pagee* which had supported the city now feasted on its fields, and the Boman feasted on them. When they were gone, the clans would have to move as well, but not yet. And when they did move, Camsan intended to accomplish something no other Boman chieftain had ever accomplished. Which, of course, was the true reason so many of the other clans' women and children were here at Sindi under the "protection" of his own clan and its closest allies.

Not that he was prepared to explain any of that to De'n. The young firebrand was too arrogant and ambitious to be admitted to all of Camsan's plans. Unfortunately, Camsan knew De'n spoke for a growing fraction of even those warriors in Sindi, so he dared not simply ignore him, either.

"Perhaps there's some point to your argument," the war leader told the younger tribesman as one of the women replaced his own wine cup. "I won't rush to attack the walls of K'Vaern's Cove, but we are Boman, and even the sharpest ax grows dull if it's allowed to rust too long upon the wall. I would not have you grow rusty when I'll soon have need of your strong arm, Knitz De'n, and there are reports of League cavalry on the land road from K'Vaern's Cove to D'Sley. Why don't you take your band and go see what's happening? If you find any of those League shit-sitters, kill them for us, and take their goods for your own. Then check D'Sley and make sure the shit-sitters aren't trying to rebuild it or something."

De'n looked at him for a long moment, obviously aware that he was about to be dispatched on a task which was little more than make-work designed to get him out from under Camsan's feet. Yet his own demands for a more active policy left him little choice but to obey, and so he stood and walked out without another word.

Mnb Trag rubbed his horns as he watched him go.

"We do need to do something soon," Trag said much more quietly to Camsan. "He's not the only one complaining."

"I know he's not," Camsan responded, equally quietly. "And I also know that if we sit here long enough, the plague demons will begin to carry off our warriors." The nomadic Boman had developed very little of the resistance to diseases which city dwellers required, particularly on a planet like Marduk, where no one had ever heard of the germ theory of disease or the necessity for public hygiene. "But if our prisoners spoke truthfully, then K'Vaern's Cove isn't nearly so well supplied as we'd feared, now is it? And," the war leader added with an evil chuckle, "I feel confident somehow that they were truthful with us, don't you?"

It was Trag's turn to chuckle. The greatest prize the Boman had taken in their entire campaign had been the capture of Tor Cant, the shit-sitter whose treachery had united the clans—however temporarily—at last. It was hard to believe that even *he* could have been stupid enough to allow himself to be taken alive, but Trag had come to the conclusion that there was nothing Tor Cant hadn't been stupid enough to do. It was a pity, in some ways, because for all of his stupidity the one-time Despot of Sindi had possessed a certain devious cunning. He might have amounted to something if he'd had a single *sekr* of brain or even a trace of backbone to go with that quality.

Fortunately for the Boman, he'd had neither. It had taken him almost six days to die, but he'd told them everything they could ever have wanted to know about his betrayals of his fellow shit-sitters before the first iron had even begun to glow. Most of the "councilors" and advisers they'd captured with him had taken their cue from their despot . . . not that their efforts to buy their lives with their information had worked, of course. But it did mean that Kny Camsan knew all there was to know about both the strengths and weaknesses of his last remaining foes.

"I share your confidence in their . . . honesty," Trag said after a moment, "and the K'Vaernian Guard is far too small to be a threat in the field. All they can do is hold their walls, and they won't be able to do even that once starvation sets in properly. But their accursed navy remains intact. Can we be certain that they'll be unable to fill their granaries?"

"From where?" Camsan chuckled scornfully. "We've destroyed all of the other shit-sitter cities around the sea and throughout the Tam Valley, and the other clans sit on their fields and devour their animals. All they can offer K'Vaern's Cove is more mouths to feed and no food to feed them with." He clapped hands in a gesture of negation. "No, Trag, hunger will begin to bite them long before the demons weaken us. Then they'll come out and fight, or they'll go aboard their stinking boats and flee, and either way, we'll take their city and burn it to the ground."

"And the League cavalry?" Trag asked.

"We'll see," the war leader said, taking a bite of half-raw *civan*. "True, the iron heads had more guts than these worthless Southerners, but there can't be many of them left. I doubt there's anything to the rumors, but we'll see. And if there isn't, we'll send some of the youngsters out to K'Vaern's Cove to see how it's defended. If it looks weak, or if they're beginning to run low on food already, we'll put in an attack to probe their defenses. But I am *not* going to repeat Therdan."

Not, at least, until I've taken K'Vaern's Cove, as well . . . and made my position as paramount war leader something more permanent, he added silently. He didn't say it aloud, although that wasn't because he distrusted Trag. His older ally knew all about his plans, he was sure, despite the fact that they had never openly discussed them, and if Trag had disapproved, one of them would already be dead.

"All right," Trag said after only the briefest moment, "but be warned. Hungry or not, those damned K'Vaernians have always been too tricky to make me happy."

"I can't believe we've gotten this close without these idiots even guessing we're here," Honal said.

After being ferried across the river, the cavalry had taken back trails up to a point just outside Sindi. Thanks to the reports from the Marine long-range reconnaissance patrols, the Northerners had been able to avoid the scattered clusters of Boman on the north side of the river between D'Sley and Sindi. Not that there'd been many of those clusters to avoid.

Sindi, the undisputed queen of the upper Tam, had originally been built on the south side of the river, but it had long since spread to both banks, taking its impressively fortified walls with it. Before the Boman came, it had been surrounded by vast fields of barleyrice, which the constant rains were rapidly destroying, now that no one tended them any longer. But its true wealth had lain in the fact that it had controlled the only bridge across the river for *hurtongs*. The bridge itself was a massive stone construction at the heart of the city, wide enough for four *pagee* or twenty warriors abreast, whose completion, generations before, had really begun the history of Sindi.

Although Sindi had drawn most of its wealth and power from its position on the Tam, the city was actually located at the confluence of three rivers. A smaller stream, the Stell, flowed into the Tam on the western side of the city, where the road to D'Sley crossed it on a narrow stone bridge and then continued on through spreading fields to the distant jungle. The third river, the Thorm, joined the Tam just upstream from the city, flowing down from the northeast and eventually becoming unnavigable not far from one of the Northern League cities.

The cavalry troopers had turned progressively more grim as they drew closer to the destroyed cities which had been their homes, but Rastar wasn't worried. He knew they were fully focused on their target, and he was confident that they understood the mission brief. Which seemed to be working out almost perfectly—so far, at least—he told himself, because Honal was right. The Boman clearly didn't have a clue that they were anywhere near. Before the barbarian invasion, there would have been Sindi cavalry patrols this far out to spot them, or at least workers in the fields, but now there was nothing at all on the north side of the river beyond the city gates themselves. All of the field huts had been burned, and nothing moved here but an occasional *basik*.

So far, so good.

"It's a *hurtong* to the gates," Rastar said. "Clande, your group will stop here and hold. Get the surprise set up along the trail, and don't let anybody we may have missed sneak up behind us, or we're all pocked."

"Yes, Rastar." The young cousin might have argued once that rear area security was hardly the job of a warrior. But the only survivors of the League of the North were those who'd learned the lessons which had made their survival possible, and the hotheaded "warrior" who would once have argued was one with last season's rains.

"The rest of you," Rastar went on, sweeping Honal's subordinate officers with his eyes, "remember why we're here, and don't get too enthusiastic. It's not like there's all that much we can really do if they're hiding inside the city, after all! We'll make a charge at the gate and see if that works. It probably won't, so we'll put some grapnels on the walls. When they start throwing their damned axes, shoot a few of them—but don't, for the gods' sake, let them realize how effective the rifles and revolvers are. When they get their shit together, we back off and taunt."

"We've heard this before, Rastar," Honal said patiently and squinted up into the gathering light as the morning drizzle began. "Let's go."

The last prince of Therdan looked at his cousin and nodded.

"Let's all be charming lures, shall we?"

"Absolutely," Honal said. "Sheffan! Front!"

"Julian," Gunny Jin whispered into his radio, "give me the Old Man."

"Pahner here."

"The cavalry are starting the demonstration, Sir."

"Good. Give me an update if the situation changes."

The massive gates shrugged off the thunderous explosion with scarcely a quiver.

"Oh, very nice," Rastar said. "They should be convinced they're impregnable now."

"Yes," Honal agreed. "And so far, we haven't even lost anyone."

That, Rastar knew, would change as soon as the sun rose above the eternal clouds. Already, the Boman could be seen on top of the high wall, running around without apparent direction. A few groups of cavalry had gotten grapnels up on the battlements and were swarming, slowly and carefully, up the lines. As the two commanders watched, a group of barbarians got one of the heavy hook-and-line arrangements unfastened and hurled it over the side. The grapnel, fortunately, didn't hit anyone, but the shower of throwing axes which followed it emptied a few saddles. Nor had all the Boman activity been as pointless as it had looked, and more than one Northerner flinched as a pair of massive hooped bombards fired from a bastion of the main gate in a huge belch of lurid flame and thick smoke. Fortunately, the Boman gunners had only a vague notion of how artillery was supposed to work, and they hit nothing. The arquebusiers who'd finally begun assembling in their covered positions were another matter, however. They were no more accurate than the bombards, individually, but there were far more of them, and more saddles began to empty, while here and there a *civan* went down bellowing in pain.

"Time to call them back," Rastar ordered.

"Got it."

The high call of the *glitchen* horn rang out through the rain, signaling for the cavalry to pull away from the walls and out of ax range, and Rastar watched with an approving eye as his troopers obeyed.

"Now to do the real work," he said with a grunt of laughter.

"They're taunting us," Mnb Trag said.

"Yes," Camsan agreed. "But *why* are they taunting us?"

The Northerner cavalry had been at it all morning. Their initial attack had been a complete failure—the bags of gunpowder had barely even scratched the gates. But the small band hadn't given up, though precisely what the idiots thought they could accomplish was beyond Camsan. They'd been riding around the walls and hurling taunts at the guards for the last few hours. No scatological or genealogical detail had been left out of the suggestions which could be clearly heard on the walls, and the taunts were working, judging by the furious anger of his warriors.

"They want us to chase them," Camsan said, "so we won't."

He turned to look back over the city with a proprietary eye. Although it had taken some damage in the sack, it was still the crown jewel of the upper Tam, with rank on rank of low stone houses rising up the central hill to the citadel. Whatever else anyone could say, *he* had taken Sindi, and the horns of that hated bastard Cant. Nobody was going to take either of those accomplishments away from him, and he'd already decided that Sindi would make an appropriate capital for the new, powerful empire which would shortly replace the weak and gutless shit-sitters who had dared to challenge the Boman clans.

But his contemplation of the future was interrupted when Trag gave a handclap of negation.

"I don't think you have that choice," the older chieftain told him, and pounded on a merlon of the granite wall with one false-hand. "If you sit here much longer, looking like you're afraid to face a couple of hundred League shits in the open, you might not have a position by tomorrow."

"That bad?" the war leader asked his adviser. Trag grunted, and as Camsan turned to look at the warriors around them, he was forced to admit that his ally might have a point. "All right, take the Tarnt'e and go chase them down. There was never a group of cavalry Boman couldn't run into the ground—not even old, worn out Boman," he added with a grunt of laughter, but Trag didn't join his amusement.

"I don't think that will work either," he said somberly. "If I go out, by the time I get back, you'll have been deposed, and Knitz De'n will have taken your place."

"But if we do what De'n wants and storm K'Vaern's Cove head on, it will be the death of thousands of them," Camsan said. "Do they want that?"

"No," the older chieftain said, "but most of them figure it'll be someone else who does the dying. Besides, what they really want, most of them, is to return to their villages. But we made this stupid pact to destroy *all* the cities of the south, which means they can't go yet, so they want to destroy K'Vaern's Cove and get it over with. They're frustrated, and that's why they want to gut these iron head pukes."

"Don't they realize that the iron heads wouldn't be riding around out there all by themselves unless they *wanted* us to come out and chase them? There has to be a reason they want to lure us away from the city, Mnb."

"Of course there does, and most of our warriors know it. But if they can't burn K'Vaern's Cove to the ground, then killing these Northerners will have to do. They know perfectly well that the Northerners want them to come out from behind the walls, and they don't care. At least it would be an honorable battle. Besides, there's only three or four hundred of them."

"That's exactly my point," Camsan said. "The Tarnt'e alone would be more than enough to crush them all."

"That's *not* the point," Trag replied patiently. "You have forty thousand warriors in this stinking city, all of whom want to kill something . . . and most of whom are starting to think thoughts you'd prefer they didn't. You think they don't know some of the other clans are beginning to mutter about how many of the women and children are here under our 'protection'?"

Camsan's eyes narrowed, and this time it was Trag who grunted a harsh laugh.

"Of course they do! Fortunately, most of them think you're only trying to keep the other clan leaders in line, and I think most of them actually admire your ruthlessness. It's what we need in a war leader. But our warriors are Boman, too, and their axes have been unbloodied too long. If you don't give them—all of them—a chance to kill something else, then they're going to start thinking very hard about killing *you*. Kny, you're one of the finest war leaders ever to think for the clans, and I believe you truly have the chance to accomplish what you and I both know you desire. But you don't pay enough attention to the way our warriors *feel*, and that's going to get you killed if you keep it up."

Trag didn't add that it would undoubtedly get him killed right alongside Camsan. Both of them knew it was true, but that didn't invalidate anything he'd just said. More than one Boman war leader had been removed by the clans if he seemed too timid, and the retirement of Boman war leaders was an . . . extremely permanent process.

"Oh, very well," Camsan said at last. "It's ridiculous to take so many to defeat so few—how many iron heads do the fools think there are to go around?—but you probably have a point. I'll give them their chance to kill something. But if I go out to play chase-the-*basik* in the woods, can you stay here with your tribe? At least I can trust you not to totally screw up."

"I can hold the city," the older chieftain agreed. "Besides, I have to admit that I'm a bit old for a *civan* chase."

Julian updated the situation map on his pad and transferred it to the captain.

"It's looking pretty good so far, Sir. The main Boman force is headed out the gates now. Only bad news is that we had another batch of barbs head southwest earlier—about two thousand. We don't have any idea where they were going or where they are at the moment."

Pahner tapped his foot on the barge deck and spat his chewed-up *bisti* root over the side.

"Have the cavalry screen echelon to the south. And throw the patrols out a little farther to keep an eye out for the strays. We need to make sure they don't show up at the wrong time."

"Not good," Kar said. "We're on a slim margin. If your 'strays' turn up during the attack, they'll make things difficult."

"Difficult, but not impossible," Pahner said. "Fog of war. You have to figure that something will go wrong even in the best case, and if that's the worst that happens, I'll be delighted. I'm more worried about them hitting us *after* the assault, anyway."

He looked out over the river. It was filled with barges and boats for over a kilometer in every direction as the army of K'Vaern's Cove made its slow way up river.

"If we get compromised from the north bank, we can land on the south side, where we've got the cavalry screen and the Marine LURPs to cover us. The only part I'm really worried about is the possibility of having this Camsan get word to his detachments too quickly and assemble the main host to come back while we're still landing, and even then the cavalry should slow them up long enough for us to finish landing or retreat."

"Or to get hit during the transfer," Bogess said quietly.

"We can break that part of the operation off at almost any time," Pahner replied with a shrug. "As long as Rastar does his job and the screen stays alert, we're golden."

CHAPTER THIRTY-TWO

"There's something very familiar about this," Honal said. "And I'm getting tired of running away from these fellows."

"Shut up and spur!" Rastar laughed. The wood line was rapidly approaching, and he hoped everything was in place. If it wasn't, things were about to get interesting.

Behind them, the Boman host was still pouring out of the city. It was going to take a while to get them all out, even with the three huge gates in Sindi's northern wall, but at least ten or fifteen thousand were already outside the fortifications. Rastar was relieved—and a bit surprised—to see that so many of the bastards were already coming after his troopers. He and Pahner had both expected a relatively small force to be sent out at first, and they'd figured that the rest of the horde would sit still until the original pursuit force suffered a mischief. But the Boman seemed to be in a bit of a hurry, and from the looks of things, at least sixty or seventy percent of all the warriors in Sindi intended to go chasing after a mere three hundred Therdan and Sheffan cavalry. It didn't seem fair.

"Horns!" Rastar called as they approached the edge of the jungle. The road, such as it was, continued on under the dense trees and tangled lianas, a muddy track that had been the main route to their former homes. In better days, it had seen regular caravans carrying the raw products of the Boman, leather and drugs mainly, to the south, and the return flow of manufactured products—jewelry and the very weapons the cavalry now faced.

The cavalry responded instantly to the call of the horns, narrowing into a double line as it approached the wood line.

"I can see the spare mounts," Honal called. "Now to get it stuck in!"

The two leaders broke to either side of the road, and Rastar dismounted from his wearied *civan* as the rest of the troopers of his "bait force" thundered past them with a yell.

"Time to pock them all!" Rastar shouted to them, swinging up into the saddle of a fresh mount.

"Give 'em hell, Sir!" one of the troopers called back, still headed for where their own remounts waited. "We'll be right behind you!"

"Up the banners!" Rastar bellowed in a grunt of laughter. "Let's get it stuck in!"

"Up the banners!" Honal passed on the order in a voice fit to wake a dozen generations of the dead as he bounded up onto a fresh *civan* of his own. He drew the first pair of his revolvers and raised them overhead.

"*SHEFFAN!*" he howled like a hunting *atul-grak*, and the voices of four thousand additional heavy cavalry thundered their own deep warcries as they burst out of the edge of the jungle behind him.

"Aha!" Camsan's head came up as the baying voices sliced through the pattering rain and he recognized the standards at the head of the charging force. "*That's* what this is all about."

"It's that stupid, gutless prince who led the escape from Therdan when he ran away," one of his henchmen grunted as he, too, recognized the banners. "Good. It's time to finish that line off once and for all."

The war leader gazed across at the standard of fallen Therdan, coming at him through the rain, and felt considerably less sanguine than the subchief.

"His uncle wasn't so easy to kill . . . or gutless," he pointed out. "Neither was his father, and I think we're about to get mauled. But you're right—we'll hunt them down at our leisure now. There's not much else to do. Besides, if we don't kill them now, they'll just be back next week."

Camsan made no effort to coordinate the actual attack. There would have been no point in trying, since Boman warriors in hot pursuit of a foe did not respond well to direction. The two or three thousand arquebusiers had already fallen begrudgingly back from the front ranks, since the rain made their matchlocks effectively useless, but the rest of the host only quickened its pace.

Camsan was right about what was going to happen to his leading warriors, but not even he realized how bad it was actually going to be. The Boman were old hands at fighting League cavalry, and they should have known better, but they were also individualists who fought as individuals. And, as almost always happened when the enemy ran away from them, they were more concerned with overtaking their fleeing foes before anyone else caught up and stole the honor of the attack from them than they were with maintaining anything remotely like a formation. The first five or six thousand out of the city gates had opened a relatively wide gap between themselves and their fellows as they pounded through the rain after Rastar's troopers, and—as also happened with unhappy frequency—they were about to get reamed when the "fleeing" cavalry turned on them, because none of their fellow clansmen were in range to support them.

It was all rather depressing to Camsan, who'd spent the last half year fighting an uphill battle to teach his tribesmen at least some modicum of caution and discipline, but it was hardly surprising. And to be fair to his warriors, they knew exactly what was going to happen. But they also knew that the rain would take most of the Northerners' wheel locks out of action, and they still boasted half again the cavalry's numbers. They were going to take losses, but they would also *inflict* losses, and they should be able to at least keep the enemy occupied and pinned down until their slower compatriots could catch up. Besides, this would be their first opportunity to kill something in almost five months, and they bellowed in hungry anticipation.

Some of that anticipation turned to surprise moments later, when the charging cavalry opened fire despite the rain. Mounted troops' wheel locks usually worked at least a little better than matchlocks in typical rain conditions, but these cavalry troopers' weapons weren't working "a little" better. They were working a *lot* better, and Camsan grunted a curse as he watched bullets slam through his warriors. The League cavalry's fire was *much* heavier than normal, and despite the bounding gait of the bipedal *civan*, it was also damnably accurate.

"How the hell are they firing those damned things in the rain?" Camsan demanded as he and the rest of the main body ran after the vanguard, and then snarled a fresh curse as Hirin R'Esa, chieftain of the Ualtha and one of the war leader's staunchest supporters, went down with a fist-sized hole in his chest. "However they're doing it, I'm glad they don't have more of them!"

"It won't do them much good now," his henchman replied with a feral grin. "They're down to ax range, now."

"What's that prayer Roger taught you?" Rastar grunted as he holstered his smoking revolvers.

"'Gods, for what we are about to receive, may we be truly thankful,'" Honal shouted back. He grinned in the human way, bare-toothed in the rain, as the troopers around him laughed.

"Whatever," Rastar muttered as he couched his lance. The rain of axes was tearing holes in his ranks, and he wasn't prepared to take *too* many casualties in what was really nothing but a giant feint.

The cavalry slammed into the first rank of the barbarians and carried them away. The Boman were already shocked and disordered by the massed pistol fire. Rastar's troopers had discharged well over twenty thousand rounds of twenty-millimeter fire into them. Firing from the back of a moving *civan* had never done much for accuracy, but the Boman had been a big target, and the avalanche of pistol bullets had killed almost a third of their front rank outright and wounded even more of them.

The Northerners' long lances easily took out the rest of the first rank. Snarling, war-trained *civan* slashed and tore as they rode over the wounded, snapping off arms and even heads with vicious delight, and the Broman howls of anticipation of a moment before became shrieks of raw agony as the survivors of Therdan and Sheffan wreaked bloody revenge. Almost better, at least half of Rastar's troopers managed to recover their lances as they slammed through the front rank, and they used them to good effect on the next, slaughtering the barbarians in front of them. And then the cavalry broke through into the gap between the Broman main body and what had been the vanguard. Two-thirds or more of that vanguard were now corpses, and aside from a few who'd been taken by battle frenzy, most of the survivors were running as hard as they could.

By Rastar's most conservative estimate, his four thousand men must have killed at least that many barbarians, and the shrieks of rage and hatred from the rest of the Boman host were music to his ears. Clearly, he and his troopers had accomplished their main goal; whatever happened now, the barbarians would never stop chasing them. Typical Boman bloody-mindedness would see to that, but it never hurt to make sure they got the hint, and Clande and the rest of the reserve were waiting to do just that . . . assuming that he and Honal could get their men back on the trail before the next wave of barbarians caught up to them. That next wave was larger—*much* larger—and for all their frenzy, Boman weren't stupid enough to offer him another opportunity like the last one. No, this wave would concentrate mainly on pinning the cavalry while other warriors swept around on their flanks, and that meant it was time to go.

"Back!" he shouted. "Sound the horns! Back to the forest. Time to run for it!"

His troopers had already managed the hardest part of the maneuver; they hadn't allowed themselves to be sucked into chasing down the fleeing survivors of their first clash. Now they responded instantly to the horn calls and wheeled once more to thunder back up the muddy road towards the woods.

"This is where it gets tricky!" Honal shouted beside him.

"Get to the front. Don't let anything slow us down," Rastar ordered, and Honal nodded acknowledgment and slapped his spurs to his *civan*. Rastar watched him go and crossed the fingers of his left true-hand in yet another gesture acquired from the humans. Timing, he thought, was everything.

The cavalry's lead ranks bogged up a bit as they reached the opening in the woods, but they were all veterans who'd been in nearly continuous battle for half a Mardukan year. Their commanders had learned their own trade well and added the benefits of human notions of discipline to their own, and they handled the maneuver with an aplomb that would have been frankly amazing before the long war against the Boman. Troops interleaved with troops, and squadrons formed into columns, until all three thousand-plus surviving riders were pounding at a gallop down the mud-slick track.

They got themselves sorted out not a moment too soon, for the second wave of Boman had kept right on coming, absorbing the fragments of the first wave as it came. The front ranks of at least twelve thousand howling warriors were fewer than fifty meters behind the rearmost trooper, and Rastar—holding his position near the rear of the column—felt a moment of intense anxiety. The barbarians were close enough to keep up a shower of throwing axes, although their accuracy left a great deal to be desired, and the slower pace the *civan* were forced to adopt as they thundered along in close proximity was allowing the Boman warriors to close the remaining range slowly.

"This is where some artillery would have been nice," he muttered to himself. But if he didn't have field guns, then he had the next best thing . . . assuming that it worked.

An ax clanged off of his backplate, and he gave his mount the spurs, leaning forward in the saddle to urge the beast onward. Another handful of his men went down, but only a handful, and the Boman were beginning to slow themselves down in turn as they packed solid in the relatively narrow slot of the track. Which was exactly what Rastar wanted and the humans had planned on.

The explosions, when they came, were like the end of the world. Rastar had never heard of "directional mines" or "claymores" before the humans came along, but he'd seen them tested in K'Vaern's Cove. It was amazing how murderous such a relatively simple concept could be, but not even the tests he'd observed had prepared him for the reality of what a few score old musket balls packed atop a half-*sedant* or so of gunpowder could do.

Clande and his reserves had been busy while Rastar and Honal trolled for Boman, and the trail was lined on either side with the infernal human devices. The troopers had placed one every two meters, and there were almost two hundred of them. The Boman were running three and four abreast as they pursued their enemies, and over six hundred of them were in the kill zone when Clande touched off the fuse and the rolling explosions marched down the trail to envelop them.

There were, perhaps, a dozen survivors.

Six hundred, or even six thousand, casualties were scarcely a fleabite against the total numbers of the barbarian host, but not even the Boman were immune to the sheer shock and horror of such heavy losses so instantaneously inflicted. The howling war cries turned to screams and shrieks, and the headlong pursuit slithered to a broken-backed halt amid the bodies and bits of bodies, shattered tree trunks and fallen branches, and the drifting smoke that shrouded the hell-spawned carnage of the ambush.

Rastar reined his *civan* back to a walk, looking over his shoulder at the destruction and agony, and bared his teeth in a hungry, human-style smile. Another small payment on the enormous debt Therdan owed the Boman, he thought viciously, and stood in the human-designed stirrups he and his troopers had adopted.

"Kiss my ass, you Boman pussies!" he shouted, slapping his rear end. "See you in Therdan—and bring your pocking friends!"

"What in the name of all the demons was *that?*" Camsan's henchman demanded as the two Boman stopped in stunned disbelief. The war leader had been no more than forty or fifty meters outside the kill zone, and he shook his head, half-deafened by the unexpected fury of the explosions.

He'd never imagined anything like the torn and mangled pieces of what had been warriors—certainly not that such carnage could be wreaked in an eyeblink! He stared at the wreckage for several moments, then shook himself again as he felt the matching consternation and disbelief of the warriors surrounding him.

He looked around quickly. The morning had not gone well. He and his warriors had killed perhaps two hundred of the shit-sitter cavalry, but their own losses had easily been fifteen or twenty times as great, and the sheer shock of this last hammer blow only made the pain of their casualties bite deeper. The clans had lost far more men in taking any one of the shit-sitter cities he'd conquered, but losses were expected when storming sheer stone walls. This was something else, and he recognized its potentially deadly effect on his warriors' morale.

"It was clever of the iron heads," he grated loudly enough to be clearly heard as he made himself walk forward into the blood and torn flesh. "Clever, but only gunpowder, not magic or demons. This is why they wanted us to follow them."

"Exactly as you *did*," a subchief accused, and Camsan turned slowly to face him. The war leader said nothing, only looked the subchief in the eye, and then Camsan's battle ax, the ceremonial ax of the paramount war leader, flashed up in a lethal arc and the subchief's head thumped heavily into the bloody mud of the track.

The silence which followed its impact was profound, and Camsan turned in place, sweeping every warrior in range with his hard gaze.

"For months you've whined and complained like children deprived of sweets because I would not lead you to battle," he said flatly. "I've warned you again and again that K'Vaern's Cove will be no Sindi—that the Cove's walls are high, and its people cunning. And for warning you, I have been repaid with mutters that I am no fit war leader. *I*, who took Therdan and crushed the League under our feet. I, who took D'Sley and even fabled Sindi! I, who have led you to triumphs our sires, and their sires, and *their* sires before them, never dreamed of!

"And now, when the iron heads rode around the walls shouting insults at you, and you demanded that we go forth and take their horns, you cry like little children because I gave you what you wished. I see that the warriors of the Boman are become *women!*"

He felt their sullen resentment, but none dared to meet his iron gaze, and he spat on the ground.

"There's no magic here, only cunning from our enemies and the foolishness of warriors who can see no response to any challenge but to rush to meet it. Do not blame me for the consequences of your own rashness! And don't think for an instant that any man who questions my decisions and my orders again will not be *atul* meat before nightfall!"

He kicked the dead subchief's head contemptuously off of the trail, and glared at all of them, one warrior staring down the shock and defiance of thirty thousand others, and the fiery elixir of his own power as he crushed any challenge to his authority filled him like fine wine. The silence stretched out, singing with tension, until, finally, he grunted in satisfaction at their submission.

"Now," he went on then, his voice calmer and more businesslike, "it's clear that the iron heads have returned to plague us, and this"—he gestured at the chaos of the ambush site—"proves that the K'Vaernian shit-sitters are supplying them with new weapons. There can be no more than a few thousand iron heads left in all the world after the feasting of our axes in their cities, but it would seem that the K'Vaernians mean to use them to bite at us. No doubt they hope to lure us into traps and ambushes like this one again and again. Perhaps they even believe that they can somehow drive us into leaving the Cove unburned if they strike us often enough.

"But we are the Boman! We are the warriors of the North, the power of the wind itself, and we will hammer our enemies into dust! We won't give these iron heads the time to sting us again and again, won't let them choose the moment at which *they* will attack *us*. Mnb Trag and his clan hold Sindi behind us, and the K'Vaernians will never risk their own precious hides beyond the safety of their walls. Nor could all the iron heads who still live take the walls against Trag and his warriors. Even the full strength of the K'Vaernians would require a siege to break those defenses, and the iron heads will have no chance even to try if we stay close upon their heels. They know that as well as we do, too, and so they will have spare mounts hidden ahead somewhere. They know us of old, even as we know them, and so they know that without such remounts they will never outdistance the Boman in the long run. They think to leave us behind here, at the beginning of the chase, or to exhaust us until we give up, but their hope is in vain, for we will take the time for a true *basik* hunt! You wish blood on your axes? Very well, I'll give it to you!"

He wheeled to the messengers who always attended upon the

paramount war leader. Picked runners all, carefully chosen from their own clans and tribes, they waited only for a nod from him to dash off with messages to any of the clan leaders, and he waved them closer.

"These new toys of the iron heads," he said, careful to put only contempt into the word "toys" and to conceal the shock he himself still felt at their effectiveness, "will be far more dangerous if they're able to choose the time and place to use them against us. So you will go to the leaders of your clans, and you will summon them to the field. We will pursue the iron heads wherever they may go, and the other clans will join us, closing in and driving them like *basik* before the beaters. Even if still more of them wait out here somewhere, and even if all of them are gathered together in one place, we'll have the numbers and the strength to sweep them aside as if they were so many grains of sand. Let them flee where they will, even unto the ruins of Therdan and Sheffan themselves! There will be no escape, and we will overwhelm them even if they find some worthless fortification to hold against us!

"Go! Summon the clans, for we have enemies to kill!"

"Christ," Pahner said. "Thirty-two thousand? What did they *leave?*"

"Far less than that," Bogess opined. The Diaspran had become Pahner's chief of staff, for all intents and purposes, as his own forces were integrated firmly into the K'Vaernian force structure, and he frowned thoughtfully as he considered the LURPs' report. "Most of the warriors would have insisted on chasing the Northerners. The Boman and the Vasin are enemies of old, with so many scores to settle that no one on either side could possibly count them all up."

"Jin says there are still some wandering around in the fields," the Marine said, consulting his pad.

"Looting," Bistem Kar said with a wave. "They'll be gone by the time we land. And we'll be landing out of sight of them, anyway."

"Something's going to go wrong," Pahner said.

"Who now is taking council of his fears?" Bogess asked with a grunt of laughter.

"Not taking council, just worrying," Pahner grumped. "And where the hell did Roger get to?"

"Start to forget our real job there, Boss?" Julian asked with a grin, and glanced at the heads-up display on his helmet visor. "Reports have him with the forward cavalry screen on the D'Sley-Sindi road. Track, rather."

"Good," Pahner said. "He's staying back like I told him to." The Marine paused and frowned. "If the report is accurate, anyway."

"Hey, Gunny! How ya doing?" Roger said quietly.

Jin suppressed his start and turned to look at the prince. The dying light of afternoon revealed Roger, lying on his stomach, covered in a gill blanket and with his face coated with camouflage paint while he grinned at the gunny's jump.

"Any news?" he asked.

"Jesus, Sir," D'Estrees said. "You scared the shit out of me. You ever heard of giving a poor Marine with a loaded rifle a little warning?"

"Gotta keep that old situational awareness, Corporal," the unrepentant prince said. "The night will soon be alive with little creepy-crawlies." He turned back to Jin. "So, what's happening?"

"Rastar says they're well into the chase," Jin replied. "The cavalry's about twelve klicks to the north, with the Boman from Sindi in hot pursuit. And it looks like this Camsan fellow's taken the bait, hook, line, and sinker." The noncom patted the directional shotgun mike on the side of his helmet and grinned. "Gave a hell of a little speech after the claymores turned about two hundred meters worth of scummies into sausage filling, Sir. Sounded to me like he figures he got his dick caught in a drill press and the only way to keep somebody from challenging his position is to go personally nail Rastar's horns up on a wall somewhere."

"So he called in the other clans?"

"That he did, Your Highness, that he did. I just hope Rastar and Honal are half as good as they think they are, 'cause if those bastards ever *do* catch up with them, it's gonna be ugly."

"Don't sweat it, Gunny," Roger advised. "As a matter of fact,

Rastar is probably at least two thirds as good as he thinks he is. Besides, we only gave him enough claymores for one good ambush. Didn't want him getting too creative on us, after all! So any other little unpleasantries he wants to send the Boman are going to have to come out of his rifles and revolvers, which ought to encourage him not to let them get *too* close." The prince shook his head. "He'll play tag with them, just like we planned, until we're ready for them to head on home, and it looks like they'll be bringing all their friends with them when they come."

"Hope so," Jin said, and waved in the direction of Sindi's barely visible walls. "Meanwhile, there's nothing stirring in Sindi Town."

"Are you out here by yourself, Sir?" D'Estrees asked.

"I dropped most of the troops about four kilometers back and came forward with half a troop of cavalry. They're back about a half klick."

"Who's in the group, Sir?" The gunnery sergeant asked. "Just Mardukans?"

"Four hundred cavalry from Chindar, four hundred or so infantry from the pikes, and Beckley's team. Oh, and Cord and Matsugae."

"You brought Kostas?" D'Estrees asked. "Don't go getting our cook killed, Sir!"

"I told him he ought to stay home in the Cove, where it was safe," Roger said with a grin, "but he pointed out that since the army now had real cooks, he could go back to being my valet. 'Just because you're sleeping on the ground doesn't mean we can't keep up appearances.' "

"Ha, that's Kostas!" Jin said. "How long you going to stay, Sir?"

"You mean potentially giving away your hide? Not long—I can take a hint. I'll head back to the troops in a minute. I just wanted to look at the city."

"What're you going to call them?" the corporal asked.

"The Mardukans?" Roger gave a quiet chuckle. "I don't know. Maybe 'Her Majesty's Own Mardukan Guards'? Whatever I call them, I need to be getting back before they come looking for me."

"Take care, Your Highness," Jin said. "And for Vishnu's sake, keep your head down and out of the line of fire."

"Will do, Gunny," the prince said. "See you in Sindi."

CHAPTER THIRTY-THREE

Mnb Trag looked out over the fields in the growing light. Somewhere to the north, he knew, were Camsan and the rest of the clans, perhaps closing in on the presumptuous iron heads even as Trag stood here on the walls of Sindi. It irked him immensely to be left behind, as if he were too old or lazy to go chase cavalry, yet he had to agree with Kny.

It was never wise to do what your enemy wanted you to do. Presumably that iron head cavalry had known the Boman would chase them, and presumably they'd also known that no heavy cavalry could outrun the Boman indefinitely. So there had to be a trap waiting for the host, and Camsan had been right to be wary.

Yet Trag knew that *he* had been correct, too. Trap or no trap, Camsan had no choice but to pursue the Northerners and destroy the challenge to his authority their mere presence represented. And whatever the iron heads had hoped to accomplish, they would fail in the end. No shit-sitter Southern army survived, aside from the relatively tiny force of the K'Vaernian Guard, and the Guard was far too weak to endanger any Boman force in the open field. So, in the end, the trappers must be trapped and destroyed. Judging by the dangerous deviousness of that first ambush, the K'Vaernians had obviously devised new weapons in a desperate attempt to make their League mercenaries more effective, and that undoubtedly meant casualties would be heavier than they ought to have been before the host managed to trap and destroy the iron heads, but their fate was ultimately sealed. And in their destruction, Camsan would add yet another triumph to the matchless string of victories he'd produced for the clans, and so further consolidate his grip upon the power he and Trag both knew lay almost within his grasp. "Barbarian" the shit-sitters called the Boman, and there was truth to the sneer, Trag admitted proudly. But "barbarians" could build empires, too.

Yet for all his satisfaction, something still felt wrong. He couldn't quite lay hold of what it was that concerned him, but it was there.

And then, as the light gathered, it became clear what it was.

A small host emerged from the forest on the D'Sley Road—small, but obviously much larger than any force the shit-sitters should possibly have been able to assemble. Block after block of infantry marched forward, moving in regular lines more precise than even those K'Vaern's Cove Guard bastards. He was too old to see what sort of weapons they carried at this range, but there were at least two shit-sitters for every warrior he still had in Sindi, and he had no doubt that they carried scaling ladders in plenty.

"Where did *they* come from?" one of his warriors gasped.

"K'Vaern's Cove," the chieftain answered. "I guess they must have put a sword into the hand of every shit-sitter who could see lightning or hear thunder and just brought them out." He grunted in laughter at the thought of the enemy's obligingness at bringing the soft, gutless—and untrained—city slugs into the sweep of his own ax. Still, it looked as if there were an awful lot of them.

"We should be able to pile them on the wall like bales of barleyrice," he said, "but it will be a fight to tell the grands about."

More and more of his fellow tribesmen gathered on the parapet as the regular ranks of shit-sitters assembled just out of bombard range. The groups walked in step, their odd march broken only when they crossed the small bridge over the Stell, and formed in neat blocks on the city's side of the stream.

"I've never seen spears that long," someone said. "You don't suppose those gutless Wespar were telling the truth when they said . . ."

The voice trailed off, and Trag grunted a deeper, harsher laugh at the edge of nervousness which had sharpened the remark.

"I've never put much faith in the lies Wespar pussies who got their asses kicked by a bunch of shit-sitters tell to cover the way they must've fucked up," the chieftain said. "And even if they were telling the truth, how would the same spears have gotten clear to K'Vaern's Cove this quickly?"

"You're probably right," one of his own tribesmen said, "but those really are awfully long *pagee*-stickers out there, Mnb."

"Maybe someone from the water boys told them how to scare the Wespar off," Trag scoffed, "but we aren't Wespar, are we? We're the Tranol'te! And even if we were Wespar, do you really think there's any way they could get something as long as those damned things up *scaling* ladders?" He laughed more loudly than ever.

"No, I don't," the tribesman said.

"Of course you don't," Trag said, and waved dismissively at the small army which had now taken up position in front of the gates on the northern side of the river, close enough that even Trag could see them clearly. "And I don't see any battering rams over there," he went on, "so there isn't really much they can do to us as long as we're not stupid enough to go out and meet them head-on, now is there?"

"I don't know, Mnb," the tribesman said. "We don't have enough warriors to man the walls. Not the way we ought to, anyway."

"Doesn't matter," Trag said confidently. "*They* don't have enough scaling ladders to swamp us, either. We've got more than enough to hold this part of the walls until the end of the world, and they don't have enough time for anything like a proper siege. Kny Camsan is out there behind them, and it won't take him long to realize why the iron heads wanted to lure us out of the city. When he does, he'll come right over them, and that will be the end of K'Vaern's Cove! All we have to do is keep them right where they are until he gets here. So get your warriors moving—we need them here on the walls!"

Messengers dashed off to summon the warriors of the clan to battle, and Trag leaned on the battlements, watching the shit-sitters. His confidence was genuine, but he was honest enough to admit that he didn't have a clue what the shit-sitters were up to as scores of them began pushing some sort of wagons up behind the blocks of infantry.

No doubt it was some new fancy trick the K'Vaernians had devised, but no trick was going to get them magically through the massive stone walls of Sindi.

"Move, move, move!"

Rus From and General Bogess were an eye of calm in a hurricane of effort as the specially trained companies manhandled the wagons into position. Those positions had been very carefully selected and surveyed by the Marine LURPs who'd kept Sindi under constant surveillance while the K'Vaernian army was equipped and trained. As well as both Diasprans had come to know their remarkable human allies, they'd been astonished by the routine, matter-of-fact way in which the Marines had roamed Sindi's environs under cover of night. Everyone knew the Boman barbarians could hear the whine of an insect's wings at seventy paces, yet the humans had penetrated effortlessly to the city's very walls, and their unobtrusively placed stakes had guided each wagon to its preselected position under the Diasprans' watchful eyes.

"Do we really think this is going to work?" Bogess asked the cleric under his breath, and From chuckled.

"Oh, I'm certain it will *work*," he said. "Once, at least, that is, given our gunpowder situation. Whether or not the Boman will cooperate by being where we want them to when it does work isn't my province, however, thank the God!"

"You're always so reassuring," Bogess muttered.

"Of course I am, that's my job!" From said cheerfully, then frowned thoughtfully. "It looks like we're just about ready," he observed. "Time for our last inspection."

"Let's get started then," Bogess replied, and the two of them separated and headed in opposite directions along the arc of wagons arranged before the northern walls of fallen Sindi.

"The bastards are up to something," one of Mnb Trag's subchiefs muttered.

"Of course they are," Trag shot back. "What? You thought they'd marched all this way just to stand there and scratch their asses at us?"

"Of course I didn't," the subchief retorted. "But I don't hear you telling us what it is they *are* up to, either!"

"Because I don't know," Trag conceded. "On the other hand, what does it matter what they're up to as long as they're out there and we're in *here?*"

He stamped a foot on the massive, solid stone of the parapet, and the subchief joined him in grunting laughter.

"The carts are laid in, Armand," Bogess said as he and From trotted up to Pahner and Bistem Kar. "The LURPs' stakes were exactly where they were supposed to be, and we're ready whenever you give the word."

"Good," Pahner replied, but his tone was a bit absent. Kar stood beside him, studying the city's walls through Dell Mir's telescope, but the Marine had the magnification of his helmet visor cranked up to give him a far clearer view than any primitive telescope could hope to match.

"They're a bit more spread out than I could wish," Kar said after a moment.

"Well, we can't expect the other side to do everything we want it to," Pahner pointed out. "And it probably doesn't matter all that much in the long run—these aren't exactly precision weapons, so there's going to be enough spread in the impact zone to cover a good bit of target dispersal. I'm more concerned about how many may still be under hard cover in the bombard and arquebus galleys. We're going to get good coverage, but we don't have anywhere near as much overhead penetration as I wish we did."

"According to Jin's count, there can't be very many arquebusiers left in the city, Sir," Julian pointed out over his powered armor's radio. "And if they aren't blind, then they must've seen all our nice scaling ladders. Which means they have to have moved just about everybody they've got left up onto the battlements to repel boarders."

"Nice and logical, Sergeant," Pahner agreed with a sour grin.

"Unfortunately, logic is still a really good way to be wrong with confidence."

"Yet I think he's right," Kar said, closing his telescope with a click.

"If he isn't, we'll find out soon enough." Pahner sighed, and turned to From. "All right, Rus. They were your babies in production, so I guess it's only fitting to let you be the one to send them on their way. Light 'em up."

"What *are* those stupid shit-sitters up to?" Mnb Trag groused. "I'm not as young as I used to be, damn it, and these old legs are getting tired!"

"Sure they are," the subchief laughed. "You're a Boman, 'old man,' so don't think you can fool *us* into thinking you need a rest! No sitting down until you've killed your quota!"

"If I must, I must," Trag agreed with a theatrical sigh, and tested the edge of his ax with a thumb. "Still, I wish the *basik* would go ahead and poke their heads up here where I can cleave them!"

"Oh, they'll be along, I'm sure," the subchief told him. "Either that, or they'll slink back downriver like the cowards they are."

Trag grunted agreement, but his attention was on those odd wagons the shit-sitters had pushed into position with such care. Now crews were stripping the canvas covers off of them, and the old chieftain rubbed at a horn in puzzlement as the pewter-gray, late-morning light gleamed dully on strange, stubby cylindrical shapes. He couldn't tell what they were made of, but there were scores of them in each wagon, arranged in some sort of wooden frames that held them upright. Each of them was perhaps a handspan in diameter, but at least as long as a warrior's forearm, and the work crews seemed to be fussing over them with a ridiculous attention to detail.

Whatever they were doing, it didn't seem to take them long—this time, at least—and the crews scampered back to their positions. In fact, Trag realized, the wagons were widely separated from the waiting shit-sitter army. The closest of them was at least a hundred paces from the nearest block of infantry, and he suddenly wondered why that was.

* * *

Rus From made himself wait until the last wagon crew had completed its work and confirmed that they were safely back behind the danger lines. Then he glanced at Pahner one more time, turned to the K'Vaernian artillerist standing beside him with a lit torch, and nodded.

"Light it," he said flatly, and the K'Vaernian touched his torch to the waiting quick match.

A small, bright, hissing demon flashed along the lengths of fuse, racing across the damp ground in a stink of sulfur, and throughout the ranks of the army, men covered their eyes or ears, depending on their individual inclinations. And then the hissing demon reached the first wagon.

Mardukan societies of all types and stripes boasted enormous and detailed bestiaries of demons and devils—not surprisingly, probably, given the nightmare creatures which truly did walk the planet's jungles. Yet not one of the collections of monsters the humans had yet encountered had included anything remotely like the Terran dragons of myth.

Until today.

The wagons seemed to explode, but that wasn't quite what had happened. Each wagon contained a wooden frame, and nested into each frame were two hundred and forty twenty-centimeter rockets. Two thirds of those rockets were fitted with time-fused fragmentation/shrapnel warheads—a bursting charge of black powder surrounded by a shaped matrix of musket balls which turned each missile into what was, effectively, a huge, self-propelled shotgun shell. The other third were pure blast weapons, with simple contact fuses designed courtesy of Nimashet Despreaux and warheads charged with two kilos of black powder each.

There were fifty wagons outside Sindi, for a total of twelve *thousand* rockets, and the blast warheads alone carried eight metric tons of gunpowder, exclusive of the propellant charges. The projectiles roared heavenward in an incredible, choking column of brimstone-flavored smoke and flame, then arced over and came screaming down. The fragmentation warheads burst in midair, and although the jury-rigged time fuses were crude, to say the very least, the vast majority functioned approximately as designed. A deluge of almost two million musket balls hammered the battlements and a zone fifty meters deep on either side of the walls, like the flail of some outraged war god that turned every exposed Boman into so much torn and shredded meat. No one on Marduk had ever so much as contemplated such a weapon, and so none of the barbarians had even considered taking cover. Instead, they'd crowded together, almost literally shoulder-to-shoulder, to await the anticipated assault, and they couldn't have offered a better target if they'd tried to. Here and there a small group or an isolated individual happened to have had sufficient overhead protection to avoid annihilation, but they represented only a minute proportion of Mnb Trag's tribe and its allies. When that dreadful broom of fire and fury swept across the walls of Sindi, almost ten thousand Boman warriors perished in a single screaming moment of devastation.

And on the heels of the fragmentation warheads, came the blast weapons. Compared to modern human weapons, the quaint, crude black powder rockets were mere children's toys, but the earth trembled underfoot like a terrified animal as those "toys" came crunching down on the walls and the buildings behind them. A terrifying drumroll of explosions threw fire and smoke, bits and pieces of barbarian warriors, roofing tiles, building stone, and shattered wood higher than the walls themselves, and the soldiers of K'Vaern's Cove looked at one another in shock and awe at the sheer havoc of the humans' weapons.

Mnb Trag never had the opportunity to share their shock and awe. Along with virtually every warrior of his tribe, he was wiped out of existence before he had time to grasp, even dimly, what horror lurked within the despised shit-sitters' wagons.

"Damn," Julian said almost mildly. "Think we used enough dynamite, there, Gronningen?"

"We can hope," the big Asgardian replied stolidly, watching the incredible pall of smoke and dust rising like some loathsome beast above the broken stoneyard which had once been the northernmost portion of the city of Sindi.

"Guess we find out now," Julian said as his HUD flashed. "Time to saddle up, troops."

Mnb Trag was dead, but by some fluke of ballistics and fate, the subchief who'd stood barely ten paces from the old chieftain still breathed. That wouldn't be true very much longer, and the subchief knew it, for he felt his strength fleeing with the blood pulsing from his savagely mangled legs. But the anesthesia of shock kept him from truly feeling the pain, and he pushed himself up onto his elbows with his fading strength and stared about him in total disbelief.

The wall itself still stood, virtually intact and gruesomely decorated with the torn and dismembered bodies of his fellow clansmen, but the neat houses and streets behind the walls had been threshed and shattered under a club of fire. Flames roared from the broken structures, bellowing and capering like demons above a broken wasteland of rubble, and the dying subchief felt an icy stab of terror as he surveyed the wreckage. Not for himself, for a man who knew he was dying had very little else to fear, but for the host following Kny Camsan in his pursuit of the League cavalry. If this dreadful devil weapon could unleash such devastation upon solid stone and masonry, what would happen if it caught the host in the open, completely without protection?

That thought shuddered in the back of his fading brain, and he turned away from the vista of ruin. He found himself facing the massively bastioned main gate of the city, instead . . . just in time to see magic.

Before the Mardukan's dying eyes, four demons appeared out of nowhere in a ripple of distortion, like the wavering of heat above a flame. They were mottled gray and yellow, with only two arms and bulbous heads and bodies, and their skins looked like wood or metal. As the subchief watched in amazement, one of them made a sword appear from nothing and struck it deep into the gate. Into the gap between the leaves of the gate, actually, and metal screamed as the demon sliced downward. Massive locking bars of bronze and iron parted like thread, and then the demon made his sword disappear, reached out to grip one huge bronze-sheathed panel in each hand, and pulled them apart.

The subchief watched in horror as a second supernatural apparition began to assist the first. Those gates were incredibly heavy, and slightly warped from the Boman's own assault on the city and the iron heads' bags of gunpowder. Dozens of stout warriors were required to open or close either one of their panels . . . slowly. But those two powerful demons, all by themselves, were—

And then, he died.

There were still a few Boman survivors, and some of them were actually on their feet as Julian threw the full weight of his armor against the gate and it came fully open. The huge hinges were twisted top and bottom, but the soft iron couldn't resist the powered "muscles" of the suits. Only the fact that, massive as they were, the suits were much lighter than the gate panels had prevented the armored Marines from flinging them open instantly, but instantly wasn't really required.

The first barbarians were already charging forward to regain the gateway, and Julian wondered whether it was courage or stupidity—or if there was a difference between them—that kept the barbarians on their feet. Or perhaps it was only the battle fury for which the Boman were famed. Not that it made any practical difference what kept the survivors coming.

The army behind him was also charging for the gates, and his HUD showed a tide of blue icons racing to support him. But the K'Vaernians had kept well clear of the impact zone, which meant they had considerably farther to go, and it was clear that the surviving barbs were going to get there first.

Not that it was going to do them a bit of good.

Julian didn't even bother to unlimber his bead cannon. He and Moseyev were still busy opening the gates, anyway, but that was all right. The only way the scummies could reach the gate was down the long, narrow gate tunnel, and anything his stutter gun could have added to the carnage of Gronningen's plasma cannon in such confined quarters would have been superfluous.

The phlegmatic Asgardian squeezed off a single shot that filled the tunnel's bore from wall to wall with a sliver of a star's heart. Half the tunnel roof disappeared as the upward-angled plasma bolt slammed into it and sliced a huge wedge out of the back face of the city wall. For a few moments, the rest of the tunnel roof looked as if it might hold, but then it, too, collapsed downward, taking half of one of the gate bastions with it. The avalanche of plunging masonry looked as if it might be going to bury the Marines, but it fell clear . . . and Gronningen's *second* shot blew straight down the gaping, roofless cut through the curtain wall which had once been a tunnel.

The bolt of nuclear fire hit the new-made rubble before it even had a chance to settle properly, and the broken walls and falling stones simply lifted back into the air. Some of their mass was converted to slightly cooler plasma, but most of it simply added its weight to the shrapnel flying from the explosion, as if the city itself was rising up against its invaders.

The same actinic fire, mixed with bits of half-molten stone, washed over the surviving Boman . . . who promptly stopped surviving.

"Krin," Bistem Kar half-whispered as the first battalion of K'Vaernian infantry slid to a skidding halt behind the armored figures it had intended to relieve. No unarmored individual was going to be able to survive in the blast-furnace fury of that shattered gate tunnel for some hours to come, and the Cove's senior guardsman shook his head in slow disbelief. The humans had never demonstrated any of their energy weapons for the K'Vaernians, who'd had only the reports from Diaspra to go on, and despite himself, Kar had never really quite believed those reports. Oh, he hadn't doubted them intellectually, but what Bogess and Rus From and other veterans of the New Model Army had described to him had been so far beyond the limits of his experience that he'd simply been unable to grasp the reality.

Now, he'd seen it . . . and he still wasn't certain he believed it. The power of the plasma cannon was even more shocking, in an odd sort of way, because it came on the heels of the rocket bombardment. The dreadful, overwhelming hiss and roar and crackle and thunder of the rockets had been the most cataclysmic thing he'd ever experienced.

In the instant that those howling missiles slammed home, he'd felt, however fleetingly, as if the very lightnings of the gods had been placed in his true-hands. Yet that single shot from Gronningen's weapon had sliced effortlessly through the massive stonework even the concussive thunder of the rockets had left virtually untouched, and the tough, confident guardsman felt something tremble inside him as he realized that every single word the Diasprans had told him was true.

He turned to Pahner and shook his head.

"Why don't you use them to clear the whole city?" he asked, jerking his head in the direction of the armored Marines, still standing unconcernedly in the inferno of the gutted gate tunnel. "We're going to take casualties in those warrens, prying the Boman holdouts out one by one."

"Power," Pahner said. "Not enough of it, that is."

"Ah," the K'Vaernian commander said with a gesture of puzzlement. "I'm just a simple old soldier, of course, but—"

"Ha!" the Marine laughed. "Some 'simple old soldier'!"

"I stand by that description," Kar said with a dignity which was only slightly flawed by the twinkle in his eye. "But, simple old soldier or not, *that*—" he waved at the gaping wound which had once been a gate tunnel "—seems ample power to deal with anything these barbarians might bring to bear."

"Not that kind of power," Pahner said. "Or, not directly, that is." The K'Vaernian regarded him with obvious confusion, and the Marine shrugged. "You know how some of the hammer mills in K'Vaern's Cove use wind power, and others use water power from your storage cisterns?"

"Yes," Kar said, his expression suddenly thoughtful. "Are you saying those things"—he nodded at the quartet of armored Marines once more—"don't have enough rainwater stored in their cisterns?"

"In a way," Pahner agreed, trying to figure out how to explain "potential energy." "The suits run on very powerful energy storage devices. We don't have many of them, and we need those we have for later use. And the weapons themselves only have so many charges, so we can't afford to use them unless we really need them. And we *are* going to need both them and all the power we've got left soon enough; there's a *real* battle waiting for us down the road."

"I can see that you wouldn't consider this a battle," Bogess said, glancing at the carnage of the gate. "But that's because we pulled the main force away from the city, *and* because the Boman were considerate enough to assemble right in the middle of our kill zone, exactly as we'd hoped. Unfortunately, we've used up the rockets now, so we won't be able to blast them this way again. Although," he added thoughtfully, "I still don't know how useful the rocket wagons would be in a real mobile battle. We knew where the city was, so we could plan exact trajectories. And better yet," he chuckled grimly, "Sindi couldn't exactly dodge."

"That's true enough," Kar acknowledged, "and it's also the reason I agreed that we should use them all now—there's not any point in holding back weapons which might not work later if their use now helps to assure a victory we have to have."

"Agreed," Bogess nodded. "But it still looks like there were at least ten thousand warriors still in the city, and that's only a small fraction of what's out tramping around chasing Rastar and Honal. Sooner or later, we're going to have to face up to the rest of the horde, after all, and I suppose that *would* qualify as a battle in almost anyone's eyes."

"I wasn't talking about the rest of the Boman," Pahner said, pulling out a slice of *bisti* root. "We haven't been totally up-front with you guys. Oh, we haven't *lied* to you, or anything like that, but we've . . . neglected to mention a couple of things. Like the fact that the port we keep saying that we have to reach on the other side of the ocean happens to be held by our enemies."

"*Your* enemies?" Bistem Kar said carefully. "With similar weapons, I assume?"

"Yes."

"God of Water preserve us," Bogess said faintly.

"Anyway, there won't be many holdouts to find in there," the Marine observed. "As you said, Bogess, most of them were right where we wanted them, waiting for us on the walls. Most of the ones we missed there got themselves killed in the gate tunnel, and the ones who didn't are probably still running . . . and will be, for a while. So keep the troops in hand and fight them through the city, but you shouldn't have that much trouble punching through. Just remember we have to get in before everybody else refugees out. And while you two get that moving, it's time for Rus to bring up the labor teams so we can get down to the real work."

"Well," Bogess said, "now I understand why you Marines don't look upon a battle with the Boman with dread. This *isn't* much of a battle to you, is it?"

"In a way," Pahner said, "but it's not just a matter of scale, you know. That—" he gestured with his chin at the huge pall of smoke and flame still billowing above the rocket strike "—is just as destructive, in its way, as any plasma cannon. It's not as . . . efficient, I guess, but those poor Boman bastards are just as much dead, mangled meat as if we killed them with bead rifles or smart bombs. Blood is blood, when you come right down to it, and it's not the thought of the battles that lie in our future that makes this any less dreadful. Not really. It's just that once you've walked through Hell a few times, it takes a lot for anything to get past your shell.

"Even something like this."

CHAPTER THIRTY-FOUR

Roger squatted by the side of the trail and tied his hair up in a knot. A *crint* called in the jungle, and he smiled.

"It's good to be back in action," he said.

"Maybe so," Cord replied repressively. "But I wish you would at least stay behind the scouts . . . as Captain Pahner instructed you to."

"I *am* behind the scouts," Roger said with a grin, and pointed to the south. "See? They're right over there."

The thrown-together force whose cavalry component had taken to calling itself—unofficially, at least—"The *Basik*'s Own" had pounded up the muddy track from D'Sley as fast as the infantry's *turom* could go while the main army made the same trip by water. Now they were about a half-day short of the city itself, and a thin line of screening cavalry stretched south from them, bending back in an inverted "L" to cover the track from just west of Sindi back to the Bay while the labor gangs who couldn't be crammed into the available water craft completed the march from D'Sley behind it.

Roger had chosen an encampment along a shallow stream that cut the track. The waterway, no more than thigh deep to the *turom*, flowed out of the jungle to join with the Tam River just to the north. It would provide a landmark to place the force around and water for the *civan* and *turom*.

The prince himself had just climbed down from Patty when Turkol Bes, his infantry commander, rode up on his *turom*, dismounted, and clutched the inside of one thigh.

"God of the Water, none of the troops will be able to fight! They'll all be too busy rubbing their groins!" he groaned.

"You'll get used to it," Chim Pri laughed as he slid off his *civan*. "After a week or so, you'll get used to it."

"How are the *turom*?" Roger asked.

"They'll be okay," Bes said. Not long ago, the young battalion commander had been a simple wrangler working on the Carnan Canal in Diaspra, but only until the Carnan Labor Battalion had been drafted for the New Model Army at King Gratar's orders. Of all the workers in the battalion, Turkol Bes had repeatedly shown the greatest ability to think on his feet and make good decisions under pressure, and promotion had been rapid.

"It's not like they're carrying much weight," the former laborer continued. "But they're not used to going so fast."

"Too bad we couldn't put you on *civan*," Chim Pri said with another laugh. "You'd really love that."

"But they needed all the spare *civan* in the Cove for the main cavalry force," Roger pointed out. "Maybe after we get them back we can upgrade."

"Oh, no," Bes said. "I'll sit on a *turom*, if that's the cost for keeping up with the *civan*-boys. But I am *not* going to try to ride one of those vile and ill-tempered beasts."

"You do whatever it takes to complete the mission, Turkol," Roger pointed out. "Speaking of which, right now we don't have one. But we can expect to get used pretty soon, I think. Now that the labor force is in Sindi, the Captain's going to start spreading the cavalry screen back out to cover the troops still working on the road gangs, and he'll need us then. Maybe even sooner. So we need to start thinking about how that might work. This is ground we could be fighting over, so I want everyone to keep a close eye on it."

The two battalion commanders traded looks.

"Do you think we'll actually be used?" Pri asked.

"Yes, I do," the prince said. "You might think you're just an oversized bodyguard, but Pahner is going to use us. Our mobility will be a key factor, if the Boman are hard on someone's heels."

He took a sip out of his camel bag, then pursed his lips and grimaced when it ran dry. It was time for a refill, but he looked at the nameless stream without enthusiasm. It was choked with mud stirred up by the hundreds of *civan* and *turom*, and although the bag's osmotic filter would take out the mud, some of the taste always got through.

"We need to keep an eye out all around," he continued, playing with the nipple of the empty camel bag. "Just because we think we know where the threat is, doesn't mean we're right."

"Let me fill that for you, Roger," Matsugae interrupted, gesturing at the camel bag. "You're just going to distract them playing with it if I don't."

"Thanks," the prince said, pulling the bag out of his day pack and handing it over.

"There *is* a cavalry screen out there," Bes pointed out to the prince, gesturing with his false-hand.

"Yes, there is," Pri said. He handed his own canteen to Matsugae at the valet's gesture. "Thanks, Kostas," he said, and looked back at the infantry commander. "It could probably stand to be pushed further out, though, if we want real security. And even if we do push it out, it could still be wiped out before we got the word . . . if there was a force coming up from the south, at least."

"So keep an eye on the terrain," Roger said, nodding in agreement. "The roads and the streams and where they are, shortcuts, and spots that would slow you down. Or slow the Boman. And most of all, make sure everyone stays on his toes."

Matsugae walked upstream, waving at the occasional soldier he knew. He recognized quite a few of the Diaspran riflemen from work details which had been assigned to the kitchen—a surprising number, really. It just showed that they'd been on this godforsaken planet too long, he thought. But he had to admit, hellhole or not, it made good people. The Mardukans were a fine race, and it would be interesting to see what Roger made of the planet after he got back to Earth.

The valet finally reached the edge of the picket lines and turned to the stream. There was a small team of scouts a bit further upstream, but they weren't fouling the water, and the hovering cavalry screen didn't seem to be doing so either. It was running quite clear, and actually a bit cool, which would help the chiller on Roger's camel bag.

He stepped onto a root and dropped the camel bag into the water. Its active osmotic system could absorb the water directly through its skin, but using the chemical filter took several hours. Fortunately, there was also a simple pump which could fill and filter it rather quickly, but Matsugae suddenly realized that although he *knew* about the pump, he'd never personally used one. He'd seen the Marines use them enough times, but this was actually the first time he'd fetched water on the entire trip; he'd had his own duties, and there'd always been someone else around to do that.

He looked down at the camel bag, fiddling with the pump fitting for a few moments until he finally figured out the release. Then he dropped the snorkel tube into the water and started pumping. To his delight, the bag started to fill instantly, and he grinned. *Got it right in one*, he thought cheerfully, watching the bag swell.

What he forgot to watch was the water.

The fastest reactions in the universe couldn't have gotten Roger across the encampment in time, and the finest neural combat program couldn't have killed the damncroc any deader than the two dozen rounds from the cavalry outpost.

None of which made any difference to Kostas Matsugae.

By the time Roger got there, it was all over but the bleeding. The *atul* had taken the valet in the throat, and even Doc Dobrescu's little black bag couldn't have done anything for the imperial servitor. More was gone than just the throat when one of the cavalrymen rolled the limp body over.

Roger didn't bother checking for life. He'd become only too intimately familiar with death, and no one could live with his head half severed from his body.

"Ah, Jesus, Kostas," St. John (J.) said, coming up behind the prince. "Why the fuck didn't you look? There's always crocs."

"I don't think he'd been outside a secure perimeter before," the prince said quietly. "I didn't think about that. I should have."

"No one can be right all the time," Cord said. He knelt by Matsugae and picked up Roger's camel bag. "Mistakes happen. You have to accept it when they do, but this was not your mistake, Roger. Kostas knew the jungle was dangerous. He should have been more cautious."

"He didn't understand," Roger said. "Not really. We all spent our time wrapping him and Eleanora in foam packaging."

"The foam packaging we should have wrapped *you* up in," Beckley said. The team leader shook her head. "We need to bag him, Your Highness."

"Go ahead," Roger said, then knelt and removed the palace badge from Matsugae's tunic. "I promise you, Kostas. No more mistakes. No more dawdling. No more dandying."

"Maybe dandying," St. John said. "He liked you to wear nice clothes."

"Yes, he did." Roger looked at the much patched chameleon suit the valet was wearing. "St. John, look in his packs. Knowing Kostas, he's got one good outfit packed. Beckley, if he does, dress him in it. Then bag him, and before you tab him, I want to say a few words."

"Yes, Your Highness," the corporal said quietly. "We'll take care of him."

The prince nodded, but before he could reply, his helmet gave the minor ping of an incoming call.

"Roger, it's Pahner. The engineers are getting down to it here in Sindi, but it looks like we're going to need a bigger labor force to pull this off. That means I'm going to have to draft more infantry, which means what cavalry we have is going to have to take on an even bigger share of responsibility for our flanks and the convoys. I'm going to have to bring them close into the road and spread them thinner to cover the extra footage, so I need you to swing further down to the south to anchor the line. I want you at Victor-One-Seven by nightfall."

Roger looked down at the body of his friend and shook his head.

"Could we have a couple of hours, Captain? We have a . . . situation here."

"Are you under attack?" Pahner asked.

"No . . . No we're not, Captain," Roger said.

"Then whatever it is, handle it and get on the road, Your Highness," the Marine said crisply. "You're a mobile unit, and I need you mobile. Now."

"Yes, Sir," Roger said quietly. He keyed off his mike and looked at the corporal. "Can the ceremony, Reneb. I promised no more mistakes and no more dawdling. Bag him and burn him; we're moving out." He switched back to the captain. "We'll be on the trail in ten minutes," he said.

"Good," Pahner said.

Rastar slid off his *civan* and moaned.

"I'd kill to be able to take off this armor," he groaned, and Honal grunted in laughter.

"You Therdan people are too soft. A mere forty *kolong*, and you're complaining!"

"Uh-huh," the prince replied. "Tell me *you're* not in pain."

"Me?" the cavalry commander said. "I think I'm going to die, as a matter of fact. Why?"

Rastar chuckled and rubbed his posterior gingerly while he looked at the stream.

"Thank goodness for accurate maps," he said. "I never appreciated them properly before."

"Yes, knowing where to water and where to hide—as opposed to where to fight—is *very* important," Honal said a bit tartly.

"Don't worry, cousin," Rastar told him. "There'll be plenty of fighting before this is done. Send back skirmishers with a communicator. Have them find the Boman, but tell them not to get too close. Just give them a few shots to sting them, then pull back. Make sure they have plenty of remounts and know where to go." He pulled out his map and studied its markings. "The turnoff for the first group is just ahead, and I especially want to know if the Boman split up when we do."

"Will do," Honal agreed. "I still say this plan is too complicated, though. Splitting ourselves up is crazy."

"We need to keep the Boman interested until it's time to lead them back home again," Rastar said, not looking up from the map, "and Boman are simple sorts. If we just run in a straight line, they may lose interest and start heading back too soon. That would be bad. But if we run all over the countryside like headless *basik*, their uncomplicated little souls should find the puzzle irresistible and keep them coming right behind us. We hope."

"Can I still not like it?"

"Yes . . . as long as you *do* it. And speaking of doing, it's time to go."

Fresh *civan* had been brought up from their string of spares while the officers talked, and Honal looked up at the towering expanse of his new mount with a sour expression.

"I don't know if I can climb clear up there," he groaned.

"Here, let me give you a boost," Rastar offered. "You Sheffan super-trooper, you."

Camsan cursed.

"*Another* group splitting off!" he complained.

"And in a whole different direction," Dna pointed out. "They must have cut their numbers by half with all this scattering."

"Hard to tell," the war leader said. "They're keeping in line to confuse our trackers about numbers, but I think you're right—there are fewer headed toward Therdan than there were."

The Boman leader rubbed a horn in thought.

"Have all of the messengers reported back yet?" he asked.

"All but the one to Hothna Kasi," Dna replied. "He had the farthest to go, but he should have arrived there by midnight of last night." The other Boman glanced up at the overcast, estimating the time. "By now, all of them should be on the trail."

"Good," Camsan grunted, "because that means all this splitting and scattering isn't going to do them any good in the end. It's just going to break them up into even smaller bits and pieces when our warriors finally start catching up with them. But I think we need to split off some parties of our own to go directly after these groups. I want to know where they're all *really* headed."

"Break up ourselves?" the scout leader asked.

"Yes. This isn't like the iron heads," the war leader said quietly. "They're being more devious than normal, and I smell a trap. Something, somewhere, is going on. Something big."

CHAPTER THIRTY-FIVE

"Damn," Beckley said. "I didn't believe it could be done."

"Neither did I," Chim Pri said.

"You have no faith in the Laborers of God," Turkol Bes told them with quiet pride. "When the God rains destruction, you have to build and repair *fast*. It's what we're best at."

The road from D'Sley to Sindi, which had been reduced to so much soupy mud by Boman foot traffic, had changed. Engineering crews, working to Rus From's careful plans and equipped with giant crosscut saws, axes, sledgehammers, and splitting wedges, had altered the landscape almost beyond recognition. Massive trees, some of them more than a meter in diameter, had been cut off close to the ground, sawn into lengths, split, and dragged out to the side of the roadbed. Wood wasn't the best material for covering a road, especially on Marduk, because it rotted and broke too quickly. But this road was being designed for one purpose and one purpose only, and it only had to hold up for a few days of heavy use.

Behind the woodcutters and splitters had come other teams of Mardukans, including civilians impressed from D'Sley and K'Vaern's Cove, leveling and grading the beaten track and filling in the deepest bogs with gravel and gabions of bundled barleyrice straw. When they finished, a third group had taken the split logs by the side of the grading and laid them down to form a corduroy road. The entire project had been one continuous motion, and now that it was done, the first wagon loads of supplies and materials liberated from Sindi were creaking along it towards D'Sley.

Ther Ganau, one of Rus From's senior assistant engineers, trotted up on a *civan* and waved two hands.

"Stay out of the right-of-way, if you will. I don't want anything to slow traffic." He gestured at the heavy flow of nose-to-tail wagons. "What do you think?" he asked Roger.

Pri looked over at the silent prince, and sighed. "Brilliant, Ther Ganau. Truly amazing. I've never seen such a sight in all my days."

Roger remained silent, and Cord dug a thumb into his back.

"Say something," the shaman hissed, and Roger looked up at last.

"Very nice, Ther," he said listlessly. "The Captain said he wants us anchoring this end of the line. Where's the best place to dig in?"

The engineer began to reply, then paused for a moment as he noted the roll of material lying on the withers of the prince's *flar-ta*. He recognized one of the humans' devices for cremating their dead, but all the people who would normally have been around Roger in the field were still there, and he brushed the question aside. He could deal with that mystery later.

"Yes, Your Highness. The Captain has called most of our infantry forward from this end of the line, so if I could borrow the Carnan Battalion for close security and push your cavalry a bit further out to the west, I'd be grateful."

"Whatever," Roger said. "Take whatever you want." The prince kneed Patty towards the river and lifted his rifle from the scabbard. Unless the Tam was totally abnormal, there were bound to be damncrocs in it.

"What happened?" Ganau asked quietly, gazing after the *flar-ta*.

"A croc got Kostas," Beckley replied.

"The God take him," the priest-engineer said sincerely. "A terrible loss."

"Especially to the prince," the Marine pointed out. "Kostas was with him for years. And he's blaming himself."

"What should we do?" the engineer asked. "Is there anything?"

"I don't know," Beckley said as a shot rang out from the river bank. "I just don't know."

The incoming call's priority code said it came from the sergeant major, and Pahner told his toot to accept it.

"Pahner."

"We have a situation with His Highness," Kosutic said without preamble. "Beckley just called it in. She says Kostas bought it this morning, and Roger's in a total funk. He's turned over his command to Ther Ganau and isn't answering calls. Reneb says he's sitting down by the Tam shooting crocs and won't talk to anybody."

Pahner carved off a slice of *bisti* root and popped it into his mouth.

"You know," he said after a long moment, "I'm trying and failing to decide which part of that I like the least."

"Me, too. I'm gonna miss Kostas' damnbeast casserole. And I'm not sure I'll be able to eat croc again."

Pahner looked out over the gathering heaps of material outside the gates. The stores of Sindi, which soon would be the stores of D'Sley and K'Vaern's Cove, were unbelievable. Despite the tremendous inroads the Boman had made upon them, the food supplies of the city remained enormous. Sindi had completed its own massive harvest just before the invasion began, and it was also a central gathering point for the products of the entire region. More than that, it seemed obvious that the rumors that Tor Cant had been stockpiling grain for at least two full harvests in anticipation of the present war had been accurate.

The result, when gathered in one place, was a truly awesome mountain of barleyrice, and the Boman had barely begun to devour it. The barbarians had been too busy eating the draft animals of the city and its satellite communities to waste much time with mere grains and vegetables. All of which meant that even with the barges which had moved the infantry upriver, there was no way to recover those supplies before the Boman returned. The barges would have time to make one, possibly two, trips, but if he committed them to that, they would be unavailable in the event that the plan came apart and a precipitous retreat from Sindi became necessary. Which didn't even consider the fact that there had never been enough barges to lift the combat troops *and* Ther Ganau's engineers.

The city's magazines had also contained several dozen tons of gunpowder, but that posed no particular transportation problems, since From and his engineers were busily expending it as they completed the destruction of northern Sindi.

If they were going to get all the other captured supplies out, though—and God knew K'Vaern's Cove could use every scrap of food in Sindi, especially if things worked out to leave a Boman field army still active in the area—then that corduroy road through the swamps *had* to be held. And while this would-be Boman Napoleon, Camsan, seemed to be chasing Rastar and Honal as fanatically as one could wish, there were still other bands of barbarians wandering around out there. If one of them should hit the convoys of wagons and *flar-ta* lumbering back and forth between Sindi and D'Sley, the results could be catastrophic. Which meant he needed Roger functional. Now.

He thought about a solution and grimaced. The obvious one—which wouldn't work—was to call Roger and tell him to get over it. The one which *would* work, unfortunately, wasn't a good answer in the long-term. The consequences could be literally cosmic, but it was the only one that might work in less than the couple of days it would take Roger to get over his funk without it.

"Eva," he said, "I'm gonna have to break every rule in The Book. As a matter of fact, I'm gonna have to throw it away."

"Okay," the sergeant major said. "What are we gonna do?"

"Get me Nimashet."

Nimashet Despreaux paused.

The prince sat on the river bank, rocking back and forth, his rifle across his lap. She knew, intellectually, that there was no way he would use it on her, but she also knew that he wasn't tracking very well at the moment. So she cleared her throat just a bit nervously.

"Your Highness?"

Roger looked out over the rippling water. He was scanning for "v"s in the fading evening light, but even as his eyes watched the stream with the alertness and intensity of the hunter he was, he wasn't really present. His mind, to the extent that he was thinking at all, was in a brighter past. A past that wasn't filled with blood and death. A past where his mistakes didn't kill people, and where all he had to worry about was getting his mother's attention, if not approval, and not completely screwing up in the process. Not that he ever had. God knew he was a screwup. He always had been. It just did not make any sense to give him the slightest shred of responsibility. All he ever did was fuck it up.

He started without turning his head when someone laid a hand on his shoulder.

"Go away. That's an order. I'm busy."

"Roger. Your Highness. It's time to leave." Despreaux wondered if she could get the rifle away from him without inflicting—or suffering—damage, then decided to shelve that question. Even if she'd been able to get the rifle, he'd still have his pistol, and facing Roger with a pistol in his hand was a losing proposition. "We need to get your cavalry into position," she said.

"Fuck it," the prince said in a flat voice. "Let Ther tell Chim what to do. And Turkol. I'm done giving orders, or even making requests. All I ever do is fuck things up. Even us."

He looked up over his shoulder at last, and the sergeant almost stepped back at his expression.

"Look at us, what there is of 'us.'" He snorted bitterly. "I can't even carry on a fucking conversation with a woman I love without totally screwing up."

"You didn't screw up, Roger," the sergeant said, sitting down at his side. Her heart had taken a tremendous lurch at the word "love," but she knew he didn't need her throwing herself at him at the moment. "I did. I realize that now. In fact, I've realized it all along—I just didn't want to admit I have, because it was so much easier to go on being mad at you, instead. But all you were trying to say was that fraternization is a bad idea, and you were right. If you don't watch it, it screws up a unit faster than anything else ever could."

"That wasn't what I was trying to say," the prince said. "It *is* a bad idea, but with so much fooling around going on in the Company, what damage could one more affair do?"

"So what did you mean to say?" Despreaux asked warily. "I assume you *weren't* going to refer to the hired help?"

"No." Roger rubbed his face and looked out on the water again. "What I meant to say was: I don't fool around. Put a period on the end of that sentence. I did a couple of times, and they were outright disasters. And I felt like a shit each time. All I could think about was that I didn't want another bastard in the world. I didn't want to betray someone like my father and mother had."

He pulled his helmet off and set it on the ground. The river bank was covered in a low, soft ground cover, somewhat like short clover, under the shade of a massive jungle giant. It was as comfortable a place as any on the planet to deal with bleak despair.

"I didn't know what the relationship was between my mother and the bastard formerly known as 'my father,'" he said. "But I did know that wondering what the relationship was, and blaming myself for whatever it *wasn't*, had to be the worst way for a kid to grow up. And there are places in the Empire where it matters how 'pure' you've been, and I had to think about that, too. Most people think I never gave a good goddamn about my obligations as a prince, but that's not true, either. Of course, it's not surprising they think that way—I managed to screw up those obligations, too, after all. But that didn't mean I didn't care, or that I didn't recognize that the risk was too great for me to justify fooling around."

"At all?" the incredulous sergeant asked. "For how long? And, I mean, uh . . ."

"I lost my virginity when I was fifteen. To a younger daughter of the Duke of New Antioch. A very ambitious daughter."

"I've heard about that one," Despreaux said carefully. The "scene" was a minor legend in the Emperor's Own and the cause of one of the few resignations of a company commander in its history. "And I've heard that nobody had ever seen you 'with' anyone else. But, I mean, what do you—I mean, that's a looong time."

"Yes, it is. Thank you for pointing that out."

"It's not good for you, you know," the Marine said. "It's not healthy. You can develop an enlarged prostate even while you're young. Sure, they can fix it, but prevention is a much, much better alternative."

"Do I really have to discuss the details of my non-sex life with you?" the prince asked. "Especially right now?"

"No, you don't," Despreaux admitted. "But didn't anybody ever talk to you about it? Didn't you have a counselor?"

"Oh, sure. Plenty of them. And they all took the same position: I needed to release my bonds to my father, put my sense of his betrayal of me behind me, and take responsibility for my own life. This is referred to as 'reality therapy' or 'quit being such a fucking whiner.' Which would have worked real well, except that it wasn't my *father* I resented the hell out of."

"Oh." The sergeant tugged at an earlobe. "That has to be weird. Everybody in the Empire regards the Empress like, well, like a goddess, I guess."

"Yep," Roger said bitterly. "Everyone but her son. I never, ever forgave her for the fact that I didn't have a dad. She at least could have remarried or something. I finally figured out that was one of the reasons I went into sports—look at all those father figures."

"Oh," Despreaux said again, and then, very, very carefully, "And Kostas?"

"Sort of," Roger said with something halfway between a chuckle and a sob, then drew a deep breath. "Kostas was hard to see as the kind of larger-than-life pattern kids want in their fathers, I guess. But in every other way that counted, he was the closest I ever got. Could have gotten, maybe. He was always there when I needed him . . . and I wasn't there when *he* needed *me*. Of course."

Despreaux's arms twitched as she listened to his ragged breathing, but she made herself pause and think very carefully about what she was going to do. The intensity of Roger's emotions, and the jagged edges of his grief and self-hatred hit her like a fist, and she was more than a little frightened by the dark, pain-filled depths which stretched out before her. But fear was only a part of what she felt, and not the greatest part, and so, finally, she gave a slight shrug and gently took the rifle out of his hands and set it on the ground. Wordlessly, she wrapped her arms around him and pulled him down to lie with his head on her lap . . . and ran her fingers through his sweaty hair as he began, very quietly, to cry.

Her own eyes burned, and she wondered how many lonely years it had been since he had ever let anyone see him weep. Her heart ached with the need to reach out to him, but she was a Marine, a warrior. She knew what needed to be said, but not how to say it, and so she crooned wordlessly to him, instead, and somehow, he seemed to understand the words she couldn't find.

"I don't know what to do, Nimashet," he told her. "I . . . I just can't kill anybody else. I've killed so many of you already. I just can't do that anymore."

"You didn't kill anybody, Roger," she said gently, the words coming at last because she needed them so very badly. "We're Marines. We all volunteered for the Corps, and we volunteered again for the Empress' Own. We knew the score when we signed up, and we could've quit at any time."

"You didn't sign up to be marooned on a planet full of four-armed barbarians while trying to protect a deadbeat prince!"

She smiled, and if that smile was a bit misty, that was her own business.

"Not a deadbeat—more like a dead-shot. Your Highness, there are so many ways to die as a Marine that it's not really funny. This is near the top of the list of odd places and ways, but it's not clear at the top."

"Kostas didn't sign up to be a Marine," he said softly. "He didn't sign on to die."

"People die all the time, Roger." The sergeant combed the tangles out of his hair with her fingers. "They die in aircar accidents, and of old age. They die from too much parsan, and from falling in the shower. They die in shipwrecks, and from radiation poisoning, and by drowning. Kostas didn't have a monopoly on dying."

"He had a monopoly on dying from my mistake," Roger said in tones of quiet, utter bitterness. "I made a simple request and didn't think about the consequences. How many times have I done that—and not just to him? How many times on this march have you

Marines been put in jeopardy—or killed—because of my stupid actions? My stupid *unthinking* actions?"

"Quite a few," Despreaux said. "But I think you're being a bit unfair to yourself. For one thing, I've talked to Turkol and Chim. You didn't ask Kostas to get you water; he *offered*. I know, I know," she said, laying one hand lightly across his mouth in what wasn't quite a caress. "That doesn't change what he was doing, or the fact that—just like always—he was doing it for *you*. But I think it does matter that it was his choice, not yours. And while we're on the subject of fairness, do you really think Kostas didn't know about the risks? Know the jungle is dangerous? Roger, he was along for every single step of the march. He was the one who oversaw the mahouts butchering the damncrocs when you and Julian had that shoot-off crossing the damned river before Voitan—you think he didn't know they lived in rivers? For God's sake, he's the one who was on safari with you on all those godforsaken planets none of the rest of us ever even heard of!"

"What are you saying? That it was *his* fault?"

"I'm saying it wasn't *anyone's* fault. Not his, not yours. He went to perform a routine task—not just for you, but for Chim Pri—and somehow, for some reason, he was too distracted to pay attention. It happens, Roger. It happens all the time, every day of our lives. It's just that here on Marduk, if your attention wanders at the wrong moment, you end up dead. You didn't kill him, and he didn't kill himself—the fucking planet did."

"And the Marines? What about *them?*" Roger demanded in a harsh, almost spiteful tone.

"Two things," Despreaux told him calmly. "One, every time you've 'put us in jeopardy' it was a relative danger. This planet is no place for a right-thinking Marine who wants to die in bed, preferably while getting a leg-over, but you didn't pick it, and you certainly didn't order us to come here. Second, a lot of those 'stupid unthinking actions' are the reason we love you. Looking at it sensibly, I guess it really isn't very smart of you, but you just throw yourself at the enemy and keep moving forward until you come out on the other side, and in some ways, Marines aren't all that different from Mardukans. We know the object is to kill the other guy and come home afterward, and we don't have any use at all for officers who keep hanging themselves—and us—out just to prove what great big brass ones they have. But for all that, we respond to COs who *lead* us a thousand times better than we do to those who send us out ahead. And whatever other faults you may have, we've discovered on this shit ball of a planet that you're one hell of a leader. You've got a lot to learn, maybe, about thinking your way through problems—I swear, if you ever faced a Rasthaus wartbeast, you'd throw yourself into its mouth and try to tunnel out the other end!—but you wouldn't do the one thing a leader can never do in combat: hesitate."

"Seriously?" Roger rolled over on his back and looked up at her, and she stroked his face and smiled.

"Seriously. The only thing a Marine truly hates is a coward. Hold still." She leaned down and kissed him. It was a hell of a bend, but she was limber, and Roger released her lips reluctantly.

"What are we doing? And how did we get from Kostas to here?"

"What? They didn't cover that in the Academy?" she asked with a soft laugh. "Call it the desire for life renewal in the face of death. A strong desire. The need to hold back the ferryman in the only way we know." She paused and ran a hand down his side. "Ten years, huh?"

Roger sat up and wrapped his arms around her. As he did, he noted that his tactful bodyguards had discreetly withdrawn out of sight of himself and their squad leader. Which made him wonder what would happen if another damncroc, assuming there were any left in the entire river after his extermination efforts, slipped up out of the water while they were engaged. Which made him wonder where his cavalry detachment had gotten to. He remembered giving the infantry to Ther Ganau, which made him wonder who was covering the supply convoys.

Which made him groan.

"What?" Despreaux asked huskily.

"Oh, God, Nimashet. We just don't have time. Where's my cavalry? How are Rus From's engineers doing at Sindi? What's happening with Rastar? Are the barges all in place, and who in hell is covering Ther's caravans?"

Her eyes flared, and she grabbed him by the front of his chameleon suit.

"Five minutes," she ground out through gritted teeth.

"More like thirty seconds," the prince told her with something almost like a laugh. "If we can get our clothes off in time, that is. But it's thirty seconds we need to *not* take. I've already lost hours with this despair shit, and we don't need to lose any more with the reverse."

She stuck her hip into his and rolled him over onto his back with the grip on his chameleon suit.

"Listen to me, Prince Roger Ramius Sergei Alexander Chiang *MacClintock!*" she hissed. "I want a promise. You can make it on anything you care to name, but you *will* make it! And that promise is that as soon as we get somewhere safe, and all the crises are past, you will take me to bed. And take your time at it. And do it *well.*" She picked him up and pounded him lightly on the ground with each phrase. "Do you swear?"

Roger wrapped his legs around her, pulled her down on top of himself, and kissed her.

"When we're back on Earth. When all of this is behind us, when we're back in the Imperial Palace, and we can be sure it's not the situation. When I'm sure that I love Nimashet Despreaux more than life itself, and that it's not unbridled lust from all the pain and death and blood. Then I'll take you—as my wife, if I can get away with it, or as a senior partner, if I can't. And I will love you until the day I die. I swear it on my dead."

She pounded her head into his breastbone.

"All I want to do is to screw you, you idiot! You're supposed to be telling me you'll love me and marry me to get me to bed—not telling me that to get *you* into bed *I* have to marry you. That's *my* line!"

"Do you accept?" Roger asked.

"Of course I do!" she snapped. "I'd have to be an idiot not to. I love you so hard it hurts, and don't think I'll get over that just because we get back to Earth. Hell, I was so far gone I loved you when you were just an overblown, brainless, arrogant prick of a clotheshorse and I damned well should have known better!"

"Speaking of clotheshorses," he said, fingering the placket of her chameleon suit, "these uniforms could use some work. That's the second thing I'm going to do when we get back to Earth." He looked into her eyes. "So we wait?" he asked in a quieter voice. "You're okay with that?"

"I wouldn't use the term 'okay,'" she said. "'Okay' is definitely not the adverb, or whatever. As a matter of fact, if there's a direct opposite of 'okay' for this situation, that's about where I am. I'm not exactly 'bad' with it, I guess, but I'm definitely sort of 'anti-okay.' On the other hand, I'm a big girl. I'll live."

Roger rolled over, then stood, and pulled her to her feet.

"You ready to go?"

"Sure," she answered sharply. "Let's go find something for me to kill before *you* start looking any better."

"Okay," Roger said with a smile. "I want you to know, I really do want you. But I don't get any easier with time."

"I've noticed," the sergeant muttered darkly. "Stubborn as a Mardukan day is long." She shook her head. "I have *never* had this much trouble getting a man to bed. For that matter, I've never had *any* trouble getting a man to bed. It was always the other way around."

"Frustration is good for the soul," Roger said. "Look at what it's done for me!"

"Yeah," Despreaux said with a sigh. "No wonder you're so dangerous. Ten years?"

CHAPTER THIRTY-SIX

Armand Pahner stood on the walls of Sindi and gazed out over the muddy, trampled fields. Work crews, wagon trains, and infantry pickets marching out to relieve other pickets stretched as far as the eye could see with a helmet visor set to max, but even as he gazed at them, the activities outside the walls weren't what occupied his mind.

He was thinking about women and children.

The Boman host traveled with all the (limited) comforts of home, including its women and young . . . and Kny Camsan's ambitions had concentrated over half the total host's dependents right here in the city. In fact, it was that bit of intelligence, discovered by Gunny Jin's LURPs and confirmed by reports from a handful of the primitive woodsmen who continued to linger in the forests, despite the Boman's presence, which had shaped the captain's entire strategy.

Pahner had given the strictest orders that every one of those dependents was to be taken into custody, and that none of them were to be molested in any way. The biannual "heat" of the Mardukans eliminated, for all practical purposes, the issue of rape from the local art of war, which—given humans' history—he thought was a very good thing. But that didn't necessarily make war nice and sanitary, and the Boman's depredations and the sheer, horrifying scale of the massacres they had perpetrated had left the locals perfectly willing to slaughter their women and children in return and be done with it.

K'Vaernians didn't have the expression "nits make lice," but there was general agreement that the only good Boman was a dead Boman, and the age or sex didn't matter.

Those qualities did, however, matter to Pahner. Leaving aside the clear proscription in imperial regulations against atrocities, leaving aside even his own personal repugnance for unnecessary slaughter, he needed those dependents. He needed them alive, and in good condition.

They were bait.

Normally, the Boman didn't besiege a city the same way a "civilized" army might have. If they failed—or chose not to—overrun its walls with their first, concerted rush, they fell back on their own sort of investment. They didn't call up the engineers to dig trench lines, and they made no effort to batter down walls or tunnel under them. Nor did they encamp outside a city's walls to hold it under a close envelopment. Instead, they just . . . existed, like some vast, slowly swarming sea which had inundated all of the lands about their enemies yet offered no fixed camps which might be assaulted to force them into battle. Their presence, and overwhelming numbers, prevented any organized movement on the part of the besieged city. Anyone trying to break out or escape was caught and overrun. Laborers trying to work the fields were massacred, draft animals were slaughtered or run off. If large forces sortied against them, they avoided their foes until enough barbarians gathered to pull them down and destroy them. If a city was weak enough, they were willing to simply pile up to the wall and assault it, but in general, they took their time and let it fester and rot . . . *then* assaulted it.

Part of the reason for that was logistical. The Boman were herdsmen, of a sort, which helped sustain their population levels, but they also depended on large areas for hunting and gathering, like other Mardukan barbarians. Even without the need for hunting, their flocks of meat animals—the closest to "farming" they came—required vast grazing areas. At home, they moved their flocks constantly, allowing the grazing in any one area to recover between visits, and they were generally forced to do exactly the same thing when they went to war, assuming they intended to actually feed their warriors. There was no way they could organize a supply train, so staying put for any extended period wasn't really practical, except for the times—like Sindi—when they were able to capture supplies someone else had stockpiled.

True, they had chosen to begin this war with a series of frenzied, massive assaults which had suffered huge casualties, but that had been because this time they were working to a comprehensive strategy which had been designed to annihilate *all* of the southern city-states, not simply to take a single town. They had recognized their need to smash the Northern League quickly, before it could recover from Sindi's treachery and its cities could come to one another's aid as they always had in the past.

The sheer surprise of their coordinated tactics had done almost as much to defeat the League as anything agents from Sindi might have accomplished, Pahner suspected, although he had no intention of suggesting anything of the sort to Rastar or their other Northern allies. After generations of fighting Boman in the same old way, no one in the League had anticipated such an overwhelming onslaught . . . and neither had the Southern city-states behind it. The terror effect of the League's sudden collapse, coupled with the sheer size of the Boman host and the fact that most of the Southerners, secure in the League's protection, had settled for modest defensive works of their own, had made it relatively simple to storm each successive city in turn, and Camsan had done just that. Sindi had been a tougher nut, but the war leader had made no real effort to restrain his warriors' enthusiasm in Sindi's case. He couldn't have, given the reason the war had been decreed in the first place, but casualties in the storm of Sindi had actually been worse than they had in the attack on Therdan. The Northerners had been far tougher opponents, but Sindi had been much larger, and its authorities had been given sufficient time to prepare before the hurricane howled down upon it.

But after Sindi, the Boman had reverted to their more normal tactics rather than attempt an extremely unwise storm of K'Vaern's Cove. The only real difference was that their capture of Sindi gave them a powerful, heavily defended forward base, and—coupled with their conquest of the other Southern city-states—enough captured food to stay in place for several months. Eventually, of course, they would eat their captured larders bare and have to begin thinking about more aggressive ways to take the war to the Cove, but until the humans and their Diaspran allies arrived, Camsan's strategy of letting the K'Vaernians rot and deplete their already limited food supplies feeding the floods of refugees had been working quite nicely. It had been almost certain that, assuming he could hold the Boman together as a cohesive force, he could have sat where he was long enough to reduce the Cove to starving near impotence and then poured his warriors over the walls the Guard would be too weakened to defend.

Which was the whole reason Pahner was out here now. Whether or not the Cove would be fatally weakened before starvation forced the Boman to move themselves, *he* couldn't wait to see the outcome. He needed to bring the barbarians to decisive battle now, so that he and his Marines could get the heck out of Dodge before their food supplements ran out, and to do that he needed to do two other things. First, he needed to present them with a threat which appeared less formidable than it actually was, and, second, he needed to give them a reason to attack that threat.

A reason like rescuing all of their women and children.

The captain didn't much like his own strategy, but it was the only one he could think of which had a chance of working within the time constraints he faced. And if there were things about it that he didn't like, *he* wasn't the one who had decided to level every city-state north of the Diaspra Plateau and the Nashtor Hills.

He snorted, once more amused by his own perversity. Here he was, protecting thousands of women and children from massacre at the hands of his own allies, and all he could think about was how despicable of him it was to use them as bait to lure their menfolk into battle. On the other hand, he suspected he was also dwelling upon that thought to avoid considering one that worried him even more, and it was probably time he stopped doing that. He shook his head, then checked the time and decided that he couldn't put it off any longer.

He drew a deep breath, sent a command to his toot to bring up his communicator, and spoke.

"Roger?"

"Here," the response came back, almost instantly, and the Marine felt his shoulders relax ever so slightly.

"You sound better," he said. "Are you?"

"It comes and goes," the prince said over the radio. "I'm tracking again, if that's what you mean. Whose idea was it to send Nimashet?"

"I felt that you were a bit too exposed," the captain said. "So I augmented Corporal Beckley's team with the rest of the squad. They'll stay with you for the remainder of the operation."

"I see." There was silence over the com for several seconds while both of them digested a great many things which hadn't been said and probably never would be. "So, how're we doing?"

"Pretty much on schedule," Pahner replied. "Eva is working with Rus on the preparation of the defenses. That only seemed to make sense, given her involvement with the artillerists. And Bistem and Bogess have their infantry fairly well organized on the approaches to the city, given that we've had to tap each regiment for a labor battalion to help out Rus's engineers."

"And Rastar?" Roger asked.

"So far, so good," Pahner told him. "He's having a bit more trouble than we'd hoped he would opening the distance between himself and their main force, and it's pretty obvious that they're trying to catch him between the pursuit from Sindi and forces from the other occupied city-states. So far, they haven't been able to hit him with anything he couldn't handle, and his ammunition supply seems to be in pretty good shape, but his whole diversion looks like turning into one big running battle."

"Are we going to have to go in after him?"

"I don't know. I hope not, and so far it looks like we can probably avoid it. But I'm keeping an eye on the situation."

"Good. And what do you want us to be doing?"

"Pretty much what you are, Your Highness. From what Beckley and Despreaux told me yesterday evening, you've got your cavalry about where I want it on that southern flank. I'm going to peel the Carnan Battalion back off from Ther's close cover force on the convoys and send it back to you. We'll let the other cavalry cover him; I want those rifles back out there with you."

"Just to keep my precious hide intact?" Roger asked a bit tartly, and Pahner snorted.

"I'm sure that's somewhere in the back of my mind," he said, "but it's not foremost. Mainly, I just want to be sure that the anchor at the far end of my line isn't going to come loose if somebody runs into it."

"I see. Well, in that case, Captain, we're just going to have to see to it that we stay put, aren't we?"

Dna Kol swallowed a bite of parched barleyrice and leaned down to suck water from the stream.

"If we don't find these damned shit-sitters soon, we head back to the city. I'm out of food and patience," he growled.

"What are they doing?" one of the warriors asked. "First they head west, like they're going back to wherever they crossed. Now they head east."

"They're scattering to avoid us," Dna Kol said. "And somewhere, they're gathering again."

"How can they find each other out here in the woods?" the warrior asked. "I don't know where I am. Oh, I could find the city easily enough if I headed in the right direction long enough, but I certainly couldn't tell anyone else how to find *me.* So how do *they* know where they are? Or where to go to find the rest of them?"

"Maps," another of the warriors spat, drawing his head up out of the stream. "Damned shit-sitter maps. They map everything. They'll know where every stream crossing is before they get to it."

"Which is how they're managing to lead us around by the nose," Kol agreed. "But we'll track them down soon enough . . . and bring the whole host down on them when we do."

"I could do with some new armor," the first warrior said. He pulled a throwing ax from its belt loop and made a chopping motion. "And I know just how to get some."

"Let's move," Kol said. "I can smell them. They're near."

Rastar ran another patch through the barrel of one of his

revolvers, examined the weapon carefully, and decided he was satisfied. In some ways, the last prince of Therdan missed Captain Pahner's pistol. It held far more rounds than the seven-shot revolvers, its recoil was less, and it was a *lot* easier to clean. But for all that, he still preferred these new weapons. There was something about the spit of flame and the trailing smoke from gunfire that added a deeper dimension to the battle. And Pahner's pistol had been too much like magic. These pistols were clearly the work of mortal hands, yet they spoke with all the sound and fury of a gunpowder thunderstorm.

"Time to change *civan* again," he announced as Honal rode up to him and reined in.

"I'm not sure I can dismount," his cousin groaned. "I *used* to think I was tough."

"I believe you mentioned that yesterday morning," the Northern leader said. He finished loading cartridges into the cylinder, carefully plugged the mouth of each chamber with the heavily greased felt pad which prevented flash-over from detonating all seven rounds at once, and began fitting the copper caps over the nipples at the rear of the cylinder. "Change your mind?"

"I think I've figured out a translation for that joke that bastard Pahner told us before we set out," Honal said in indirect reply as he slid gracelessly out of the saddle and fell onto his back. The *civan* delicately stepped away as a groom came up to unsaddle it.

"Oh?" The prince finished capping the cylinder and swung it back into place and looked up inquiringly. The humans' toot translations were usually excellent, but they made a hash of jokes . . . which had been obvious in the case of Pahner's statement.

"You just have to make a terrible pun out of it, and it's really quite funny," the Sheffan cavalry commander said, still laid out flat on the ground. "If, of course, you haven't spent three days at a fairly constant trot. Try it this way: 'A Manual for Cavalry Operations, Forty *Kolong* a Day, by Princely Arseburns.'"

"Ah!" The Therdan prince gave a grunting laugh. "Har! That's pretty good, actually. Feel better?"

"No," his cousin said. "I have princely arseburns. I have armor chafe. I have dry-slime. And I think my legs just fell off."

"Nope," Rastar said with another grunt. "They're still there. Hey, think of how the *civan* must feel."

"Pock the *civan*," the cavalry commander said with feeling. "When we get back to K'Vaern's Cove, I swear I'm going infantry. If I never see another *civan* again in my life, it will be too soon. I'm going to personally eat every one of them I've ridden in the last three days. It'll take a couple of seasons, and I think I've already killed two the cooks didn't get gathered up, but I'll get all of the others. I can do it. I have the determination."

"We have lost quite a few," Rastar said softly. "A lot more than I'd like, in fact. But as long as they hold up for the last run, we're golden."

"Not necessarily," Honal said, finally sitting up with another groan. "One of my scouts caught a group on our back trail."

"*Now* you tell me?"

"They're a few hours back," Honal told him unrepentantly. "But we do need to ready a reception."

Dna Kol paused at the edge of the clearing. The spot was a regular stopping place on the Sindi-Sheffan caravan trail, an open area created by a thousand years of caravans' cutting undergrowth for firewood, and a medium-sized, fordable stream ran through it. A heavy rain was falling, reducing visibility, but it was still clear that more iron head cavalry than he ever wanted to see again waited on the far side of the clearing.

"Crap," he snorted. "I think we've been suckered."

"There's more of them moving off to the right," one of his followers said. "Let's hammer this group before the others get into position."

"I think we're the ones who're going to be hammered," the subchief said. "But that does seem to be the only option."

Rastar grinned in the human fashion as the Boman burst from the tree line, screaming their tribal war cry. His only worry had been that they might move back into the trees, taking cover from the cavalry's fire, but perhaps the pounding rain explained why they hadn't. Surely, by now, the Boman must have realized that the League troopers' new firearms were remarkably unaffected by precipitation! Still, he supposed the ingrained habits of decades of experience against matchlocks couldn't be overcome in a mere three days.

"Load up, but hold your fire!" he shouted as he spurred his *civan* into the clearing. "I want to try something."

He drew up, turned his *civan* to present its flank to the barbarian line, and pulled out four of his eight pistols as the Boman charged to get into throwing ax range. His true-hands pointed right and left, to the outside of the charging barbarian line, while the false-hands pointed at its center. He let all four eyes defocus, drew a deep breath, and opened fire.

The astonished barbarians' charge shattered as all four pistols blazed simultaneously and the accurate, massed fire piled up a line of bodies for the following warriors to stumble over.

The prince's grin was a snarl through the thick fog of rain-slashed gunsmoke as he spun his *civan* and galloped back through the positions of his waiting cavalry.

"Okay," he called, smoking pistols held high, "now *you* can try!"

He holstered two weapons and started reloading the other two as the cavalry about him began to fire.

"Wyatt who?" he grunted.

"Are you going to get all the supplies out?" Roger asked over his helmet com.

"I sure hope so," Pahner replied with a snort. "Although we're retaining a good bit more than I'd originally planned. Got to feed these women and children something."

"I'm surprised the troops are staying in hand so well," Roger said, studying the video feed from the captain's helmet and taking in the orderliness of the city's occupiers.

"Me, too," Pahner admitted. "I'd assumed at least a twenty-five percent loss rate from AWOLs in the city, but we're at nearly one hundred percent present as of the morning report."

"That high?" Roger sounded surprised, and Pahner chuckled.

"Bistem Kar gave them an incentive," the Marine explained. "Before he released the troops to glean, he paraded them in front of the huge piles of stuff from the main storerooms and promised each of them a share on return. Some of them never even left—why go hunting through the city, when you can be handed a bag of gold and silver for staying put?—and the rest came back soon enough."

"That Kar is one smart cookie," Roger observed with a chuckle.

"That he is," the captain agreed. "And there's an important lesson here, Roger. Smart allies are worth their weight in gold."

"So what's the game plan at your end?" the prince asked.

"Rus's people are recovering from their engineering efforts. As soon as they have, I'm sending half of them back to Tor Flain to man the D'Sley defenses for him and help Fullea cross load the Sindi loot from the river barges and caravans to the seagoing vessels for transit to the Cove. The other half will move over and begin helping to load the barges from this end."

"And Bistem and Bogess?"

"I'm putting half of their people on the stores, and the other half on security. We're going to have Boman filtering back from the north soon, and I want a good security screen dug in to deal with them until we're ready."

"And after that, we wait," Roger said.

"And after that, we wait," Pahner confirmed.

Kny Camsan's head went up as he heard the firing to the north.

"Another skirmish, while all the time this group gets smaller and smaller and further and further away," he growled.

"What else can we do?" one of the subchiefs asked. "We have to run them to ground."

"Of course we do," the war leader said, "and we can. I have yet to find a group of *civan* that can outlast the Boman over the long run. But they're scattered all over the landscape, and we've been letting them dictate where we go by chasing directly after them. No more! Tell the warriors to spread out and head back towards the southeast. Instead of chasing them, we'll sweep on a broad front while the other clans join up with us. When our full strength is assembled, we'll be a wall, moving through the jungle, and whenever we encounter one of these accursed groups of theirs, we'll hammer them into the earth!"

"That sounds better than chasing along their back trail day after day," the subchief agreed. "But we're running low on food."

"We are the Boman," Camsan said dismissively. "The host can go for days without, and when we've run them down, we'll fill our bellies on the meat from their *civan* and go back to Sindi in triumph."

"Some of the host have tired of the chase. They're already going back to Sindi."

"Fine by me," Camsan grunted. "I didn't want to chase these shit-sitters in the first place, but be damned if I'll head back now until I have that Therdan pussy's head on a spear!"

CHAPTER THIRTY-SEVEN

"Armand?"

Pahner looked up in surprise as Eva Kosutic stepped into his commandeered office in the Despot's Palace of Sindi. He hadn't actually seen her face-to-face since their arrival here. They'd stayed in touch through their coms, of course, but the sergeant major had been buried in her own portion of the preparations for the "Sindi Surprise Party," as most of the army was calling the battle plan, which had kept her busy with the engineers and the artillery corps. It wasn't her physical presence that surprised the captain, though; it was the tone of her voice and her expression. He hadn't seen a grin that huge since well before Bravo Company ever heard of a planet called Marduk.

"Yes?" he replied, arching his eyebrows, and her grin got even bigger.

"Just got off the radio with Doc Dobrescu," she said, and laughed. She didn't chuckle—she *laughed*, with a bright, almost girlish delight that deepened his surprise even further. "He's got some . . . interesting news," she added.

"Well, would you care to share it with me, or are you just going to stand there with that stupid grin all day?" he asked just a bit tartly, and she laughed again.

"Sorry, Boss. It's just that I've always known His Evilness had a really perverse sense of humor, and now He's gone and proved it!"

"And how, if you ever intend to get around to it, has he done that?"

"You know that little job you gave the Doc? The one that's had him running everything he could get his hands on through the analyzers?"

"Yesss," Pahner said slowly, leaning further back in the camp chair behind his desk.

"Well, he just hit pay dirt," the sergeant major told him. "He's found something the nanites can process into the protein supplements we've got to have."

"He *has?*" Pahner snapped back upright in the chair.

"Yep, and you'll never guess where he found it," Kosutic said with another huge grin. Pahner cocked his head demandingly, and she laughed once more. "You remember that poison gland in the *coll* fish? The one that's absolutely lethal to any Mardukan, no ifs, ands, or buts?" Pahner nodded, and she snorted. "Seems the Doc remembered how Radj Hoomis failed to poison us and said, what the hell, let's check it, too. And when he did—"

She shrugged, and Pahner stared at her.

"Let me get this straight," he said slowly. "This deadly poison no one else on Marduk can eat is like . . . like *cod liver oil* for humans?"

"Not a bad analogy at all," she agreed with a nod. "From what he's saying, it tastes just as bad—or even worse. But all his tests say it's the real stuff. Of course, it won't work for anyone who doesn't have the full nanite loadout, but when you couple it with apsimons, the troops—and Roger—are good to go almost indefinitely. And we've got enough regular supplements to keep everyone who doesn't have the full spectrum nanites going for a good year or more, as well. Which is what I meant about His Evilness and His sense of humor."

"Hmmm?" Pahner was still too busy grappling with how Dobrescu's announcement had changed his constraints to realize what she was saying for several seconds, but then he laughed harshly. "I see what you mean," he said, shaking his head slowly. "We agreed to kick off this entire operation, built the damned army, pissed off every merchant in the Cove, turned K'Vaernian society on its ear, pushed the training, drove everyone into the field, and set up this whole trap just because we were running out of supplements and couldn't afford to wait around. And now we find out we've got all the time in the fucking world!"

"Absolutely," she agreed with a laugh of her own.

The two of them stared at one another for almost a full minute without saying another word, and then Pahner sighed.

"I wish we'd known sooner," he said slowly. "Kostas would be alive right now if we hadn't had to go back into the field, for one thing. But at the same time, maybe it's for the best. If I'd known about this, I would've been a lot more willing to sit things out and look for other options as the safer way to get Roger home, and if I'd done that, there wouldn't have *been* a K'Vaern's Cove in another six months."

"From what we've seen of these Boman bastards since we actually hit the field, I think you're probably right," Kosutic said more somberly, "and I wouldn't like that. I've decided I can really get along with these K'Vaernians, almost as well as with Rastar and his *civan* boys. So I guess I'm glad we didn't leave them in the lurch, too. And speaking of Rastar," she went on, changing the subject, "just how are he and Honal doing?"

"Don't know," Pahner admitted, and checked the time on his toot. "They're about due for another check in, but the last time I talked to them, even Honal was starting to sound a little frayed around the edges."

"Honal? The original Mardukan Hotspur?" Kosutic chuckled. "That'll be the day!"

"It looks like they're spreading out," Honal said. The most recent group of Boman to encounter his troopers were stretched out on the ground, riddled with pistol bullets or spitted on lances and sabers. This time, however, almost a dozen of his own men were down to keep them company on their trip to Hell. "This is the largest bunch we've run into yet."

"And I think they're closing in on us," Rastar agreed unhappily. "They're getting thicker as we head south."

The native prince eased himself in the saddle and looked around. It was raining again, which didn't do much for visibility, but he was reasonably confident of his present location. Thanks to the fact that each group to split off from the main force had included at least one trooper with a human communicator, he also knew roughly where all the rest of his men were. The good news was that his entire force should be reformed within the next several hours. The bad news was that the Boman seemed to have figured out roughly where he was headed for his rendezvous.

"We're not going to be able to make it back to Sindi," Honal said. "Are we?"

Rastar pulled out a map and grimaced accusingly at it, although it really hadn't told him anything he didn't already know.

"I don't know," he sighed. "We're so close I hate to give up. I don't doubt that they'll go ahead and head back for Sindi even without us to chase, but if we have to give up on the city, we'll have to head all the way up to the Sumeel Ford, instead, and that means heading up the Tam to the Chandar Fords. We'd be completely out of it. By the time we could cross the river, we might have to head all the way to Nashtor to avoid the Boman."

"So much for that plan, then," Honal said. "And I don't know that we could make it, anyway. The *civan* are just about worn out."

"I know," the prince said. He grimaced again, and keyed his communicator. "I think we need to tell the captain."

Pahner looked at the map and managed not to swear. It wasn't easy. From the reports, there was no way the cavalry on its own was going to break through the Boman who'd swept around to get between it and Sindi. Only a fraction of the total Boman force had managed to bottle them up, but a fraction was all it took, when they'd been outnumbered the whole time by nearly thirty-to-one.

If he sent them east, on an end run to the fords on the upland plateau, they would be out of play for the entire battle, depriving him of the huge bulk of his cavalry. That probably would have been endurable, given the battle he intended to fight, but it would cost him any real possibility of a pursuit if—when—the Boman broke. Worse, it was almost certain that all or some of the main host would go right on chasing them. Not only would that mean that whatever percentage of the barbarians kept chasing the cavalry would miss the reception he'd so carefully prepared for them here at Sindi, but it was also likely that the Boman would manage to run them down before they could reach safety.

Yet there were reports of Boman everywhere between Rastar's force and Sindi, not just farther out, where the cavalry was in light contact with the barbarians. Some of them were even starting to hit the guards he'd pushed out from the northern gates of the city, and he had damn all information on their numbers. If he sent out a relief force to rescue Rastar, he risked having it defeated in detail by an enemy whose strength he was unable to accurately evaluate.

He gazed at the map for several more silent moments, then straightened and turned to his command group.

"Bistem, you have the most forces present and on security," he said. "Take all the Diaspran forces that aren't broken up as stevedores, add them to First Division, and go relieve the cavalry. Take Julian and his team, as well. We'll worry about power for the armor later."

"Yes, Captain," the K'Vaernian commander said. "We won't fail."

"Make sure you don't," Pahner said, "and don't stint the fire. We've been saving the full power of the rifles for a surprise, and I think it's about time to start showing these bastards how surprising they are."

"Yes, Captain." The K'Vaernian gave a human-style nod, ducked out of the command tent, and started forward, calling for messengers. Pahner watched him go, then keyed his communicator again.

"Rastar, I'm sending out a relief force. The K'Vaernians are going to head for your position. Dismount and fight as infantry and push your way through to link up."

"Yes, Captain," the distant prince said over a background crackle of pistol fire. "The woods are thick enough out here that we've already had to dismount, but we can't keep our flanks secure enough to push forward. I've tried twice, and been badly outflanked each time. If you don't mind, I think I'll wait for the K'Vaernians to draw some of the attention off of us."

"Do as you see fit," the Marine said with a face of stone. Clearly, it was getting tight in the woods. "The relief column is on the way. However, be aware that if more forces press down on you, I might have to tell them to retreat."

"Understood," the embattled prince said. "We'll try to cut down the opposition as much as possible. Rastar, out."

Pahner looked around the fields before the city. The piles of cured leather, sacks of barleyrice, cloth, coal, ores, charcoal, refined metals, and a thousand and one other things vital to K'Vaern's Cove's economy were being slowly reduced by the line of bearers carrying them to the barges, the caravans of packbeasts, and the long line of wagons creaking down the corduroy road. Whatever happened here, the Cove desperately needed those supplies if it was to survive while its trading partners rebuilt themselves from the ruins. Yet every one of the stevedores loading the booty was also a soldier who was as much out of the battle as if he'd been shot through the head.

He could take some of them off of the loading duty, but that would slow down the loading operation. Which would be fine, if his overall plan worked. But as Rastar's predicament pointedly illustrated, plans had a tendency to spring leaks, and if the master plan collapsed, the Cove would need those supplies worse than ever.

Finally, he decided to take the gamble. The majority of the Boman were on the north side of the river, but they clearly were closing in on the cavalry, which had turned out to be too good as bait. There should be enough pickets covering the northern approaches to the city itself, even after Kar's departure, to hold anything else which might come at them from that direction. The caravan route to D'Sley on the south bank couldn't boast anywhere near the same amount of security, but it was covered by its own thin cavalry screen, and it seemed—so far, at least—to be isolated from the main threat area. If there were any formed Boman on the south side of the river, they couldn't possibly be present in numbers as great as those to the north, and the screen would just have to take them on as they came.

"Rus, get in the middle of that," he said, gesturing to the lines of Mardukans loading stores, "and see if you can find some way to speed things up."

"Will do," the engineer said.

"Come on, Rastar," the captain said quietly. "Keep your ass alive until Bistem can drag your butt home."

Honal swung out the cylinder of his revolver and grunted.

"I love these things. Where has Pahner been all my life?"

"Flying between suns, according to the Marines," Rastar said, hammering a stuck bullet out of the barrel of one of his own pistols. The cartridge had succumbed to the eternal humidity, despite its flashplant wrapping, and the damp gunpowder had only sparked enough to drive the slug into the barrel. "I wish he were here at the moment, though. What a screwed-up situation."

More Boman had trickled up behind the cavalry unit, encircling it. Fortunately, most of the force had reformed before the Boman pinned it, which had at least prevented the detachments from being annihilated in detail. The bad news was that it put them all in one place, which meant that better than three thousand riders and nearly eight thousand *civan* were trapped in a single pocket which the barbarians could now close in upon. Most of the true war *civan* were on the perimeter, squatting like ostriches on nests as cover for their riders, and the cavalry had managed to fell trees to simultaneously expand their fire zones and form a crude abattis covering most of their front, but the eddies of barbarians were sweeping inexorably closer.

Honal took another breath and squeezed the trigger.

"Got you, you Boman bastard," he muttered, then chuckled sourly. "You know, much as I love these revolvers, I could wish we had more rifles to go with them!"

"Some people are never satisfied," Rastar grunted. "We've got a helluva lot higher rate of fire than rifles, and with all these pocking trees, it's not like the bastards are out of range when we see them at all!"

He got the barrel cleared and closed the cylinder once more. There'd been times during the pursuit when he would have agreed wholeheartedly with Honal, but there simply weren't enough rifles to go around. Dell Mir's simplified cartridge design had allowed the humans to somewhat better Rus From's original estimates on the numbers of rifles which could be supplied with ammunition. Instead of five or six thousand, K'Vaern's Cove had managed to put eight thousand into the field, but that still fell far short of any number the K'Vaernians and their allies would have liked to see. It also meant that virtually the entire production of rifles had gone into the hands of the infantry units, who—if everything worked out the way it was *supposed* to work—would be doing the majority of the fighting. Rastar's troopers had been issued only four hundred of the new weapons. On the other hand, they'd had six thousand revolvers—virtually the entire production of that weapon.

They'd also gone through well over two thirds of their total ammunition by now, but Rastar decided not to think about that just at the moment.

"Oh, I'd never want to trade my revolvers in," Honal told him, eyes searching for another target. "I was just thinking that if we had more rifles, that would mean we also had more rifle*men* to carry them. Which would be very comforting to me right now."

"To me, too," Rastar admitted. "But I think there's a fair chance that we'll be seeing them sometime soon."

"I hope so," Honal said more somberly. "And I think I'm glad about who the Captain chose to send to relieve us. If *I* had to choose between Bogess, bless his thick head, or Bistem Kar, I'd take Kar any day."

"I have to agree," Rastar grunted, "but I wish he'd hurry up and get here." The Boman were massing for another attack as he finished reloading his pistols. "It's not like we've got an infinite amount of ammunition."

"He'll be here soon," Honal said. "Quit fretting."

Krindi Fain clasped all four hands behind him and stepped in front of Lieutenant Fonal. The adviser sergeant turned his back so that the company of forming infantry couldn't see what he was saying and cleared his throat.

"You need to quit fretting, Lieutenant."

"Is it that obvious?" the officer asked nervously.

"Yes," Fain said. "There are many ways to lead well, and twice as many to lead poorly. Looking nervous and uncertain is in the 'twice as many' category."

"So what do you suggest, Sergeant?"

"Take a breath, look at your map, and don't rub your horns every few seconds. There's a worn patch forming. Laugh. You can talk to the troops, but only about stuff other than whether or not they're ready. Your best bet is to stand there like a rock and just look as certain as the rainfall. If you go talk to Colonel Tram or General Kar for a moment, then come back and look really relaxed, it would help."

"But what about getting the company ready? We've got half a platoon missing!"

"Leave the worrying about that to Sergeant Knever. Either he's the right man for the job, and the company will perform for you when you need it, or you should have replaced him before now. Either way, it's too late to be thinking about changes. And if we have to leave without half a platoon, we leave without them."

Fonal started to rub a horn once more, then checked the movement.

"How can you be so calm, Sergeant? There are a lot of Boman out there, and not many of us." The officer leaned closer. "We're going to get slaughtered, in case you hadn't realized it," he hissed.

The sergeant tilted his head to the side and studied the lieutenant.

"Would you prefer to round up the missing ranks, Lieutenant?" he asked, wondering what the response would be. He wasn't very surprised, unfortunately.

"Frankly," Fonal said, squaring his shoulders, "if *we're* missing half a platoon, I suspect most of the other units in the regiment probably are as well. And it would be a good idea if an officer stayed behind to gather them up and send them forward."

"You have a very good point, Lieutenant," the Diaspran said. "Could you excuse me for a moment?"

Fain gestured at Erkum Pol and walked over to the quartet of armored Marines.

Julian was monitoring the commander's briefing. Kar had been handed a difficult tactical problem and not much time to solve it, but he was going about the preparation as professionally as anyone Julian had ever seen. Some of his regimental and battalion commanders, on the other hand, didn't seem all that happy about the mission, so the NCO wasn't feeling particularly happy in turn when someone rapped on his armor to get his attention.

"Hey, Krindi. How they hanging?"

"One lower than the other, as usual, Sergeant," the Mardukan answered soberly. "We've got ourselves a little situation over in Delta Company. The company commander just told me he thought it would be better if he stayed behind and rounded up stragglers."

"Oh, shit," Julian said. "Anybody hear him?"

"Aside from Erkum and me? I don't think so."

"Good," Julian said. "I won't have to kill him."

The Marine thought about it for a moment. The only person who could relieve the commander—and that commander definitely needed to be relieved—was Bistem Kar, but the K'Vaern's Cove Guard commander was far too busy to bother with a single cracked officer.

"Tell the company commander that, pending confirmation from General Kar, he's temporarily assigned to rear detachment duties. He should report to General Bogess while the rest of the force is in the field."

"Are we going to be able to get away with this?" Fain asked. "I mean, I agree and everything, but can we get away with it?"

"I can," the Marine said. "I'll tell Pahner about it, but that's about all I need to do. You don't send an officer out if he can't keep it together in front of the troops. Maybe you make *him* a troop, but that's for later. And I'll explain it to Kar and the guy's battalion commander when the time comes."

"Last question," Fain said. "Who takes the company? There's no subordinate officers—just a sergeant seconded from the Guard, and he's running around getting everybody in line and making sure they all have ammo."

Julian was just as happy that there was no way to see into his armor as he grimaced. After a moment's additional thought he gave an equally unseen shrug.

"You take it," he said. "Tell the sergeant that you're standing in until a qualified officer can be appointed. I'll get with Kar right after the meeting and tell him what's going on."

"Joy," Fain said sarcastically. "You know, if I'd known this day was going to come, I'd never have taken that pike from you."

"If *I'd* known this day would come, I never would've handed it to you," Julian said with a laugh.

"They're moving out now," Roger said, picking at the food in his bowl. The new cook simply didn't have Matsugae's way with Mardukan chili.

"That's half the force," Despreaux said, doing a quick count with her own helmet systems. "Who the hell is guarding the store?"

"There are still seven regiments in and around Sindi, even if two thirds of their personnel are busy humping crates. South of the city? Us. There are six, maybe eight hundred cavalry in the screen from here to the D'Sley swamps, with a few pickets to the east. If anything ugly comes our way, of course, the troops acting as drovers and mahouts will do their best, but they're going to be pretty scattered out. And then there's the crate-humpers back at Sindi."

"Just getting them into formation would take a couple of hours," Beckley put in. "By the way, I'm glad you two finally kissed and made up."

"Is that what we did?" Roger asked, regarding the corporal with a crooked eyebrow.

"According to the pool it is," Beckley replied with a complacent smile. "Won me almost five thousand credits, when I get home to collect it, too."

"I thought you looked revoltingly cheerful, you greedy bitch," Despreaux said with a grin.

"Me? Greedy?" Beckley shook her head mournfully. "You wrong me. I'm just delighted to see that, once again, the course of true love cannot be denied."

"Let's hope not, at any rate," Roger said, suddenly somber. "It would be nice if *something* about this trip stayed on course."

CHAPTER THIRTY-EIGHT

"Where in the hell did all this shit-sitter cavalry come from?" Sof Knu demanded, glaring at the ten- or fifteen-man cavalry picket from the undergrowth while rain drizzled down from an ebon sky.

"It must have been the 'marsh gas' we were chasing," Knitz De'n replied.

The last five days had been a period of utter frustration. De'n's tribe had arrived on the K'Vaern's Cove road to find absolutely no sign of any iron head cavalry, although there had been some tracks, washing away in the rain. They'd found a few of the damned wood runners and tortured them for information, but most had denied knowing anything, no matter how much they screamed. Finally, one had admitted to seeing some cavalry, but the place he claimed to have seen them was so close to Sindi that De'n had ordered his torturers to give him special attention to punish his lies. But the worthless creature had continued to shriek the same lie over and over again until he died, so the subchief had decided he had no choice but to check it out . . . only to find these damned patrols between him and the city. The only good thing was that the shit-sitters hadn't spotted him in return. Yet.

"We can sweep them aside easily," Knu said. "Just give the word."

"The word is *given*," the subchief growled, pulling out a throwing ax. "As soon as the tribe is assembled, we'll run right over them. And anything else that stands in our way."

"What was that?" Roger looked up from his map and cocked his head.

"What was what?" Despreaux asked. "I can't hear a thing but the rain."

"Shots," the prince replied. "To the southwest." He stood up, trying to triangulate the source by turning his head from side to side, but the brief crackle of gunfire had already died.

"Somebody shooting a damnbeast?" Chim Pri suggested uncertainly.

"Maybe one of the cavalry pickets," Roger said. He looked out at the rain-soaked, night-dark woods and shivered despite the unending Mardukan warmth. "Chim, saddle up. I want you to head southwest and see what you find. Push skirmishers out front, but find the picket that was shooting if you can, and find out what it was shooting at."

"No more shots," Turkol Bes pointed out.

"I know," Roger said wiping the rain out of his face. "And I don't care. I still want to know what they were shooting at."

"I'm going," Pri said, looking into the water-filled, Stygian blackness. "But if it's trouble, you'd better be ready to follow us up sharpish."

"We will," Roger assured him, keying his helmet com. "Sergeant Jin?"

"We heard it, too, Sir," the gunnery sergeant said. The majority of the LURP teams had been left out to supplement the cavalry screen. "It was almost due west of us. All we could hear were the shots, but it sounded like one of the screen patrols ran into something heavy."

"*Atul*?" the prince asked, and over the radio, Jin could hear Mardukans bellowing what sounded like orders in the background. Clearly, the prince was on the ball.

"I don't think so, Sir," the NCO said. "I was just about to call it in to Captain Pahner when you called me."

"Right," Roger said, and Jin could almost hear the wheels turning. "I'm pushing my cavalry down there to see what they find. I'll go ahead and orient the Carnan that way, as well. Call the Captain and give him a situation report. MacClintock out."

The NCO smiled in the darkness. Whatever was going on in the deep woods seemed to have galvanized the prince, thank God. He truly sounded like himself for the first time since Matsugae's death . . . and that was the first time the gunnery sergeant had ever heard Roger refer to himself unthinkingly as a MacClintock.

Patty burbled unhappily as the mahouts threw on her harness.

"I know, girl," Roger said, soothingly. He patted her behind her armored ruff. "I know it's dark. Deal with it."

It *was* dark—very dark. The double cloud layer had set in with a vengeance, and the moons weren't even up above it. Once they got away from the fires, most of the force would be nearly blind. The cavalry would be depending on their *civan* to find the way, and many of them would get lost. But the *civan* would eventually find their way back, at least. The same could not be said for the infantry.

He looked up to see Bes coming towards him in a way which demonstrated the point. The infantry leader had been reading a map in the tent, and now, in the shadows of the *turom* assigned to the mobile unit, he was walking with all four arms thrown forward, questing for anything which might loom unseen in his way.

"Over here, Turkol," Roger said. His own helmet systems, of course, made the area almost daylight-bright . . . which gave him an idea.

"God of Water, Your Highness," the infantry commander said. "How are we going to find our way through this?"

"I was just thinking about that," Roger told him. "I think I'll have to break up my Marine squad and let each of them lead a section of the column. We'll move in line until we find out what's happening, and each of the troops will have to hold hands with the men in front of and behind him."

"Okay," Bes agreed, his eyes starting to adjust at least a little. "The good news is that the Boman don't like to move in the dark, either. And they do it slowly. I'll go get the troops lined up."

"And I'll get the Marines," Roger said.

"*No!*" Despreaux snapped. "We're your bodyguard, not seeing-eye Marines!"

"Sergeant Despreaux, that's an order," the prince said coldly, "and if I bring it to Captain Pahner's attention, which I should *not* have to do, he'll back me on it. We may very well have a hostile force of unknown size on our flank, and no forces on this side but *us.* I don't have time to debate with you."

"Who covers your back, *Sir?*" the squad leader demanded.

"Two Marines," Roger answered, "one of whom will *not* be you. And you won't be leading a group, either, nor will I. That leaves eight. Go get them ready, and have them report to Turkol. We need to have left already."

Despreaux threw up her hands.

"All right, all right. I get the picture. Yes, Sir, yes, Sir, three bags full. Just do me one favor, Your Highness."

"What?"

"Don't go riding into the middle of a thousand Boman screaming a war chant, okay?"

Roger snorted. "Okay. And do me one favor back."

"What?"

"Don't get yourself killed. I've got plans for you."

"Okay," the sergeant said. "I'll be going now."

Chim Pri reined in at a small stream and strained to hear. The jungle was always alive with sound, yet this time there was something extra. The rain had stopped, temporarily at least, but a wind was blowing through the treetops. It probably presaged yet another rainstorm, which would be irritating enough, but it was also blowing noisy spatters of water off of leaves and vines. It made hearing difficult, yet there was something else, another rustling half-lost in the background sound, but there.

He turned around and realized he could barely see two mounts behind him.

"First three troopers. Move forward and see what that is. And try not to get yourselves killed."

A trio of *civan* trotted obediently forward, and he heard one of the all-but-invisible troopers grunting in laughter.

"Yes, Sir. We'll try real hard not to get killed."

"You'd better," the cavalry commander said with a grunt of his own. "Anybody who gets killed tonight is going on report!"

It took only a few moments for the *civan* to thread their way between the trees. But their approach, quiet as it was, was detected, and the night rang with barbarian warcries from hundreds of lungs.

"Gods of Fire and Darkness!" Pri snapped. "What in the three hells did we run *into?*"

One of the troopers he'd sent forward let loose with all seven shots in one of the newly issued revolvers, and the brilliant lightning bolts of the muzzle flashes showed the cavalry commander dozens of barbarians . . . and probably hundreds more behind them.

"Spread out!" he shouted. "I need some sort of accurate count!"

The commander spurred his *civan* to the south, searching for the tail of the barbarian column as the Boman charged straight into the swirling cavalry of the *Basik*'s Own. Finally, as the shots rose to a crescendo, he decided he'd seen enough.

"Sound the recall!" he ordered the hornmen, who'd somehow kept up through the woods. "Sound a general retreat. Hopefully, they'll fall back to the infantry."

He picked the communicator off his breast as he turned to the northeast, wondering how to tell Roger that the entire force was apparently cut off. Behind him, the horns began to sound.

The enemy was upon them.

"Well, gentlemen, this is what happens when you draw to an inside straight," Pahner said.

"It might not be that bad," Bogess said. "If it's a small force, we can beat it off."

"According to Chim Pri, it's at least a thousand or two thousand," the Marine said, "and our last sizable cavalry force—his—is scattered through the woods and all mixed up amongst them. So it's not going to be easy to stop them."

"Should we stop the loading?" Rus From asked.

"Not unless we have to," Pahner said. "Pull one regiment off of loading duties just in case, but basically, it's up to Roger now. If he beats them, we'll continue as we're going. If he's forced out of position or flanked, we'll start pulling troops off of loading to form a front facing towards D'Sley." The Marine paused and shook his head. "Did I just say what I think I said?"

"You said we should pull a battalion off of loading and that it's up to Roger," Bogess said. "Is that what you mean?"

"Yes," the captain said with a grimace. "I'm supposed to be protecting *Roger*, not the other way around. This is *not* going to look good in my report."

"You have to write the report for it to look good or bad," Rus From said with a grunt of laughter. "Let Roger look out for himself."

"Lord, Lord, Lord," the Marine groaned. "His mother's going to kill me."

Roger dropped his pad into its pouch and shook his head. He already knew the terrain, and there was nowhere to anchor his flank. There was a stream not too far behind them, though, that would work to control the line.

"Turkol, we're backing up to the far side of the stream. Put one company in reserve, spread the other three in a line, and start working out a light defense work. Have them dig in good; we're not backing up any further."

"Got it," the infantry battalion commander said. "What about the flanks?"

"If we can get the cavalry back in, we'll have it cover them. Until then, I'll split the Marines and put them in place as security teams." He thought about it for a moment more, but there wasn't much else to do. "Move."

★ ★ ★

"Roger," Pri said into the communicator, "where the hell are you? And where the hell am I, for that matter?"

"Do you remember crossing a small stream on your way out?" the prince responded, gazing at the icon the location transponder in Pri's communicator had thrown up on the map on his pad.

"Yes, I'm on the same trail we followed on the way out, I think." The cavalry commander looked around. He heard occasional pistol shots behind him, but he had at least half his command regrouped.

"We're setting up on the stream. Are you in contact with the Boman?"

"No," Pri said. "Not as an organized body, at least. Some of my people are still out there, and I can hear them shooting, but it's blacker than the inside of an *atul*'s nest, and I can't see crap. We broke contact as soon as we realized we were outnumbered, though, and I'm pretty sure my stragglers all know which way to head."

"Well, get back down there. Stay together this time, and hit them hard, then fall back in contact. We need them to come to us from the direction of our choice, and the only way to make sure they do is for you to lead them right in. We've got you on our pads and helmet HUDs, and Despreaux or I can guide you, roughly, at least, if you lose orientation on our position."

"Got it," the cavalryman said, glad to have orders, even if they were mildly crazy. "You do realize that there are over two thousand of them, right?"

"Fine," Roger said. "Just get them to the stream, and Turkol will do the rest. Oh, and when you get close, you'd better start sounding your horns."

Roger strode along the line of digging riflemen and grinned.

"I thought you New Model Army boys could *dig!* What are you, a bunch of women?"

A shovelful of wet dirt, half mud, came flying out of the darkness and hit his chest in answer.

"We're so good we can hit you in the dark, Sir!"

"As long as you can hoist them as well as you throw them," Roger said with a laugh. "We've got about two thousand Boman coming at us, so I think you're going to appreciate a wall in a little bit."

"Don't worry, Your Highness," one of the riflemen said. "We're not afraid to die for the God."

A quote came to mind. Roger couldn't remember who'd said it, but it sounded like Miranda MacClintock.

"You're not supposed to die for your God, soldier. You're here to make sure the other poor sod dies for *his*."

"Nice," Bes said as Roger walked back to the command post. The low wall and fighting trench the soldiers were erecting was backed with a small bastion for the commanders. Considering that they'd only been working on it for half an hour, it was quite an accomplishment.

"It was a quote," the prince admitted. "I swear, every good military line has already been used by somebody." He looked at the developing defenses and shook his head. "Very nice. I suppose if we can't win with this, we don't deserve to. I wonder how it's going north of the river?"

CHAPTER THIRTY-NINE

"Yes, Sir. I understand," the sergeant said.

"If I had a 'qualified officer' to replace you with, I would," the Marton Regiment's adjutant said. "To tell the truth, if I'd had a qualified officer to replace Lieutenant Fonal with, I would have."

"Yes, Sir. I understand."

"You don't sound like it," the battalion commander put in with a serious expression. "You sound petrified."

"I'll handle it, Major Ni," Krindi Fain said. "I'd just expected to be replaced. At most, I'd figured I'd handle the route march. But fighting them? I'm not sure I know how."

"Just do what you're told, soldier," the CO said. "I'm giving you a temporary rank of full lieutenant. You taught most of them the drill, so don't tell me you don't know it yourself. Just do what you know."

"Yes, Sir," the Diaspran began again, then checked himself. "I really do understand. And will comply."

"Okay," Ni said with a gesture of support. "Get to it."

Fain found himself walking back through the temporarily stopped division, wondering where and how he'd gone wrong.

"What's wrong, Fain? You look like somebody shot your dog."

He looked over at Julian and made a gesture of resigned horror.

"I'm in command of the company."

"Yeah," the Marine said. "I thought that might happen."

"I'm not real sure about this," Fain admitted. "It's a lot of responsibility."

"So was the training you gave them," Julian pointed out. "Same deal. Just get up there, and do what comes natural. Remember every good leader you've ever known and copy them. Slavishly, if you have to. And never let them see you slime." For some reason, the Marine found this last humorous.

"Okay," the Diaspran said.

"Here." The human dug into a pouch and pulled out a twisted piece of metal.

"What's this?" Fain asked, turning it over and over in a true-hand.

"First battle I was ever in," the Marine said, "I caught that piece of shrapnel. I held onto it for good luck. I sort of figured if I had it, I'd never get hit again. Don't know why. But it's always been a lucky piece for me."

"What are you going to do without it?" the Diaspran asked.

"I'm not going to need it for this battle," Julian said, tapping his armor. "The Boman hasn't been born that can crack this stuff. You take it. I'll be okay."

"All right," Fain said. "Thanks. And may the God of Water protect you."

"It's not me you have to worry about," the squad leader said, hefting his stutter gun.

Kny Camsan grunted in laughter.

"So that's what those shit-sitters were doing! There's an army back at Sindi, and they were trying to get back to it."

"That's nothing to laugh about," a subchief said sharply. "All our loot is back there, not just the loot from Sindi. And our women."

"Sure," the war leader replied with another grunt. "And so are ten or twelve thousand warriors with Mnb Trag to keep them on their toes. Which means their stupid army is still going to be sitting in front of the walls waiting when we get back. This was just a big spoiler raid. They wanted to suck us away from Sindi so they could get the rest of their army into position."

"Maybe," the subchief said. "If that was the idea, it worked, though."

"Of course it did," Camsan agreed. "And how much good is it going to do them? We've got the entire host almost fully assembled now, and the shit-sitters aren't just outside their walls, they're outside *ours,* with every warrior we have ready to come right up their backsides. They probably figured that they'd get all of our warriors out of Sindi to chase their cavalry, but they didn't, and their smart-ass plan has them stuck out where we can get at them in the open!"

"Maybe," the subchief repeated. "But we're having a hard enough time with these shit-sitter cavalry. Those new weapons of theirs are tough."

"Not tough enough now that we know where they are and what they're trying to do," Camsan shot back. "When we overrun the iron heads, we'll take their new weapons for our own. And then we'll overrun their army at Sindi and take *their* weapons, too. And when we've done that, there will be no army to man the walls of the Cove, and we'll overrun *them*, as well!"

"Let's hope it goes that way," the subchief said gloomily, "but so far, the iron heads have been doing much better out of this than we have."

"Listen up!" Bistem Kar's powerful voice boomed over the gathered infantry division. "So far, this whole war has been going for the Boman, but we're taking it to them now. The only thing that stands between us and victory is that the cavalry is trapped in there."

He gestured over his shoulder to the deep woods.

"We're going to go in there and find them. It won't be hard." There was an uneasy chuckle at that, for the crackle of gunfire was clear in the distance. "Then we're going to open up a hole and let them out. Then we march back to the city.

"I won't kid you; this is going to be a tough fight. But we can do it. All you have to do is aim low and obey your officers. Now, let's go give the Boman a little taste of what war with K'Vaern's Cove means!"

"Lieutenant Fain," the battalion CO said, "we've been tasked with putting out a company of skirmishers. Do you know the difference between skirmishing and regular fighting?"

Light was just beginning to filter through the trees, but there still wasn't enough to see your hand in front of your face, much less distinguish a white thread from a black. The entire march from the city had been made in inky darkness, and only the sheer insanity of it had prevented complete disaster. After all, the Boman had known no one would be crazy enough to try it, so why bother to set up ambushes along the route? Now, with dawn approaching, the infantry was arrayed to pry the cavalry out of its trap. If it could.

"Skirmishing means to spread out and move slow," the Diaspran said in reply to the question. "Move from cover to cover. You're trying to find the enemy force. When you do, you engage them at maximum range from cover. You try to slow them up and figure out how they're deployed, but you can't let yourself get pinned down by them, or they'll kill you."

Major Ni sighed.

"As I suspected, you know far more about it than my other company commanders. Congratulations, you just volunteered."

"Sir, this isn't a skirmisher unit," the Diaspran protested. "You use woodsmen for skirmishers. Or trained forces. It's a job for . . . crack shots and experts!"

"Nonetheless," Ni said with a gesture of command. "Get out in front."

Fain went trudging back to his new company, wondering how to pass on the word.

"Straighten up," Pol said. "Don't let them see you slime."

"Where did you hear that?" Fain asked. It was more words than Pol usually used in a week.

"Sergeant Julian," was the only reply.

Fain started to think about that. How would Julian handle the situation? Well, first of all the sergeant would be hard as nails. No protests would be allowed. Julian would explain what they were going to do in a way that made clear he was a past master of the technique . . . whether he'd ever heard of it before in his life or not.

Fain had trained with the Marton Regiment, so he knew, in general, who were the crack shots. There were quite a few who were good in Delta Company, and that was important with skirmishers.

Before the recently promoted lieutenant knew it, he'd practically walked into his formation.

"All right, you yard birds!" he snapped. "We've been detailed as skirmishers. And *we're* going to show the rest of these shit-for-brains what that means . . . !"

Roger had just taken a sip of water from his camel bag when the skirmishers pelted back from their sentry posts.

"Here they come!" one of them shouted as he tumbled over the hastily constructed wall.

The former laborers of the New Model Army had worked hard through the night, and the fortifications were as well constructed as anyone could have done in the time available to them. They consisted of a shallow wall and a trench behind the stream, all covered by a thin line of infantry pickets. Most of the cavalry had made it back and was forming up at the rear, and as soon as Pri pronounced them ready, they would head for the flanks to reinforce the Marines.

Cases of spare ammunition and rations from the pack *turom* were spaced along the wall, runners had been assigned, and most of the pack animals—including a recalcitrant Patty—had been sent to the rear, up the road towards Sindi, to clear the fighting position.

All that was left to do was fight.

"Captain Pahner, Roger here," Roger said into his radio, considerably more lightly than he actually felt. "We're about to engage an estimated two to three thousand screaming barbarians. I have, as usual, created numerous bricks without straw. And might I say once more how incredibly much fun this whole Mardukan Tour has been. We really must try it again sometime."

Despite himself, Pahner chuckled, but the chuckle had a grim note.

"Just finish them off and sit tight," he said, "because it doesn't look like I'm going to have anyone to send you for a while. The north bank is heating up."

* * *

One of the skirmishers paused, raised a hand, and made the sign for lots of good guys. Then he corrected it to bad guys.

Krindi Fain grunted and motioned for the spread-out company to move over to the left. The Marines had a term for the movement he wanted, but at the moment, he couldn't think what it was. The idea, though, was clear. When they opened fire, the Boman would know they were being attacked, and if the skirmishers attacked from right in front of their own main force, the Boman would know where their enemies were and where to counterattack. But if the skirmishers moved over to the side, the Boman might be suckered into attacking in the wrong direction.

In which case, they were *basik* on toast.

Most of the lead scouts, all people who'd at least been in the woods a couple of times, started making signals that they were seeing Boman, and Fain waved the rest of the company to a halt. Clearly the enemy was concentrating on the cavalry, but sooner or later they were bound to notice the force at their back. It was time to get it stuck in, so he grabbed a messenger and scribbled a note.

"Verbal to the Major. Tell him we're engaging . . . enfilading the Boman from the west flank."

"Enfil . . . enfol . . ."

"Never mind. Just tell him we're hitting them from the west. Get going."

The messenger disappeared into the undergrowth, and Fain looked around. He caught the company's sergeant's eye and made a gesture across his throat, followed by a complicated and terribly rude one.

Time to get it stuck in.

Honal looked up at the sudden sound of a light crackle of riflery from the south.

"About time," he grunted.

The Boman had gotten increasingly aggressive even as windrows of their dead built up around the perimeter. The undergrowth beyond the crude abattis was now so shot torn that the jungle forest had been opened up from the ground to about five meters up, and it was all swarming with Boman.

"Just in the nick," Rastar agreed, tightening a bandage around one of Honal's upper arms. "Spread the word to get ready to move out. When we do, I want the sick, the halt, the lame, and the dead on saddles. And we need to be ready to cover the retreat. These bastards are going to be really irritated to see us leaving, and it isn't going to be easy to convince them to say goodbye."

Fain looked to both sides. The Boman in front had gone to ground under the hail of fire from the skirmishers, but more were probing around the flanks.

"Tell First Platoon to fall back and south," he said, and turned to Erkum Pol. "Get the reserve to the south and make sure our way home stays open. Don't let them run, and make sure they shoot low."

"Okay," the private said, and loped off.

"Come on, Major," the newly promoted company commander whispered. "Where's the rest of the pocking army?"

"Colonel," Bistem Kar growled, "what seems to be the problem?"

"I'm ordering my lines, General," the Marton Regiment's commander said. "It will take a bit more time."

The officers of the regiment were in a huddle by the side of the Therdan-Sindi trail, and it was apparent from their expressions that the K'Vaernian commander had appeared in the midst of an argument. A heated one, from the looks of things, and that was never good news in a combat zone.

"Ask me for anything but time," he muttered. Unfortunately, Colonel Rahln, the regimental commander, like too many of Kar's senior officers, was not one of his long-term Guard officers.

The field army had been organized into five divisions, each of three regiments, plus the attached League cavalry. Each regiment consisted of one four-hundred-man rifle battalion, two four-hundred-man pike battalions, and two hundred-man companies of assegai-armed spearmen for flank protection. That meant each regiment represented almost a third of the entire prewar Guard's manpower, and there were fifteen of them in the army. Kar had kept command of the First Division for himself, and he and Pahner had at least managed to ensure that all of the other divisional commanders were Guard regulars. But despite everything they'd been able to do, all too many of the regimental commands had gone to political cronies of influential councilors or merchants, and Sohna Rahln, the Marton Regiment's CO, was one of them. Prior to the war, Rahln had been a merchant involved in several businesses, notably shipyards, but not a sailor . . . and definitely not a soldier. The appointment had been a sop designed to persuade him to support the operation, and now it was endangering it.

"Colonel Rahln, could I speak to you for a moment in private?" the general rumbled.

"I have no secrets from my officers," the former merchant said loftily, and Kar gritted his teeth. One thing he particularly disliked about Rahln was that, like many of the wealthy political appointees scattered through the force, he could never quite seem to forget his prewar contempt for the Guard. After all, if the Guardsmen hadn't been stupid—or lazy—they would have gotten *real* jobs during peacetime, wouldn't they? "You can have your say here."

"All right," Kar said. "If that's the way you want it. We have skirmishers out there, from *your* regiment, who are in contact with the enemy and need your support. We have cavalry trapped out there that needs to be relieved. You have the point regiment, and you are personally responsible for the movement of your units. You will begin the assault in the next ten minutes, or I'll have you shot."

"You can't do that!" Rahln snapped. "I'll have you broken for even suggesting it!"

The K'Vaernian general reached out and lifted the lighter officer into the air by his leather harness. The colonel squawked in shock at the totally unexpected assault, but his shock turned to terror as the Guard officer flipped him over a hip and then slammed him onto the ground on his back so hard that everyone within three meters actually heard the air driven from his lungs.

Kar dropped to one knee and took the colonel by the throat with one false-hand.

"I could squash you like a bug," he hissed, "and nobody would care. Not here. Not in K'Vaern's Cove. Now get a spine, and let your officers—who, unlike you, know what they're doing—get to work!

"Nine minutes," he added, with a shake of the throat.

"Are you sure that was a good idea?" his aide asked as they headed back to the command post.

"The only problem with it was getting that cretin's foul slime on my clean harness," the general snorted. "His battalion commanders are professionals. If he leaves them alone, he'll make the deadline. But cut orders to replace him with Ni if he continues to fuck up. And send a team of Guards . . . with revolvers and a watch."

CHAPTER FORTY

Fain looked around. The remnants of his company were gathered by the side of another of the numerous streams found in the Sindi Valley. They'd managed to pull out of the developing pocket, but they'd left some bodies behind. Pol was here, though, with the reserve which had hammered the Boman trying to flank them from the south. The company had found it necessary to watch its footing on the way out to avoid tripping over the bodies of dead barbarians.

The brass, naturally, had failed to provide a map, so Fain had only the vaguest notion of where they were. He did know, however, that the Boman had pulled back for the moment. They were maintaining their perimeter around the trapped cavalry, and they appeared to think the skirmishers were the only threat. That was nice, since it presumably also meant that the barbs still didn't have a clue where the *real* threat was coming from, which was precisely what Fain had hoped he and his people would accomplish.

The only problem was that they weren't skirmishing anymore. He needed to keep the Boman aware of Delta Company's presence if he wanted to keep them from figuring out where the rest of the relief force was, and he knew it. But he also knew that, ultimately, raiding on the flanks like this didn't do any good, however much it confused the enemy, unless there was an immediate follow on assault, and an assault was exactly what had failed to materialize. It was obvious that if the company went back, the Boman would be on them like *atul* on a stray *turom*, but unless the rest of the regiment got its head out of its ass and actually moved when he headed back in, it would only get his people killed without even doing any good.

It wasn't supposed to work this way. There should have been an assault. The Major had *said* there would be an assault, not just his single company thrown out here in the middle of nowhere without support.

It wasn't supposed to be this way, and he hoped it was going better elsewhere.

"Captain Pahner, Roger here."

The voice sounded in the captain's mastoid implant, and he keyed his helmet.

"Ah, Prince Roger! Still alive, according to the little chip in my brain which I suspect detonates if you die."

"I see everyone is in a good mood," the prince said. In the background, Pahner could hear continuous and heavy rifle fire. "I'd like to revise that previous estimate of mine. Make that three thousand-plus Boman."

"I really love this business," Pahner said conversationally. "I know that no plan survives contact with the enemy, but have any plans ever gone this awry?"

"I'm sure they must have," Roger said in an encouraging sort of way. "Somewhere. But I digress. I don't suppose you have anything resembling a reserve back there?"

"Actually, I did," Pahner said. "I'd detached half the laborers back to combat duties. But I just sent them north of the river to back up Bistem. It would take at least a couple of hours just to get them back to this bank, much less to your position. Why?"

"Just wondering," Roger said, and Pahner heard the distinct sound of a bead pistol firing. "We got a bit flanked here."

"Roger," Pahner said in a very calm voice, "are you surrounded?"

"I prefer to call it a target-rich environment," the prince replied. "But the good news is that they seem bound and determined to wipe us out rather than bypass us and head for the city or the D'Sley road. So we're succeeding in our mission, aren't we?"

"But I'm not," Pahner said calmly, very calmly. "I'm pulling the rest of the infantry off of the stores."

"Yeah, well, don't bother on our account," Roger said. "You couldn't get infantry here for hours, and this is gonna be over, one way or the other, in another thirty minutes."

Roger ducked as Despreaux fired over his head. Particles of black powder stung the back of his neck, the muzzle flash singed his ponytail, and only his helmet kept him from being permanently deafened.

"Careful there, honey!" he said. "I've always wondered what a toot looks like, but I don't want to look at my own."

"Screw you, Your Highness," the sergeant said as a rifle volley hammered the latest charge into offal. "That one was too close."

"Not so bad," Bes said, sticking his head out of the slit trench they'd gouged out of the muddy earth behind their original positions. "Would have been nice if we'd been able to hold the original line, but this one isn't bad, except on the flanks."

"Speaking of which," Despreaux said. "Reneb, check in. Everybody still here?"

"Still here," the team leader confirmed. "No casualties in the team so far, and we're piling them up."

"Same here," Roger said, looking out of the slit trench.

There were only twelve humans in the entire force, but each of them had begun the day with thirty ten-round magazines for their new rifles. They were conserving that ammunition as much as they could, letting the Mardukans' single-shot rifles carry most of the fight at long range. But whenever the barbarians began another charge, the sheer volume of fire from those magazine-fed rifles and the cavalry's revolvers wreaked dreadful carnage.

The ground on both sides of the trench for as far as Roger could see into the jungles was littered with Boman bodies. The barbarians had learned that the only way to get into ax range was to charge forward blindly, seeking to break through the fire zone by sheer weight of numbers. A few times, it had gotten down to hand-to-hand, but even there the Carnan Battalion and the *Basik*'s Own had managed to hold their own, and the assaults had been repulsed.

"Here they come again!" Bes shouted, closing his rifle breech and firing at the first of the charging Boman.

This time the barbarians had managed to coordinate their attacks, which made things tougher. They came from both sides, but not directly at the flanks, which probably would have rolled up Roger's entire embattled position. The prince looked to the nominal "rear" and shook his head as the aiming reticle appeared in his vision. He tossed his magnum to Cord, who'd become quite a respectable rifle shot himself, drew his bead pistol once more, took up a two-handed stance, and began a timed fire sequence. One shot per second cracked out for each of the fourteen seconds it took the Boman line to reach the trench, and each shot took out a barbarian.

The riflemen to either side, Marine and Mardukan alike, had been hammering out fire in both directions. The rifles' black powder filled the little clearing with gray-white smoke and a smell like the breath of Hell itself, and as the Boman jumped into the trenches or struck down with their two-handed battle axes, it seemed as if Lucifer had arrived in person.

The majority of the defenders switched to their long bayonets, and Despreaux blocked the swing of an ax, buttstroked the axeman in the groin, and then ducked as Turkol Bes bayoneted someone over her shoulder. She sprang past him as Cord missed a block and was slammed into the wall of the trench. The bleeding shaman had been the last thing between Roger and an ax-swinging Boman easily as large as Bistem Kar, and the sergeant felt an instant of pure despair as she realized she could never reach him before he reached Roger.

Patty had been sent back with the other pack animals, but Dogzard had evaded all efforts to corral her and send her back, as well. As the barbarian's ax rose for the fatal stroke, ninety kilos of hissing lizard ripped into his leg from the side. The dog-lizard's attack slowed the Boman just enough for Roger to twist sideways and get a shot in. The hypervelocity bead took the axeman almost dead center, but despite the slamming impact, the barbarian still managed one last swipe at Roger. The prince blocked the blow with the sword in his right hand, then stepped out of the way as the giant toppled at his feet.

The axeman had been the last enemy alive in the trench, and Roger stepped back again as a pair of Diaspran infantrymen heaved the body out of the trench and added it to the parapet of corpses.

"God damn these stupid, four-armed bastards," Despreaux cursed wearily, wiping blood out of her eyes. "Don't they know when they're beat?"

"Sure they do," Bes grunted in laughter. "Almost as well as oversized *basik*."

Knitz De'n grabbed both his horns and shook them back and forth in anger. A scout had just brought back word that Sindi had actually fallen—that the city was being looted to the ground and that all of their women and children had fallen into shit-sitter hands—and this tiny group had repulsed *five* charges by the finest ax wielders in the Valley of the Tam. It wasn't possible.

"One more time," the subchief hissed. "One more charge, and we can destroy them all."

"No, we can't," Sof Knu said flatly. "These new arquebuses of theirs are impossible, and they fight like demons. Let us go west; surely some warriors must have escaped the fall of the city. We can find them—join with them, and harass these K'Vaernians. Harass them, and pull them down like *kef* do a *turom*. It's how we always face greater forces."

"No!" Knitz De'n shouted. "We'll kill them here and now! This is our land, taken by our arms, and no one will take it away!"

"Do as you wish," Sof Knu said, "but I'm leaving, and taking my warriors with me. I'm not insane."

The ax entered between Knu's shoulder and neck, almost severing his right true-arm. He fell, and Knitz De'n dragged the ax free with a wrench and waved it in the air.

"Do any others dispute my right of command?" he snarled, looking around the group of sullen barbarians. "One more charge!

Into the face of death I fly! With the heart of an *atul* and the strength of the *pagathar! Wesnaaar!*"

"I don't believe it," Despreaux said, and Roger looked up from bandaging Cord.

"This is a joke, right?" he said as he watched four Boman charge out of the brush. The unsupported quartet was about as much threat to the combat veterans dug in to await it as a similar number of children.

"Either berserk, or doing it for honor," Pri said. He gave the barbarians another look and grunted. "Berserk."

"Well? Is anyone going to shoot them, or are we just going to let them kill us all?" Despreaux asked tartly.

Four bead pistol shots cracked out before a single rifle could speak, and the Boman flew backwards in explosions of gore.

"What?" Roger said, holstering the pistol and returning to his *asi*'s bandage. "Like that?"

"Yeah," Despreaux said quietly into the sudden silence. "Like that."

"You know," the prince said, never looking up from the bandage, "one of these days, I'm going to be in a fight where I don't kill anything."

"That'll be the day," the sergeant replied sadly.

"You know, this could turn out to be a nice day after all," Krindi Fain said as regular volleys started hammering to the east.

Despite the lack of support, the former sergeant had sent snipers forward to peck at the Boman line. The response had been violent, but uncoordinated, with nearly three hundred Boman chasing the snipers into the woods . . . where the survivors of his hundred-man company had finally ambushed them at the edge of a thicket. The company's fire had piled up most of the barbarians for very little loss, which had been one of the first things to go right all day. But nice as that had been, the sudden, massive firing crashing out to the east now was the most blessed sound he'd ever heard.

"Our job's done," he said. "Let's go find the good guys. And for the God's sake, keep an eye out! The Boman are going to be swarming around the flanks, and we don't want to get shot by our own people, either!"

"Can we loot the ones we killed, Lieutenant?" one of the troopers asked.

"Not until after the battle," he snapped. "Now let's move out while the moving's good."

"But we're gonna retreat," the trooper protested. "We won't be able to get nothin'."

"You're gonna get my foot up your ass if you don't shut up," Erkum Pol said. "You heard the Lieutenant. Move it!"

"Time to leave, people," the company commander said, pointing slightly to the south of the firing. "About there should be good."

"Right there!" Rastar shouted as the *civan* lurched to its feet. He spurred to the west, revolvers streaming smoke and flame. Half a dozen of his troopers rode with him, their massed fire tearing a hole in the Boman line, and then all of them dodged aside as the herd of stampeding *civan* thundered past them.

The loose *civan*, driven by Honal and a dozen more mounted troopers and maddened with fear from the firing and blood smell behind them, smashed into the already breached Boman line, throwing it even further into chaos. The regular volleys from the south, when most of the previous firing—light as it had been—had come from the south*west*, had thrown the enemy totally off balance. Caught between two fires, the barbarians on the south side of the perimeter hadn't known which way to turn.

The barbarians on the other three sides had no such doubts. They charged forward when they saw the cavalry slipping out through the hole in the line, but only to run into regular, slamming volleys of aimed rifle fire. The three thousand cavalry in the pocket had been low on ammunition, and barely a tenth of them had been armed with rifles. The men of the five rifle battalions Bistem Kar had peeled off and assigned to Major Dnar Ni, who had replaced the recently deceased Colonel Rahln as CO of the Marton Regiment, suffered under no such handicap. There were two thousand of them, and they slammed volley after volley into the packed barbarians. The four-armed Mardukans could load, prime, and fire their weapons without even lowering them from the firing position, and their rate of fire was incredible by any human standard. The Boman were crowded so closely together a single bullet could kill or wound as many as three, or even four of them, and each rifleman was sending six aimed rounds per minute straight into them. Not even the famed Boman fighting frenzy could carry them forward into that vortex of destruction, and the warriors in front of the firing line were driven to ground.

The warriors to either side of the relief force riflemen spread wider, seeking to find and envelop their flanks, only to encounter assegai-armed spearmen and recoil afresh.

"Message to Colonel Des," Kar said. "He's to refuse his right flank and withdraw. Same message to Colonel Tarm, but he's to refuse his *left*."

The K'Vaernian general looked up with a nod as Rastar reached his command group and reined in.

"Prince Rastar."

"General Kar," the prince said with a matching nod. "Nice of you to show up."

"Had a few problems with a subcommander," the K'Vaernian admitted. "They're solved. How many are we looking at?"

"Not the entire host, thank the gods." The cavalry officer slid off his *civan*. "I think Camsan figured out where we were headed sooner than we'd planned. Whatever happened, he scattered his own troops and the first ones to reach him through the woods here in an effort to keep us from getting back to Sindi, and that's all we've got to worry about right this minute. The rest are still back there, coming down from the north to join up. Only a few of them actually found us, I think, but that, unfortunately, seems to include Camsan himself, so the coordination's been fair. And all the rest of them are undoubtedly coming on from behind him."

"As long as it's not the full hundred thousand already, we should be fine," Kar said. "We need to retreat smartly, though."

"Oh, yes," Honal agreed fervently, riding into the conference. "I don't want to spend another night like that last one."

CHAPTER FORTY-ONE

"This is actually beginning to look halfway decent," Pahner said.

"I'm glad to hear it," Rus From said. The Diaspran who'd become the chief field engineer of the K'Vaernian army stretched wearily. "We managed to get almost all of the exposed stores aboard the boats and sent them off downriver," he reported. "There's still a lot to go, but it's all on the south side of the river now, behind the surprise."

"Good," Bogess said. "Now if we can just get the army back together here before Camsan turns up—and assuming, of course, that Bistem gets back here intact—things will definitely be looking up. And it looks like Roger has smashed the Boman to the south quite handily."

"Yep," Pahner agreed. "Gotta love competent subordinates. Of course, that begs the question of who's the subordinate in this case. Speaking of which." He keyed his communicator. "Prince Roger, Captain Pahner."

Roger groaned as the attention signal pinged.

"Roger," he said. "Take that however you prefer."

"I hate to break this to you, Your Highness, but I need you to bring your butt back to Sindi. I imagine we'll be entertaining the main host here sometime tomorrow morning, and I'd like you to be present for the party."

"Gotcha, Captain," the prince said with another groan, and surveyed the troopers lying all around the reclaimed original trench line in exhausted heaps. No doubt it was all dreadfully untidy, and not at all the way it was supposed to be according to The Book, but at least all the bodies were out of the trench, and all the wounded had been bandaged.

"We'll head out in a few minutes," Roger went on. "But be aware that we had to send all of our *civan* and *turom* back already, so we're on foot. That's going to slow us down."

"Understood," Pahner said. "I'll send some troops out to meet you with your mounts. Move out, Your Highness."

"Roger, out." The prince smiled as he got to his feet. "Take that however you prefer," he whispered, and then poked the sergeant who'd lain half-asleep beside him with a toe. "Despreaux! What the heck are you doing lying around snoring when your prince is in danger?"

Krindi Fain wasn't lost, he simply didn't know where his battalion—or his regiment—had gotten to. No one else seemed to know either, but, since seeing their company commander stumbling around in the middle of a retreat looking for their parent unit would be a bad thing for morale, he'd parked the company with the supply packbeast guards and gone a-hunting.

He also wasn't asleep, simply sort of numb. Which was how he came to be walking with his eyes sort of closed when he slammed into the obstacle.

"What are you doing here, soldier?" Bistem Kar's aide-de-camp demanded as the acting lieutenant bounced off of him, and Fain's eyes went wide at the sight of all the brass standing about.

"Krindi Fain, acting lieutenant, Delta Company, Rifle Battalion, Marton Regiment!" he said, snapping a salute. "I'm looking for the Battalion, Sir!"

"Fain?" Kar himself rumbled. "Weren't you an instructor sergeant not too long ago?"

"It's a long story, General," the braced acting lieutenant said. "I think I'll let Major Ni and Sergeant Julian explain it, if I may, General!"

"Delta Company?" one of the other officers said. "I thought that was Lieutenant Fonal. I was surprised he got picked to command those skirmishers on the southwest flank, but that was you, wasn't it?"

"Yes, Sir," Fain said. "We're just trying to find our way home now, Sir."

General Kar grunted in laughter.

"That's the best description of this madhouse I've heard yet," he said, and his command staff joined his laughter. Fain was pretty sure that his participation in their humor wouldn't be appreciated, but he was too tired to really care, and he raised all four hands, palms upward in a purely human gesture.

"I'm just trying to find our unit, Sir," he said tiredly. All these clean staff officers, who'd undoubtedly had to suffer through a hot breakfast and forego the pleasure of being covered in smoke stains and blood, were making his head ache.

"Not anymore," Kar said. "Go back, get your people, and bring them up here, instead. I'll be moving around, but I'm sure you can find the headquarters. I'm sorry there's no sleep for any of us, but make sure they get a bite to eat . . . and then replace the command group security company. *Colonel* Ni is just going to have to figure out how to spare you, because I'd rather have combat-proven veterans watching my backside!"

"Thank you, Sir," the former NCO said.

"No," the general said firmly. "Thank *you*. When we hit the Boman, they didn't know which way to turn, and that was due in large part to you. So thank your company for me. When we get back to Sindi, I'll do it personally."

"Yes, Sir," the acting lieutenant said. "I better go get the Company."

It took hours to retreat through the trees. The Boman seemed endless as the long Mardukan day wore on; for every one they killed, two more seemed to spring up out of the earth. The cavalry was essentially useless, since not only were its *civan* all but exhausted, but it lacked the clear space to work up to a charge even if they hadn't

been. The few mounted troopers with rifles had been sent to fill gaps in the line, but Rastar and Honal kept one troop in the saddle, ready to plug any sudden holes.

The pikes weren't much more use than cavalry in the close confinement of the jungle, but the assegai-wielding spearmen proved their value again and again during the chaos and confusion of the withdrawal. The Boman probed around the flanks, and even turned them a few times, only to be driven back and pounded into the ground. It seemed, as the choking pall of gun smoke rose like thick fog through the canopy, as if the withdrawal would never end. The nightmare struggle, crash of rifles, scream of bullets, and shriek of the wounded and dying were all part of some eternal, unending purgatory from which there could be no escape, and all anyone knew of it was the tiny part that he himself endured.

But, in the end, the withdrawing regiments finally reached the edge of the trees, and the whole, dreadful engagement could be seen.

Pahner saw it from the walls of Sindi, and shook his head as the units began to emerge. Bistem Kar had pulled out most of his dead, and all of his wounded, and he'd taken a fraction of the casualties he should have. Of course, he'd had an enormous advantage in terms of his troops' weapons, but Pahner suspected that the K'Vaernian general would have succeeded in a battle against an equally armed force, as well. There was a name that hovered on the edge of his consciousness, something about a wall. That was what Kar reminded him of, a stone wall nothing could break, even as he moved his units like dancers in a thunderous ballet of battle.

The pike battalions came first as the K'Vaernian forces began to clear the edge of the jungle. It was clear to Pahner that Kar had been forced by the combat environment to reorganize his forces on the fly, and the rifles continued to fire further into the jungle as the pike units shook out into line and dressed ranks. From the looks of things, they hadn't been heavily engaged in the previous fighting, and it was likely that the Boman had not yet discovered just how hard a target an unshaken wall of pikes was.

As the pikes settled into place, other units began to emerge from the jungle. Rastar's cavalry came first, much of it dismounted by now. The wounded and the dead came next, covered by walking wounded and spearmen. The riflemen came last of all, falling back with an iron discipline Pahner could feel all the way from the walls. It was a discipline he and his Marines had trained into them, but he knew only too well how that discipline could have vanished if the troops had feared for one moment that their commander was irresolute. Obviously, they had no such fear where Bistem Kar was concerned.

The trickiest moment came when the pike blocks had to open ranks to let the riflemen pass through, but Kar managed the maneuver so adroitly that the Boman never even seemed to recognize the moment of opportunity.

By the time the Boman realized what was happening, the retreating army had reformed itself into a huge, hollow square of pikes. In effect, there were no flanks for the barbarians to attack, any longer, and the entire formation marched slowly but steadily towards the gates of Sindi. Time and again, masses of Boman swept outward, hooking around in an effort to find an open flank to exploit, only to find themselves held well beyond hand-to-hand range by the pikeheads while aimed volleys tore them apart. Once or twice, enough barbarians managed to circle around the pike square to bring it almost to a halt, but each time, Kar concentrated his riflemen to bring a devastating fire to bear and literally blasted a path through them.

In the end, even the Boman were forced to admit that they could not overwhelm their enemies, and the triumphant relief force broke free of the sea of barbarians and began to funnel back through the gates while a steadily contracting shield of pikes, covered by rifles on the ground and on the walls alike, held off the barbarians' last, despairing charges.

Throughout the endless, exhausting day, Krindi Fain had stood at the edge of the command group and watched the general work. Kar had stood still and calm, hands clasped behind his back, and only occasionally snapped out an order. But whenever he did give an order, aides and messengers scurried to obey.

Fain didn't have to worry about that, though. He'd deployed his company around the general, and that was that. The new company commander realized that his own blundering into the group around the general was at least partially to blame for the change in his command's assignment, since it had pointed out a certain weakness in Kar's security arrangements. There was no way he should have been able to, more or less, sleepwalk past the command group's previous guards, and he was determined that no one else would sleepwalk past *him*. Not that it required a great deal of personal effort from him. Delta Company's skirmishers, their rifles held muzzle-down and to the left, like some of the Marines, glared balefully at anyone who approached the general. Nobody was going to sleepwalk past *these* guards.

That eager alertness had left Fain free to watch the progress of the battle, and he'd recognized that in Bistem Kar he saw someone operating on a level of competence he could recognize and appreciate but never hope to approach himself. Now he watched the Boman attacks trickle off as darkness finally fell and the last of the relief force, including the command group, withdrew behind the walls of Sindi.

Kny Camsan stood in the evening rain and stared in disbelief at the walls of Sindi.

It couldn't be true. It was impossible! Yet the evidence was there before his eyes, impossible to deny.

He had trusted Mnb Trag to hold Sindi in his absence, and he wanted to blame the old chieftain for failing him. But no one could look at those walls and blame Trag. Even all that the shit-sitters had done to the host throughout this long and terrible day paled beside what they'd done to Sindi. Camsan could not imagine what had torn and ripped the massive walls that way, but there were dozens of breaches through them—huge wounds through which the shit-sitters must have stormed to wrest the city from Trag and his warriors.

"What do we do now?" one of the other chieftains demanded harshly.

"We gather our numbers throughout the night," Camsan replied, never taking his eyes from the ravaged walls of the city which was to have been his capital.

"And what then?" the chieftain pressed, and Camsan turned to face him.

Tar Tin was of the Gestai, one of the larger Boman clans, and the Gestai had been among the most restless under Camsan's leadership. Tar Tin himself was a chieftain of the old school, one who believed in the exalted power of the battle frenzy to carry warriors to victory over insurmountable odds, and that made him dangerous. Worse, he'd been one of the stronger supporters of the war leader Camsan had replaced after the debacle at Therdan, and his resentment at being pushed aside by those who'd supported Camsan ran deep.

"And then we pin the shit-sitters and starve them," Camsan said sharply.

"And starve our women and children right along with them?" Tar Tin more than half-sneered. "Truly a plan of rare genius!"

"It's the only way!" Camsan shot back forcefully. "The losses we've taken charging into their guns again and again today are proof of that!"

"I say that it is *not* the only way," Tin spat. "The shit-sitters themselves have broken and torn the walls which might have held us out, and they hold our women and children hostage against us. Do you think that they'll hesitate for a moment to kill those women and children—the women and children you gathered together here that they might be '*safe*'—once they realize they themselves are doomed? We must attack—*now!* We must storm through the gaps they made for us in their own foolishness and overwhelm them before they destroy the entire future of the Boman!"

"That is madness!" Camsan protested. "Didn't you see what their new weapons *did* to us in the forest? Don't you realize that if they can tear such rents in walls of stone and mortar, they can do far worse to our warriors if we allow them to catch us in the open? No, we must find another way!"

"We must *attack!*" Tin snarled, even more loudly. "That's what true Boman do—they charge, and they die. And then other Boman charge over their bodies, and still others, until a charge strikes home and we triumph!"

"We've lost thousands this day!" Camsan snarled back. "And if we assault those walls, today's losses will seem as nothing. It will be Therdan all over again, only many times worse. What good will we do our women and children by charging to their rescue only to be destroyed ourselves? Do you think the shit-sitters will hesitate to kill them once they've destroyed the host, and the threat of our vengeance no longer hangs over them?"

The war leader clapped his hands in a gesture of violent negation.

"To charge a prepared enemy with the weapons these shit-sitters possess would be as stupid as it would be pointless! We must find a better way!"

"It is your 'better ways' and your clever stratagems which have killed more of us than anything else," Tar Tin said in a flat, deadly voice. "I think you have lost the respect of the clans. This disaster is *your* doing, even more than the shit-sitters'."

The Gestai chieftain stepped back and raised his hands.

"Who is the origin of our grief? The walls of the city lie broken and open! Our warriors lie dead on the field for nothing! Whose hesitation and refusal to overwhelm K'Vaern's Cove gave the shit-sitters the time to prepare these 'new weapons,' and who led our warriors out to face them while our women and children were stolen from us?" Tin glared savagely at Camsan, and his voice dropped to deadly softness as he repeated, "*Who is the origin of our grief?*"

The other chieftains gathered around the argument. Most of them were far older than Kny Camsan, and more than a few had resented his relative youthfulness when he was named war leader. They'd supported his ascension after Therdan because the horrible casualties suffered trying to storm that city's walls had been enough to frighten even Boman. But now, with casualties almost as heavily piled on the field and scattered through the jungle, and with the bulk of the clans' women and children in the hands of shit-sitters, they were willing to consider another change.

"What do you think they're doing over there?" Roger asked wearily.

His mobile force had reached Sindi shortly after nightfall. Even many of the infantry had learned how to doze in the saddle now, for utter exhaustion was an excellent teacher, yet Chim Pri and his cavalry had somehow managed to dress ranks and trot jauntily through the southern gates under their snarling *basik* standard. Now the prince stood on the battlements, most of his weight propped on a merlon while he and Pahner gazed out across the fields.

"Jin has a LURP team keeping an eye on them," the captain said now. "We can't get close enough to tell exactly what's going on, even with the directional mikes, but it sure sounds like they're having some sort of deep and meaningful discussion, complete with lots of threats. I imagine they're discussing a possible change in the chain of command, and, frankly, nothing would please me better. This Camsan character is much too flexible and innovative a barbarian to make me happy."

"You really think they'll come at us again in the morning?" Roger waved at the heaps of Boman bodies, clearly visible to both of them thanks to the magnification of their light-gathering helmet visors. "After we did that to them in the open field?"

"I've done everything I can think of to encourage them to, at any rate," Pahner replied. "We used up almost a dozen charges for the plasma cannon blowing those nice, wide breaches in the wall, and I'll be extremely disappointed if it doesn't occur to any of them that they've got all sorts of ways into the city now. And the fact that all their women and children are in here should suggest to them that it would be a good idea for them to come and rescue them."

"And if they don't?" Roger asked. "What do we do then?"

"If they won't come to us, then we go to them—in a manner of speaking. I'll blow the Great Bridge behind us to maroon them on the other bank of the river, then head south with their women and children in the middle of a pike square, if I have to. They'll probably find a way across the river eventually—I'm sure they'll build rafts, if nothing else—but I figure we can make it almost all the way to D'Sley before they can get onto this side in any strength. There's enough left of the walls there, especially with the repairs Tor Flain, Fullea, and their people have been making, to hold easily with the rifles and the new artillery, and we'll still have their women and children as bargaining counters.

"In some ways, I'd have preferred to do that from the beginning, because whatever happens, it's going to be ugly if they come at us tomorrow. If we could get their dependents back to D'Sley and *make* them talk to us, and if it were handled right, by someone like Eleanora, it would probably offer the best way to settle this whole thing without huge additional casualties for somebody. Unfortunately, I didn't think we'd have time to hang around and handle the negotiations ourselves, which would have meant leaving it all up to the K'Vaernians, and much as I've come to like and respect most of them, I don't think that would've been a good idea. Even the best of them are still a bit too prone to simply slaughter their enemies and be done with it for me to feel comfortable about leaving so many thousands of noncombatants in their hands. Now that Dobrescu's come through with his *coll* liver oil extract, we could probably take the slower route . . . except that everything is already dug in and ready here, and there's too good a chance the bastards would manage to get across and swarm us in the open on the way back to D'Sley."

Roger turned his head and gazed at the captain's profile. Armand Pahner, he had discovered, was as complex a human being as he'd ever met. The captain was one of the most deadly people the prince could imagine, with a complete willingness to destroy anything or anyone he had to in order to complete his mission and deliver Roger alive to Earth once more. Yet for all his ruthlessness, the Marine was equally determined *not* to destroy anything he could avoid destroying. The prince had discovered enough about his own dark side, here on Marduk, to know how easy it would have been for someone in Pahner's place to become callous and uncaring. The Boman were only barbarians, after all. Why should their fate matter to a civilized man whose entire objective was to get off their planet in the first place?

Yet it did matter to him. As he stood there on the battlements beside Roger, Pahner had all the pieces in place to trap and destroy the Boman host. Not simply defeat it, but *destroy* it, in a massacre which would make today's casualties look like a children's pillow fight. The captain had worked for weeks to plan this operation, driven his Marines and his allies mercilessly to prepare and execute it, and he was determined to drive it through to a conclusion. No doubt many people would have believed that his determination sprang from a desire to stamp out the Boman once and for all, but Roger knew better. That determination sprang, in fact, from a desire to *spare* all the Boman that he possibly could. It was a recognition that the Boman would never concede defeat until they were made to do so, and that the only way to make them was to crush them militarily, with all the casualties and carnage that entailed. But the only way to prevent Pahner's allies from truly destroying the Boman by massacring the women and children who represented the continuation of the clans, was to force the warriors to admit defeat.

And so, in a way, the only way to save the warriors' families was to kill the warriors themselves, and that was precisely what Armand Pahner was prepared to do.

CHAPTER FORTY-TWO

Kny Camsan turned his face to the North as the gray light of a rainy Mardukan dawn filled the skies. Somewhere up there, young warriors were being born. In the far hills, shamans were placing their infant false-hands on the hilts of knives and slicing the palms of their true-hands to introduce them to the pleasure and the pain of battle. Somewhere, young hunters were tracking *atul* for their first kill.

Somewhere, life went on.

The ax didn't quite sever his head from his shoulders. That was a bad omen, but it wasn't allowed to delay the ceremony of investment of the new war leader, and Tar Tin, the new paramount war leader of the clans of the Boman, was anointed in the blood of his fallen predecessor, as tradition demanded.

Tar Tin lifted the blood-smeared ceremonial ax over his head and waved it at the far battlements.

"We will destroy the shit-sitters who befoul this land! We will retake the city, retake our women and our children, retake all that booty they would plunder from us! We will destroy this shit-sitter army to the last soul and level K'Vaern's Cove to the very earth and sow it with salt! We shall cleanse these lands so that treacherous shit-sitters across the world tremble at the very name of the Boman and know that treachery against us is the way of *death!*"

The chieftains and subchiefs assembled around him cheered and brandished their battle axes, and he pointed once more at the battered walls of Sindi.

"Kill the shit-sitters!"

"They seem upset," Pahner observed.

The captain, Roger, and Julian's entire surviving squad stood in the cellar of a large, demolished house in the northern portion of Sindi. The hurricane of the rocket bombardment had turned this entire part of the city into uneven mounds and hills of rubble, and the flourishes which Rus From's engineers had inflicted, with artful assistance from touches of Gronningen's plasma cannon, only completed the air of devastation. There was absolutely nothing in the area to attract the attention of any Boman warrior, which, of course, was the entire object.

"I think you might say 'upset' was just a *bit* of an understatement," Roger said judiciously, striving to match the Marine's clinical tone.

"You're probably right," Pahner conceded, "but what really matters is that they seem to have themselves a new commander, and, as Poertena would say, he's a 'pocking idiot.'"

This time, Roger only grunted in agreement. There wasn't much of anything else to say, as the two of them watched their pads display the torrent of red hostile icons streaming towards the breaches left so invitingly in Sindi's walls.

Roger watched them for a few more moments, but his eyes were drawn inexorably towards the clusters of blue icons waiting for them. Those icons represented the rifle and pike battalions who had the hardest job of all, and he wondered what was going through their minds as they hunkered down in their rough fieldworks and waited for the onslaught.

Krindi Fain was quite certain that it was an enormous honor to be selected as the commander of Bistem Kar's personal bodyguard. With a whole three hours of sleep behind him, he almost felt alive enough to appreciate the honor, as a matter of fact. Unfortunately, there was a downside to his new assignment, as the echoing war cries and the thunder of the Boman's drums brought forcibly to mind.

The general wasn't quite in the most advanced position his troops occupied, but his dugout of rubble and sandbags came close enough to make Fain very, very nervous. Of course, the lieutenant—his "acting" rank had been confirmed before he turned in last night—understood why Kar had to be where he was. After yesterday, the Guard commander enjoyed the total trust—one might almost say adulation—of his troops, and their confidence in their commander had to be absolute for this to work. Which meant they had to know that "the Kren" was there, sticking his own neck into the noose right along with them.

This leadership crap, Fain thought, for far from the first time, was an excellent way to get killed.

"They're coming through about where we figured, General," Gunnery Sergeant Jin announced. The gunny and his LURP teams had been called in during the night and redistributed to put at least one Marine with helmet, pad, and communicator with each regimental commander and Kar. Now the noncom pointed to the pad open on the rickety table at the center of the dugout, and Fain managed—somehow—not to crane his neck in an effort to see the display himself. Not that it would have helped much if he'd been able to see it; unlike Kar and his staff, Fain hadn't learned to read the display icons the others were now peering at so intently.

"They seem to be throwing more of their weight on the west side than we'd anticipated, General," one of Kar's aides pointed out, and the huge K'Vaernian grunted in agreement.

"Doesn't matter in the long run," he said, after a moment. "They still have to come to the bridge if they want to get to the other side. Still, we'd better warn Colonel Tarm to expect more pressure sooner than he anticipated."

"On it," Jin said laconically, and Fain watched his lips move soundlessly as he passed the message to the Marine attached to Colonel Tarm's regimental CP.

"Looks like they're slowing up a little," someone else observed, and the entire command group grunted with laughter which held a certain undeniable edge of tension.

"No doubt they're confused about why no one's shooting at

them," Kar said after a moment. "What a pity. Still, they should be running into the expected resistance just about . . . now."

A distant crackle of rifle fire broke out with perfect timing, as if the general's comment had been the cue both sides awaited.

"Contact," Julian murmured so quietly that Roger was certain the intel sergeant didn't even realize he'd spoken aloud. Not that any of the Marines in the cellar had needed to be told. They were watching their pad displays as the probing tentacles of Boman warriors ran into the first strongpoints and battle was joined.

"What do you make the numbers, Julian?" Pahner asked.

"Hard to say exactly, Sir," the NCO replied, "but I don't see how it can be much more than sixty, sixty-five thousand."

"Did we really whittle them down by forty percent in one day?" Roger wasn't quite able to keep the disbelief out of his voice.

"Probably not," Pahner said. "Oh, we could have come close to that, but it's more likely that they've got a lot of stragglers who are still heading in. They might even have a few chieftains or subchiefs who've decided not to participate in this little party, whatever the new management wants. Still, it's enough to get the job done, don't you think?"

The leading waves of Boman ran into a blizzard of rifle fire and died.

Rus From's engineers had sited the strongpoints with care. Wherever possible, they'd placed the rubble revetments where sunken lanes through the ruins would inevitably channel the heads of any invading columns into heavy interlocking fires, and the riflemen and spearmen manning those entrenchments took brutal advantage of their positions. The broken streets of Sindi ran red with barbarian blood, and fresh clouds of smoke and brimstone rose above the ruins as torrents of bullets hammered through flesh and bone.

The Boman shrieked enraged war cries as their point elements recoiled, but *all* they did was recoil. The clans had experienced what the new rifles could do the day before, and they were as prepared as anyone could be for the carnage they faced today. No one had ever accused the Boman of cowardice, and their frantic need to rescue their women and children drove them forward even more savagely than usual.

But for all Tar Tin's determination to storm the shit-sitter positions regardless of cost, he wasn't an utter fool, and even if he had been, many of his chiefs and subchiefs were not. They knew that driving directly into the fire zones of their entrenched enemies would invite casualties not even they could endure, and so they drew back and probed, looking for ways to bypass the dug-in defenders and get behind them.

As it turned out, there were many bypass routes. Sindi had been an enormous city, by Mardukan standards, and the full strength of the K'Vaernian army would hardly have sufficed to cover its interior in depth once the walls were lost. There simply weren't enough bodies in Bistem Kar's divisions to do that, which was why he and Pahner had placed his people in nodal positions covering primarily the approaches to the Great Bridge. They'd also paid meticulous care to planning and marking retreat routes through the rubble, complete with two alternates, for every unit. When the Boman managed to begin working their way around a position's flank through the broken stone and wreckage, the infantry manning it simply fell back—promptly—to the next prepared position on its list.

It was a dangerously complicated maneuver, requiring discipline, communication, and perfect timing, and only the army's faith in Bistem Kar and the electronic wizardry of the Marine communication links and remote sensors scattered through the ruins made it possible.

"All right, gentlemen," Kar said, looking around his command group as the last infantry battalion between them and the Boman began to fall back, "it's time we were going, too. Lieutenant Fain, if you please?"

"Yes, Sir!" Fain threw the general a salute he hoped didn't look *too* relieved and nodded to his top sergeant. The top nodded back, jerked his head at First Platoon, and Delta Company formed up in a ferocious, bayonet-bristling moving perimeter around the command group as it fell back towards its first alternate position.

"We're on our way, Captain," Fain heard Kar telling Pahner over the communicator clipped to the general's harness. "So far, they don't seem to suspect a thing."

The long morning wore away in a nightmare of thundering rifles, screams, smoke clouds, and carnage. It was impossible for any Boman chieftain to form a clear picture of everything that was happening, but certain essentials were clear enough.

Whatever the shit-sitters had done to Mnb Trag and his warriors when they took the city away from him, it had changed the northern portion of Sindi beyond all recognition. The Boman were hardly city dwellers to begin with, but the tortured wasteland of broken walls and roofs, heaps of rubble, and fallen timbers had obliterated the landmarks many of them had learned to recognize during their months in the city.

Yet in many ways, that actually favored them, for the burned-out shells of buildings and the haphazard heaps of stone helped to conceal and cover them as they probed for ways around the shit-sitter strongpoints. They were taking losses—hideous losses—as they stumbled into one entrenched position after another, but they were also driving the shit-sitters inexorably back. The broken city deprived the shit-sitter riflemen of extended fire lanes and left no place for those deadly pikes to deploy, and the force of Boman numbers gradually forced Bistem Kar's troops back, and back again, and back yet again.

Exactly as Armand Pahner had planned.

"And now," Bistem Kar murmured, "comes the *difficult* part."

Krindi Fain could hardly believe his ears, yet he knew the general was serious. The long, bitter battle had reached the approaches to the Great Bridge. In fact, most of the surviving infantry had already retreated across it. But Kar had retained his own First Division to cover the final withdrawal, and Colonel Ni's regiment had the honor of forming the division's rearguard.

The afternoon was mostly gone, and evening was coming on quickly, but the Boman seemed inexhaustible. The God only knew how many thousands of them had already been killed, but it seemed not to have fazed them in the least. Probably that was because, despite their casualties, they'd been so successful in driving back the K'Vaernian forces. Whatever their losses here in the city had been so far, they were lower than the casualties they'd taken in the jungle the day before, and unlike yesterday, they had a clear meterstick—the ground they'd gained—to prove they were winning.

They had also been killing K'Vaernians, Diasprans, and Northerners. Fain didn't know what total casualties were, but he knew they'd been painful. The worst had been the loss of the entire rifle battalion from the Tonath Regiment when a Boman thrust broke through more quickly than anticipated and cut its carefully planned retreat route. The rest of the regiment had tried desperately to cut its way through to rescue its comrades, but the attempt had failed, and General Kar had ordered the surviving Tonath battalions to fall back. It had taken his direct order—repeated twice—to convince them to break off, and they'd retreated only sullenly even then, but they must have known it was the only thing they could do.

The loss of four hundred riflemen, along with the regimental commander and the human Marine private who'd been his communication link to headquarters, had been more than merely painful, but they were scarcely the only losses the army had suffered. The best estimate currently available was that the defenders had so far lost almost twelve hundred men, almost as many casualties as they'd suffered in the all-day fight in the jungle. Yet severe as those losses might be, they were a mere fraction of the casualties the Boman had taken, and they were also the grim but necessary price the army had to pay to bait Captain Pahner's trap. Coupled with the ground the Boman had recaptured, they "proved" that the "shit-sitters" were being driven back, with no option but to continue to yield ground.

Now the trick was to get the rearguard across the Great Bridge intact and without discouraging the barbarians' enthusiasm for keeping up their attack.

The command group was already at the northern end of the bridge, awaiting Colonel Ni's troops. Captain Pahner had been pressing General Kar to fall back earlier, but the K'Vaernian Guard commander had politely but firmly resisted the human's pressure. He would retreat only with the last of his own troops, and that was the way it was.

Fortunately for Fain's peace of mind, those final troops were falling back rapidly, and the moment of the general's departure was at hand.

The lieutenant looked out over the Great Bridge and shook his head in admiration. The troops retreating across it presented a picture of absolute chaos, obviously jostling and shoving one another in their desperate haste to escape the oncoming Boman. Of course, the effect would probably have been somewhat spoiled for an observer with an eye to detail, because none of those "fleeing" soldiers had thrown away their weapons, which was almost always the first thing troops did when they'd truly been routed. Aside from that minor detail, however, the picture could hardly have been more convincing, and Fain hoped that whoever was in command of the Boman had an excellent view of it.

But the rearguard couldn't afford to present the same picture of confusion, and as Colonel Ni's reinforced regiment came into sight, it was obvious that it wasn't going to.

The northern end of the Great Bridge opened into a large plaza or square, and the Marton Regiment moved slowly but steadily backward across it. Both pike battalions were in line, facing north and three ranks deep to hold the Boman beyond hand-to-hand range. The assegai companies had each been reinforced by a hundred and fifty dismounted, revolver-armed League cavalry, each with at least two pistols, which gave each of the assegai companies almost as much close-in firepower as the regiment's rifle battalion. One of the reinforced companies of spearmen covered each flank of the pike line, while the rifle battalion moved wherever it was needed to pour in a heavy fire and drive back particularly enterprising Boman thrusts.

"Nice, very nice," Kar commented to an aide, and Fain was forced to agree. Which didn't keep him from clearing his own throat pointedly from his position at the general's elbow. The K'Vaernian turned and cocked his head at the lieutenant, and Fain gestured at the bridge.

"Sir, I imagine that Colonel Ni would be just as happy if we would get out of his way and give him room to maneuver his troops."

"My, how tactfully phrased," the towering Guard commander murmured with a grunting chuckle. But he also nodded, much to Fain's relief, and the Diaspran lieutenant muttered a silent prayer of gratitude to the God of Water and nodded to Sergeant Knever once again.

The command group moved out onto the bridge, conspicuously isolated from the rest of the army as the "panicked retreat" of the previous units streamed towards the southern bank of the Tam. Fain would have been considerably happier if the general had kept a bit closer to the troops who'd preceded them across the bridge, but Kar was in no hurry. In fact, he had a distinct tendency to lag behind even his aides-de-camp and his message runners while he watched Ni's troops falling back to the bridgehead. The barbarians seemed determined to prevent this final group of shit-sitters from escaping their vengeance, and groups of them charged forward despite the surf roll of rifle and revolver bullets, screaming their war cries and hurling throwing axes even as they were hammered down. Troopers were going down, as well, most wounded, rather than killed, especially among the pikemen, but the regiment's discipline held, and the Boman were losing at least three for every casualty they inflicted, even now.

Which didn't mean that they couldn't still overwhelm the regiment by sheer weight of numbers, Fain reflected, and dropped back beside Kar once again.

"Sir, the General might want to move along a bit faster," the lieutenant suggested diffidently.

"In a moment," Kar replied with an impatient wave.

"Sir, the General keeps saying that," Fain pointed out. He watched another wave of Boman crest and die less than twenty meters in front of the retreating pikes, and beckoned unobtrusively to Erkum Pol, who sidled closer.

"I'll retreat when I'm ready to, Lieutenant," Kar rumbled in a deep, repressive tone. "It's not going to do the Regiment's morale any good to see me go scampering off to safety, you know."

"Sir, with all due respect," Fain said diffidently, "I'm sure the Regiment would be very relieved to know you were out of harm's way. And whether they would or not, Sergeant Julian told me that Captain Pahner wants your butt at the reserve command post *before* the Boman come across the fucking bridge. That's almost a direct quote, Sir," the lieutenant added in an apologetic but politely firm tone.

"I said I'll come in a moment," Kar said even more repressively, and Fain shook his head.

"Erkum?"

"Yeah, Krindi?"

"Escort the General across the bridge," the lieutenant said flatly.

Bistem Kar's head snapped up, and for an instant, his eyes narrowed dangerously. Then they swiveled to Pol, who stood a full head taller than even his own formidable stature, and something like an unwilling chuckle escaped him.

"All right, Lieutenant," he told Fain wryly. "I'll go. I'll go! Who am I to argue with the mighty Erkum Pol? I don't want to get laid out with a plank!"

"I wouldn't hit *you*, General," the private said reproachfully.

"No doubt," Kar said, laying one hand on the towering Diaspran's upper shoulder, and then gathered up the rest of his command group with his eyes. "Gentlemen, Lieutenant Fain would appreciate it if we'd all step briskly along." He made a shooing gesture with both false-hands and flashed a bare-toothed human-style grin. "No dawdling, now!"

"Press them! *Press them!*" Tar Tin howled as the final band of shit-sitters retreated onto the bridge. The new war leader was trapped well back from the van of the host, but he could see the Great Bridge from his vantage point atop a collapsed house. And if he couldn't get at the shit-sitter rearguard now, he'd been in the forefront of the warriors who'd overwhelmed the trapped arquebusiers, and his ceremonial battle ax ran red with their blood.

The battle frenzy hadn't quite claimed him, but he felt the exaltation and the fire blazing in his own blood. They were only

Southern shit-sitters, true, yet they'd stood and fought as courageously as any iron head—indeed, as any *Boman*—and the honor of their deaths filled his soul.

It had been a good battle, a great one whose grim glory the bards would sing for generations, and despite the host's losses, victory was within their grasp. However courageously the shit-sitter arquebusiers might have died, Tar Tin himself had seen the panic and terror with which the other shit-sitters had fled across the bridge. He knew the signs—he'd seen them often enough on many another battlefield. That was a broken force, one whose leaders would never convince it to stand if he could only hit it again, quickly, before it had time to untangle itself and find its courage once more.

"Once across the bridge, and the city is ours once more!" he shouted, brandishing his battle ax and waving still more of his warriors into the assault on the stubborn shit-sitter rearguard.

The host attacked with redoubled fury, but the shit-sitters were fully onto the bridge now, and it was no longer possible to threaten their flanks. The ones armed with those long, dreadful spears thickened their ranks, presenting an impenetrable thicket of needle-sharp points, and withdrew at a slow, steady pace. It was impossible to get to hand strokes with them, but at least the thicker formation also blocked their infernal arquebusiers, and the Boman pressed them harder, showering them with throwing axes. The shit-sitters' raised shields were a roof, rattling under the keen-edged rain of steel, and here and there one of them went down. But there were always other shit-sitters ready to drag the wounded to safety, and the slow, sullen retreat continued without breaking or wavering.

Tar Tin snarled, for he wanted that rearguard crushed, yet despite his frustration, he was satisfied enough. The shit-sitter rearguard might be retreating in good order, but it *was* retreating, and rapidly enough that the host would still arrive on the other bank before the rest of their broken army could reform.

"All right, people, let's get into our party dresses," Pahner said, and the squad of Marines around him reached for their helmets.

Roger reached for his along with them, and reflected that it was just as well that he'd spent so many days marching around the jungle in his own powered armor before the company left Q'Nkok. It had given him the opportunity to thoroughly familiarize himself with the armor's capabilities and limitations. He was still far from competent by the standards of the Imperial Marine Corps, and he knew it, but at least he was confident of his ability to move wearing the stuff.

The Marines obviously shared his reservations about his other abilities where the armor was concerned, for the plasma cannon with which his armor had originally been armed had been replaced with a bead cannon. The "stutter gun" was a thoroughly lethal piece of hardware, but its current loads, although ruinously effective against unarmored barbarians, would *not* take out a suit of IMC combat armor. He supposed that he might have felt a little offended by their evident concern over where his fire might go, but all he really felt was relieved.

All around him, helmets were being affixed, and he watched the HUD come up in his own visor as the helmet sealed to its locking ring. Most of the really power-intensive systems remained on off-line standby, but the armor was live, and a slight shiver ran through his nerves as he reflected upon the destructive power massed in this cellar.

As Pahner had told Rastar on the day the Northern cavalry first joined forces with the Marines, they had sufficient spares and power for two uses of the armor, and this, the captain decided, was the right place to expend one of them. Roger knew that the Marine had considered using the armor in an open field fight, but the Boman had been too dispersed. The Marines would have exhausted their power packs before they could have covered even a fraction of the host's geographic dispersal.

Which had been the entire reason Pahner had constructed the elaborate trap called Sindi.

The Marton Regiment passed the midpoint of the Great Bridge. From its central span to the northern bank, the bridge was a solid mass of Boman, pushing and shoving at one another in their determination to reach the hated shit-sitters. It was a terrifying sight, viewed from the south side of the river, and Bogess and Rus From stood watching it with a sort of awed disbelief.

The bridge was clear between the retreating K'Vaernians and the south bank, and the reinforced regiment was a minuscule force opposed to the thousands upon thousands of barbarian warriors struggling to reach and kill it. The fact that it was exactly what they had planned for and wanted to see didn't make the sight one bit less frightening, and the two Diaspran leaders turned their backs upon it by unspoken mutual consent.

Instead of watching the grim, steady retreat, they let their eyes sweep over the surprise awaiting the Boman on this side of the river.

The original architects of Sindi had built a massive, separate gatehouse and bastioned keep to cover the Great Bridge's southern end. Beyond the gatehouse was another square, even larger than the one at the northern end, and beyond that were the first rows of houses and shops. The city's street net was as tangled and convoluted as that of any other Mardukan city, and even the broader boulevards were scarcely anything which might have been called wide open, but the designers had seen no reason to build massive curtain walls along the southern bank of the Tam. The only way an attacker could reach that part of the city was across the Great Bridge itself, so the powerful gatehouse blocking access to and from the bridge was really all the protection the city had required against assault from that direction.

The current landlords had made a few changes, however. Rus From's engineers had used old fashioned sledgehammers and charges of the black powder liberated from Sindi's own magazines to demolish whole blocks of buildings on the southern side of the square, effectively extending the plaza almost another full kilometer to the south. But if they'd given it more space to the south, they'd compensated by using the rubble produced by their demolition exercises to build stone walls, six meters high and three meters deep across every street and alleyway giving access to the square. Then they'd loopholed the inward-facing wall of every building still standing around the entire perimeter of the square and reinforced most of *those* walls from the inside with sandbags, for good measure. They'd left two of the main boulevards unblocked on the square's south side to permit the retreat of their own troops, and aside from the Marton Regiment, the entire army had now disappeared through those openings.

Through those *previous* openings, to be more precise. No sooner had the last "fleeing" infantryman passed through than the engineers had sprung into action once more. The walls of sandbags they'd assembled across the boulevards weren't quite as tall as the stone walls blocking the other streets, but they were just as thick . . . and each of them had embrasures for six of the new "Napoleons" from the cannon foundries of K'Vaern's Cove.

The general and the cleric regarded those grim preparations one last time, and, almost despite themselves, felt a moment of something very like pity for their enemies.

Krindi Fain heaved a sigh of relief as General Kar and his command group climbed the steep stairs to the top of the bastion and joined Bishop From and General Bogess. He would have been even more relieved if the gates and gate tunnel hadn't taken their own share of damage from the humans' plasma cannon. Although he understood why it was just as important for the defenses on this side of the river to have been "wrecked," it still would have been nice to be able to close a good, sturdy gate of bronze-sheathed ironwood against the shrieking hordes of Boman warriors, especially with the security of both senior Mardukan generals and their chief engineer to worry about.

He made a quick inspection of his troops' positions and felt a surge of pride. His men had to be at least as nervous as he was, given that they'd been less thoroughly briefed on the plan than he, but every one of them was exactly where he was supposed to be, already laying out his cartridge box. If everything went the way it was supposed to, the rest of the regiment would retreat into the gatehouse bastions along with Fain's own company, and if the main gateway had been blasted to bits, the gates and firing slits protecting the bastions were completely intact. They certainly ought to be able to hold out against anything the Boman could do for hours, at the very least, and that should be ample time . . . assuming the plan worked the way it was supposed to.

* * *

"Now! Drive them *now!*"

Tar Tin's shout was as hoarse as the scream of a newly branded *sorn*, but he was hardly alone in that. Every chieftain and subchief was shrieking the same message, goading their warriors on, and the war leader laughed in savage triumph as the host's leading warriors drew closer and closer to the southern gatehouse. Even from his own position on the north bank, the damage that gatehouse had suffered when the shit-sitters seized the city was clearly evident. What should have been an all but impenetrable barrier had been opened like a gutted *basik*. All they had to do was to drive these last, stubborn shit-sitters through the shattered tunnel and the city would be *theirs*.

"About *now*, I think," Captain Armand Pahner murmured as the blue icons of the Marton Regiment crossed the green safety line projected onto his HUD, and his toot transmitted the detonation code over his armor's com.

The micromolecular detonator had been designed to handle anything from highly sophisticated chemical explosives to small thermonuclear devices. The design team which had produced it had never even considered the possibility that it might be used for something as crude as black powder weapons, and they might have been offended by such a plebeian misuse of their ultrasophisticated brainchild.

Pahner could not have cared less about that. All he cared about was that it did precisely what he wanted it to do and ignited the quick match fuse running to the five hundred black powder claymore mines emplaced along the west side of the bridge.

The mines didn't detonate simultaneously. Instead, a rolling wall of fire and smoke raced clear across the bridge from just beyond its midpoint all the way to the northern bank of the river.

"Now!"

Colonel Ni's deep-voiced shout rang out, and every one of his pikemen squatted as if simultaneously stricken by diarrhea. The six hundred or so Boman who'd been outside the claymores' kill zone were too stunned by the cataclysm behind them to react, although there was very little they could have done, anyway. As the squatting pikemen cleared their line of fire, four hundred riflemen and three hundred revolver-armed cavalrymen opened fire at point-blank range. The bridge was so narrow that the K'Vaernians' and Northerners' ranks could be only twenty men across, but they could fire three ranks deep, and as each group of sixty fired, it squatted in turn to clear the fire of the group behind it. The firing sequence began with the cavalrymen; by the time it reached the second group of riflemen, there was not a single living, unwounded Boman on the entire length of the Great Bridge.

Sergeant Major Eva Kosutic paced back and forth along the gun line atop the rubble-built wall on the western side of the square. She hadn't been happy about being stuck here in the city while the troops were actually engaged in the field, especially when Roger and his Mobile Force had been fighting for their lives. But she was about to make up for her recent inactivity, she thought, listening to the crashing thunder of the Marton Regiment's volleys with a cold, thin smile.

"Load with grape," she told the gunners she and her initial cadre of naval artillerists had trained, and her smile turned even colder and thinner as she considered the surprise present they had for the Boman.

"Beware of Armaghans," she told the distant barbarians softly. "Especially when they bear gifts."

Tar Tin stared in horror at the Great Bridge.

Half a kilometer of Boman warriors—almost six thousand of them—had been ripped apart and strewn in bloody wreckage all along the northern half of the bridge. No doubt the host had lost many more than that during the fighting across the city, but not in such an eyeblink of time. Not so . . . horrifically. One moment they'd been living warriors, fierce and proud, screaming their war cries as they surged forward to close with their shit-sitter enemies; the next, they were so much shredded meat and blood, blown and splattered across the paved roadway. Blood ran from the bridge's storm drains, not in trickles but in streams that *splashed* into the river below and dyed it until it looked as if the Tam itself were bleeding to death.

And even as he stared at the carnage and destruction, even as the shit-sitter rearguard turned and jogged into the shadows of the broken gate tunnel, yet another huge explosion roared through the humid air. He watched the cloud of smoke and dust billowing up from the middle of the center span and hammered the edge of his ceremonial ax on the heaped stone upon which he stood, screaming his fury. The accursed shit-sitters had blown up the bridge behind themselves! Despite the panicked rout of almost their entire army, they were going to escape him because some demon among them had planned even for this contingency!

Curses and howls of baffled rage rose from thousands of other throats as the rest of the host realized the same thing. Warriors shrieked promises of dire vengeance, promised the gods the slow, lingering death of whatever shit-sitter had planned that ambush and that escape from their wrath.

But then the dust and smoke began to dissipate, and all of the curses, all of the shouts, faded into a breathless silence as the Great Bridge emerged slowly from the haze once more.

Tar Tin realized that he was holding his own breath, leaning forward, staring with hungry eyes as the bridge reemerged, pace by pace. Perhaps, if the gap wasn't too wide they would still be able to get across. Perhaps a temporary span, or—

A shout of triumph arose—first from one throat, then from a dozen, and finally from thousands. *The bridge stood!* The shit-sitter explosion had blasted away the raised stone guard walls on both sides, and taken a ragged bite out of the eastern side of the roadbed, but that was all. *All!*

"Now you will all die, shit-sitters!" Tar Tin screamed jubilantly. "So clever you were—so brilliant! But nothing stands between you and our axes now!" The paramount war leader of the clans raised his ax of office overhead in both true-hands, and his voice rang out like the trumpet of the war god.

"Forward the clans! Kill the shit-sitters!"

★ ★ ★

Armand Pahner inhaled in deep satisfaction as a fresh wave of Boman began thundering out onto the gore-splashed roadway of the bridge. His greatest fear had been that the barbarians would refuse to thrust their heads into the trap awaiting them on the south bank of the river. He'd had no choice but to set up the claymore ambush, because it had been imperative that there be a clean break between the K'Vaernian rearguard and the first ranks of barbarians to cross the bridge. The rearguard had to have time to file through the bastions' gates and bar those openings behind them, because he'd dared not let them into the killing ground with the enemy still in contact. Any force small enough to fit onto the bridge would have been easily outflanked and destroyed once the Boman had room to deploy around them, and the rest of the waiting troops couldn't have fired on the Boman without killing their own rearguard. Not to mention the fact that any premature firing might warn the barbarians of what was coming in time for them to refuse to cooperate. Yet even though he'd had no option but to place the claymores, he'd been more than half afraid that if the ambush worked, the Boman would recoil, refusing to continue their advance lest they run into additional, similar ambushes.

The only answer he'd been able to think of was to make the Boman think the defenders had done their level best to destroy the bridge entirely. The theory had been that the barbarians would figure that they wouldn't have tried to destroy the bridge, unless they'd been afraid of being pursued. From which it followed that this was the ideal time *to* pursue them. And so Corporal Aburia had worked with exquisite care to prepare a black powder "demolition charge" which would look spectacular as hell, do a fair amount of superficial damage, but leave the bridge structurally intact. He'd been a bit anxious about asking the corporal to tailor that precise a charge with something as crude as black powder, but she'd come through with flying colors.

Now he watched the bridge filling once again with close-packed Boman, and keyed his communicator.

"Here they come, Eva," he announced over the dedicated channel to the sergeant major. "Don't let anyone get too eager."

★ ★ ★

Honal stood peering through the firing slit in the wall of what once had been a shop of some sort. He had no idea what sort of goods it had sold, nor were there any clues to give him a hint. All that was left was a large, square, empty room with heavily reinforced stone walls. Well, that and the swivels, mounted on heavy timbers, driven into the ground, which the K'Vaernian Navy had contributed to the campaign.

The Sheffan nobleman rested one proprietary false-hand on the swivel beside him. For all intents and purposes, it was a small muzzle-loading cannon with a shot weight of no more than a single human kilo which took its name from the way it was mounted aboard K'Vaernian warships, which had a habit of mounting a dozen or so of them along each rail as antipersonnel weapons. Julian had taken one look at them and pronounced that they were the galaxy's biggest muzzle-loading "shotguns"—whatever a "shotgun" was. Honal didn't really know about that. All he knew was that this particular swivel was going to help him extract his long awaited vengeance for murdered Sheffan, and he showed his teeth in a snarl any human might have envied.

Bistem Kar watched from atop the gatehouse bastion as the unending tide of Boman swept towards him down the bridge. It scarcely even hesitated when it reached the area Aburia's charge had damaged, and the general's growl of satisfaction rumbled deep in his throat as the barbarians kept right on coming.

"Lieutenant Fain!"

"Yes, Sir?"

"Lieutenant, those bastards may get suspicious if we just welcome them into our parlor, but I don't want to put down enough fire to discourage them, either. I think one company of really good shots ought to be just about right. Would you happen to know where I might find one which would be interested in the job?"

"As a matter of fact, General," the Diaspran lieutenant told him with a slow smile, "I do. Company! Action front!"

★ ★ ★

Tar Tin snarled as the first shit-sitter arquebus fire began to crackle from the bastions to either side of the broken gatehouse. So, some of the rearguard had had the presence of mind to position themselves there in an effort to delay the host's pursuit of their fleeing fellows! It was a courageous decision, he conceded, since they could not have an unlimited supply of ammunition and whatever happened to the rest of their army *they* were certain to be dug out of their positions eventually and killed. But it was obvious that there weren't enough of them to stop the Boman. Dozens of warriors fell, or plunged over the side of the bridge into the Tam, as bullets struck them down, but even as dozens fell, hundreds continued to charge forward at a run, and already the host's fleetest warriors were passing through the broken gatehouse.

The bridge was theirs! The bridge was theirs—and soon all the rest of the city, and their families, and their stolen booty would be theirs once more and K'Vaern's Cove would be doomed!

Eva Kosutic watched the barbarians spilling into the enlarged plaza like a dark, living tide pouring into a dry lake bed from a sluice gate. They came onward, waving their axes, screaming their war cries, and she felt her gunners stirring uneasily. Not nervously, really—more . . . impatiently. They wanted to open fire *now*, but she only stood there, hands clasped behind her, and waited for the lake to fill.

Sna Hulf of the Ternolt Clan of the Boman charged through the ruined gate tunnel, howling his war cry. The exultation of battle carried him forward like a man possessed, eager to prove his courage and punish all shit-sitter treachery. He'd never experienced anything quite like the charge across the bridge, never been part of such a focused, unstoppable surge. It was as if the bridge were a narrow streambed, and the host a mighty tide driving through it, gaining speed as its bed narrowed until it erupted from the far end of the channel with a force nothing could resist! The weight of all his fellow warriors, of all the clans, thrust him forward with the massive momentum of literally kilotons of bone and blood and muscle.

Yet even in his exalted mood, he realized there was something strange and different about the square at this end of the bridge. It was larger than it had been the last time he was here, and all of the streets leading off of it seemed to have disappeared. And there were *holes* in the walls of all the buildings. And what were those shit-sitters doing on the platform atop the wall where the main boulevard had been?

He stared at the shit-sitters—the only ones he could see—while the momentum of his fellows propelled him forward into the square. They stood behind some sort of strange, two-wheeled carts which supported metal tubes of what looked like dark bronze. The tubes were long, and slender, unlike anything he'd ever seen before, yet there was something about them . . . something familiar, if only he could place it . . .

"I've never seen so many Boman in such a small space in my entire life," Honal remarked to Rastar and Chim Pri.

"Like a stock pen full of *turom* at branding time," Pri agreed, rechecking the priming caps on one of his revolvers.

"And one big pocking target," Turkol Bes added. The commander of the Carnan Battalion had borrowed one of the Marines' repeating rifles and had at least forty magazines piled up in front of him. The weapon was ridiculously small for him, but that was all right with Bes.

"And one big pocking target," Rastar agreed grimly.

"They're starting to slow down, General," Krindi Fain remarked, and Kar nodded in agreement. The general had Dell Mir's telescope back out, and was peering towards the northern end of the bridge.

"I imagine the square is beginning to fill up, Lieutenant," he said almost absently. "Even with all the pressure coming from behind them, they can only cram so many bodies into so much space." He chuckled evilly. "Of course, we're about ready to begin making room for more of them, aren't we?"

"General, Colonel Ni reports that some of the Boman are beginning to try to force the gates into the bastion," one of Kar's staffers announced, and the general shrugged.

"I suggest you tell him not to let them do that," he said in mild tones, still peering through his telescope. "Although," he added dryly, "I imagine they'll have something else to distract them very shortly."

"Armand, we're just about full here."

Pahner grinned at Kosutic's pointed tone. The sergeant major would never come out and admit that she was feeling antsy, but her use of his first name in front of the troops, even over the dedicated command circuit, was a dead giveaway. And looking at the congested horde of red icons packing tighter and tighter together in the square, he could hardly blame her. The remote imagery from her helmet showed him a vast sea of Boman, surging this way and that while those closest to the edges of the huge mob began to hack at the barricades with their battle axes. They weren't going to get through that stone any time soon, but he didn't want them to get any ideas about helping one another swarm over their tops, either.

"How many do you figure are still on our side of the river or the bridge, Julian?" he asked.

"Call it ten or twelve thousand on the bridge, and another ten or so on the approaches," Julian replied after a moment.

Pahner frowned slightly. He'd calculated that the Boman could fit a maximum of about forty or forty-five thousand into the square beyond the gatehouse, but he didn't really think there were that many already in it. Call it thirty thousand, he decided. If Julian's estimate was correct—and Pahner rather thought it was—then the Boman were down to no more than fifty-two thousand, little more than half the size of their host before the campaign began. If things went according to plan, those on the bridge and already in the square were toast, but there was no way the limited number of suits of powered armor available to him was going to be able to simultaneously seal the bridge and round up anyone who wasn't already on it. Which meant that at least ten thousand of the barbarians were going to escape, and he hated that.

His frown turned into a grimace and a snort as he realized he was actually upset by the idea of inflicting "only" ninety percent casualties on his enemy. Hubris, he decided, wasn't something a Marine needed to go around encouraging, and a mere ninety percent casualty rate ought to be enough to encourage even Boman to behave themselves in the future.

"All right, Eva," he said soothingly. "If it will make you feel any better, go ahead and get started."

"Gee, thanks," she said sarcastically, then turned to the gunners on the platform with her, and the captain heard her over the still-open com-link.

"Open fire!"

Sna Hulf had been shoved almost directly up against one of the stone walls fronting the square by the unendurable pressure of the warriors behind him. One or two of his fellows had already lost their footing and disappeared under the shrieking, ax-waving ocean of warriors. He had no doubt that they'd been trampled into paste, and the pressure around him was becoming distinctly unpleasant, but he couldn't take his mind off those bronze tubes.

If they'd been fatter and ringed with reinforcing hoops or bands of metal, he would have been tempted to think they were bombards. But no one had ever mounted a bombard on a carriage like *that*, and no one had ever cast a bombard that skinny for its length. It was ridiculous. And yet . . . and yet . . .

He was still pondering the conundrum when Eva Kosutic's order reached her gunners.

The gun platforms had been very carefully designed. Aside from the twelve guns in the sandbagged barriers built to close the two avenues by which the retreating K'Vaernians had cleared the square, each battery was at least six meters above ground level, and the gun platforms themselves sloped upward towards the rear, so that the guns' point of aim, at maximum depression, was well below the level of the batteries on the opposite side of the square. After all, no one wanted any friendly fire casualties.

But if no one wanted friendly casualties, there were going to be plenty of *unfriendly* ones. Each round of grapeshot consisted of nine individual shot, each fifty millimeters in diameter, and there were a hundred and eighty-two guns. Just over sixteen hundred iron balls, each seventy percent the size of a pre-space baseball, ripped into the packed Boman. Anyone who got in the way of one of them simply exploded in a spray of crimson and shredded flesh, and each of them blasted its way well over four hundred meters into the stunned mass of warriors.

No one ever knew how many thousands of Boman died in that first salvo, and it didn't really matter. Even as the artillery opened fire, riflemen and revolver-armed cavalry rose atop the walls around the square, or stepped up to the loopholes, and the six hundred Navy swivels mounted behind other loopholes belched fire and smoke. The swivels were loaded with canister, not grape, and each of them sent one hundred and thirty-five musket balls screaming into the Boman.

Honal shouted with delight as he touched off the swivel. The concussion as hundreds of field guns and swivels and thousands of rifles and revolvers simultaneously opened fire was like the blow from some mighty hammer. The deafening waves of sound and overpressure seemed to squeeze the air out of his lungs, and the brimstone stench was shot through with lurid tongues of flame, like some demon's paradise turned loose on mortal beings.

To either side of him, Rastar, Chim Pri, and Turkol Bes stood at their own loopholes, blazing away with the same manic grins. Honal's assistants stepped forward and began reloading the swivel, and the cavalryman drew two of his own revolvers and emptied them through the swivel's firing slit while they worked.

Shrieks and screams of terrified agony came from the slaughter pen into which the Boman had been herded, and hell-spawned night enveloped the scene of horror as choking clouds of smoke devoured the light.

Tar Tin was halfway across the bridge when the terrible explosions began on the far side of the gatehouse. The mighty stone structure of the Great Bridge itself seemed to quiver and pulse underfoot with the fury of the shit-sitters' fire, yet even through the dreadful thunder he could hear the despairing shrieks of the warriors trapped and dying under it.

Horrified understanding smote him as the choking pall of powder smoke rose above the far end of the bridge, and a fist seemed to close about his heart as he realized Kny Camsan had been right all along. To charge headlong against the shit-sitters' new weapons was to die, and he had been fooled—duped by shit-sitter cunning into doing just that! He still couldn't see what was happening in the square ahead, but he didn't need to see to know that the disaster to which he had led the clans was complete.

All about him, other warriors heard the sounds of slaughter and realized, as he, that the shit-sitters *wanted* them to continue their charge forward to their deaths. For a few moments, the pressure of those behind kept them moving forward anyway, but then even those at the very rear of the column realized, however imperfectly, what was happening. The pressure eased, and the flow of movement across the bridge began to reverse itself.

"Okay, troops," Pahner said to the armored members of Julian's squad. "Time to push the little dogies along."

The true purpose of the armor was far less to wipe the Boman out of existence than to break the back of the remnant's morale.

It worked.

The armored Marines, concealed by the sophisticated chameleon systems of their armor, had actually passed through the rearmost stragglers of the Boman host without being detected. They'd split up, spreading out to cover as many as possible of the streets, alleys, and avenues leading into the square on the north bank of the Tam with at least one Marine, and now they advanced, firing as they came.

A tidal wave of flechettes, cannon beads, and plasma bolts erupted out of nowhere, tearing lethal holes through the Boman who had just begun to retreat from the holocaust on the *other* side of the river, and it was too much. Not even Boman battle frenzy could support them in the midst of such supernatural devastation and horror, and the warriors began throwing down their weapons and groveling on the ground, anything to get out of the hail of terrible, terrible death from the invisible demons.

★ ★ ★

Honal sent yet another charge of canister blazing through the loophole, and reached for another pair of revolvers. He stepped up to the opening and opened fire, watching still more of the trapped, screaming Boman fly back from his fire in splashes of red, and he laughed with an edge of hysteria. It was like killing *basik*. He could probably have wandered in with a *club* and killed the Boman—they were that broken.

His revolvers clicked empty, and he snarled in frustration at the interruption of the terrible frenzy of slaughter. He swung out the cylinders and began stuffing fresh cartridges into the chambers. He recapped them, closed them, and began firing yet again.

"Cease fire, Honal," someone said in his ear.

"What?" he asked, picking another target and squeezing the trigger. The Boman blew sideways, disappearing into the heaped and piled corpses of his fellows, and someone hit Honal on the shoulder.

"*Cease fire!*" Rastar shouted in his ear.

Honal gave his cousin an incredulous glance, unable to believe what he was hearing, then looked back out the firing slit. The terrifying warriors of the Boman were a pitiful sight, most of them trying desperately to cower behind and under the piles of their own dead, and Rastar shook him by the shoulder.

"Cease fire," he said in a more nearly normal voice. "Despreaux says to cease fire. It's all over."

"But—" Honal began, and Rastar shook his head.

"She's right, cousin," the last prince of Therdan said. "Look at them, Honal. Look at them, and remember them as they were when they came over our walls . . . and as they will never, *ever* be again." He shook his head again, slowly. "The League is avenged, cousin. The League is avenged."

Tar Tin stood trapped in the center of the bridge, watching the destruction of his people's soul. The pride of the warrior people who had always triumphed, for whom defeat had never been more than a temporary setback and a spur to still greater triumph, died that day before his very eyes, and he knew it. Whatever might become of the pitiful survivors of the clans, they would never forget this disaster, never again find the courage to take the shit-sitters by the throat and teach them fear. *They* were the ones who would cower in terror from this day forth, hiding in the shadows lest the terrible shit-sitters come upon them and complete their destruction.

And it was he, Tar Tin, who had led them to this.

He knew what the clans would require of him—if they still possessed the spirit to demand a war leader's death. And he knew what they would *expect* of him, yet try as he might, he could not force a way through the defeated warriors about him to attack the shit-sitters and force them to kill him. He could not even sing his death song, for there was no enemy to give him death with honor. There was only shame, and the knowledge that the warrior people, terror of the North, would be warriors no more forever.

He looked down at the ceremonial ax in his true-hands—the ax which had been borne by the war leaders of the clans for fifteen generations, and which had finally known defeat and humiliation. His hands tightened on the shaft as he pictured the shit-sitters' gloating pleasure at claiming that emblem of Boman pride as a trophy to hang upon a palace wall in some stinking city, far from the free winds of the hills of the North.

No! That much, at least, he would prevent. In this, if in nothing else, he would prove himself worthy of his war leader's title.

Tar Tin, last paramount war leader of the clans of the Boman, clutched his ax of office to his chest with all four hands and climbed upon the parapet of the Great Bridge of Sindi. The water of the Tam ran red with the blood of his people below him, and he closed his eyes as he gave himself to the river.

CHAPTER FORTY-THREE

Poertena tossed down a single card.

"Gimme."

"Never draw to an inside straight," Fain said, flipping a card across the table. "It just won't work."

"A week," Tratan said. "A *week* he's been playing, and already he's an expert."

"It won't," the company commander said.

"We've got the masts almost finished," Tratan said, changing the subject, "and the last of the spars will be ready next week. Now if you hull pussies would ever get finished . . ."

"Real woodwork takes time," Trel Pis said. The old K'Vaernian shipbuilder scratched his right horn as he contemplated his cards. "You can't rush perfection."

"We gots tee last load o' planking from tee mills yestiday," Poertena said. "Tomorrow we starts putting it up. Every swingin' . . . whatever gets to put up planks til we done. T'en we parties."

"So next week the Prince has his yacht?" Fain asked. "Call. Pair of twos."

"Or tee week after," Poertena said. "We gots to set up tee rigging, an' t'at takes time. An' tee new canvas ain't ready yet, neither. Four eights. Gimme."

"If he was a Diaspran, I'd never believe it," Tratan said, throwing down his hand.

"Natural four?" Fain said in disbelieving tones.

"Hey," Poertena said. "If you gots tee cards, you don't have to draw to a straight. It's only when you pocked you gots to do t'at."

"Sergeant, could you take a look at this?"

The humans hadn't tried to explain the nature of the listening post to their hosts. The Mardukans had remarkable facility with gross manufacture, but the minute the word "electronics" was used, it became supernatural. So instead of trying to explain, Pahner had just asked for a high, open spot on the western wall, and left it at that.

Julian walked over from the open tower where the rest of the squad was lounging in the shade and checked the reading on the pad.

"Shit," he said quietly.

"What's it mean?" Cathcart asked, tapping a querying finger on the flashing icon.

"Encrypted voice transmission," Julian said, crouching down to run expertly through the analysis.

"From a recon flight?"

There was an unmistakable nervous note in the corporal's voice, and Julian didn't blame him. The entire company had known since the day they left Marshad that someone from the port had discovered the abandoned assault shuttles in which they'd reached the planet. The scrap of com traffic they'd picked up from the pinnace which had spotted them had been in the clear, which hadn't left much room for doubts. But it had also been *only* a scrap, and what no one knew was what whoever was in control of the port had done about that discovery since. It was unlikely that anyone would believe a single company of Marines could survive to get this far, but it certainly wasn't impossible.

"Don't know if it's a recon flight," he told Cathcart after a moment, "but whatever it is, we're close enough to pick it up. Which means they're close enough to see us . . . if they look. Or hear us, if we're careless with our radio traffic. "

"Saint?" the corporal asked, glancing at the sky.

"Civilian," Julian replied. "Standard program you can download off any planet's Infonet."

"That's good, right?" Cathcart said. "That means the Saint blockade might have been lifted. It might be a freighter or something."

"Yeah," Julian said. "Maybe." He tapped the icon, and it flashed red and yellow. "On the other hand, pirates use the same program."

Cord had considered himself a scholar in his day. And a poet. So when O'Casey set her toot to the task of accurately translating the long-ago log of the only ship known ever to have crossed the ocean, it was as a scholar that Cord had offered his assistance.

But it was with the mind of a shaman that he finally read the words which had been written on the crumbling leather leaves of the ancient log.

"Upon the forty-sixth day of the voyage, in the first quarter after light, there was a vast boiling upon the sea, as of a giant swell of water. All who were not employed upon the oars gathered on the starboard side to observe as another boil came up, and still another, each closer to the ship and apparently approaching rapidly.

"Just as the fourth boil of water was observed near alongside the starboard beam, there was a great shudder from below, as if the ship had struck a hidden reef.

"Master Kindar called to back all oars, but before any action could be taken, a vast mouth, as wide as the ship was long, opened up, and the bow of the vessel dropped into its maw.

"The jaws closed upon the ship, tearing it asunder and taking away many who had run forward to see the apparition. Many others, especially those along the sides, were thrown from the shattered remnants.

"I stood my post upon the rudder deck as the ship began to roll to the side. There was more screaming forward, as the ship shuddered again, and it was apparent that the beast had taken another bite, but it was out of my view.

"I clung to the rudder as the ship rolled, and then lashed myself to the starboard bulwark as the fragment continued to float. Forward, I could hear the screams of others caught in the water, and again and again the creature crashed against the remnant of the ship, until it

became either sated or disgusted with the fare. Perhaps it was the latter, for it has been ten days now, and it has not returned.

"The cook and I are the only survivors of the good ship Nahn Cibell. The wind and tide drive us slowly onward across the endless ocean. I have written all that I know. I hope to speak to my wife at the end of this voyage, and to see my young.

"But it is very hot upon the sea. And we have no water."

Roger sat on the end of the dock and looked out over the small cove. He could hear the party getting into swing behind him, but for the moment he was content just to watch the sun descending over the K'Vaern Sea.

He rubbed the cover of the bag, and unrolled it. The jeweled badge of an imperial servitor glittered in the fading light, and he unpinned it from the bag and held it up in one hand. He ran the forefinger of his other hand lightly, gently, across it, then drew a deep breath and pinned it very carefully to the breast of his own chameleon suit. He gave it a single, almost tender pat, and then returned to the bag.

One end held a lump, and he unsealed the bag and gently picked out a handful of fine ash.

"Oh, Danny boy," he whispered, and his hand moved, sending the fine drift of ashes out over the water while the words of the ancient paean to love and loss whispered out under the cry of four-winged avians whose like had never been dreamed of on Earth.

> "Oh Danny boy, the pipes, the pipes are calling,
> From glen to glen, and down the mountainside.
> The summer's gone, and all the flowers are dying.
> 'Tis you, 'tis you must go, and I must bide.
> But come ye back when summer's in the meadow,
> Or when the valley's hushed and white with snow.
> 'Tis I'll be here in sunshine or in shadow,
> Oh Danny boy, oh Danny boy, I love you so."

"Roger?" Nimashet put her hand on his shoulder. "Are you coming? This is your party, too."

"I'm coming." He stood and dusted off his hands. "I suppose that food is as good a way to celebrate him as any."

Prince Roger Ramius Sergei Alexander Chiang MacClintock, Heir Tertiary to the Throne of Man, took one last look at the gentle swell surging across the reef at the entrance to the cove. Then he turned and walked back to the restaurant, hand in hand with a sergeant of Marines, and the fine film of ash still clinging to his palm mingled and spread between their hands, unnoticed.

Behind them, the ashes slowly mixed with the salty sea and floated out on the tide of two moons. Floated out on the tide to wash upon distant shores.

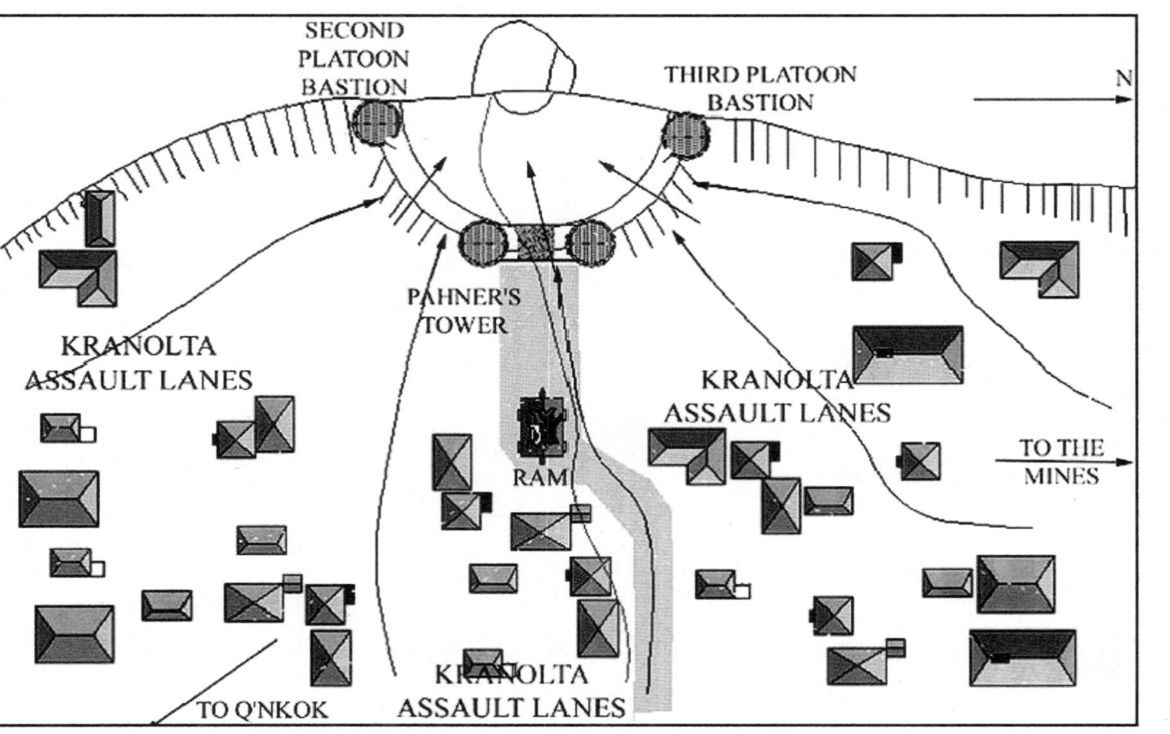
SECOND
PLATOON
BASTION
THIRD PLATOON
BASTION
N
PAHNER'S
TOWER
KRANOLTA
ASSAULT LANES
KRANOLTA
ASSAULT LANES
TO THE
MINES
RAM
KRANOLTA
ASSAULT LANES
TO Q'NKOK

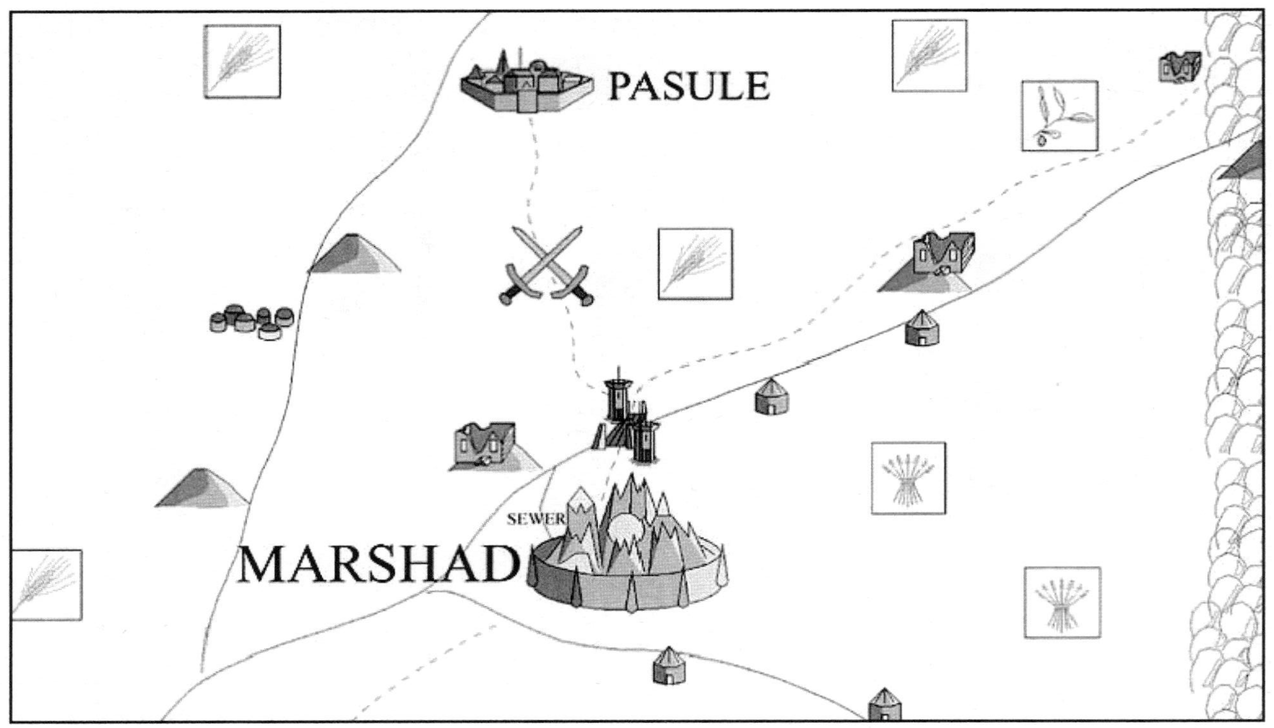
PASULE
SEWER
MARSHAD

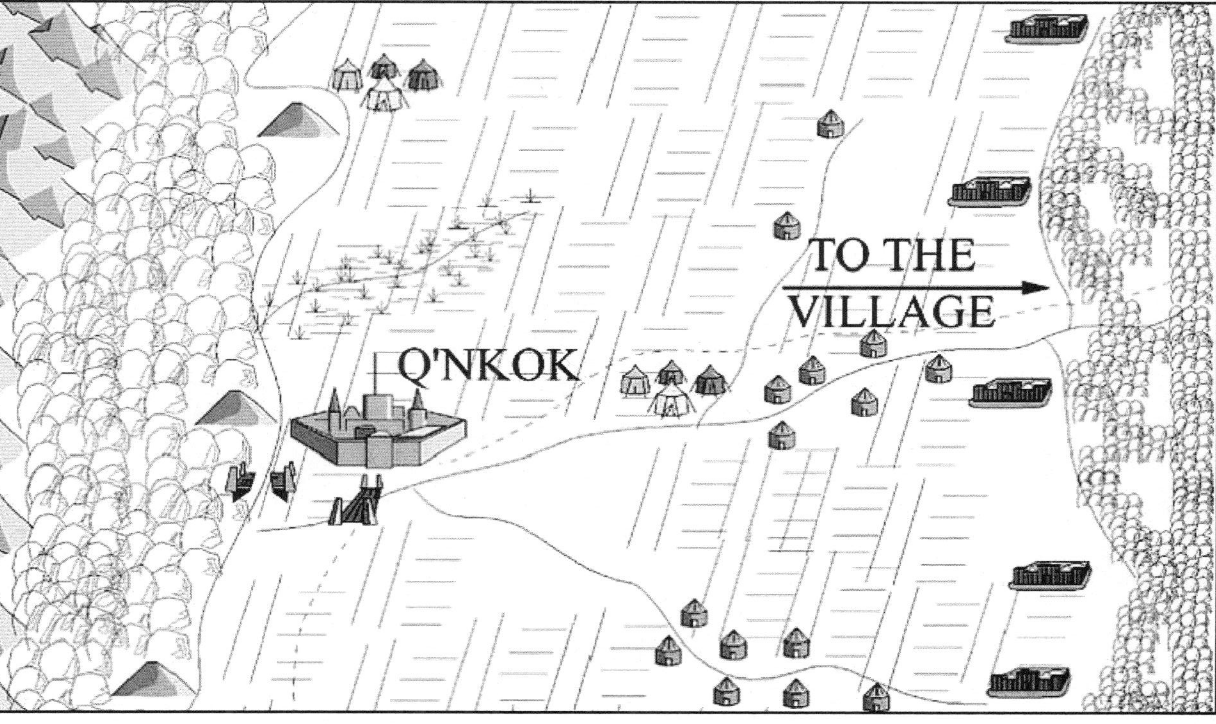
Q'NKOK
TO THE VILLAGE

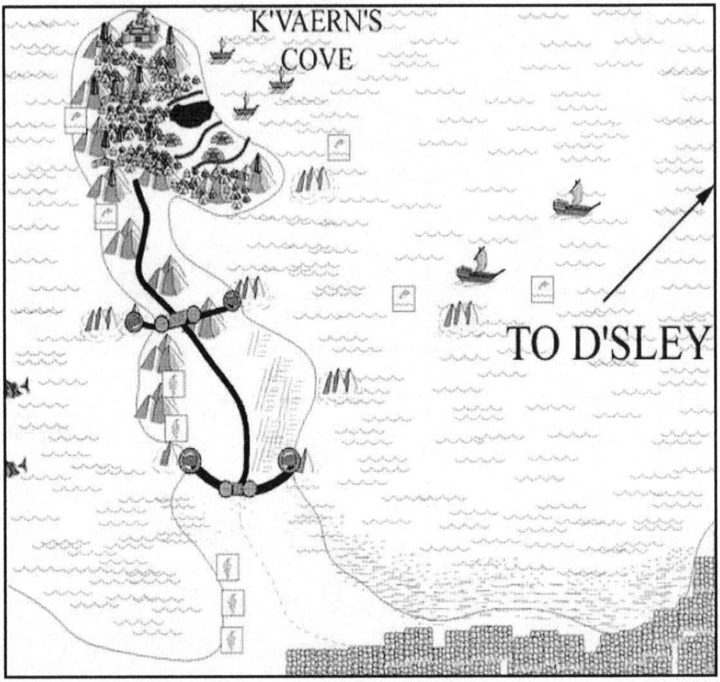

K'VAERN'S COVE

TO D'SLEY

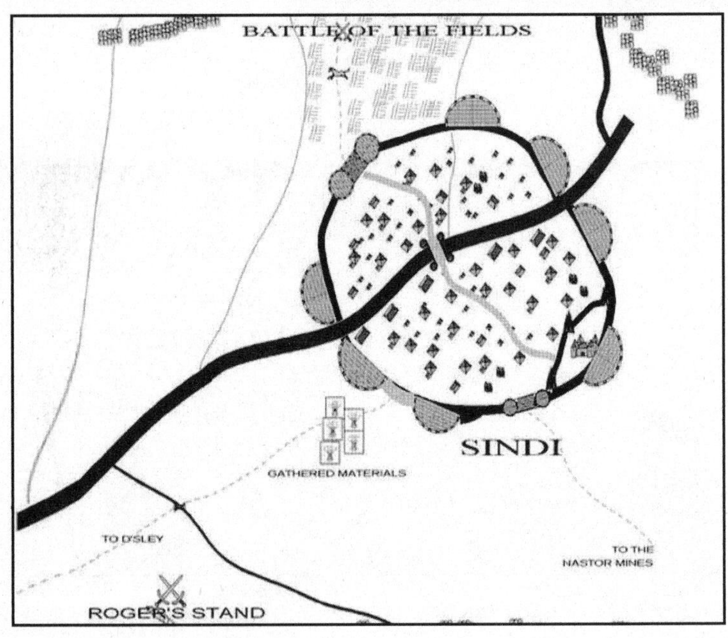